ALLISON M. AZULAY

Destined

Ex Tempore Series: Two

Destined is a work of fiction. Names, characters, places and incidents are products of the author's imagination or are used fictitiously. Any resemblance to actual events or locales or persons, living or dead, is entirely coincidental.

https://www.allison-m-azulay.ca

ISBN 978-1-989215-00-5 (softcover)
ISBN 978-1-989215-69-2 (ebook)

Cover Design by SelfPubBookCovers.com/RLSather

Published in Canada by Allison M. Azulay

Table of Contents

DEDICATION

For Sandy and Sherri, extraordinary women.

CHAPTER 1

Ladies of the night

The house looked like any other on the avenue: a red brick Victorian set back amid rose bushes, oaks, and maples that dwarfed the patch of well-trimmed lawn bordered by cutting flowers grown for the interior vases. By night, colours had faded and shadows had blackened to contrast feathery strips of vegetation and sharp angles of structures silvered by the touch of the gibbous moon.

A brick walk lay arrow-straight between the front stoop and the wrought-iron fence, the gates of which had been left open in apparent forgetfulness. The entry alcove bore a discreet candle sconce in one corner, affording enough light to show the location of the bell pull without revealing the identity of callers to passersby and neighbours.

Pull the bell he did, once his fumbling fingers found it. Michael MacGregor swayed as he waited. The damp air filled his

nostrils with the scent of roses, and he hazily noticed that a dog barked twice somewhere nearby as a two-horse carriage rolled along the packed dirt of the street.

Presently Madame Maxine, dressed as always in black-lace finery and, as always, smiling genially below cold eyes, opened the door and ushered him to the parlour.

As elegant as the outside, the interior might have been the well-appointed receiving room of any residence in the neighbourhood, and the finely dressed company would have done any fashionable home proud.

Alderman Struthers and the Honourable Howard Jenkins, member of the Legislature, waxed political in a pair of wine velvet wing chairs by the fireside. The banker Thomas Cavendish languished on a chaise longue of peach brocade, while Nathaniel Bennett and Donald Merrick, seated at opposite ends of a wine-and-cream striped sofa, haggled over the cost of shipping silks the latter wished to import from China.

The distinguishing feature of the place was the female members of the household: Apart from Madame Maxine—who flitted about, chatting with guests or directing the young ladies or giving instructions to black-liveried servants—the women strolled or lounged in a state of undress that was emphasized rather than covered by colourful silk dressing-gowns draped casually about their shoulders and lying open to reveal their corseted attributes.

Having left the arms of Miss Dorothea, the blonde still in her room above, Benjamin Levinson drifted into the parlour, his silk cravat hanging loosely over his partially buttoned shirt and waistcoat. Immediately, Thomas Cavendish hopped up, strode to the stairwell, and climbed the steps toward his own long-awaited appointment with Miss Dorothea.

As the banker passed, Michael MacGregor gripped the jamb of the broad parlour entry and surveyed the females on offer. The little ones, as always, flinched at sight of the huge Scot. The older, more experienced, and amply endowed Miss

Margaret, however, wandered his way with a knowing smile and slid a plump arm around his waist.

"Will you come with me?" she asked rhetorically as she led him to a back room on the ground floor. One day, he thought dully, he might see the upper levels of the establishment. If he ever arrived in a sober state.

∞

MacGREGOR STOOD braced by the closed door and watched dazedly as Miss Margaret loosened his tie, unbuttoned his vest, and opened his flies. That done, she sauntered to the posterbed, slipping off her robe and tossing it onto the cushioned bench as she passed her dressing-table. Without preamble, she lay on the bed and spread her legs. The Scot stared at her crotch, its brown fur exposed by the strategic slit in her bloomers and illuminated by the rosy glow of a pink-shaded oil-lamp resting on the vanity table.

The middle-aged blonde waited expectantly as her client reached into the blue frock-coat he still wore and retrieved his pocketbook. He pulled out a few bills and stuffed the wallet back into its place. After a moment, he pushed himself from the wall and staggered to drop the money among the bottles of perfume on the mirrored table before he lurched the few paces to the bed.

He collapsed upon her, groped her breasts a moment, and then he reached to fumble with his member. He fisted himself several minutes with increasing frustration and frenzy, and finally he lay limp, breathing in choked sobs as Miss Margaret absently stroked his oiled black hair.

Suddenly it was more than he could bear: that cool, impersonal sympathy. Michael MacGregor pitched himself up, rolled to sit at the edge of the bed, and backhanded the woman across the face.

"Stupid whore!" he yelled.

He tried to stand, but his legs gave out under him and he

fell to the floor with a crash that almost drowned her outraged scream. In seconds, the door was thrown open and Madame Maxine stalked in behind two enormous brutes in black.

Before the madam could inquire, Miss Margaret shouted, "He hit me!"

"Did he pay you?" the madam demanded.

"Yes, but not enough to cover this!" The prostitute indicated her reddened cheek.

"Out with him!" Maxine ordered, and the two bouncers hauled him up with vise grips on his arms and rough supporting holds under his shoulders. Before they could remove him, the madam searched his jacket, rifled his pocketbook, and replaced the wallet empty.

As her men dragged him through the hall and out the rear exit, she called after, "And don't ever darken my door again, you Scotch bastard!"

∞

DUMPED INTO a narrow alley between tall buildings that stretched above into blackness, Michael MacGregor clutched the top of a stone plinth and struggled up out of the dirt and trash to lean against the near wall. He felt the limestone hard and irregular against his back and head. He had lost his hat, he now recalled, but where and when, he did not know. Perhaps in the carriage that had brought him here, or in a tavern, earlier.

A yowl and answering mews to the right told him an alley-cat hunted relations rather than rats, and he muttered envious congratulations under his breath. A pool of light beyond that end of the passage illuminated a wide street he guessed to be King. He turned right and staggered out in search of a drink.

He wandered, disoriented. In the dim light from widely spaced streetlamps and the brighter glow of the moon that climbed in the east, the tall buildings all looked alike to him, and none looked as they likely did in the day, stark shadows

changing their apparent shapes. Fog was seeping into the city from the lake, and the sight of it oozing along the dirt of the road filled him with an increasing unease.

A turn brought him to a small square lined by shops, their darkened windows revealing nothing of their wares or quality. Silence lay as heavily as the encircling shadows; he would find no tavern here. Choosing an alley at random, he stumbled on.

Soon, he found a street he recognized by the milling mollies and the stench of low ale and cheap cigars. A boy in a voluminous skirt and *décolleté* bodice that displayed his hairless chest sashayed toward the Scot, mist eddying about him as he moved. Panic gripped Michael MacGregor's gut. He whirled and half-ran to another alley that he knew would take him to MacDonald Park, leaving behind the sound of the molly's disappointed "Bitch!"

The park was in sight, its beckoning grass and bushes lit by a streetlamp, when the first blow hit him. MacGregor had not yet dropped to his knees from the impact of the bludgeon to his back when a vicious kick hurled him sideways. A sharp pain stabbed through his shoulder when he struck a brick wall and then fell to solidly packed dirt, but he had no breath with which to cry out.

Hands molested him, turning him, holding him down, and rifling his pockets.

"Bloody empty!" cried one of the ruffians on finding the pocketbook. The man flung it to the ground and kicked MacGregor in frustration.

"Look!" exclaimed another. "'E's not even done up 'is flies, the pervert! Prob'ly just come from 'is molly-whore."

A menacing voice said, "Mebbe we should teach 'im better'n spendin' 'is coin to practise the Devil's ways."

MacGregor closed his eyes, his mouth curling weakly in a sardonic grin at the irony that he should be killed by footpads mistaking him for a sodomite.

"Maybe you should mind your own business."

The new voice was feminine, MacGregor thought. Not a molly but an actual woman. Before he could make sense of the impression, shuffling and curses brought him to the realization that the bandits had turned their attention to her.

His menace now tinged with derision and lewdness, the gang's leader said hoarsely, "An' what would a *respectable lady* such as yourself be doin' walkin' the backstreets at night?" His emphasis on the words clearly conveyed he thought her anything but.

MacGregor tried to push himself up, but pain stabbed through his shoulder once more. This time, he did cry out.

One of the thugs turned back and aimed a kick at him, but MacGregor managed to grab the foot with his uninjured limb and unbalance the man. The hoodlum toppled. A thud when the thief's head hit the brick of the opposite wall was smothered by the noise of another struggle. The Scot turned his bleary gaze from the still body of his attacker to the darkness of the alley. He could see movement that obscured details as efficiently as the lack of light.

Scrapes and scuffles, a metallic sound, and an odd whirring he could not identify came from the dusky passage. He tried again to get up, this time rolling first to the less painful side. As he staggered to his feet, the yelps and thwacks that had made him fear the woman would be beaten to death ended abruptly. He reached for the wall to keep him upright, and he stepped toward the middle of the alley. At a light clinking followed by faint footfalls, he stopped. Out of the murk, she appeared, her white hair a nimbus the unearthly glow of which made him wonder if this were all some strange dream.

"Aagh!" The pain put paid to the notion that he was only dreaming.

"I'm sorry," said the woman, pulling back from her attempted embrace. "You're injured, aren't you?"

"Mmm," MacGregor managed to utter through clenched teeth and tight lips.

She reached carefully to put an arm around his waist. As she urged him toward the park, stooping to grab up his wallet on the way, she said, "We'd better get well away before they wake up. They won't be pleased with either of us."

∞

ON THE FAR SIDE of the park, in a location hidden from the alley by hedges and thickets, the woman examined his arm in lamplight blurred to a nebulous halo by the fog.

"Dislocated," she said, her tone matter-of-fact.

"Aye," he murmured.

She started at the sound and looked up into his face. A series of emotions he did not understand flickered through her eyes. She swallowed visibly. At last, she licked her lips, nodded in some unspoken decision, and commanded, "Sit down. I'll put it back."

She helped him to his knees on the grass within the hazy orange circle of gaslight. He braced himself, but she said, "Try to relax. Tensing will only cause you more pain."

He took a deep breath and let it out, slow and tremulous, forcing himself to ease his muscles. She spread the lapels of his coat and, ever so gently, pushed the fine wool jacket over his shoulders. Once it was removed, she disappeared behind the hedge. MacGregor gaped in astonishment, wondering what she was about. Before he could reach any conclusion, she reappeared lugging a flat and obviously heavy stone and carrying white cloth draped over her shoulder.

"Let your arm drop," she ordered as she approached. After setting the rock by his knee, she eased the cloth—one of her underskirts, he now saw—up under his injured arm to the armpit and tossed its ends over his shoulder.

Then, she squatted beside him with feet planted apart in most unladylike fashion and retrieved the rock as she said, "I'm going to put this into your hand. I know it sounds crazy, but if

you take the weight of it onto your arm, your joint will pop back into place."

He swallowed and nodded, instantly regretting the movement. When she slid the stone between his hand and thigh and placed it into the curl of his fingers, he gripped it, wincing at the discomfort even that small motion caused him. Carefully, the woman balanced the slab in one of her hands and gathered the ends of the skirt in the other.

"Ready?" she asked, still holding the weight.

"Yes," he said.

The woman released the rock, allowing him to take its weight, and simultaneously propelled herself to a stand while tugging upward on the skirt at his shoulder. A jolt shot through him; it tightened his fingers in reflex and forced out a grunt. Then, breathing heavily, he dropped the stone, and he rubbed his newly restored joint gingerly.

"I'll be damned!" he exclaimed in a whisper.

The woman smiled.

"My home is just across the creek," she said. "I'll give you something to help you heal, and you can make your way to your own home from there, after you've rested."

Once more, she helped him up and put an arm around his waist to support him as he walked.

"What's your name?" she asked casually, steering him across the street.

"Michael MacGregor," he replied politely. "I thank you for your assistance...Madam." He decided not to seek amity, nor to inquire into her private business in echo of the thug's words. Whoever she was, he would likely never see her again.

Genially, the woman introduced herself and answered his unspoken question, "Mrs. MacGregor. Anne MacGregor. No relation, I'm sure. I was on my way home from work."

He observed, "It's a dangerous business for a woman to walk the streets at night, whatever her work."

As they turned into a side lane, she replied, "True. I don't

always take that route. But I'm glad of the whim that bade me take it tonight."

"Hmmph," he responded, not sure he should be grateful that she had saved his life.

∞

HAD SHE NOT walked these streets so often, she might have strayed, her mind awhirl and the mist thickening. The man beside her was a stranger. Yet he was not.

Anne stole a glance. His hair was cut short and pomaded in the manner of the times, but even tousled and dirtied it gleamed purely black in the moonlight that occasionally penetrated the brume. His eyes, she had seen in the lamplight of the park, shone a familiar limpid lapis blue. Lush jet lashes defined those beautiful orbs and the thick brush of his black brows hedged them. He was not bearded but shaven, and the strong lines of his jaw harmonized with the straightness of his nose.

Though now stooped from pain and drunkenness, he was clearly long and lean and broadly built. At times, when he swayed or stumbled, she had difficulty keeping them both upright.

He wore not a kilt but a trouser suit in fine wool, its jacket in the extended length common to gentlemen, its lapels wide and sharply pressed, and its buttons satiny silver. His silk shirt and double-breasted jacquard waistcoat further proclaimed his wealth and status, along with what had once been highly polished shoes. A blue silk cravat that matched his eyes hung loosely at his neck, a diamond stick-pin intermittently peeking out among its folds. Even the man's hands, large and fleshy, bore the buffed and manicured stamp of the elite.

But for all the differences, he was the image of her late husband, Alex.

∞

AS THEY WALKED in silence through avenues and lanes, the dawn twilight began to cast its blue glow over the city, revealing the change to poorer housing. He smelt the transition, too: The freshness of leaves and the perfume of flowers faded, soon overpowered by the fetid odours of backyard flocks and infrequently emptied privies as well as the stench of the small river they now crossed. His own back-alley reek blended with the ambient airs.

Michael MacGregor appraised his companion. She was most likely a charwoman, he thought. Perhaps one who cleaned office buildings after the day staff finished their work. Older than himself, by her manner and by the silver hair, though her face did not bear the lines he would have expected to accompany such snowy tresses.

Now that his head had cleared of its liquored fog, he noticed the odd garments she wore: This woman's clothing pre-dated even his mother's. Something from another century, he reflected, as images from a book of European history and from paintings in museums flashed into his mind. Her low-necked bodice would have been *de rigueur* a hundred years ago, or even fifty, but now it marked her a harlot.

She wore no hat, and her shoes were simple, flat felt slippers, neither laced nor buttoned. That too was peculiar. And when the morning's glow illumined bunched white linen protruding at the edge of her sleeve cap, he recognized a style common to the eighteenth century. How very strange.

"This way," she announced, and she turned from the bridge thoroughfare to a broad lane less travelled by carriage and wagon, judging by its grassy mat. This area smelled fresher than its surroundings, he noted, inhaling with pleasure the scent of herbs and flowers, trees and shrubs. As they trod the meandering byways, he caught traces of chicken and goat, sheep and cow, but on the whole, the air had a refreshing cleanness, and he wondered why one of the poorer districts should smell better than its middleclass counterpart a stone's throw away.

Finally, the woman pushed a picket gate inward. It creaked open and then clacked closed behind them as they entered the yard. With no bricks or flagstones, the path to the door was merely well-trodden grass, a smaller version of the public lane. The wooden steps and porch creaked under his weight; it occurred to him he might fall through, if the boards were weak enough from age, but they held.

He glanced about. The property defined by the low, whitewashed palisade was by no means generous, but it was brimful of vegetation, and wooden boxes below the windows sprouted greenery and blooms, as well. The little clapboard house was whitewashed and trim outside and, upon entering, he found it clean and tidy within. It did not surprise him that a bowl of apples lay on the bare pine table and a vase of wildflowers sat on a small desk.

"I'll show you to the privy," said the woman as she set a newly lit candle upon the table. She strode to the back door made in Dutch style with a window in its upper half bearing cotton lace curtains strung on a wire, both rectangles of cloth now shoved to one side. Just beyond the door, on the back porch, the woman opened a shed attached to the house and gestured for him to enter.

"Toss some of the leaves in after you're done," she said, pointing to a basket next to the seat. "And wash your hands in the basin."

MacGregor eyed the basket and its faintly fragrant contents, and then glanced at the bowl in the corner, sitting on a shelf alongside a tall ceramic container with spigot, and flanked by towels on wooden racks. When he looked back, the woman had gone. He closed the door to the little hut that, unlike most privies, was bright with moonlight that streamed through one of three high windows. It smelled earthy, rather than noxious, and its broad bench and high ceiling gave a sense of spaciousness found more often in the grand indoor water closets of the wealthy than in the outhouses of the poor.

The Scot relieved himself and shook his member to expel a clinging drop; then he tossed a handful of leaves and petals from the basket into the privy's hole. He had turned to the door, but he remembered her admonition to wash his hands. It was a peculiar demand, given that his whole body reeked of the filth into which he had fallen, but he supposed that he should follow the rules of the stranger's household.

When he returned to the kitchen, the woman—Anne, he recalled—gave him a minuscule dose of liquid remedy squeezed from a dropper. The medicine tasted of nothing but water and a barely discernible hint of brandy, he noted perplexedly as she led him upstairs to a bedroom. After setting the candle on one of the small bedside tables, she helped him to undress to his waist.

The welts that he could see on his side were already blue. He felt her fingertips gently sketch their extent and probe the ribs at his back.

"Does this hurt?" she asked.

"No."

She moved round to his side and probed again.

"This?"

He caught his breath. "A little."

She glanced up into his face, but quickly looked back to continue her examination, urging him toward the light with gentle pushes as she scanned. At last, she said tentatively, "I don't believe your ribs are broken. Nor cracked. But bruised, certainly, along with this other bruising."

She stepped back and faced him squarely as she warned, "Take note of the colour of your urine. If you see blood, go immediately to Dr. Edward Hanes; he has an office on Queen Street, two blocks west of Bay. He's the best physician I can recommend for such matters."

MacGregor nodded, briefly wondering how she would know the city's physicians well enough to determine their relative quality. But her concern for his wellbeing seemed sincere, and he felt oddly touched by it.

She added, "And I suggest you keep your arm in a sling for several days to ensure you don't overtax the shoulder while it heals."

Again he nodded. When she insisted that he remove his lower garments, however, he balked. The small bedchamber contained no screen behind which he might hide himself.

"I'll turn my back for the sake of your modesty," she assured him, suppressing an amused smile, "but everything must be cleaned of this awful stench. Rolling in alleys leaves...a distinct impression."

When she turned away, he heaved a sigh, stripped off his shoes and hose, trousers and drawers, and dropped them by the pile of his belongings next to her. He could not argue with her assessment that his clothes were high-smelling. He guessed that the ordure in the backstreets included several types of animal as well as human waste, and not a few varieties of rotting vegetables, most of them sulphureous.

He scrambled into the bed, nearby, and covered himself as she bent to pick up his clothing. He stretched under the blanket and sheet, enjoying the softness of her mattress and the smell of summer meadows that wafted from the linens. He should have washed, he thought hazily. Then, he thought no more.

CHAPTER 2

By the light of day

B loody hell," Anne muttered as she carried the foul-smelling garments and accessories out of the room. "Bloody hell," she repeated, descending the stairs in a cloud of reek.

The man had clearly fallen into filth in that alley. And maybe in another street or alley before that. Moreover, he was an habitual drunk; he exuded that sour stink of liver-strained liquor that oozed from the pores of someone who drank heavily and often, and had been doing so awhile. Years, perhaps.

She sighed as she dumped the clothes into the yard. He was young; he was well off; and he was beautiful. *What could have turned him into an alcoholic?* she wondered.

When she returned to the house to gather soap and other paraphernalia she required, her belly suddenly liquefied. She trembled violently, and she gripped the cupboard to brace herself.

It's him.

There could be no doubt that this man was the newest incarnation of her belovèd. How he had come to be here, what his life had been until now, she did not know. Nonetheless, he was—regardless of his current name—her husband, Alex MacGregor.

But he did not know her.

Still shaking, she brushed away the tears that had filled her eyes, straightened, set her lips firmly, and picked up her dish of soap.

∞

IN THE WELL-HOUSE, in the light of a single candle, Anne worked the long wooden handle of the pump and water began to spurt fitfully and then gush steadily from the device's metal spout into the kettle. She filled two iron pots and lugged them to the small outdoor kitchen she had built behind the house. Once fires had been set ablaze in the belly of each of her pocket-rocket stoves (a late-twentieth-century technology named for the sound produced as the wood burned), she went back to the pump to fill her laundry tubs.

There was no point in separating the articles, she decided. They had all been immersed in liquid filth and smeared with various soft and solid materials. Indeed, her own gown now bore splotches of crud from contact with his clothing; so, she stripped off her skirts and bodice to wash them, as well. She started by soaking all and rubbing out the worst of the substances while the water in her kettles boiled.

After two changes of water, she dropped the sopping apparel onto the grass and cleaned the tubs with soap before refilling them and adding boiled water. It took several more scrubbings with an assortment of tools and soaps to extract the stains of excrement, tomato, chewed tobacco, blood, and something she did not recognize.

Finally, as the rising sun lightened the sky, she set her three-legged iron cauldron over her stone-lined pit and filled the vessel. She lit tinder and gradually fed sticks to the flames below, bringing the water and the clothes soaking in it slowly to a rolling boil. Once the garments had been thoroughly heat-disinfected, she let the fire die and left the water to cool.

A few more items remained: She picked up the man's shoes and carefully washed the scum from uppers, heels, and soles. After a thorough polish with lemon rind to remove the odours that still clung, she wiped the inner surfaces with a rag dampened in lemon water and fished the laces from the cauldron to squeeze out excess moisture and push them through the eyelets of his footwear. Finally, she placed the shoes by her desk. Then, she took more lemon rind to the leather tabs of his suspenders, to the calfskin pocketbook, and to the gold watch, before deciding she had done as much as she could to salvage the man's belongings.

Exhausted, she trudged through the garden to pick a few leaves here and dig a couple of young roots there to fill her belly. At last, she climbed the stairs and lay next to him. He stank, but she could scarcely smell it, now.

She stared at this stranger in her bed, with his broad brow and smooth cheekbones and with his angular jaw shadowed by black stubble. Gazing at his familiar countenance, she remembered a henge, a ring of standing stones upon a windswept hilltop in the Highlands of Scotland where she had literally run into a man from the past who soon became the love of her life.

And as she began to drift off, she remembered....

∞

A lifetime ago, mid eighteenth century
ANNE LOUISA Hurley Grégoire MacGregor ran headlong through the underbrush toward the river.

"I follow Big Alex. I see Redcoats come with fire-sticks," young Red Fox had told her, panting from his desperate run for help. "Many Redcoats," he had said with a gesture she knew to indicate at least a dozen men. He had pointed. "That way. Where the river is shallow."

Her heart pounded in her chest and blood roared in her ears as she plunged through the forest toward the ford, the skirts and bodice laces of her long blue gown catching on twigs, and her stays, though loosened, digging into her flesh with the effort to breathe more deeply. A hawthorn speared and ripped the linen lace from the ruffle of one of her elbow-length sleeves.

How had they found him? And what were they doing so deep in French territory?

An ugly suspicion wormed through the back of her mind, one catalyzed by the memory of a furtive split-second glance by Two-Toes Larocque on the occasion of their first encounter, and his later attitude toward Alex. What had the bastard done?

Shouts ahead. A scream. A deep, resonant bellow that could only come from Alex. A shot. And three more, almost simultaneous.

Oh, God! They've shot him!

More shouts and shots as Anne flew, whipped by bramble and bush, stumbling on rocks. Her foot caught a protruding root, and she pitched into a mass of ground hemlock that hid a small boulder. She nearly blacked out at the pain when her torso impacted the jutting granite and snapped woody evergreen branches. The corset had saved her from impalement on the low shrubs, but her eyes welled with tears at the certainty something had torn inside her. Cursing, she scrambled up to hurtle once more through the forest. She had no time, now, for anything but Alex.

Finally breaking through a screen of cedar, ash, and willow, she careered into a pair of redcoats, toppling with them down the incline to fetch up at the water's edge. Rough hands seized her arms and hauled her up. Another hand grabbed her by

the hair and jerked her head back as Lawrence Sydenham stepped around to lean so close she felt his breath on her cheek. The fair-skinned officer, bewigged under his bicorne, examined her as though she were a strange, unfamiliar bug.

"I know you, don't I?" he said at last. Shaking his head, he remarked, "Had I only known how close Alex was, in that pitiful public house in Scotland, I certainly would not have let that MacPherson whelp get in my way."

He stepped back and jutted his chin in a wordless order. At once, the soldiers holding her wrenched Anne around to see Alex lying sprawled supine on the shore, half submerged, his long locks floating like black seaweed in the blood-reddened water, his plaid-draped chest stilled, his eyes staring sightlessly, his broadsword and claymore clutched in his hands. Two-Toes stood over him, leering at her, and a pair of redcoats lay dead nearby. Though tears blurred the image, it had already been burned crisply into her brain.

The Englishman grasped her chin and pulled her face toward him. Smiling maliciously, Sydenham said, "I would have preferred to take my time with your husband, Madam, but failing that, I shall have to make do with you."

Anne stared impassively into his cold, blue eyes. She had lost everything. She no longer cared what the redcoats would do to her.

THE SKY WAS GREY with impending rain as the clatter of the soldiers' hurried withdrawal died away. The river lapped against the shore, babbling over the rocks of the shallows and rippling against her right side. The *ki-ki-ki-ki* of a hawk-owl drew Anne's dull eyes up to catch a glimpse of its flight. She coughed weakly.

Her vagina burned with the battering it had received, and her shoulders and back throbbed where her flesh had been driven, again and again, against stones and pebbles lodged beneath her.

Anne slowly pushed herself up out of the mud, the grit of

wet sand clinging to her skin and clotting her hair. The tears that had long ceased and dried up to encrust her eyes and cheeks and temples now gushed forth anew at sight of Alex, lying still where they had left him.

Half-blinded, she struggled to her knees and crawled to him. She cradled the spiritless body of her husband, clad in the brown and beige tartan of his kilt, and wept until she could cry no more. Then, as rain and night fell, she dragged him up to higher ground. There, she dug his grave with her hands, scratching the cold soil until spasms in her belly forced a tiny lump of flesh out into the world to be buried with his father.

AS MORNING twilight washed the sky with pearly grey, Anne scrubbed her legs of blood. Then, she hung her husband's dirk on her belt next to her own and strapped his *sgian dhu* to her left thigh. Leaving his claymore and her smaller broadsword to stand as a pair of steel crosses at the head of the rock-covered grave where he and his son lay, she took up his basket-hilted blade, shoved it into its scuffed leather sheath, and slung Alex's baldric obliquely across her back and chest to carry his weapon just as he had always done.

Tugging the sword-belt, she stood tall and determined. She was ready.

ANNE DARTED through the woods guided by shafts of moonlight that penetrated the conifer canopy. Cries of alarm faded into the night as she raced from the Ojibwe settlement. No one would follow before morning, she knew, for there would be questions as to why the Métis and the Redcoats, alone, had been killed and marked. Before dawn, she would have reached the river and the hidden canoe.

She crossed the stream by skipping from boulder to boulder at the head of the whitewater before the bend. Her broadsword jounced as she hopped, throwing her off-balance at first, and she tottered a moment before stepping onto a flat-

topped slab. Once she picked up speed, though, bounding the closely spaced clusters, she sailed across with ease. The moonlight now winked in and out as clouds scudded from the north, making the journey through the forest slower and more treacherous. Nonetheless, she pressed on over the frozen ground, her crystallized breath trailing behind like puffs of tobacco smoke.

Three hours later, she topped a rise and recognized the small lake nestled in a dell. On the opposite side, she would climb the ridge and then descend to the canoe at the headwaters of the river, as planned. She spotted her Odawan friend on the far crest, waiting for her by an outcrop that cleaved the forest cover, and she waved to him.

On the strand below, she unslung her burdens and placed them on the prepared balsam fir log. As she pushed it into the water to float it to the small island more than halfway to the other side, thunder rumbled and the sky unleashed a sleety deluge.

Her friend Little Feather had warned her that, according to the lore of the local people, the island was a place of bad magic. That was why she had chosen this route: Given the island's reputation, none would follow beyond this point, perhaps thinking her an Underwater Panther or other form of spirit that had avenged itself against some slight by the foreigners and the Métis.

Once on the rocky islet, she hauled the log up onto shore and dragged it through the trees toward the opposite side. She was sopping and she was sweating. She was also tiring: Rage, the need for retribution, and the exhilaration of success had long since diminished and been supplanted by a renewal of her grief. Perhaps that was why she ignored the electrical tingle that grew as she trudged among the pines: To be struck by lightning seemed a fit end to her life and a means to rejoin Alex and Seumas.

She broke out into a broad clearing with a huge, slate-

grey outcrop at its centre. She started across and, suddenly, she stepped into Hell.

ANNE TRUDGED the dirt road she had found upon escaping the island. There had been no sign of the canoe or of Little Feather, though she had not truly expected to find either. She had no idea *when* she was, but the road's plain dirt and wagon ruts suggested she had not gone far into the future. At least, not as far as her own time.

She arrived at a crossroads. She looked to her left, then to her right, then ahead. She sighed and, for no particular reason, she turned east.

∞

Present day, late nineteenth century
DANGER...TERROR...screaming...screaming....

Michael MacGregor woke with a start to the sound of children screeching and laughing somewhere nearby. Drenched in sweat and trembling, he blinked and glanced about, having no idea where he was. At a slight movement beside him, he turned to find a white-haired woman who seemed vaguely familiar lying beside him.

The ache in his shoulder brought it all back: the whore, the mollies, the alley, the thugs, the woman. He made to get up and realized he was naked. How had that come about? Oh, yes: She had insisted upon cleaning his clothing. He wondered if she was a professional laundress, or merely motherly and kind. For a moment, he also wondered if they had had relations, but he instantly dismissed the notion.

Taking care to move slowly—not only to avert waking her, but for the sake of his aching head, his brain feeling too big for his skull thanks to an unknown quantity of whisky and wine—he rose and searched for the chamber pot. Finding none, he took the cotton kimono from the hook in back of the door and wrapped himself to go to the outhouse. The robe was small, but

roomy enough by design that it covered him sufficiently.

He found the privy beside the back door and remembered his previous experience of the chamber. It smelled...clean. He recalled that strange impression from the night before—or was it this morning—and he wondered how the woman managed to keep it so fresh. Surely the nightsoil wagon did not come more often to her home than to the other houses in the city?

He sniffed his chest and grimaced. He smelled worse than this outhouse.

When he had emptied his bladder, he stepped out into the late morning sun and looked about. A few yards away, he noted the cauldron. From here, he could see the blue of his jacket floating inside the iron pot. Wisps of steam told him the water was still too hot to attempt to retrieve his clothes.

It occurred to him he should telephone his father and have a fresh suit sent...where? He had only the vaguest recollection of where he was. Nonetheless, he went in search of a telephone, only to find no such modern convenience. He had, in fact, expected as much, but had held out the faint hope that a woman of such limited means might have chosen to obtain one despite the cost.

Again, he noticed his own stench. He looked around but saw no sign of water access in the house. With a scowl and a huff of annoyance, he stalked outside and searched for a well or springhouse. He spotted a likely shed and stepped in to investigate. To his relief, it contained a well-pump.

Taking one of the tubs that lay draining on the grass outside, he filled it with water. When he tried to haul it to a vine-covered arbour next to the little summer kitchen, he was instantly reminded of the woman's admonition to avoid straining his injured shoulder. After a moment's thought, he fetched another basin to the arbour and used a bucket to empty the contents of the first vat into the second. At last, he availed himself of the soap he had seen in the house, removed the femininely flower-printed robe, and set about scouring away the night's

degradations.

∞

STANDING ON the flagstone floor of the arbour, the Scot finished his ablutions by scrubbing the cotton kimono that had taken on the sour air of his body. Once that was done, and the robe was hung on a protruding stick to dry, he scooped water from the tub with the bucket and doused himself. He snorted and gasped at the shock of the cold water; then, he shook himself like a dog, scattering droplets.

All at once, he became aware that someone was watching him.

Grabbing the kimono to hold over his private parts, Michael MacGregor whirled, face fierce, ready for confrontation. To his astonishment, seven young boys stood by the porch, observing him with expressions ranging from embarrassment to shock to curiosity to suspicion. He gaped at them, nonplussed.

"What you doin' here?" the eldest inquired discourteously. The lad's sharp eyes, cocked eyebrow, and belligerent stance indicated he did not expect to hear a satisfactory answer and absurdly intended to defend the lady of the house against a grown man who towered over him.

The other boys looked from their leader to the stranger, their attitudes not aggressive but expectant.

MacGregor swallowed and pursed his lips. Even injured, he was sure he would have no difficulty defending himself, but he had no wish to fight children. After a mere second's thought, he said simply, "The lady, Anne," her full name came back to him, "Mrs. MacGregor," he cleared his throat, "was kind enough to help me when I was injured, last night."

The older lad looked him up and down, blatantly disapproving of the intruder's nakedness. MacGregor wondered if these children were the woman's sons. That would certainly explain the hostility. But he had seen no beds for children in the

house, and none of the boys resembled her in the slightest. Nor one another, for that matter.

Then—belatedly—the Scot wondered if this Mrs. MacGregor had a living husband and, if so, whether such husband might arrive without warning to find a naked man in his yard, clutching his wife's kimono.

"You'll be gettin' dressed and leavin' then," said the oldest boy, his tone allowing for no options.

"Well," MacGregor explained sheepishly, feeling as though he faced an Inquisition, "I'll have to wait upon my clothes. They're in that cauldron over there. Mrs. MacGregor washed them."

"Well, we'll see if we can help," said the lad with a sardonic smile. He marched to the cauldron, placed a foot at its lip, and shoved to topple it and spill its contents upon the grass. Then, he picked up the still-steaming apparel and tossed the lot toward MacGregor.

"There ye go." After shaking his hands briefly, the boy stood, stone-faced and with arms akimbo, and watched implacably as the intruder wrung each of the sopping garments.

Trying not to flinch at the scalding torrents expressed from the cloth and flowing over his hands, MacGregor cursed under his breath and shot frequent angry glances toward the lad who regarded him through steely eyes.

Finally, the Scot hung the lady's dripping skirts and bodice over a line behind the arbour and donned his wet undershorts and trousers. When he finished buttoning his shirt and gathered his vest and jacket and stockings, the smallest boy asked, "Were ye in a fight?"

"'Course 'e was," said a dark-haired and dirty-faced boy. "Ye saw the bruises, clear as day."

MacGregor let out a long exhalation and admitted, "I was attacked by a man with a cudgel."

"Ahh!" three of the lads exclaimed with knowing nods. One added, "Robbers."

"Don't matter," said their leader. "He's off home, now." He locked eyes with MacGregor. "Ain't ye?"

"Yes," the Scot hissed, suppressing his anger with difficulty. For a brief second, he wished they were his own children so he could take a switch to them. He instantly dismissed the notion, though, telling himself he would rather die childless than lay claim to such spawn. He stalked to the house and took the stairs two at a time to seek his shoes, peevishly making no effort to be quiet.

The woman stirred and sat up, blinking and rubbing her eyes. "Did you sleep well enough?" she inquired through a yawn as he knelt to look under the bed.

"Where did you put my shoes?" he demanded, and he immediately regretted his rudeness. He closed his eyes and reined his emotions.

Her voice betrayed no hint of offense when Anne answered, "They're downstairs by my desk. Your wallet, suspenders, and watch are there, too, on the desktop."

"Thank you," he said quietly. Only now did he recall, with self-deprecation, having seen his belongings there while searching for a telephone.

The woman's brows shot up when she noted the cling of his clothing. "You're all wet! You can't go like that!"

"I've outstayed my welcome," he replied politely as he rose and headed for the door. Before exiting, he half-turned, bowed his head, and said, "Thank you for your kindness. I'll take my leave."

MacGregor padded downstairs and briskly buttoned on his suspenders before sitting upon a wooden stool to pull on his socks and shoes and tie his laces.

"Where's my kimono?"

He glanced up to see the woman scanning the room in a sleepy haze. She wore nothing but a threadbare undergarment and he could see the outline of her body. He looked away quickly and said, "I wore it to go outside. I've washed it and left it

hanging in the arbour. I'll fetch it for you."

"Oh, I'll get it," she said, walking toward the back door.

"No!" he cried, springing to his feet.

She stopped and stared at him, eyes wide with surprise.

He explained, "You don't want to go out undressed. Your boys are out there."

He slipped past her and into the yard to retrieve the robe, squeezing out as much water as he could before bringing it inside to hand to her.

"Thank you," she said, gazing at the damp garment with some dismay. She shook it out and put it round her shoulders but left it hanging loose.

"Thank you, Mr. MacGregor," she repeated.

He gazed into her upturned face. She did not have the sort of beauty that was currently in fashion, but her quiet loveliness appealed to him. Drawn into the amethyst of her eyes, their true colour revealed by daylight, he felt he could sink into those pellucid pools and float there forever.

A scuffling noise drew him from those purple depths.

MacGregor turned to find the boys standing on the veranda, peering through a window. As he turned back, he felt the eldest lad's gimlet eyes boring into him. In reluctant farewell, he lifted the woman's hand to kiss her knuckles in a courtly gesture.

"It is I who must thank you, Madam," he said quietly. "You saved my life." With a glance to his attire, he smiled wryly and added, "Not to mention my clothing."

To his astonishment, she blushed. What surprised him even more was the pleasant tingle her response aroused in him. He cleared his throat and stepped back, suddenly diffident.

"Oh, my goodness!"

She now noticed his hands, red and blistering. "Come with me," she demanded. She tugged his sleeve and marched him to the well-house, where she filled a white enamelled pan with water.

"Put your hands in this," she instructed as she placed the basin on a wooden slab set into the low south wall of the summer kitchen.

He might have refused, but her manner communicated plainly that she would brook no argument. When he complied, the palliative effect of immersion in the cool water weakened his knees. He leaned against the half-wall to take some measure of support, and he closed his eyes in near bliss.

He breathed in deep, ragged gasps and huffs, recognizing only now how much pain the wash-water had caused him. As he relaxed with the easing of the burn, it occurred to him that he had become habituated to suppressing pain, by one means or another. The futility of the activity that had come to define his life struck him with an impact like a blow to his head.

The woman's gentle voice opened his eyes. "Take this," she said.

He accepted the droplets of remedy that she expelled from a glass tube into his mouth.

Then, she changed the water twice before allowing him to leave. With a final inspection of his hands, she advised, "Wash your hands in cool or tepid water for the next few days. Don't burst the blisters; let them heal of their own accord. And you can expect the skin to peel."

"Yet again, I must thank you," he said. He did not want to leave, but he had no excuse to stay. And from the corner of his eye, he saw the agitated squirming of the eldest of the seven boys.

"Good day," he said abruptly. With a curt nod, he pivoted and strode past the children, along the side of the house, through the gate, and into the street.

He had found his way to King Street by the time he realized he had forgotten his pocketbook and watch.

CHAPTER 3

Family matters

Anne turned aside to yawn. The boys accepted her assurance that the stranger they had found in her yard was merely someone she had rescued last night. They demanded details, of course, and she gave them an abridged version of the relevant events.

The eldest of her students, Jack O'Reilly, eyed her a moment with lips pressed tightly. He seemed to be deciding whether to ask something. In the end, he simply huffed and seated himself on the edge of the porch. At that, the other lads joined him, and all then pulled out from their back pockets the copies of their penny novels.

They always sat side by side like seven birds on a wire, she noted with a smile. They were her little flock.

Jack resided in a crowded house with extended family that included several aunts and uncles, three of his grandparents,

both parents, and almost thirty children of various ages—his siblings and cousins. It was not surprising that his hand-me-down shoes were stuffed with newspaper to cover the holes in their soles and to fill the space his still-growing feet did not, that his trousers hung too short, that his threadbare shirt and pants sported several patches and mismatched buttons, and that his curly red-brown hair had been hurriedly cropped to keep it out of his eyes. Nor was it surprising, given the common attitude toward bathing, that neither his clothes nor his body touched water, much less soap, with any frequency, though she had taught him to wash his hands before meals.

The other boys were no different in appearance or habit. But two lived on the streets, taking shelter in discarded boxes, unlocked sheds, or entry alcoves, depending on weather and degree of police forbearance. The youngest, Geordie, lived in a brothel with his mother. And Terence lived with his widowed mother and six sisters.

"Very good, Geordie," Anne said with a smile when the exceptionally bright redheaded child finished a chapter of *The Unlikely Adventures of Morgan the Pirate*. "Larry?"

Geordie handed his book to his friend, who dutifully began to read aloud the next chapter. In the interests of economy, she had asked each lad to purchase a different book so they could enjoy several stories at the cost of one. Being boys, they had chosen tales of pirates and American outlaws, but she had been amassing a modest personal library of classics by Jane Austen, Jules Verne, the Brontë sisters, Shakespeare, and Chaucer for future use, to round out their reading.

A warm breeze lifted strands of her hair to fly around her face. She brushed them away absently as she paced in the sunlight and listened to the *Unlikely Adventures*. Her kimono, a delicate blue floral print, flowed and flapped as it dried in sun and air. Unlike boys from more prosperous neighbourhoods, these lads took no notice of her scanty apparel, used as they were to seeing sisters, mothers, neighbours, and local whores in

various stages of undress.

Jack's behaviour today, however, signalled a growing interest in her quite out of tune with their relationship as teacher and student. His voice had begun to crack, and his chin had sprouted fine hairs foreshadowing the facial evidence of sexually mature masculinity soon to come. When she caught his surreptitious glance, she casually drew her kimono back from its billowing flare to lap modestly in front. No, she had best not appear in less than full dress from now on.

When the boys came inside to cipher on her chalkboard, she slipped upstairs to don a calico frock.

∞

"WHAT THE DIVIL!" Joseph MacGregor's eyes flew wide at sight of his son. Then, they narrowed.

"Drunk again and whorin', I suppose." That he had slipped into a broader Scots accent than usual was clear indication of his annoyance.

"I was robbed," Michael told his father, hoping to stave off a lecture.

"By the whore or her pimp?"

Hermione MacGregor's dismayed cry came from behind. "What on earth?"

Michael turned to find his mother and sister standing in the doorway of the parlour. Both gaped.

"He was robbed," the elder MacGregor replied quickly, with a piercing glance toward his son.

Immaculately arrayed, as always, Elizabeth eyed her brother's wrinkled raiment and said, "That does not explain what happened to your clothes. Did you fall into the lake?"

"Something like that," Michael replied evasively.

His mother slowly shook her head as she surveyed his disreputable attire. She heaved a sigh. The plump little woman, her winsome face softly lined with her years and haloed by a

loose upsweep of her grey hair, looked up into her son's eyes and said judiciously, "See if Ford can do something with your suit, dear."

He leaned to kiss her cheek. "Yes, Mother."

With a chastened glance toward his father, Michael left his family and ran up the stairs to his room. He stripped hurriedly and piled his clothing on a chair for the valet's care. When he opened his armoire to take a clean set of drawers and an undershirt, he spotted his bruises, reflected in the mirror inside the door. Only then did it occur to him that no one had asked if he had been injured. He suddenly wondered if they cared.

He shook his head to dispel the uncomfortable notion and went to the bathing room to wash off the dust of the day's walk and subsequent open-carriage hackney ride.

Wrapped in his blue silk robe, he stood at the window to gaze out to the sprawling gardens and orchard of his family's estate as his valet and one of the footmen filled the bathing tub with water. He surveyed the formal knot garden toward the side; the kitchen and herb garden off the rear door; the beds of everlastings his mother tended personally; the roses; and the orchard of apples, pears, plums, and cherries edged by espaliered grapes and set off by an evergreen hedge. With regret, he realized he had always taken for granted the fecundity around him. Gardeners kept the lawns cropped and weeded the many beds, while arboriculturists tended the orchard and the trees along the drive from the road. His father also employed groundskeepers to manage the acres of native forest that edged the rear of the property. Joseph MacGregor liked to wander the wood, at times. Said it reminded him of the Old Country. But Michael thought that even his father paid little heed to the beauty of his lands.

On the other hand, the strange woman from The Flats clearly cared for her own yard and house with love and appreciation. During his walk toward home, he had noted that

her neighbours also treasured their small homes and properties, rentals though they might be. He reflected that, for all his family and their wealthy friends and acquaintances spent fortunes to keep up appearances, they did not truly value the richness they possessed.

He heard the door close. Turning back to his bath, Michael regarded the room's striped blue silk wallcoverings edged by braid above the polished oak wainscot; the gleaming silver candle sconces and white tapers; the Persian carpet that covered most of the waxed oak flooring; the mahogany table and blue plush récamier; the bank of chiffoniers and closets that held his suits and shirts, cloaks and shoes, and the various expensive sundries of his lavish wardrobe. To his mind's eye he recalled the whitewashed walls of the woman's bedroom, decorated only with pale, stencilled vines and leaves and flowers above the dado; the plain divan on which she slept, and the quaint quilts by which it was covered; the small bedside tables with wooden candlesticks; the pine armoire and pine-framed standing mirror; the old wooden chair; the hooks on the wall and door that held some of her clothing. Never before had he perceived the dignity of simplicity. He suddenly felt ashamed of the opulence around him.

How often had he seen poverty, even destitution, in his travels? He had felt sorry for those without means, and he had occasionally given money to a beggar or food to a waif. How pitiful those token efforts now seemed, meant more to assuage the conscience of one with too much than to truly help anyone. He sighed at the realization there was, in fact, little else he could have done in the circumstances, for the ways of the world made poverty and oppression inevitable. Even a rich man, alone, could not feed and house and clothe the teeming masses.

He shook his head as if to erase the subject from his mind and he pulled off his robe to toss it onto the récamier.

∞

LYING AGAINST the high back of the porcelain bathtub, Michael MacGregor closed his eyes to enjoy the heat of the water penetrating his aching muscles and the scent of the steaming liquid infused with the herbal salts that he had purchased during his last visit to Montreal. His knees stuck out of the water, of course, he being far too big for even the largest available cleansing vessel, and he rested his blistered hands upon the curled upper edges. But most of him was immersed. He rubbed his shoulder.

As he settled to soak and to inhale the restorative vapours with their balsam scent, the image of the white-haired woman in her shift drifted into his mind once more. Behind his eyelids, he could see the shape of her breasts...her buttocks...the small round of her belly...the hint of fur between her legs....

His eyes opened wide and he looked down. To his astonishment, his body had responded to the memory.

He leaned back, closing his eyes again, and pictured her vividly. This time, he stroked himself.

∞

ANNE WAITED in the foyer of the mansion as the butler went in search of Michael MacGregor. The house was every bit as fine as she had guessed it would be: Black marble bordered the gleaming black-and-white speckled terrazzo floor of the vestibule. Fine, snowy gypsum plaster coated the walls and ceiling embossed with bas-relief squares and diamonds that decorated the cornice and defined the medallion that set off the base of the enormous crystal chandelier. On the walls, silver girandole sconces held beeswax candles that, even unlit, imparted a faint honeyed scent to the house, and gilt-framed paintings displayed images of bucolic tranquility. A bench sat by the front door, its padded seat covered in dusky blue velvet and its graceful polished-oak legs shining in the light from the leaded-glass windows flanking the entry. Opposite the door and

curving majestically, a grand staircase climbed to the upper floor.

Anne had been examining one of the paintings closely when an inner door opened and a diminutive man emerged from one of the rear rooms. He looked her up and down with a coolly appraising eye as he approached.

"Can I help you?" he inquired in a tone that suggested he did not think so.

"Thank you, no," she answered with a smile. "A gentleman—the butler, I suppose—has gone to find Mr. MacGregor for me."

The portly grey-haired gentleman with sharp pale-blue eyes and conservative dark-grey suit of high-quality wool cocked a bushy eyebrow and said, "I am Joseph MacGregor."

Anne curtsied and replied, "I am pleased to meet you, sir. But it is Mr. Michael MacGregor I seek."

From the staircase, a resonant baritone declared, "And you have found him."

Anne turned to see her erstwhile houseguest descend wearing a clean and pressed grey suit and a warm smile. As he came toward her, arms outstretched to take her hand, the butler who had accompanied him strode to stand by the door.

With a faintly censorious edge in his tone, Joseph MacGregor asked his son, "Do you know this woman?"

Michael's voice betrayed no emotion as he politely introduced her. "Mrs. MacGregor, may I present my father. Father, this is the lady who saved my life and mended my arm."

That took Joseph MacGregor aback.

Anne raised her eyebrows disapprovingly at Michael to say, "Though I note that you have failed to take my advice and keep your arm in a sling for a few days."

Michael put a hand to his chest and bowed contritely. "Indeed, I had forgotten. I shall remedy the situation straight away."

"Speaking of remedies...."

Anne reached into the leather pouch suspended from her

belt and retrieved a small dropper bottle. She uncapped it and instructed, "Sit down, please."

To Joseph MacGregor's wide-eyed shock, his son obediently sat on the bench by the entry door. As Anne approached, Michael opened his mouth to allow her to squirt two drops of liquid under his tongue.

Collecting himself, the elder MacGregor stepped forward and said brusquely, "I am sure we are grateful for your help, Mrs. MacGregor. But I am afraid we must prepare for this evening. We are expecting guests." At his nod, the butler opened the door.

"Of course," said Anne.

But rather than leave immediately, she replaced the bottle into her purse and reached into her side pockets. "I actually came only to deliver these." She produced the watch and pocketbook that had been left on her desk.

"Thank you," Michael said gratefully as he rose and took back his belongings. He protested, "But you should not have walked all this way just to return these. I could have come for them."

"It was no trouble," she assured him. "A friend of mine drove me in his hackney cab. But now I really must go. My employer will be expecting me."

Michael rushed to offer, "If your friend has already left, perhaps I can drive you to your destination?"

Joseph MacGregor opened his mouth to object, but Anne's reply cut him off. She said, "That won't be necessary, but I thank you for offering."

∞

SHE CURTSIED to him and to his father, an antiquated gesture that brought a charmed smile to Michael's lips, and she turned on her heel to march out the open door, head high. He chuckled softly as he watched her descend to the waiting hackney with the

air of a queen about to embark on a journey through her realm.

Once the butler had closed the door behind her, Joseph MacGregor said in an uncomplimentary manner, "What an extraordinary woman!" He remembered his son's earlier statement and asked incredulously, "You say she saved your life?"

"Yes, she did," Michael replied as he turned to the MacGregor patriarch. "And she tended my injuries. And after what I do not doubt was a long day's toil, she cleaned the filth out of my clothes. Now, she has come far out of her way to return the belongings I had left behind out of forgetfulness."

He glared at his father and demanded, "So what exactly is it about so kind a woman that you do not approve?"

Joseph MacGregor worked his mouth a moment, returning his son's scowl. At last he spat, "She looks like a whore!"

Michael took several breaths, remembering the Spartan little house, the threadbare shift, and the manner of their meeting, before he said quietly through clenched teeth, "She is poor, Father. That does not necessarily make her a whore."

Still glowering into his father's eyes, Michael MacGregor commanded, "Harris! Get me a sling, if you please. My arm needs to be kept bound while it heals."

Without another word, he returned to his room.

∞

ANNE'S HEART LIFTED and lightened her step as she walked into the garment factory. He had been glad to see her. She knew it.

She allowed herself a tiny glimmer of hope.

∞

WHEN HE CAME down to dinner, Michael MacGregor sported a sling over his black dinner jacket. The valet, Ford, had fussed

about, pulling the ends of his employer's white silk tie out from under the sling and generally trying to make a silk purse out of the enormous, white-cotton sow's ear.

"There's naught more I can do, My Lord," Ford had said dejectedly.

Michael had let the "My Lord" go by. It was always a measure of the man's agitation that he fell back on the term he had used so many years to address his former master, the late Earl of Something-or-other. The valet was fastidious to a fault, and the younger MacGregor's habits frequently gave the man heartburn.

"It'll do," Michael had told the servant kindly. "It's my fault I got injured, not yours."

The valet's grunt had indicated his certainty that his employer's appearance was his responsibility alone, even when said employer did stupid things such as falling off a horse or getting attacked in a back alley. After all, he was a valet; it was his job to make the gentleman look presentable.

Leaving behind Ford's dismay, Michael had hastened downstairs. Now, he entered the drawing-room to face the censure of his family.

"Oh, Michael, do you *have* to wear that dreadful thing?" Elizabeth wailed, clearly presuming he did not.

"It's only for a few days," he told her, trying to restrain the choler his sister invariably aroused in him. "To let my shoulder heal."

Elizabeth pouted and said petulantly, "I do believe you do these things just to embarrass me!"

"Oh, yes," he said drily, "I got myself bludgeoned and nearly killed just to make your life a misery."

Before his sister could snap an indignant reply, Harris announced the arrival of the first guests.

∞

"GOOD HEAVENS!" Miss Jaclyn Orwell exclaimed in wide-eyed horror at his explanation for the sling. "How perfectly terrible! My goodness, it's not safe in the streets anymore!"

Seated across the dining table that had been formally draped in heavy white linen and white crewel lace, the daughter of Reginald Orwell placed a delicate hand to her chest in token of distress. *And,* Michael thought, *to draw attention to her bosom.* He had seen this bit of theatre before: the batting of the eyelashes, the coquettish little smile, the hand to chest, the fan placed to draw the eye to a handsome feature or waved to flutter a curl of hair.

He forced a smile as he wished his parents would stop foisting heiresses upon him. He reached for his crystal goblet filled with rich red wine, but stopped, his fingertips barely contacting the smooth pentagonal stem that rose to curving calyces below the gracefully rounded bowl of the glass. After a moment of inner struggle, he pulled his hand back and picked up his stylishly embossed sterling silver fork, instead, and scooped up a mouthful of whipped potato.

The conversation turned from crime in the streets to a new showing at the art gallery. While participating in the discussion, Joseph MacGregor furtively watched his son's actions and expressions. Michael felt his father's scrutiny and glanced toward the head of the table. Quickly looking away once more to avoid those expectant, demanding, disapproving eyes, he reached again for the wine, and again he hesitated. He closed his eyes and swallowed.

His mouth had gone dry but his belly felt fluid. He set down his utensil and stared at his plate, no longer hungry. He wanted a drink. He wanted to drown himself in alcohol.

And yet....

He regarded Miss Orwell out of the corner of his eye, taking care not to draw her attention to him. She was prettier than most of the women (girls, really, for the most part) that his parents had presented for his consideration. She had a smoothly

oval face, sparkling brown eyes, and shiny golden hair. The shape suggested under her gown was certainly feminine.

But she did not appeal to him. Just as her predecessors had not appealed to him. And the whores had not appealed to him. Not one.

He remembered the molly the previous night. And he remembered another night, in another town, another man....

He stared at the glass of wine before him: waiting, ready, its ruby gleam promising oblivion. He wanted to take it and toss it back and follow it with a decanter of brandy and a bottle of whisky.

And yet....

He saw in his mind's eye an image of the glass upturned and become old-fashioned, gathered skirts spread over a woman's form, the gown ballooning from her waist. And when he looked up from that imagined waist to the face above, he glimpsed a glory of white hair framing kind violet eyes and a warm smile. His mind drifted to the woman in her shift, sunlight behind her, her body a shadow beneath the thin cambric.

Suddenly, he realized his own body now revealed his thoughts. He hoped he could stifle his response before it became necessary to stand.

CHAPTER 4

Comedy...

Mother and Father were pleased. Despite his best efforts to discourage her, and with substantial aid from his father, Miss Orwell had backed Michael into a corner and arranged for him to escort her to the regatta in two days' time.

Elizabeth was downright ecstatic: Kenneth Armstrong had proposed to her sometime between the dessert course and the coffee. How the lawyer had managed that, Michael did not know, but his sister now floated on air and even kissed her brother in greeting as he entered the morning room for breakfast. She had not found romance particularly agreeable, but perhaps marriage would better suit her, Michael thought. Though he had his doubts about her intended, he decided that he honestly wished his sister well as he stepped to the buffet to fill a plate.

Seating himself in his usual chair at the round, linen-

draped table, Joseph MacGregor announced, "Michael, I'd like ye to come with me to the distillery at week's end."

Michael blinked at his father in surprise. He asked, "Why?" Though there had always been a tacit understanding that he would join the firm someday, the elder MacGregor had never before asked him to take part in the business.

"It's time ye learned how things are done, my boy."

My boy. His father had not called him that since he had gone off to university and come back a drunk. And he had not called his father "Da" in even longer.

"If you wish," Michael replied uncertainly as he set his plate and cup upon the table and took a seat. He abstractedly gulped his tea and found himself choking on the scalding liquid. Coughing and sputtering, eyes watering, he leapt up, ran to the oak sideboard, and drank directly from the silver ewer of water Harris always placed there.

Elizabeth giggled. "Oh, Michael! You are so funny!"

"Are you all right dear?" his mother asked.

Michael looked from his mother to his sister to his father to Harris, whose usual air of disapproval had been replaced by stolid forbearance. The small sunny chamber with lace-lined bow windows and cheery floral wallpaper, sparkling with the rose-painted crockery and silver tea service used for private family meals, seemed suddenly surreal.

"Fine," Michael said at last.

He sat down to his breakfast, completely baffled. By the time he finished the scones and jam, eggs and ham that he had chosen from the buffet, he had concluded that either his family was under some spell, or the prospect of finally marrying Elizabeth off had lifted a great weight that had long oppressed the household.

∞

HIS HANDS FELT stiff, the skin too tight, and gripping the reins

reminded him of his exposure to scalding wash-water the day before. Smiling sheepishly, he had to admit to himself that he had not improved the situation by immersing his hand in the steaming bathwater, later, as he indulged his fantasy.

No, he could not take his horse. Leaving the stallion to the groom, Michael went in search of the coachman.

He had intended to go to the Yacht Club to speak to his best friend Evan about the regatta. Or rather, about Jaclyn Orwell. Instead, on impulse, he called to the driver, "Take me to The Flats."

The coachman turned on his bench to stare at his employer's son incredulously. "Sir?" He obviously believed he had misheard the instruction.

"The Flats," Michael repeated.

The man twitched his eyebrows and muttered something under his breath as he turned back to drive into one of the poorest districts in town, this one beyond the madhouse.

∞

WHEN THE LITTLE clapboard house set off by a whitewashed picket fence came into view, Michael called, "Here! Stop here!"

The driver reined his horses to a halt and made to wait at the roadside. But his passenger gave him a five-dollar note and bade him return to Rosemont.

"I'll be fine," Michael assured him when the man protested. "I know my way home."

The coachman grimaced in consternation. Then, he shrugged both shoulders and eyebrows with an expression that conveyed, *If the gentleman wants to risk himself in such a place, who am I to argue?* His backward glance as he drove away said with equal clarity, *I'll be reading about him in the morning papers.*

Michael chuckled as he watched after the receding vehicle. George Combie, like the other members of the MacGregor household, considered all but the more affluent parts

of town to be dangerous slums best avoided. The coachman made no demur when his employer's son asked to be taken to Madame Maxine's establishment, or to any of the hotels and taverns he frequented, even though Michael often found, on the morning after, that a hackney driver had taken advantage of his drunken state to give himself a very large tip from his customer's pocketbook after depositing him in front of his home in Rosemont. Moreover, the younger MacGregor had occasionally been accosted and robbed in the "better" neighbourhoods. Nonetheless, the prejudice against poor districts persisted even among the serving staff.

When the carriage disappeared beyond a bend, Michael turned to the house. Inhaling deeply, he straightened his grey suit jacket as best he could and tugged at his sling. With another determined breath, he pushed the gate open and strode to the front door. There, he wavered, fist up to knock but unmoving.

Doubts raced through his mind: *Perhaps she is merely kind and has no interest...Perhaps she is married; she did call herself "Mrs."...Perhaps she thinks me too young for her...Perhaps —*

A cough came from behind. He turned to find an old woman in an embroidered drawstring blouse and patched skirt peering at him from the other side of the fence. The knobbed knuckles of one hand encircled the ball of a black stick that tapered to its point at her bare feet, while the bony fingers of the other hand scratched at her hip. The freshening wind whipped strands of grey hair away from her face, and she stared through jet eyes in a heavily creased countenance. Her jaws champed in a chewing motion.

"Lookin' for Herself, air ye?"

"Uh, I'm looking for Mrs. MacGregor," he replied, not sure if his erstwhile saviour and "Herself" were one and the same.

"She's at the crick," said the old woman.

She stopped scratching long enough to point in the direction of the specified watercourse, and the Scot assumed she

referred to the Bow, which meandered by this and three other neighbourhoods. His coach had crossed it on the way here.

Now absently swatting at a fly, the beldame added, "Wi' the younguns."

"With her children?" he asked with brows raised, not sure he wanted to know the boys he had seen belonged to Anne.

"Ain't hers," the woman stated, and she spat on the ground.

To his relief, the Scot saw that the old woman had not actually been gnawing food or tobacco. He averted his gaze from the splotch of spittle that glistened on the grass.

Wanting to be clear, he asked, "Not hers? The lads are not her children?"

The hag shook her head. "Ain't got none o' her own." She grinned: a wide, nearly toothless smile under sharp eyes. "Ain't got no man, neither. You lookin' to set that to rights?"

She appraised him, up and down, an action that made him feel completely naked. He swallowed and stammered, "Th- thank you. I'll...I'll just go."

"Go that way. Take the path," the old woman directed, pointing again toward the "crick." A low rumble gurgled up from her belly as she turned and sauntered away, leaning on her stick with each step.

Michael hastily glanced down toward his flies to see if they were open, or worse, if his desire had manifested physically. He let out a long, tremulous exhalation when he realized he had not disgraced himself. Then, he stood staring after the old crone. Her deep chortle had ripened to a high-pitched cackle by the time she stepped into a weather-greyed wooden house across the lane and two doors over.

Discomposed, the Scot went in search of the white-haired woman, wondering how it was that her elderly neighbour seemed to know exactly what he was thinking. And why she called Mrs. MacGregor "Herself."

And what the devil was "Herself" doing anywhere near

Bow Creek, a malodorous open sewer pouring into the lake?

∞

THE INDICATED direction brought him to a well-worn footpath between a pair of log houses blackened with age. The narrow passage took him past rustic sheds and outhouses; thatch-roofed chicken coops and dovecotes; several intersecting lanes and more homes; a stack-walled barn; and a broad three-sided pole building with shake roof that appeared to combine the functions of smithy, bedchamber, stable, and storage shed. Just beyond, a small patch of meadow bordered an open forest.

Paper birches, their white skins curling in strips, and grey-barked speckled alder bushes edged the wood, giving way to taller elms, ashes, aspens, poplars, and the odd evergreen cedar that shaded an understory of white-flowered dogwood; shrubs of currant and wild raspberry; feathery ferns; and in glades that afforded more light, a few stunted crabapples dotted with pink blooms.

The shrill rasp of cicadas rose above his footfalls, and the poplars and aspens rustled with the breeze. He dodged to avoid the spreading, spiny leaves of a thistle beside the path, a monstrous thing almost as tall as he. Ahead, the voices of children mingled with the burble of the stream.

When he emerged from the wood, Michael found the white-haired woman standing in the middle of the rivulet, her skirts hiked up but their hems dragging in the water, nonetheless. Around her, the lads he had encountered in her yard frolicked alongside several more boys and a few girls. High-pitched squeals erupted when two of the younger boys began to splash the three smallest girls near the shore.

"Oy!"

The possessive lad from the day before had noticed him. And was not happy to see him. The woman, on the other hand, smiled with pleasure when she spotted the visitor. She waded

toward shore, to the evident dismay of the lad.

His heart now racing, Michael stepped into the sunlight beyond the fringe of willows. Suddenly, his foot slid on something slick and shot out from under him into the air. He landed hard, on butt and back, with a thud and with breath forcibly expelled in a bass grunt. The children shrieked and chortled in hilarity, the eldest boy's guffaws especially loud and derisive. Michael pushed himself up, angry and humiliated, and with a fleeting rue at the knowledge that Mr. Ford would be most displeased upon seeing the grass stains his trousers and jacket had surely acquired.

"Oh, my goodness, are you all right?"

Anne MacGregor knelt beside him and looked into his face, her own anxious. Michael MacGregor melted, her gaze instantly dissolving all of his embarrassment. He thought he could bask in the warmth of her glow all his days.

A nearby shuffle broke the spell. The children had come forward, gathering close and gawking curiously.

"Whozat?" asked a little girl in loose green dress and once-white apron. Her unbound brown curls floated in her eyes and cascaded over her shoulders.

"Children, this is Mr. MacGregor," their caregiver announced. She stood and offered a hand to help him up.

In an attempt to recover some dignity, he chose to forgo the aid and got his feet under him despite the constraint of the sling. The eyes of the smaller children rounded with awe and their necks craned upward as he rose to tower above them.

One of the little ones asked, "Is he your bruver?"

"No, dear," Anne replied. "He just happens to have the same last name."

"Oh," the dark-haired little boy responded as he looked the newcomer up and down, simultaneously boring a small forefinger into his nostril. He removed the digit from his nose and opened his mouth, but stopped, finger poised, and closed his mouth once more. Grimacing, he eyed the little greenish lump on

the end of his nail, glanced up to Anne, and then rubbed the finger on his trousers, instead.

"I was told I'd find you here," Michael said to Anne as he tore his appalled gaze from the little nose-picker. "May I ask what you're doing?"

"Finding rocks," a boy in grey wool trousers patched at both knees promptly replied.

"What kind of rocks?" Michael asked.

"River stones," said another child, similarly vague.

The woman smiled and explained, "We look for anything interesting: jasper, quartz, gold."

"Gold?" the Scot exclaimed, and his eyebrows jumped toward his hairline.

"You never know what will wash into the creek," Anne said with a mischievous wink and a shrug.

Michael scanned the small stream. To his surprise, the waters here flowed clear and smelled fresh. He guessed it must be a tributary, rather than the Bow. He asked, "May I join you?"

Before the eldest lad could object, Anne said, "Of course." She gestured toward the rivulet and then strolled ahead as the youngest children raced back to the centre of the stream.

Though his friends happily returned to their pastime, the jealous adolescent lingered to glower at the Scot when Michael MacGregor removed his sling and coat and sat on a squat wooden chair, one of three mismatched seats placed near the bank. Michael pulled off his shoes and socks and rolled up is trousers, pointedly ignoring his pubescent rival as he prepared to join this peculiar group in hope of acquainting himself with and perhaps ingratiating himself to the intriguing woman who had aroused feelings of which he had thought himself incapable.

CHAPTER 5

...and tragedy

The adults and children waded along the creek, peering into its pellucid waters in a desultory quest for any treasures that might be hidden among the cobbles and under the silts of the streambed. The little ones frequently plucked coloured stones and brought them for inspection, bearing each one in cupped palms as though it were a rare diamond. Anne always smiled and scrutinized the pebbles, identifying the mineral composition and ascribing some mystical quality to the material or the shape. The pleased youngsters pocketed their prizes and went in search of more.

The older children had learned to be more selective. They squatted to sift soil and stones through their fingers, occasionally studying a pebble closely or holding it to the light.

"I have to admit I am surprised," Michael told Anne. "I have seen Bow Creek where it flows into the lake. It's...hellish."

Anne confirmed his earlier supposition: "This is actually a tributary, one of the headwaters of the Bow. Its official name is the very unimaginative 'Short Creek,' but everyone here calls it the 'Sweetwater' because it's pristine along its whole length.

"Unfortunately, the Bow is another matter. People don't appear to know enough not to dump sewage and industrial wastes into the waters they will be drinking."

Michael conceded, "You're right. It makes no sense, but people do it anyway. And now, our tax money will be wasted trying to reclaim the lakeshore that should never have been allowed to become so filthy in the first place."

Two of the tots approached, both wanting Anne's attention. Michael observed in admiration as she fussed and praised and taught bits of geology and philosophy in the guise of play.

And he wriggled his toes, revelling in the sensation of the sand squishing between them. It made him feel a child, again, himself. He breathed with delight the warm summer air, and he basked in the midday sunshine, smiling to himself regretfully at the realization how long it had been since he had last partaken of such simple pleasures. Sophistication was a poor substitute, he decided.

Larry, a dark-haired ten-year-old, brought a rock to him, and Michael picked it up in his free hand. He turned it this way and that, enjoying the cool smoothness in his palm and noting the yellow-grey colour and the dull lustre under the sheen of moisture. He said, "This is limestone."

"Limestone," Larry repeated. He looked at Michael and asked, "What's it good fer?"

In a lecturing tone, as though he were back in school enlightening a first-year, Michael enumerated the possible uses: "Constructing foundations and buildings, laying road base and cobbles, making quicklime, purifying iron in a blast furnace. Artists sculpt it or make white pigment out of it. The softer type is what we call chalk. And sometimes limestone has jasper or

flint in it, as well.

"This," he said as he handed it to the boy, "would make good road or garden gravel."

Larry nodded, committing the information to memory. He bent to put the rock back, but changed his mind and stuffed it into his pocket.

A sharp crack startled flocks of starlings, jays, and crows from the nearby trees.

"What the devil!" Michael exclaimed as all glanced about in puzzlement. "Get down!" he shouted as he dived into the water. "Everybody down!"

Another crack rang out, and another, as Anne and the children followed his example. All but one.

"Geordie!" Anne cried when she saw the boy still standing, facing the wood, agape and eyes wide in astonishment. "Geordie!"

She scrambled up and ran to him as the little redhead began to collapse in slow motion. She caught him in her arms and held him. Then, she screamed in horror. And screamed again in anguish.

Now beside her, Michael murmured, "Jesus!" He saw the red stain spreading on the child's shirt and the lifeless eyes that had frozen in an expression of bewildered surprise. "Jesus!"

Snorting in rage, he whirled, ripped off his sling, and ran in the direction of gunshots that repeated twice more.

∞

ANNE HELD the small body in her arms and rocked, sobbing. The other children gathered around her, weeping in fright and grief.

"What'll we tell his mam?" Jack asked, his voice cracking plaintively.

Anne could not answer.

A raven cawed harshly. The cicadas took up their tuneless

song. Wind whispered in the trees. The creek rippled calmly on. And the soul of a child vanished from the world.

∞

MICHAEL MacGREGOR ran as a man possessed, heedless of rocks and rubbish beneath his bare feet. He crashed through the undergrowth and exploded into the meadow beyond the riparian strip of forest, racing past a row of straw-filled targets. At a distance, a large gaggle of men milled blithely. He could hear their banter and laughter, and he could see the rifles that they brandished insouciantly.

One of them noticed him and waved. Momentarily, the whole group turned to gawp as he hurtled toward them. When he came close enough to see their faces, he recognized almost all. And he saw their surprise turn to alarm at his expression.

"You bastards!" he shouted as he careered into their midst and ripped rifles from the hands of the two nearest, slamming the weapons to the ground with enough force to break the stocks and ignoring the jolt of pain in his shoulder. Two men dropped their guns in startlement and backed away in fear. A fifth, holding his weapon loosely at his side, demanded, "What the hell do you think you're doing, MacGregor?"

"You murdered a child, you stupid bastards!"

The men froze.

"Oh, God!" someone murmured.

Slinging his rifle over his shoulder, George Bates demanded in a tone of negation, "What are you talking about?"

"There are children by the creek and you killed one of them! Have you not the sense to pay attention to where you shoot, you stupid bastards?" He glared at Bates who, as a weapons dealer, should have known better.

The one he did not know declared dismissively, "Impossible. They don't have such range."

Michael snarled, "Perhaps you'd like to come and explain

that to the child's mother before she buries her son."

"Oh, God! Oh, God!" the moaner repeated.

Bates wiped a hand over his mouth and muttered uncertainly, "Christ!"

Michael whirled and stalked back toward the creek. Behind him, the unfamiliar man called, "You'll pay for these."

Michael did not turn or break stride as he shouted, "Fuck you!"

∞

WHEN HE RETURNED to Sweetwater Creek, the Scot found Anne still sitting in the stream, holding the child and dazedly rocking to and fro. The other children stood helplessly about her, weeping. He waded to them and caught a whiff of voided bowel as he approached: the smell of death. Gently, he lifted Anne, grasping her shoulders and propelling her toward the bank.

"Where is his home?" he asked quietly.

The eldest boy, the one Anne had called Jack, answered, "The cathouse on Poplar. His mam works there."

Michael requested, "Would you lead the way, please, Jack?"

Jack drew himself up, nodded manfully, and picked up the little girl in green. Following his example, Larry and Ian scooped up two more of the small ones while Terence, Kevin, and Rob each took the hand of another two youngsters. Then, the mournful band proceeded to Poplar Lane.

∞

THE FACES of the brothel denizens dropped when Anne entered with the small red-haired bundle in her arms, guided by a tall, grim stranger and followed by more than a dozen children. All were soaked, and Anne's and the children's cheeks were stained with tears.

The madam swallowed visibly and then collected herself

to snap her fingers at one of her girls in a wordless command. The other women disappeared beyond doorways and up stairs as their employer ushered the sad little procession into the bordello's parlour.

Michael guided Anne to the chintz-covered settee. Then, he turned to Jack and suggested quietly, "Perhaps you'd better take the children home. I must tell Geordie's mother what happened, but there's no need for the rest of you to stay."

Jack looked at Anne, still swaying and tears still streaming down her cheeks.

"I'll see Mrs. MacGregor gets home," Michael assured him.

"Somebody should stay with her," said Jack uncertainly, torn between the needs of his teacher and those of his young charges. His tight-lipped glance to Michael silently but emphatically qualified, *Somebody else.*

Michael drew a deep breath and let it out slowly. More than anything in the world, he wanted to spend the night with this woman. But now was not the time. He said, "There's an old lady near her house who may be persuaded to take care of Mrs. MacGregor. The one with the black cane."

Jack stared at him, assessing. Finally, he nodded acceptance of the plan and herded his playmates out the door.

∞

SEVERAL MINUTES after the departure of the children, a disgruntled salt-and-pepper-haired longshoreman in nankeens stamped down the steps from the upper floor, swearing as only dockworkers swear and pulling on his brown shirt. He stopped dead at sight of the child cradled in Anne's arms and the grief on her face. Subdued, he crossed himself, swallowed, and exited without another word.

Several more minutes passed before a redheaded woman came down the stairs wearing a hastily donned dress and a

baffled expression, accompanied by the whore who had been sent to fetch her. On seeing her child, the mother emitted a wail that started low and rose in both pitch and volume. She ran to the boy and took him from Anne's arms.

Instantly, Anne came out of her stupor. She embraced the howling mother and held her tightly as they rocked together. Then, she sent the elder (and, by appearances, more intelligent) of the brothel's two bouncers for the undertaker and asked the madam to bring the police.

Now fully dressed, the ladies of the house began to drift into the parlour. One stood next to the redhead, opposite Anne, to console the sobbing mother. The rest sat in silence, weeping.

Standing just outside the broad opening to the lounge, Michael MacGregor watched the women as they mourned for the little boy. All of these whores cried as an aunt or sister would cry for the loss of a beloved child. He had seen so many prostitutes, yet never before had he recognized them as people, as ordinary women, perhaps even as ladies much like his own mother and sister. And suddenly he felt ashamed that he had ever dismissed such women as mere trash.

∞

THE UNDERTAKER arrived first. After a quick appraisal of the situation, he knelt before the redhead, Mrs. Monaghan, and promised to provide her child the very best care. When he rose, he nodded to the big Scot, his expression conveying his uncertainty as to how the stranger fit into the scheme of things as well as startlement at the blisters on the large hands. Then, the mortician stepped to the door just as a policeman entered with anxious expression.

"Constable O'Toole," the grizzled undertaker greeted the newcomer.

"Mr. Jessop," the officer acknowledged unhappily. "A sad day, sir."

"That it is," the elder man replied softly.

Wearing the dark-blue uniform and helmet of the city's constabulary (the high-necked wool jacket leather-belted at the waist and secured with closely spaced metal buttons; the hard, domed hat bearing a large silver badge and a black chin strap), the young man pulled a pad and pencil from his pocket to record details of the incident. His hands trembled noticeably, and Michael frowned, wondering why. Dismissing the matter as probably attributable to inexperience, the Scot strode the two paces to the entry to introduce himself, "I am Michael MacGregor."

He reached for his calling cards and belatedly remembered he had left his coat, and his pocketbook and shoes, by the creek. After cursing under his breath, he said quietly, "Mrs. MacGregor and I both witnessed the...the accident."

Constable O'Toole leaned closer to whisper, "Miss Hetty says he was shot."

"Yes," both Michael and the undertaker replied.

The constable looked from one to the other and glanced toward the child in the mother's arms. He murmured, "I've sent for Detective Morgan. He may want an autopsy performed."

Michael informed the policeman, "There were over a dozen men with rifles in Mercer's Field, very likely trying them with intent to purchase. I can give you most of their names but I do not know which weapon fired the bullet that killed the boy."

"Mercer's Field," said the Constable, tapping the top of the pencil against his chin thoughtfully. He looked at Michael and asked, "Gentlemen, would you say?"

Michael nodded. "To a man."

The constable grimaced and sighed. He said, "I'd best go speak to the detective."

After the policeman left and closed the white-painted door soundlessly behind, Mr. Jessop mumbled, "So there may not be an autopsy after all."

Michael regarded him sharply, but realized at once that

the undertaker was probably right. Rarely was a wealthy man taken to task even for outright crime, much less for an accident, no matter how tragic the consequences. And the police were not likely to expend resources to discover the identity of the man whose careless stupidity had resulted in the death of a prostitute's child.

Not wishing to intrude upon the ladies' grief, the two men waited discreetly in the entry. Michael gazed from the threadbare carpet that lay before the door, to the worn wooden treads of the narrow staircase, to the faded wallpaper with its floral design. Cheap paintings hung along the hallway, on the walls of the parlour, and above the fireplace; a mishmash of inexpensive cotton prints upholstered the chairs; tawdry knick-knacks dotted the mantel and side tables: This place was a far cry from the luxurious and tasteful style of Madame Maxine's. Yet, strangely, the Scot felt more comfortable here than he had ever felt in the more elegant establishment—notwithstanding the current circumstances.

The madam had gone to the kitchen and now returned bearing tea on a brass salver. With a lift of her chin, she gestured to a wooden box-bench beside the door, and she handed cup and saucer to the Scot and to the undertaker as they sat. Without offering cream or sugar, she turned to bring the tray into the parlour.

Michael set the steaming drink on his knee and leaned against the wall. Through half-closed eyes, he observed the scene in the next room, wondering what might have become of the little red-haired boy had he lived to manhood. The Scot had known the child only a few hours, but considered him bright and good-hearted. The lad's circumstances, of course, as the son of a whore and growing up in poverty, would have limited his prospects. But some had overcome similar impediments to become men of prominence. This child would never have that chance.

He took a sip of the tea to distract himself from an

unbidden and uncomfortable evaluation of what he had done with his own potential.

"Mercer's Field," the undertaker muttered.

Michael looked to the man, and he suddenly wondered the same thing: "How could a bullet have travelled across the field and through the wood to kill the boy?"

"How far would you say those men were standing?"

"Too far," Michael recalled. "Unless...."

"Unless what?" came a feminine voice.

He glanced up at Anne in surprise; he had not heard her approach. Turning his attention to the question, he shook his head in perplexity. "I don't know," he said, not wishing to express the notion that had occurred to him. "I suppose it might be possible for a bullet to travel that far, with enough propellant. And the rifles looked like a new design."

"But you'd think it would have struck a tree, even so," Mr. Jessop remarked. "That patch of woodland is not wide, but it's dense."

Anne closed her eyes a long moment. When she opened them, she said in a low, doleful voice, "Miracles can happen. For better...and for worse."

∞

AS LUCK WOULD have it, Detective Morgan was not a man who deemed the social elite sacrosanct. The dark-haired and dark-eyed policeman in brown suit with matching vest listened solemnly to the witnesses. From a respectful distance, he studied the small lifeless form cradled in the arms of its mother as the redhead rocked with dull eyes and tear-stained cheeks. Afterward, he returned to Michael to ask for the names of the men in Mercer's Field, and he ordered an autopsy. When Mrs. Monaghan roused from her stupor and jibbed at the idea, he assured her that the coroner should be able to verify the cause of death and extract the bullet with minimal intrusion upon her

son's body. He further gave the young widow his word that the procedure was necessary in order to find the culprit and bring him to justice.

The distraught woman mulled his statement several minutes. At last, she nodded assent and allowed little Geordie's remains to be taken to the morgue.

CHAPTER 6

Madness

To his surprise, Michael MacGregor found his shoes, socks, and jacket lying where he had left them by the creek. His frock-coat had been rifled, though, for it was no longer laid neatly across the back of the chair. He immediately opened his wallet. As he had suspected, the money was gone. He gathered up his belongings with the intent to carry them as he took Anne home at once, but she stepped into the creek and began to wander about, apparently searching for something in the very spot where the boy had been shot. Rather than ask her purpose, the Scot decided to put on his hose and shoes while she performed whatever ritual of mourning she required. When he had shod himself and donned his jacket, he found her still roaming, seemingly aimless. He settled into the rough chair and waited as the sun sank behind the trees.

All of a sudden, she bent to extract something from the

water. After the merest glance at the object, she put it into her pocket and strode to him.

"I'm ready," she announced.

Without comment, he rose and followed her as she walked slowly along the narrow path back to Cedar Lane.

∞

THE SUN HAD SET and the western horizon had cooled from its previous blaze of orange to a watery cyan hue by the time they reached the little clapboard house behind the whitewashed picket fence. At the gate, Michael grasped Anne's hand and kissed it in farewell.

"Please don't leave," she whispered.

He clasped her hand in both of his. Reluctantly, he said, "I shall fetch the old lady from up the street, here." He nodded toward the house the crone had entered. "She could stay with you, that you not be alone."

Anne stepped forward and placed her free hand on his cheek.

"Please?"

Her supplication wrenched his heart.

"I should not," he whispered, still torn between desire and decency.

Wordlessly, she gripped his hand and brought him inside.

∞

ANNE RETRIEVED a cutwork cloth from the side cupboard and spread it over the table, smoothing it with care. She set a simple white plate and plain steel fork and knife at each end of the pine rectangle and pulled one of her mismatched pressed-back chairs from the side to position it at the place setting nearest the back door, opposite a similar seat already situated at the other end. In the centre of the table, she laid a dish of butter, a tiny bowl of sea salt, and a pepper grinder. She noticed her guest's surprise at the

last, for pepper was one of the more expensive spices and a grinder found more commonly in the households of Mediterranean immigrants than in the homes of British families.

"Sit, if you wish," she said softly, gesturing toward the chair nearest him. "I must go outside to fetch the food, and I'll put on a kettle for tea."

He nodded, and she stepped out to her back yard to gather vegetables from the garden for their evening meal.

∞

MICHAEL STOOD by the front door and watched as Anne silently fetched this and placed that. He might have offered to help, but the slow, ritualistic quality of her motions stayed him and he simply observed, perceiving that to interfere would be to profane something sacred.

When she took a basket from atop a hutch and went out to her garden, he followed, but remained on the back porch and gazed after her as she plucked young leaves and sprouts, small potatoes and peas from the round beds scattered throughout her property. She lit a fire in a stove built into the shingle-roofed open structure of the summer kitchen, before washing her produce with a tender touch. Then, the spuds and kettle she set to boil, and she began to shell the peas with actions adroit and rhythmic. Once the legumes were potted and placed over the fire, she gathered the greens into a bowl, added a few colourful blossoms, and drizzled the salad with bottled liquids he guessed to be oil and vinegar.

The potatoes cooked quickly, and soon she brought the plain repast inside to the dining table.

They ate without conversation, and when the meal was done, she collected the dishes and took them outside to wash them in an enamelled basin. Again, the Scot merely watched as she performed her domestic tasks in a manner that conveyed a sense of sacrament.

Once all had been cleaned and dried and carried inside to be put away in cupboards, Michael said quietly, "I'll go fetch your neighbour, now."

He turned toward the front door, but a touch to his shoulder stopped him. Stepping around to his front, Anne took his hands in hers and gently kissed each in turn. Then, she led him up the stairs.

∞

HE MADE NO DEMUR—indeed, he did not move, as though in a dream he dared not disturb lest it vanish—as Anne slowly undressed him and then herself. Button by button and layer by layer, she removed all that separated them. He watched her, so mesmerized he noted not the knife sheathed at her thigh.

When the last scrap of fabric had slipped to the floor and she had released her hair from its bonds, she hugged him.

At the sensation of her skin against his and the scent of her hair and body, the Scot's rapt fog quickly dissipated with the heat of his rising passion. When she nuzzled his chest and caressed his buttocks, his every hair rose to her touch, his manhood stiffened, and his heart quickened. He slipped his fingers through her hair, and his breath came fast and shallow as he sought her lips. He began his own probing with tongue and hands and, soon, he could stand it no more.

Grasping her by neck and bottom, he laid her crosswise upon the low divan. He knelt at the bedside, parted her thighs, and pulled her hips to him. As though Heaven itself were blessing their union, a beam of moonlight through the window pointed the way, and Michael penetrated her with a catch of his breath. In moments, he poured himself into her.

Panting, he held her to him, his large hands planted on her hips and his eyes closed as he clung to the euphoria of satiation. Gradually, respiration and heart slowed and at last he opened his eyes to look upon the first woman he had ever loved.

Her hair gleamed silver in the light of the rising moon and its waves spilled across the quilt. She gazed at him, a little smile curling her lips, and she reached invitingly. With one hand pressing her buttocks, he kept her impaled; with the other, he pulled her up and into his embrace. But he had grown soft and she was wet; he slipped out of her as they kissed.

"Damn!" he murmured. "I wanted to stay inside you forever."

She grinned. "That door is not locked."

"Thank the lord!" he exclaimed happily, and he pushed up to roll them together onto the bed. Then, his hands roved as he tasted her again. "I want to know every part of you," he whispered hoarsely.

"The desire is mutual," she assured him.

∞

MICHAEL MacGREGOR lay still beside Anne, imbued with a certainty, a knowledge of belonging, and the long-fractured pieces of his being coalesced into a unified whole. For years, he had thought he would never know the love of a woman. For years, he had believed himself unnatural, as the bastards had always told him he was and as his experiences had seemed to confirm. Now, he knew truth.

He gazed at her sleeping countenance, pale in the celestial light that shone through the dormer window, her lips bearing a hint of smile. He drew a wisp of hair away from her face and kissed the silky tress before laying it by her ear.

As he stared at this slumbering angel, he felt his heart full for the first time.

No, he did not belong to them. He belonged to her.

∞

ANNE WOKE to a tickling on her lips and discovered Michael, beside her, caressing them with a feathery touch. She smiled.

"Did you sleep well?" she asked as she turned to cup his cheek.

"Better than I've slept in years," he murmured.

Her breath caught and her heart leapt at the fondness in his eyes. She blurted, "I so love you, Alex."

He froze, and she instantly realized her mistake. In his eyes she saw the thoughts, the disappointment rippling through his mind, and she rushed to stave off disaster. There was only one thing she could say, though she knew it could backfire and drive him away.

"I'll have to get used to calling you Michael, now. I called you Alex for so long."

He stared and frowned, astounded and baffled.

She held his eyes and declared, "You were once Alex MacGregor, my husband. Now, you are Michael, as you were more than once before you became Alex."

His frown deepened and he shook his head as though certain he had misheard her words.

"No, you heard rightly," she assured him.

He pulled back and regarded her warily. She stared into his eyes, open to his scrutiny.

He said slowly, "You are saying that you believe I am your dead husband come back to life." He swallowed visibly.

"I am not mad," Anne insisted. With wavering confidence, she amended, "At least, I don't think so."

She took a tremulous breath and explained, "I know that religions—Western religions, at any rate—teach that we have only one life of the body and all else is existence in Heaven or Hell or whatever. But I am certain that is not true. The Eastern religions speak of reincarnation. And I have reason to believe they are correct."

He continued to stare at her an extended moment, digesting her words. At last, he asked, "Why?"

"Why do I think so?"

He nodded, not taking his eyes off of her.

She inhaled deeply once more before the next plunge: "I can see souls."

He tilted his head as though viewing her from a different angle might reveal a truth he had not yet seen.

She said, "I know it sounds preposterous, but I have seen two of you in the same time period—the same soul in two different bodies." She added in a tone resigned to future difficulty, "How *that* came about is, well, something for another discussion."

He tilted his head the other way and narrowed his eyes, clearly thinking her mad.

She sighed and closed her eyes. Then, she opened them to fix his.

"Dammit, Michael, I don't think I can prove it to you. I can only tell you what I believe: that we have loved many times in the past and will love again in the future." She sighed once more. "If you find it offensive, or think me insane, there is nothing I can do about that."

She sat up and turned away to climb out of bed; his hand on her arm stopped her. When she looked back, he searched her eyes for a small eternity. At last, he set his jaw and said, "Perhaps you are mad. And perhaps I am. But I do not want to lose you, mad or no."

Tears filled her eyes. She flung herself into his arms and clung to him, sobbing, as he held her and kissed her crown.

∞

MICHAEL MacGREGOR smiled inwardly and suppressed a chuckle at the irony of the situation. *Only I would fall in love with a madwoman,* he thought. *Not to mention a woman older than I. And one Father and Mother will certainly not approve.*

Despite his efforts, the chuckle escaped. She felt it erupt in his belly and looked up anxiously. He smiled and stroked her lovely, soft hair. She smiled back shyly, hopefully, her tears

gleaming in the morning sun.

Lord, how he wanted her!

His hands drifted over her body and his mouth again sought hers.

∞

MICHAEL CREPT UP behind and wrapped his arms around Anne as she stood in her kimono at the little stove in the summer kitchen. Nuzzling her ear, he whispered, "What is finer than a barely dressed, round-arsed woman and a bowl o' parritch?"

She giggled. "You sound more Scotch by the minute."

"I am Scotch," he said. "Born, if not bred."

"Oh?"

"I was born there, raised here in childhood, and later schooled in England and Scotland."

She turned in his embrace to look up into his face. She said, "Well, that explains a few things." Something occurred to her. She asked, "Do you speak Gaelic?"

"No," he admitted. "It is not encouraged, here or there."

"I'll teach you what I know," she promised.

He smiled and kissed her.

"Hm-gmmm!"

They turned to see Jack standing at the corner of the house, glaring at Michael MacGregor. Furious, the lad shouted, "Ye said ye'd leave her be!"

Anne stepped between them. "I asked him to stay," she told the boy.

His face contorting with rage and disappointment, Jack railed at her, "I shoulda known ye'd be a whore like all the rest!" He whirled and ran out into the street and on toward the creek.

Anne heaved a great sigh and bowed her head.

"It's my fault," said Michael. "I told him I'd have the old woman stay with you."

"It's not your fault," Anne insisted. "This has been

coming for a while. Sooner or later, I'd have had to refuse him."

"Still," said Michael, "I took advantage of you in your grief. It was indecent. I should have waited."

She turned to him, tilted her head, and chuckled softly. With eyebrows raised, she said, "As I recall, it was *I* who took advantage of *you*."

"Well," he said, blushing, "I could have stopped you."

She stepped forward and put her arms around his waist. Gazing into his eyes, she said, "I'm glad you didn't."

He, too, was glad. He kissed her.

∞

WHILE MICHAEL DRESSED, Jack's face came back to his mind: the boy's pain and anger and thwarted desire. As he pulled on his socks, that image transmuted to one of his father wearing a similar expression of outrage and disappointment the first time he came home drunk, dragged by acquaintances who had brought him from a whorehouse. How many times had he seen that paternal disapprobation and censure? It had always made him feel a failure. But of course, he had had reason to consider himself one, regardless of his father's opinion.

He glanced toward Anne, by the wardrobe, lacing her stays. His lips curled in a wry smile at her absurdly anachronistic costume. Everything about her was peculiar. It occurred to him that he could not imagine any time or place in which she would fit...blend...belong. She was unique. And in truth, he was also a fish out of water.

The memory of her gaffe in calling him by her husband's name returned, emptying his belly. His instant reaction had been a sense of betrayal, of disillusionment more profound than anything he had ever experienced. But her explanation....

He was convinced she believed what she had told him: that he was her husband of old, returned to her in a new form. But by everything he had been taught, such a thing was not

possible.

Watching her coil her hair into a knot at the nape of her neck and pin it in place, he realized he truly did not care if it was possible or if she was mad. She was his, and he was hers.

"Let's get married," he said abruptly. "Today."

She turned to look into his face, hers surprised. After a mere moment's hesitation, she said, "All right."

∞

VIRTUALLY EVERYONE, certainly the mayor and council, had gone to the regatta. The town hall was nearly deserted, though a clutch of ladies stood just inside the entry handing out Temperance leaflets, each woman dressed from chin to toes in exhibition of puritanical zeal. They made no effort to hide their disapproval of Anne, she with cleavage displayed proudly.

Michael drew his intended through the maze of hallways, scanning the brass signs on each door until he found the one he sought.

Inside the registrar's office, waxed dark panelling that matched the lobby and corridors shone along the lower third of the twelve-foot walls, and simple white plaster topped the oak wainscot. Opposite the entry, two clerical desks were set squarely to face the door. Behind them, two flags (the Union Jack on the right and the Red Ensign, unofficial flag of the country, on the left) draped colourfully from wooden poles in the rear corners, separated by two banks of double-hung windows stretched across the outer wall. The city's coat of arms dominated the left side-wall, while a portrait of the queen, lovingly framed in polished walnut, hung on the right.

Echoing the wainscot, an oak half-wall severed the space and confronted those who entered. Discreet doors allowed staff access at each end, and a wood-framed glass window jutted above the countertop to symbolically isolate the bureaucrats from the public while enabling them to serve the citizenry. One clerk

stood behind it today, at one of the two narrow openings in the glazing.

There were three other couples ahead, waiting to apply for licence to wed. When their turn finally came, Michael and Anne stepped to the wicket hand in hand.

The clerk peered at them through his spectacles, noting the fine cut and high quality of the Scot's mid-grey suit with its broad lapels and pewter buttons, and cocking an eyebrow in surprise and undisguised disapprobation at Anne's well-worn blue gown with its deeply *décolleté* neckline. Nonetheless, he filled out, stamped, and signed their papers and, when asked, directed them to the Justice who would officiate their wedding.

∞

TO THE JUSTICE'S consternation, Anne neglected to include a promise to obey as she repeated the vows. But her hands and voice trembled; so, after a moment's pause and a gesture from the groom, he dismissed the oversight and simply continued the ceremony.

He did, however, sputter in shock, his eyes wide, when Anne quickly pulled the ring from her fourth finger and gave it to Michael to place onto her hand once more. In apology, she told the official, "We forgot to buy a new ring. This was the one my late husband gave me on our wedding day."

The Justice looked to Michael, who shrugged in casual acceptance of his predecessor's token of troth. After a moment of blinking and throat clearing, the discomposed official got on with the business at hand.

Slipping the violet band onto Anne's finger, Michael began, "With this ring...."

At sight of the circlet of which he had previously taken no notice, he stopped, eyes wide, and stared until the Justice ahemmed and brought him out of his startlement. With an unsettled glance to the man and back to the ring, the Scot gazed

into Anne's eyes, swallowed, and murmured, "With this ring, I thee wed."

His countenance expressing bafflement, the officiant hurriedly finished the ceremony as though to forestall another disconcerting interruption. After pronouncing the couple man and wife, he instantly snapped his book shut and pulled a handkerchief from his pocket to wipe his brow.

"*Husband* and wife," Anne corrected.

Stifling an urge to chuckle, Michael turned her away before the Justice could protest her impertinence in attempting to alter the prescribed wording. As they exited the room, she said, "Well, it's only common sense. He can't declare us man and woman, because God did that; so, he must call us husband and wife. It's a matter of proper terminology."

Michael tried very hard not to laugh as he replied, "Yes, dear."

∞

AFTER A PASSIONATE interlude in the only unlocked and unoccupied place Michael could find in his hasty search of the public building, the newlyweds left to spend much of the day making arrangements to include Anne on the Scot's bank accounts and to pay his creditors, most of whom had remained in their respective shops rather than attend the festivities along the river. Once his long-neglected responsibilities had been discharged, he took his wife shopping for new and up-to-date clothes. She allowed him to buy her two unpretentious gowns, but insisted on purchasing bolts of fabric and spools of thread in lieu of more ready-made frocks.

Now, they came to Rosemont. It would be easy enough to pack his belongings and take them to her house, he had told Anne. After all, no one was home. Even the servants had gone to the regatta.

Or so he had thought. To his surprise, Michael found the

valet in his room.

"Sir!" Ford greeted him in astonishment. "I thought you had stayed at your club for the night and gone straight to the boat races."

"No, Ford," Michael replied. After taking a deep breath, he announced, "I got married."

Ford blinked several times. Then, collecting himself, he rushed to pump Michael's hand. "Congratulations, sir!" He leaned to look behind his employer and asked, "Is your lady to be moving in today?"

"Actually, Ford, I'll be moving into her home."

Ford gaped, his mind working furiously behind the grey eyes.

Realizing what the man must be thinking, Michael said, "I will not be able to take you with me, but I understand that my sister's fiancé will be moving into this house. I'm sure he'll need your services."

Ford exhaled in a relieved sigh. Then, he asked with alacrity, "Shall I help you pack, sir?"

∞

ANNE AND MICHAEL took his trunks to Cedar Lane and rushed to bring everything inside. They had been in and out of the house several times, already, fetching and carrying. But now, as the sun sank behind the trees and houses hugging the southward curve of the lane, they faced each other on the front porch, about to step into their home, officially, as a married couple. Michael had intended to scoop Anne into his arms to carry her over the threshold, but she stopped him.

"There's one thing more I'd like to do," she said, taking his red and blistered hands and gently kissing each of them.

"What is that?" he asked, wondering what else might be required.

"Another rite," she told him. "In the Gaelic."

"I don't speak it," he reminded her.

"Just repeat the words," she insisted. "I'll translate as we go."

They stood, hands clasped, and spoke the ancient words, the very words Alex had once taught her:

"This day we are joined as husband and wife,
"Enriching our clan with new hearth and home.
"You cannot possess me, for I belong to myself,
"But, while we both wish it, I give you that which is mine to give.
"You cannot command me, for I am a free person,
"But I shall serve you in those ways you require
"And the honeycomb will taste sweeter coming from my hand.
"I pledge my love to you, and all that I own.
"I promise you the first bite from my plate, the first sip from my cup.
"I pledge that your name will always be the name I cry out in the night,
"And into your eyes will I smile each morn.
"I promise to honour you above all others, and
"I shall be a shield for your back as you are for mine.
"We will remain, forevermore, equals in our marriage,
"And our never-ending love shall be renewed in our life yet to come.
"This is my wedding vow to you."

Michael gazed into the eyes of his bride, feeling that, somehow, these strange words had more meaning, more validity than the legal service with its officials and documents and stamps. Now, they were truly bound, he and this woman.

He kissed the ring on her hand, that tiny circle from his dreams, and he gathered her into his arms to carry her directly to their marriage bed. And when he lay beside her, afterwards, listening to the slow rhythm of her breath as she curled next to him, he dared to imagine that—just perhaps—there could a

happy ever-after even for him.

∞

YOUNG JACK GREETED THE NEWS of their marriage with a kaleidoscopic range of emotions reflected in his face, from shock to anger to relief to disappointment to acceptance. At last, he stoically extended his hand to congratulate the winner of the fair damsel.

"I ain't sayin' you're the better man," the lad declared. "But I know I ain't old enough to take care o' the lady, myself, and it was decent o' ye to make an honest woman of 'er. She could do worse, I s'ppose."

"That's big of you to say," Michael responded solemnly, shaking the boy's hand and forcibly suppressing an urge to laugh.

The other children rushed out excitedly to spread the word that Herself had married a giant from The City. Thereafter, the rest of Anne and Michael's day was filled with greetings from well-wishers come to get a glimpse of the stranger in their midst. By late afternoon, Michael MacGregor had heard several neighbours refer to him as "Himself." And the old lady from across the lane cackled all the way home once more.

∞

STANDING BESIDE HIS NEW BRIDE in the foyer of his father's house, Michael took a deep breath and smiled down at Anne, now dressed demurely in a richly hued blue gown of fine summer-weight wool with high, lace-trimmed white collar and moderately bouffant sleeves. After a quick squeeze of her hand to reassure them both, he opened the drawing-room door.

He greeted his family formally, "Mother, Father, Elizabeth." He nodded to his sister's fiancé, "Mr. Armstrong." After raising Anne's hand to kiss her knuckles, he announced, "This is my wife, Anne."

Harris stood as though turned to stone. Hermione MacGregor paled and sat down. Elizabeth dramatically pretended to faint onto the settee and her intended rushed to pat her hand anxiously. Joseph MacGregor sputtered, livid with rage.

The elder MacGregor fulminated, "Are you mad? It's bad enough you disgrace us by leaving Miss Orwell high and dry to miss the regatta, after promising to accompany her—"

Michael interrupted equably, "As I recall, it was *you* who made the promise, Father."

Joseph MacGregor sputtered again before continuing his rant with renewed vigour, "You disappear for days on end. And you throw over the daughter of a prominent member of the community for this, this...gold-digging whore!"

His face dark, his voice a quiet menace, Michael spat the words, "Do not...*ever*...speak of my wife in that manner again."

Equally quiet and with furious venom, Joseph MacGregor said, "I should ha' left ye on that bloody hill with your dead mother!"

The words had the impact of a lightning strike. It seemed as though no one dared even to breathe for several minutes.

"What the hell do you mean by that?" Michael demanded.

He caught a wordless exchange between the people he had thought his parents. Anne pressed closer to him.

"Joseph—" Hermione started, but her husband cut her off with an abrupt wave of his hand.

Eyes like daggers, Joseph MacGregor said, "I found ye in the West Highlands, on a hill, a babe in the arms of your dead mother among a pile of rocks."

"Standing stones," said Anne in a strange hush.

Michael looked at his wife uncomprehendingly. She appeared to be staring into an inestimable distance.

Joseph MacGregor also noted her tone and expression. He frowned and regarded her quizzically. His voice wary, he asked, "You know the stones of Dùn-Draoidheil?"

"I know them," she said in a whisper, her gaze still far away.

Now anxious, Michael asked, "Anne, what is it?"

She looked at him and smiled, one of those Sphinx-like smiles that lent an impression of immense age, as though she might be as old as the world itself. She cupped his cheek and whispered, "Someday, I'll tell you, my love."

He put his hand atop hers and kissed her palm, searching her eyes. But he found no answer to his question.

Recalling the beginning of this conversation, he turned to his erstwhile father and demanded, "When were you planning to tell me I am not your son?"

Hermione MacGregor spoke up. "There was no need to tell you. We had raised you from infancy and you were our child in every way." She turned to her husband and finished angrily, "And there was no need to tell it now!"

Her hesitance evincing fear of the answer, Elizabeth asked, "Am I your daughter?"

Hermione turned to her with a deeply affectionate smile. "Yes, dear," she said. "You are our daughter. It was after you were born that I...." She closed her eyes, unable to say the words.

Softly, Joseph finished for her, "Lost our boy and took fever. And then could not bear another child."

He approached his wife and put a hand gently on her shoulder. She placed her hand over his, tears filling her eyes.

His voice flat, Michael said, "So I am a foundling."

Why had he not recognized it before: his family—those he had thought his family—all brown-haired and pale-eyed and small, while he stood out in contrast like the ugly duckling? The realization settled in his gut like a stone. Michael turned to Anne, at a loss even to know what he felt much less to communicate it.

She seemed to know his heart. She said quietly, simply, "We have each other."

They left the MacGregor house as they had entered it: husband and wife, hand in hand, on their own.

CHAPTER 7

Indignities...

The inquest had been scheduled for the day after the regatta. Dan Doherty, Larry's father, drove Anne and Michael to the courthouse in his hackney cab early that morning. Anne had dressed in a sober grey gown with a high, rounded collar and a black bow at the neck. A grey bonnet hid her hair, and a small black reticule held her pocketbook and handkerchiefs. Michael, also in charcoal grey, wore a black armband over his suit jacket. On the steps, a pair of eager young reporters badgered them with questions, but received only Michael MacGregor's minatory stare.

Like the town hall, the courthouse had been furnished with dark, panelled wainscot. The corridor's oak plank floor gleamed under layers of polish, reflecting the glare of purple-hued electric arc-lights that had recently been installed at intervals along the high ceiling. Portraits of former judges shared

wall space above the wainscot with lithographed maps and sepia-toned photographs of prominent landmarks. Rarely aired, the place smelled of the perspiration of the thousands who had passed through these halls, as well as of subtler scents of floor wax and the musty odour of paper and books. Detecting a hint of ozone, the Scot glanced to the lights and wondered briefly what price might come with "progress."

Michael held Anne's hand as they sat on a long bench abutting the wall of the passage beyond the lobby. A few clerks hurried by from time to time, each carrying files under an arm, while a cluster of bailiffs chatted at the far end of the hallway, awaiting the commencement of official sessions.

Anne's shoulders heaved slightly with the sobs that she tried to suppress, and Michael squeezed her hand in token of sympathy and support. She tried to smile up at him, but her face only contorted with pain. Seeing it, he released her hand to put his arm around her shoulder and pull her to him. Then, he handed her a handkerchief and she dabbed her eyes. She had cared deeply for the child, he realized, and he grieved for her loss, wishing he knew some way to comfort her.

Considered old enough to testify, Jack, Ian, and Larry arrived later. The boys came to sit next to the MacGregors, each lad wearing his best (meaning cleanest and least tattered) trousers and shirt, with a vest to cover his suspenders. Together, the five waited in glum silence amid the increasing bustle of clerks and lawyers, witnesses and plaintiffs, constables and reporters, some of whom hastened to a destination while others merely milled outside the courtrooms.

At last, the group from The Flats was called.

Behind his raised walnut desk in the smallest of the courtrooms, Justice Edwards listened intently to the evidence provided by the coroner, Dr. Howard Thorne, pertaining to the death of George Patrick Monaghan, aged five. The judge cocked an eyebrow as Detective Morgan, undeniably middleclass in his short, high-buttoned, and narrow-lapelled brown suit and plain

vest, described the location of the boy's demise and the weapons that had been fired in Mercer's Field. The senior Justice pursed his lips as he listened to the testimony of the three boys. Then, he nodded attentively as the MacGregors each described their recollection of the events surrounding the child's death.

Finally, Jonathan Rogers stepped up on behalf of the sportsmen of Mercer's Field to say that, owing to their not having been present at the scene of the accident, they had declined to attend the inquest on the grounds that they had no relevant testimony to offer. The lawyer ended his speech by handing to Justice Edwards a list of the names of those who had been in Mercer's Field on that day, with the assurance that the *gentlemen* in question—he emphasized the word—would be happy to make themselves available if officially requested to do so. The judge perused the document, eyebrows rising at the names he read there.

After setting the list aside and clearing his throat, Justice Edwards declared that George Patrick Monaghan had died by misadventure. The gavel dropped with a bang.

∞

"MISADVENTURE? What does that mean?" Jack asked as they descended the courthouse steps.

Michael stated angrily, "It means that the judge has ruled it an accident with no one to blame."

Jack fumed, "That ain't right! Them rich bastards kill't our Geordie!"

Resting a hand on the boy's shoulder, Anne said circumspectly, "We do not know that, Jack. It's possible that it was pure accident rather than negligence on someone's part."

Michael interjected, "It's also possible there is something else at work here."

Larry frowned as he asked, "What d'ye mean?"

The Scot voiced the doubt that had been plaguing him: "It

seems odd that a bullet could have come all the way across the field, through the woods without hitting a tree, and fly straight to Geordie."

He looked to his wife at the sudden tightening of her hand in his. She quickly looked away, but he had seen in her eyes a deep distress at his words. As much for her benefit as that of the boys, he added in a more hopeful tone, "And by the look on the detective's face, I do not think he will let the matter lie without further investigation. He will discover the truth."

"Good," said Jack. The other boys grunted similar sentiment as they piled into Dan's cab, the four-seat hackney waiting in tandem with Ian Farrell's carriage for two.

∞

"ARE YOU SURE you want to go alone?" Michael asked as he and Anne entered the factory where she worked. He surveyed the scuttling men and boys hauling bolts of fabric and boxes of unknown articles. A pair of dark-haired men who were clearly brothers rolled a rack laden with enormous coils of cloth from out of one doorway into another, nearly upsetting a lad bearing a stack of flat paper boxes that rose to almost hide his eyes.

"I think I should," Anne answered. "It will be fine. Mr. Drew can be quite reasonable." She hoped that her words had sounded convincing, but Michael's cocked eyebrow told her that her true assessment of the man had crept into her voice.

Anne smiled up at her husband sheepishly and stood on her tiptoes to kiss him. Then, she skirted the bustle of the vestibule to hike up the long, narrow, steep flight of stairs that led to the office of her employer.

∞

WATCHING AFTER his wife as she skipped up the steps and out of sight, Michael felt his gut tighten. Her manner had told him she expected to be berated by her employer for failing to report

for work the two nights previous.

Had his father—Joseph—not reacted so violently to their marriage, Michael would have insisted his wife resign her position immediately, perhaps to preside over the establishment of a new home and household in Rosemont or Glenwood. But his future was now in doubt, and what earnings Anne gleaned might well be needed to sustain them until such time as he gained a position in one firm or another.

An unbidden voice from the furthest recesses of his mind reminded him that his reputation for drunkenness and the gossip of his marriage to an "unsuitable" woman would likely hamper his efforts to find employment. His belly sank as he took stock of the meagre resources that remained to him.

∞

AT THE FIRST of the closed doors in the cramped dark corridor, Anne knocked above the brass plate proclaiming the name of the room's occupant: Samuel Drew, proprietor.

"Come!" his muffled call beckoned.

When she entered, Drew glanced up, a sheaf of papers in each hand and piles littering the entire surface of the desk illuminated by a brass oil-lamp with glass globe and brass shade. The prematurely balding, middle-aged man squinted, not recognizing her, and asked, "Can I help you, Madam?"

"I wanted to apologize for not coming in to work, the last two nights," Anne told him. "There was...a death."

His eyes flew wide when he recognized her voice. He regarded her a moment. Then, he contracted his lips into a disdainful pucker and frowned. "Oh, it's you." He looked away, setting down the sheaf in his right hand and picking up a pen. "You're fired."

He held the batch of papers in his left hand high, as though to prevent it from being sucked, as through a vortex, into the morass on his desk. With his right, the pen in his hand, he

hastily pulled out a drawer and extracted a book, slapping it on top of the clutter and opening it clumsily.

After a moment's indecision, glancing from his handful of papers to the book and back again, he dared to press the edge of his left hand on one side of the bankbook. He carefully printed the counterfoil and then the cheque before scrawling his signature on the latter and initialling the former. Finally, he tore away the cheque.

"Your wages," he said, holding the slip out to her. Pointedly looking her up and down, this time with a hint of lewdness in his eyes and in the curl of his mouth, he added, "Though it appears you have other sources of income, Mrs. MacGregor."

"As a matter of fact, I just remarried," she told him coolly as she snatched the cheque. She glanced at the sum and then fixed him with a cold glare. "But I am sure this will cover the cost of the funeral."

He frowned. "Your husband's?"

"No. The boy who was shot."

In her peripheral vision, she caught his shocked expression as she whirled to exit the open door.

∞

"I AM NO LONGER employed," Anne informed her husband grimly as they escaped the commotion of the garment factory and turned up the street crowded with workers and tradesmen.

Michael made no comment. He merely pulled her close and put his arm round her shoulder protectively, steering her out of the way of oncoming traffic as they negotiated the narrow passage between red brick buildings. Smoke issued from chimneys above to fill the sultry air with haze in the unseasonable heat wave that had descended upon the city. The stench of sweating labourers competed with the reek of refuse and industrial vapours as the early afternoon sun raked the

streets and alleys from a cloudless sky.

Where the street widened into a square, Michael drew Anne to sit on a public bench. He twisted on the wooden seat, clasped her hands in his, and looked into her eyes to say, "I will take care of you."

He hesitated, swallowing and glancing around at passersby, before he continued, "I know my fa—"

He stopped abruptly, inhaled slowly, and then amended, "Joseph MacGregor...will cut off my allowance. But I still have a small income from investments made when I was in the Army, and I will find work."

He fixed her eyes once more, squeezed her hands, and said earnestly, "I promise you."

Anne smiled and assured him, "I do not doubt you, Michael." She withdrew a hand to caress his cheek and added, "And I know that we will live well enough without your...your father's money."

He searched her eyes, marvelling at the certainty he found there. And he prayed that he could live up to her expectations.

∞

AFTER EXCHANGING their formal apparel for clothing more comfortable in the day's oppressive heat, Michael and Anne strolled arm in arm along the grassy lanes and streets of The Flats, smiling and waving to neighbours they passed. Occasionally, someone engaged them in conversation— commenting about the weather, seeking Anne's advice about crops or ailments, or discussing politics—but for the most part, the newlyweds simply enjoyed each other's company.

They wandered the meandering ways lined with houses that ranged from brick to log to clapboard to cob constructions, some painted or lime-washed; some with silvered or blackened wood; some two-storey; some single with an extra half-storey

formed by the attic, as evidenced by curtained windows below roof gables. To Michael's amazement, even those dwellings that had been allowed to age naturally bore the signs of care and upkeep more frequently seen in the "better" parts of town: Roofs varied in colour where new shingles lay next to older ones. Many windows gleamed, freshly washed, above flower-filled boxes. And gardens, while not of the orderly formal designs favoured by the wealthy, invariably overflowed with flowers and vegetables, herbs and fruits. Every yard had a few trees, and every house had a welcome mat. He wondered at the pride with which his neighbours lavished their homes when, only a few miles away, the people of The Warren and other poor and working-class districts lived in squalor that could not be explained solely by the negligence of landlords.

Eventually, Michael and Anne returned to Cedar Lane and took the path toward the creek.

When they emerged from the forest, the sun had dropped low enough to plunge the stream into shadow. Nonetheless, cicadas trilled on the far bank where scattered rays pierced the near canopy to beam across the open expanse and spotlight a bushy willow or a tall aspen.

An old-timer from Willow Bend sat alone in one of the creekside chairs, absently holding a fishing pole aloft, its line drifting on the current as he stared into the water. At their appearance, he glanced up, startled out of his reverie.

Recognizing them, he smiled and said genially, "Ev'nin' to ye."

"Caught anything, Mr. Flynn?" Anne asked, grinning.

"Nothin' but wee buggers ain't worth keepin'," he replied. He nodded in greeting to Michael and sat back to resume his peaceful pastime.

Anne and Michael turned upstream, hand in hand. The rivulet narrowed, its volume diminishing as they approached its source. Here, the air smelled of fresh water and sun-scorched leaves and grass, with the occasional whiff of wood-smoke from

the cooking fires of The Flats. This was the edge of town, with nothing beyond but forest and meadow between the isolated working-class community and the rail lines in the west. Northward, the tributary of Bow Creek divided them from a few small farms and from the large private sporting club known as Mercer's Field. To the east lay the Bow. And to the south, a broad avenue separated The Flats from a private hospital with extensive grounds, followed by a section of the railroad, a scatter of industrial buildings, and the lake that stretched to the horizon.

At last, when they passed the spring that gave rise to the Sweetwater, Michael broached the subject that had weighed on his mind all day. He said quietly, "After the funeral, I will go into the city and seek work."

Equally hushed, Anne asked, "What kind of work?"

"I have no idea," he admitted. "I have education, but few skills. It had always been assumed that I would eventually take over my...Joseph's business."

He sighed, "I may have to learn a trade if I cannot find a position in a bank or something of the kind."

"You'll find something," Anne said with confidence. "And I can seek another job. There are plenty of new buildings that need cleaning."

"I willna have ye be a drudge!" Michael barked.

As he visibly struggled with his pride, Anne hurried to explain in conciliation, "I meant only that I would be willing to help, if you should receive low wages at first."

She cupped both his cheeks and held his gaze as she added, "Marriage is a partnership. We must work together and help each other."

She whispered, "Please let me help."

He stared long into her eyes. Finally, he sighed and said, "If needs be."

∞

THEY WERE WITHIN sight of their cottage when Anne tapped Michael's arm. In a low voice, she said, "There is someone watching the house. A stranger."

In the dim of twilight, Michael scanned the way ahead and spotted the man standing too casually under a maple tree at the edge of a dooryard across from their home.

"His soul is black," Anne whispered.

Michael looked to her, his brows raised in surprise at the statement, but the hairs on his own neck and arms had stiffened at sight of the slim, sandy-haired man. As the couple drew closer, the outsider lit a pipe, pretending to take no notice of them. Michael saw his quick glance, though, and he saw the scar on the left hand, a white slash across the sun-browned skin, catching the light of the flame as the man set match to tobacco.

The Scot studied the stranger, memorizing the arch of his brow, the line of his jaw, his stance as he leaned against the tree. Yes, he would know this man if he saw him again.

The MacGregors turned into their own yard.

Keeping the suspicious character in his peripheral vision, Michael escorted his wife into their home. Inside, he glanced around to assure himself no one lurked within. Then, he locked the doors and went ahead to check the upper floor before allowing Anne to enter their bedroom.

While she undressed, he returned to the ground floor and peered out the window. The stranger continued to lean against the maple and stare at their house until a group of O'Reillys ordered him to move on.

CHAPTER 8

...and indecencies

As promised, the coroner had merely extracted the bullet that had killed the child and made his report based on a superficial examination—the piercing of the small chest having undoubtedly been sufficient to take the youngster's life. That formality concluded, Detective Morgan released Geordie's body to the care of Mr. Jessop.

Laid out in his little pine box in St. Anthony's, the boy looked like a sleeping angel, none of the trauma of his brief life and violent death in evidence. Everyone in The Flats, Catholic or Protestant or Jew, attended the funeral. All day, family and friends and neighbours braved a thunderstorm and subsequent intermittent showers to solemnly parade past the coffin, many stopping briefly to kiss the little face or to lay a hand on the breathless chest.

Anne stood by Sarah Monaghan, an arm around the

woman's shoulder, while Miss Hetty, on the other side, held the grieving mother's waist and kept her supplied with fresh hankies. Michael remained at the back of the church with Geordie's best friends: Jack, Larry, Ian, Kevin, Rob, and Terence. The motley group of boys kept vigil all day, stepping outside only to relieve themselves, while their respective families milled nearby in a show of support for the children who had experienced such a distressing loss.

In the evening, Father O'Donnell performed the service and led the procession to the gravesite. Tall enough despite his age, Jack took a place among the pallbearers and marched with head high and cheeks tear-stained as his father looked on with pride for his son, as well as with sorrow for little Geordie and his mother.

Once more, the mourners walked past, this time tossing flowers and handfuls of damp dirt onto the coffin. When the last had gone by, the priest nodded to the digger whose job was nearly done. As the churchyard caretaker finished burying the child, Father O'Donnell gave one last blessing and bade the widow Monaghan go home. Anne, Miss Hetty, and the ladies of the bordello escorted the still sobbing Sarah while Michael brought up the rear.

Halfway to the house on Poplar Lane, a neighbour rushed to meet the residents of the cathouse. Gesticulating wildly, the man said, "You gotta come quick! You's been robbed!"

"What?" All else driven from her mind, Miss Hetty ran to the brothel, most of her employees following close behind in a flurry of skirts.

"How could anyone do such a thing?" At the end of her tether, Sarah Monaghan glanced from Anne to Michael to her friend, Donna, at her side. Her voice trailed to a whisper and tears flowed anew. "How could they?"

Anne and Michael exchanged a look of shock and incredulity. Sobering, and gripping Sarah's hand tighter, Anne said, "Let's just get you home. Nothing else matters."

When they arrived at the stone dwelling, they found Miss Hetty muttering angrily and stomping from room to room, assessing the damage. Not a stick of furniture had been spared: knick-knacks and paintings had been tossed to the floor, porcelain smashed, chairs and tables upturned, stuffing ripped out of seats and sofas.

Louise O'Malley tripped and barely caught herself as she flew down the stairs. She shrilled, "They've ruined the beds! And our clothes are everywhere!"

Miss Hetty said something very uncomplimentary in the Irish and raced to the upper floor to see for herself.

One of the bouncers had fetched the policeman who had attended the funeral. The two men stepped through the open front door, stopped, and gaped.

"What in the name of...!" Constable O'Toole shook his head, aghast. Spotting Sarah Monaghan, he rushed to her to say, "I'm so sorry, Mrs. Monaghan. What a terrible thing to happen, on top of...of everything else. Ma'am, if there's anything I can do for you, I'd be most pleased if you'd call on me."

Sarah Monaghan forced a smile through her tears.

Anne glanced at Michael and raised her eyebrows in a wordless question. At her husband's nod, she turned back to Sarah and asked, "Would you like to stay with us tonight? This is all so much to deal with."

Sarah looked from Anne to Michael to the Constable before she took a deep, resolute breath and said, "I've lost me boy! I'll be damned if I'll be driven out o' me home, too!"

She strode toward the stair, turned about with eyes flashing fiercely, and looked to each of them again as she said, "I thank ye for your kindness. But I shall stay here and look after me own."

With that, she pressed her lips together defiantly, gave a curt nod, whirled, and marched up the stairs with head high.

"What a woman!" Constable O'Toole murmured in admiration.

Michael said, "If you should need to speak to us, Constable...."

"I'll know where to find you," said the officer, touching the rim of his helmet in a gesture of appreciation and respect as well as farewell. When he turned away, he pulled a pencil from one pocket and a notepad from another.

Anne and Michael had just stepped out to the brothel's shaded veranda when Jack came running up. "Missus!" he cried breathlessly. "You's been robbed!"

Having heard, Constable O'Toole ran outside. He demanded, "Them, too? Who else?"

Jack shook his head, gasping for breath. He wheezed, "Don't know, sir."

"All right, lad," said the beat cop, "I want you to go check the neighbourhood and find out."

Jack nodded and hurried away as fast as his lungs would allow, passing Detective Morgan, who arrived on his bicycle with two more constables in tow. "What is it now, Patrick?"

"Robberies, sir," O'Toole answered. "Two that I know of, so far. I've sent a neighbourhood lad to see if there've been any more."

Michael put in, "If you don't need us here, we should go home and see what may have been taken."

"Good idea," Morgan agreed. "I'll come by in due course."

As they rushed home, neither Anne nor Michael voiced what was on both their minds: that the two places little Geordie had most frequented had been ransacked on the day of his funeral.

∞

"NOTHING," MICHAEL TOLD Detective Morgan. He gestured to the drawers pulled from cabinets, the contents scattered across the floor. "They made a mess but took nothing."

"Looks just like the cathouse and the other three homes," O'Toole observed in puzzlement.

"Searching for something," Morgan stated with grim certainty.

"While everyone was at the funeral," Anne murmured. She swallowed visibly, her face doleful.

"It seems as though it must have something to do with the boy's death," O'Toole remarked, "but what could that be? He was scarcely five years old."

"Which came first," Michael mused aloud, "the chicken or the egg?"

Both Anne and Detective Morgan shot him a sharp glance, but the policeman instantly turned pensive as he pondered the implication. Anne, on the other hand, whirled and began to put her cupboards to rights with zeal.

"Detective," Michael asked with a brief, baffled glance to his wife, "was anything missing from Miss Hetty's? Or the other houses?"

"A pair of earrings and a necklace from Miss Hetty's. Nothing from the other homes, as far as anyone has told us," Morgan replied.

The Scot frowned and stared at the man with a perplexed expression. "They took costume jewellery that can't be worth more than a few dollars, if that?"

Morgan nodded. "Does seem odd, doesn't it? Especially when I have no doubt there are much better pickings in this house?" His probing tone begged an answer.

"Much better," Michael confirmed. "All upstairs and none taken." The Scot thought aloud, "They wanted something they suspected Geordie had." With brows high, he speculated, "And the jewellery theft at Miss Hetty's may not be related; perhaps someone else took advantage of the robbery to pilfer coveted items." Many times, in one red-light district or another, he had heard harlots squabbling over trinkets.

Constable O'Toole rubbed his chin and pursed his lips

with an expression that indicated he had a fair idea which of the inhabitants of the bordello might have sticky fingers.

Morgan said, "If that be the case, the brothel, I can understand; it's where he lived. But why here? And why the other houses?"

Michael told him, "Because Geordie was one of the lads Anne has been teaching to read and write."

Constable O'Toole knew, "And the other homes that were searched each belonged to one of the boy's friends, sir. Though the O'Reillys suffered no intrusion."

As she shoved a drawer back into the side cabinet, Anne pointed out in an irritated tone, "The O'Reilly house is never completely empty. And their dog would have attacked any stranger who violated its territory, thus raising the alarm."

Morgan nodded thoughtfully and decided, "Perhaps I'd better speak to the other lads you teach."

Anne grunted acknowledgement but did not look up as she gathered the papers and envelopes strewn on the floor about the desk. Eyes narrowed, Michael watched her a moment before escorting Morgan and O'Toole to the door.

When the policemen had left, Michael frowned in bewilderment as his wife slammed this and banged that in her ferocious tidying. He wanted to ask what vexed her so, but the ire she radiated decided him to wait until she had calmed.

Finally, by the time all had been straightened, Anne's motions had slowed and her manner had become dispirited rather than angry. When she began to set the table in preparation to make dinner, Michael took the plates from her and set them aside to gather her into his arms. At once, she began to weep uncontrollably. He held her and stroked her hair until, as twilight cloaked them in darkness, she settled. Then, without a word, he led his wife upstairs to their bed.

∞

THE NEXT DAY, heavy rain drove everyone indoors after church. Street kids Kevin and Rob had returned to the city following the funeral and could not be found, but the youngsters of The Flats who had been Geordie's frequent companions sat stiffly on Anne's mismatched kitchen chairs, the four as skittish as though they had been summoned before a Grand Inquisition. She brought each a cup of freshly brewed chamomile tea to ease the tension in the room.

Constables O'Toole and Ryan stood by the back door with pencils poised to record testimony. Michael MacGregor leaned against the wall beyond the small potbellied cast-iron woodstove, by the stairwell, his long legs crossed at the ankles as he fiddled with his watch. Keeping the pine table that was topped only with Anne's simple white tea service between himself and the boys, Detective Morgan began his series of questions. Probing gently, always watching their eyes and their posture, he delved into the activities of the lads and their late friend. Occasionally, he repeated a query in a new way, or asked a different boy.

Nothing the lads related shed any new light on the events of the past week. But Anne noticed something about Terence O'Grady that puzzled her. After a time, Detective Morgan straightened to ease his back and pulled a handkerchief from his coat pocket to wipe across his perspiration-dotted brow. Anne took the opportunity to ask a question of her own.

"Terence," she said, coming to kneel beside him so that she could study the boy's eyes, "why do you have two books in your pants pockets?"

Terence looked down and kicked his legs nervously, as he had done unceasingly through the interrogation. With head bowed, but daring a glance aslant into Anne's eyes, he chewed his lips a moment and then said, "Geordie give it me."

Morgan stopped, his handkerchief still in hand. The two constables looked up. Michael straightened, alert, and slipped his watch into his vest pocket.

Anne asked, "May I see it?"

Terence reached to pull a battered penny novel from his left rear pocket. He said, "He found it on the ground where his mam lives. Outside the privy, he said. He figured, 'Finders keepers.' We was readin' it."

Anne opened the paperback volume with its lurid cover drawing and flipped through the pages.

"It's got writin' in it or somethin'," said Terence, "but we was only readin' the printed parts."

Anne rose to bring the book to Paul Morgan. Michael and the constables peered over his shoulders as the detective inspected the markings jotted in black ink in the borders of the booklet.

"Some kind of code," Morgan surmised. He looked up and asked, "Terence, was it?" When the boy nodded, he continued, "Terence, when did Geordie give this to you?"

"When we was goin' to the crick," Terence replied. "Afore...." He swallowed and bowed his head once more.

Anne recalled that neither boy had carried a book at the creek; they must have hidden it in Terence's "secret stash" behind the smithy shed. She asked, "Did Geordie say when he found it?"

Terence shook his head.

Detective Morgan puckered his lips a moment. At last, he said, "That'll be all, lads. Thank you for answering our questions."

Three of the boys leapt up and hurried out the front door, but Jack hesitated. He asked, "You think somebody kill't Geordie for that?" He jerked his chin toward the book.

"We'll see, son," said the detective. "It's too soon to be certain. But we'll look into it."

Jack nodded acknowledgement and followed his friends.

When the boys had departed, Michael asked quietly, "Detective, were you able to identify which gun fired the bullet that killed Geordie?"

Morgan glanced up at him and said, "Not yet. We've

asked the sportsmen to bring in their weapons for testing. They refused, but I've convinced Judge Anderson that it would be in the interests of justice to rule out the possibility of another weapon, fired from closer to the creek. He's issued a warrant." The detective smiled wryly and added, "Of course, it may be difficult to test the *broken* rifles."

Michael blushed and nodded penitently.

CHAPTER 9

Dreams and nightmares

He woke from a tantalizing dream of love, his member erect and throbbing. Lying in the dark behind Anne, spoon-fashion, Michael cupped her breast, pressed himself against her, and kissed her crown.

"Are you awake?" he whispered. He thought he could feel her smile.

"It's a little difficult to sleep with such distractions."

He snuggled closer and nibbled her ear, making her giggle. She squirmed against him, and he tickled her to make her do it again. When his attentions sent her into gales of laughter and made her kick and writhe, he grasped her wrists and held them. Shifting atop as he pulled his wife onto her back, he parted her legs with his knee and manoeuvred between them.

"I think you're awake now," he said.

Breathing in gasps and half-giggles, she asked facetiously,

"And why do you want to wake me, sir?"

He kissed her thoroughly in answer.

∞

AS HIS PULSE and respiration slowed, Michael rolled over onto his back. Anne turned to curl next to him, reaching her arm across his belly.

"That was worth waking up for," she purred.

Michael chortled. Closing his eyes, he let out a long exhalation and savoured the sensations in his body: the lingering tingles, the satisfaction of completion, the warmth of her next to him. And those other feelings: of belonging, of gratitude, of—he had to admit—pride at having pleasured her.

"Glad you married me?" she asked rhetorically.

He chuckled again. Then, he said seriously, "I thank God every day."

"So do I."

"Anne?"

"Yes, my love?"

"What are standing stones?"

He felt her start at the question. But she settled once more, shifting closer to lay her head in the hollow of his shoulder. After a deep breath and a slow exhalation, she spoke.

"They are markers."

He waited.

After what felt to him an interminable pause, she went on, "What they mark—the standing stones and other ancient signposts—are points of power. Places where strange things can happen."

This time, he could not wait. He prompted, "What kind of strange things?"

Again, she inhaled deeply. "People disappear."

Before he could query further, she continued, "Some do. Not all. Many are not affected, apparently. And some are

simply...changed, in mind or body. Others are injured or even killed in those places."

"Like my mother," he realized.

"Yes," Anne said. "That would be my guess."

After another pause, she explained, "The places of the stones—it's always stones of some sort, in some configuration, you understand, because nothing else lasts—the places marked by stones, and other places that are not marked, or are no longer marked, can be found all over the world."

"Points of power," he murmured. "Do you know what they do?"

"Yes. That is to say, I know what the ones I have experienced do. I have heard of still more that have different functions."

"Functions?"

Though it was too dark to see, she rose on her elbow as if to look into his eyes. She said, "The one at Dùn-Draoidheil moves people through time."

Michael swallowed. His body tingled and a shiver shot up his spine.

He repeated quietly, "Through time."

With a sigh, she said, "Yes. I have been through time...more than once. And I know that there are other places that transport a person across great distance rather than across time. That is how Alex and I came to be on this continent. We came directly from Scotland."

It was too preposterous. And yet she believed it, he knew.

Anne said, "I told you I have seen two of you in the same time. It was just before Culloden. There was one of you born into that period, and another who had come to that century through Dùn-Draoidheil. Two men. Two different bodies. But the same soul.

"One died soon after Culloden. Alex died later, but still well over a hundred years ago.

"And now I find you: brought again to a time not your

own."

Michael licked his lips. His mouth felt dry. He did not want to believe, yet he had to ask.

"Do you know what time is my own?"

"No." She added, "Besides, you grew up in this time. So, from a certain standpoint, this *is* your time."

That made sense. Then, it occurred to him to wonder, "Have you been alive all this time, since Culloden?"

If so, that would make her....

"No," she replied. "I stepped through another power point, quite by accident, and ended up in this time. Or rather, I came through five years ago."

He realized, "That's why you have clothes from another century." And then he gasped, "Good lord, you were at Culloden?"

"Yes," she told him. "We only just made it away. You were...*Alex*...was badly wounded."

"What time do you come from? Originally?"

She paused a small eternity. At last, she whispered, "From the future."

∞

"MICHAEL! WAKE UP!"

He sat bolt upright, panting hard, his heart pounding. Like a hunted animal, he glanced wildly about the room, its pale furniture and whitewashed, flower-stencilled walls dimly visible in the light from the lunar sliver.

"It's all right, Michael," Anne said soothingly. "You're all right. It was a dream."

He turned at her voice and blinked, eyes round as he stared, half-seeing. Gradually, he focussed. He reached trembling hands to touch her face, the softness of her skin an anchor to keep him from falling again into nightmare.

Anne rose onto her knees and embraced him, stroking his

sweat-soaked back and running her fingers through his hair. She held him and murmured to him until he came to himself and hugged her, his grasp so tight she could hardly breathe.

She clasped his head with both hands and kissed his face.

"What is it, my love?" she asked in a whisper. "Can you tell me?"

He relaxed his grip and glanced into her eyes. Looking away again, he said dismissively, "I get nightmares, sometimes, that's all."

Anne regarded him a moment before she said, "I have noticed that. But tonight was worse."

Michael took a deep breath and gazed into her eyes once more, his face a portrait of fear and desperation. "There's something I must tell you."

∞

ANNE HELD HER HUSBAND in her arms, rocking him as he sobbed. Her own tears flowed down her cheeks into his hair.

After a long time, he pulled away, reached for the handkerchief she always kept at the bedside, and blew his nose. He bowed his head in shame and turned from her. His voice barely above a whisper, he said, "I canna blame ye if ye want to leave me."

Anne blew her nose on the sheet and tried to get herself under control. At last, she stepped off the bed and came round to plant herself in front of him. Taking his face into her hands, she forced him to look up at her. She held his eyes and said each word distinctly: "I will never leave you."

He clung to her and wept again.

∞

MICHAEL WOKE from his doze to find Anne crying out breathily in her sleep. He shushed her, stroking her hair. She did not waken, but she fell silent and lapsed into a fitful slumber. By

the wan light of the approaching sunrise, he watched as she jerked and gasped, still assailed by unseen monsters.

He regarded her in awe. From the first night they met, she had proved competent, capable, subtly powerful. Even in the depths of her grief for the child Geordie, there had been a strength within her. Now, he saw her vulnerability, and he wondered what terrors so haunted this quietly formidable woman.

She twitched and whimpered softly, his lover, his wife, and he knew he must be strong for her.

He had always thought himself a weak man. But for her, he wanted to be strong. For her, he thought—for the first time—that he *could* be strong.

Tenderly, he pressed her cheek to his chest and held her. She reached for him, still in sleep, and she calmed. His heart filling with gratitude and gladness at the love she expressed even now, he closed his eyes and listened to the steady rhythm of her respiration.

CHAPTER 10

Interviews and evaluations

A nne sent her husband off with a hearty breakfast to see him through a day in the city. He had argued that he should wait, that she was in danger from the man who had been watching their house. In her turn, she had insisted that the people of The Flats would come to her aid if the need should arise. Finally, after twenty minutes of futile attempts to justify remaining home, he relented. He donned his mid-grey suit and left the house, exasperated, to find Dan Doherty waiting to drive him to town.

Anne smiled and waved to him as he rode off, and then she surveyed the neighbourhood before stepping back inside.

She had just begun to wash the morning's dishes when she felt it: a sudden sharp prick in her belly. She closed her eyes and took several slow, calming breaths. Behind her lids, she searched inward, scanning her womb.

Her eyes still closed, both hands on her convulsing abdomen, she laughed and sobbed as tears of joy flooded her cheeks.

∞

"ET TU, DOHERTY?" Michael remarked when he found the man casually sitting atop his hackney cab as though he had just happened to have nothing to do but wait at the MacGregors' gate.

"Eh?"

With a sigh and a shake of his head, Michael climbed aboard the rig and said, "I assume you know where I'm going?"

"You're dressed to go to court or to Parliament, ain't ye? Which one'll it be?"

"Let's try the bank district, first, shall we?"

Michael settled into the cab and waved to his wife in reluctant farewell. He wanted to stay with her, and he worried all the way to town, taking no notice of the view along the way. His gut clenched whenever he thought of Anne alone, easing only slightly when he remembered the boys.

"I cannot be here all of the time," he had told the lads on the day of the funeral. "Someone needs to watch after Anne. This man, the stranger, may intend her harm."

The six had nodded solemnly, the lines of their mouths set in resolve to protect Herself.

Jack, of course, had suggested that the man should meet with an unfortunate accident and the other lads had eagerly concurred, but Michael had vetoed the proposal. Instead, he had suggested they watch the man—carefully, for he was quite likely dangerous—to see if he might have any confederates, or if he might take an unwholesome interest in anyone else in the neighbourhood, such as Mrs. Monaghan. The boys had seen the wisdom of the plan and agreed.

The shouts of a newsboy brought him back to the present.

As the hackney turned from King Street, Michael forced down another strong impulse to rush back to The Flats, telling himself, *She'll be fine. Our neighbours think of her as kin. They'll take care of her.*

Abruptly, a second mental voice intruded, one he had been trying to keep under lock and key: *Yes, she's fine. And the real reason you want to go back is your worry you won't be able to provide for her. That you're useless and will soon have the proof of it.*

He swallowed, his gut tightening at the fears that had escaped their imaginary box to confront him, and he roused, grateful for the distraction, when he suddenly recognized around him the Bay Street buildings he knew so well. The cab pulled up in front of his bank, and Michael disembarked after a brief argument with Dan Doherty, who finally accepted compensation for the ride. The Scot hoped such tiresome token debate would not accompany every service he engaged in The Flats.

As the horse-drawn carriage drove away with a new client (the ever-practical Mr. Doherty taking advantage of proximity to a streetcar stop), Michael inhaled sharply and strode the twenty-odd paces to the Exchange house down the street.

∞

ANNE HAULED the bucket of hot, soapy water into the house. On her knees in the entryway, she pulled her brush from the pail and began to scrub the grey-painted floor. She hummed happily, turning the rhythmic circular motions into a sort of dance as she scoured with brush and wiped with cloth. In time, the dance became trance and, for perhaps a half-minute, she took no note of the taps at the door. Finally, the insistent knocking penetrated her awareness.

Scrambling up and wiping her hands on her apron, she craned to see out the window nearest the door. A buggy stood in the street, drawn by a fine sorrel horse. She looked down: The floor of the entry was still wet.

As the knock came again, Anne raced out the back way and around to find Joseph MacGregor huffing impatiently. He turned as she stepped onto the porch.

"I'm sorry," Anne said politely. "I had been working and I didn't hear you at first."

He examined her: old blue dress with low neckline, rumpled apron, wisps of hair falling about her face, reddened hands. He said, "Cleaning, I suppose."

"Yes."

He pursed his lips and champed for a moment, his deeply creased cheeks twitching, before he said sharply, "I expect you think I'm going to capitulate. That I'll take Michael back and take *you* to the bosom of our family."

"No," Anne said evenly, countering the ferocity of his gaze and tone with the mildness of her own. "I think you'll disown your son in spite because he did not choose to marry for money."

Joseph MacGregor's eyes flew wide, and he sputtered in astonishment at her turning of the tables.

Before he could reply, she added, "Which is fine by me. We can do quite well without your wealth and your pretentiousness. You think we are not good enough for you. *I* say you are not good enough for us."

With head high, she pivoted and marched off to finish her housework, leaving her father-in-law to fume impotently on her porch.

∞

MICHAEL WALKED out of the Exchange not certain what he felt. There was a sense of deflation at being rebuffed. And a disappointment at failing to acquire one of the more lucrative positions available to a man of his education and accustomed status. But there was something else: an unexpected relief. Upon reflection, he realized that the marble and brass, oak and walnut,

all the trappings of wealth had oppressed him, made him feel trapped in a cold, empty world of numbers and ostentation.

Then, his fears resurfaced to prey on his mind: Fears of failure. Fears that he was truly the incompetent, feckless, useless wretch his father's—no, Joseph MacGregor's—disappointed eyes had so often declared.

Hands balled into fists at his sides, he closed his eyes and swallowed. *No*, he told himself. *I am not—will not be—useless.*

With a deep breath, he surveyed the buildings around him. No, he must try again.

∞

HE HAD INQUIRED at every bank, law office, trading house, and accounting firm in the district. All had claimed they had no positions available, though he knew a few had been lying. Once more, he forcibly suppressed that taunting voice inside his head.

Suddenly, he wondered if he was being blackballed. And if so, by whom?

It occurred to him that his father—stepfather, foster-father, whatever the man might be called—was not the only person who considered him feckless. Nor was he the only one Michael had annoyed. Certainly, Miss Orwell's father might wish to avenge his daughter's sense of slight. Indeed, tales of Miss Orwell's own vindictiveness now came to mind, though he thought her influence limited to the distaff side of the social elite. Her father, on the other hand, had many friends.

And then there was George Bates and his sportsmen. Many such men would go to great lengths to punish someone who had caused them even minor inconvenience.

He sighed. Perhaps he should ask Evan. If anyone had his finger on the pulse of the city, it was Evan Sydenham.

∞

ANNE HAULED the bucket of dirty water to the yard and

poured it out near the dripline of one of the thirstier trees bordering her small property. She returned to find Jack fidgeting uncertainly by the corner of the house.

She had noticed for several days, by the way that he had hastily averted his eyes whenever she looked his way, that something had been on the adolescent's mind. Apparently, the time had come. "Spit it out, Jack," she commanded.

The boy took a deep breath and asked fiercely, "Does he hurt ye?"

Anne stared, taken aback. With a perplexed frown and a little shake of her head, she said, "No, Jack. He is a kind and gentle man. Why would you think he hurts me?"

Jack swallowed and searched the ground at his feet as though for the right words to express himself. At last he looked up and blurted, "But he's so big!"

Anne tilted her head and pressed her lips into a moue as she regarded the boy. After a moment's thought, she raised her eyebrows questioningly and said slowly, "You don't mean his height and breadth, do you?"

Jack blushed scarlet and quickly bowed his head. He admitted, "I seen him...naked without no clothes. That first day."

Anne bit her lip to stifle a smile. Then, she stated quietly, firmly, "No, he doesn't hurt me."

Jack looked up, round-eyed, and protested, "But...but...he's so *big!*"

At this, Anne stepped forward to clasp the boy's hands in hers and said, "And for many women—perhaps most—he would, indeed, be too big for comfort. But for me, he fits just right."

Jack's eyes widened even more. "But...you're *small!* I mean, so much smaller'n him!"

Anne smiled. "I may be small on the outside, but I'm large enough on the inside. Like that magic house in the story I told you."

When he did not appear convinced, she went on to

explain, "People come in all sizes; that's plain enough. But what is not so obvious is that the outside does not necessarily reflect the inside. Or in the case of men, the overall size does not necessarily match the size of their private parts. I think you've probably noticed that."

Jack frowned and tightened his mouth into a thin line as he compared this statement with his own observations.

"In a way," Anne mused, "a big man—I mean a man whose privates are very big—such a man is at a disadvantage. There may be few women who can accommodate him. On the other hand, a small or average man will fit many women."

Jack recalled, "My da says it ain't the size o' the wand that matters."

"Your da's right," she told him, "in the sense that it is not the size that pleases a woman."

"What is it, then?" Jack's face instantly revealed his mortification that he had said that aloud.

Anne grasped his chin and lifted his face to look into his eyes. She said quietly, assuredly, "If you want to please her, you will find a way."

∞

"OH, MY, WHERE DO I BEGIN?" Evan Sydenham, Viscount Danford, exclaimed as he took a snifter of brandy from the waiter's tray and inhaled its fragrance. The moderately tall, blond aristocrat, eldest son of an earl and diplomat, leaned back into his wing chair, draped one arm over the upholstered side as he held up his goblet in the other, and shook his head in mock censure at his friend.

The gentlemen's club, discreetly housed in a grey stone Victorian on a quiet side street a short walk from the newly built Legislative Building, had been Evan's second favourite haunt from the day he had arrived in the city. His favourite had always been the Yacht Club, that establishment being more tolerant of

the sort of boisterous behaviour to which Evan was prone. But this staid club offered the finest array of wines and brandies in town, perhaps in the province.

Here, in The Study, clusters and pairs of wing chairs, some in plush green velvet and some in striped satin, all protected by snowy antimacassars, huddled here and there around the oak-panelled and Persian-carpeted room, ready to envelope members in a perception of privacy as they sipped imported brandy or good scotch. A low conversation drifted down the hallway and disappeared as the Honourable Howard Jenkins and the Honourable Adam Lewis took their Tory discussion from the foyer to the dining-room.

The scent of the brandy triggered a craving for spirits, and Michael realized he had not had a drink in days. Despite his longing, he decided that today was not a good day to indulge.

"Just tell me, Evan," he said wearily. "Is it...Father?"

"No, actually," said Evan after tasting the brandy. "I do believe he's the only one who *hasn't* got it in for you, dear boy."

Michael leaned back and heaved a sigh.

"And me, of course," Evan added with an ingratiating smile and a graceful gesture. He eyed Michael a moment before he asked with an air of casual interest, "Is she worth it?"

The Scot gave his friend a penetrating stare. At last, he said quietly, "Yes."

∞

AS THE SUN LOWERED toward the western horizon, Michael walked back toward King Street. He could take a hackney, but he wanted time to think. Evan had gaily enumerated the entire list of his enemies, often specifying the transgressions for which he was now being punished (aside from his marriage, which had apparently been the last straw in the eyes of many). No one was willing to do him any real harm, lest Joseph MacGregor change his mind and bring him back into the fold. No one except Miss

Orwell, that is. On the other hand, a word here or there that prevented him from taking a position in any prominent business could easily be dismissed as bad luck.

That left only trades and labour, all of which would provide a modest income at best.

Strangely, Michael felt as if a weight had been lifted from him. At least he knew who his enemies were and how far they would go. With the possible exception of Miss Orwell. He dismissed the socialite to return to a contemplation of his options.

Trades. What skills could he offer?

Just then, he saw a man hovering at the edge of a building under construction. Michael surveyed the foundation, set in its rubble-filled trench, and the beginnings of the stone walls above the plinth. On impulse, he strode purposefully to the man who had stooped to measure the wall with a collapsible rod.

"Excuse me," said the Scot as he approached the broadly built, middle-aged, brown-haired man in sturdy blue dungarees and a tan vest over a yellow cotton shirt. "Can you tell me who is constructing this building?"

The man straightened and said, "I am."

Heart quickening, Michael inquired, "Do you have use for a stoneworker, sir?"

The man eyed him, taking in his size and build, and his suit. He asked, "Are you asking for yourself, by chance?"

Michael nodded. "Yes."

"You look a gentleman. What experience do you have?"

The stonemason's mien was wary but not dismissive. Taking heart, Michael eagerly described his education in geology and his Army service. He emphasized his summers in Cornwall building dry-stone walls, and his stint in Egypt building an infirmary.

"Let me see your hands," the man demanded.

Michael extended his hands for inspection, explaining self-consciously, "I scalded them recently." On an optimistic

note, he added, "But they're healing well."

The builder examined them briefly and said, "You may have done a little heavy lifting in the past, but you've a gentleman's hands, now. What makes you think you can do an honest day's work?"

Michael flinched at the stinging words. But necessity trumping pride, he said in all sincerity, "I have a new wife and no income to speak of. I'll work as hard as needs be to do right by her."

The man pursed his lips and considered a moment. At last, he offered his calloused hand and said, "The name's Jake Trevelyan. Be here tomorrow morning, seven sharp."

CHAPTER 11

New beginnings

Anne collapsed on her husband's chest, breathing tremulously. As she lay astride and above him, Michael maintained his grip on her buttocks, softly kneading her flesh. He wondered how long he would be able to enjoy her passion and his own before it became necessary to abstain.

A child. In truth, the possibility of having a child of his own had never occurred to him.

A realization stabbed him. His voice breaking with his heart, he whispered, "I have no name to give him."

Anne pushed up on her hands and looked into his eyes. "Yes, you do," she told him firmly.

"I have Joseph's name," he responded desolately.

"It's also your own," said Anne.

He shook his head and closed his eyes, perceiving himself unable to make his meaning, and his pain, clear.

"Michael, look at me," Anne commanded.

When he opened his eyes, she fixed his gaze with her own. She said, "You are a MacGregor. I know it. "

He frowned and searched her eyes. "How can you know? Did Fa...Joseph say so?"

"He didn't have to," Anne replied. "I knew it from the moment I touched that bit of old plaid among your belongings."

Michael thought a moment before he recalled, "My swaddling-band?"

"Actually, by the size of it, I think it was your mother's earasaid."

He objected, "No one's worn an earasaid in over a century."

Anne conceded, "Nor will they, for a while yet. But it's a MacGregor pattern, in a sett not yet invented. And that earasaid has passed through a time field."

He regarded her a moment before he asked tentatively, "You can know that by touching it?"

"Yes," she told him. "Passage through time leaves a kind of signature. A...vibration. An energy. I suppose I can feel it because I've jumped through time repeatedly, myself. I recognize that trace."

Michael mulled the matter. Certainly, a tartan, wherever or whenever its origin, could be considered proof of clan affiliation, he assumed. Scottish associations had been proliferating throughout the world, and plaid designs, once outlawed, were now approved by the clan chiefs and registered officially. His heart lightened as he gradually accepted her assertion about his ancestry.

At last, he said, his voice low and full of hope, "Then our child shall be James Alexander MacGregor." Why he had chosen that name, he did not know. But it felt right to him. He smiled at the prospect of christening his son, and he pulled his wife into his arms.

As he held her, it occurred to him to wonder, "What is it

like to move through time?" He could not bring himself to fully credit it as possible, but he enjoyed the fantastical notion, rather as one would relish the absurdities of a yellowback novel.

Hushed, she said, "If there is a Hell, it is within that space that is not space, that time that is all time and none. It is Chaos, where nothing is as it should be. And it is filled with the screams of the damned."

Michael's arms tightened around her, protecting and clinging. His wife had a frightening way of making the impossible all too real.

∞

ANNE SMILED to herself at the name Michael had chosen for their child. He could not know that he—as Alex—had also chosen James, or rather the Scottish variant of James, as the name for his son. She marvelled that Michael was at once so different from and yet so similar to Alex.

As she lay in her husband's arms, her nose tickled by the curly black hairs of his chest, she recalled the words, long ago, of an old woman who had told her, "You will have a child. You must have faith. The right time will come."

She had thought, once, that the right time had, indeed, come. She and Alex had felt such joy, then, as they looked forward to the birth of Seumas. But fate had played a cruel trick in the form of Lawrence Sydenham.

Anne prayed that no such impediment would mar her happiness with Michael. She wanted nothing in the world more than to bear little James Alexander MacGregor.

∞

HE HAD THOUGHT to slip out while Anne slept, but Michael emerged from the outhouse to find her waiting her turn. She kissed him lovingly, and then, without a word, slid past to close the door of the little-house behind her.

Smiling happily, realizing he was glad of her company, he took the stairs two at a time to dress for a day of hauling and placing stone. When he returned to the kitchen, he discovered his wife had set the table for breakfast, going so far as to put a lace cloth under the chargers and a vase of flowers in the centre. A shallow bowl of newly gathered honey in the comb sat next to the salt server and the butter dish. He checked his watch and stepped out to the back porch, into morning twilight's glow. Anne's humming drew him beyond the well-house to a garden where she gathered herbs and just-ripened serviceberries. All around, the air was filled with the twitters of wakening birds and the freshness of a wakening world.

The kettle began to whistle. Leaving his wife to her task, Michael hastened to the summer kitchen to pour the boiling water into the waiting teapot. He lifted the lid of another pot that shared the little stove to find the porridge had started to thicken. He stirred it with a paddle from a crock of wooden implements, and he inhaled with delight the aromas of bubbling oats; steeping tea; and the yard's bounty of sprouting greenery, burgeoning flowers, and summer's first ripening fruits.

Though his belly fluttered with nervousness in his desire to make a good impression, today, on the job, Michael knew he felt a deep contentment: This life with the woman he loved was the idyll he had never dared dream he could live.

When Anne joined him, he folded her in his arms and kissed her tenderly before carrying the oatmeal to the house as she followed with the tea and the basket of garnishes for their breakfast together.

∞

MICHAEL STEPPED into the early morning sunshine and joined the men of The Flats off to work in the city, each carrying a lunch bag and flask. His neighbours glanced at his muslin sack and his attire (his oldest blue flannel sporting trousers, pale-blue linen

shirt, brown vest to cover his suspenders—they being considered underclothing and thus unfit to be seen in public—and sturdy brown walking shoes) and nodded their wordless greetings. None commented, but he felt their approbation: He was one of them, after all.

With each block, the numbers of workmen grew, some carrying the tools of their trade. As they trooped across the wooden footbridge, out of earshot of still-sleeping children, jovial chatter began.

Giovanni Cacciotti ventured to inquire, "MacGregor, sir. Where do you work?"

"You have no need to call me 'sir,' Mr. Cacciotti," he responded, glad he recalled the man's name. "But to answer your question, I hope to work for Mr. Trevelyan, the stonemason. He's giving me a trial, today, on Draper Avenue."

A chorus of ahs and a nodding of heads nearby greeted his announcement. The news rippled through the crowd and, presently, a man jogged from behind to fall into step beside the Scot.

"Hear you're workin' for Trevelyan?"

Michael said, "I hope so. I start today."

The man sidled and extended his hand, introducing himself. "Michel Villeneuve. Dey call me Mike." He added, "I work for Trevelyan. On de Draper projec'."

"Good to meet you," Michael acknowledged with a smile of genuine pleasure. Knowing someone at the site made his first day on the job just a little less daunting.

Another man stepped up. "Goin' to Draper, are ye?"

Mike Villeneuve answered for him, "Yep. New man startin' today."

The second worker offered his hand. "Rob Donnelly."

"Michael MacGregor," he replied, shaking the hand firmly as he recognized his next-door neighbour. He looked from one to the other. "How long have you worked for Mr. Trevelyan?"

"T'ree years," said Mike Villeneuve.

"Six for me," said Donnelly. "Hooked up with'm when 'e first came to town. Treats 'is men good."

Several heads bobbed in agreement.

By the time Michael reached the streetcar stop on the western end of Queen Street, seven men had joined him. At least two dozen more, headed in the same direction, climbed aboard the spanking-new electric vehicle with them, while the rest of the local working men dispersed north or south to other destinations, or waited for the next eastbound car.

∞

THE GONG of the clock tower in the distance signalled noon. Without need of command, the men set down their tools or burdens, collected their prepared lunches from the pile under the shadow of an oak on the edge of the adjacent property, and moved off to sit in open spaces here and there about the site to enjoy a brief rest and a much-needed meal.

Those who had ridden the street rail with him gathered around Michael in the shade of the oak as he opened his sack and retrieved the flask Anne had packed for him. He gulped the sweet ale and stuffed a bannock into his mouth, grateful for her foresight and providence.

Chewing a bite of the sandwich his own wife had made for him, Mike Villeneuve asked, "So, how did ye come to meet Herself?"

Michael smiled to himself at the strange cross between low French and local Irish that distinguished the man's accent. He answered, "She rescued me from thugs who were about to kill me."

"Mmm," the man responded in unison with several of the others.

Mick McGee said, "Heard it was somethin' like that. You've the air of a drinker."

It was not censure, exactly. But Michael recognized the tone of a father having a word with the errant beau of his daughter. And he knew, having been informed ever so discreetly by Ford (and much less discreetly by Elizabeth) that he smelled of the booze he had imbibed.

He asked point-blank, "Do I still smell of it? I haven't had a drink in days."

"Aye, it'll take a while to pass," Rob Donnelly told him knowingly. With a sly grin, he added, "Not that most of us don't smell o' the *aqua vitae* from time to time."

Guilty snickers rippled through the group, and Pat O'Connell started to choke. Helpful hands clapped him firmly on the back until he coughed up a morsel of chicken.

Deliberately casual, Marc Desrosiers said, "I hear'd you be the son o' Joseph MacGregor."

Michael gritted his teeth. Reining in his initial angry response, he said more sharply than he had intended, "I'm not his son."

"Didn't like you marryin' Herself," Mick McGee surmised, an edge of affront in his worldly-wise tone.

"No, he didn't," Michael admitted quietly.

Rob Donnelly waxed philosophical: "Well, they say a good woman's a pearl o' great price, and I've no doubt you've taken yourself such a pearl, whatever your kin may think."

At that, Michael smiled. "Yes," he said. "She is...a gem."

∞

ANNE HAD BEEN sweeping the front porch when a well-appointed carriage rolled into view and stopped in front of her home. The coachman hopped down to open the door for Hermione MacGregor. As her mother-in-law approached, Anne set the broom aside and strode to the gate.

"To what do I owe the pleasure?" she asked coolly.

Hermione stood outside the closed gate and regarded her

daughter-in-law a moment, taking in the odd garments, white hair, and patched apron. At last, she heaved a sigh, looked into Anne's eyes, and said, "I wish to speak with you."

After a brief evaluation of the woman, Anne unlatched the gate and drew it back, gesturing toward the front door. As the liveried driver took his seat to wait, the MacGregor matriarch walked up the short path to the porch and into the home of her son and his wife.

Hermione scanned the plainly furnished room with undisguised curiosity and some surprise. Anne pulled a pressed-back chair from beneath the kitchen table and held it as the woman sat. Then, she fetched glasses from a shelf and a pitcher of freshly made, sweetened spearmint tea from the screened and barred window on the north wall (the glazed casement she had fitted with a horizontal board to form a two-tiered cold cupboard that served the function of a refrigerator).

"Thank you," said the matron as she accepted the proffered beverage. She sipped it, savoured its flavour a moment, and admitted, "It's quite good," before she set down the glass and squared her shoulders.

"You gave Joseph quite a turn," the woman said with a hint of amusement. "Not many people stand up to him."

Anne smiled wryly. "I suspected as much." The distiller had a bulldog look and manner that, no doubt, intimidated many.

Hermione MacGregor took another sip of tea before proceeding. With an air of decision, she fixed the gaze of her son's wife and asked straight out, "What do you want?"

Anne regarded her through narrowed eyes before taking a deep breath and saying, "From you, nothing. From Michael, everything."

The woman blinked several times before recovering to ask tartly, "What do you mean?"

Anne chuckled briefly, but her smile faded and she held her mother-in-law's eyes as she said in a firm, quiet voice, "What

I want is a husband who loves me and accepts my love in return. A man with whom to spend my days and my nights and my life. A father for our child." In an unconscious reflex, she touched a hand to her belly. "That's what I want."

Hermione MacGregor's eyes widened at the protective, motherly gesture and she blinked again. She swallowed, and she looked up from the cradling hand to the steady eyes of the woman who had captured her son's heart.

After a moment, she asked primly, "Is it Michael's?"

"Yes."

They held each other's gaze a long time. Finally, the matron said in a whisper, "I'll speak to Joseph."

∞

MICHAEL COLLAPSED onto the back porch, legs stretched out into the grass. He stared dully at the tray of food as Anne positioned it and stabilized its uprights on either side of his lap. The smell of the hot daube and fresh bread set his mouth to watering, but he made no move to take up the utensils.

Anne knelt beside him. After a moment of stroking his hair, its perfect black now whitened with stone dust, she kissed his gritty temple before settling herself to the task of feeding her exhausted husband. She picked up the spoon; scooped vegetables, beef, and broth; blew softly across the steaming stew; and brought the spoon to his mouth. When he opened his lips at the touch of the steel utensil, she poured the food onto his tongue.

Patiently, mouthful by mouthful, Anne fed him as she soon would feed their child. Then, she brought water and cloths and washed him where he sat, pulling off his sweat-soaked and grimy garments and wiping him down with firm but gentle strokes.

When Anne laid him back so as to remove his shoes, socks, trousers, and drawers, he let her strip him and tend him in

loving, silent service. Once he had been bathed, she bandaged his blistered and abraded hands and administered drops of her remedies. Finally, she rubbed his skin with an herbal lotion to ward off mosquitoes and wrapped him in a sheet where he lay.

Michael blinked blearily. He had never been so tired in his life, not even during his first weeks in the Army when the sergeant had taken the recruits, carrying heavy packs, on full-day hikes up and down hills. Of course, he had been younger, then, and still fit from his rowing days in school.

He thought absently that he should feel humiliated at being spoon-fed by his wife, but he was too exhausted even for that. Indeed, he was amazed and grateful at her patience and kind attentiveness. For a moment, he tried to imagine Elizabeth in a similar circumstance, and he pitied his sister's future husband.

As he lay on the back porch, covered in herbal scent and cotton sheet under the stars, muscles aching and skin scraped, he realized that he had never felt happier. His eyes closed of their own volition, and he dreamed of stone and earth and an unending walk in the Highlands.

∞

"I'VE NEVER done this before," Anne admitted nervously.

"If you want me to—"

She rushed to insist, "No, no. I can do this. I'll be careful."

Michael sat still and watched his wife approach with the razor. He could see her fierce concentration as she forced her hands to steady and she focussed on the point where blade met flesh. Had he not already cut himself trying to shave with arms that shook with the effort, he would try again.

He felt weak and helpless. He felt ridiculous. And he felt ashamed that he had let himself deteriorate to such a degree. Father—Joseph—had warned him of the price of debauchery. Now, he wished he had listened.

He could only hope Anne's liquid remedies would work quickly.

∞

BY WEEK'S END, Michael could feed and wash and shave himself. His hands had calloused; the signs of the earlier scalding had diminished; the scrapes and cuts were healing well; his sunburnt skin had begun to bronze. Although his muscles still ached, the pain had eased and the sharp spasms had ceased. To his relief, he was becoming inured to the physical demands of his trade.

Bathed, and clad in his silk robe, he stood on the back porch and gazed at the stars. Anne came to join him, smelling of her cucumber soap and wrapped in her cotton kimono.

In the dark of the moon, with no earthly competition along the lampless streets of The Flats, the array of celestial lanterns above glittered keen and bright. A soft, warm breeze fluttered raiment, lifted wisps of unbound hair, and blew the scents of summer's bounty about them. No dog barked. No cat yowled. No child cried.

"I've been thinking," Michael whispered as he stepped behind and put his arms around his wife, one spanning her chest and the other cradling her waist. He pulled her close against him.

"Have you?" she responded. "And what have you been thinking?"

He said, "I think...that it has been six days since I last made love to you."

"Indeed, I do believe you are right," she said. "Whatever shall we do about that?"

He reached under her kimono to cup her breasts, and he leaned to nibble her ear.

∞

"SHALL WE GO to St. Anthony's today?" Anne proposed as she

buttoned the front of her grey gown.

Tying his peacock-blue silk cravat, Michael frowned, perplexed. "We're not papist. Why would we go there?"

A week earlier, they had attended the tiny, white clapboard church with empty steeple that served all Protestant denominations on Sundays. But at this suggestion Michael suddenly wondered if, indeed, his wife *was* papist. He turned to ask cautiously, "Are you...?"

Pushing the top fabric-covered button of her dress into place and arranging her collar, Anne smiled and said, "I do not believe in popes."

Michael let out the breath he had not realized he had been holding. While he felt no aversion to Catholics, personally, he knew well the climate of intolerance among many in the city.

Anne went on, "Nor do I believe in bishops or reverends or priests or rabbis or imams."

At his dumbfounded gape, she explained, "I believe in God, not in religion. Not in organizations that take on a life of their own as centres of political and social and, truth be told, financial power instead of spirituality."

Michael regarded her thoughtfully a moment before turning back to the mirror to insert his emerald tie pin. He contemplated the notion a full minute before asking with what he hoped was a casual air, "Are you Christian?" He focussed on her reflection in the long, pine-framed looking-glass hinged on bowed legs with extended feet.

Anne tilted her head and fixed his eyes through the reflected image. She said, "I have read the Christian bible and many other holy books. I find truth in all of them. And history, some of which is appalling. And questionable ideas, as well.

"As for the words attributed to Christ," she added, "I find those profound, though often misinterpreted and misunderstood by both adherents and opponents."

Michael turned to her and clasped her waist, looking deeply into her eyes. He said, "You are a very unusual woman."

All of a sudden, a realization struck him: "You're attending both churches to bridge the gap and bring the people of The Flats together!"

He gazed at her through new eyes, round with amazement and appreciation, and he now understood why everyone in the neighbourhood referred to his wife as "Herself." As she smiled up at him, he nodded awed understanding.

And hoped he could live up to the responsibilities of his unintentionally acquired role as "Himself."

∞

WHEREAS THE LITTLE white Trinity Church overlooked the banks of the Bow, St. Anthony's stood upon the highest elevation in The Flats, a low rise on the western edge of the district. Built primarily from the grey mud excavated for its foundation, its unfired bricks lovingly handmade by parishioners, the Roman Catholic church's solid façade and soaring bell-tower dominated the little community. Only the asylum on the southern border of The Flats rose taller at a full five stories, its forbidding stone exterior sequestered behind high limestone walls and surrounded by sweeping tracts of lawn.

Anne and Michael walked arm in arm along the grass-and herb-filled lanes, joining the throng that wended its way to St. Anthony's. They greeted their neighbours genially and waved to those headed in the opposite direction. When they reached the churchyard, they paused outside to chat with the small cluster of elders who habitually entered the church last.

When the perpetually mourning-draped Mrs. Anna Maria Gisella Madonna Buzzetti finally tottered into the church, supported on one side by her son, Marco, and on the other by her grandson, Luca, the gaggle at the door stepped in behind and took seats in the rearmost pews.

At home, Anne had shown him how to make the sign of the cross; so, Michael dutifully tapped forehead, chest, left

shoulder, and right shoulder along with the congregation and knelt on the wooden boards set before each bench when everyone else did. He watched Father O'Donnell perform the rituals of this unfamiliar faith. And he marvelled that, on this warm day, the priest barely perspired under the many layers of the traditional vestments: long black cassock; white linen amice to cover the everyday clerical collar; snowy, ankle-length alb with modest lace edging at the hem and sleeves, its midsection girdled with a white, tasselled cord; long stole round the neck, crossed over the chest and secured by the cincture, the stole's ends hanging just above the hem of the alb; and finally, the cape-like chasuble, the outer garment proclaiming the priest's status as celebrant.

Michael understood little, the Mass being entirely in Latin, and although he had studied the ancient language in school, he was not accustomed to hearing it spoken with such fluency. But for all its strangeness, he found the Catholic service unexpectedly moving.

Neither partook of the Eucharist, but when the collection tray was passed around, Michael and Anne each contributed to the parish coffers. And on the way out of the church, they placed money in the poor-box under the approving eye of the almoner.

∞

"I'M STARVING!" Michael exclaimed as they strolled Aspen Alley. Waiting until after church to break his fast had seemed unfair to him ever since he was first required to forgo the Sunday-morning meal in childhood.

"You're in luck," Anne told him cheerily. "Eddy Jackson needed to cull two of his steers this week. I have beef roasting in the pit."

"Thank you, God!" he said with no irreverence.

Michael had noted that, among his wife's many peculiarities, her cooking habits were perhaps the most

anomalous. In the yard, she had built a rock-lined pit, covered when not in use, that served a variety of purposes, including the boiling of laundry and the firing of pottery as well as the roasting of meat. In the summer kitchen, next to a wooden counter, sat two little clay stoves she called "estufas," the pair sometimes linked by a thick slab of iron plate laid across them. Opposite, on the north wall stacked with cordwood on its outside, a cob oven baked bread and bannocks, while an open trough topped by a removable iron grid—an adaptation she termed a "barbecue"—seared both meat and vegetables. At times, she nestled a Dutch oven among the coals to cook a stew or soup.

This arrangement, he had come to realize, was their only functional kitchen. The space in the house would be more appropriately labelled a dining-room, though Anne often washed dishes or churned butter on the countertop, there. He wondered whether she considered it a hardship to cook outdoors in the cold of winter. And he shook his head in amazement at the memory of her running through rain to fetch a pot of hot water for tea.

When they turned into the curving Cedar Lane, he stopped dead. His father's—Joseph MacGregor's—carriage-and-four waited in front of their gate.

"What does *he* want?" he said with a trace of the anger that had flared within him to clench his gut and curl his fingers into fists.

"We'll soon find out," Anne replied phlegmatically.

∞

JOSEPH, HERMIONE, and Elizabeth MacGregor, and Kenneth Armstrong sat stiffly in the wooden chairs arranged on three sides of the table. Facing them, Michael reached into the fruit bowl atop the low cupboard by the back door and bit into an apple as his stomach complained at the further extension of the night's fast. He said nothing, merely leaned against the corner cabinet bridging the east and north walls as he eyed his visitors

coldly. All waited for Anne to return with tea.

When the mistress of the house had finally returned and served the steaming Oolong, the infusion accompanied by a small pot of honey and a tiny pitcher of fresh goat milk fetched from across the street, she stood with her husband and waited expectantly. The guests each sipped tentatively, clearly anticipating that the fare would be below their standards, but their expressions lightened with surprise at the taste of the hot beverage. Hermione added milk. Kenneth added a substantial dollop of honey.

After one more sip, Joseph MacGregor set cup into saucer and both onto the table. He inhaled long and deeply, looked into Michael's eyes, and said grudgingly, "I may have been hasty and unduly harsh when we last had words."

Michael stared at him a moment. Then, he surveyed the faces of the other three and glanced at his wife, her smile encouraging, before he licked his lips, took a deep breath of his own, and said, "At least I know who I really am."

"No, Michael!" Hermione expostulated. "You are our son. You always have been, since...we first found you."

"Aye," Joseph stated with a tightening of his jaw. "You are, my boy."

Elizabeth spoke up, her shrillness belying her words, "We want you to come home."

Michael's lips drew into a wry smile at her ambivalence. Then, sobering, he said quietly, "This is my home, now."

Kenneth Armstrong remonstrated, "Surely you can't be serious. Why on earth would you want to remain in a slum?"

"It may be a slum to you," Michael said equably, "but I have made friends here." He took Anne's hand and smiled down at her, adding, "And this is my wife's house. Our home." He turned back to conclude, "I like this place and this neighbourhood, and I will not leave."

Hermione sighed. Despite their personal preferences in the matter, Elizabeth and Kenneth huffed and squirmed in

agitation at what they clearly considered an absurd decision. Joseph cocked an eyebrow.

In afterthought, Michael grinned as he mentioned one final consideration: "Besides, Ford will be much happier not having to make me presentable."

Joseph now said pragmatically, "Well, I daresay you are closer to both the distillery and our warehouses."

Her countenance evincing worry, Hermione turned to her husband to protest, "But Joseph, the baby...."

Kenneth Armstrong started. He looked from Hermione to Anne.

Anne's voice rang clear and firm: "The baby will be fine. Affluence guarantees neither health nor safety." She added with a cynical smile, "And what breeding tells is all too often some rather shocking secrets."

Hermione frowned. She sounded truly baffled when she asked, "What do you mean by that?"

Anne opened her mouth to speak, but Michael cut her off with a firm squeeze of her hand. He said, "She means that even the best families have dirty laundry they do not want aired in public. Skeletons in the scullery, bastards in the buttery, and so on."

Joseph nodded, pursing his lips. He said judiciously, "That's true enough."

At this juncture, the patriarch stood and announced, "Wherever ye may choose to live, Michael, I'd like ye to come to work with me at the distillery."

Kenneth Armstrong gave his future father-in-law a sharp glance, but said nothing.

Michael faced his father squarely, took a determined breath, and said, "I appreciate your offer, Fa—"

He reflected a moment before he amended quietly, "Joseph."

Another pause. The older man worked his lips, struggling uneasily with the changes in his relationship with his adopted

son.

Finally, Michael said, "I cannot accept your offer." Before Joseph could object, he explained, "I have taken employment with a master stonemason. I must at least finish this job before I contemplate other work. I have given my word."

Joseph worried his lip another moment before he sighed and acknowledged, "Aye, if ye've given your word, ye must keep it, to be sure." He added, "But will ye at least consider coming to the distillery once your obligation is discharged?"

Michael nodded. He said, "We'll see...Father."

"Good...good." Joseph MacGregor looked from his son to his wife and daughter. Then, with a small bow to Anne, he said, "We thank you for your hospitality. We must be off. We're expected at the Jenkinses' for dinner."

The members of the party rose and dithered a moment, Kenneth Armstrong gulping down the last of his tea and Elizabeth straightening her skirts primly. When the four took their leave, Anne and Michael accompanied them to their coach and watched as the boxy vehicle, its windows reflecting gold in the afternoon sun, lumbered away and turned onto Sumac Street.

When his kin were out of sight, Michael embraced his wife—his new family—and held her tightly.

CHAPTER 12

Brotherhood

Rob Houlihan and Kevin Kelleher materialized as if by magic when Anne retrieved the roast beef from the pit. Both orphans who lived in the streets, they seemed to have antennae sensitive to meals home-cooked by soft-hearted women. Indeed, that was how Anne had come to meet the scruffy boys: She had baked bread in her newly built summer kitchen and, when she pulled the loaf from the oven, had turned to find two youngsters looking up at her through doleful puppy eyes, hungry and pathetic.

After a time on their own, the lads had developed both a wariness of strangers and a sense of independence, neither of which would allow fosterage or adoption, even by loving families. They had chosen to remain brothers-by-choice and live wild. Now and then, Anne and other ladies of The Flats gave them new or serviceable hand-me-down clothes and footwear

when they outgrew the old. And Anne had persuaded them to join the rest of her students and learn to read, that they might someday make a future off the streets.

No one asked how they fed themselves when not in The Flats. Everyone suspected they had learned to pick pockets, or pilfer small items from stores, or run errands for some of the less scrupulous men in town. No one wanted to know for sure: Poverty has its own protocols.

Anne spread a blanket in the shade of her cherry tree and placed the platters and bowls of food in the centre, within the ring of plates and utensils. When Michael arrived, bearing the jug of sweet ale from the cold pit next to the foundation on the north side of the summerhouse, he cocked an eyebrow at the boys sitting cross-legged on the quilt, stuffing rolls into their mouths.

Anne smiled sheepishly. "Guess who's come to dinner."

Michael shot her a jaundiced scowl and sat down to the long-awaited meal.

Kneeling, Anne took fork and spoon to transfer salad from the large bowl to each of the plates. The boys peered suspiciously at the greenery presented to them and poked it to see what lay hidden among the leaves. When they found bits of fruit and flowers and boiled egg, they looked at each other with raised brows and wide eyes. Once a dollop of dressing had been spooned atop the salad, and a buttered oatcake, baked new potatoes, and bite-sized pieces of meat had been placed around it, the boys looked at each other once more, this time with broad grins. They immediately attacked the ring around the green.

The lads had polished off all but the salad before they even looked up from their plates. Each took a gulp of the sweet ale that had been poured for them, and now observed the adults. They glanced from their hosts to each other and back again as Anne and Michael speared leaves and petals and chunks of fruit to eat them with relish.

After a wordless exchange consisting mostly of eyebrow shrugs, each of the boys reached tentatively for a leaf and tasted

it. They glanced at each other and shrugged their shoulders noncommittally. Undecided, they tried a petal. Then a slice of egg. Then a few berries. By the time they had concluded that they did not like this strange food, they had emptied their plates.

When Rob and Kevin left—hurriedly, before they could be induced to take part in such abhorrent rituals as washing dishes or, Heaven forbid, bathing—they stuffed their pockets with the remaining oatcakes and scones (in the interests of leaving no food to rot, of course) before dashing away.

Michael shook his head as he watched after the scampering rapscallions. Clearly, he already had extra mouths to feed.

∞

JACK AND LARRY appeared in early evening, after the Carey funeral, to report that the blond stranger had been spotted again, this time at the cathouse. He had caused no trouble, according to Miss Louise, but the boys had followed him to a tavern on Front Street called the "Cup and Star."

"A bad place, that," said Jack. "Constable Ryan says so."

"Why does he say that?" Anne wondered.

"Dunno," Jack replied with a shrug. "But that's what 'e says."

"Sounds familiar," Michael murmured, straining to recall where he had heard that name.

"Da says there's Fenians go there," Larry told them. "Leastways, there use' to be."

Michael recalled, "That was it! The newspapers claimed the Bluebottle Riots started there, back in seventy-eight! There were rumours the Fenians had stirred it up, but there was no evidence to support the claim."

Anne observed, "Such a group often gets blamed falsely just because of its reputation. On the other hand, they may well have contributed to the riots for their own purposes."

Nodding to himself, Michael thought aloud, "And they could be back in the country, up to no good."

All of a sudden, he and Anne looked at each other, eyes wide with realization, and said simultaneously, "Geordie's book!"

∞

CONSTABLE PAUL McMURTRY, new to the constabulary, listened with pouting lips and dubious stare as Anne and Michael relayed the information gleaned by the boys. When he did not even write down what they told him, they exchanged annoyed glances and summarily dismissed the man by saying a prim, "Good night, Constable." Abruptly, they turned to go inside.

Muttering profanities under his breath, the policeman stepped off the porch into the twilight beyond the rectangles of candlelight from the windows. He had almost reached the gate when Larry and Jack came running.

"Missus, Mister!" they called together from up the lane. By the time they arrived, panting, Anne and Michael had already shoved past the disgruntled cop to meet the boys in the street.

"Come quick!" Larry rasped, pointing toward Sumac Street.

Anne and Michael raced along the road, followed closely by the winded boys and, after a bout of indecision, by the constable. Gestures from the lads headed them this way and that until they reached Trinity Church.

"Inside," Jack called hoarsely.

The door stood ajar. Michael pushed it open and stepped in ahead of Anne to scan the single room beyond the little vestibule. In the dusky interior illuminated only by pale moonbeams through the west windows and the open doorway, he glimpsed nothing but the rows of benches and the pine table that served as the altar. Then, a whimper drew him and Anne

forward.

Past the front pews, Kevin and Rob lay hunched on the age-greyed floor, trembling violently, breathing in ragged gasps, the tracks of tears staining their dirty cheeks. They now smelled of more than their usual ripe odour of unwashed boy. Vomit and urine, blood and street ordure had been added.

Anne and Michael stepped around and each knelt to the children.

"What's going on? Who are they?" demanded the constable when he saw them.

"Local boys," said Anne. With an angry glare, she added acerbically, "Clearly, none of your concern."

McMurtry flinched as though she had slapped him. Anne merely turned to murmur softly to the children, stroking their hair.

"Come, we'll take you home," she said. "We'll keep you safe."

When Michael tried to pick him up, Kevin wailed and pulled away, curling into himself.

"Oh, Jesus!" the Scot murmured. He knew. When he looked to Anne, he saw that she knew, too.

Anne leaned down and whispered to Kevin, "It will be all right, Kevin. I will bring you home and we'll take care of you. We'll bring you and Rob home."

Michael moved round to offer help to Rob, instead; he was grateful that the boy accepted his aid. Meanwhile, Anne pulled Kevin to a stand and put an arm around his waist to support him as he walked unsteadily. They had got as far as Cottonwood Crescent when Dan Doherty arrived with his cab and drove them, and Jack and Larry, the remaining distance to Cedar Lane.

Constable McMurtry was left to find his own way.

∞

"I'LL GET BEDDING. We'll set them on the floor," Anne called back as she ran upstairs. When she returned and spread two blankets on the painted planks, Michael and Dan Doherty eased the young lads down. Both boys immediately curled into foetal position.

Before Anne could throw another pair of coverlets over them, Larry exclaimed, "They're bleedin'! Look! Their bums!"

"Jesus save us!" said Doherty, and he crossed himself. He put a protective arm around his son and held him close.

Jack dropped to his knees on the quilt and leaned down to gaze into Rob's face. "Who done it?" he asked in outrage. "We're gonna get 'em, Rob! Just you tell us who!"

Rob shook his head weakly and wept.

"Perhaps he doesn't know, Jack," Anne said quietly as she covered the children. "Give him time."

Jack's own tears flowed. He blinked them back and stifled furious sobs as he rose and stood with body rigid and hands curled into trembling fists at his sides.

Kneeling, but not daring to touch them, Michael assured the boys, "It will get better. In a while, it will get better. It'll stop hurting."

He closed his eyes tightly against the memory of his own pain and the certain knowledge of theirs. Tears rolled into the stubble on his chin.

Anne brought several remedy bottles. Gently, she pulled open each boy's lips to squeeze in two drops of one of the liquids.

"What's that?" Larry asked.

"Arnica," said Anne. "For healing. I'll give them some other remedies, as well."

Dan Doherty asked, "Will they heal? I mean...." His voice trailed off.

Michael looked up into the man's face. He locked eyes with Doherty and shook his head, his countenance forlorn.

"Oh, Jesus!" the coachman breathed, realization dawning. He crossed himself again.

∞

WHEN KEVIN and Rob had finally fallen into fitful sleep, Michael left Anne to sit by them as he accompanied the other boys and Doherty out into the night air. At the gate, the four stood a long time in anguished silence as the crescent moon set in the west.

At last, Michael turned to go back to the house. On impulse, Doherty reached out to press his arm, stopping him. Michael waited as the hackney driver started to say something, then hesitated, and finally gave it up, bowing and shaking his head.

Jack had pieced together the clues. As Michael turned away once more and walked to the porch, the boy whispered to his friend's father, "But how could somebody do that to Himself? He's so big!"

In the quiet of the night, Michael had caught every word. He stopped at the stoop and said softly, "I wasn't this big when I was eleven."

They heard him.

∞

MICHAEL LAY behind Anne on the floor in the dark, the two of them facing the wounded children and hearing them start and cry out faintly in their sleep.

When he finally drifted off, Anne heard her husband make the same noises, an echo of shattered innocence.

CHAPTER 13

Questions

Word had already gone out. Michael noticed the covert glances and the outright stares as he walked through The Flats and across the bridge to the streetcar pickup. Some faces expressed pity, some suspicion, some revulsion, some curiosity. His gut tightened with every block as the unnatural silence, the unspoken questions assaulted him.

At the construction site on Draper Avenue, he worked without words, nodding at directions, and avoiding conversation. But he noticed the whispers of his colleagues, and he caught the sly glances. At one point, early in the morning, Jake Trevelyan remarked the unusual quietness of the crew, but received no answer to his veiled inquiry.

The distant clock-tower had struck nine when Detective Morgan and Constable David Baker arrived on their bicycles and asked the site manager for a word with Michael MacGregor. On

seeing the policemen park their cycles, Michael finished placing the stone he had fetched from the rock pile and strode to streetside before summoned.

"Detective, Constable," he greeted them with a token brush of his cap brim.

"Ah, good!" said the detective. "I am sorry to intrude upon your workplace, but I must ask you some questions, sir." He gestured toward the far walk, and the three gathered under an elm on the other side of the street.

When they were out of hearing range, Detective Morgan stated, "I understand you had some difficulty with a pair of boys."

This was not the matter the Scot had expected to address. Michael frowned slightly, and then said with barely controlled anger, "The boys had been raped." He added, "And none too gently."

The officers exchanged looks that conveyed surprise, shock, and annoyance before settling into dour determination.

Morgan got to the point. "Did they say who did it?"

"No," Michael replied. "They did not seem to know, when asked. But they were in shock, I think, and may be able to at least describe the men, in a day or two." He added, "My wife is taking care of them as we speak."

"Right, then," said the detective. "We'll call around tomorrow to see if they've anything they can tell us." He added through his teeth, "And in the meantime, I'll have a few words with Constable McMurtry."

Before the detective could take his leave, Michael asked, "Did the constable happen to mention the other matter?"

Half-turned away, Morgan looked back and raised his eyebrows, "Other matter?"

Michael pressed his lips together and snorted in gruff irritation. "My wife and I told him last night what the local boys—you know them, Jack and Larry—what they had discovered about the stranger in the neighbourhood."

The detective quickly flipped through his notebook and said, "Oh, yes. The blond stranger you mentioned. Has he been seen again?"

"Yes," Michael told them. "He availed himself of the services of one of the ladies on Poplar Lane, and the boys followed him back into the city, to a place called the 'Cup and Star.'"

"The Cup and Star," Baker repeated.

At the man's tone, Detective Morgan asked, "Is there something special about the place, Constable?"

Baker nodded affirmation. "Yessir. It's...known to be favoured by...Irish Catholics." The constable's face showed his uncomfortable awareness that his superior was of the Irish Catholic persuasion.

Michael mentioned hesitantly, "It may be nothing, but there was once talk that the Fenians had used it as a...a base of operations, I suppose you'd call it. But that was a long time ago. In seventy-eight."

"Nevertheless, it might explain the code in the penny novel," Morgan thought aloud, grimacing as he made a note in his booklet and then stuffed the pad and pencil into the inner breast pocket of his jacket.

With a deep inhalation, the detective extended his hand and said, "Thank you, Mr. MacGregor. You've been most helpful." He added grimly, "I only wish we could meet under better circumstances, on occasion."

"Agreed," Michael said quietly as he shook the detective's hand.

"And do give my respects to your wife," Morgan added politely, bowing his head slightly and pinching the rim of his dark-brown fedora in farewell.

∞

THE COURTEOUS demeanour of the police officers had altered

the attitudes of many of the stoneworkers, and after the constable and detective rode away, the mood of the worksite lightened. Furtive mumblings became open chatter, and men looked Michael in the eye once more. To his discomfort, though, the usual lunchtime clusters coalesced into one large, closely packed mass centred on him as the crew broke for the midday meal. Even Trevelyan came to sit beside him.

Not given to mincing words, the boss asked what was on everyone's mind. "So, what's this about some lads bein' sodomized?"

Accepting the inevitable, Michael took a deep breath and explained the grisly events of the night before.

In his heavy accent and his clumsy manner, Johann Bucholtz said, "You of such things know. When a child you were?"

Michael stared at him and swallowed, forcibly suppressing the memories and emotions that threatened to overwhelm him whenever he spoke, or even thought, of "such things."

Finally, his voice soft and tremulous, he said, "I know more than I wish to know of such things. And yes, I was a child."

He bit into his sandwich savagely. No one said another word throughout the meal break.

∞

FOR ONCE, the boys did not complain at being immersed in warm water and scoured with soap. Rob and Kevin simply sat still as Anne lathered and rinsed their bodies and hair, taking careful note of the bruises and cuts, and adapting the pressure of her massage to the degree of damage where she washed them.

She rubbed infusions of larkspur and calamus into their hair and combed out the lice and fleas with which they had become infested. And she bandaged their wounds and plied the lads with more remedies. All the while, she hummed and sang

softly. The music calmed the boys.

Their clothes, she burned. Wrapped in towels, the lads watched impassively from their perch on the back porch as flames engulfed the rags in the stone-lined pit. The blaze had not yet died down when a delegation of women brought trousers and shirts, socks and shoes, suspenders and hats to be tried on and adjusted for fit. While the boys accepted the kindly attentions in unresponsive silence, the ladies stretched garments to compare length; gently pulled sleeves onto the boys' arms as they would dress an infant; rolled socks and pushed them over toes and heels; and placed shoes against feet, sole to sole, to determine suitability before sliding on a correctly sized pair and lacing them up.

In frilled rose gown with matching jacket, and shading herself with ruffle-edged parasol, Miss Hetty "happened" to stroll by the house that lay almost a mile from her own, and offered warm jackets from her collection of found items, should the boys need them come autumn. As the women of The Flats concluded their ministrations and gathered up any items too big or too small, ready to return to their homes, Anne thanked her neighbours for their assistance and their generosity.

Turning her attention to the quilts, she used a pair of sticks to pick up the now flea- and lice-ridden coverlets to set them into a cauldron full of water and light a fire below. Then, as the bedding boiled, she fed the boys freshly baked bread with butter and jam, a bowl of newly ripened serviceberries from her garden, and cups of mint tea with honey. Only when the lads had finished their repast did she venture to ask gently, "Are you ready to talk about what happened?"

Dressed in their new apparel and seated on the back porch, the two glanced to each other. Kevin chewed his lip and Rob cleared his throat. Both fidgeted with their shirt buttons.

Rob inhaled deeply for three breaths before he said at last, "We was workin' near the opry when some swells nabbed us. Said they'd let us keep the money if we did somethin' fer 'em.

Then, they took us to a place nearby, in an alley, an'...."

He looked up into her eyes, his own imploring, "We—we thought they wanted us to run an' fetch somethin'...or—or...mebbe...mebbe show 'em where the best whorehouses was, or...."

He bowed his head and wept, his shoulders heaving up and down with the sobs. Kevin sobbed, too, at the recounting.

Anne asked softly, "How many of them?"

Rob lifted three fingers.

Her own face was wet as Anne squeezed drops of remedy into their mouths and sent them to lie in the shade, in the hammock strung between the maple and the cherry.

∞

THE REST of the day was quiet, with the heavy silence of men pondering matters that disturbed them profoundly.

"I hope the lads'll be all right," said Rob Donnelly as the streetcar glided to a stop. "If you and your wife should need any help...." He let the offer dangle.

"Thank you," Michael responded when they alighted at the western end of King Street. "We may need it." He shook his head and said sadly, "But I don't know how much we can do for them."

As they walked westward, joining other gaggles bound for home, Mike Villeneuve said, "I'll 'ave me wife send around some extra food. We 'ad a fine harvest o' peas."

Pat O'Connell piped up, "And we've an old hen ready to drop. She'll be for the pot."

Pressing his mouth taut, too overwhelmed to speak, Michael could only nod his thanks for the benevolence of his neighbours.

∞

WHEN THE BOYS had finally been put to bed on a fresh mat of

blankets, Anne and Michael sat on the edge of the low front porch, leaning together and encircling each other with their arms. The half-moon shone overhead and the stars glittered against the black of the sky as mosquitoes whined hungrily but stayed out of reach, repelled by the lotion the pair had slathered over exposed skin.

Michael nodded a greeting as Old Sean Flynn sauntered by with fishing pole resting on his shoulder, and the elderly man touched his cap in reply.

"Swells," Michael muttered.

"In the Opera district," Anne reiterated.

"Jesus!" the Scot whispered, wondering which among his former friends and acquaintances were rapists of children.

∞

DETECTIVE MORGAN knocked on her door at nine in the morning. Anne stepped out to the porch and apprised him and Constable O'Toole of the information she had gleaned so far, before bringing them into her home to question the boys.

All through the interview, Anne stood between Rob and Kevin, they seated on kitchen chairs, she firmly holding a small hand in each of her own. Detective Morgan spoke gently and took pains to tread delicately around the issue of pocket-picking, making it clear to them that he was more interested in the crimes of the men than in the boys' petty thievery.

Occasionally, Constable O'Toole asked for clarification of some point, claiming he could not keep up with their speedy answers as he recorded them in his notebook. He licked his pencil and contorted his face when he wrote, feigning great concentration. At his antics, the boys emitted giggles and relaxed by increments.

When he had learned as much as the boys could tell him, Detective Morgan promised to send an artist to draw the men from the boys' descriptions. As the policemen headed to the front

door, Kevin asked meekly, "Detective, are you related to Morgan the Pirate?"

The man's brows reached for his hairline and he gaped in surprise. After a moment of discomposure, during which Constable O'Toole's attempts to suppress a grin failed utterly, the detective answered, "Very likely, lad. Every family has its bad apples."

At that, he popped his fedora onto his head and hurried past O'Toole and out the door.

∞

THE EXASPERATED artist produced rather indistinct portraits of the three rapists. The boys had contradicted each other repeatedly, and neither could recall any of the faces clearly, perhaps confusing the features of one man with those of another. But they finally remembered that at least one of the men was foreign, and most likely two.

"Did they sound French?" Anne asked.

"No," Rob replied. "Didn't sound like Mr. Villeneuve, a-tall. Nor Mr. Cacciotti, neither."

Kevin spoke up quickly, "Sounded like Mr. Bucholtz. Sorta. One of 'em, anyway."

"But not exac'ly," Rob added.

The descriptions and sketching continued another half-hour before the artist gave up.

When she saw him to the door, Anne asked the man to give Detective Morgan the new information about the pederasts. The grey-suited artist nodded curtly and tapped the rim of his black bowler before hurrying out to his bicycle with an expression of dismay.

Standing at Anne's side in the doorway as the man rode away, Rob whined despondently, "We didn't tell 'im right."

At the boys' dejection, Anne said encouragingly, "Don't worry. You'll remember better in time."

"Did anybody ever hurt you like that, Missus?" Kevin asked.

Taken aback by the question, Anne frowned and brushed an imaginary bit of lint from his shoulder. Avoiding his eyes as her own suddenly watered, she swallowed hard and whispered, "Yes."

Seeing her distress, so much like their own, the boys flung their arms around her and hugged her tightly, trying not to weep. She returned the embrace.

∞

THROUGH SUPPER, Rob and Kevin avoided Michael's eyes and spoke only to ask for a second helping of oatcake. The Scot tried to make light conversation, telling jokes he had heard from the stoneworkers and describing the process of erecting a building, but the lads did not respond. When Anne carried the dishes to the summer kitchen and began to wash them, he took the opportunity to discover the reason for the boys' reticence.

"Is it me?" he asked. "Are you afraid of me, now?"

The boys' eyes widened in surprise. They glanced to each other and then bowed their heads, shaking them in negation.

"What is it, then?" the Scot pressed. "Please tell me. Have I done something?"

The heads, still bent, shook again.

Michael regarded them helplessly a long moment as they swung their legs, crossed at the ankles, back and forth beneath the flat wooden seats of the chairs. A fly buzzed around his face and Michael irritably swatted it away with his hand.

Anne's voice drifted through the open Dutch door. She was singing a Gaelic ballad, its strains accompanied by a clinking of crockery and occasionally punctuated by the bark of a dog somewhere in the neighbourhood. He smiled, thinking what a wonderful mother she would be to their child.

The realization struck him with the force of a slap across

the face: She was like a mother to them! Perhaps Rob and Kevin saw him as a father of sorts. He recalled his own father and the chasm that had opened between them, filled with all Michael had never been able to convey as well as with the disapproval that had long emanated from Joseph MacGregor.

Once he got his emotions under control, the Scot pushed the table aside and knelt before the boys to take a hand of each into his own. He swallowed visibly and drew a deep breath.

"Long ago," he said quietly, "a bad man did to me what those men did to you."

The boys looked up, eyes round with astonishment. They listened as he went on.

"Not once, but many times," he told them. "He was a powerful man, and I dared not tell anyone what he was doing, for I knew they would not believe me. I knew they would listen to him, instead."

Tears had begun to roll down his cheeks. He released the boys' hands to pull a handkerchief from his pocket and blow his nose. The lads wiped their own noses with their sleeves as wetness overflowed their eyes.

Michael pressed on, "I tried to tell my father, to write to him, but he never wrote back and I believed he was ashamed of me. And worse...."

He took a deep breath and let it out in a long, tremulous sigh before continuing, "The man would tell me, every time he took me...he told me it was my nature. That I was...that I would always be different. And I believed him."

He rubbed a shirt-sleeve across his eyes, leaving behind a streak of white stone dust.

"I believed him," he whispered, "because, even when he hurt me, he could make me feel...."

He swallowed and straightened as anger surged.

"I did not know," he said vehemently. "I thought—and he told me—that, if he could make me feel...good, that...that I was like him. Different. That I was not meant to love a woman. That I

could never feel so good with a woman. That I was meant to be...used.

"That was why, I thought...." He stifled a sob before he finished, "Why my father was ashamed of me. And that was why I tried to kill myself in war, and later in drink."

He closed his eyes and bowed his head under the weight of years of desolation. His chest and belly shuddered with barely suppressed sobs, and his fists tightened with the effort to control himself.

Rob asked, "How...how did you know...that you weren't...?"

Michael looked up into the boy's eyes. His smile a pained grimace, he whispered, "It was Anne."

He glanced over his shoulder and listened a moment. She had begun a new, unfamiliar tune: *"It's the way you love me that makes me sigh...."*

Turning back to the boys, his fond smile softening and brightening his face, he affirmed, "It was Herself. I loved her from the start. I wanted her, as I had wanted no other woman. And no man...."

He did not finish that statement. Instead, he murmured, "I knew I was meant for her alone."

Michael rose and looked down into the faces of the boys. He said with assurance, "I did nothing wrong, and neither did you. What they did does not make you like them. You have no need to be ashamed."

The boys nodded understanding, their faces and demeanour lightening at the lifting of their burden. And Michael realized that the telling had lifted his own.

He turned toward the Dutch door that led to the rear yard, but turned back at a recollection as the boys hopped off the chairs.

"Now, about the picking of pockets," he said sternly, raising a finger and cocking an eyebrow in disapprobation.

The boys bowed their heads once more and grimaced

guiltily.

∞

THE LADS HAD BEEN tucked into their bed by the front door—now kept locked—when Anne filled the bathing tub Michael had placed near the summer kitchen. She set kettles on the stove and then poured the boiling liquid into the vat to bring up the temperature of the chilly well-water.

Michael stripped down, peeling off the shirt and trousers and underthings impregnated with dust and sweat from his day's toil. Watching his wife prepare the bath, he wondered whether she hauled buckets and kettles of water into the house in the long, cold winters of this country. He decided he must find a way to lighten her load. An indoor pump, perhaps.

A north wind cooled the evening air. Michael inhaled deeply. Rain. There would be rain by morning.

A firefly glimmered in the dusky underbrush, that cultivated copy of a forest understory surrounding the fruit and nut and sap trees that all but enclosed the small property. Another phosphorescent beetle flickered. In moments, dozens more joined them.

Soon after their wedding, Anne told Michael she had planted all but four of the trees and all of the shrubbery when she purchased this land less than five years ago. Gazing up at the canopy dark against the tints of grey and lavender that washed the sky, he marvelled that such recent additions had grown so quickly. He wondered what magic she used to encourage their development.

Stepping into the arbour to scrub away the day's dirt before soaking in the tub, Michael smiled to himself. More than once, he had heard Anne described as a witch by the people of The Flats. Not in a fearful or hateful way, but with respectful awe. As he poured a bucket of water over himself, gasping and snorting at the shock of sudden cold direct from the well, a vision

came to his mind: a memory of Anne walking Dan Doherty's sick horse through her garden, last week, and plucking sprigs from any plant the sorrel nibbled. She then brewed a batch of medicine from the herbs and mixed it into the gelding's water. The next day, the horse was fine and frisky.

Yes, she was a witch, he decided as he cleansed his body with her homemade soap. His smile broadened and his rubbing slowed to a sensual massage as he watched her undress to begin her own ablutions.

Oh, yes. She is magical.

∞

TWILIGHT DEEPENED to dusk. Anne stepped into the tub, between Michael's knees. He reached up to grasp the cheeks of her rump and leaned to kiss her bush. She obligingly tilted her pelvis when his mouth and tongue probed below, searching for her sweet spot, and she gasped when he found it.

"Come," he whispered, shifting to make room.

While he leaned back, she moved to straddle him. His hands glided to her hips and he pulled her to him. Then, she gripped and positioned his phallus, and both of them groaned when she slid down to sheathe him.

Out of the corner of her eye, Anne saw them: two pairs of eyes watching from the porch. She leaned to whisper in Michael's ear, "We have an audience."

She pulled back and indicated the direction with a dart of her eyes. Smiling, she mouthed, "What shall we do?"

Michael slid his fingers through her hair and drew her face to his. He murmured, "I suppose they may as well learn this way as any."

He kissed his wife deeply. Then, he put his feet under him, found his balance, and rose, hands under her buttocks to keep her impaled. She tightened her legs and arms around him as he stepped out of the bathtub and brought her to the grass.

There, he knelt, set her down, and proceeded to give the curious boys a long, slow, thorough demonstration of a man's marital duties.

CHAPTER 14

News

"MacGregor!"

Michael MacGregor and Archie Burton had been sorting the new load of stones by size, placing the largest in piles within easy reach of the building's walls and turning the best face out. Jake Trevelyan liked a neat worksite, and Michael and Archie were not only strong enough to haul the heavier stones, but both had dry-stone experience and knew how to shape a wall. Further, both had an eye for the aesthetics of the rock faces and for pleasing arrangement of colour variations.

When the boss called, the two had been organizing the new batch of raw material for three hours, stepping gingerly in the mud from the predawn rain. Now, Michael set down the blue-grey slab he had just picked up, and he manoeuvred among his co-workers, dodging a wheelbarrow full of mortar and sliding on the slick clay soil on his way to meet his employer. As

the Scot passed the street face of the partially constructed building, Trevelyan looked up from the architectural drawing he held against the wind, caught Michael's eye, and jerked his head toward a group of boys standing in the road.

Michael frowned uncertainly, wondering who these children might be. On his approach, however, Jack stepped out from the centre of the gaggle and waved with a lopsided grin.

"Jack," Michael greeted him with a smile, surveying the lad's companions. None were familiar. "What brings you here?"

The boy told him, "I been tellin' the lads, here, about Rob an' Kevin. An' 'bout the cove as has been hauntin' The Flats."

Michael nodded vaguely, unsure what exactly this had to do with him and why it was important enough to bring to his place of work.

Jack explained, "See, me an' Larry an' the lads, here...well, we know each other, see. An' we...uh...we work together from time to time."

A picture of juvenile street crime flashed into Michael's mind, along with memories of newspaper articles and Temperance League leaflets about the deplorable state of the city's youth. He pulled his mouth into a wry smile at the sudden realization he stood face to face with, and lived next door to, some of the delinquents.

"Well," Jack went on, "we all been on the lookout for the foreign swells what hurt Rob an' Kevin. An' th'other fellah, too."

A stab of apprehension clenched Michael's gut. His jaw tightened, his eyes sharpened, and his face set. But he awaited the boy's conclusion.

"We think we found two o' the swells, an' we seen th'other fair-haired fellah on the docks with some sailors—they ain't English, by the way. Nor Irish, nor Scotch. Saul, here, thinks they're mebbe German."

He finished, "So, we was wonderin' what we should do now."

The boys regarded him expectantly.

Michael took a deep breath. What would German sailors be doing on lake boats? he wondered. Everyone knew that intergovernmental talks about opening the St. Lawrence to ocean vessels had stalled. Only small, shallow steamers plied the waters from Montreal into the Great Lakes.

He considered the matter a minute before he said, "First of all, I don't want any of you taking chances with these men. They're bound to be dangerous. Perhaps even deadly."

The boys sobered. Street life had accustomed them to peril, but such had rarely included more than the risk of a beating or of imprisonment in an orphanage or workhouse.

Michael rubbed a hand over his face, smudging the grey-white stone dust that caked his skin, and regarded them a moment more. Presently, he asked, "Do you think you can find out who the swells are? Their names?"

The boys looked from one to the other. A lanky teenager with a shock of rust-coloured hair suggested, "We could mebbe steal their wallets."

Michael nodded thoughtfully. "They may keep calling cards there that would identify them, though there's no guarantee of it." He glanced at the speaker and then to the others and said, "But if you can get near enough, without being noticed, to hear them called by name, that would be even better. That would ensure we have the right man...men."

The boys looked to one another once more. Several tightened their lips and nodded in wordless acknowledgement that it could be done.

"As for the other matter," Michael added, "if you can find out which ship the sailors came from and where the other man stays, that would be helpful."

"We'll do that," Jack assured him. "We ain't gonna let none o' these buggers get away with messin' with our own."

All the boys nodded emphatic accordance.

"No, we won't," Michael agreed. As they turned to leave, he admonished, "Do be careful, lads."

Again, they nodded to him, flashing grim smiles.

"Oh, and Jack."

The named boy raised his eyebrows in question.

Michael said, "If you should happen to see Detective Morgan, I'm sure he'd like to know what you've told me."

Jack grinned broadly. Then, as one, the urchins whirled and sprinted down the street.

∞

THE SKY LOURED, threatening further rain, but the morning passed without the expected showers and another course of stone had been laid by the time the clock tower struck twelve. Michael placed the rock he had picked up back onto the pile and sauntered to fetch his lunch bag. As had become his custom, he joined the group of men that comprised his friends from The Flats.

Mick McGee remarked casually, "So, now you're the Pied Piper, eh?" His raised brows then curled into a frown and he grimaced in dismay when he peered at the soggy sandwich he had pulled from his flour-sack bag.

After gulping a swig of Anne's home brew, Michael replied, "The boys want to be helpful. I expect that will keep them too busy to do anything that would land them in jail. For a while, at least."

"Better watch it, lad," said Pat O'Connell with a grin. "Next thing ye know, your house'll be full o' strays."

"It already is," Michael admitted. "Young Rob and Kevin stick to Anne like glue."

Rob Donnelly said, "Well, they're safer in The Flats than downtown."

"Yes," Michael agreed. "And Anne may need the help, as her belly grows."

All heads within earshot bobbed up in surprise.

"She's in de family way, den?" asked Mike Villeneuve.

"Yes," Michael confirmed with a smile of happiness and shy pride.

Pat O'Connell shook his head and chortled. Through his laughter, the older man said, "You're quick, ye are, lad." He wheezed with mirth.

Several men nearby clapped the new father's shoulders in congratulations. In minutes, the news had spread throughout the crew.

∞

CONSTABLE O'TOOLE swallowed a bite of bannock and a sip of tea at the kitchen table. A brass oil-lamp perching atop the cupboard by the back door added its smoky odour to the sweet scent of the single, columnar beeswax candle on a blue stoneware dish in the centre of the undraped pine table. The two small flames cast a glow that faded toward the children lying on blankets by the front door. Rain pelted the shingled roof and the exposed west wall, and thunder grumbled in the distance. A moment later, a flash that shattered the blackness outside and a sharp crack and deep boom that rattled the windows in their frames announced the arrival of the storm.

Kevin started in his sleep, but did not wake. And Rob rolled over, pulling the quilt half-off of his bedmate.

"This is delicious, Ma'am," O'Toole said quietly.

"Thank you, Constable," Anne replied in a whisper.

"You said you had news?" Michael prompted, his own voice hushed.

"Mm. Yessir," said the young police officer. He hastily swallowed and licked his lips to catch the last of the crumbs. "It's about the penny novel. Seems the writing in it—the handwriting, that is—seems it's in Russian. Only, maybe in code or something, because the words don't make sense in themselves, apparently. Something about blue skies, and suns, and stars, and the price of eggs."

Michael and Anne looked to each other, both frowning in mystification.

Anne said, "German sailors, Russian writing in a code, a man Miss Hetty says is definitely Irish and who frequents an Irish pub...." She glanced from her husband to the constable and back again. "What can it all mean?"

Eyebrows raised, Michael shook his head in bewilderment and replied, "Damned if *I* know."

Her downcast gaze scanning the table but seeing the small face and flaming hair of her former student, Anne added in a low, sad voice, "And why did Geordie have to die for it?"

Seeking to give what comfort he could, Michael gripped his wife's hand firmly as tears spilled from her eyes.

Constable O'Toole pushed away his plate, leaving a half-finished bannock. He rose with troubled countenance as he prepared to brave rain and storm and night to return to his stationhouse.

CHAPTER 15

Menace

A nne woke with a start. Stars. She had been dreaming of stars. But there had been nightmare in those Morphean nebulae.

The rain had stopped, and the nocturnal silence roared in her ears.

Michael stirred, snuggling closer and smacking his lips. She pressed back against him, and he murmured contentedly in his sleep. He was so warm, and he smelled of their passion and of his own musky maleness. She wanted to drift into slumber, wrapped in his heat and scent, but her mind now raced, frantic in its erratic leaps.

Blue skies and suns. Eggs and money. Russians and Germans. A pub and a ship. Foreign pederasts. An Irishman with a black soul and a taste for whores. A penny novel with jottings. Riflemen in the meadows. Shots in the woods.

And Geordie.

She opened her eyes. A dim radiance gradually intensified outside the north window, and the droplets that clung to the little square panes twinkled like tiny stars.

Stars. The Cup and Star. Prussian sailors originally from a ship known as the Northern Star, out of Amsterdam and docked in Halifax. And words scribbled in Russian that translated, she knew, as "little sun" and "evening star."

A *frisson* swept coldly up her spine. Moving slowly, she manoeuvred out from under her husband's embrace and slid off the bed. Quietly, cautiously, she crept to her old cedar-lined wardrobe, now sandwiched by Michael's trunks, and opened its upper doors. The right leaf squeaked on its hinges and Michael tossed in the bed. She waited until he had settled.

When he lay still, Anne located the waist-tied cotton pockets she always wore beneath her old dress, the canvas pouches now stuffed behind her husband's suspenders on a middle shelf. After pinching both bags to determine which held it, she reached into the right pocket and pulled out an egg-shaped ball, perhaps an inch and a quarter through its length, its surface smooth and cool. Tiptoeing to the window, she held the cabochon up to the light to see the white asterism in its blue depths: the star sapphire she had plucked from the creek the day Geordie died.

She held it a long moment. Then, she put it back into her pocket and dressed to make breakfast.

∞

ANNE HAD SENT Rob and Kevin off to the creek, asking them to watch over the little ones who liked to sneak away from home to play in the mud and water. She smiled at the memory of the boys' eagerness to take this responsibility. They no longer clung to her in terror as they had the first few days. She smiled, too, at the knowledge that Michael had helped himself as well as the

boys when he revealed to them the secret he had guarded so many years. He now carried himself with greater ease, and he smiled readily since the lifting of his own burden. Even his aura had lightened, no longer dimmed by the shadows of fear and shame and self-hatred.

Having the house to herself, Anne pushed desk and table together to make a larger workspace and began the process of pressing her lovely new fabrics. The chore required attention but little thought, leaving her mind free to contemplate the significance of the sapphire.

Clearly, the gem was no river-washed pebble, no accident of Nature. It had the feel, as well as the appearance, of one cut and polished by a jeweller. How had it come to be in the Sweetwater?

An image of Geordie on his final day came to her: His hip pocket had bulged roundly. At the time, she had thought nothing of it; the boys often picked up odds and ends of all sorts, temporary treasures that fascinated for a day or two and were quickly supplanted by a new prize. But his pocket had been empty when she had held him in the creek and when she had carried him to his mother.

Later that day, in her grief-stricken daze, she had sought that ovoid object, needing a small token of her little favourite to cherish in remembrance. She had found it by its shape and recognized it by its resonance. Once she had sequestered it in her pocket, it had remained there, a subliminal comfort.

Until today. Now, the gleaming little rock sat in her pouch with the weight of a boulder.

The child must surely have found the stone in or near the brothel just as he had found the penny novel, Anne reflected. Some fool—very likely the blond stranger and almost certainly in a drunken muddle—had left both behind. Then, Geordie, being as bright, inquisitive, and attracted to shiny objects as any jackdaw, had simply salvaged what had been lost.

Whatever their purpose, both book and bauble would

have been valuable enough to retrieve. And apparently valuable enough to kill for. The horrifying hypothesis she had been avoiding for two weeks crystallized in Anne's mind: Had sweet Geordie been murdered simply as a diversion to allow someone the freedom to search for the novel and gem?

The sound of shots echoed in her mind. Shots from the distant past. And several shots by the creek: One had been louder than the others. Though she had buried that anomalous perception, unable to make sense of it in her grief, it had pounded against its mental coffin, demanding release. Again and again, she had ignored its persistent banging, unwilling to allow that ghastly insight to disinter itself. Now, it rose to haunt her.

"Missus! Missus!"

The urgent call from the back porch wrenched Anne from her reverie. Running to the door with heart in her mouth, she found little Becky O'Malley panting, the tot's eyes like saucers.

"What is it?" Anne demanded.

The frightened redhead pointed toward the creek and said through laboured breaths, "Bad...man!"

"Stay—No! Go home!" Anne called as she dropped the cooling sadiron in the grass and ran headlong toward the Sweetwater, her heart racing as fast as her feet.

Carrying a basket of laundry, one end balanced on her hip, Mrs. Roarke called after Anne in alarm as Herself flew past. Behind, other shouts rose, but Anne merely sprinted onward, down the street, along the alley, through the wood, until she broke out into the clearing on the bank of the creek.

"Ah, there ye are," called the Irishman in a genial tone that did not match his sharp gaze. He grinned sardonically from the centre of the creek, clasping Rob to his side, fingers entwined in the lad's hair, and holding a knife to the boy's throat.

On the right, Anne saw Old Sean Flynn sitting in his usual spot, his fishing pole dangling in the creek. But when she approached, an odour of faeces and urine and a growing pool of blood below his chair told her that the old-timer was not asleep,

as his bowed head and slack posture suggested.

Her every nerve screamed as Anne stepped into the water, eyes fixed on the blond villain. He wore brown trousers rolled to his knees; his pale-blue shirt bore a white tab collar and wooden buttons; his tan vest hung open; and his beige wool cap sat slightly askew. Next to him, Rob Houlihan stood rigidly, the whites of the boy's eyes showing all around his coffee-coloured irises. He swallowed repeatedly as he watched her wade slowly toward them. The other children, also round-eyed, huddled several yards away, downstream, shaking in helpless terror.

"Why don't you let the children go," Anne urged calmly, knowing the man would refuse.

Sure enough, he said, "Well, there's no need, now, is there, Missus?" He raked her with his eyes and pursed his lips speculatively.

"What do you want?" she spat.

His gaze rose to hers and held it, his smile fading. "I think ye may know, already, Missus." He jerked his head toward the children and continued in his conversational manner, "See, the weans, here, seem to think ye know all there is about rocks an' stones. So, I'm thinkin' ye maybe found a special one. One that was lost."

He tilted his head and regarded her with a penetrating and expectant stare.

Anne took a deep breath. She said, "So, you want me to look for your lost stone."

"Already looked," he replied. "So, as I say, I think ye found it and took it." His voice sharpened to a whip-crack when he snapped, "I want it now."

Reverting to his casual air, he said, "Or shall I look...elsewhere?" He tightened his grip on Rob's hair and pressed the knife-point deep enough to produce a trickle of blood. The boy squeaked in pain and terror.

"Fine," Anne flared. She reached into her pocket.

"Uh-uh-uh!" the man cautioned. "Nice an' easy."

Seething, Anne inhaled slowly and obeyed, reluctantly bringing the little blue egg into the light and presenting it in her upturned palm. She said, "Now, let him go."

"You ain't givin' the orders, sweetie," he said. "Come."

Anne waded on, still holding the sapphire as on a platter. When she came within a couple of yards of the man, he abruptly shoved Rob away toward the other children and gestured for her to come closer.

Her gaze locked with the Irishman's as she edged forward, Anne saw peripherally that young Rob stumbled and staggered to join the gaggle of girls and boys. Kevin put his arm around his friend as Rob held a hand protectively over the puncture wound that trailed a sanguine seepage.

"Don't even think o' runnin' away, now, lads," the foul man warned. Though his eyes remained fixed upon Anne, he pulled a pistol from behind his back and aimed it toward the little ones.

"An' you, Missus," he said, his mouth curling into a sneer, "get on your knees."

Anne knelt. Her belly liquefied as he closed the gap between them, shoving the knife into its sheath at his belt and grabbing the stone from her hand to tuck it into his shirt pocket.

"There's no need for you to rush away, now, either."

He added in a menacing tone, "An' don't be tryin' any tricks unless ye want another one o' your weans to take a bullet. Maybe go right through an' hit two or three, at this range."

He said imperatively, "Ye know what to do."

Anne's hands trembled as she stretched her arms, reaching to unbutton his flies. She pulled the trouser fronts away to find he had already stiffened. And she found something more: a chancre on his penis. The man had syphilis. She knew the terrible effects of prenatal exposure to the disease. What she did not know with certainty was whether she could protect her child from it if she were exposed. There was only one way to ensure the baby's safety.

When she hesitated, the Irishman demanded harshly, "Get on with it."

"Can't you at least let the children go?" she pleaded, letting her hands drop to her sides.

"Well, now," he replied, "you bein' a teacher, seems to me only natural ye should teach 'em a woman's job."

Tears rolling freely down her cheeks, Anne inched forward on her knees. Suddenly, she lurched and cried out.

"Quit your stallin'," he spat.

"I hurt my knee on a rock," she protested. Leaning back on her haunches to reposition her feet, she raised one knee and rubbed it conspicuously, breathing in tremulous sobs. The other hand slipped between the folds of her skirts and through the pocket-access slits at her hip.

"I'll hurt more'n your knee if ye don't—"

She snatched her *sgian dhu* from its accustomed hidden sheath at her thigh and stabbed upward as she leapt to her feet, calling, "Ruuun!"

The knife slashed skirts and sliced flesh as the children scattered, the gun went off, birds shot out of the trees, and the man screamed.

The Irishman staggered back, face struck with an expression of astonishment. He glanced down to find blood oozing from his penis. Snarling now, he whipped the gun barrel toward her, but she tackled him. As they fell back into the water, the pistol fired once more.

Anne bashed the man's face with the pommel of her *sgian dhu* and pushed up to stumble away toward shore, where several mothers poured from the path to embrace the fleeing children. Behind her, she heard a whooshing sound as the man rose out of the water. Ahead, she saw the widening eyes of her neighbours.

Just then, Constable O'Toole charged from the forest, nightstick in hand, shouting, "Halt! Police!" He stopped short, eyes popping wide.

A click came from behind. Anne whirled to see the

Irishman pull the trigger again. And again. Abruptly, he spun and ran, bleeding from penis and nose, and he crashed into the underbrush on the far side of the creek.

"Are you all right, Ma'am?"

Anne turned to find Constable O'Toole putting an arm around her shoulder, his face full of concern.

She felt as though she was falling, and she saw a crow flying, its path strangely vertical.

∞

A JERKING. Hands lifting her. A burning. Swaying. Voices. Burning still. Darkness.

Anne floated toward consciousness, though she could not summon the strength to open her eyes. Something was wrong: A sense of distress filled her. Then, suddenly, she realized the distress was not her own. She reached out to the child within, caressing and assuring with her thoughts as she examined embryo and womb. When she knew all was well with both, she visualized the baby in her arms and sang him to sleep.

Once the child had settled, she drifted back into insensibility.

∞

ANNE OPENED her eyes to Michael's anxious face above her. He caressed her cheek with a curled forefinger as he held her left hand in his own.

"Anne—Anne, stay still, my love." His voice betrayed worry even more clearly than his countenance.

Anne blinked. She blinked again. She said, "I'm all right."

"No, you're not," he insisted. He glanced back over his shoulder as the portly Mrs. Bannion came forward with dropper bottle in hand.

"Now, open up," said the old lady as though she were speaking to a child.

"It's one of your remedies," Michael assured her.

Anne opened her mouth and rolled back her tongue to accept the drops.

"Very good," said the woman. "Now, you just rest, dear. The doctor is on his way."

"What doctor?" Anne asked, alarm pushing through the haze. She attempted to rise, and she grimaced at a stab of pain.

"Dr. Hanes," Michael answered, instantly pressing her shoulder to the bed. "I know you think well of him; so, I sent for him."

"Why—why do I need a doctor?" she asked.

"You were shot, dear," Mrs. Bannion informed her.

"I was?" Fuzzily, she realized what that disturbing sensation had been: that sharp jolt, and the burning in her side.

"The bullet passed through, and it's a small wound, but...."

Michael's attempt to reassure her apparently did nothing for his own confidence. He blinked back tears, and she saw the tracks through the stone dust on his face, the bronze trails left by earlier lachrymation.

She smiled weakly and murmured, "I'll be all right, my love."

He clasped her hand in both of his and kissed her fingertips.

Memories floated to the surface and she asked, worried now, "Are the children all right? How is Rob?"

"They're fine," Michael told her. "They've had a terrible fright, but none are hurt." He amended, "At least, not badly."

"Mr. Flynn," she recalled in distress.

"He's been sent to the city morgue," Michael stated, and he kissed her hand again. "The children said he'd been killed some time before you arrived. You couldn't have helped him."

Tears slid down her temples to pool in her ears. Anne whispered, "I should have known."

Michael leaned close and muttered fiercely, "Don't you

dare blame yourself! You saved the children!"

"They might have been killed," Anne now remembered, realizing the risks she had taken.

"They weren't," Michael said firmly. "And you damned near were."

"He has syphilis," she whispered, her tears flowing again. "I couldn't let him...."

Michael's grip tightened on her hand. "You did what you had to do," he whispered firmly. "You did the best you could." His own cheeks gleamed with renewed tears.

All at once, Anne began to snicker silently.

Michael frowned with bewilderment. "Are you laughing?" he asked, astounded.

She could not answer. Michael chuckled, despite himself, as her fizzing mirth built to bursts of soundless hilarity interspersed with grunts and grimaces of pain.

Through gasps and wheezes, she tried to answer. "I just...remembered...."

She giggled again, and she squeezed her eyes shut, doubling over with the stab brought on by her laughter. After a moment, she opened her eyes and continued breathlessly, "When...I last saw...the bastard, he...he was...."

Another quiet fit interrupted the explanation. At last, she calmed enough to say, "He was running through the bush...with his cock hanging out of his pants...." She squeezed her eyes tight to suppress another spasm and continued, "He was...running through poison ivy."

Michael's rumbling guffaws joined her peals of high-pitched hysterics, bringing a thunder of feet on the stairs as well-wishers and caregivers ran to investigate the uproar.

∞

MICHAEL SHOOK his head, amused and amazed, despite his worry, that even such a laughable incident had struck his wife so

funny as to render her inarticulate and to make her giggle through pain. When Anne had settled and the crowd had filtered down into the kitchen and the yard, he blew a long, slow exhalation. His own laughter had drained away the gut-clenching tension that had set his every nerve alight from the moment he saw Jack hurtling along Draper.

"Mister! Mister!" Jack had shouted from down the street.

At the desperate call, Michael had dropped his mortar board and trowel and run to meet the lad at the sidewalk. The boy had hopped off his bicycle in his rush when he reached the construction site, and he had allowed the two-wheeler to glide on until it struck the kerb and flipped into the dirt by the road.

"We lost 'im! He got away from us, an' —"

"Who?" Michael had demanded as the other workmen stopped to listen, some coming forward.

"The stranger." Jack spoke rapidly through laboured breath. "He come to The Flats, to the Creek, an' he shot Herself!"

"Oh, God!"

Michael's face had revealed his horror, at which Jack had rushed to add, "She's still alive, Mister. The constable got her home, but she's hurt bad."

With no thought but the need to go to Anne, Michael had run down Draper, heedless of the calls from behind him. Only when Jack had appeared alongside on the bicycle did he come to himself enough to hear the lad offer the bike. He had nodded wordlessly, stopped to take it, climbed aboard, and pedalled as fast as he could to reach his wife's side, taking shortcuts through a small park and over lawns to bring him to the footbridge closest to Cedar Lane.

At the front door, Constable O'Toole had greeted him and immediately suggested Anne be taken to hospital.

"No," Michael had replied as he climbed the stairs three at a time. "She would not want that." He had recalled vividly Anne's scorn for a certain physician they had passed in the courthouse on the day of the inquest. Though considered by most

to be at the top of his profession, the leading surgeon in the largest local hospital had apparently earned her distrust and contempt.

Michael had knelt by the bed as Mrs. Bannion and Mrs. O'Reilly lifted the blood-soaked chemise and washed the wound.

"Sir," Constable O'Toole had insisted, quickly and abashedly turning away from view of the half-naked woman to focus on her husband, "she needs medical attention."

Gathering Anne's near hand into his own, Michael had nodded and said, "There's one doctor she trusts." He had closed his eyes and frowned, trying to remember the name she mentioned when they first met.

"Janes or Banes or something," he had said uncertainly.

"Dr. Hanes," the constable had guessed. "I know the man. I'll send for him right away."

Michael had simply nodded, and stroked his wife's temple, and watched the local women work as the outward expression of his fears flooded his face.

∞

DR. HANES examined the handwritten labels of the remedies that had already been administered. After questioning all who had given Anne care, he produced from his black leather bag a brown bottle of his own and gave her two drops.

Michael watched as the tall, lean physician dressed in impeccable charcoal-grey wool suit and white silk shirt, silver hair at his temples lending him an urbane and distinguished air, unwrapped Anne's wound and peered closely at the torn flesh. The long, manicured fingers probed gently as the man's cool blue eyes scanned tissues and monitored reactions. After his assessment, he applied a fresh dressing with ministrations that seemed downright tender.

Seized suddenly by a surge of jealousy, Michael asked sharply, "How is it you know my wife?"

The doctor's thin brows rose in surprise at the Scot's tone. Then, his eyes narrowed a moment in penetrating evaluation. Finally, Hanes said, "We worked together a few years ago, I as physician and she as a practical nurse."

"She is not a nurse," Michael pointed out.

"At that time, she was," Dr. Hanes insisted evenly. "I should say, more correctly, that she volunteered her services when such help was desperately needed. You may recall the factory explosion in eighty-nine?"

"I was in England, but I heard the news from my father," Michael replied with a nod.

"Not all of my colleagues appreciated your wife's gift for healing," the doctor continued as he checked Anne's pulse. "But I was deeply grateful for it. Otherwise, we would have lost many more than we did.

"She was tireless," he said with open admiration. "Dressing wounds, fetching water, washing both floors and patients, feeding those who could not feed themselves...." His voice hushed as he added, "Sitting with the dying."

He turned to Michael and said quietly, "You are a lucky man."

The two men locked eyes a moment.

Then, straightening and adopting a more professional tone, Hanes added, "And Anne is a very lucky woman. Although she needs care, the wound is not as serious as it might have been. I see no reason to hospitalize her as long as the wound is cleaned and re-bandaged daily. I will see to it."

Michael nodded and said quietly, gratefully, with a sense of shame at his previous attitude, "Thank you, Doctor."

CHAPTER 16

Recovery

Jake Trevelyan came by on the first night to tell Michael he should take whatever time he required in caring for his wife; his job would be waiting when he was ready to return to it. The older man said little more, but he clearly understood the young husband's worries and his need to watch over the woman he loved.

The ladies of The Flats created a committee to see that food was provided daily and the household duties were fulfilled at the little clapboard house on Cedar Lane. Morning and evening, worried friends and neighbours stopped by to ask after Herself and to discover if anything might be needed.

Detective Morgan stationed armed men throughout The Flats in case the Irishman should return. Unofficially, local men formed a citizens' army of the unemployed to supplement the police presence. Working men also took turns on patrol when

they returned from their shifts. Young children were kept indoors, and women and older children were escorted when they left their homes.

The tension in The Flats was tangible.

∞

MICHAEL NODDED politely to the police officers he passed in the early morning. Striding Willow Bend, he tapped his hat-brim to eighteen-year-old Miss Evelyn O'Grady and said, "Good day," as he overtook her. The prim young woman, dressed in pleated blouse with bouffant sleeves, ankle-length skirt, buttoned shoes, and flat-topped straw hat with bow to match her skirt, on her way to her new job in the department store downtown, smiled at him, but raised both eyebrows and gaped when Himself turned into Poplar Lane.

Michael MacGregor felt other eyes upon him as he marched alone along the notorious little street to its principal residence. And he felt a sense of grim amusement that he should be so discomposed by the disapproving glares of his neighbours while on his way to perform an innocent errand, given that he had frequented bawdy-houses for less noble cause and had cared not a whit who saw or took exception.

At the door of the bordello, he knocked too loudly, as though conspicuousness might make his presence appear innocuous. Regretting the folly, he chuckled to himself as he waited in the shade of the broad porch, where a round-topped pedestal table and cushioned wicker chairs lent a homey air to the only hospitality business establishment in The Flats.

The tall, yellow-grey fieldstone house with white gingerbread adorning its eaves sprawled among rose bushes and lawns planted by the original owners. Officially two stories high, its steeply sloped roof afforded a third floor with space enough for extra bedrooms—a feature as prized by the current inhabitants as by the large family that had lived there for four

generations. Michael wondered whatever became of the farmer and his family.

Presently, a swarthy woman in the simple dress of a drudge opened the half-glazed door, its window curtained with lace. She said, "Nobody's up, sir. But I'll fetch Miss Hetty for ye, if ye'll wait a bit." She stepped back to allow him to enter.

The maid offered him a seat, but he stood and fiddled with the slouch hat he had doffed at the door, holding it by the brim and nervously turning it round and round. He noted that the furniture damaged when the place had been rifled on the day of the funeral had been replaced by newer items, and the already eclectic mix of colours and prints now had an even greater variety. Broken knick-knacks had simply been removed, leaving the mantel and side tables bare of all but a few lamps, candles, and ash cups, while the three paintings that had not been destroyed had been hung as before. The carpet had clearly been cleaned, the previously dirt-drabbed swirls of colour now brightened and the fringe combed. And new curtains adorned the windows.

Miss Hetty appeared in a flowing silk chinoiserie dressing-gown left open to reveal her lace-edged chemise and bloomers. Her eyebrows rose at sight of him, and she quickly scanned his form to judge which of her girls would most suit his size.

With ingratiating smile, she said, "I think Marion would be pleased to accommodate you, Mr. MacGregor."

Blushing, Michael informed her, "Actually, Miss Hetty, Anne sent me."

When the madam's eyebrows rose once more, even higher, and her eyes widened in astonishment, he rushed to assure her, "Not for that. It's about the man who shot her. He has syphilis."

At that, the madam crossed herself. "Jesus, Mary, and Joseph!" she exclaimed in dismay. "Is she sure?"

He suppressed a surge of anger and replied through

clenched teeth, "Apparently, she got a good look and, yes, she's sure."

"Oh, the bastard!" Miss Hetty cried. "As if I don't have enough trouble keepin' these girls clean!"

Michael told her, "Anne says eating Roquefort cheese every meal for a week will kill the syphilis. But you'll have to eat plenty of yogurt, too. Something about the cheese interfering with digestion."

"Roquefort. That's the mouldy cheese, isn't it?" asked Hetty.

"Yes," he affirmed. "She says it's that particular mould that will kill the disease."

"Hm," Hetty snorted. "I suppose it can't be worse than mercury injections."

Michael added delicately, "She also suggests your customers should be informed and given the cheese—at least those you've seen since the...the bastard came, and...."

He took a deep breath before finishing quickly, "That you should suspend business until you've killed the disease."

He grimaced apologetically at the financially inconvenient ramifications of his message.

Miss Hetty heaved a doleful sigh. After a moment's consideration, she asked, "Can it really be cured?"

Michael nodded. "She says it can. It just takes a lot of cheese and a little time."

Miss Hetty sighed again. "Good thing I keep records o' who comes when," she muttered.

When Michael turned toward the door, she said brightly, "If you ever decide to come back for another reason," her smile broadened and she looked him up and down lasciviously, "I'm sure we can...help you."

Michael blushed once more. He swallowed visibly and said, "I appreciate the offer, Miss Hetty, but I'm a one-woman man."

"Pity," she replied on a wistful sigh.

∞

CONSTABLE RYAN'S footsteps on the stairs woke Michael from his doze. His head shot up from the mattress and he blinked drowsily. Sitting up in his chair and peering about, he wondered how long he had slept. Slanted sun still shone through the east window. *Couldn't have been long,* he thought.

He leaned forward again and gently pushed a strand of hair from Anne's temple. She stirred but did not wake.

"Excuse me, sir."

The young officer hesitated.

"What is it, Constable?" Michael asked softly.

"There are some people at the bridge, sir, wanting to come here to see you."

"People?" Michael blinked again and squinted blearily.

"They say they're your parents, sir," Ryan informed him. "They're pretty insistent, but we have strict orders not to let anyone into the neighbourhood unless they live here. And with the militia walking about with clubs and chains and such...."

Michael nodded and heaved a sigh. As he rose, he said, "I'll go talk to them. The bridge, did you say?"

"Yes, just the other side of the main bridge, sir. In a coach."

∞

MICHAEL STRODE across the widest link between The Flats and the city. This was the one bridge broad enough and sturdy enough for vehicles; the other passages all accommodated only foot traffic and the bicycles of the constabulary and the few residents who could afford such modern contrivances.

Coming from town, a wagon lumbered over the arched stone crossing, driven by Miss Hetty's bouncers and drawn by two black Canadiens, the horses' characteristically long tails nearly trailing in the layer of dirt that covered the roadway. When the buckboard went by, Michael smelt the distinctive tang

of Roquefort and he smiled to himself at the memory of his morning visit with Miss Hetty.

On the far side of the Bow, he saw the MacGregor equipage, its coachman waiting patiently. A few yards away, Joseph MacGregor stood nose to nose with an unyielding constable, shouting and gesticulating to no avail, his tall hat askew and his face beet red with outrage. Nearby, on the opposite side of Bridge Street, a cordon of officers barred a gaggle of reporters, some holding notebooks and pencils while others wielded large, boxy cameras and hand-held flash pans. All of the journalists strained toward the unfolding drama, attempting in vain to push past the constables.

His mother's anxious face peered out the rear window of the coach as Michael approached. Suddenly, she noticed him and her expression transformed, softening in a smile of relief. Waving to her, Michael jogged the last third of the bridge and bypassed his father and the police officer to help her out of the carriage. He held her hand as she hiked her skirts to daintily step down to the wooden running-board, and then he lifted her in an affectionate hug. Several flashes announced that their photograph had been taken.

"Michael! Michael!" Joseph MacGregor called as he strode to his son.

"My boy," the elder man said breathlessly when Michael turned to him, "we came as soon as we heard." His voice sharpened as he added, "But these...*constables*...wouldn't let us see you!"

His son knew the grizzled Scotsman's emphasis of the word replaced the appellation he would have preferred to use, one guaranteed to excite the ire of the policemen. But even in anger, Joseph MacGregor knew better than to antagonize the authorities: A copper's power had its limitations; nevertheless, he could cause substantial inconvenience if he turned his mind to it.

Michael set his mother on the ground and addressed both of his parents. "They're doing what they've been ordered to do.

And with good reason."

Joseph made to protest, but Michael cut him off with a quick gesture. "The neighbourhood is not safe, especially for strangers," he pointed out, explaining, "There are armed people everywhere and the place is a powder-keg."

He smiled appreciatively as he added, "I am glad you thought to come, but it would be better if you stay home, for now. There's nothing you can do here."

His mother asked anxiously, "Your wife...?"

"She is alive, and in care of an excellent doctor. You know him, I believe. Dr. Edward Hanes."

Joseph nodded, "Good man, yes."

His mother persisted, "And the child?"

"The bullet passed nowhere near the child, thank God," Michael replied. "And Dr. Hanes is very optimistic about Anne's recovery." A trace of fear flickered across his face, but his parents did not seem to notice.

Hermione sighed and smiled again, her alarm assuaged. She said, "I'm so glad, Michael."

Joseph offered, "If there is anything we can do—"

"I'll let you know," Michael promised him. After a moment's pause, he said, "Now, I must get back to Anne."

"Of course," his parents said in unison.

He hugged them both, and then he strode across the bridge, picking up speed as he headed home, heedless of the shouts of the reporters and the clap and crackle of the photographers' flares.

∞

EACH DAY, after the doctor tended Anne's bandages and pronounced her condition improved, Rob and Kevin, Jack and Larry, Ian and Terence took turns reading to her. Michael noted with a hint of fatherly gratification that their articulation meliorated by increments as each recited chapters of *Sense and*

Sensibility. When Anne drifted to sleep, he encouraged them to proceed.

"She'll hear you," he assured them. "Go ahead."

So, the lessons continued and the lads felt useful. Indeed, they were soon joined by younger children whose mothers had come to help Anne. The boys accepted at once the role of teacher to guide the new students.

Today, as Jack coaxed Dorcas O'Herlihy to sound out a word, Anne smiled faintly at Michael and squeezed his hand. Their wordless exchange lightened his heart: Pale as she was, Michael could see she was healing. He stretched out his other hand to rest lovingly on her belly.

∞

OLD SEAN FLYNN'S body was released from the morgue. The coroner had taken pains to examine him thoroughly, though the knife wound from the rear that had penetrated the man's left lung and sliced a major blood vessel had been quite sufficient to kill him. For the sake of the Flynn family, Mr. Jessop had done his best to hide the signs of murder and of autopsy.

Anne demanded that Michael take her to the funeral. After much wrangling, he reluctantly agreed to escort her to the burial site for the interment, but refused, absolutely, to allow her to sit through the entire service at St. Anthony's. He also insisted that she remain in her nightgown and robe, rather than fuss with restrictive clothing that no one would see under her blankets anyway.

To create a mobile seat for Anne, Mr. Bucholtz had very cleverly affixed two bicycle wheels to a broken armchair; Michael did not ask where he found the wheels. Today, the Scot decided to put the rig to the test. Once his wife had been wrapped and placed comfortably, he pushed her along the most level sections of the rain-washed streets to the small cemetery beside the Catholic church. On the way, he glanced frequently toward the

low, grey sky and prayed that the showers that had sharpened the scents of blossom and leaf, grass and herb would not return before he could bring her home.

Murmurs of surprise rose when the MacGregors entered the churchyard, but quieted again when Father O'Donnell cleared his throat loudly. Anne sat straight in her wheelchair as the priest intoned and as Michael held an umbrella over her against a slight drizzle. By the time the first handfuls of dirt were being tossed onto the pinewood coffin, however, Michael noticed that Anne had slumped; her energies were flagging. He leaned down to whisper, "Can you hold on a little longer? Or shall I take you home?"

She smiled up at him weakly and squeezed his hand. "I'll do," she murmured.

Nonetheless, Michael immediately scooped dirt from the nearby mound and helped her to toss her handful. That done, he hurriedly wheeled her away toward the road.

Dan Doherty caught up and said, "If I'd known ye'd be comin' I'd ha' fetched ye meself."

Michael replied with a rueful smile, "If I'd known we'd be coming, I'd have hired you."

"Well," said Doherty, "we can fix that right now. Stay here."

The cabby waved a restraining gesture and ran across the street to his rig. A few moments later, he wheeled it around and brought it to a halt in front of Anne's chair. Michael knew how tired his wife must be that she made no demur, but allowed herself to be lifted and deposited into the carriage. There, her husband gathered her into his arms to keep her steady as Dan Doherty drove them home.

"I'll fetch back your chair," Dan told them as he opened the cab's door for his passengers.

"Thank you," Michael replied. Carrying his wife, he stepped down to the lane.

The hackney driver rushed forward to open and hold the

gate of the picket fence for them. Then, the man ran ahead and opened the front door, as well, and Michael bore Anne directly to her bed.

After checking her bandage to assure himself she had not reopened the wound, he fetched dry blankets to cover her fully and tucked them close around her. Then, he sat by her side, holding her hand, and he brushed her hair away from her face, letting it fall lightly over her ears the way she liked it. Her respiration slowed to a steady rhythm as she drifted to sleep. The clatter and curses when Dan tripped and dropped the chair onto the porch did not wake her. Nor did the violent thunderstorm that swept through during the night.

∞

"MY HEAVENS, you heal swiftly, Madam!" Dr. Hanes exclaimed when he removed the bandage. He gingerly touched the red marks that lingered at the site of the wound, glancing up to see whether she felt pain. She did not flinch.

"I do feel much better," Anne assured him. "In fact, I would appreciate it if you would tell the ladies and my husband that I can get up and use the privy by myself."

The doctor sat back and pursed his lips as he eyed her. "I'll make you a deal," he said at last. "I'll tell the ladies that you are strong enough to sit up and to go to the privy on your own, but you are to rest for another week at the least."

Anne pouted peevishly a moment. Then, she asked hopefully, "Can I at least sit out in the sun?"

Dr. Hanes grinned and relented, "All right. I'm sure sunlight and fresh air would do you good."

"Thank you, Edward," she responded gratefully.

The physician wrapped her middle with clean, loosely woven cotton. Then, he pulled his stethoscope from his bag, set the wings into his ears, and placed its metal button upon her abdomen.

Michael stepped into the room, waiting at the doorway and watching anxiously as the doctor continued his auscultation. Several minutes later, Hanes pulled down the folds of Anne's white linen gown to cover the bandage and her belly. Finally, he administered a drop of remedy.

As the doctor rose to leave, Anne asked with a glance toward Michael, "Could you please reassure my husband that I'm fine?"

Michael shot her a narrow glare.

Dr. Hanes nodded and replied, "I will let everyone know what I have told you." As he turned, Michael came forward to meet him. "Your wife is doing exceptionally well," Hanes affirmed.

Michael took a deep breath and relaxed. He nodded and said with an appreciative smile, "Thank you, Doctor."

The physician reached to clap Michael upon the shoulder and draw him toward the door. He said, "I'd like to speak to you and to the ladies who have been tending your wife."

As the men descended the stairs, Anne smiled happily.

∞

MICHAEL RETURNED and scooped Anne out of bed to take her to the back porch. He still held her as though she were fragile china, she noted as they descended to the kitchen, but she made nothing of it.

"I'll fetch the blankets," said Mrs. Roarke as she dashed past them and up the stairs.

"In the meantime, I'd like to use the privy," said Anne when she and her husband exited the back door. She specified firmly, "By myself."

"I'll be here if you need help," Michael replied in a tone that indicated he thought she would require it. He gently set her down to stand for herself.

Anne stepped inside the backhouse and closed the door.

Her hands trembled as she reached to open the lid of the toilet seat, and she sat at once, feeling the strain on muscles unused for a time. The wood felt hard under her, yet more forgiving and certainly warmer than the enamelled metal bedpan the doctor had appropriated from the hospital for her use.

A small dark spider crept in short jumps along the inner wall to the fixed translucent window that passed soft, hazy light between the privy and the kitchen. Cicadas shrilled nearby, and a bee buzzed next to the screened window at the side of the hut where nasturtiums climbed a trellis. Anne stayed awhile in the little-house, enjoying the privacy, until Michael's worried knock and anxious call hurried her.

Walking gingerly to the chair as Michael hovered, prepared to catch her if she fell, and as Mrs. Roarke held the blankets ready, Anne protested, "You really don't need to fuss so."

Kathleen Roarke reproved, "Dr. Hanes said you'd say that. And he said to tell you not to tire yourself as you've a wont to do."

"Hmph," Anne grunted in annoyance. Nonetheless, she sat still and allowed herself to be swaddled and coddled.

Michael perched on the porch, at her feet, with a hand on her knee, and he studied her a long moment. He asked softly, "Are you sure you're all right?"

Anne wriggled an arm free of the multicoloured quilts to grasp his hand and give it a quick squeeze. "I'm not in perfect working order," she admitted, "but I'm ready to start getting back to normal."

At his hesitant expression, she added, "Slowly. A little at a time."

Michael nodded and pulled his mouth into a tight smile.

They sat together in silence in the shade of the porch, enjoying the warm day, the gentle breeze, the scents of the flowers, the rustle of the leaves of tree and bush. When their neighbour left to tend her own household, Anne called softly,

"Michael, there's something I want to talk about."

He looked up, expectant.

"You should go back to work."

His face hardened instantly. "I'll not leave you alone and helpless," he exclaimed. His unspoken "again" hung in the air between them.

Anne inhaled slowly and curled both her hands around his. She fixed his eyes and said, "It was not your fault. If you had been here, he would have shot you. We both know that."

Michael looked away, resisting her logic. Anne bent forward, bringing her face closer to his. When she reached to cup his cheek and pull his eyes back to her, the motion wrenched a soft groan of pain from her lips.

At once, Michael rose and protested, "You mustn't lean that way! I can see it hurts you." He gently pressed her against the chair and stood to tower over her so that she must look up to him.

He said, "I can't leave you while that man is still at large."

Grasping his hand again, she said earnestly, "Please, Michael. You need this."

"We don't need the money," he insisted. "There's enough left—"

"It's not the money, my love," Anne put in. "And there are armed constables and neighbours all through The Flats. Not to mention the fact that the police are scouring the city for the man."

"They haven't found him yet," Michael said bitterly.

"I don't think they will."

He regarded her uncertainly. "Because he's got the stone and probably left the city to sell it," he assumed.

"Maybe," she replied. "Though it's possible the buyer was already here."

They remained silent a moment before she restated quietly, "You can go back to work and return to normalcy. You'll feel better for it, my love."

Michael squatted beside her once more and kissed her hand. After gazing up into her eyes for a time, he sighed and nodded reluctant acquiescence.

∞

NO ONE COMMENTED upon his appearance among them as the men of The Flats headed for work early Thursday morning. Michael caught up with Mike Villeneuve and soon found himself surrounded by his fellow stoneworkers.

When they reached the worksite on Draper Avenue, he was amazed how high the neat stone walls he had helped to build had risen. They were now wrapped in a grid of wooden posts and beams and platforms and stairs. He tossed his lunch sack under the oak tree with the rest and reported to the boss for the day's assignment.

Soon after, he joined his friends on the scaffold to raise another course on the walls of the Taft building.

∞

WHEN DETECTIVE MORGAN visited, Anne was sitting on the back porch in a large rocking chair provided by Mrs. Bucholtz, her legs wrapped in two coverlets courtesy of Mrs. Johannsen and Mrs. Murdoch, and her shoulders draped with no less than three woollen shawls from the same ladies.

"How are you feeling, Ma'am?" he asked as he removed his brown fedora and set it on the end of the porch. He always wore dark brown, Anne noted. Though, in all likelihood, she reflected, he could afford only one suit on policeman's pay.

She looked back over her shoulder to the half-opened Dutch door before whispering confidentially, "Well done is how I feel. In fact, nearly burnt to a crisp." She waggled her elbows and shoulders so that the shawls slid out of place to expose her cotton-clad torso, and she inhaled with exaggerated relief.

In the house, Mrs. O'Malley hummed as she chopped

vegetables and scraped them into a tall pot. Mrs. Bannion swept the painted floor with enthusiasm.

Detective Morgan smiled humorously and remarked, "I see you're being well cared for."

Anne said loudly, "I'm so well cared for, I'll likely end up in an early grave!"

She winked and grinned as Mrs. Bannion stomped to the back door to say, "More like you'll put yourself there, Missy, with all your tryin' to do for yourself and your man as if ye were right as rain instead o' shot half dead and in the family way, besides."

With a huff of irritation, the woman set the broom against the wall, opened the lower half of the door, and marched to her patient to pull the shawls back into place. She scolded, "Now, don't you be givin' yourself the pneumonia." With another snort of motherly annoyance, she whirled and strode back inside to finish her sweeping.

Anne and the detective grinned to each other.

"So what brings you to The Flats?" Anne asked.

The detective clasped his hands behind his back and announced, "We found the Irishman last night."

Both sweeping and chopping stopped abruptly. Two sets of feet padded to the back door.

"Where?" Anne inquired.

"Washed up just west of the Durham," Morgan answered. "Shot. The coroner figures he's been dead since a little while after you last saw him."

"The price of failure in his line of work," Anne surmised. "Or perhaps he was not sufficiently wary of his associates."

"Odd thing, though," said the detective, "He'd had a hell—a...nasty rash, too."

Anne grinned as she said, "*That's* the price of running through poison ivy with your trousers half off."

"Mmm," said Morgan with a slight shudder. He cocked an eyebrow as he said drily, "Can't say he didn't deserve it."

The man glanced toward her and then away, with the air of one trying to decide how to say something. Finally, with an attitude of delicacy, the detective asked, "I understand there was a jewel?"

Anne smiled coolly. She admitted, "There was. I had picked it up out of the creek the night...."

A sob caught in her throat. She collected herself and continued, "The night Geordie died. It had been in his pocket."

Morgan opened his mouth to respond, but she cut him off as she went on.

"I didn't know what it was, at first," she explained. "It had been late when I found it, and I didn't really look at it." She closed her eyes and suppressed another sob before she added quietly, "I just wanted something of him...to remember him by."

"I see," the detective responded uncertainly.

Anne looked up and told him, "I kept it in my pocket, you see. And I didn't even think about it until the dream."

Morgan frowned. "Dream?"

She said, "A dream about stars. After the discovery of the Russian words. And when I woke, I remembered the stone. That was the night before...."

She gestured toward the wound and Morgan nodded understanding.

Her brows furrowing, Anne speculated, "Perhaps I had caught a glimpse of the asterism, the star within it, but didn't realize what I had seen until the image came back in the dream."

She regarded the detective and assured him, "I had intended to bring you the stone once Michael came home that day...but I never got the chance."

"Perhaps you could give it to me now," said Morgan lightly.

Anne gaped, brows rising in surprise. She stated, "I don't have it. The Irishman took it from me."

The detective pressed his lips together and ground his teeth, his jaw twitching, his eyes downcast.

Anne said, "I take it you didn't find it on the man."

"No," Morgan confirmed sourly. "So, I suppose his confederates stole it."

With eyes narrowed, he searched her face.

Anne responded to his unspoken question, "The last time I saw that stone, Detective, he had taken it from me and put it into his pocket."

Morgan heaved a sigh. "The Chief Constable will not be pleased." He glanced about absently for a moment before he added with barely stifled anger, "And someone has got away with theft as well as murder."

"And perhaps more. The book and code suggest the stone was not merely stolen for cash but was meant to fund something," Anne thought aloud.

"But what?" Morgan wondered.

Anne replied on an exhalation, "We may never know."

The detective nodded, resigned to the insolubility of the case. He picked up his hat, bowed his head, and said, "Good day, Mrs. MacGregor. I do hope you recover fully soon."

He donned his hat and started toward the front yard, but stopped and turned back to face her. Hesitantly, he said, "There is just one more thing, Mrs. MacGregor."

"Yes, Detective?"

"I understand you had a...weapon—a knife—with which you...defended yourself?" He rushed to add, "And the children, of course."

"Yes."

She waited.

After a moment of working his lips, he asked, "I also understand that little Becky O'Malley found you at home, and that you ran directly to the creek. So, I was wondering," he looked her in the eye to finish, "how it is that you happened to be armed?"

A small smile spread across her lips as Anne said, "Detective, since the war, I have not felt dressed unless armed."

Morgan stared, nonplussed. After a moment in which his mind visibly ran through the possibilities, he frowned perplexedly and asked, "And what war is that, Mrs. MacGregor?"

Anne's smile broadened as she held his eyes. "Good day, Detective."

CHAPTER 17

Celebration

The withdrawal of the armed police officers sparked a night of gaiety as the residents of The Flats relaxed at last and belatedly celebrated Dominion Day. Ale and cider, whisky and homemade wine flowed throughout the district. On every street, firecrackers popped and sparklers fizzed to the delight of young and old.

Michael wheeled Anne, wrapped in a quilt, to the party at the corner of Cedar and Sumac. Mrs. O'Reilly Senior immediately brought them glasses of the lemonade that was usually reserved for children, the sweet-tart drink she had ladled from the large enamelled bowl set on a tree stump. Meanwhile, one of the Mrs. O'Reilly Junior handed them plates of roughly cut sandwiches fetched from the table placed by the low white board fence that surrounded the whitewashed, shake-clad home of the Bucholtz family.

With Mick McGee on fiddle, Marc Desrosiers slapping spoons, Ian Farrell playing flute, and dusky Tim Peckham pounding a homemade drum, something akin to music was achieved. Children and adults hopped and danced on the sward to the sprightly sounds as the sun sank westward.

Anne and Michael were sitting together in the shadow of an old oak, enjoying the spectacle, when a small, tight procession approached from beyond the next intersection. Eyebrows rose and curious expressions followed Kenneth Armstrong and the MacGregor family as the finely dressed outsiders skirted the dancers and slipped past the row of emptied kegs to greet their kin. Elizabeth clung to her fiancé's arm as though afraid she might be grabbed and manhandled, perhaps kidnapped or killed, by the locals. The lawyer stood stiffly, acting the brave protector.

Hermione embraced Michael at once and then gushed over Anne, promptly taking Michael's seat to stay by her daughter-in-law's side and to hold her hand in her own white-gloved grasp. She smiled and chatted, quite at home, and was soon joined by Maeve Doherty and Tess Tulan, who deposited themselves upon squat stools to flank the MacGregor women.

As the conversation instantly turned to babies and children, Anne detected a hint of Welsh lilt in Hermione's decidedly English speech, and she wondered how the woman had met her husband. While still listening to her mother-in-law, Anne caught snatches of other conversations and noted that each member of the family spoke differently: Hermione's English pronunciation, Joseph's Scottish burr, Elizabeth's clipped colonial accent. And then there was Michael, who, as she had discovered in the course of their time together, sounded Canadian in casual conversation, English in formal discourse, Irish when joking, and Scottish when angered or upset. She smiled to herself at how much he sometimes sounded like Alex.

∞

JOSEPH CLASPED Anne's hand and made polite inquiries after her health before turning to survey the festivities with the air of a king observing his subjects. Michael stood by him, introducing neighbours who strayed within range. A few of the local men greeted Joseph with deference that told Michael they worked at the distillery, but most merely shook his hand and eyed the MacGregor patriarch with curiosity. Their brows rose as they glanced from Michael to Joseph and back, their gaze then jumping to Hermione and to Elizabeth, obviously comparing Himself with his family and finding the differences surprising.

Mrs. O'Reilly Senior and her unmarried daughter Alice (the spinster notorious for the temper that matched her fiery hair) brought refreshments to each of the newcomers, smiling and chatting to them as though they were old friends. Elizabeth hesitantly took a glass of lemonade and pulled her mouth into a smile below timid eyes. Kenneth sniffed his glass suspiciously and then downed it.

Dan Doherty presented a stein of ale to Joseph, which the latter gratefully accepted.

"Never did like lemonade," the grizzled Scot said as he handed his glass of sugary yellow liquid to a passing child. Becky O'Malley was more than pleased to oblige the elderly gentleman by drinking his share.

Joseph glanced at his son's glass. As he pulled a silver flask from his inside pocket, he asked, "Want me to sweeten that?"

"No, thank you," said Michael. "I haven't had a drop for some time and I don't plan to start."

As he replaced his flask, Joseph remarked casually, "Odd thing for a distiller to be a teetotaller...But not unheard of."

"I'm not a distiller," Michael said quietly.

"Not yet."

They stood in silence awhile, tapping their feet to the beat of the lively Irish tune and sipping from their respective mugs.

After a time, Joseph looked to his son and said

conversationally, "I understand you work for Jake Trevelyan."

"I do."

Joseph nodded. He said, "I always wondered why you insisted on attending that school in Glasgow instead of the one in London...And spending your summers in Cornwall, of all places."

"I like rocks," Michael said simply.

"Mmm," Joseph responded. "Trevelyan tells me you'd make a fine master stonemason, if you put your mind to it."

"That's kind of him." Michael did not quibble over his father's speaking to the man. He supposed he would do no less than investigate the employer of his own son. That thought brought another to mind.

"Father," he began tentatively.

Joseph looked up at him.

"I don't know whether I'll join the business, but my son...."

Joseph said firmly, "My grandson will inherit whatever I have."

Father and son locked eyes a long moment. Finally, Michael nodded acknowledgement and gratitude. Then, both turned back to watch Jack O'Reilly comically dance a jig with all three of his little sisters.

At that moment, out of the corner of his eye, the younger MacGregor caught Kenneth Armstrong's stare. He turned to the man, about to include him politely in conversation, but the lawyer abruptly looked away. Michael frowned and blinked perplexedly.

As Armstrong leaned to mutter something to Elizabeth, avoiding her brother's eyes, Michael shook his head and dismissed he sister's aloof fiancé with a sigh.

∞

THE NEXT DAY brought a parchment envelope hand delivered

by one of the MacGregor footmen. Anne opened the door to find the black-clad young man gazing after one of the O'Reilly girls as she carried a multicoloured bundle of rags home to be cut into strips and sewn into a rug.

Anne interrupted his speculations. "Yes?"

The handsome blond turned back, dutifully smiled, and handed her the envelope. "From Mrs. MacGregor," he told her.

"Thank you," Anne replied.

She watched the footman as he retrieved the bicycle upon which he had arrived and mounted it to pedal toward the city. Suddenly a little dizzy, Anne clutched the doorjamb and shook her head. When the vertigo passed a moment later, she closed the door and returned to the kitchen table to resume her sewing. She sat in the rocking chair Michael had purchased for her, finding that its wide seat, enfolding arms, and thickly padded cushions made it more comfortable than her other chairs, these days. Ensconced, she opened the wax-sealed envelope to pull out an embossed invitation to the engagement celebration of Elizabeth Abigail Moire MacGregor and Kenneth Oliver David Armstrong, two weeks hence.

She set the invitation on the table and picked up the silk bodice she had begun to sew as Mrs. O'Malley brought in a pot of tea from the summer kitchen.

∞

ANNE'S BROOD gathered round her to sit in the afternoon sun. The girls wore long printed frocks and white aprons, while the boys wore coloured shirts with trousers held up by suspenders crossed in back and buttoned to their waistbands. Her six eldest—Jack, Larry, Ian, Terence, Rob, and Kevin—all wore flat caps with stiff, fabric-covered peaks above the brow, like the men of The Flats. Today, none wore shoes.

In a sky deep blue with shreds of white cloud, the sun shone hot and bright. The cicadas' song was the only natural

sound, though from the summer kitchen a clang of pots and several colourful Irish phrases announced canning preparations by two of the young Misses O'Reilly. Early beets, baby carrots, and cauliflower would be pickled, today, along with a bumper crop of cucumbers. And a portion of the harvest of blackberries, mulberries, serviceberries, and strawberries would soon be turned into jelly and jam.

The day's heat had its own scent, not quite overpowered by the ripening tomatoes and basil, thyme and savory, nor by the floral perfumes of rose and violet, cicely and sweet pea. On the other hand, Larry's dog, Mose, still reeked of his recent encounter with a skunk.

"Eew!" Katie O'Reilly complained. "For the love o' God, Larry, get that cur away!"

"He hardly smells a-tall anymore," Larry protested.

"Ye mean, ye canna smell 'im for your nose is burnt clean away by the stench," said Patsy O'Reilly.

The sisters stood with hands on hips, giving Larry the glare popularly known as "the evil eye." After a full minute's brave attempt to withstand the withering stares, the lad relented and stalked to the front gate, whistling for Mose to follow.

The younger children sniggered when Larry urged the dog to find squirrels. That particular game, so loved by Mose, had led to the calamitous confrontation that now left its offensively odorous stamp on the mutt. Deterred by neither previous nor potential disaster, the dog eagerly raced off to do his master's bidding.

"Where's Mister?" asked Dorcas O'Herlihy when Jack returned from the house with the leather-bound copy of *From the Earth to the Moon*. She had become used to seeing Michael at Anne's side.

"He's gone to the city," Anne told her simply.

As Jack sat down on the grass and opened the book, Anne announced, "There is something I want to tell you all."

The children looked to her with raised-brow surprise and

with curious expectation.

Gazing from one to the other round the circle, starting from her left and ending to her right, Anne said, "I want you to know that I am very proud of you." She looked again to Becky O'Malley, to Rob, and to Kevin to say, "You have been very brave." Then, she looked to Jack, Larry, Ian, and Terence to add, "And you have been very helpful."

She scanned the entire group once more and said, "I could not ask for better friends, or for better students."

The small children squirmed with happiness at such praise. Blushing, the older boys smiled shyly at the unaccustomed gift of laudation.

"And Mrs. Villeneuve says there will be berries and cream with tea, today," she added.

When the children's cheers died down, Anne straightened and looked to Jack. She asked, "Now, where were we?"

CHAPTER 18

Revelations

Michael sat in the shade of an elm at the back of the Draper property and stretched his legs. Mick McGee flopped down to his left, Marc Desrosiers to his right. Seeking a space out of the sun, Mike Villeneuve nearly tripped over the Scot's long limbs. He grunted and settled himself by the large feet.

Not shy, Pat O'Connell lightly kicked Michael's boot and said, "Oy, make room, ye great behemoth!"

Michael grinned as he pulled his legs up and crossed them. He quipped, "It's not my fault God was so generous when he made me."

Pat retorted, "Ah, but was 'e generous where it counts, boyo?"

Michael reddened, cursing himself for walking into that one so readily. To cover his embarrassment, he opened his

muslin sack and extracted the lunch Anne had made for him despite his protests that he could feed himself.

Rob Donnelly piped up, "Oh, to be sure, the Good Lord has been more than bountiful in every respect."

Michael's blush deepened, and he bit savagely at a chunk of cooked chicken Anne had provided as the men glanced to Donnelly and back to him. It occurred to the Scot that Donnelly's house lay next to his and Anne's, and that its second storey might well afford a comprehensive view of their property. And the O'Reilly house was even taller.

"And how would ye know that?" asked Mick McGee. "Is there somethin' ye should be tellin' us, Rob?"

Donnelly grinned from ear to ear and shrugged noncommittally. Michael wondered with chagrin how many times his neighbour had witnessed the newlyweds enjoying a "wee tussle" in the backyard. In future, they would have to be more discreet.

Abruptly, Michael stopped chewing and craned to see around Mike Villeneuve. He had spotted the lanky amble of Jack O'Reilly and now waved to the boy.

"What brings you here?" he asked as Jack casually squeezed himself between Villeneuve and O'Connell and sat down. The Scot handed the lad a boiled egg.

Jack smacked the egg on his thigh and began to peel it. He did not look up as he announced, "Me an' the lads got a couple o' names fer ye."

Along with the other men, Michael waited, watching as Jack finished peeling the egg and popped it whole into his mouth.

When he had chewed and swallowed, the boy said, "Von Ratzenhausen and Skavronsky."

Blanching, Michael set down his chicken and swallowed hard. He knew the German to be a margrave, a man of considerable rank, wealth, and influence in his own country. And he knew Skavronsky, too: He had met the man in England, in a

circumstance he would rather forget.

∞

DETECTIVE MORGAN frowned. "You know these men?"

Michael kept his eyes on the yellow-and-white gingham tablecloth as he pressed a crease apart, his outspread hands pulling in opposite directions on the flat of the table. "I know one, and I know *of* the other," he said, stroking the fabric repeatedly as though the motion could erase his memories as well as the fold line.

Sitting next to her husband, Anne reached out to clutch one of his hands and grip it tightly. The detective noted the supportive gesture and glanced curiously from Anne to Michael.

When neither MacGregor looked up or spoke further, Morgan summarized, "So, we've a German and a Russian, both wealthy, both pederasts, and both here under diplomatic aegis." He added, "Though their purpose in coming to this country is not clear."

Michael said, "My friend only knew that one or the other intended to buy something, but he doesn't know whether it's land or some other form of investment."

"And this friend?"

"Also a diplomat," Michael prevaricated.

Detective Morgan grimaced and sighed. "Well, should your friend discover anything more, I'd appreciate hearing of it."

Michael assured him quietly, "If I find out more, Detective, I'll tell you."

As Morgan rose to leave, Anne frowned and thought aloud, "Is it possible that the object of purchase was the sapphire?" She looked from her husband to the detective and added, "And if so, why are they still here? Surely, they must have it."

Michael suggested, "Perhaps there's a further exchange involved." His jaw tightened and he said through his teeth, "Or

perhaps they haven't got all the pleasure they intend from this country."

The detective assured him, "We'll make certain their particular pleasure is difficult to come by." Behind him, Constable O'Toole nodded emphatically.

Michael regarded Morgan. Then, he turned to smile grimly at Anne and put her hand to his lips.

As husband and wife gazed into each other's eyes, slipping into a private world, Detective Morgan set his hat upon his head and wordlessly ushered Constable O'Toole out the back door.

∞

MICHAEL TOOK a seat by the broad, panoramic east windows of the Yacht Club, acutely aware that the written invitation, complete with the seal of the Earl of Heth, constituted the only reason the concierge would allow a dust-covered tradesman to enter the building, much less the saloon.

Viscount Danford sauntered into the dining-room, its glazed east and south walls overlooking the River Durham and the lake, respectively, and its west windows affording a view of the tennis courts and the sunny rose garden beyond. As usual when he haunted the Yacht Club, the Englishman wore his white silk shirt open, jauntily exposing his graceful neck and a hint of his hairless chest. Today, the shirt accompanied his tennis breeches, their snug fit emphasizing his pert bottom.

Evan, Lord Danford, plucked a crystal wineglass from the tray of a passing waiter as he surveyed the diners. When he spotted Michael MacGregor, his lips spread into a broad grin and he strode directly to deposit himself into the empty *fauteuil* across the small, linen-draped table from his friend.

"The prodigal doth return!" Evan exclaimed with a sweeping gesture. He frowned as he eyed the glass in front of Michael, and he leaned to get a closer look. With a wrinkling of

his nose, he asked incredulously, "Is that lemonade I smell?"

"It is," Michael confirmed with a wry smile.

"Has you on a short leash, does she?" Evan remarked with a sardonic edge as he leaned back and sipped his rosé.

Michael noted that the man always inhabited a chair as though it were a throne. He replied, "I *choose* not to imbibe."

"Of course, dear boy," said Evan with a significant look and a manner that conveyed disbelief.

Michael returned the look and affirmed, "Anne has never asked me to desist. In fact, we've never spoken of it at all."

"Mm, she *is* good," said Evan. "Most women hound a man to death. She's got you thinking it's *your* idea."

Michael heaved a sigh and shook his head in exasperation. He did not expect Evan would ever understand how he felt about Anne. And for the first time, he actually pitied the man he had always admired—a man so sophisticated of habit and cynical of disposition that he might never experience love.

A waiter placed menus and glasses of ice-water before them. Neither of them spoke for several minutes as they perused the list of the day's fare. A sense of estrangement filled the air between them.

Finally, Evan's countenance softened. He said seriously, "I was sorry to hear of your wife's...accident. I do hope she is well."

Michael's voice was hushed when he responded, "She is, Evan, and thank you. She'll be able to attend Elizabeth's engagement party."

"Well, that is good news," Evan said brightly. Catching a glimpse of someone behind the Scot, he added caustically, "Though some will not be pleased to hear it."

Michael asked, "Should I look?"

Evan grinned and told him, "No. It's only Jaclyn Orwell. She's sending evil thoughts your way."

Michael smiled sheepishly. "I'm not sure I don't deserve them."

"Of course, you don't," said Evan, leaning forward to slap Michael's hand lightly. "She only wanted you for your money, anyway." Sitting back again, he added drily, "Ironic, isn't it?"

The waiter returned.

Michael folded his menu and said, "I'm not hungry, thank you."

Evan retorted, "Nonsense." He glanced up to the server and said, "We'll both have the sole."

Michael protested, "No, I'm not hungry."

Evan shooed the waiter away with a wave of his hand and scolded, "You mean you're too poor to pay for yourself and too proud to let me pay for us both." He sipped his wine and then set the glass on the table with a peremptory tap. "Really, Michael! Don't be bourgeois. You know how I hate to eat alone."

Now, Michael leaned back. He said, "All right, Evan. If you insist."

"I do."

With a quirk of his eyebrow, Michael commented, "You know, most people only hate to *drink* alone."

Evan flashed his polished teeth in a broad smile and said, "I can drink anywhere, anytime. But eating alone gives me indigestion."

Michael joked, "Maybe you should get a wife."

Evan's blaring hoot drew the startled stares of the entire room, and a few beyond the door. To Michael's amusement, the Englishman fizzed in a paroxysm of mirth until tears came to his eyes. When at last he quieted, he whipped a handkerchief from his sleeve, dabbed at his eyes, and blew his nose noisily. Then, as he dropped the sodden cloth onto the window ledge, he sighed regretfully, "Oh, Michael, I shall miss you."

Michael started. "Where am I going?"

"Not you. Me," Evan told him. "It'll be announced soon. I am to be attaché to the ambassador for Brazil."

"Congratulations!" said Michael with sincerity. "When?"

Viscount Danford's face fell. He said, "Two months."

"Isn't it what you wanted, Evan?" Michael asked gently, frowning in perplexity at the man's dolorous expression. "A career in diplomacy?"

"Hell, no," Evan replied emphatically. "It's what my father wants. So, now I am to spend my best years in some godforsaken tropical country. And a papist one, at that."

"You hate our winters," Michael reminded him.

"But I love you."

Michael caught his breath. Then, he blinked. Then, he swallowed.

The waiter set plates of steaming fish before them, but neither man ate a bite.

∞

"I NEVER KNEW," Michael told Anne in a whisper. "I—I never guessed."

He was still in shock.

Sitting on the edge of the front porch next to her husband, Anne rubbed his back soothingly with one hand as she gripped his clasped hands with the other.

"What did you say to him?" she asked quietly.

Michael snorted in remembered astonishment. "Nothing," he answered. "I couldn't say a thing!"

He shook his head and closed his eyes tightly. "He's always been my best friend. I never guessed that he could be...that he could be...."

Anger bubbled up and he spat the words, "That he could be one of *them*."

"I don't think he is," said Anne.

Michael turned on her. "How can you say that?" he demanded. "He's...he's—"

"A homosexual, but not a rapist."

Michael jerked as though she had slapped him. He stared at her, eyes wide, astounded and uncomprehending.

"Think about it," Anne persisted. "You didn't know because he made no advances toward you. He must have realized you could not accept them."

Michael turned away, his eyes darting here and there in visible manifestation of the search of his memory. He licked his lips and took a deep breath. Finally, he acknowledged, "That's true. I don't think he would ever have hurt me."

"No," said Anne. "At least, not intentionally. And not in that way."

Closing his eyes, Michael lifted his face skyward. When he opened them, he noticed the clouds as though for the first time.

"It's beautiful," he murmured. "The sky. The clouds." He surveyed the trees, the nearby houses, the flowers in their yard, and he added, "This country."

He looked to Anne, at his side. "You."

Turning his gaze to his hands, their fingers spread wide on his knees, a recent cut dark with clotted blood and the week's bruises yellowing, he said, "Today—before he told me—I felt sorry for him because I thought he'd never know love."

His face contorted to a pained grimace and he whispered, "But perhaps it's worse to know a love you can never have."

Michael stared into Anne's face, his own countenance bereft. He said sadly, "He was my friend."

She said, "He *is* your friend."

Michael gathered her hands into his and kissed them. After a moment's reflection, he nodded and agreed, "He *is* my friend."

∞

ANNE MARVELLED that a man so buffeted by life as her husband could remain so naïve. Though she had not met the viscount formally, she had seen him downtown, one evening, and had guessed at once that the Englishman's affections would

never be invested in a woman.

When Michael kissed her hands fervently, she kissed him back, and then led him up to their bedroom, wondering at the strange twist of fate that had made a Sydenham her husband's best friend, and at the karma that had turned hate into love.

CHAPTER 19

Intrusions

I don't want to hurt you," Michael whispered.

Wordlessly, Anne continued to unbutton his shirt, and then moved on to his flies. He was hard, as he had been many times in the last weeks. This time, she would give him what he needed. As she pulled down his trousers and drawers, she rubbed her face against him.

"Oh, lord, don't do that!" he protested. But he made no attempt to stop her.

∞

MICHAEL STOOD motionless as Anne undressed him. He so yearned to make love to her and yet he so feared to do it. She was injured, he had told himself again and again. He could damage her, and perhaps the child as well.

But when she massaged him with her face, her smooth

skin setting him on fire, it was all he could do to hold himself back. His legs trembled with the combined effort of standing still and stopping the rush that wanted to erupt at her caresses, the rush so long denied. He closed his eyes in concentration; his breath came in laboured gasps.

Suddenly, he opened his eyes in astonishment and looked down to find Anne embracing him with her mouth. He gaped as her head bobbed rhythmically, slowly sliding up and down. Of its own volition, his hand moved to rest on her crown. She could not take the whole of him, but her attempt was all that was needed to loose the flow that had been dammed inside him. He groaned at the sudden release.

As he panted above her, she pulled away, straightened, and wiped her lips with the back of her hand. On impulse, Michael bent to grasp her face and plunged his tongue into her mouth that he might taste himself in her — salt in her sweetness. Strangely, he found it intensely erotic.

"I didn't know a woman could do that," he whispered as he then fumbled with her buttons, his earlier hesitance supplanted by avidity.

"Really?"

Her surprise astounded him.

"Truly," he affirmed. "I thought it was something only men do."

She swatted his too-eager hands away and finished undoing the buttons of her gown. As soon as the fastenings were freed, he hastily shucked her outer shell and pulled her to the bed. Anne settled herself to lie in the middle of the mattress and lifted the hem of her shift as Michael climbed onto the divan and manoeuvred between her legs.

She said, "I would have thought you'd have experienced it with a prostitute.

"I was always drunk," he admitted contritely. "I suppose they didn't think it worth the effort."

Anne reached up to take his face into her hands. She

murmured, "*I* think you're worth it."

Michael sank to press himself against her, and he kissed her long and deeply. He kissed...and caressed...and loved his wife...and fell asleep wrapped around her.

∞

RAIN BEATING on the window pane pulled him toward wakefulness. Michael reflexively cuddled closer to Anne and sighed, unwilling to pass out of the realm of his happy dreams. After a time, though, the lashing roused him enough that he batted his eyes sleepily and stared at the window.

For a moment, he thought he should get up and dress for work. Then, he remembered yesterday: He had gone to the Yacht Club to see Evan on Saturday evening. And then Anne had reminded him of the joys of being a man.

He contemplated the revelations of the day before: How had he failed to recognize Evan's propensity? Now that he knew, he realized the signs had always been there, from the first day they met....

∞

England, 1878

THE PAPIST CHURCH bell rang in the distance, calling the devout to early Mass. Michael stumbled up the steps in the dark, willing his muscles to take him to his room, to his bed, to oblivion. His hand scraped the stone wall as he climbed, and he stubbed his left foot against the next riser, pitching forward to slam his face against another and bang his knees on the hard edges of the steps.

Fresh tears of pain wetted his face as he pushed himself up. He staggered to the landing and out into the corridor. His mouth tasted of foulness and puke, and he wanted to vomit again. Groping along the hallway, he came to the sixth door and gripped the metal knob with hands still sweating and shaking so

badly he could barely turn it.

Inside, he fell against the door, closing it with a thump and a click. His head swam and throbbed, and he dived for the chamber pot that gleamed dully in the morning light that penetrated the ancient square panes coated with the film of coal smoke, within and without. He made it in time to empty what remained of his stomach contents into the pot.

When the retching finally stopped, he collapsed against the wardrobe and sobbed.

He did not know how long he had been sitting there before he realized he was not alone. A stirring, he thought: a stirring in the bed had alerted him to the presence.

"Who's there?" he demanded, both fearful and angry. "What are you doing in my room?"

"Not to put too fine a point on it, old boy," said a pleasant English voice, "but you're in *my* room."

Michael looked about anxiously in the growing light. Suddenly, he noticed the azure silk dressing-gown draped over the wooden chair, and the pile of books scattered haphazardly on the desktop. His robe was brown wool and his own bureau was always neat.

A figure rose from the curtained bed and stepped out into the light. A young man, he saw. A student like himself. But a smaller, slighter, and younger lad of fair skin and hair and of aristocratic demeanour.

"I—I—I," Michael stammered in confusion, "I'm sorry. I...I s-see now that I've made a mistake. I...m-must have missed my floor...or perhaps I'm in the wrong wing. Is this Pritchard Hall?"

"No, it's Danford Hall," said the blond boy. He came forward and extended his hand. "I'm Evan Sydenham." With an apologetic tone, he added, "Also known as Lord Danford. Viscount Danford."

Michael grasped the hand and got his feet under him. As he stood to tower over the other, he said, "Michael MacGregor's

my name. No titles. Not even an 'Honourable.'"

Evan Sydenham's eyes had grown as the intruder rose, and he now exclaimed in awe, "My...God, you're big!"

Michael's mouth curled into a little smile. As he released the viscount's hand, he replied, "I suppose it's my Highland blood."

Then, he noticed the bulge below the young man's pyjama shirt and panic gripped him. He said hastily, "I'll just be going, then," and he strode to the door.

"Drop by anytime," Evan called after him invitingly as Michael exited and raced away.

∞

Present day

MICHAEL SMILED abashedly at the memory of his reaction to Evan's morning erection, his own now clamouring for attention. He kissed Anne's hair and inhaled her fragrance as the wind rattled the bedroom window. Slowly, tentatively, he probed her, all the while stroking her ever so gently. To his delight, her hips invited him, rotating in tiny circles and pressing her roundness into the crook between his thighs and belly. Her eyes remained closed, but a little smile played at her lips.

He let out his breath in a long, tremulous sigh as he slid into her waiting passage, its depths wet and warm. He murmured hoarsely, "I hope you'll pardon my intrusion, Madam."

Anne responded with a quiet chuckle, and her gyrations intensified.

∞

MICHAEL LAY on his side, propped on one elbow, his head nestled on his palm as the opposite hand rested on his wife's belly. Supine, Anne placed a hand on his and gazed into his eyes.

He could lie like this forever, he thought, basking in the

love that radiated from her as light from a star. She filled him with peace, and with hope for the future, and she asked nothing but the love he gladly gave her.

The purple of her eyes fascinated him. He had neither seen nor heard of such eyes before. They reminded him of the amethyst geodes he had studied in Scotland, while her hair called to his mind the glowing white skies of the Highlands. Indeed, there was a wildness about her that evoked those ancient moors and windswept mountains. And suited this infant country, as well.

A draught from the window lifted a wisp of her silvery hair and he pushed it behind her ear. When she returned the favour, securing one of his jet locks, he smiled broadly, and she did the same.

"I must go to the privy," she announced. "But I think we might stay home from church, today."

He grasped her hand and kissed her palm. "A capital idea."

His own bladder needed emptying, but he lingered in bed to watch her rise and wriggle out of her shift with motions and a view of her arse that stood him anew. She donned the kimono she always kept in back of the door, and she floated out of the room.

He closed his eyes and snorted in annoyance at his wilful member. He had all day to satisfy "John Henry," as she had named it. But he had better piss before he burst.

∞

STEPPING OFF the back porch into the rain, Michael glanced about, acutely aware—thanks to Rob Donnelly—that the screen of trees and bushes that lined the property did not entirely obstruct the neighbours' view. He sprinted barefoot across the patch of grass and around the serviceberries, juneberries, currants, and blueberries that grew among the staggered trees

just inside the six-foot-tall raspberry hedge that fenced the east side of the yard. On his way by, he snatched ripe fruit from this bush and that, to pop the sweet and tart treats into his mouth.

As he sheltered under the spread of a beech, Michael surveyed the area, evaluating the degree of privacy. When he had assured himself he could not be seen, he relieved himself at last, the easing of pressure almost as delicious as seminal ejaculation. Business complete, he removed his robe and hung it over a low branch. After a quick shower in the rain beyond the beech's dripline, he stepped back under the umbrella of leaves and rubbed himself down to strip away most of the liquid that clung to his skin and hair. Then, he plucked more berries from nearby bushes to fortify himself for the morning's agenda, admiring, as he did so, his wife's ability to pack such abundance into so small a space.

Ready, he wrapped himself in his robe to make the dash back to the porch. As he slipped the blue silk over his arms, he remembered its origins: Evan had given it to him as a Christmas present in the last year of their boarding-school days together. The viscount had had it made specially, in a hue that matched Michael's eyes.

Michael swallowed, remembering with a pang of regret Evan's face that winter morning: the look that had gone unrecognized, expressing feelings and desires that would be forever unrequited. He suddenly wondered if that was the lot of the homosexual. For Evan's sake, he hoped not. For his own, he thanked God once more for Anne.

∞

THE CEASELESS RAIN drummed upon the roof, and the beat of gusting winds echoed the rhythm of his thrusts when he took her again. And again.

"You're sure?" Michael asked as he positioned himself. Reluctantly, he offered, "I can do it myself."

His concern for Anne urged him not to impose himself so; his lust for her spurred him to revel in her until she begged him to stop.

"I'm sure," she whispered.

"Oh, God!" he moaned as he entered her for the fifth time.

∞

MICHAEL LIT the bedside candle and set the match in the bowl left for that purpose. He crawled back into bed to watch the tiny light flicker gold across Anne's skin, her face and form pink with the glow of satiation. That rosy flush communicated fulfillment, and he so delighted in seeing this proof he had pleased her that he hesitated to pull the sheet to cover them.

The scent of beeswax and candle smoke mixed with the smells of their sweat and passion, and with the damp that had permeated the house.

Anne rolled to her side, her back to him. The motion he knew as an invitation to spoon with her brought the still-red scars of the bullet's passage into view. Michael touched them gently, front and back, a small expanse of pristine flesh between. He had a similar pair of marks on his right thigh where a Mahdist had shot him during a battle in the Sudan.

He kissed Anne's temple and pulled the sheets up. As he lay snuggled behind his wife, memories came, unbidden, of the many times he had tried and failed to meet death. And of the reasons why....

∞

Scotland, 1880

"MISTER MacGREGOR! I have your assignment here."

Michael's gut clenched at the call of his professor. Sweat dripped down his sides as he preceded the slender, slightly dishevelled man with tea stain on his white cotton shirt and beige vest into the cramped office, its yellowed walls lined with shelves

packed so tightly with books that they bowed and threatened to break. The tiny transom above the dark, narrow door and the single tall latticed casement on the leeward side of the building allowed little airflow, and the room always smelled musty and close.

He had thought it would be different in Glasgow. He had been wrong.

When the door clicked shut, Michael's heart and gut lurched in unison. He did not turn, but only stood by the boxy oak desk strewn with pens and piled with papers and files.

The man stepped up behind him and reached around to lift his waistcoat. The long, cool fingers unbuttoned his flies and waistband and suspenders, and then slid inside the top of his trousers and under his shorts to tug both down to his knees in a swift, practised jerk.

"Bend over, there's a good lad," the velvet voice commanded casually.

Closing his eyes, Michael did not move. He said, "I don't want to."

"Of course ye do, lad," the voice said unctuously. "It's only natural."

A hand reached around and grabbed him, hard. Michael flinched at the pain and pitched forward, knocking a jar of pens to the floor and scattering a pile of papers as his hands flew out to brace him.

"Much better, that's a good lad."

The painful grip eased and the hand began to stroke him softly. He tried to will his cock to remain limp, but the traitorous appendage stiffened under the man's caresses.

"Yes," said the soft, triumphant voice. "You see? It's in your nature."

One hand continued to massage his front while the other shifted to the back and fondled his scrotum a moment. After a brief respite, Michael felt the fingers, now oiled, parting his cheeks. He squeezed his eyes tightly shut against the inevitable

penetration.

Tears of humiliation leaked from the corners of his eyes as the man stroked and thrust and sated himself.

After a groan of completion, the voice taunted him again, "Oh, yes, you're a pretty lad...And we mustn't forget *your* pleasure, must we?"

The smooth, oily hands did their work, and Michael left the professor's office with his assignment in hand and wishing for the thousandth, or maybe the ten thousandth time, that he were dead.

∞

Present day

FOR AN INSTANT, Michael wondered if he clung to Anne only to prove himself a proper man. Memories then flooded into his mind: of the day's lust, of their prior lovemaking, of the evening bath when he first knew he truly wanted her, of the violet eyes that had so captivated him....

No, he loved her. In every sense.

∞

"WE SHOULD PUT out the candle," said Anne.

"Am I too hideous to look at, now?" Michael teased.

Anne shifted, turning onto her back. Her mien tender, she gazed at him, caressing his familiar broad brow, smooth cheekbones, and angular jaw. Her fingers stroked the bristly roughness of his stubble, and traced the line of a thick eyebrow.

"You are beautiful," she whispered raptly. "You take my breath away."

Michael asked quietly, "Do I look so much like him?"

Her expression sharpened, and his face showed his regret of the impulsive question. She regarded him a long moment.

"You still think I love you only because you look like Alex?"

He swallowed visibly as she held his eyes, but he said nothing. She sighed.

At last, Anne cupped his cheek and said, "As I told you before, you *are* Alex. And you are Michael. And you are the many others before that."

"Many others," he repeated.

Anne said firmly, "You have been many men. And you will be many more. And I will always love the infinite variety of you."

He blinked, abashed, and he swallowed again.

Anne smiled, slipped her fingers through his hair to grip the back of his head, and said, "Kiss me, you fool."

She pulled him to her and tasted his lips once more.

∞

WHAT HAD HE been thinking? he wondered as he blew out the candle. Why in God's name had he been so stupid as to ask that?

He knew the answer: He was jealous. Jealous of any man—of every man—she had ever loved. He wanted to be the only one.

And yet...she seemed to truly believe he *was* the only one.

I will always love the infinite variety of you.

He found himself wondering: Had he been someone else? Had he loved her before, another self in another time?

Then, he wondered: Had he loved another Anne? Would he—could he—love her again, in another form?

Would she look the same in another life? Would he? Would he know her?

He hissed a light nasal snort. *Impossible,* he told himself. She was his for this life and that was all that mattered.

He drifted to sleep, to dream of a hill in the Highlands and of Anne leaping out of a rock and into his life.

CHAPTER 20

Engagements

W e've received an invitation to Miss Hetty's," Anne announced when Michael walked in the back door.

Her husband stopped dead. "Miss Hetty's?"

"Yes," Anne confirmed. "Any idea why?"

Michael thought a moment. Then, he shook his head slowly and said, "Not a one, unless she wants to thank us for curing her girls."

Anne told him, "The invitation is not exclusively for us. Apparently, the O'Reilly's and the Doherty's have been invited as well."

"Then, damned if I know what it's about," he said as he dropped his empty lunch sack on the hutch and bent to kiss his wife.

"Mmm," she said, licking her lips. "Limestone. Fifty million B.C. Very good year."

Michael grinned and straightened. "Is that an indication you want me to bathe?"

"Right away," she replied. "The party is tonight."

∞

MICHAEL LINKED Anne's arm with his as they walked from their home toward Poplar Lane. On the assumption that the occasion must be special, she had dressed in her blue gown and he had donned his light-grey suit and blue silk tie.

When his wife refused to take either her wheelchair or a hackney cab, Michael told her he wanted to enjoy the evening air. Thus, they set out early, well before the designated time, so that they could stroll unhurriedly. Both knew his true motive was concern that she not tire herself.

"I'm not an invalid, you know," Anne said as they stepped through their gate into Cedar Lane. The westering sun cast an orange glow across the houses, gardens, and avenues of The Flats, and gleamed in golden reflections from windows here and there.

"Of course you're not," Michael replied lightly. "But it's a lovely evening and we should enjoy it. Autumn will come soon enough."

"I love you," Anne said softly.

He looked down to see her fond smile, and he matched it with one of his own. He grasped her hand and squeezed it gently. Then, they sauntered in silence all the way to Poplar.

∞

THE BROTHEL'S PARLOUR had been decorated with balsam boughs and sprays of roses. Imported bayberry candles lit every wall and surface, scenting the air with their tang, and so bright was the room that its windows beckoned, visible from the far end of the street, even as the sun set in a final flare of brilliance.

Miss Hetty immediately brought Anne to a huge plush

wing chair in the corner. As Michael took up a protective stance by his wife's side, the madam rushed to greet the Dohertys and the Farrells.

The maid, Rachel, and the cook, Hannah, both in black dresses and white ruffle-edged aprons, brought out trays of little cakes decorated with dustings of sugar and drizzles of sauce in various colours. As she scanned the selection, Anne guessed the flavours to include chocolate, lemon, strawberry, caramel, and mint. She chose one sprinkled with red and bit into it to discover it was, indeed, a strawberry confection. Michael sampled the caramel cake and accepted a glass of lemonade instead of wine as neighbours dressed in their Sunday-best crowded into the house of ill repute. The noise level rose with each addition, and so did the heat.

Some of the men seemed familiar with the establishment, though a few of the younger husbands pretended no knowledge of the bordello and its notorious inhabitants. The women, on the other hand, openly surveyed the place they had never dared enter: some disapprovingly, some apprehensively, all curiously taking in the furnishings and decorations, the resident ladies and their colourful *décolleté* gowns. With admirable discretion, the prostitutes addressed each new arrival as though meeting the gentleman for the first time.

"Michael. Mrs. MacGregor," Dan Doherty greeted his neighbours genially, a tankard of frothy ale in hand.

"Mr. Doherty," Anne acknowledged with a nod and a smile as Michael inclined his head in salutation.

"Quite the turnout," said Patrick O'Reilly, clan elder, also holding a stein. "Though for what I don't know." He spilt a bit of brew when one of his sons pushed past and jostled him. "Oy!" he admonished. "Watch where ye step, ye lout! Don't be wastin' good drink!"

"Don't be drinkin' more'n your share!" his wife scolded. Her face transforming from censure to kindliness, the tall wiry woman turned to Anne and asked, "And how are ye, dear lady?

Are ye healin' all right?"

"I'm very well, Mrs. O'Reilly, thank you," Anne replied. "I'm well taken care of." She clasped Michael's hand and smiled up at him. He beamed and bent to kiss her knuckles.

"And so ye are," said Dottie O'Reilly with an approving nod, and she placed her hand on the shoulder of her significantly shorter husband with a warm glance of affection to him.

A tinkling sound drew everyone's attention as Miss Hetty tapped a silver spoon against her wineglass. When all eyes were upon her, she set her flute and spoon on the mantel and announced, "Ladies and gentlemen...we're here to celebrate the engagement...."

The madam raised her arm and beckoned. Constable O'Toole, wearing a vested civilian suit of dark-blue serge with maroon bow tie, stepped forward shyly, blushing and holding the hand of Geordie's mother, who wore a simple, modest, round-collared green gown that complemented her fiery hair.

Miss Hetty finished, "Of our dear friend Constable Patrick O'Toole to Mrs. Sarah Monaghan."

The madam immediately began to clap her hands enthusiastically. At once, the other ladies of the brothel joined her. Rising, Anne quickly followed suit and called, "Bravo! Brava! Congratulations!"

The rest of the room, hesitant at first, took up the call. Soon, the happy couple were being drawn into a gender-polarized series of felicitations, the ladies of The Flats gathering round Sarah Monaghan, the men taking turns slapping the constable on his back and shaking his hand.

"I'll be damned!" whispered Michael.

"It's been a long time coming," Anne assured him. Her face fell slightly as she murmured, "A pity it didn't happen sooner."

"Go," Michael urged. "Time for Herself to bless the bride."

Anne grinned and then made her way toward Sarah as

Michael offered his best wishes to the district's favourite police officer.

∞

AS THINGS SETTLED, the men removing to the front porch and dooryard while the women remained in the parlour, Constable O'Toole bashfully accepted the ribald jests of his fellows. Himself accustomed to tactless and even malicious gibes, Michael brought a large glass of Miss Hetty's whisky to fortify the flustered young man.

"Thank you, sir," said O'Toole gratefully.

"You looked like you could use it," Michael replied with a grin that expressed both amusement and compassion. He raised his half-full glass of lemonade and toasted, "Slainte."

The constable nodded, raised his own glass, and then took a large gulp. When he coughed and sputtered upon swallowing, Michael slapped his back.

"All right there, Constable?" the Scot asked with a combination of humour and concern.

His eyes tearing and his face flushed, O'Toole said hoarsely, "H-hm—Yes, sir. Just not used to strong drink."

"I'm getting *un*used to it, myself," Michael admitted.

Overhearing, Denny O'Reilly said, "A teetotalin' Scot? Are ye Presbyterian, then?"

"No," said Michael. "But I've drunk more than my share for too many years."

"Aye," said Tom O'Reilly, returning to the veranda after an indiscreet piss among the rose bushes, "I heard ye was a drinker before ye come to The Flats."

Old Patrick O'Reilly put in sagely, "A good woman can turn a man from evil ways."

"Ain't worked for you, Pop," said Patrick the Younger, not at all jocular.

Heading off a potential Donnybrook, Denny piped up,

"Well, there's no harm in an occasional draught of the water o' life, now is there?" He clapped Young Patrick on the shoulder, hard, and forcibly steered his irascible brother toward a group of men by Miss Hetty's gate, saying "Why, even your favourite football player takes a nip now and then, does 'e not? What's 'is name, again?"

"Phew!" exclaimed Constable O'Toole as the two O'Reillys joined a lively debate about the prospects for the Dominion Championship. "Thought for a minute, there, I'd have to go back on duty!"

"Agh!" Old Patrick declared with a dismissive wave. "That lad's always been full o' piss an' vinegar!" He peered into his empty stein as though he might find something in it if he looked hard enough. Disappointed, he said on a sigh, "Must get meself another ale." He strode purposefully to the door and tripped on the sill as he entered the front hall.

Tom observed, "I think I'd better go with 'im. It don't take as much as it used to, to put the old man four sheets to the wind. And there'll be Hell to pay if Mam sees 'e's had too much." He rushed after his father, leaving the Scot and the groom-to-be on the veranda.

Glancing about to assure himself none would hear, Constable O'Toole cleared his throat and leaned close to ask Michael with diffidence, "Sir, I wonder if I might have a word with you alone? Privately, I mean." He panned the clusters of men nearby.

Brows high in surprise, Michael blinked and then suggested, "Shall we take a walk around back?"

"I think that'd be good, sir," said O'Toole with an air of relief.

They strolled, drinks in hand, off the porch, around the side of the former farmhouse, past a shed, and into a small, night-blackened garden beyond the row of outhouses installed to accommodate up to five customers or residents at once. As they passed the privies, it occurred to Michael that the O'Reilly family

could use such a setup. And then he wondered if they had already built one, given that at least three of the O'Reilly men were regular clients of Miss Hetty's girls.

By unspoken agreement, the Scot and the constable stopped under a cherry tree. Fireflies winked about them in echo of the stars above, and crickets chirped invisibly in the moonless dusk that was pierced, in the distance, by bright squares-within-rectangles of candlelight emanating from the lower floor of the brothel.

"What did you want to discuss, Constable?"

"Well, sir," O'Toole started hesitantly. He paused a moment before he resumed with obvious discomposure, his accent increasing with his distress, "I've been wonderin'—that is, I've heard things an' I was hopin'—"

The young man swallowed hard and fidgeted, unable to continue. Michael imagined he must be blushing purple from head to toe. Fortunately, darkness hid the man's mortification.

"Constable, are you asking me about your wedding night?" he guessed.

"Well...um...yessir."

Michael turned a spontaneous chuckle into a cough and said, "Mm. Too much sugar at the bottom of the glass." He hoped the man could not see that he had not taken a drink. And he grinned wryly at the irony that he should be considered an authority on the arts of love after only a few weeks of marriage and an adulthood of inexperience with women.

He said, "I'm no expert, you understand—"

"Beggin' your pardon, sir, but that's not what I've heard."

Taken aback, Michael snorted a half chuckle. What could he have heard? he wondered. And from whom? Rob Donnelly immediately came to mind. The man had no shame.

"Well," Michael said with modesty, and with more than a little annoyance with the village gossipmonger, "regardless what you may have heard, I can only tell you what little I know. And that is: that you have to let the woman lead you. Listen to her,

pay attention to what she says and does, and be guided by her reactions to what you do. If you love her, you'll want to please her. And you'll find that giving her pleasure is very erotic.

"Then," he added, "Nature will take its course...Does that answer your question?"

"Uh, mostly, sir," said O'Toole.

"What else do you need to know?" Michael asked, hoping he could give suitable counsel.

After a long, uncomfortable moment, the bridegroom said, "It's just that...."

He pressed his lips together tightly, and then finally admitted, "Well...the lady—Mrs. Monaghan—has so much more experience than I do."

Michael put a reassuring arm around the constable's shoulder and urged him back toward the brothel's dooryard. He said, "Mrs. MacGregor also had far more experience than I, when we married."

The younger man was astounded. "Truly, sir?"

"Truly," Michael affirmed. "Fortunately for us men, women are very patient and forgiving creatures."

∞

ANNE COULD NOT help noticing that Sarah Monaghan frequently glanced to her with an expression that encompassed diffidence, embarrassment, uncertainty, and entreaty. During a lull in conversation, she approached the redhead. Feigning fatigue, she smiled apologetically and asked, "Mrs. Monaghan, would you be so kind as to help me to the privy?"

"Of course," said Sarah, her smile evincing relief as well as concern.

When they had reached the back porch, Anne paused and pointed wordlessly. She had spotted Michael and Patrick O'Toole heading for a garden beyond the latrines. When the men had gone well out of earshot, Anne led Sarah to a secluded space at

the side of the house.

"What did you wish to ask me?" she wondered.

Even in the dark, Anne knew the woman was reddening. She guessed, "Are you, by chance, a little concerned about your...experience...relative to your future husband's?"

"Yes," Sarah responded with shame.

"Sarah," Anne said firmly, "Patrick would not have asked you to marry him if your manner of making a living disturbed him. It's not as if he is unaware, now, is it?"

"True," the woman admitted. "But—"

"Moreover," Anne continued, "I do believe he's asking my husband's advice on this same matter as we speak." She grinned as they entered a pool of light from the kitchen window. "I suspect he wants to live up to your expectations."

Sarah Monaghan stopped and gaped in surprise. "My expectations?"

"Of course," said Anne. "He wants to please his wife. As it should be."

Sarah's gaze wandered as she contemplated this unexpected revelation.

"There is one thing, though," said Anne.

"Yes?"

Anne pursed her lips and took a deep breath. At last, she said, "If you want to erase your past in his mind and your own...to truly start anew...."

She paused a moment and looked into the prostitute's eyes, seeing there a hopefulness that wrenched her heart.

She said, "At the first opportunity—it does not have to be your wedding night, but as soon as you can manage it—sleep together under the stars.

"I know it sounds odd," she allowed, "but the ritual of declaring your love, with God and the heavens as your witnesses, will help you both to put the past behind you."

Sarah Monaghan nodded slowly as she absorbed Herself's wisdom.

When the light of decision dawned in the woman's face, Anne hooked her arm with Sarah's and said, "Now, about that visit to the privy...."

∞

ANNE HAD carefully washed and pressed her husband's best evening outfit: black trousers and matching jacket with tails and silk-faced lapels, white silk shirt with tall collar and turned-down points, white silk jacquard double-breasted vest, white silk bow tie, and white brushed-cotton gloves. She had polished his best shoes to a mirror shine and cleaned his gold watch. His jet evening cape, lined with silk, and his top hat had been prepared as well.

Hanging his vestments in readiness, she pictured him in his finery: He would be so handsome. She only hoped he would not be exhausted from his day's work.

With a dreamy smile, she returned to her sewing. Her new gown needed last-minute adjustments.

∞

"WHAT DO YOU THINK?" Anne asked as she twirled to show her husband the view from all sides.

With the help of the young Misses O'Reilly and Mrs. Roarke, she had used the bolt of emerald silk to fashion a simple, sleeveless gown with gathered skirt, fitted bodice, and sweetheart neckline. Per the custom of the times, she wore full-length white satin gloves, buttoned at the wrist. Her shoes were plain jet leather pumps, buffed to brilliance. And her adornments included silver filigree combs, pearl ear-drops, and the choker necklace she had made so long ago in the Highlands: a river-washed blue topaz cabochon fastened with a braid of her own silvery hair.

When he simply stared, wordless, Anne prompted anxiously, "Michael?"

A smile spread slowly on her husband's lips and he said, "I think I'm going to have a problem all night." He rushed to pull her into his arms and admitted, "For I'd like nothing better than to take it off you, bit by bit."

He nuzzled her ear, and she squirmed and giggled.

∞

THE CREAM OF SOCIETY had been invited to the gala held at the Carleton Hotel. Guests wandered from the ball room to the nearby Regency dining-room and back as an orchestra in black tails and white ties played Strauss, Ravel, and Tchaikovsky for the dances. During interludes, a pianist entertained with Liszt, Chopin, and Debussy solos.

Throughout the grand hall, glittering crystal sconces and chandeliers glowed with the beeswax and bayberry candles that had not yet been replaced by electric lights. Rose bouquets, some yellow and some pale pink, competed with the sweet scents of the candles, but both were soon overpowered by a mix of exotic perfumes and perspiration as the city's elite crowded into the Empress Room for the reception.

Most of the men dressed as Michael did, though few looked as dashing in Anne's opinion. A handful boasted the coloured sashes and brooches that marked them diplomats or members of one European aristocracy or another. Several wore the scarlet tunics of the British Empire soldiery, with collar pins indicating rank, shoulder braid proclaiming formal dress, and ribbons and medals on display.

The ladies had decked themselves out in silks and laces, feathers and beads, jewels and gilt. Many had rouged their lips. All but Anne had dabbed themselves with scent. Most, including Elizabeth MacGregor, seemed to be in competition for the most lavish costume.

Michael linked Anne's arm with his with a proprietary air, though, by the hungry stares of many women they passed,

Anne thought she had more cause to keep a grip on her husband than he on her. Nonetheless, she smiled winsomely as he introduced her to his acquaintances on the way to join his family. For the most part, the men regarded her speculatively but behaved with civility. The women, on the other hand, treated her with barely veiled scorn.

At sight of her son, Hermione MacGregor rushed to embrace him and her daughter-in-law, kissing each in turn and praising Anne's gown. Leaning close, she added in a low voice, "I do so admire your restraint, my dear. So many of these young women gild the lily until the flower is utterly hidden."

Anne murmured, "I've always agreed with the Japanese that less is more."

"Less is more," Hermione repeated. "How clever. And so very apropos."

Anne added sincerely, "And may I say, Mrs. MacGregor, that your own gown is lovely." She had noted that Hermione MacGregor tended to understatement in her attire, and tonight the matron wore a gown so like Anne's that one might assume they had hired the same dressmaker. The primary differences between them were the colour (Hermione in lilac silk) and the more modest neckline and short, puffed sleeves of the little woman's frock.

"Oh, do call me 'Mother,' dear," Hermione insisted.

"If you wish...Mother," Anne responded with a ruffled smile. It felt odd to address Michael's mother so, for the woman was surely younger than she was. But then, the MacGregor matriarch would not know that.

Hermione drew her son and daughter-in-law to the reception line. "Come, my dears, you belong with the family."

Michael stood astern of the receiving row while Joseph MacGregor took the bow. Elizabeth and Kenneth Armstrong, installed amidships, were bounded by Hermione and Anne. Slowly, the guests floated by to greet their hosts and congratulate the betrothed couple.

A brown-eyed blonde with daggers in her eyes squeezed Anne's hand too tightly and smiled too brightly to Michael. "Michael, my dear," the socialite addressed him with deliberate familiarity and with a suggestive glance toward his wife.

"Miss Orwell," Michael said as he took the hand that she offered with coquettish batting of her eyes and with her opened fan placed strategically to emphasize her bosom. He bowed slightly, his smile coolly polite, and he shook her hand almost imperceptibly.

Anne made no effort to suppress her amusement at the young woman's theatrics, which entertained the fair-haired man next in line. He introduced himself, "Evan Sydenham, Mrs. MacGregor."

"I am very pleased to meet you, Lord Danford," she responded as she shook his hand firmly. "Michael speaks so highly of you."

"Does he?" said the viscount, taken aback. Recovering, he said, "I am pleased to hear it."

"Evan," Michael welcomed his friend warmly, taking his hand and shaking it with both of his. "Thank you for coming."

The two men stood with clasped hands a long moment in wordless exchange. It gratified Anne that their friendship would not be lost, despite the knowledge that now existed between them. She had been shocked and disconcerted when she first learned that Michael had befriended a Sydenham. But now that she knew more of this man and saw what passed between him and her husband, she realized that Evan Sydenham was very different from his ancestor.

A colonel and a member of the Legislature stepped up. She turned to greet them cordially.

Suddenly, Michael tensed, and Anne followed the direction of his hard stare toward men farther down the reception line. Her husband quickly looked away, focussing on the person before him, and he forced a smile as a plump politician offered a beefy hand and introduced his equally

corpulent wife. But Anne narrowed her eyes and gazed at the two approaching diplomats with their broad sashes and preposterously ornate badges. They appeared to her as a pair of black holes blotting light and life. One extended his hand to her and flashed an ingratiating smile. She neither took the hand nor returned the smile, but only glowered at the man with revulsion. His face hardened, and he glared into her eyes as she stared back unflinchingly in a contest she would not allow him to win. Finally, he snorted, seething, and he turned to Michael. At once, his face drew into a sneer as the second villain bypassed Anne to join his comrade in confronting her husband. Both older men offered their hands. Michael refused to reciprocate, merely staring at them in disgust.

"Surely you'll oblige an old friend with simple courtesy, my dear boy," said the first, a moderately tall man Anne guessed to be in his sixties, with wavy grey hair and the pallid skin of the inveterately dissolute. His stout companion, a little younger but with the same look of dissipation and disdain, muttered something in German.

Michael said in a low, dangerous voice, "I am not your dear boy. You are not my friend. And you will leave this place now."

Michael's tone and manner had attracted the attention of the next people in line and that of his family, as well.

The first roué laughed. "Oh, dear Michael, you are so amusing."

In full voice, Michael demanded, "Get out, you filthy sodomite bastards!"

Even the pianist stopped playing his background music as everyone turned to witness the developing disturbance.

"How dare you address your betters so!" railed the Prussian.

With volume rising to a bellow, Michael retorted, "The lowest rat or cur in this city is better than the likes of you! You are rapists of children!"

The entire room drew an audible breath in shock.

Before either man could reply, Michael continued, "Some fool may have given you diplomatic immunity, but such contrivances cannot erase your guilt. You are a disgrace to your respective countries, and you disgrace all men."

The slim man sneered, "Do you think you're different? Any man can have you!"

Michael's punch sent the Russian flying several yards, and would have sent him farther had it not been for a wide-eyed waiter who was knocked to the floor in a shower of wine, crystal, and silver as guests scattered with startled shrieks. The margrave made a prompt strategic withdrawal and, as he hissed obscenities in Prussian, pulled his associate from the tangle with the waiter and up to a tottering stand.

In one last attack of venom, the Russian count spat through his cut lip, "You will pay for this, putain!"

Along the rapists' path, everyone stepped back to give them a wide berth as they fled.

Silence fell upon the room. No one moved, as though even their breath were checked by some magic.

Finally breaking the spell, Viscount Danford said in typical British understatement, "What a disagreeable pair."

Anne suppressed a chuckle but gave him a grateful smile for his quick wit in placing blame upon the diplomats. She appreciated his loyalty to Michael, and she thought he would make a very good diplomat, himself.

Michael had begun to tremble. Anne took his arm, holding him firmly, and she smiled up at him in support and reassurance.

Joseph came to his son. He asked hesitantly, "Michael, do you know those people? How...?"

Anne spoke up, "They raped two young boys of our acquaintance. The police have been on the lookout for those men; though, unfortunately, all the constabulary can do is try to prevent the perverts from harming other children."

A shocked murmur rippled through the room at this news.

Then, Elizabeth displayed a lack of savoir-faire so acute as to cross into obtusity by whining to Michael, "How could you ruin my engagement party?" Anne now saw the self-absorption that Michael had described in his sister.

Kenneth Armstrong added hastily, "What did he mean, 'Any man can have you'? And why did he call you a 'putain'? Isn't that French for whore?"

Anne replied angrily, "They have been raping young boys a very long time. Them, and other men like them. They point the finger, but it is they who are whores."

Joseph gasped in realization, "Oh, God!" He swallowed and murmured, "Michael...Why did ye not tell me?"

Tears filling his eyes, his hands curling into fists, and his jaw tight with the effort of control, Michael responded in an anguished whisper, "I tried."

Joseph frowned and squinted, uncomprehending.

Hermione rushed to embrace her son. Her shoulders shook with her sobs as she attempted belatedly to comfort him.

Kenneth Armstrong persisted, "Well, I can understand such a thing happening once...." He let the implication hang in the air.

Anne tilted her head and examined the lawyer for the first time. On close inspection, she saw a shadow shrouding his aura. And a very dark patch that struck her as cancerous, growing malignantly.

She turned on him. "Rapists prey on children—or other victims—because they can. Often, they take positions that allow them repeated access to their prey, and they invariably blame their victims for these crimes.

"Further," she stated loudly, "and especially when children are involved, they try to convince their victims that it's their own fault. That they are different. That they bring it upon themselves. That they deserve mistreatment.

"Worst of all," she surveyed the crowd with an accusatory glare, "idiots blame the victims, as well—either to give themselves an opportunity to look down their nose at someone else, or because, in their cowardice, they want to convince themselves that their personal sense of purity somehow grants them immunity from such depredation."

She panned the audience once more, slowly, and stated in a crisp, clear voice, "Anyone can be raped. And anyone who says otherwise is a fool...or a rapist."

Viscount Danford clapped his gloved hands and called, "Well said, Madam! You are quite right. The world would be well rid of such men as Skavronsky and Von Ratzenhausen."

Someone else cried, "Hear, hear!"

Applause and shouts filled the hall as people hurriedly aligned themselves with the viscount's sentiments. And Anne brought Michael to a chair as Evan signalled the orchestra to resume.

∞

WHEN ANNE WAVED to a waiter, the man rushed to bring a tray full of wine goblets to Michael, who stiffly lowered himself onto one of the pale-blue, velvet-covered Queen Anne chairs lining the walls. Hermione MacGregor and Evan Sydenham took seats to flank Michael as Anne knelt before him.

With trembling hand, he took a glass and sipped the champagne. It tasted sour and sweet, and the bubbles irritated his tongue and his nose. He tossed back the remainder.

Michael knew the attentions of his wife, mother, and friend were kindly meant and showed their acceptance and support of him, but he dearly wished he could disappear. He would have run into the street, could he trust his legs to carry him.

How many times had he felt so weak, so helpless, since...?

∞

England, 1873

MICHAEL MacGREGOR ran along the corridor to his morning class. He had overslept and the professor would be cross. He hoped his stomach would not growl, for he had missed breakfast, as well.

He opened the door, turning the knob carefully and pushing gently so as to make no noise; nonetheless, Professor Giles's raised eyebrow and cold stare assailed him. Michael swallowed visibly and scurried to his desk as his classmates tittered. There, he sat rigidly, grateful to be seated in the last row. In only a week at the prestigious West London boarding-school, he had managed to earn two tawsings and a hundred lines. He prayed Mr. Giles would be lenient. And he prayed the headmaster would not write to his father.

As the professor droned through the lesson, Michael gradually relaxed. Perhaps the Classics teacher had already forgotten his tardiness, he thought hopefully. However, when the man stopped him on his way out the door, his hopes were dashed.

"See me after the supper hour, Mr. MacGregor," the professor demanded.

"Yes, sir," Michael replied dejectedly.

HIS BELLY FELT full of wriggling worms as, after dinner, Michael followed his teacher from the classroom to the west door. It would be a tawsing, he was sure, though he did not know why the professor had not done it in class, or taken him to the headmaster's discipline room.

The man opened the door and held it for him. As he stepped out into the evening air, cool and damp with fog, Michael had a sudden foreboding, a sinking in his gut that he could not understand.

"This way," said the professor sharply.

Michael asked hesitantly, "Where are we going, sir?"

"We have an engagement," Giles replied unhelpfully.

Michael sighed, more convinced than ever that he was in for a tawsing. Or maybe a caning. That thought set the inhabitants of his belly to furiously agitated writhing.

The teacher led him along a path that meandered through a rose garden and past the tennis courts and rugby fields to a cottage. Though he could not see it clearly in the growing dark and thickening fog, Michael guessed it must be the little thatch-roofed stone building on the edge of the wood. He wondered who lived there, and he wondered why the professor would bring him there for his punishment.

Light shone from the rows of square panes to left and right of the plain wooden door in a diffused glow visible only within ten yards of the cottage. Pea soup, Michael remembered. A pea-soup fog, his father had called the dense mists that blanketed the city from time to time. As he peered into the grey around him, he knew he could easily become lost in those eerie vapours.

The professor lifted and tapped the old iron knocker. Presently, a tall, thin, smiling man opened the door and let them in. A shiver slid along Michael's spine and the worms in his belly slithered even faster as he entered the little house ahead of Aldus Giles.

"What have we here?" said the tall man. He grasped Michael's chin and squinted at him the way the biology professor peered at bugs in bottles. The man's skin was cold, and his touch made Michael's flesh crawl.

"Mm," murmured the goateed foreigner as he looked Michael over. The man's dark-brown, wavy hair softly gleamed in the firelight, and he smelled of pomade and sandalwood and wine. "Very nice. Pretty eyes. And his hair, so black and beautiful, puts me in mind of my Andalusian."

To Michael's relief, the man released his chin. But he then walked around behind and, renewing Michael's distress, fondled his bottom as the Classics teacher announced, "Mr. MacGregor, this is Count Ivan Mikhailovich Skavronsky, an extremely

in the mornings and sometimes in the night, and the man's attentions felt strangely pleasurable in a disturbing way—somehow different from when he touched himself. As the count suckled him, the sensations intensified, building...building....

All at once, the man stopped and stood up. Michael's willy felt harder than it had ever been, purplish red and throbbing, and he wanted more. Somehow, he needed more.

"Your turn," the count told Michael as he motioned for the professor to come forward.

Both men unbuttoned their flies and removed their lower clothing as Michael glanced from one to the other, uncertain what was expected of him.

The count took a jar from the bedside table and uncorked it to release a strong, oily scent perfumed by some unknown flower. He scooped a dollop of the grease and rubbed it onto his willy, a long thing as hard and red as Michael's own. The prospect of being asked to lick that grease made Michael want to puke.

The professor's penis, too, stood erect. "Come," Giles demanded as he sat on the edge of the bed. "You know what to do."

Reluctantly, Michael squatted in front of the teacher and mimicked the actions of the count, stroking and tonguing. Abruptly, the professor grabbed his hair and ordered, "Take it into your mouth, boy." Giles leaned back, still clenching Michael's hair and forcing him to rise and stoop forward in order to comply.

Bent over his teacher's body, with the count now gripping his buttocks, Michael suddenly felt electrified with terror. He tried to pull back and stand, but the professor pressed him down, filling his mouth to the point of gagging. Immediately, something large and solid pierced his bum.

Michael screamed.

HIS CHEEKS were wet, his eyes dull, his backside on fire from

the pounding and ripping, his mouth fouled with the men's emissions and his own vomit. But his willy felt wonderful.

"There. You see, boy?" said the professor when his stroking had done its work. "You like it, don't you? It's your nature to be loved by men."

Confusion engulfed him. Michael retched again.

∞

Present day

HIS MIND returning to the present, Michael heard Evan assure him, "I'll wire my father at once and ask him to make an official complaint to their embassies demanding the removal of Von Ratzenhausen and Skavronsky. Under the circumstances, I doubt there will be any resistance from the ambassadors."

Michael nodded his thanks.

Anne asked gently, "Shall I take you home?"

He nodded again.

CHAPTER 21

Fire!

Michael groaned as he stretched out on the bed. His earlier rage and humiliation had been subsumed under a pall of depression and tension that tightened every muscle and sinew.

"Turn over," said Anne. "I'll give you a massage."

"I just want to sleep," he replied wearily.

"This will help," she assured him, taking his near hand and pressing her thumbs along each finger and into his palm.

His eyelids fluttering, Michael moaned at the release effected by her ministrations.

"Turn over," she repeated when she had kneaded both of his hands.

He complied, and she began a leisurely, thorough manipulation from wrists to shoulders, from toes to buttocks, and along his back and neck. As she pushed here and squeezed

there, pinched and pummelled, his eyes drooped and his mind floated...drifted....

∞

ANNE WORKED her husband's flesh slowly, rhythmically, in a loving devotion. She pushed aside the memory of the black soul who had abused her belovèd and her outrage at what Michael had endured to concentrate on filling him with peace as she released the dam of morbid feelings within his cells.

In her mind's eye, she envisioned an outflow of inky energies draining the fear and shame and anger from his body even as an inflow of pure light imbued him with joy and serenity. Her inner voice sang him a ballad of love, though outwardly she massaged in silence.

When she had reached up from his feet to the level of his heart, she moved to work from his scalp to his neck to his shoulders and back to his heart. Then, she rolled him over into the middle of the bed (with effort, for he lay limp, now) and gently rubbed little circles from his hairline to his eyes and from his jaw upward. At last, she smoothed carefully around his closed eyelids and around his lips.

He had begun to breathe in deep, rhythmic respirations well before she kissed him lightly and pulled the coverlet over him. She tiptoed to the rocking chair, wrapped herself in a quilt, and settled to sleep.

∞

SOON AFTER their wedding, Michael had come home from Draper Avenue to find a note left on Anne's blackboard telling him she had been asked to visit the ailing Mrs. Carey, grandmother-in-law of Rob Donnelly. Rather than wait at home, he had decided to call on his new friend and neighbour.

"She's been right as rain all her life," Rob told him when he arrived. "But she took a turn today, sudden-like. An' now,

Father O'Donnell is givin' 'er the last rites."

"I'm so sorry," Michael responded. "You know if there is anything Anne or I can do...."

"It's good of ye," Rob replied softly. "Though there's little enough to do when the Lord calls."

Michael and several O'Reillys waited on the porch with the men and boys of the Donnelly family as the younger Donnelly females brought ale and cold tea. One by one, those of Rob's construction colleagues living in The Flats joined them, along with several other neighbours well acquainted with the elderly Mrs. Carey.

When his duties had been performed, Father O'Donnell took air among the men and accepted a pint from Rob's youngest daughter. He shook his head sadly and said, "It's a shame, Rob. She looks not to last much longer."

Rob nodded, his mouth set grimly. His youngest son began to cry.

"There, lad," the priest assured with a hand on the youngster's shoulder. "She's going to Heaven, you can be sure of that."

Rob knelt to hug his son. "An' she'll be watchin' out for us all from there." He held and rocked the boy awhile.

When the child settled, sniffling noisily and sighing, his father said, "Go on, now, an' say your goodbyes to Gran."

Rob signalled to his other sons and daughters as he rose, and all six accompanied the youngest into the house.

When the little ones had left, the priest remarked with a perplexed expression, "Odd. She keeps saying, 'Fire, fire,' over and over."

Everyone stiffened. Most of the buildings of The Flats were made of wood, and certainly their roofs and gardens were flammable. While the local houses were not as closely packed as those in the district known as The Warren, it would be all too easy for fire to spread throughout the neighbourhood and render everyone homeless. Many remembered and all had heard of the

Great Fire of 1849 that had destroyed most of the city's core.

A shriek came from a second-floor window. "Fire! Fire!" screamed the old woman.

A shiver ran up Michael's spine at Mrs. Carey's dying words.

∞

"MICHAEL, WAKE UP!"

A persistent jostling gradually brought him out of a fiery dream to groggy consciousness.

"Come, Michael, get up!"

"What is it?" he asked in sudden alarm. The sense of danger from his dream had invaded his wakefulness.

"Gasoline!" Anne told him urgently. "I smell gasoline! We have to get out of the house!"

A whoosh and roar wrenched him to full awareness as orange light glowed with increasing brightness outside the bedroom windows that his wife must have closed only now. Anne left him to rummage through the armoire and trunks and, without looking to see where they landed, she tossed clothes at him. He hastily pulled on a pair of pants and gathered the rest in his arms as she donned a dress and grabbed other items to drop into the quilt that lay over the rocking chair.

Noxious, hot smoke billowed up from below, invading the bedroom through the spaces around the door. A crash of shattered glass split the infernal rumble and the floor began to smoulder.

"Anne, leave everything!" Michael shouted above the din, tugging at her arm.

A glance toward the east dormer revealed golden tongues lapping the glass: They had little time. Coughing as the heat and fumes seared his lungs, he ran round the bed to the north window. Stumbling through the murk, he reached the gable wall and pulled the glazed leaf of the casement fully inward to unlock

and push out its screen. There, he found flames climbing the sides of the privy as well, but the back porch had not yet been engulfed.

Michael bundled his garments into a ball and hurled them toward the well-house. Racing back to his wife through the thick, choking haze, he picked her up peremptorily by the waist, hauled her clutching her oddments, and deposited her on the windowsill. Holding the wad in her arms, Anne scrambled out onto the roof of the back porch.

She called, "Hurry!" as she skipped to the edge and jumped out of sight. Dusky vapours had begun to rise from the shakes.

Michael pushed one leg out the little window and eased his head and torso through the cramped opening as the blaze slithered toward him. With one bare foot on the scorching shingles, he gripped the jamb and shifted his weight. All of a sudden, the roof gave out under him and he plunged to the porch below, enveloped in flames.

He heard Anne scream as he rolled with all his might to fall off the edge of the porch, his trousers afire and his hair and skin singeing. A bucketful of water drenched him, then another, and another, as hands dragged him away from the house.

In the orange light about him, Michael saw three figures rushing from the well-house with pails and tubs, desperately dousing the primary conflagration as well as the peripheral flares that threatened to spread destruction to the outbuildings and vegetation, thence to the neighbouring houses. More people, most of them half-dressed or in nightshirts, joined them as the neighbourhood roused to meet the crisis.

Anne gently washed Michael with cool water from which he detected a trace of herb, or perhaps of flower: something vaguely familiar. Then, she administered drops of a remedy and helped him into his shirt.

Steadying, Michael rose and joined the bucket brigade as Anne took a turn at the well-pump. The flurry of activity grew as

the number of volunteer firefighters increased.

Soon, the urgent clang-clang-clang of a bell announced the imminent arrival of the Fire Department's wagon. Though none slackened their efforts, tension eased ever so slightly at the advent of the professional firemen. Luckily, the roads had been dry and the horse-drawn vehicle had navigated the city's streets and lanes without becoming mired in mud.

The dark-uniformed firemen quickly attached their hoses. Then, two of them grasped the horizontal bar at the rear of the wagon and furiously pumped water by hand as the others held the hoses and directed the nozzles. In a moment, a gush from the tanker threw liquid upon the roof. A second tanker joined it, and the first wagon left to refill at the hydrant near the asylum. Everyone worked feverishly as flames spread and sparks flew and inferno consumed the house at Number 10 Cedar Lane.

Eventually, the blaze began to dwindle.

∞

SMOKE-BLACKENED MEN, Michael among them, shook hands with the city's firefighters as the professionals prepared to withdraw the two horse-drawn tankers to Station Number 4 across the bridge. Soot-smeared women gathered their wide-eyed children and shooed them toward home and their beds now that cool, soft morning twilight supplanted the harsh ruddy glare of the fire that had finally been extinguished. Choking stench lingered, and smoke adhered to the morning mist of dewdrops in a blanket of miasmal smog.

Many offered beds for the night and beyond, but Anne and Michael declined, not wishing to impose themselves upon their friends, nor to choose among them. Instead, they gratefully accepted promises of help to rebuild as they expressed their thanks and said their good nights.

While her neighbours dispersed, Anne stared forlornly from the street at the charred ruin that had been her home, now a

skeleton of beams and posts black against the lightening sky. Tears blurred the heartbreaking view and she made no effort to check them as her husband stepped up beside her.

After a moment of silently shared misery, she gazed into Michael's face. There, she saw sorrow change abruptly to wrath and, to her horror, decision.

"No, Michael!" she pleaded. "Don't go!"

He turned to her, eyes wild, and demanded, "How can you ask it? Do you expect me to do nothing when those bastards burn our home and try to murder us?"

"No, I...."

Eyes squeezed shut against the image inside her head, face contorted in the pain of remembrance and fear, she sobbed. Balling her hands into fists in an effort to control herself, she looked up into his eyes and blurted, "I can't...I can't watch you die again."

∞

MICHAEL SCOWLED at his wife. He wanted to shake her. He wanted to hit her. He wanted to scream.

She stood there, looking at him and seeing another man, and she had the gall to expect him to let Skavronsky get away with fucking him again!

He whirled and stormed away. He had got to Sumac when he stopped, spun, and stalked back. She had crumpled to the grass in the middle of the lane, quiescent, no longer weeping. He loomed over her, trembling with barely contained rage.

Through his teeth, he said, "I...am...sick...of hearing about your dead husband. I am sick of—"

She stared up at him. Without fear. Without anger. Without entreaty. In her face he saw only a sadness so profound it struck him like a blow. And suddenly he saw her through eyes his own and yet not his own, not here and now: He saw her cradling a body, *his* body, riddled with wounds and bleeding

into water.

His knees gave out under him and he sat down hard. He could feel those wounds: four to the chest, two to the gut, and one—the fatal one—to the neck, severing his artery. Glancing down and putting a hand to his throat, he found no blood, no wounds. Disoriented, he shook his head to dispel the sensations he should not be able to feel. He looked at Anne and saw her in her shift—in another, clean, pale-blue shift fastened with buttons down the front—smiling at him as she stood on a mountainside he had never seen but knew to be in the Highlands.

"You know, don't you," she said quietly.

Her voice brought him to the present time and place, and he realized she was regarding him with an expression he could not fully fathom. There was love in it, and grief, but something more. Acceptance? Surrender? Recognition?

The meaning of her words came to him.

"Did he...?" He paused and started again. "Was I shot? In the neck?"

"Yes," she answered softly.

"By redcoats."

"Yes."

"Evan was one of them."

"Evan's ancestor."

He looked at her in anguish as he said, "And they raped you. Next to me. By my body."

"Yes," she confirmed. "And then I killed them all."

She inhaled deeply and said on a resigned sigh, "I know you must deal with Skavronsky and his confederate, though it will not be as simple a matter as it was all those years ago."

She looked into his eyes and whispered, "If you'll let me, I'll help you."

He reached to cup her face in his hands, and he gazed into her violet eyes with the certain knowledge of love both old and new. Then, he gathered her to him, wishing he could undo what had once been done, and understanding, now, the strange

sadness that had filled her eyes when she first beheld him.

∞

A CROW LANDED upon a charred beam. All at once, there was a creaking, then a squeal, then a reverberating crash when a piece of the upper floor collapsed as the bird flapped away with a startled, indignant cry.

Wrapped in Michael's arms, he sitting and leaning cautiously against the beech that had escaped both fiery sparks and pails of water, Anne sighed. The sun had risen some time ago, but The Flats slept: everyone but Michael and Anne, who were as exhausted as anyone else, yet unable to fall into the healing oblivion of slumber. Even the church bells remained silent today, for the priest and preacher had battled the fire alongside the members of their respective flocks.

Anne sighed again.

Michael kissed her head and assured her, "We'll rebuild."

"I know," she replied sullenly. Heaving yet another sigh, she complained, "But I'd just finished making that dress."

A rumbling chortle rose from Michael's abdomen, growing louder and louder and shaking him in a helpless fit of laughter that infected Anne.

As his mirth diminished, she turned within the circle of his arms. Looking up at him sheepishly, she pointed out, "Well, it took me almost three weeks!"

She grinned as he erupted in another bout of hilarity.

∞

THE SUN HUNG mid-sky when Dan Doherty pulled his rig up in front of their gate and hopped down to saunter into the yard, assessing the damage as he passed the remnants of the house. Upon seeing Anne and Michael near the rear fence, he strode purposefully to them.

"I was figurin' ye'd mebbe want to go stay wi' your

family," he said. "Thought I'd take ye, that bein' so."

"That's kind of you, Dan," said Michael as he shifted, suddenly and painfully aware how long he had been in the same position and pressed against the tree.

Anne scrambled to her feet and Michael rose as well, both brushing away soil and grass as they stood and stretched stiffly.

Michael glanced to his wife and suggested, "Perhaps we should." He touched her belly and added prudently, "Living rough while we rebuild may be too much hardship, in your condition."

Anne placed a hand over his, fondly. She said, "We will need new clothes, as well as building materials. But...." Her smile faded.

At her hesitation, he prompted, "What is it?"

Anne said with an attempt at delicacy, "I'd rather not go to your parents' home."

At his startlement, she rushed to explain, "It's not your parents that concern me. Nor your sister. It's Kenneth Armstrong."

Michael cocked an eyebrow and regarded her a moment. Finally, he frowned and asked, "Why?"

"He's...." she started, but with a quick glance toward Dan Doherty, she changed tack and said, "There's something wrong about him. I can't tell you what. It's just a feeling."

"That's Armstrong the lawyer?" asked Dan.

"Yes," Michael confirmed.

"Hmph," Doherty grunted. "He's a lawyer, ain't he? Ain't many o' them's worth the powder to blow 'em to Hell with. Ain't even good tippers, most of 'em."

Michael grinned at the driver's evaluation. He had to admit that he had never much cared for Armstrong, himself. And the previous night's shenanigans had won the man no favour. The memory of the ball gave him an idea.

"We could ask Evan to put us up a day or two," he suggested. "At least until we clothe ourselves." Another thought

occurred. "And he may be able to help with that other matter."

Anne smiled. "Evan's it is."

CHAPTER 22

Angle of incidence

The hackney cab wound its way through the broad, tree-lined, macadamized avenues of Rosemont and up the long, cobbled lane to Hampton House, residence of the British consul. Dan Doherty guided his brown mare and sorrel gelding around the curving drive and through the arched, two-storey *porte-cochère* that protected the entry of the castellated mansion and provided a balustraded balcony for the uppermost floor.

A footman rushed to open the door of the cab and help its occupants to step down. As Anne and Michael alighted, the black-liveried servant quickly stifled an expression of astonishment. Anne guessed that there was little the man had not seen in service with Viscount Danford; nonetheless, the arrival of a half-dressed couple in singed and soot-streaked garments and carrying a small bundle of belongings was clearly not a common occurrence.

"Thank you, Samuel," said Michael as the footman showed them into the library.

"I'll tell His Lordship you're here, Mr. MacGregor," Samuel assured them politely.

Anne wandered the capacious room with its bright bay windows and soaring, floor-to-ceiling bookshelves. Persian carpets in shades of red and gold covered expanses of parquetry and cushioned the footing of the sumptuous sofas and graceful desk, the latter's top inlaid with ivory and tortoiseshell. She had begun to read individual titles of the leather- and buckram-bound books when Evan Sydenham breezed into the room and stopped dead.

"Oh...my...God!" he exclaimed at sight of them. His eyes wide, he asked, "What in the name of Heaven happened?"

Michael replied through clenched teeth, "Someone doused our house with gasoline and set it on fire."

Evan stared at him a horror-filled moment. Finally, he surmised, "Skavronsky."

"That would be my guess," said Michael.

Eyeing the bundle Anne carried and the dress she wore, its smoke-stained fabric bearing char-edged holes here and there, smaller versions of the seared breaches in Michael's ragged attire, the viscount remarked, "I take it you are wearing most of your extant worldly possessions."

"Indeed," Michael confirmed. He admitted, "I hoped you might put us up for a few days while we sort ourselves out." Through his teeth, he added "And that you might help me with a little matter of revenge."

A naughty smile spread slowly across Evan's face. He said, "What a delicious idea."

∞

AT EVAN'S INSISTENCE, emphasized by a conspicuous sniffing in their direction followed by a pronounced moue of distaste,

Anne and Michael bathed while the cook prepared luncheon and while the maids readied a bed. Evan's valet and one of the maids provided clean attire. To Michael's surprise, the viscount had kept a full suite of his clothes, left after a weekend of debauchery over a year before. Still stinging from his burns, the Scot eschewed suspenders, tie, vest, and jacket, opting instead to wear only the trousers, cinched by a belt borrowed from a burly groundskeeper, and the filmy silk shirt, the latter with its collar open. Anne made do with the black dress of a maid, sans apron and cap, and also sans shoes and stockings, her feet being larger than those of the household's distaff residents. Lacking her pins, she braided her hair on one side, her tresses now restored to pristine whiteness, and she tied the tail with a black ribbon.

The viscount joined them on a wide terrace that faced a purple-themed formal knot-garden hedged with evergreen English boxwood. The freshening breeze wafted the sweet scents of lavender and violet, bergamot and potted heliotrope across the cut-stone terrace, and pigeons cooed on the closely cropped lawn, nearby.

Furnished solely with one damask-draped round table and three tapestry-covered chairs, the terrace stretched along the entire rear of the residence under a high arcade that formed a balcony above. French doors and tall windows pierced the brindled stone walls at regular intervals, the fenestration a symmetrical arrangement of white woodwork and small square panes.

On the table, gleaming silver cutlery cast in elegant curves flanked fine bone china edged in gold, while cut-crystal goblets held water and wine. Two footmen brought platters of fruit and cheese and linen-lined baskets of bread, and then discreetly disappeared.

As Michael held her chair, Anne seated herself across from their host. The luncheon began with a mildly uncomfortable silence, no one quite sure where to look or what to say. All three focussed on the repast until Michael spoke up.

"Evan," he said lightly, "in all the years I've known you, I do believe this is the longest you've ever been silent—barring those occasions on which you were asleep or passed out, of course."

Evan grinned. He riposted, "How would you know, Michael? You were asleep or passed out much of the time."

"Touché," said Michael, raising a goblet of water in acknowledgement of point scored and then taking a swig.

Evan watched him drink the innocuous liquid. With a brief glance to Anne, he studied his friend several seconds. Then, dispensing with preliminaries, the viscount cut to the core of the present situation: "What would you like to do to Skavronsky et al?"

Michael took a deep, slow breath and looked from Evan to Anne and back. He said, "I'd *like* to kill them. But I can't imagine how I could get away with that."

Evan leaned against the cushioned rear of his chair and tented his hands, putting the forefingers to his lips. He said cryptically, "It would not be impossible to arrange."

With a penetrating stare, Anne asked, "By whom?"

Evan smiled but said nothing.

Michael asked suspiciously, "Are we talking about hiring local thugs?"

"No need," said the viscount with that enigmatic smile. He picked up his wineglass and raised it in a brief salute before quaffing its contents.

Now, Michael leaned back and regarded his friend. He tilted his head, narrowed his eyes, and pursed his lips. "You know something," he guessed.

"That I do," said Evan as he deposited the empty goblet on the table. A footman appeared as by magic and replenished the wine.

When they were again alone, Anne wondered aloud, "Would this 'something' you know have anything to do with an Irishman who turned up dead a couple of weeks back?"

Evan's smile broadened. He said, "It happens that one of my...acquaintances...has become aware that a certain gem has gone missing. A gem that was meant to fund a...revolution, of sorts. A gem Skavronsky wants very badly." He cocked an eyebrow at Michael.

"So," Michael said slowly, "if someone were to find the gem...."

Evan finished the statement, "The Russian could be lured into the open."

Anne asked, "You wouldn't happen to know what this revolution is meant to accomplish? And against whom?"

Inhaling the fragrance of the refilled goblet, Evan said, "It seems that the current Tsar of Russia annoyed a number of men when he refused to uphold his father's creation of a council of advisors one might describe as a kind of parliament. Instead, the new Tsar chose to maintain his autocracy."

Michael concluded, "So men with ambitions for power found themselves thwarted and want to change that outcome."

Anne conjectured, "And a king so threatened would take most unkindly to the men who want to usurp his power and, possibly, to kill him in the process."

Michael asked the viscount, "Does your acquaintance have access to agents loyal to the Tsar?"

"He does," Evan verified.

Anne said, "I assume the Irishman was a go-between. Perhaps he acquired the gem in the first place. But what have the Germans to do with this?"

"Wheels within wheels," said Evan. "They buy the gem for a covetous collector, thereby establishing a relationship with him; they fund the assassination, destabilizing the Russian government at arm's length without precipitating a war; and they give their own government a reason to rescind the recent legalization of trade unions."

"By inventing proof the assassination was—will be— carried out by unionists," Michael guessed.

Anne said, "The Irish connection might have been part of that supposed 'proof.'"

"I believe so," said Evan. "But we have one problem: In order to entice Skavronsky, we need him to believe we have the gem."

Anne smiled. "I think that can be arranged."

Michael eyed his wife. Voice questioning, he said, "You know where it is?"

"I can guess," she told him. "But I'll have to look."

Evan put in, "And if you can't find it?"

Anne glanced from one to the other and replied, "They are bound to know I had it. They could be convinced I still do."

Michael reacted immediately and strongly. "No! I won't have you risk yourself! You don't know these men."

Anne responded acerbically, "You mean, the men who shot me, and then burned me out of my house in the middle of the night?"

Turning in his seat and grasping her hands, Michael said intently, "I've nearly lost you twice already. I won't risk you and our child again."

Anne said quietly but firmly, "Michael, I'm healed. And it's you that has blisters from the fire." She glanced down in abstraction and thought aloud, "Which reminds me, I must give you more remedy, soon."

Michael suddenly wondered, "Where did you get it? The medicine? Was that what you brought from the house?"

"No," she said. "I kept some in the well-house, as well. And in a few other hideaways."

"A lucky foresight," Evan remarked. He added soberly, "But Michael is right. We must not put you in harm's way."

Anne suggested, "Perhaps this friend of yours could convince them he got it from me?"

Evan nodded thoughtfully. "Yes," he said. "That would explain the stone's reappearance without drawing either of you into it directly, and simultaneously give him excuse to make

contact."

Michael wondered, "Why not let them think it came from the Irishman? That he sold it for himself?"

Evan replied, "It is not as probable that O'Leary would have betrayed them at this late date, when he could, more easily, have done it much sooner." He added, "No, I believe they'd be more readily convinced that your wife—being, in their minds, a peasant, and therefore as corrupt as themselves—sold the gem cheaply, and in secret, perhaps to buy a dress or pay a debt. That would explain both O'Leary's not having it when they killed him, and its being obtained by another party."

Michael said, "And I suppose that if Skavronsky thought I was connected to the gem's resurfacing, he'd become suspicious and perhaps not take the bait."

Evan nodded.

Anne said, "They'll soon enough know they failed to kill us. Do you think they'll try again?"

Michael and Evan exchanged uncertain glances.

Evan said prudently, "Best we distract them with the gem as soon as possible."

∞

"OPEN UP," Anne commanded as she removed the dropper from the brown bottle.

With gleaming brass telephone earpiece to his ear and its long-necked stand in his hand, Michael squatted by the desk in the library to bring his open mouth within reach of his wife's remedy dispenser. Once the drops had been administered, he stood and waited expectantly for a voice to sound on the other end of the line.

Abruptly, he spoke into the circular, hornlike voice transmitter atop the brass base. "Harris, this is Michael MacGregor. I'd like to speak to my father, please."

During another pause, Anne slipped out of the room and

returned to the bedchamber that had been made ready. She placed her glass bottle into its slot in the box she had retrieved from the well-house, and she set the case beside the pockets and empty sheath and oddments she had managed to secure before the escape from her erstwhile home at Number 10 Cedar Lane. She closed and locked the cherry-wood armoire, and then stretched out on a tufted couch by one of the tall casements.

Her eyes traced the pompom-festooned gold braid that edged the heavy, bottle-green brocade draperies, the silk panels hanging from a rod beneath the matching valence and pooling on the floor. More pompoms dripped from the sashes that reined each curtain panel. Between the windows, a gilded vitrine of curios echoed a high, figured chest of drawers that stood against the opposite wall, perched on slender, curving legs atop claw feet.

Muffled footfalls marched past the bedroom, and a pigeon landed on the sill of the open window to serenade her with its throaty cooing.

Warmed by the afternoon sunlight, Anne drifted to sleep staring at a porcelain figurine glazed sapphire blue.

∞

HIS FATHER'S GRUFF, "Halloo," from the other end of the telephone line roused Michael from his musings on the luncheon conversation.

"Father," he responded, "I wanted to apprise you of the situation before you hear of it from someone else: Our house was set afire and we've been burned out." He rushed to assure, "We're all right. I'm a bit singed around the edges, but otherwise well enough. And Anne is fine." He concluded, "We're at Hampton House, for the moment, but I was hoping to meet with you as soon as I might."

Stung, Joseph MacGregor asked, "Why did ye not come here, to your home?"

Michael answered, "That's what I want to discuss with you. I can borrow Evan's grey. May I ride there now?"

"Of course, of course," said his father, puzzled. "Do come. Will you bring your wife?"

Michael noted with irritation that his father still did not use her name. Suppressing the emotion, he said evenly, "No. She's resting. I'd like to speak with you alone."

When he replaced the earpiece on the telephone base, he turned to find Evan watching him. The viscount asked, "Are you going to tell him what we plan?"

"No," Michael replied. "The fewer people who know, the better."

"Agreed," said Evan. "And do you wish Anne to abide here?"

Michael thought a moment. At last, he said, "My mother would certainly prefer that we live with my family. She's quite taken with the idea of a grandchild. And I'd like to keep Anne out of our business with your acquaintance.

"On the other hand," he said, "Anne is uncomfortable with my sister's fiancé. And I know she'll want to get back to The Flats to rebuild the house as soon as possible. She won't stay long in Rosemont. But I'll speak to my father on the matter and ask him to look after her.

"As for myself," he added, "I'd like to remain here tonight, if you agree. As much as I hate to be apart from Anne, I want to distance her from what we must do, and we have a lot to discuss."

"A sensible precaution," said Evan. "And I'll have my tailor come to fit you for some new clothing."

The two regarded each other wordlessly for a moment. Finally, Evan said, "I'll have Henry saddle the grey."

∞

STILL MINIMALLY dressed, and mounted on Evan's gelding,

Michael trotted up the elm-lined lane of his parents' Stuart Avenue home and round to the stables. There, Albee Ross took custody of the horse.

"Good to see ye, sir," said the horsemaster. "Ain't been the same without ye."

Michael smiled wryly and replied, "You mean you're no longer winning bets what state I'll be in when I return home."

Albee grinned and said with his usual irreverence, "Like I said, sir, ain't been the same."

Chuckling, Michael strode to the rear of the country house, its mottled fieldstone and white gingerbread lending a rustic air to the abode of the family that had built an empire on the importation and distilling of whisky. Joseph MacGregor would protest modestly at the use of so grand a word as "empire," but in truth his business spanned two continents and included full ownership of two distilleries and dozens of warehouses, as well as shares in four more distilleries and no less than five shipping companies.

Slipping in the back door, the prodigal son playfully kissed the plump cook who had tried for years to fatten him and who now squealed with feigned annoyance. Exiting the kitchen, he winked at his mother's prim and very startled lady's maid, the staid brunette on her way to the laundry, and he squeezed past a footman bearing a tea tray before passing through the doors that separated the servants' realm from the master's.

In the library, Michael found his father sitting at his desk, pretending he had not been waiting for his son's return.

"Hello, Father," said Michael.

When he glanced up, Joseph's simulated surprise gave way to genuine astonishment and alarm at his son's appearance. The open shirt revealed several blisters on Michael's chest in addition to those on his face and hands. And patches of eyelash, eyebrow, and scalp hair had been seared to cinders, leaving them much shorter than the adjacent, pristine jet filaments.

"Mother of God!" Joseph exclaimed. He rose and came

round the desk to get a closer look. Not daring to touch his son, he said, "When ye said the house had caught fire but you were fine, I'd thought...." Too distressed to finish, he merely gaped at the evidence of the night's calamity.

"I'm well enough," Michael assured him. "I can't stand to wear more than a shirt just now, but Anne's been tending me and the pain is much diminished.

"It could have been worse," he added in a tone of pragmatic resignation.

Joseph stared. "The fire was deliberately set?"

"Using gasoline," Michael confirmed. "Fortunately, Anne recognized the smell before they put a match to it. That's why we were able to get out. She woke me."

"But ye were burnt," said Joseph, pointing to the blisters.

"I fell through the porch roof into the flames," Michael told him. "But I rolled out, and neighbours doused me with water and pulled me clear."

Joseph nodded, distrait. "Good. Good. That's good."

Michael waited. He had not seen his father this upset since the warehouse fire that killed eight workers who had tried and failed to nip the blaze in the bud. He knew Joseph would hear no more until he had settled.

At last, the older man's distraction turned to anger. Eyes fierce, he looked to his son and demanded, "Who did this?"

Michael prevaricated, "People who will soon pay, Father. I don't want you to worry about that."

"Not worry? What d'ye mean?" said Joseph.

Michael told him, "I mean that I know who did it and I have a plan to deal with the matter. But I don't want to involve the family."

Joseph guessed, "It's those bastards who ruined Elizabeth's party, isn't it? Those perverts who—who...." He could not bring himself to speak the words.

"Yes," Michael confirmed. "But there is more to this than what is between me and Skavronsky. That's why I will take care

of it myself. There are dangerous people involved, and they've already killed one man besides setting fire to my house."

"Whatever you're plotting, you can't do it alone," said his father.

"I won't be alone," Michael assured him. "Evan will help me. And we will be joined by some of his associates. You don't want to know who."

"Ah," Joseph said with a nod of understanding. He was aware of the sort of shady characters that haunted the periphery of the diplomatic world. He had met a few, himself, during the early days of his career, when he had made more than a few enemies of his own (as Michael had once learned from Evan's father).

Michael said, "That's why I'd like you to take care of Anne until this is done."

He and his father locked eyes a long moment. At last, Joseph nodded and said, "Of course, my boy. We'd be happy to look after her." He added, "And I know Hermione will be very pleased."

"There is one more thing," said Michael. "About Kenneth Armstrong."

His father's eyebrows shot up in surprise. "Oh?"

Michael said quietly, "I don't trust him." He let out his breath in a huff, shook his head, and added, "I can't explain why. I just don't. I realize it may not be possible to prevent his visiting Elizabeth, but I do not want him near Anne."

Father and son regarded each other once more. At last, Joseph pursed his lips, nodded, and said, "I'll bear that in mind."

The elder MacGregor accompanied his son to the stable to see him off. When they had ambled out of earshot of the household, the patriarch asked quietly, "Why could ye not tell me, son?"

Michael looked at him. There was no reproach in his father's voice. The younger MacGregor swallowed and turned away, pushing down the rush of resentment to prevent its

seeping into his tone as he answered, "I tried. I wrote to you. When you did not answer, there seemed no point in speaking of it further."

Joseph frowned and blinked, baffled. He protested, "I received no letters from you at all, for quite some time, even though I wrote many, myself, as did your mother and Elizabeth. I was vexed at first, and then worried. I telegraphed to inquire, but the headmaster assured me it was common for boys to forget to write home in the excitement of their new surroundings."

Michael's mouth curled and his belly convulsed in a fit of silent, bitter laughter as hot tears welled at what he now recognized as obvious: The bastards had stolen his letters. So, in his adolescent naïveté, when he received no response to his desperate pleas to come home, he had thought....

At the realization, he wondered how much of what he had believed all these years had been predicated on false assumptions and on the lies he had been told. And how much had been based purely on his own shame and disgust for what he thought he was.

His voice rising from a pit of infinite sadness, he said, "They deceived us both, Father."

Joseph shook his head in deprecation and whispered dolefully, "If only I'd known."

∞

ANNE TWITCHED her nose and shifted. Again, something tickled her, and she wiggled her nose and shook her head. When it happened once more, she fluttered her eyes, opening them with effort, and she gazed blearily about. As she focussed, her husband's grinning face came into view beyond the tail of her braid wielded by his hand.

"Wake up, my wee Hieland faerie," he whispered.

She smiled. "Are we going home?"

"First, we'll take tea with Evan," he told her as he put a

hand under her shoulder and helped her up. When he had brought her to a stand, he added, "Then, you'll go to my parents' home."

Her eyes sharpened. "Me. Not you."

"I want you kept safe," he said. "I've asked Father to look after you until this is done—and, no, he does not know exactly what I intend to do...only that Evan will help me."

"I need to go to The Flats," Anne insisted. "Today. Before nightfall. To the creek."

"You think the stone is there," Michael realized.

"It has to be."

Michael regarded her a moment. Then, he said, "After tea, we'll go. We'll have Evan's carriage take us there, and then on to Stuart Avenue."

"I won't stay there long," Anne warned.

"I know," he replied. He lightly stroked her nose with his forefinger. "But long enough to trap Skavronsky and put this behind us."

He took both her hands in his and kissed them, each in turn, saying softly, "I don't want you to be alone."

"Very well," Anne agreed reluctantly. She encircled his waist and gently hugged him. When she pulled back, she said, "I love you."

"I'll never love anyone else," he replied, and he kissed her deeply.

∞

"WAIT HERE," Michael told the coachman. "We'll be a while."

The man nodded acknowledgement and climbed down from his bench as Anne and Michael took the path toward the Sweetwater.

Jack appeared out of nowhere and joined them. He asked, "Why ye goin' to the crick?"

"To search for something that went missing," Michael

answered.

"Ain't nobody gone back since Herself was near kill't," the lad told them. "On account o' things comin' in threes." He mused, "But I guess the fire makes three, eh?"

"I guess it does at that," said Michael. He added, "Let's hope that puts an end to it."

"Mm," Jack grunted agreement.

The three on the path soon became four, then six, as the other members of the recently named "Four Horsemen"—Jack, Larry, Rob, and Kevin—filled out the rank. (Terence had taken a job shining shoes in the city to help his widowed mother support his sisters, and Ian now sold newspapers on Queen Street.)

"You got a new dress," Larry observed, looking Anne up and down.

"Borrowed," she said.

"What are those?" asked Rob, pointing to the canvas pockets she wore tied at her waist, white pouches over the black of the maid's uniform.

"My pockets," she answered. "I usually wear them inside, but today I'm wearing them outside."

"Didn't know ladies had pockets like that," said Larry.

"Most don't," said Michael. He added with a wry smile, "Not anymore."

Anne grinned. She responded, "Not all change is for the better. Sometimes, the old ways are the best ways."

Kevin peered at the blisters he could see on Michael's hands and face. He asked, "Does it hurt?"

"Not so much anymore," Michael replied. "Thanks to Herself." He smiled at the appellation.

They walked in silence the rest of the way through the woods to the streambank. There, the wooden chairs still sat at the water's edge, orphaned and unused since the death of Old Sean. Already barefoot, Anne stepped directly into the water and waded to the centre.

"What's she lookin' fer?" asked Kevin.

"A stone," said Michael. "A special one. And if she finds it, those bastards that hurt you will pay for what they did."

Rob suggested eagerly, "Maybe we should help look."

"Whoah!" Michael cautioned, arms out, stopping the boys' advance into the water. "You know the saying about too many cooks spoiling the broth?"

"We ain't cookin'," Kevin pointed out.

Michael suppressed a smile and explained, "If we all wander about in the water, we'll stir the mud and get in one another's way and none of us will find our feet, much less a tiny stone."

The boys grimaced, unable to refute their elder's logic. Reluctantly, they stood by and watched Herself peer into the water, searching the creek-bed and soaking her skirts.

Presently, Anne stooped and scooped something out of the water. She held it to the light.

"Is that it?" Michael called.

Anne shook her head mutely, then slipped the object into one of her pockets and continued her search.

The boys glanced from one to the other, up to Michael, who appeared as perplexed as they, and back to Anne. Kevin sighed.

A moment later, Anne bent again and retrieved something that flashed blue in the waning sunlight. "Got it!" she called as she deposited it into a pocket.

Michael and the boys heaved a collective sigh of relief.

Anne was on her way back to them when she stopped, reached into the creek once more, and came up with a long, pointed object that glinted silver as she flicked her wrist to examine it from different angles. She started to hike her skirt, but catching sight of the boys, she turned about to face away and bent to sheathe the *sgian dhu* on her thigh. That done, she straightened her skirts, whirled, and marched to her waiting men with a satisfied smile.

"That's your knife, ain't it?" Jack inquired.

"Isn't it," Anne corrected. "And, yes, it is."

Michael began to say something, but thought better of it. He shook his head, shrugged what was left of his eyebrows, and followed her back to the coach. It seemed unladylike for a woman to go about armed, but he supposed that none of the ladies he knew had lived through a war. And none need be ready to defend themselves, as his wife did. His gut tightened at the thought, and he prayed Evan's plan could be put into effect quickly.

∞

HARRIS HAD JUST opened the door of the house in Rosemont when Hermione MacGregor rushed to embrace Anne, then her son, with effusive greetings. She clasped Anne's arm and brought her to the drawing-room, seating her on a tapestried settee and covering her legs with a woollen throw—despite Anne's protests—before ordering a tray brought with tea and biscuits. She all but ignored everyone else, chattering one-sidedly with her daughter-in-law and deciding which shops they should visit in order to replenish Anne's wardrobe and to purchase a layette for the baby.

Standing with his father, Michael shook his head and raised his brows in amusement. He murmured, "I've never seen Mother so happy."

"Not since you and Elizabeth were wee bairns," Joseph agreed.

Elizabeth clearly did not enjoy playing second fiddle to anyone, much less to an upstart sister-in-law with peculiar taste in clothing. She sat with her betrothed on a nearby sofa and exchanged mutterings with him as her mother organized the week's agenda around the interloper.

Michael eyed his future brother-in-law, noting the furtive glances toward Anne and overhearing the censorious remarks in concurrence with Elizabeth's grumbling. He did not want to

leave his wife here alone, but he comforted himself that Armstrong was not yet a part of the household.

"I'd better get back to Hampton House," Michael told his father without enthusiasm.

At that, Anne leapt up, dropping the blanket and quickly apologizing to Hermione as she hurried to her husband. She urged him, "You'll take the medicine I gave you?"

"Yes," Michael assured her as he gathered her into his arms. "And I'll see you soon." He kissed her deeply, and for so long that Joseph cleared his throat to remind them they were not alone.

Michael released his wife and backed away toward the door, holding her with his eyes until Joseph, tugging at his sleeve, brought him out to the foyer.

In the antechamber, Michael's father suggested, "You could stay here. I can see it pains ye to leave her."

"No," Michael replied with a sigh. "There are things I must attend to at once." He turned toward the door that would lead him through the servants' area and out to the stables, but turned back. He said quietly, "Thank you, Father."

Joseph pressed his lips into a smile and said, "We'll take care of your wife. Do what ye must do, my boy."

CHAPTER 23

Windows of opportunity

Michael pulled the sapphire from his pocket and presented it to Evan. The viscount weighed it in his hand and stroked its smoothness. Then, he brought it to a candle on the escritoire, put a jeweller's monocle to his eye, and examined the gem in the light.

"Perfect," he murmured in awe.

As he handed it back to Michael and put the ocular on the desk, he added, "I've seen larger. But none as flawless. It will fetch more than enough to hire a brace of assassins."

Michael asked, "Have you contacted your acquaintance?"

Evan answered, "He's on his way as we speak."

The two wandered out of the library, along the main corridor with its console tables and its portraits framed in gilt-wood, through the drawing-room full of plush chairs, and onto the terrace. A footman appeared with a glass of Chablis and a

glass of lemonade.

As the two friends walked through the garden in the cool night air, Michael wondered, "Does your father know about this?"

Evan replied, "Father chooses to know what he needs to know, and chooses not to know what it does not serve him to know."

Michael remarked, "How...diplomatic."

"Quite."

Michael asked hesitantly, "Does he know...?" He let the question dangle, knowing no way to express its intent without giving offence.

Evan finished for him, "About my...affections?" When Michael nodded, the viscount sighed. "That's one of the things it does not serve him to know."

They had strolled desultorily among the carefully arranged and tended flowerbeds in silence for some time when Michael said quietly, "I'm sorry, Evan."

His friend responded sadly, "I've always known, you know. That it's not in your nature. That you couldn't...feel anything for me but friendship. It's why I never pressed you."

They had walked another minute before Evan admitted, "Funny, though. Somehow, I never expected you to find someone like Anne: someone you could truly love."

He added softly, "I didn't realize I could feel so jealous."

∞

HEADING FOR THE CITY, Michael borrowed trousers and shirt from a lanky groundskeeper. His own part in the conspiracy to destroy Ivan Skavronsky had been fulfilled last night when he told Evan's associate all he knew of the Irishman, the gem, the margrave, and the Russian count.

The nondescript man, whose name was not revealed and who Michael guessed to be a spy, had listened intently and

accepted the sapphire. The three had discussed the strategy in some detail, though there were clearly nuances that the British agent preferred to keep to himself. Things must be set in motion at once, the man had said, because Skavronsky and Von Ratzenhausen had already booked passage to Europe in the belief that their original plan had been scuttled. The British spy would get word to his Russian counterpart and then arrange a meeting with the roués today. Michael had asked to be kept informed of progress, and he had offered whatever assistance he might be in a position to provide. When the meeting ended, dawn had already painted the sky a pale grey, and he had been obliged to take his leave.

As he munched the apple Lord Heth's cook had given him as a token breakfast before his departure, he wished he could participate in trapping the sodomite and his confederates. But he knew direct personal involvement would jeopardize the desired outcome. He sighed with resignation. Arm's-length justice would have to do.

The Scot had decided to spend the day on Draper Avenue, with a brief side trip to Market Square to purchase new working garb; in the evening, he would return to Anne. He strode toward the stables to borrow a horse, but to his astonishment, the consul's carriage was waiting. Evan's blond pate poked out of the window and he beckoned wearing a broad grin.

"I thought I'd accompany you," said the viscount.

Michael returned the grin and inquired knowingly, "Who do you plan to wake from a sound sleep?"

"I think I'll breakfast on Cleve Avenue," Evan replied.

Climbing aboard the coach-and-four, Michael warned, "The concierge will not be pleased. And there may be no cooks at this hour." He knew the Britannia Club had rooms for overnight guests—he had used them, himself, on occasion—but few of the members were early risers and breakfast was usually served well after nine o'clock.

Viscount Danford said breezily, "Then, I shall make do with coffee and brandy. I'm sure Broderick can manage that."

Michael shook his head and chuckled. Evan liked to keep people on their toes and, wherever he went, serving staff considered him the bane of their existence.

With a lurch, the carriage pulled away to drive into town.

∞

HERMIONE MacGREGOR could be a force of Nature when she put her mind to it. The matron marshalled daughter and daughter-in-law, shopkeepers and seamstresses as though mounting a military campaign. She wanted dresses and hats, shoes and smallclothes, coats and gloves for Anne, and she wanted blankets and gowns, bonnets and booties for her unborn grandchild.

Elizabeth took every opportunity to purchase new items for her own trousseau and criticized Anne's conservative taste. But she became as enthusiastic as her mother in providing for the layette of her future niece or nephew. For her own part, Anne allowed them to lead her about and, other than refusing excess ornamentation such as absurdly bouffant sleeves or cascades of lace, she accepted their gifts with gratitude, graciousness, and, though she hid it, amusement.

Having been outfitted in a white blouse with no more than the merest hint of lace, a lemon skirt with more gathering than Elizabeth considered chic but in a very fashionable ankle length, a matching lemon jacket with basque, buttoned shoes in buff, a broad-brimmed straw hat banded with white and yellow, and dainty white lace gloves, Anne twirled for her in-laws and bowed appreciatively to the staff of Northway's department store.

"Oh, my goodness, dear," said Hermione, "you do look fetching in that hue!"

"It does suit your colouring," Elizabeth admitted

charitably, feeling more comfortable with a companion who now attracted the right sort of attention and in whose company she was not ashamed to be seen.

Holding at arm's length as if it might be flea-ridden the black uniform Anne had been wearing when she arrived, one of the sales girls asked, "Would you like me to dispose of this for you, Madam?"

"Oh, no!" Anne answered. "Please wrap it separately so that I can return it to Viscount Danford's household. I borrowed it from one of his maids."

"Oh, of course!" said the young woman hastily at mention of the viscount. Any friend of the British consul's family instantly gained status in the eyes of both staff and nearby clients, and any peculiarity of circumstance was immediately dismissed. The girl rushed away, now holding the maid's dress as though it were a precious object.

"Shall we adjourn to the Tuscarora for luncheon?" asked Hermione.

"That would be lovely," said Anne.

The Northway staff bustled about, packaging the MacGregor purchases as Hermione wrote a cheque for the manager.

∞

ANNE, HERMIONE, and Elizabeth had just disembarked from their coach in front of Tuscarora's (one of the city's finer restaurants), when Detective Morgan called and waved from across the street. At Anne's suggestion, her companions continued into the elegant dining establishment while she waited for the policeman.

"What brings you here, Detective?" she inquired once he had successfully navigated the cart and carriage traffic of Queen Street.

Bowing his head and touching his fedora's brim to her in

polite greeting, Morgan replied discreetly, "I have a number of cases to investigate." His tone and countenance now curious, he asked, "I understand there was a fire Saturday night? That you've lost your home?"

"Yes," she answered. "I'm staying with my husband's parents, for the moment; though, I hope to begin new construction soon. My mother-in-law has been kind enough to bring me to town to replenish my wardrobe."

He scanned her quickly and said with a smile, "Indeed, you look particularly well in your new dress, if I may be so bold."

"You may, and I thank you," she responded with a smile and a nod.

The detective cleared his throat and said delicately, "The, uh, fire marshal has reported that the blaze that took your home was the work of an arsonist, yet you and your husband have not brought this to my attention." There was an obvious question in the statement.

"No," said Anne. "We have been a little preoccupied, as you may well imagine."

"Of course," he said hastily. He added, "Perhaps you would like to make an official complaint today?"

Anne smiled and regarded him a moment before replying, "Detective, I believe the matter will resolve itself without the need to burden the constabulary."

Morgan said guardedly, "I hope your husband does not intend to take the law into his own hands."

Anne told him, "No. Others will deal with the situation."

The detective cocked an eyebrow. He asked tentatively, "These...others...would not happen to be members of the diplomatic corps?"

Anne quibbled, "I don't believe they can rightly be called 'members.'" She smiled enigmatically as she added, "Though I'm sure they travel in the same circles."

Morgan nodded thoughtfully. Turning to leave, he

paused, looked back, and said, "I do hope I will not have to investigate another murder."

Anne responded, "Perhaps any...unpleasantness...will not take place within your jurisdiction."

He regarded her narrowly a moment. Finally, he pinched his hat brim in farewell and sprinted across the street to rejoin Constable Ryan.

∞

ANNE WAS JUST about to enter the Tuscarora when someone called, "Mrs. MacGregor!"

Anne stopped and turned toward the sound. "Yes," she said questioningly as she scanned for the person who belonged to the voice.

A vaguely familiar young man in light-brown trousers and slightly darker brown jacket dashed from a nearby doorway. Below his tweed cap, projecting curls of his nut-coloured hair shone in the sunlight, and his cleanly shaven face bore the dark-red evidence of a razor nick on his chin. With pencil and pad in hand, the man tipped his hat as he came forward and said, "John Devereux, Ma'am. Is it true that your husband was buggered by Count Skavronsky?"

Anne's countenance hardened instantly. Her tone equally adamantine, she said, "You must be a reporter. Even lawyers aren't so rude."

"Guilty as charged, Ma'am," he said with a chastened smile.

Anne recalled where she had seen him before: He had attended the engagement party in the guise of a waiter. She said acerbically, "You're out of uniform. Do you work in the Tuscarora, as well? Or do you only dress up as a waiter to crash parties to which you have not been invited?"

"I'm just breakin' into the business, Ma'am," he admitted apologetically. "Thought I'd write an article about the grand

affair to impress the editor."

"Which paper?"

"The *Evening Star*, Ma'am."

Anne summarized, "A brash young reporter and a brand-new newspaper, both looking to make a name for themselves." She fixed him with a gimlet eye and added, "At anyone's expense, no doubt."

The young journalist squirmed, but as she turned away, he sidestepped to put himself in her path and said with blatant accusation, "People don't take kindly to sodomites, as you may imagine."

Noting the startled expressions on the faces of passersby, Anne grabbed the reporter's sleeve and pulled him into the restaurant, her teeth gritted, her nostrils flared. Surveying the spacious entry lounge, she spotted a divan against a panelled wall, away from the door, the diners, and the maître d'hôtel. She dragged the young man to it and, with a curt gesture to him to take a seat, she parked herself on the bench upholstered in gold plush.

Seething, Anne regarded him narrowly for a moment. She said quietly but emphatically, "My husband has never been a sodomite. As for Count Skavronsky, I'm sure you heard that he did not deny the same charge against him."

Devereux took an audible breath, hesitated a heartbeat, and then said in a low voice, "Thing is, Ma'am, I've heard recently that there have been attacks against young boys. Mostly street lads no one cares about. But I also understand you and your husband took two such lads into your home. You can see how that might look, given what the count said about Mr. MacGregor."

Anne said firmly, "It is precisely because my husband understands what it is like to be victimized that he has told the police about the count's crimes. It is thanks to him that the police have been doing their best to prevent further attacks, though, unfortunately, their recourse is limited because of the rules of

diplomatic privilege.

"As for the boys," she added, "I believe he has helped them more than anyone else could, simply because they know, through him, that their experience is not unique and that they are not abnormal. Nor should it make them pariahs."

She concluded, "And I am happy to report that they are doing well and playing with their friends again."

Devereux pondered her assertions. Then, he said, "You stated, the other night, that the count has been preying on boys for a long time."

"Him, and others like him," Anne confirmed. "Rape is not a new phenomenon in any form, Mr. Devereux."

"No, I don't suppose it is," he said, blushing at her directness.

"Would you like to speak to our boys?" Anne asked suddenly.

The reporter started. He stammered, "Ye-Yes, Ma'am. That—that would be...I mean—"

"I can't guarantee they will agree," she warned. "But I'll ask them if they'll accept an interview about their experience." She thought aloud, "Perhaps it would help other boys, and girls, to come forward if they are being abused. They, too, would know they are not alone and not to blame."

She looked at him and added, "And perhaps, by bringing it into the open, victims and their families will be able to heal."

Devereux said, "Most people would rather hide such things under a rug." He admitted awkwardly, "In truth, I'm not even sure my editor will want to print an article that suggests such things happen here, in this city, and not just in Europe."

"Then remind him that's precisely why predators get away with their crimes," Anne said firmly. "Hiding things under a rug does not make them go away.

"Mind you," she added in a tone of warning, "I do not want to see such an article creating a witch-hunt against homosexuals. Not all who are homosexual are rapists. Just as

many rapists are not homosexual. And some rapists do not discriminate, but prey on both genders, on any target of opportunity. You need to make that clear."

The young man regarded her with something approaching awe. He asked incredulously, "You speak of such things with your husband?"

Anne replied, "My husband and I can speak of anything. But in point of fact, I knew of such matters before I met him."

"There you are!" Hermione called from the door to the dining-room. "My dear, we were worried. You're taking so long." She eyed the reporter censoriously as she approached.

"I apologize, Mother," Anne responded. "I was explaining something to Mr. Devereux and became quite distracted."

"Well, you must come and dine with us, my dear," Hermione insisted as she urged her daughter-in-law to a stand. "You're eating for two, now, remember."

Anne smiled and said, "Yes, of course, Mother." She started toward the dining-room, but stopped to ask, "Do you have a card, Mr. Devereux?"

"Uh, yes, Ma'am," he said, searching his pockets as he stood. He produced a bent piece of paper and handed it to her. "You can leave a message there," he said obligingly. "And thank you, Ma'am." He touched his cap.

Hermione drew Anne away, advising on the suitability of various items on the menu as Anne secured the reporter's calling card in her purse.

∞

MICHAEL SQUEEZED between Pat O'Connell and Jake Trevelyan and opened the paper bag of cheese and bread he had picked up on his way back to Draper from the clothier. (He had managed to purchase only one pair of pants, the only pair long enough in the leg. The trousers were an ugly yellow-grey, but

they fit. He had had as little luck with shirts, but at least the blue cotton he found comprised a wide enough neck and broad enough back. He had rolled the inadequate sleeves rather than button the cuffs that ended well above his wrists, and he had tucked the ungenerous shirt-tails under his waistband.)

"Any idea who torched your house?" asked Archie Burton.

"A good idea," said Michael. "But I'll have to leave justice to those who can dispense it."

"Mm," said Rob Donnelly. "Hope they catch the bastards. I've got scorched shingles on my own roof, thanks to them."

"I'll pay for the new ones," Michael offered at once.

"Agh!" said Rob with a dismissive wave of the hand, "You've got a whole house to build. Don't be tryin' to mend mine, too."

Jake Trevelyan offered, "We'll have stone left over from this project. Enough for a foundation, maybe. You're welcome to it for cost."

"Thank you," Michael said gratefully. "I'm not sure what we'll need, yet. I'll have to go through the wreckage to determine what is salvageable."

"Take your time," said Trevelyan. "We won't be finishing this place for another month, anyway."

As the conversation turned to a discussion of the problems of the Taft design with its rear turret and ornamental stonework, Michael's attention drifted to thoughts of Anne. He smiled to himself, realizing he missed her already despite having been away from her only one night.

∞

SITTING IN ONE of the semicircular burgundy-upholstered booths of the Tuscarora's dining-room, Anne shifted uncomfortably and grimaced. She found the seat too high and too wide. Furthermore, her bladder had begun to protest the

three cups of tea she had drunk to wash down the oily taste of the fish.

Interrupting Hermione's discourse on the sleeping habits of babies, she said, "Excuse me, Mother. I need to find the privy right away."

"Oh, yes, of course!" said her mother-in-law. She confided in a low voice, "I had the same problem during both my pregnancies." She pointed, "There's a lavatory off the foyer. Do you want me to come with you?"

Anne smiled and said, "No need. I'll find it."

She manoeuvred out of the booth and strode purposefully to the entry. A quick survey of the oak-walled lobby revealed several doors but no sign indicating the washrooms; so, she asked the maître d'hôtel. The man promptly directed her to the last room on the left along a corridor hidden behind a door opposite the entrance, and she sped off to find the first available toilet.

Inside the ladies' room, a richly wall-papered lounge contained a chaise longue, a walnut dressing table with mirror and upholstered bench, and an overstuffed chesterfield dotted with deep, button-filled indentations. Beyond, a marble counter and sinks lined one wall of the lavatory proper, while commodious cubicles hid flush toilets on the other. The first stall was empty, and Anne hastily sequestered herself to heed the call of her bladder.

A few minutes later, much relieved, she exited the washroom and started back to rejoin Hermione and Elizabeth. She had just passed a tall man headed in the opposite direction when a hand grasped her waist from behind and another clasped a folded handkerchief to her nose. She smelt chloroform.

∞

MICHAEL RECOGNIZED his family's equipage as it clattered up Draper at high speed. His heart leapt to his throat and he

raced down the two flights of the scaffold, pounding the planks and the treads of the stairs to the startlement of his fellow workers.

"Michael!" his mother called from the open window of the coach even before it stopped. "They took her! She's gone!"

He reached the door of the carriage, heart pounding, and demanded, "Who took her? When?"

"She went to the lavatory," Elizabeth told him excitedly. "But she didn't come back. Then, I went to fetch her and found this." She held up a small white bag.

Michael frowned and squinted uncomprehendingly.

"It's her new purse," Hermione explained. "It was on the floor of the corridor outside the ladies' room at Tuscarora's."

"How long?" Michael asked.

"We came as soon as we realized," Hermione assured him. "She's not gone more than a half-hour."

Jake Trevelyan had come up behind. "Go," he said.

Michael called to the driver, "The Tuscarora," and climbed into the carriage as the coachman flicked the reins and cracked his whip.

CHAPTER 24

Desperate measures

At Hermione's insistence, the maître d'hôtel had called both the police and her husband while she fetched Michael. Now, the members of the MacGregor family and the police converged on the Tuscarora and brought bedlam to the restaurant. Constables interviewed guests and waiters. Detective Morgan questioned the MacGregor women and the doorman. Joseph tried to comfort his distraught wife and daughter. And after telephoning Hampton House, Michael collapsed on the divan, elbows on his knees and holding his head in his hands.

"There he is!" Hermione shrilled, pointing to a startled young man. "It was him!"

A constable grabbed the man and roughly pulled him to Morgan as Michael sprang to his feet.

"What have you done with my wife!" Michael demanded.

"Your wife?" the man said in alarm and confusion.

"What have you done with her?" Michael bellowed, grabbing the man by the collar.

"Mr. MacGregor!" Detective Morgan snapped. With a restraining hand on Michael's wrist, he insisted, "Please let us handle this."

"I didn't do anything," the man protested. "I just asked her some questions and gave her my card. She said she'd try to arrange an interview for me."

"When was this?" the detective demanded.

"Couple of hours ago," said the reporter. "I haven't seen her since. I went back to Front Street."

"Then why are you here, now?" Morgan queried suspiciously.

"I was following a guttersnipe," Devereux answered. "For my story. Then, I saw the police arrive and all the hubbub; so, I thought I'd find out what's going on."

"A guttersnipe," Michael repeated to himself, thinking: *The boys might have seen something.*

Abruptly, he ran outside and scanned the street. On the boulevard lined with abutting flat-roofed, three- and four-storey brick and stone buildings, ladies in bonnets and gentlemen in tall hats strolled the sidewalks. Hackneys waited at troughs; some drivers chatted together while others solicited fares aggressively. A policeman patrolled without hurry farther on as one shopkeeper swept the walk before his establishment and another pulled a striped awning to shade his storefront. Two men perched on a wooden bench set against a brownstone, reading newspapers as young boys buffed their shoes vigorously.

Wagons and buggies drove by on the dusty roadways, obscuring the view over the way, and a streetcar stopped to take on passengers who sprinted across the avenue to reach the rail line. Straining to see past the traffic to the far side of the street, Michael noticed a small, darting form. And another.

The Scot hastened forward. Spotting a familiar gamin lounging near the display table of a flower shop, he dashed

across the road, barely averting collision with the oncoming streetcar tethered to the overhead electrical line. When the lad saw the big man running toward him, the child ran, on instinct.

Michael called, "Jack's friend! I need to talk to you."

The waif slowed and hesitated, glancing back warily, ready to slip into an open door or a nearby alley. He squinted, trying to place his pursuer. Suddenly, his face lightened in recognition and he turned to meet Michael.

"Ye're Himself, ain't ye?" he said.

"Yes," Michael confirmed. "I need your help. Someone has kidnapped my wife." He specified, "Herself."

The boy's eyes flew wide.

Michael asked, "I need you to find out if anyone saw her. She was taken from the Tuscarora about an hour ago."

"I'll tell the lads," the boy promised.

As the urchin darted off, Michael remembered what his mother had told him and called, "She was wearing a yellow dress today."

The boy acknowledged with a wave and ducked down an alley.

∞

ON HIS WAY back to the restaurant, Michael spotted Dan Doherty's cab at one of the public troughs. The hackney driver was conversing with another man as their horses watered. Seeing Himself lope toward him, the cabbie waved, but his smile faded at Michael's expression.

"Somebody's taken Anne," Michael told his friend when he reached him. "About an hour ago, from the Tuscarora. We have no idea who took her or where."

Doherty's eyes rounded in shock, then widened further with inspiration. He said, "Mose! I'll fetch Mose. If there's any trace, he'll find it."

With that, he hopped onto his seat and reined his horses

out into the street, cutting off an empty dray and earning a honk of annoyance from the horn of a black, narrow-wheeled automobile driven by a goggled and duster-clad man of means.

∞

HER EYES FLUTTERED as Anne woke. She peered into the pitch black around her, wondering where she was and why she felt so woozy. She tried to get up, but found herself checked by the pain in her head and the straps on her arms and ankles. Recalling the moment of terror in the corridor outside the loo, she tugged at the restraints. They would not give. Her breath came short and she struggled with increasing desperation in her attempts to escape. Her gorge began to rise.

A part of her recognizing the need to quell the panic that had set her senses alight and threatened to banish all reason, Anne lay back and breathed deeply, forcing herself to calm. *Nothing would be served by giving in to the fear,* she told herself firmly. She knew she must relax and think, thus to find the solution that would surely present itself.

As she got her breath under control and loosened her taut muscles, she became aware of sounds nearby. When she focussed on the muffled voices beyond the door, they came clearer.

"I'm telling you, I can't admit the woman without proper authorization," said one.

Another voice, this one familiar, said, "I'm not asking you to."

"Don't ask me to kill her," said the first.

"I'm not asking that, either. Just make sure she doesn't have this baby, or any other."

"An abortion?" the first exclaimed in horror.

The second said sardonically, "Let's not pretend it would be your first, Doctor. Just see to it. I'll take care of the rest."

The first voice lowered slightly and said, "It'll have to be tonight, after the day-staff leave. I can count on Nurse Jones to be

discreet, but I can't be sure of the others."

"Fine," said the voice Anne now realized belonged to Kenneth Armstrong.

Again, her heart began to pound.

∞

"I CANNOT ALLOW a dog in this restaurant!" said the maître d'hôtel haughtily.

"I am going to find my wife," Michael declared through his teeth, "and I don't give a damn whose dinner is upset!" He gestured angrily, and Dan brought Mose into the Tuscarora despite the steward's sputtering protests and the gasps of clients.

Dan rubbed the dog's nose with the black uniform Anne had worn. Then, he allowed Mose to smell her purse. Letting out the leash, he followed as the hound sniffed here and there through the lounge, through the restaurant, pausing at the booth where the MacGregor women had dined, and meandering back through the corridor and the ladies' room.

Hands tightened to fists, barely breathing, Michael watched the glacial process, all the while wanting to scream at the dog, at his parents, and at God. But in truth, he most blamed himself. For leaving her alone. For bringing this danger upon her. For everything. Who could have abducted her but Skavronsky?

He had telephoned the gentlemen's club, to be directed back to Hampton House. To his surprise, Evan was certain that the Russian could not have done it, even through others. Then, who? And why? Or was Evan mistaken?

Mose suddenly let out a yelp and headed for the exit. Dan opened the door, and the dog led Dan, Michael, Jack, and Larry, the other three MacGregors, Detective Morgan and Constable O'Toole, and the reporter down the street and around a corner to a horse trough. There, Mose circled again and again. He had lost the scent.

∞

FOOTSTEPS.

With a scratching, a click, and a high-pitched whine, the door opened and a woman bearing a lantern entered from a dark corridor. By the lamplight, Anne saw her prison: a compact, whitewashed room with cement floor and one tiny, blackened window. A simple table sat next to the wall on her right, and a cabinet stood in a corner.

The woman wore a white nurse's uniform with kerchief and apron. Plump and middle-aged, of brusque manner and saturnine countenance, she checked Anne's restraints and pulse. There was no warmth in her eyes, and her spirit appeared as a small, dull glow centred in her abdomen.

She was about to leave when Anne said, "I need to go to the privy."

The woman pouted her lips and snorted. She said with resigned annoyance, "I'll fetch a bedpan."

Anne sighed as the nasty nurse exited and closed the door. Of all days to leave her *sgian dhu* behind!

Not that she could have known. Nor could she have used it when someone came from behind with chloroform to quickly overpower her and render her unconscious, she reminded herself. Moreover, had she worn it, "they" were likely to have found it when they strapped her to this bed. And she would not have been able to access it even if they had overlooked it, trussed, as she was, like a Thanksgiving turkey.

Would anyone find her?

Certainly, Hermione would have raised the alarm by now. But who would search for her here—wherever here was? And who would guess that Kenneth Armstrong had orchestrated her disappearance?

Judging by the conversation she had overheard, the lawyer did not want her killed outright, which suggested he thought even *she* would not know he was responsible. Perhaps he expected her to be unconscious throughout her incarceration. Or at least unable to identify anyone who could tie him to the crime.

Or perhaps he meant to keep her here, in secret, with none the wiser.

If no one came...if she was trapped forever in this place...if her baby was murdered and her womb damaged...if she never saw Michael again....

Tears filled her eyes and her belly convulsed with the sobs she could not suppress as she anxiously wondered how long it would be till the shift change.

∞

MICHAEL WAS ABOUT to smash his fist into a stone wall in rage and frustration when Jack shouted, "Oy! Davey!"

The Scot whirled to see a spindly lad in dirty grey trousers and a shirt patched so many times its original colour was indistinguishable. Trailed by two more ragamuffins of equally tattered appearance, the boy dodged a cart and a cab to cross to the trough.

"Ho, Jack!" said Davey upon arrival. He pointed to his companions and said, "Zeke, here, says 'e saw a lady in yellah looked like she fainted, an' a fellah put 'er in a carriage an' drove 'er away."

"Where did they go?" Michael asked urgently.

Zeke pointed west, "That way."

"But there's more," said Davey triumphantly. "Walt, here, seen 'em cross over to The Flats. An' she was still fainted."

Detective Morgan asked, "The Flats? Are you sure?"

The boy named Walt nodded emphatically.

Dan said dubiously, "Nobody in The Flats would harm Herself."

"It's where they went," Walt insisted. "A lady in yellah, with white hair but not old-lookin'."

"Oh, God," Michael breathed. "It's her."

Dan protested, "But it can't be The Flats. Somebody'd see her an' word would spread."

Eyes widening in horror, Michael recalled, "The asylum!" It was the one place across the Bow where Anne would not be known and respected.

Detective Morgan ordered, "O'Toole, get Justice Edwards."

"Right away, sir," said the constable as he ran to the nearest call box.

Morgan assured Michael, "She can't be committed to the asylum without the judge's authorization. And he won't grant it without proper cause and request of the family."

At a terrifying suspicion that had formed in his mind, Michael objected, "What if someone is willing to commit her without authorization? Or to fake the papers?" Not waiting for an answer, Michael raced for his father's buggy.

Joseph MacGregor ushered his wife and daughter back toward the coach the women had taken for their day's outing. Dan and three of the boys dashed for his hackney. Detective Morgan ran to the entrance of the Tuscarora, where he had left his bicycle. Zeke and Walt disappeared into an alley. And after a moment of looking uncertainly from one departing group to another, John Devereux followed Constable O'Toole.

∞

THE NURSE finally returned with the bedpan and a helper who, but for her darker colouring, might have been Nurse Nasty's twin. One dour woman released the ankle and wrist straps while the other held Anne tightly, preventing escape.

Maintaining a firm hold, the brawny women set the hapless prisoner upon the basin and waited for her to finish. Then, they manoeuvred the pan out from under her and strapped her down once more. They managed the entire procedure without a single word.

When the door closed behind them, Anne lay still and concentrated on slowing her heart rate.

Someone will come, she told herself. *Michael will come.*

∞

FLOATING...drifting...higher....

Anne ascended through a roof and up among clouds heavy with moisture. *They should release their burden,* she thought dreamily and, as if she had waved a magic wand, they did.

She wandered higher still, straying into the blackness of space...through a sea of asteroids glinting dully in the light of the sun, the fiery ball small and yellow in the distance...out among stars that glittered like tiny gems—

Anne opened her eyes.

"'Little sun' and 'evening star,'" she said aloud, echoing the penny novel's jotted code. Could it have meant the *Evening Star* newspaper?

And could "little sun" allude to another newspaper? There was no daily in the city called *The Sun.* At least, not yet. But perhaps it was code for *The Globe*?

And what of "the price of eggs" and "blue skies"? Could that mean there would be a message hidden in the market advertisements and the weather forecast?

Or perhaps the stock reports and the shipping schedule?

It made a certain sense: clandestine communications between parties that did not know one another, or could not meet openly, yet had a common goal.

But she could tell no one her supposition while trapped in this place.

∞

THE SKY OPENED and soaked the city. The torrential downpour quickly liquefied all dirt streets that had yet to be macadamized, to mire coaches and carriages, carts and wagons. Even Detective Morgan's bicycle bogged in the slurry that, less than an hour before, had been a dusty thoroughfare.

Michael ran his hands through his hair and over his face to press away the water that dripped into his eyes. From here, he could see his father's coach two blocks back, mud halfway up the wheels. Dan's hackney, weighed by several boys and the dog, was nearer, but little better off.

He could not wait. Michael hopped out of his stranded buggy and slogged through the muck toward the bridge. It had occurred to him that there was one person who might find the means to illicitly lock Anne in the madhouse: bloody Kenneth Armstrong.

CHAPTER 25

Asylum

Dammit to hell!" Michael spat as he sank into a squelchy pocket of muck. He tugged and reefed, but stuck fast.

"Damn you, God!" he roared in desperate frustration.

"I should think you'd be praying for His help, not cursing Him," Detective Morgan scolded as he caught up to the Scot. He bent to pull at the mired leg.

"Wait," said Michael. He grimaced as he pushed up onto his toes, sinking deeper but succeeding in his purpose: to orient his foot vertically.

Dan arrived and stooped under Michael's shoulder to support his opposite side as the detective and Michael pulled simultaneously on the bogged foot. Slowly, with much grunting and sweating, and with a slurping and sucking sound, the leg rose. When the trapped foot suddenly came free with a smack, all

three men toppled sideways into the mud. Despite Herself's peril—or perhaps because of the tension engendered by it—Jack, Larry, and Davey snickered as they aided the men scrambling to their feet. Meanwhile, Mose skipped from man to man and boy to boy, sniffing and barking anxiously.

Chest heaving with the labour of his struggle, Michael wiped a muddy hand across his sweating brow, smearing brown across the bronze. His saw his father, trailing a way back, locked arm in arm with his mother on one side and his sister on the other. For an instant, Michael marvelled at Elizabeth, who normally would rather be dead than dirty, especially in public, as she now stumbled doggedly along in muddied skirts.

The thought vanished as urgency seized him once more. He must get to Anne.

∞

ANNE CURSED herself for having drifted off. She knew that emotional turmoil induced exhaustion and the hormonal changes of pregnancy also took a toll, but she needed to remain alert. How long had she slept?

Marshalling her mind's functions, she slowed her respiration and her heart and she focussed intently on her goal. Nearby, the door opened; light entered and intensified; people bustled about. But she kept her eyes closed and continued to concentrate on the ground beneath the floor.

She searched deep, deeper, and found a crack. Tracing its path, she came upon a fissure and followed its extent until she was satisfied it would do.

A clinking and muffled voices in the room threatened to distract her. Forcing herself to ignore them, Anne gathered her strength and beamed all of her thought, all of her will, all of her being to the fault in the earth below.

∞

WITH ITS STONE BASE, the bridge afforded easier walking. The men, boys, and dog picked up speed and ran across, only to slow again when they reached the street on the other side.

Farther on, as they turned into the short road that led to the mental institution, they met a group of men and women hobbling in the opposite direction. Hospital workers on their way home, Michael realized. Good. Perhaps there would be fewer to oppose the rescuers.

Then, it occurred to him that one of these people might have seen Anne. On impulse, he grasped a woman by the arm as the groups intermingled. He said, "Excuse me. Have you seen a woman in yellow brought into the hospital? Quite likely unconscious."

The navy-caped and white-kerchiefed nurse regarded him warily and said, "I am not at liberty to discuss our patients, sir."

Detective Morgan peeled away his left jacket front to reveal the muddied badge pinned to his vest as he said, "I am Detective Morgan. We have reason to believe this man's wife has been abducted and brought to the asylum, though by whom and to what end, we do not yet know."

The woman's brows rose and eyes widened. She swallowed and said, "I have seen no new patients, sir, but I do not work in admitting."

"She may not have been admitted," said the detective.

The woman's eyes grew wider still.

"Miss Horton? These people botherin' you?"

A large, burly man in white uniform and brown jacket and cap eyed the motley group of strangers suspiciously as he came to the nurse's side.

"They say a woman's been kidnapped and brought to The Cedars, Ethan," she told her protector.

"Ballocks!" said the man.

"It's true!" Jack insisted.

Davey said sagely, "There's bad business goin' on in

there."

A crowd had formed as the asylum workers stopped and listened curiously.

Morgan called out, "I am a detective with the city's constabulary. Has anyone seen a white-haired woman in yellow frock brought into the hospital, probably unconscious?"

Startled faces looked at one another. The nurses and orderlies exchanged mutters, and many among the hospital staff shook their heads.

The MacGregors had caught up at last. Hermione pleaded, "My daughter-in-law is with child. We must find her and bring her home safely."

Miss Horton's shocked gaze leapt to another nurse, who returned a significant look.

Seeing the interchange, Michael demanded, "What do you know?"

When the nurses hesitated, Detective Morgan warned, "I'd advise you to be forthcoming. A woman's life may be in danger."

Miss Horton said, "It's only rumour, you understand." Once more, she glanced at her colleague. Then, she took a deep breath and continued, "But it's been said that Dr. Desmond sometimes performs abortions in secret."

In horror, Michael and Hermione cried as one, "No!"

Astounded, Joseph said, "How is that possible?"

The big orderly guessed, "There's a wing ain't been used much. With the doors closed, nobody'd hear a thing."

"Take us there at once!" Morgan commanded.

∞

A NURSE CARRYING towels started and screamed when the front door burst open and people poured into the square, white-painted lobby, followed by a dog. The dark-uniformed duty guard jumped up from behind an oak desk, baton at the ready,

but he froze when the detective showed his badge and the brawny hospital attendant said authoritatively, "This way."

To the astonishment of the handful of night staff, some thirty people stamped through the corridors, trailing mud on the cement floor as they followed Ethan. Michael MacGregor, eyes blazing and face dark with rage and determination, kept abreast of the leader, bashing in the doors that separated sections as soon as the orderly unlocked them.

Behind a numbered door, a woman wailed as they passed by, an anguished sound that wrenched Michael's heart and gut. Another woman, farther on, shrieked repeatedly. From some rooms, he heard moaning, from others, sobs. He wondered if any of these women deserved to be here. And the thought of Anne's being trapped in this place sickened him.

They had just entered another corridor when Mose began to yelp.

∞

"SHE LOOKS ASLEEP already," Nurse Nasty observed.

"Well, she won't be for long once we start; so, we'd better sedate her," said a man's voice—the same voice Anne had heard in converse with Kenneth Armstrong.

She must keep her wits, Anne knew. She redoubled her efforts. In her mind, she maintained her focus on the fault, seeing its shape and the texture of the surrounding rock. She pictured the earth moving.

Abruptly, the rock of her visioning lurched, one side of the fissure sliding a millimetre, then a centimetre, then several more. She felt a burst of energy, and she heard a rending as stone surfaces met and scraped over one another. Thunder resounded through the cement and mortar of the building. The table to which she had been strapped shook. Metal objects clattered. Something fell with a clang and Nurse Nasty screeched. A thunk, and another, preceded the sudden dimming of the light in the

room.

"What the hell?" exclaimed the doctor as he stumbled and clutched Anne's leg to steady himself.

A crash brought blackness.

∞

THE FLOOR MOVED. At least, Michael *thought* it moved.

A growing rumble, a smash, and a clang set women to howling and squealing behind their locked doors. A rolling table in the hallway shimmied sideways as Mose barked excitedly.

"Earthquake," said Detective Morgan.

"*Beira!*" Michael breathed. To the orderly, he called, "Hurry, man!"

The burly attendant ran down the corridor and Michael raced after him with Detective Morgan close on his heels. They turned a corner to be brought up sharply at the first of two sets of windowed doors, in series, six feet apart. Ethan unlocked the first and then scrambled to find a separate key for the second. When he opened the inner door, a scream pierced the emptiness beyond. Michael hurtled down the dark hallway toward the sound that trailed and vanished as he approached the end of the passage barely lit by a lamp someone behind had thought to fetch. At the renewal of the scream, he turned to a door on his left.

He rotated the knob. The door gave easily and opened upon a scene of struggle as Anne, bound to a narrow table in the centre of a tiny chamber, twisted and wriggled against the restraining hands of a hefty nurse and a doctor, both in white aprons. A single candle burned on a tall chest in the far corner, revealing surgical instruments and more candles scattered across the floor, along with a brass lamp, its glass chimney shattered and its oil leaking slowly onto the cement to taint the air with a smell of kerosene.

Too enraged for words, Michael grabbed the doctor by

the shoulders. The startled man cried out in surprise as Michael tossed him toward the corridor, where he fell into the waiting arms of the hospital attendant and the handcuffs of Detective Morgan.

Seeing the intruder's wrathful expression, the nurse's eyes popped and she uttered a strangled squeak. Keeping the table between her and the Scot as he rushed to his wife, the doctor's assistant tried to escape, only to be nabbed by Dan, Jack, and Joseph when she reached the door.

Outside the room, the detective officially arrested the nurse and doctor as approximately thirty bedraggled witnesses muttered their shock and derision and as Mose yapped and growled. Inside, Michael quickly unbuckled the straps that held Anne and gathered her into his arms. His own tears flowed as she wept in his embrace. And he held her and rocked her for a long, long time as the thunder beneath his feet subsided.

Thank you, God, he said under his breath. *Thank you.*

∞

THE ORDERLY was waiting patiently in the corridor, candle sconce in hand, when Anne and Michael finally emerged from the little room.

"Everybody went to the Great Hall," the burly attendant informed them. "Your kin an' all. I'll take you."

"Thank you," Michael said with a grateful smile. "For everything." He held out his hand and added, "I'm Michael MacGregor."

The orderly shook the hand and introduced himself. "Ethan Parish, sir."

"Ethan, this is my wife, Anne."

"Thank you Ethan," she said sincerely.

The big man pulled off his tweed cap, bobbed his head, and replied shyly, "Ma'am."

Then, the attendant turned and led them through the

winding ways of the institution to a large open chamber full of chairs and tables. Meant for daytime activities and visits with relatives, the room's bank of casements on the outside wall permitted penetration of exterior light to brighten the space, while glazing along the upper half of the inside wall allowed staff to monitor patients' activities and visitor's safety from the corridor. Candlesticks had been provided to illuminate the hall for the unaccustomed evening guests, the tapers' meagre light glowing gold in the cold whiteness of the room.

"Miss Horton," Ethan called when he brought in his charges, "What happened to the doc?"

Miss Horton informed him with relish, "Some constables came and took him and Nurse Jones away to jail." She squirmed with her attempt to suppress a giggle.

Hermione and Elizabeth MacGregor, both looking exhausted, sat nearby with several nurses in a circle of plain wooden chairs. All were drinking tea. At once, Hermione forced herself up and came to Anne and Michael. "My dear, how dreadful! Are you all right?"

"Yes, Mother," said Anne. "I'm a little tired, but I'm fine."

"They didn't...?" Hermione could not say the words.

Anne assured her, "No. They didn't harm the baby. They would have, had you not come when you did."

"I'm so glad you're safe," the matron said as she hugged her daughter-in-law. Tears dotted the corners of her eyes and she dabbed them with a handkerchief as she stepped away.

"You look tired, yourself, Mother," said Michael. "Do sit down."

"No," said Anne hastily, glancing from her mother-in-law up to her husband. "There is something both of you need to know. I must speak with the detective."

∞

JOSEPH MACGREGOR stood in the far corner of the hall with

Detective Morgan and Constable Ryan, where the policemen interviewed members of the asylum's staff. Dan Doherty and the boys had disappeared, presumably to retrieve Dan's cab and to send the dog home. As the rest of the MacGregor party approached (minus Elizabeth, who remained with the nurses), Morgan dismissed the man he had been questioning and motioned toward a group of simple, sturdy chairs set round a small bare table.

"Do you know who abducted you?" the detective asked once all had seated themselves.

"Yes," said Anne. "That is to say, I know who instigated it. I only glimpsed the man who chloroformed me in the Tuscarora. He came up from behind."

"It was Kenneth Armstrong, wasn't it? The instigator," Michael presumed.

"No!" cried Hermione in horrified disbelief.

"Yes," Anne confirmed. "I heard him order the doctor to abort the baby and ensure I could never have another child."

"Bastard!" Joseph exclaimed as Hermione, in wide-eyed shock, covered her mouth with her lace-edged handkerchief.

Michael's grip tightened on his wife's hand.

Anne continued, "It seems the doctor has performed abortions before. I suspect Kenneth blackmailed him into doing his bidding."

Morgan asked, "You heard Armstrong. Did you see him?"

"No," Anne admitted. "But I did recognize his voice."

Morgan took a deep breath, clearly concerned as to the relative weight of such evidence in a court of law. He shook his head faintly, perhaps dismissing the matter until another time, and inquired further, "Do you have any idea why Mr. Armstrong would do such a thing?"

"Money," spat Joseph MacGregor with disgust. "He probably hoped he and Elizabeth could provide the only heir to my fortune, and thus secure his control of it."

Morgan nodded thoughtfully. Then, he asked, "Is there anything more you can tell us, Mrs. MacGregor?"

"There is one more matter. *Another* matter," she said. "It came to me while I was alone in that room." She leaned closer and said, "I think I've figured out the purpose of the notes in the penny novel."

Detective Morgan's eyebrows shot up. So did Michael's.

∞

IT WAS FULL DARK by the time they left The Cedars. The day staff had drifted away long since; constables had come and gone; the board of the asylum had been apprised of the arrests and its members had hastened to The Cedars to make strenuous assurances of their ignorance of Dr. Desmond's activities as well as profuse apologies to the MacGregor family. Finally, Detective Morgan had decided he could do no more here, today, and bade the Scots good night.

When the outsiders passed, the janitor cast angry glances toward them, uttering obscenities under his breath as he scrubbed the filthy floor of the lobby. The guard, on the other hand, bowed obsequiously and opened and held the large entry door for them as they stepped out into the night.

The MacGregors strolled the gravel path that led to the asylum's gates. A wind had come up, gradually drying the landscape as it snatched up the vapours of the day's downpour, leaving the air fresh.

Elizabeth sniffled as she clung to her father's arm; her parents had broken the news of her fiancé's treachery and unworthiness. At first, she refused to believe that her precious Kenneth could be a villain capable of so dastardly a plot. However, the appearance of Constable O'Toole forced her to accept the truth. Grinning triumphantly, the constable brought word to Detective Morgan in the gathering-hall of the mental institution: Kenneth Armstrong had been caught red-handed

with falsified commitment papers.

By the time O'Toole reached Justice Edwards, the judge had already signed and stamped the documents with their fake medical evidence and forged family signatures. O'Toole notified the station at once, and the constabulary immediately began the search for the lawyer. But the hunt ended quickly: Unfortunately for Armstrong, his buggy stuck in the mud on his way from the office of Justice Edwards. There, in the middle of a major intersection, Constable O'Toole himself apprehended the solicitor and confiscated his files as evidence.

"Worse luck for Mr. Armstrong, I expect the whole affair will be in the papers," the constable reported. "That young journalist—the one from the Tuscarora—was right there when I arrested the man." He added in an aside, "I think he's got a nose for news, that one. Even managed to hail a photographer of his acquaintance and got a photograph of Mr. Armstrong in handcuffs. That'll make the front page, for sure."

At that, Elizabeth had swooned.

∞

JUST OUTSIDE the gate, the MacGregors found Dan Doherty waiting for them in his hackney cab.

"There's good news and bad news," he said casually from his perch. "The bad news is Your Lordship's carriage is still stuck fast in the mud. Both of 'em." A grin spread across his face as he added, "The good news is, mine ain't." He tipped his hat to them.

After stifling a chuckle at his neighbour's opportunism, Michael suggested, "Father, why don't you take Mother and Elizabeth home? Anne and I can stay here in The Flats for the night."

"Oh, to be sure," Doherty readily confirmed. "There's many as will gladly take Himself and Herself into their home. And they've their own place, as well, o' course. Not that there's much left of it."

Elizabeth asked with some annoyance, "Why do people call you 'Himself' and 'Herself'?"

Dan volunteered the answer: "Well, that's because Herself has always taken care o' the people o' The Flats, as befits a fine lady what cares for her manor-folk. And Himself, o' course, is Herself's man. Not to mention a mite more refined than most of us as live in The Flats."

"A mite, perhaps," said Michael with a self-conscious smile. Glancing down at his mud-caked clothes by the light of the asylum's gate-lamps, he added, "Though you wouldn't think it to look at me."

"Are you sure you won't come home with us, dear?" Hermione pressed her daughter-in-law.

"This *is* my home," Anne responded. She looked up at her husband fondly and corrected, "*Our* home."

Michael grasped a loose wisp of her hair, its filaments sparking gold in the lamplight. He gently curled it behind her ear and lovingly caressed her cheek. As they gazed into each other's eyes, the other MacGregors discreetly climbed into Dan's rig and headed for Rosemont.

∞

THE ODOUR of charred wood still pervaded the area, but Anne and Michael decided to sleep under the stars on their own land rather than impose themselves upon any of their neighbours at this late hour. First, though, they picked berries and herbs, tomatoes and leafy greens from the garden, as neither had eaten since lunchtime. Thereafter, bathing—albeit cursory and in cold water—took precedence over sleep, and Anne washed her shift and stockings for the morning as Michael scrubbed his own filthy garments.

Raiding yet another hidden cache, this one in the summer kitchen, Anne produced a bottle of liquid remedy as well as a soothing ointment for her husband's healing skin. She spread the

sweetly scented oil with a gentle hand, and she inspected the remaining blisters by the light of a taper from the well-house.

Three quilts had escaped the fire (they had been hanging on the laundry line over the rearmost garden bed, behind the well-house), but only the one sheltered by the majestic oak at the fenceline had escaped the deluge. The dry blanket served as their mattress beneath the oak.

"Are you cold?" asked Michael as he lay next to his wife and pulled her close. "I'll wrap this thing around us if you like."

"I'd rather you wrap *yourself* around me," Anne replied, and she snuggled close, kissing his neck and caressing, barely touching, his back and buttocks. She added mischievously, "If you feel up to it."

He responded with kisses and caresses of his own, his body already demonstrating how "up" he was.

∞

THE TWO LAY swathed in the quilt, Michael holding Anne in his arms and gazing at the moon, its perfect half-circle occasionally dimmed by puffs of cloud. He murmured, "I knew you were in terrible trouble when the earth shook." He looked tenderly into her face and added, "My *Beira*."

"You remember," she said.

He stroked her hair and replied, "Some things."

He gazed at her awhile and then he said, "I remember that I called you that. And that you could call upon the earth to shake and call forth precious stones from the water.

"I don't understand it," he admitted. "But I know you are my *Winter Goddess*. My *Beira*."

She said softly, "And you are my sun and moon...the light in my skies and the love that warms my heart."

CHAPTER 26

Rebounds and tangents

Birds twittered and flitted, and a calf somewhere nearby lowed for its mother. The pale, cloudless sky held a greenish cast in the glow after sunrise, and the milky half-moon overhead had begun its descent toward the west. Below, in his usual routine, Old Mose marked the fences of Cedar Lane as his territory and sniffed about curiously for sign of visitors and interlopers.

Clothes still damp, Michael felt comfortably cool as he stepped out of his gate and joined the rest of the men headed for work in the early morning. Word had spread—most likely thanks to the boys, he thought—about the kidnapping and arrests of the day before. The Flats were abuzz with the news, and everyone inquired after Herself and her child, and after his poor, betrayed sister.

"Ach! It's a sad business," said Mick McGee as they

reached the river.

Pat O'Connell said philosophically, "Money is a mixed blessing, to be sure. There's always someone wants to take it from ye."

All around, nods and murmurs expressed agreement.

"Have ye thought what ye'll do about your house, there, Michael?" asked Rob Donnelly

"We haven't had a chance to discuss it," the Scot admitted. "But I was looking over the wreckage, this morning, and the foundation seems in good shape." He added, "Though I thought it might behove us to expand a little, with a baby on the way."

"An' likely many more in future," Rob grinned.

Michael blushed as chuckles rippled among the group of labourers crossing the bridge over the Bow.

∞

"MacGREGOR," SAID TREVELYAN, shaking his head, "I can't decide whether you're the luckiest or the unluckiest man I've ever met!"

"I'm not sure, myself," Michael admitted.

"How is your wife?" the Cornishman inquired.

"Well, thank you," the Scot answered. "She's taking stock of what remains of our house and resources." He added, "I feel better knowing she's among friends. And several local lads are keeping an eye on her."

"Good, good," said his employer.

It eased Michael's mind that, according to Rob Donnelly, the nightly watch that had slackened after the discovery of the body of the Irishman had been reinstituted after the fire. Three attacks in six weeks had decided the people of The Flats that the city was not as safe as it once was.

After a thoughtful pause, Jake Trevelyan clapped his hands and called to the milling men, "Let's get to work!"

Michael climbed the scaffold to see how much damage yesterday's unexpected downpour and earthquake had caused.

∞

AN UNFAMILIAR carriage rolled up the lane and stopped at the gate, drawing Anne's gaze. She smiled as Hermione and Elizabeth alighted from their hired cab.

"Welcome!" she called as she dodged around a pile of debris and approached wearing the lemon outfit from the day before.

"Oh, my dear!" Hermione cried in dismay at sight of the charred ruin. "How dreadful!"

The matron kissed her daughter-in-law on both cheeks and stepped back to stare again, eyes wide and shaking her head at the blackened framework that had once been a house.

The driver unloaded boxes Anne recognized as the clothing Hermione had bought the day before. She picked up several and fetched them to the shelter of the summer kitchen, which had survived the fire with only minor damage to a section of its shingles. Once the man had been paid and discharged, Hermione and Elizabeth followed Anne's lead and brought two large cartons each, holding them by their crossed cords. When all the packages had been safely stored out of the weather, the three stood once more before the remains of the house.

"Whatever will you do?" Elizabeth exclaimed, appalled at the mess she beheld.

"We'll rebuild," said Anne phlegmatically. Surveying the site, she mused, "A little bigger, I think. With better insulation and a new room for the baby."

She began to see it in her mind: the structure, the layout, the central masonry heater-cum-cookstove. The new house would be compact, but efficient and cosy. She smiled and nodded to herself.

"What are you smiling at?" Elizabeth asked, mystified.

Anne grinned happily and said, "I was envisioning the future. It will be perfect!"

Elizabeth cocked an eyebrow and looked dubiously from her sister-in-law to the wreckage and back. But Hermione pressed Anne's hand and said, "I'm sure it will be, dear." The matron pinched her lips together; inhaled a deep, determined breath; and declared, "We came to help. What would you like us to do?"

∞

DIVESTED OF BONNETS and jackets, jewels and dainty gloves, and wearing aprons and kerchiefs and sturdy workgloves borrowed from the elder O'Reilly women, Hermione and Elizabeth joined the ladies of the neighbourhood to carefully clear the small bits and pieces from within and around the burnt hulk. The larger timbers would be dismantled by the menfolk, later, and salvaged for whatever use the scorched wood could serve.

Anne had propped the spring-hinged gate open with a rock to make entrance and egress easy. From their gleanings, the women formed neat piles of wood chunks, graded by size, outside the fence where anyone could take what they wanted as they passed. A few children had already absconded with scraps for their private hoards, and a few more were examining the debris for choice pieces of their own. Mose sniffed about the heaps briefly, and then wandered away to find toys of the animate variety. Anne shook her head and chuckled as she watched after the mutt, wondering what he would get up to today.

The Four Horsemen sauntered into view, and Anne hailed them with a wave. As she strode to meet the boys, they jogged toward her, and all gathered in the middle of the grass-covered roadway as calico-clad adolescents Katelyn and Moire O'Shaunnessey passed, urging their family's two goats and four

sheep toward the better browsing in the Commons on Spruce.

"I have a proposal," Anne announced. "For Kevin and Rob."

"Uh-huh?" Rob responded curiously.

She preambled, "You do not have to do this, if you prefer, but I said I would ask."

The boys nodded understanding.

Anne explained the purpose and process of an interview with the journalist, stressing that they had the right to refuse to answer any question at any time, and the obligation to be as truthful as possible when they did answer.

"You don't have to mention picking pockets," she told them. "And I would advise you not to speak of that, else you might get yourselves into trouble."

She added with a stern countenance and dry tone, "And as always, I also advise you to find *legitimate* means to earn your living."

The urchins squirmed guiltily under her knowing gaze.

She glanced toward Larry and Jack, who avoided her eyes, before she smiled to Kevin and Rob once more and continued, "So, take your time to decide, and then tell me what you want to do. If you accept the proposal, I will arrange for Mr. Devereux to meet with you at a time and place of your choosing."

Rob and Kevin exchanged looks and shrugs, and Rob said, "Okay."

"Okay, yes, or okay, you'll think about it?" she queried.

Kevin asked, "Will ye come with us?"

"If you like," she responded. "In fact, I think it best that you have someone with you."

"How about us?" asked Jack, gesturing to himself and Larry.

"Why not?" she said.

"Then, we'll do it," Rob decided with an emphatic nod. "If you come, and Jack and Larry, too."

"Tomorrow?" Anne asked.

"Here, tomorrow," Rob agreed.

Larry and Jack and Kevin nodded accord. Jack said on behalf of all, "'S'okay by us."

Anne told them, "Then, I'll write a letter immediately, and you can take it to Mr. Devereux at the *Evening Star*."

∞

ANNE SENT three of the boys—Jack would not leave her—off to Front Street with a letter written on a sheet of stationery from Hermione. Along with cheese from the well-house and bottles of sweet ale salvaged from the former cold pit, she had packed newly ripened peaches, cherries, and mixed berries for the lads' bagged lunch. (By the grace of God, only a small patch of herbs near the summer kitchen and the flowers and vines edging the house had suffered from the blaze; the rest of the garden had survived.)

Anne had just come back to make a lunch for Hermione and Elizabeth and Jack, as well, when a spell of dizziness struck her. She shook her head. When her vision began to blacken, she reached out and caught someone's arm.

"Missus!" Patsy O'Reilly cried, grasping Anne and stumbling with her. "Mam!" the girl screamed.

Several hands took hold of Anne and eased her to the ground as she tried to blink away the darkness. Gradually, the vertigo eased and her sight returned. She smiled faintly up at Hermione's anxious face and made light of the matter. "That was...unexpected."

"I do wish you'd come home with us," her mother-in-law urged as she patted Anne's hand. "All of this danger and hardship has surely taken a toll. You need to rest."

To Anne's surprise, Elizabeth echoed her mother's sentiments. "Let us take care of you. You work too hard."

The eldest Mrs. O'Reilly concurred. "You do at that, Miss

Anne," she said in a motherly tone of reproof. "Ye've been shot, kidnapped, and burnt out o' your house—not to mention married and put in the family way—and that's more'n a body should have to put up with in a lifetime, much less the space of a few weeks!"

"I see your point," Anne responded with a sigh. She promised, "I will take it easy."

"Hmmph!" said old Mrs. Bannion with a wry sneer. "In a pig's eye, ye will!"

Anne shot her an abashed—and guilty—grimace.

"It's settled, then," said Hermione peremptorily. "You will come home with us when the driver returns, and I'll see that Michael knows where to find you."

Anne protested, "But I have harvesting to do. And canning and drying for the winter. And building anew. I can't just up and leave my home."

Hermione replied, "We can come back each day and help you do a *little*," she emphasized the word, "at a time."

Katie O'Reilly volunteered, "And we can help."

"Certainly," said the eldest Mrs. O'Reilly. "We can all pitch in." She quoted, "'Many hands make light work.'"

The neighbourhood women nodded and called their endorsement of the plan.

"All right," Anne acquiesced. "But I'd like to stop by Draper Avenue and tell Michael, myself. I don't want him to worry."

"Very well," said Hermione. "The carriage will return mid-afternoon. We'll ask the driver to take us by way of the construction site. In the meantime," she added firmly, "you will rest."

Anne heaved a tight-lipped sigh.

∞

THE OTHER WOMEN had gone home to feed children, finish

housework, and accomplish whatever else they needed to do during their day. Now, while harvesting lunch, Anne showed Hermione and Elizabeth around her little property as Jack stood guard at the gate.

"Is that a beehive?" asked Elizabeth incredulously, pointing to a whitewashed cube on the edge of the garden, the box shaded by raspberry and blueberry bushes.

"Yes," Anne confirmed as she plucked luscious peaches to place in her basket. "Every garden needs its pollinators. And the busy little darlings provide me with honey and wax, besides."

The three strolled on, Elizabeth nervously putting distance between herself and the hive while following her mother and sister-in-law. They picked berries and ate them on the spot; discussed the medicinal and culinary uses of various plants; and admired the beauty of the grand oak with its dense canopy, the red-dotted cherry skirted by diverse bushes speckled with the colours of their ripening fruits, the stately conifers that guarded the northern flank, and the thick hedge that held back the winds of autumn and winter.

When they had come full circle, Hermione gestured to the oblong projection jutting from the main foundation and asked, "What was there?"

"The privy," said Anne to the astonishment of her in-laws. She stepped closer and peered at the black earth within the rectangle.

Elizabeth sniffed cautiously and said, "It doesn't smell like a privy."

"Did you add lime?" asked Hermione.

"No need," said Anne, astounding her guests once more.

Unable to see anything on the surface, she fetched a long stick from the pile of kindling in the summer kitchen and returned to poke about in the bottom of the demolished outhouse.

"What are you looking for?" asked Hermione.

"Worms," said Anne.

"Worms?" Elizabeth whispered to her mother, but Anne overheard.

Straightening, Anne said, "I think some of them managed to burrow deep enough to survive the heat." She smiled cheerily, "So, I'll be able to replenish the herd when we build the new privy."

Hermione and Elizabeth exchanged glances evincing their suspicion that Anne, hatless throughout the morning, had stayed in the sun too long.

Ignoring their worried expressions, Anne explained, "Manure management is best done Nature's way. After all, Mother Nature has been doing it for a lot longer that we mere mortals have."

"Worms," Hermione repeated thoughtfully.

"Worms," Anne confirmed. "They eat the manure and turn it into black gold: excellent compost for the garden." She glanced at the contents of the box and added judiciously, "I'll dig that out and apply it before we begin construction. It may have been sterilized of the beneficial microorganisms that normally inhabit the soil, but it will provide minerals for the beds, nonetheless."

Elizabeth asked uncertainly, "Don't you mind doing such work?"

Anne replied with a shrug, "Better than sitting on my fanny doing nothing at all." She immediately regretted the flippant remark when Elizabeth blushed. Too late to take it back, though. In compensation, she added with a smile, "Besides, you'd be amazed how satisfying such activities can be."

Waxing philosophical, she said, "Maintaining a connection with Nature is a way to connect with God, the Creator of Nature."

She added pragmatically, "It's healthy exercise, as well. The trick is simply recognizing the difference between useful work and useless toil. The best way to prevent exhausting and

unnecessary labour is to think first before acting: Decide what you actually need; figure out how to let Nature do most of the work; put in the initial effort to create your system; and then enjoy the little that's left for you to do."

Elizabeth protested, "But you don't have any of the labour-saving new inventions I've seen in the catalogues and shops."

"I do not put faith in engineers and scientists," Anne replied. "They come up with elaborate schemes to outwit or dominate Nature—which they can never do. At least not for long, and not without paying a heavy price, sooner or later.

"And whenever some salesman tells me he can save me labour, I know his product is going to cost a lot of money and create some other kind of problem as yet unforeseen.

"Besides, the more of such devices you have, the more storage space you need for them."

"You sound like William Morris and the people of the Arts and Crafts movement," Hermione remarked.

"Why, thank you," said Anne brightly. "I suppose I do share some of their attitudes and beliefs."

"I like Morris prints," Elizabeth put in. "In fact, I plan to paper my room with one of his designs."

"You must show me. I'm very partial to his style, myself," Anne replied, seeing an opportunity to change the subject, mend her earlier *faux pas*, and encourage her sister-in-law. She hooked her arm with Elizabeth's as they walked toward the blanket for their picnic lunch. "Michael tells me you have a talent for needlepoint. You must show me your projects, as well."

Out of the corner of her eye, Anne saw Hermione's smile.

∞

THE AFTERNOON SUN cast stubby shadows that pointed northeastward by the time the Four Horsemen gathered at the gate. Larry handed Anne the note she had written to John

Devereux. On it, the reporter had scribbled his assurance he would come to The Flats on the morrow, midmorning.

"So," Anne told the lads, "make sure you are washed and wearing your best duds in case he brings a photographer. You want to make a good impression."

"You think he might take our picture?" Rob asked eagerly.

"He seems to be a man who understands the value of an image; so, he might," Anne answered. She added, frowning thoughtfully, "While I'm not sure of the wisdom of displaying your likenesses under these circumstances, I suppose the men who harmed you already know what you look like, anyway.

"*But*," she warned with a raised finger and elevated eyebrows, "it will certainly make many other people aware of you, as well, and force you to stay on the straight-and-narrow."

The boys' expressions took a wary turn as all pondered the ramifications of publicity. When Anne turned away and winked at Hermione and Elizabeth, the ladies stifled smiles.

∞

MICHAEL WAS on his way back from the bank of latrines at the rear of the property when he noticed the coach that had pulled up in front of the Draper worksite. He started when Anne opened the door and stepped out of the carriage to address Jake Trevelyan, the master stonemason readily identifiable by his sheaf of blueprints and commanding mien. After a brief exchange with her, Trevelyan scanned the area and, spotting Michael's approach, waved him forward.

"I'm sorry to disturb you at work," Anne apologized, "but I wanted you to know your mother has insisted I come home with her."

Hermione debarked from the cab to advise her son sternly, "I will not have Anne stay alone, with no one to notice or help if she should faint again."

"Again?" Michael repeated in alarm.

"It was nothing," Anne assured him hastily, with a dismissive gesture. "Just my body adjusting to pregnancy." With a glance to her mother-in-law, she admitted, "But I can't expect the ladies of The Flats to hover over me night and day; so, perhaps it is best that I have company, in case it should happen again."

Michael grasped her shoulders and said firmly, "Yes, you most certainly should." He pulled her close and hugged her tightly, wanting to protect her from all harm. Whoops and whistles erupted from his coworkers.

Releasing his wife, Michael watched as she climbed into the carriage. He remained at the street edge, gazing after the receding vehicle until it turned out of sight. Finally, with a sigh, he went back to work.

∞

WHEN JAKE TREVELYAN blew his whistle to end the work day, Michael gratefully brought his tools down from the top scaffold to ground level and deposited them in the shed at the rear of the property. He stretched strained muscles as he bade good night to departing colleagues who lived in The Warren (the city's repository for new immigrants) or in the more prosperous, middleclass Westdale.

He had joined the men heading for The Flats when he spied the elegant palomino and its blond rider approaching from the north and leading a grey gelding. Shaking his head and smiling, he hailed Evan.

To his friends from The Flats, Michael said, "Seems I have a ride directly to Rosemont, tonight. Please give my regrets to Dan Doherty. I'll have to make it up to him another time."

Goodbyes ensued, and the men of The Flats ambled south. When Michael waved in farewell, he caught sight of a rig parked two blocks away. He frowned as he peered at the empty

buggy, its sorrel horse and its configuration familiar. Then, he shook his head dismissively as he thought, *There are plenty of carriages and horses like Father's. He never leaves his office this early on a Tuesday.*

Michael turned and strode to meet Viscount Danford.

∞

IN THE PARLOUR, Elizabeth produced from the chiffonier a book of wallcover samples to show Anne. She leafed through the swatches, enthusing over this one and that one, waffling as to the best choice.

When her mother repaired to the kitchen to discuss the dinner menu with the cook, Elizabeth begged Anne, "Do come up to my room. It's so important to see the colours in the proper light."

"Of course," said Anne, and she allowed herself to be led by the hand up the stairs and along the carpeted corridor to her sister-in-law's bedchamber.

The room's tall casements had been left open to the summer air, screened only with white lace curtains. The heavy cream silk draperies, gathered by matching tasselled silk cords, pooled on the dark walnut floorboards visible beyond the edges of the golden knotted-pile carpet adorned with graceful vines and flowers. Above, swagged silk valances hung below a smoothly undulating plaster cornice that complemented the white-painted baseboard and window mouldings.

Crewel lace edged the snowy ruffles of the pillow and bolster casings and the linen square that topped the cream silk jacquard cover of the night table. More creamy silk upholstered the dressing-table bench and the couch, the latter's gently curved back merging into a tightly rolled end. The bed's puffy duvet and flounced skirt of cream-coloured satin shone softly in the afternoon sun.

Brass candlesticks and toiletry trays echoed the yellow

tones of the carpet, while gilt-edged porcelain containers and jewellery boxes painted with gold swirls repeated both the room's primary and secondary hues.

At the foot of the bed, a large satinwood chest had been incised with twisting intaglio designs. The honey-oak armoire and commode, the chestnut dressing table, and the cherry-wood secretary with companion chair all bore pleasingly simple lines, while the dark gleam of the walnut bedstead proclaimed it the most important furnishing in the room.

Anne surveyed the boudoir, its surfaces touched by the sun's warm glow. It cried out for something to clothe its uncomfortably naked plaster walls.

She gazed thoughtfully at the carpet and asked, "Could you show me your favourite samples again?"

Elizabeth brought the book of swatches and opened it in turn to each of the patterns that most attracted her.

"Let's place them against the walls," Anne suggested. "To see them in the actual intensity of light they would receive."

They tested the designs, one at a time and on every wall. Then, they examined them again.

Finally, Anne said, "Personally, I'd go with the artichoke pattern. The colours reflect those of the carpet in subtler shades, and the lines and curves most closely resemble those of the carpet." She looked to Elizabeth and asked, "What do you think?"

Elizabeth compared the swatches to the floor covering once more before concluding, "I think you're right. It is the best match." She whispered, "It'll be beautiful." Then, she broke into tears.

Anne quickly took the book from her sister-in-law to set it on the chest. She hugged Elizabeth and rocked her until the younger woman stepped away to blow her nose on a hankie pulled from her sleeve.

As Elizabeth settled slightly and inhaled in sniffling gasps, Anne drew her to the bed and sat her down. She perched

alongside and put an arm around the young woman's shoulders. Then, she waited.

After a long, tearful silence, Elizabeth lamented through renewed sobs, "He never loved me, did he?"

Anne gently pushed a stray wisp of brown hair behind her sister-in-law's ear and said, "Probably not." She added quickly, "But that does not mean you are unlovable. It just means he was the wrong man."

"But there are no other men," Elizabeth wailed. "And I am over thirty."

Anne suppressed a chuckle and said, "I am a lot older than that. And do you mean to tell me that, in a city with a population of nearly two hundred thousand, at least half of them male, you think there is no possibility for a woman as pretty as you to find a husband?"

Elizabeth blinked at her, taken aback. She stammered, "But—but—"

She glanced about as if the words (or perhaps the man) she sought might be lying on the carpet.

Recognizing her sister-in-law's concern, Anne said, "Just because you have met few candidates in your parents' social circle does not mean they do not exist somewhere else." She advised, "Don't limit yourself to rich men. Finding a good one is more important."

Elizabeth blinked at her again and swallowed. Then, she blew her nose once more. Finally, her robin's-egg blue eyes round and childlike, she asked in a tiny voice, "Do you think I could ever find someone who would love me the way Michael loves you?"

Anne cupped Elizabeth's face in her hands and gazed into the younger woman's eyes. She said firmly, "Yes, I do."

∞

IN HIS SMALLCLOTHES, as Anne called them, Michael stood

stock-still in the middle of the drawing-room of Hampton House while the tailor wrapped the graduated tape around his chest, then around his waist, then around his neck. After several more horizontal measurements—and some clucking at the expansion of Michael's shoulders, biceps, and thighs—the tidy little man moved on to the more stable vertical dimensions. When he had finished, he stepped back and eyed Michael critically, his lips pursed and his head tilting back and forth as he surveyed the Scot from toe to crown and back.

"Grey, I think," Antonio Abruzzi said aloud to himself in his thickly Italian accent. "And blue. Not brown, no. Unless—"

His eyes widened and lit with inspiration as he exclaimed, "The new bolts from Roma! I think there is one that would match the bronze of your skin. Bellissimo!"

With that, the tailor pivoted on his heel, scooped up his samples from the plush settee, and rushed away in a flurry of tape and fine woollen fabrics.

Rising from his gold damask-covered *bergère* beside the marble fireplace, wineglass in hand, Evan commented, "You always bring out the best in Signore Abruzzi. He enjoys dressing you."

Michael refrained from replying that Evan enjoyed the view of him half-naked. He now remembered with discomfort the many times his friend had accompanied him to his fittings. But he also remembered something else....

∞

England, 1879

MICHAEL MacGREGOR raced across the moonlit quadrangle and into the rear door of Pritchard Hall. Trembling from weariness and impotent rage, he climbed the stairs toward his room. When he exited the stairwell, however, he saw his door ajar and a light shining within.

He stood a long moment, unable to bear the thought of

what awaited him there, but uncertain what to do. He reached out to brace himself against the wall, suddenly feeling too weak to support his own weight.

A memory came to him: the young man, Evan, whom he had met last year. They attended different classes and rarely crossed paths, but the lad was always friendly toward him, unlike many others. And Michael knew where his room lay.

It was a desperate plan, but it was the only one he had.

He crept back into the stairwell and headed for Danford Hall.

DID HE DARE knock at this hour? He tried the knob, instead, and found the door unlocked. He supposed Lord Danford felt secure enough to forgo locks and keys, unlike himself. *Not that locks do me much good,* he thought angrily. Slowly, carefully, he pushed the door inward and peered around it.

The full moon illuminated the chamber brightly, bringing lighter objects into sharp relief against the dark floor and furnishings and the panelled walls. As he remembered, the lad kept a messy desk and tossed his garments about carelessly.

A lump in the bed stirred and then settled.

Michael swallowed. Then, plucking up his courage, he slipped inside and quietly closed the door. After another moment's hesitation, he stepped to the bedside rug and lay down upon the floor. Hard and cold though it was, it seemed far preferable to the alternative.

He closed his eyes.

MICHAEL WOKE sweating and panting. He looked down. Though he could not see the evidence in the shadows by the bedstead, he knew he had wet himself. It invariably happened when he dreamt that particular dream: a ring of purple crystal that he held in his hand and placed on the finger of a woman. At least, he *thought* it was a woman, though he never saw her clearly. What he recalled, always, was the ring and the erotic

feelings it evoked.

He lay back on the rug and closed his eyes, seeing that strange stone circlet in his mind. And as always when he pictured it, he hardened and throbbed again. He opened his flies and stroked himself, wondering why that image affected him so. Soon, he lost himself in that lovely gem and in sensations real and imagined.

Despite his attempt to be silent, a moan escaped him as he spilt himself once more. Still breathing tremulously, he opened his eyes to find, above, a shadowed face looming over the side of the bed.

He started. "Jesus!"

As he calmed himself, remembering where he was, he stammered, "Uh-uh—s-sorry, Evan. I-I-"

"No need to explain," said the lad. "We all do it." He added drily, "Though we usually do it in our own room. You aren't lost again, are you?"

"I, uh, couldn't go to my room, tonight," Michael replied lamely. "And I couldn't think where else to go. I figured I'd sleep here and leave before you woke." Apologetically, he said, "I'm sorry I disturbed you. I'll just...just go."

"Don't be silly," said Evan. "You're here. You might as well stay. Why don't you get into the bed? It's big enough for us both, if not comfortably so."

"I'm all right here," Michael protested.

"Nonsense," Evan retorted. In a fatherly tone, he commanded, "Come and get under the blankets before you catch your death." He held up the duvet and sheets in invitation.

After a moment's vacillation, Michael pulled off his shoes and climbed into the bed as Evan shifted to the other side.

"Thank you," the Scot whispered when they had both settled.

"Good night," Evan whispered back.

WHILE EVERYONE else went to breakfast, Michael sneaked

back into Pritchard Hall and, to his relief, found his room vacant. He washed and changed and gathered his books and pens, and then he headed for his first class of the day. On his way along the crowded corridors, he smiled to himself in gratitude for the kind young viscount who had asked no questions, but merely offered the comfort of his room to a stranger.

AS HE PASSED Evan in the study hall, Michael smiled appreciatively and nodded his thanks once more. Then, he slid into one of the empty seats by the window and opened his book to begin his assignments. Other students found the exterior walls too chilly to work comfortably, but Michael did not mind the cold even in winter. He sought the brightness of the daylight that streamed through the diamond-paned casements even on cloudy days. In truth, he also preferred the sense of solitude he found at the table where no one else worked.

Suddenly, a shiver ran up his spine, one that had nothing to do with the temperature of the air. A hand came to rest below his back with all too much familiarity, and Professor Goddard hissed angrily at his ear, "Where were you last night?"

"Michael!"

Startled, Michael looked up to find Evan Sydenham coming to sit beside him. The junior professor straightened and stepped back a pace as the young viscount noisily plopped his books and papers on the dusky old table that shone with years of wax polish. The lad subsided onto the next stool with a deep sigh. Then, to Michael's surprise, Evan turned to place one graceful hand on his and said, "Thank you for helping me, last night."

Lord Danford leaned closer and, briefly squeezing Michael's hand before releasing it, said, "It was most enlightening. I do hope you'll help me again, dear boy. I'm afraid mathematics is not my forte."

The professor pivoted and stalked away.

When the man was out of earshot, Michael whispered

gratefully, "Thanks."

"Never did like that man," Evan whispered back. He opened his own book and chose one of his pens.

After that day, Evan always sat by the windows with him. And the remainder of Michael's final year in boarding-school was the most peaceful he had known since he had come to England.

∞

Present day

SAMUEL APPEARED from nowhere to replenish Evan's goblet. Michael wondered where the Hampton House footman hid himself, for there were no alcoves in the spacious drawing-room filled with comfortable chairs and couches hemmed by wainscoted walls crowded with painted landscapes and still lifes in the styles of the Old Masters. (The consul's residence was an homage to the Old Country and the old ways. Only the dining-room had been decorated with the vibrant works of Canadian artists in a tip of the hat to the young nation.)

As he quickly donned his outer garments, Michael inquired, "What do you think of this newspaper connection?"

"Coded messages in the gazettes?" Evan responded to the diversion. "Very likely. Though deciphering them could be a problem if we do not even know which section might contain the cryptogram. Nonetheless, I've passed on the information and my contact will look into it."

"When will Skavronsky leave?" Michael wondered.

"A week Friday," Evan answered. "And he's taken the bait."

Michael said, "He knows about the stone."

"A meeting has been arranged for tomorrow."

Michael exhaled slowly. He said, "Thank you, Evan." He gazed into his friend's eyes and added meaningfully, "For everything."

Viscount Danford regarded him a moment. Then, he smiled faintly and lifted his glass as he replied softly, "You are most welcome, dear boy."

∞

UNLIKE HARRIS, whom Michael had passed as he entered his father's house, the chambermaid's eyes flew wide at the bulge under Michael's trousers. But like the butler, she instantly averted her gaze. After a brief and abashed curtsy, the freckled and reddened young woman hurried from the bedroom and left the couple alone.

Anne was only partially dressed, readying for the late supper (the evening meal was always postponed on Tuesdays and Wednesdays when Joseph MacGregor stayed in town until well past six o'clock), and Michael did not bother to do more than unbutton his own flies. At once, he kissed her crystal wedding band—the violet circle he had never replaced—and abruptly pressed her against a clear space on the wall. He lifted her underskirts and, after a few moments of nibbling her earlobes and fondling her lower lips to open and wet her, he inserted himself and took her with the same fierce ardency that had seized him at sight of her ring on their wedding day.

After the official ceremony, he had made love to her in a broom cupboard, the only unlocked and unoccupied room he could find in the public building. He had shoved several mops into a corner, pressed her against the wall, lifted and pierced her as she had encircled him with both legs and arms.

Now, as then, he thrust ever deeper, carried away by his desires. Now, as then, she urged him not to stop. Now, as then, he obliged until she finished in a shudder and a moan, precipitating his own climax. And now, as then, gripping her buttocks, he stood panting with his wife as the last spasms emptied him, and he thanked God that he was a man.

CHAPTER 27

Moving on

J oseph brought home a copy of the *Evening Star* as well as his usual *Daily Globe*. Surrounded by advertisements on the front page of the *Star*, a photograph of Kenneth Armstrong—in handcuffs and flanked by two constables—bore the headline: CAUGHT IN THE ACT! The story of the kidnapping, attempted abortion, rescue, and subsequent arrests was told in lurid detail next to an ongoing account of the plight of striking mill workers, both articles continuing on the next page. Brief reports of the earthquake and storm turned up on page three.

After supper, by the drawing-room fireplace with its smoothly carved oak mantel and gleaming brass screen, the MacGregor patriarch sat in his favourite wing chair and read aloud the article pertaining to his family.

"The scandal is all anyone will talk about for months," Elizabeth whined as, nearby, she resumed her needlework.

"Oh, I wouldn't be too sure about that," said Anne from her perch next to her husband on the sofa by the windows. "With all this labour unrest, and no less than eight dailies competing with one another for readership, I expect there will soon be another scandal to eclipse this one."

"Well, yes, but...." Letting the words trail, Elizabeth sighed and sulked.

Anne guessed, "You mean that everyone at the Yacht Club will continue the gossip."

Elizabeth grimaced and heaved another sigh in confirmation.

"Don't fret," Anne responded, taking Michael's hand and smiling up at him. "You never know where you'll meet the right man." Fixing her husband's gaze, she grinned and said, "It could even be in a filthy alley in the middle of the night."

He brought her hand to his lips and kissed it. "Luckiest night of my life," he said.

From their chairs by the fireside, Joseph and Hermione exchanged smiles. Elizabeth sighed wistfully and threaded another colour onto her needle.

∞

MICHAEL HAD LEFT word with the staff to see that he woke before sunrise, as they did. In the event, he rose on his own, wakened by the brightening dawn twilight through the open window. To the surprise of the servants, he and Anne joined them for a breakfast of simple oat porridge and fruit fresh from the orchard. When they finished, Anne fetched more fruit while Michael made his own sandwiches, wrapped them in waxed paper, and stuffed them into a muslin sack alongside a flask of water.

After topping up his lunch bag with her harvest, Anne kissed her husband goodbye and watched from the lane as he rode off on Evan's grey. When he had turned into the road and

disappeared from sight, she walked back to the kitchen to arrange an early breakfast for Hermione and Elizabeth. If her in-laws insisted on keeping her close, they would have to keep up with her.

∞

THE FAMILY COACH and Joseph's buggy had been rescued from the mud and returned for cleaning and repair, but although the grooms and driver had worked well into the night, the coach's rear axle still needed replacement. And so, the three MacGregor women once more hired a hackney cab to take them to The Flats.

Today, Hermione and Elizabeth wore more practical garments: their simplest, oldest dresses; straw hats; aprons borrowed from their maids; and sturdy gardening gloves. They even stopped to purchase flat-soled shoes on the way. To the shock of the shop's proprietor, Anne chose sandals from the men's stock. Becoming accustomed to her daughter-in-law's idiosyncrasies, Hermione took the matter in stride.

When the cab pulled in front of the gate, all three women gaped as they disembarked. The house was gone: Not a sign of it remained except the stones of the foundation and plinth that traced its outline.

Mr. Tighe, one of the resident in-laws of the O'Reilly household, hobbled toward them, supporting himself on his thick, dark cane. Smirking smugly, he said, "Thought ye'd be starin' at that great heap o' cinders for a while yet, eh?"

"However did you get it down and cleared so quickly?" Anne asked, amazed.

"'Twas O'Connell an' Villeneuve come up wi' the idea," he said. "'Jus' take out the load-bearin' timbers,' says they." He added in a confidential tone, "'Course, 'tweren't near so easy as it sounded. Donnelly damn near got hisself crushed."

"Is everyone all right?" Anne gasped in alarm.

Mr. Tighe waved a hand and puffed dismissively. "Oh, aye," he assured her. "All's well. Donnelly just got hisself a good scare is all. Make 'im a mite less careless in future, I expect."

Noting how the man leaned on his stick, Anne asked, "And how's the leg, Mr. Tighe?"

"Ach!" he waved again. "Just acts up a bit when the weather's turnin'. Don't fret yourself."

Anne made a mental note to send home with Jack a bottle of remedy. She did not ask where the timbers went; she was sure they would be put to good use.

∞

THE MISSES O'REILLY happily joined the MacGregor women to harvest and clean, slice, and lay out the bounty of the little property for drying in the glazed contraption Anne had rigged for the purpose. It had been stored in a shed over winter, and retrieved and used recently by the O'Reilly and O'Shaunnessey families. Now, it was hauled to squat in the middle of the vacant space left by the destruction of her house, there to glory in the sunlight all day, with nothing to obstruct the solar rays that powered convection airflow through its black-painted interior.

"Oh, it's been workin' fine, Missus," said Katie as she slid a tray screened with sturdy netting and topped with bush cranberries and mulberries into the rear chamber of the device. "We dried more'n a peck o' currants and the same o' blueberries last week."

"Good," said Anne. "Until construction starts on the house, I think we should leave it here and everyone can use it as they need." She thought a moment before she added, "Once we begin to build, we could, perhaps, put it in the Commons. By then, the sward will be grazed to the nub, so there will be no worry about animals getting into it."

"Except raccoons," Patsy pointed out. "The little buggers can unhitch the door."

"That's one of the reasons to empty it before nightfall," Anne reminded her. She looked to Hermione as she added, "The other being that an overnight rain could spoil the batch."

"Does it have some sort of fan?" asked Elizabeth as she searched for evidence of mechanical parts.

"No need," said Anne. "The sun and Nature do the work."

She pointed to the screened opening at the bottom front and explained, "Fresh air is drawn in here by the heating of the air along the chute."

Gesturing up the inclined inky channel under the glazing, to the top of the device, she continued, "Which rises to flow into the body of the dryer."

Anne stepped around to the back, where a tall, vertically oriented box abutted the sloped section in front. She finished, "And down through the food, cooling as it goes to this exit." She pointed to another screened opening, this in the rear wall below the door that allowed access to the column of trays on horizontal runners.

"How simple!" Hermione exclaimed in admiration. "Wherever do you get these ideas, my dear?"

Anne admitted, "They are not all my own. Many have been used for centuries in other lands, other cultures."

"Like the little stoves," Patsy knew. "The ones that ladies in," she said the word slowly and carefully, "Brah-mah-poo-trah make."

Nodding, Anne specified, "Except, they make theirs in the ground, while I've created mine in clay so that I can stand while I use them."

"Have you been to India, my dear?" asked Hermione.

"No," Anne answered. "But I knew someone who had been." She added, "I take knowledge where I can find it."

Just then, the Four Horsemen arrived, all of them washed, combed, and wearing their cleanest trousers and shirts. They had even buffed their shoes to a dull, mottled shine.

"How handsome you look," Anne greeted them, smiling.

The boys responded to the praise with shy grins and squirming.

Katie warned, "Don't be swellin' their heads, Missus." She slipped behind her cousin and playfully grasped Jack's pate with both hands as she said, "They're big enough as it is."

Jack wriggled out of her grasp and tried to muss her hair in return. A small scuffle punctuated by shrill squeals and giggles ensued.

"Oy!" Larry called. "There 'e is!"

Everyone looked to see John Devereux and a companion arriving by hackney. Jack quickly pressed down his hair, and Katie straightened her dress and apron.

∞

ANNE SAT ON the ground under the shade of the crabapple tree that had grown spontaneously next to the small cluster of pines and spruces in the southwest corner of her lot. Her crossed legs spread her skirt and apron to form a nest in which washed peaches waited to be peeled and sliced. She deftly cut wedges, leaning forward to allow the sweet juice that dribbled along her hands and wrists to fall into the large, white-enamelled bowl that held the chunks. The pits and peels, she tossed into another, smaller, wooden bowl. Eventually, the seeds would be planted somewhere in The Flats.

From her position, Anne could see and hear the boys and Devereux. More importantly, the lads could see her and know she was there, should they need her advice or assistance. Or just a sense that they were protected.

The photographer, a Mr. Benjamin Ogden, took a picture of the four boys and the O'Reilly sisters standing under the shade of the oak, the composition lending to the portrait both a familial and a bucolic air at odds with common Dickensian notions about the worth of disadvantaged children. As the interview

progressed, Mr. Ogden strolled the lane, occasionally stopping to take another photo of something or someone. Anne noticed, though, that he often glanced toward Elizabeth, who hovered within earshot of the boys and their interlocutor.

Anne watched her sister-in-law pretend to pick berries while she listened intently to Rob and Kevin as they described their horrifying ordeal at the hands of strange men in an alley. Tears flowed down Elizabeth's cheeks, mirroring those of the boys. At one point, she turned away, dropped the basket of fruit, and disappeared among the bushes. In a little while, she returned, eyes red and swollen, wiping her mouth with a handkerchief. Seeing Anne, she strode directly to her brother's wife and sat down at her side.

"I didn't know," Elizabeth whispered remorsefully through renewed sobs. "All this time, I just thought he was spoiled because Father doted on him." She wept bitterly.

After a time, she gazed into Anne's eyes, her own plaintive, and asked, "How could we have known?"

Not waiting for an answer, she looked away, eyes downcast, and continued, "And how could he have borne it? To be...to endure such a thing and be unable to tell anyone? To have lived with the shame all these years?" She broke down again.

"I treated him so badly," she whispered, her shoulders slumping under the burden of guilt and her own shame as she continued to cry.

Patsy came to fetch the bowl of peach pieces. She glanced uncertainly to Elizabeth and then to Anne. When Anne shook her head solemnly to indicate there was nothing the girl could do to help, Patsy left quietly with the fruit, the knife, and the pits.

Keeping her sticky hands out of the way, Anne sat up and put her arms around her sister-in-law's shoulders as the younger woman shed tears of regret and sympathetic anguish for her brother. Soon, Hermione joined them and took over the comforting of her daughter.

∞

THE O'REILLY and Donnelly families provided a feast for lunch. A half-dozen chattering ladies spread blankets; deposited baskets; laid out plates and cutlery and mugs; opened bottles of sweet ale and fruit wine; and passed around platters of cooked meats, cheese, and boiled eggs, along with bowls of fruit, salad herbs, and homemade dressings.

Anne smiled and winked at Hermione when Mr. Ogden inserted himself between Elizabeth and the eldest Mrs. O'Reilly. The young man, suited in light-brown twill that closely matched his tightly waved, chestnut hair, extended his hand to Miss MacGregor and introduced himself politely. He spoke well, evincing education, as he asked her questions and described his work at her urging. Not handsome, yet attractive, with slightly crooked nose that had probably once been broken, and with soft blue eyes, the photographer smiled at Elizabeth with warmth and conversed with enthusiasm that augured courtship. Again, Anne and Hermione exchanged pleased smiles.

Across the colourful patchwork quilts, the four young lads clustered together. Their shared tears had dried and their spirits had revived. Now, they wolfed down their meal as though they had not eaten in days and expected never to eat again. The dowager Mrs. O'Reilly cocked an eyebrow and shook her head; she had seen more than her share of growing adolescents consume enough to choke the average adult.

The reporter, bracketed by the eagerly attentive Misses O'Reilly, called to Anne, "Mrs. MacGregor."

"Yes, Mr. Devereux?" Anne replied with raised eyebrows.

"I was wonderin' if I might have a word with ye," he said, his accent thickened by the day's association with so many Irish immigrants. He added, "After lunch, o' course."

"Of course," she responded, and she speared a bite-sized strawberry with her fork.

∞

A LEOPARD FROG hopped by, golden-brown and dark-spotted against the green of the herbage, the two yellow folds that ran along the length of its back glinting in the sun as it fled. Above, a bluebird, its reddish-brown breast and white belly visible from below, called a melodious *turee* as it banked toward the north. Across the street, the bright yellow of a goldfinch flashed among the white-barked birch trees clumped near the spreading maple at the edge of the Bannions' yard.

Anne opened her gate and walked through; John Devereux followed. As they strolled slowly along the lane, cicadas shrilled in the afternoon heat that intensified some odours and suppressed others.

"What would you like to know?" she asked.

He said, "First, I'd like to say that you were right: The boys have recovered remarkably from what was clearly a hellish experience. Having the support o' family—or, in this case, good friends—seems to have played a vital part in that recovery."

"Vital indeed," said Anne.

The reporter drew a long breath. Abruptly, he inquired, "What is it like to be with a man who's...who's...?" Words failed him.

"Who has been with men?" she finished for him. "Is that what you want to know?" She did not ask whether the question was posed purely for his personal enlightenment.

"Yes," he admitted uncomfortably.

"You are, of course, assuming I have a basis for comparison."

"I heard you had been married before."

"Yes, I was." She had no intention of going into the details of *that* subject.

Anne thought a moment, stepping around a recently deposited cow-pie glittering with the green and blue iridescence of flies in the sunlight. Finally, gazing to the horizon, she said, "I

cannot know what my husband experienced or what he feels. But I can tell you that he has suffered from nightmares much of his life and that they have grown fewer, and less intense, since we married.

"I can also tell you, from my own experience, that he is as lusty a man and as good a lover as any I have known."

Stopping and turning to face Devereux, she looked into the reporter's eyes and said with certainty, "And he loves me."

They stood, eyes locked. At last, the young man nodded. "Thank you," he said softly.

When they wheeled across the street and headed back toward Number 10, Anne and Devereux found the Four Horsemen shadowing them. Anne stifled a grin.

"Seems we've been chaperoned," said the reporter with amusement.

"They're very protective," Anne acknowledged, adding, "It's a common trait in a close-knit neighbourhood like this one."

Devereux asked curiously, "Is that why you live here? When you could live anywhere you choose?"

Anne cocked an eyebrow and regarded the man. He had been digging, she realized. She said simply, "I like it here. These are good people."

They walked through the gate as Jack held it open for them.

∞

AS MESSRS. DEVEREUX and Ogden prepared to leave in Ian Farrell's cab, the photographer disengaging from his conversation with Elizabeth most reluctantly, Anne spotted a familiar form loping along the lane.

"What are you doing home so early?" she asked as she ran to meet Michael. "Not that I'm complaining," she added quickly as she threw her arms around him.

Her husband lifted her from the ground and kissed her

long and deeply. Finally, he set her down and, with a brief buss, announced, "I'm fired."

Anne's eyes flew wide. She blinked and gaped incredulously. Then, her expression transformed to one of perplexity when Michael's lips spread into a broad smile.

Finally, her husband explained, "It seems my father has had a little talk with Jake Trevelyan."

As the hackney rumbled by, Michael pulled Anne to him again, one hand cupping her head and the other arm reaching around her waist. Planting a foot forward for balance, he drew her backwards and he bent to kiss her as though he had not seen her in years.

Supine, Anne let her arms fall back as she entrusted herself to his and gave herself up to his kiss.

∞

ANNE AND MICHAEL packed Elizabeth and Hermione into Dan Doherty's carriage and sent them on ahead with a promise to come to Stuart Avenue in time for supper with the family. The O'Reillys and the boys retreated hastily upon Michael's homecoming, with a pledge from the Misses O'Reilly to return before dark to package the fruit currently drying in the black box.

"They know us well," Anne commented as the neighbours scattered unbidden.

"Mmm," Michael concurred as he nibbled her ear and brazenly fondled her behind, pressing her against him.

"Isn't this a little public even for us?" she protested as he nuzzled her neck and set her hips rocking. She moaned breathlessly at his caresses.

"I guess we'd better go inside," he agreed reluctantly. But he made no immediate effort in that direction. Finally, after licking her neck sensuously to elicit another groan of pleasure from his wife, he asked, "Is there room in the well-house?"

"We'll see," she replied, and she moaned once more as he

kissed her neck ever so lightly from shoulder to ear.

∞

THE LITTLE HUT proved less convenient than hoped. Laden shelves lined all the walls, and the off-centre pump, its long handle and curved spout at unfortunate heights, left little floor space for the MacGregors' purpose. After a cursory inspection, Michael closed the door and pressed Anne against it.

When he lifted her skirts and touched her nether lips, to his delight he found her already wet and receptive. She helped him unbutton his flies and he quickly penetrated her.

"Ow!" he cried, and he clutched his head, pulling away abruptly. "Damn! I hit the lintel," he said crossly, with a minatory glare at the offending beam.

Anne surveyed the well-house again as Michael rubbed his pate. "Sit," she commanded, pointing to the floor.

Michael regarded the pine boards dubiously, but squatted and positioned himself as best he could. First, he set his back to the wall, his crown barely beneath the lowest shelf, but that left no room for Anne's legs. When he moved out into the open, there was little space for his own long limbs, what with the diminutive dimensions of the shed and the assorted paraphernalia piled in its corners. Not only was he forced to bend his knees, but his trousers, strategically dropped for vertical pursuits, now constrained his movement.

After tossing tubs and pails outside and hurriedly unlacing and removing his shoes, Michael roughly tugged off his pants and stuffed them under his backside as he arranged himself once more. He sighed; it was not ideal, but it would have to do. At least he could move freely.

When he looked up to beckon her, Anne stepped astride him and lowered herself, taking to her knees and manoeuvring to slide over him. But to his annoyance and embarrassment, he had begun to soften.

Undeterred, Anne rubbed herself against him and gazed into his eyes with that look, that hunger that so enthralled him. He hastily unbuttoned her blouse and pulled at her garments until he had freed her breasts, their flesh swollen and warm and their nipples and areolae grown a darker pink with pregnancy.

Her breath came short at his touch and she cupped his head, urging him on when he bent and teased her nipples with his tongue. He was throbbing, now, but he wanted more than a "quickie," as she described their more expeditious copulations.

She rose on her knees and reached down to grasp him. He allowed her to sheathe him, enjoying her heat and her tightness as she slid onto his phallus, but he gripped her waist and prevented her attempts to ride him. Instead, he rocked his hips, slowly, pushing himself inside her as he watched her face. Her eyes closed, and she savoured the sensations, as he did, but with an urgency that he suddenly found exciting. He wanted to tantalize her, and the thought set his balls aching with need. He stopped.

Anne opened her eyes. "What are you doing?" she demanded.

"Come," he commanded hoarsely as he pushed her back and off of him so that he could attend to her breasts once again.

"Michael, please," she whispered, catching her breath as he stroked her gently.

"Turn around," he said. "On your knees."

She obeyed, and he lifted her skirts to bare her buttocks. She never wore bloomers, and it pleased him that she was always accessible. To him.

"Oh, lord!" she breathed when he tickled her pudenda. "Now, please!"

He rose to his knees and inched inside her, incrementally, relishing the thrills that shot through him with her every motion as she rotated her hips to entice him. When he had plumbed her depths fully, he eased himself into a slow, steady rhythm.

Her little noises became more desperate and he found it

increasingly difficult to hold back. But he restrained himself and slowed even more.

"No!" she cried.

He chuckled. Part of him wanted to give her mercy; part of him did not.

"You bastard!" she swore.

"Tch, tch," he clucked, stopping entirely. "Is that a way to talk to your husband?

"Damn you!" she said, angry now.

He moved again, his thrusts glacial.

A moment later, she pleaded impatiently, "Please."

"Well," he responded with exaggerated reluctance. "If you ask nicely."

"Please," she repeated softly, and the supplication in her tone stabbed him: It echoed of his own, long ago.

"Oh, God!" he groaned. His voice desolate, he said, "I'm so sorry, Anne."

How could he do to her what they had done to him? Closing his eyes against sudden, contrite tears, he withdrew and murmured, "I don't deserve you."

Anne turned around to stare at him, her expression perplexed, then distraught. He had sunk to his haunches. She scrambled forward to embrace him, and she clasped him to kiss his face...his eyes...his mouth.

"Please tell me, my love," she urged.

"It's—" he started, but shook his head, too ashamed to speak the truth. He squeezed his eyes tightly and tears rolled down his cheeks. He repeated in a whisper, "I don't deserve you."

"How can you say such a thing?" she demanded.

He all but shouted, "You don't understand!" He closed his eyes again and curled his hands into fists, trembling in the struggle to rein himself.

"Then, tell me, please," she implored quietly. "Please let me help." She pulled his head to her breast and stroked his hair,

rocking him as she would a child.

Michael put his arms around her and clung to her as if she were a lifeline in a gale. For that was how he felt: adrift in a storm of conflicting emotions and desires, some of which he did not want to own. Yet they were his, and he cried out in frustration and rage at the confusion within him.

Anne simply held him and kissed him, murmuring softly and stroking his hair. After a long while, he relaxed into a kind of dull stupor, exhausted to insensibility.

Sitting back, Anne cupped his face in her palms and asked in a low, gentle voice, "Can you tell me now?"

He looked up into her eyes, his own filling again. His whisper bleak with humiliation, he admitted, "He made me beg."

He instantly closed his eyes, unable to bear hers lest he find there the very shame and revulsion he felt.

To his astonishment and dismay, she guessed, "And you wanted to make me beg."

He stared at her a brief moment, then quickly glanced away. He muttered, "You should leave me."

"Bullshit!"

He gaped at her once more, this time bewildered and at a loss to respond to her anger.

"Bullshit!" she repeated. "I will not leave you!"

He protested, "But I can't help myself. I wanted to...to...."

"I know," she said softly. She took a deep breath, fixed his eyes, and asked, "Do you think no one else has such feelings? Thoughts they would rather no one knew? Thoughts they'd rather not have?"

He frowned, and swallowed, considering her words.

Anne told him, "Most people have fantasies of one sort or another. Many feel embarrassed by or even ashamed of some of them."

Michael insisted, "I don't want to treat you the way they treated me." He bowed his head. "But...."

"But such fantasies can be exciting," she finished for him.

He glanced up at her and then away, not sure whether her knowing was a comfort or a further dishonour.

She clasped him to her again and kissed his head. "Oh, Michael," she said, "I love you."

He simply held her, accepting the solace of her embrace. Gradually, he became aware that her strokes and kisses of comfort had altered to sensual caresses. He looked up into her face and saw, once more, that hunger he had recognized earlier.

Her whispered "Please" instantly brought back his lust, and he scooped her into his arms. Forcing his mind and its baffling contradictions away, he let his body's needs come to the fore. Hands and tongue demanding, he explored her, owning her, and revelling in that intimate possession.

Lifting her as he pushed up onto his knees, he commanded, "Turn around."

When she did, he impaled her abruptly and she gasped. Keeping her pinned, he leaned back on his haunches and pulled her upright, her back arched, to caress her proud breasts. Slowly, he began to thrust, just a little.

Again, she whispered, "Please, Michael."

With a kiss to her temple, he rose onto his knees in the little hut, leaning over her, his front to her back, and he finally gave her what they both needed.

∞

OUTSIDE, as the neighbours sat down to their dinners, Anne and Michael stood together, back to front, he with his arms around her and chin resting on her head, she grasping his forearms. They gazed at the emptiness that had once been their home.

"What will you do now? Anne wondered.

"Father wants me to work with him. Now. Tomorrow," he said.

"Do you want to?" she asked.

He thought a moment before he replied, "I think I do." He

added, "I always expected to, sooner or later. But now that it comes to it, I know I want to help him."

"Good," said Anne. "It's important to do what makes you happy."

"And you?" he asked. "Are you happy?"

"Yes." She turned her head and leaned back so that she could look up into his face. "Yes," she repeated, her smile tender.

He smiled, too, in joy.

CHAPTER 28

The price of eggs

Dan Doherty happily drove Herself to Rosemont, with Himself riding the grey alongside. In the city, the driver whistled gay Irish melodies, reverting to a low hum when Michael stopped to buy a copy of the *Evening Star* from a lad on Bay Street. When they reached the outskirts of town, the cabbie belted out bawdy ballads as Anne giggled and Michael joined in, his baritone harmonizing with Doherty's tenor. Occasionally, as they passed, a farmer or groundskeeper glared or grinned, but most out this way lived well off the road among cultivated trees and an assortment of outbuildings.

At Hampton House, Anne remained with the hackney carriage under the *porte-cochère* while Michael reined the grey gelding around to the stables. As expected, Evan met him there, wineglass in hand, sauntering from the manor house to the long outbuilding with his usual insouciant air.

"I hear you'll be joining your father at the distillery," said the viscount.

"How did you hear so soon?" Michael demanded, astounded that his personal business should already be public knowledge.

"I hear everything, dear boy," Evan replied with a smirk. He added, "You're not the only one with friends in low places."

"Speaking of persons in low places...." Michael said with a significant look as they started back toward the mansion. He waited as they walked, knowing his friend would not reply until they were alone.

When they were out of earshot of the stable hands, Evan announced, "The sale has taken place and money has been exchanged. Notes, that is."

"Already? How much did it go for?"

"The final price was two and a half million francs," said Evan.

Michael whistled in surprise. He had not realized the gem was that valuable.

The viscount added, "It probably could have fetched more, given that the collector is nouveau riche—and *very* riche at that—but the Russian was so anxious he capitulated by early afternoon."

"I take it your friend demanded a finder's fee?"

"He settled for five percent. I'm told Von Ratzenhausen got fifteen."

"Leaving more than enough to hire several assassins."

"Indeed," said Evan. "I expect it's meant to buy the help, or at least the inaction, of a few key generals, as well."

Michael asked hesitantly, "What was Skavronsky told about the finding of the stone?"

Evan grinned, "Perhaps that's the best part. He thought exactly as we expected: that your wife found it and sold it for a pittance. Apparently, it seemed to tickle him that he was taking it from you, especially when told you've fallen on hard times."

"It would," Michael said through his teeth.

"Indeed," Evan remarked. "He is almost as obsessed with you as Professor Giles."

Michael glanced to him sharply. He had never told Evan of his experiences at school, though he realized his friend had certainly heard the rumours. He wondered if the viscount considered his own feelings a perverse obsession.

They rounded the boxwood hedge, slipping through a narrow, white-arched gate, and they strolled the private garden next to the house. Michael breathed deeply of the floral perfume as he quelled the rage that had risen at the knowledge of Skavronsky's triumph, false and fleeting though it might be.

At last, as they reached the terrace where he and Anne had dined with the viscount, Michael inquired, "What next?"

Evan said, "The Tsar's agent has witnessed the deal made for the sapphire."

When Michael raised both eyebrows in query, the viscount explained with an amused smile, "The negotiations took place in a house of ill repute with a rather ingenious feature: a half-silvered mirror through which the room in question can be viewed surreptitiously. One can only guess what purpose it was meant to serve."

He grinned lewdly as he added, "And how exactly my acquaintance came to know of it." He pursed his lips speculatively for a moment, and then shook his head in a dismissive gesture.

Getting back to the subject at hand, he said, "The Tsar's agent may have been skeptical to begin, but now, Skavronsky will be watched very closely."

Michael nodded thoughtfully.

"You realize," Evan cautioned, eyeing the Scot, "whatever happens to Skavronsky will in all likelihood take place in Europe or Russia, after his confederates have been identified."

Michael sighed. "I know." He looked at Evan questioningly. "You will let me know, won't you?"

"Of course I will," said the viscount. "Such a tale needs a final chapter."

Motioning toward the French door and stepping inside, he added, "As for Von Ratzenhausen, his part in this has come to the attention of certain...friends...of the Irishman."

He smiled wickedly as he remarked, "It's a very long voyage back to Europe. Anything can happen at sea."

Michael scrutinized his friend through narrowed eyes. As they strode the corridor to the main entry of Hampton House, he said, "I do believe you're enjoying this, Evan. You may have missed your calling."

"Well, dear boy," Evan replied, "as it happens, I have been giving that matter some thought."

"Oh?"

Stopping short of the double front door, the viscount said, "It occurs to me that diplomatic service is fraught with intrigue. And affords a certain...scope...that I find interesting."

Michael smiled wryly as he said, "So, Brazil doesn't sound so bad after all."

"I would have preferred to stay here," Evan admitted. "But I suppose that situation has its difficulties, as well."

The friends regarded each other for an uncomfortable moment. At last, Evan gestured and the footman opened the door. The viscount stepped out to greet Anne genially as Michael followed.

∞

"MacGREGOR HOUSE," Dan Doherty announced as he wheeled his hackney cab in front of the entrance.

"Don't let my father hear you call it that," warned Michael. "He detests that sort of pretension." He did not mention that his father actually insisted upon other pretensions. Joseph MacGregor was a self-made man and, as such, prided himself on his impoverished roots even as he lavished himself and his

family with the trappings of wealth and social position.

Michael helped Anne from the carriage and paid Doherty generously, at which the cab driver made a vociferous but token protest before stuffing the cash into his pocket and, with a tip of the hat, snapping the reins to drive back toward town.

"Come and get dressed for dinner!" Joseph called from the doorway.

"What are you doing home so early?" Michael called back.

"I'm not early," his father retorted with a disapproving scowl. "You're late." He broke into a grin as his son and daughter-in-law climbed the steps. "But I expect *you'll* be the one staying at the office, soon enough."

Anne said with mock severity, "Now, don't you be keeping my husband so wrapped up in work I never see him, Joseph MacGregor."

The patriarch replied with a tolerant smile, "My dear, I'll consider myself lucky if I can keep him till the whistle blows."

∞

AT TABLE, Michael gaped, marvelling as he gazed at his wife. Anne wolfed down the lamb rissole and stewed vegetables as though she had not eaten in a week.

At her son's amazement, Hermione MacGregor said, "I was the same. Ate like a horse."

Her husband joked, "Thought I'd have to slaughter one to feed ye." In an aside to Michael, he said, "We hadn't two pennies to rub together, then."

"I feel as though I could swallow a cow—or a horse—whole," said Anne as she sliced through the rissole's crisp, flaky pastry with her fork. "It hit me this evening. I don't recall ever being so hungry, even when food was scarce."

"It will pass," Hermione assured her. "Though I can't say how long that will take."

"Soon, I hope," said Anne. "I don't want to end up being wider than high."

Elizabeth commented cheekily, "With Michael's offspring in your belly, I expect you will be, anyway." Her father hooted agreement.

Michael tilted his head and stared at Anne, picturing in his mind's eye his wife fat, with plump cheeks and dimpled hands and roundness everywhere. Anne noticed his gaze.

"What?" she asked. "Have I slopped food on myself?" She looked down to her blouse and, finding no crumbs or splatters, anxiously patted her mouth and chin with her napkin.

Michael grinned. He confessed, "I was imagining you wider than high."

She wrinkled her nose at him, but her pouting grimace had a little smile behind it.

"Don't worry, dear," said her mother-in-law sagaciously. "A few years of running after a hearty, headstrong child will have you slender as a willow."

From the opposite end of the table, Joseph smiled at his wife as he put in, "Though a little meat on a woman is not unwelcome." He raised his glass of wine as in a toast and then sipped, still grinning and openly regarding his wife across the row of porcelain-and-gilt serving dishes and the bowls of freshly cut rose blossoms that lay between them. Hermione blushed.

Noting his parents' affections, Michael smiled to Anne, certain he and his wife would share such lasting love and desire. She smiled back, chewing, and her eyes told him she was thinking the same.

∞

FEELING HEAVY with satiation and sleepy besides, Anne subsided onto the plush sofa by one of the bay windows of the drawing-room. Michael sat beside her and she leaned into his arm.

"I love you," he whispered, and he kissed her hand.

"Ditto," she replied.

"Ditto?" he repeated with a quizzical expression.

She grinned, "I know. I say the strangest things."

He grinned back and bent to give her a quick buss on the lips.

Across the room, reading the *Evening Star* in his burgundy velvet wing chair by the fireplace, Joseph frowned and remarked, "This new paper of yours certainly harps on what it calls 'the plight o' the working class.' Not certain I agree with their so-called solutions. Sounds radical to me. And we know from what goes on in France where *that* can lead."

Seated on the opposite side of the fireplace in her matching chair, embroidering a white lawn handkerchief by the light of a globular glass-and-brass kerosene lamp set on the side table that stood as the twin of her husband's, Hermione said in a placating tone, "I'm sure there won't be any beheadings and massacres here, dear. We are a much more stoic and level-headed people than the French."

"There are plenty o' Frenchmen in this country," Joseph reminded her. "Not to mention Spaniards, Italians, Chinese, and God-knows-what-else." He muttered to himself, "And then there's the Irish." His fluted face puckered in disapproval. "Always talking about revolution."

Anne giggled. Then snorted. Then shrieked with helpless laughter as everyone regarded her with brows raised in question, her husband and in-laws exchanging looks of bafflement among themselves. Tears seeped from the corners of her eyes as Anne shuddered in mirthful spasms. Finally, after several minutes, she began to settle.

Michael asked curiously, "What amused you so?"

She said through her snickers, "A Scot—a MacGregor, no less—complaining that the Irish want to revolt against English oppression."

She collapsed again into gales of laughter.

∞

REDCOATS, MICHAEL REMEMBERED. He—as Alex MacGregor—had been murdered by English redcoats for wearing a kilt. For being a Highlander and proud of it. And before that, he had fought the English and been wounded at Culloden, Anne had told him. She had actually taken part in the Rising of 1745. He realized: *Of course, she would see Scots as revolutionaries. As freedom fighters. Perhaps as heroes, even in defeat.*

He held her as she shook in his arms, still giggling convulsively at the irony of his father's words.

Michael did not think himself a hero. Certainly not a revolutionary. How often had he submitted to another form of English oppression—though, in truth, his tormentors had not always been English. Indeed, one had been Scotch. The memories tightened his gut.

Anne must have felt his sudden tension. She quieted quickly and looked up to search his eyes. He forced a smile, but he could see her countenance now held concern.

Joseph interrupted by crossing the room to shove the *Evening Star* under Michael's nose. "Revolution is bad for business," the patriarch said gruffly, and then returned to his chair.

Grateful for the diversion, Michael opened the newspaper and began to peruse its pages. The nearby cluster of candles did not illuminate as well as the lamps on the tables next to the armchairs of his mother and father and sister, but they sufficed. And he preferred their mild scent to the sharp odour of burning kerosene.

Anne leaned and slipped under his arm, resting her head against his chest to read with him while he held the pages toward the light. As his father had indicated, there were several articles about labour unrest, strikes, and poor working conditions. Michael wondered what conditions he would find at his father's factory.

Soon after he had folded the sheets and turned to the final page, Anne pointed to a poem within a rectangle, the short verse titled "Blue skies of summer." She traced the lines of print with her finger and Michael squinted to read it, too:

> **The price of eggs has risen,**
> **Conditions all are met.**
> **We sail to autumn glory.**
> **The little sun must set.**

Anne chuckled. "It's no Enigma Code, but I suppose they think no one would understand."

Michael decided not to ask what an "Enigma Code" might be, but said, instead, "Alerting someone—someone here in the city—that the assassination is to proceed." He concluded, "They expect to be in power by fall."

Anne said, "The board is set and the pieces are moving. Remember, remember, the fifth of November."

Michael looked down to his wife and smiled wryly. "Indeed," he said. "Another gunpowder treason and plot."

"No shortage of them, to be sure," she remarked.

"Did you see that one, too?" he wondered in a whisper. If she had travelled through time repeatedly, as she had said, she might have witnessed all manner of historic events.

"No," she responded quietly. "But I saw the movie."

He blinked. Again, he decided not to ask.

∞

ANNE WOKE to a lightening sky and a heaving stomach. She managed to hold the latter's contents just long enough to retrieve the old chamber pot from under the bed. Kneeling on the carpet, dribbling saliva that tasted of bile, she wiped her mouth with the back of her hand and waited for her heart to stop pounding like a jackhammer.

"Are you all right?" The worry in her husband's voice echoed the concern in his face as he peered at her from the bed.

"I just need some water," she said.

Michael leapt up and fetched the decanter and glass from the table next to her side of the bed, pouring as he turned to her. He leaned down to give her the water, and she grasped the glass with trembling hands.

Once she had taken several gulps, she set the drink on the floor and said, "Morning sickness. I was hoping I would not experience it." She did not say aloud, *Again.*

Michael reached to push strands of hair away from her sweat-dotted face. He said, "Perhaps you should stay home, today, and rest."

She took his hand and held it to her cheek as she smiled and assured him, "I'll be all right. It passes quickly enough. And I may not be sick again today." She brightened and said, "Perhaps ever!" With that, she grinned, crossed the fingers of both hands, and crossed her eyes.

Michael chortled and then kissed her forehead.

When he attempted to take away the chamber pot, she slapped his hand and insisted, "It's my mess. I'll clean it up."

∞

A GREY DAY and a steady drizzle outside the window greeted Michael and his father when they met for breakfast in the morning room. Joseph raised his eyebrows questioningly at his son's attire: clean but simple blue cotton shirt and sturdy yellow-grey trousers.

"I thought we'd go to the office together," the elder MacGregor said uncertainly.

"We will," Michael told him. "But I figured I'd take time to learn the jobs on the floor and get to know the men."

Joseph nodded thoughtfully. He said, "Good idea." Then, smiling proudly, he added, "A good way to start, my boy."

∞

JOSEPH INTRODUCED his son to the foremen in each section of

the distillery and then brought him back to Colum MacTavish to learn the various processes involved in making mash.

Unlike his competitors, Joseph MacGregor had resisted mechanization of his business. His were old-fashioned operations, using methods learned in Oban and Crieff, Pitlochry and Kirkwall, in the days of his youth. Although other companies put out staggering quantities of liquor, Joseph produced whisky of a quality among the finest in the world.

At MacGregor's Highland Distilleries, men soaked the grains with warm water to start the germination process, raked them on the malt floor to spread them evenly and to turn them as they sprouted, and fed the fires of the kiln to dry the grains before the maltings were ground to grist.

More men tended the iron mash tun, stirring the grains, adding hot water, and sieving off the liquid wort into the containers called underbacks.

The wort was then collected into the deep wooden vats known as washbacks, there to be mixed with yeast. Soon after, the froth that bubbled up violently, rattling and shaking the vats, had to be skimmed off lest it spill over.

Once fermentation had subsided, men transferred the wort to the stills, first pouring it into the copper wash-still with its copper "rummager" chains on the bottom that prevented burning of the solids as the enormous kettle was heated from below. Then, the second distillation of the liquids took place in the smaller copper spirit-still. The gleaming pot slowly brought the temperature up and vaporized alcohols to float into the attached lyne arm, and then along it into the loops of thin copper condenser coils set in water.

Each step was monitored to ensure it took place at the proper time, and to allow undesirable elements to be drawn off. Then, the equipment was cooled and cleaned before the whole process started over again.

For each batch of whisky, oak barrels charred on the inside and previously used for sherry were filled for the aging

that would mellow and round the flavours. Joseph stored his barrels not the minimum of three years, but for twelve full years. And a few batches were aged fifteen years.

Finally, the matured whisky was diluted, bottled, labelled, crated, and stored until shipped.

All told, from distilleries to warehouses and docks, hundreds of men owed their living to Joseph MacGregor. Today, Michael MacGregor joined them, hauling sacks of grain that would be soaked, spread, and sprouted in dark warmth.

∞

AFTER A MORNING of carrying heavy burlap bags from the delivery wagons to the malt floor, Michael, dusty and reeking of sweat, wandered into a crowded, open-ended courtyard with his lunch sack to sit in an empty space on a low bench protruding from the longest of the three pale stone walls. Wooden benches and a few tables had been set out in the yard; all had become dark-grey with age and corrugated with exposure to the elements. Everything was wet with rain, but the men were soaked with sweat, anyway, and sat wherever they found room.

"You're the new lad," said a rufous-haired man wearing a loose tan vest with his white shirt and his nankeens. He leaned and extended his arm in front of the man between as he introduced himself, "D'Arcy Sloan."

Giving the offered hand a firm shake, Michael said, "Michael MacGregor."

Sloan's face hardened and he pulled his hand away abruptly. "The boss's brat, then." He spat contemptuously, "Slummin'."

"I'm learning the trade," Michael replied equably. He held the man's dark-brown eyes as he added, "As a boss's brat should."

"Eh, if it isn't Himself!" called Sean Quinn as he approached with a broad grin and a patchwork lunch bag.

"Tradin' stone work for an honest livin', air ye?"

"Mr. Quinn," Michael rose to greet him with a warm smile and a hearty handshake. "I didn't realize you worked here."

"Oh, aye, goin' on five years," said the man from The Flats.

"You know this man?" Sloan asked Quinn suspiciously.

"He's Herself's husband, he is," Quinn informed his co-worker loud enough for all to hear. "And a neighbour o' mine." Of Michael, he asked, "And how is your lovely wife? I hear she took a turn the other day."

"She seems well enough," Michael answered. "Though she was sick this morning."

"Oh!" said Tsi-Guy Villeneuve. "She got de pukin', eh?"

"I'm afraid so," Michael replied grimly. "She worries me."

"Agh!" said Quinn with a dismissive wave. "My wife puked for nine months straight and still popped out the wee one wi' no trouble."

"I'm glad to hear it," said Michael, allowing himself a tentative hope that Anne, too, would fare well—though he would rather not see her go through months of morning sickness. He added, "My mother is keeping a close eye on her."

"Good, good," said David O'Byrne, smelling of alcohol and yeast as he sidled up and clapped Michael on the shoulder. "Always good to have the older folks about when a woman is in the family way. Have ye any plans for the new house?"

"Anne has it all in her head," Michael replied as he took a seat once more, this time between Quinn and Villeneuve.

As the men of The Flats formed a knot around him, discussing women, house-building, and whisky while they ate their homemade lunches, Michael noted the uncertain looks on some of the other men, and the outright hostility of Sloan.

He had been used to that stare of loathing at school, and had known the reasons for it, then. But he did not understand

this man's instant dislike of him, given that none he had met so far seemed unhappy in their work or upset with his father. He decided D'Arcy Sloan bore watching.

∞

HERMIONE BOUGHT them all aprons of their own, this morning: two each, so one could be cleaned while the other was worn. *Always practical, Hermione,* thought Anne. Another stop in town had been required, as well, to purchase large sacks of salt and sugar for preserving processes.

Now, the MacGregor matriarch discussed canning methods with the dowager Mrs. O'Reilly while everyone else fed the fires, fetched water, cleaned and pitted, peeled and cut, stewed and stirred. The day was too wet and overcast to use the Big Black Box or its progeny in other yards; so, making jam and jelly, preserves and pickles occupied the ladies who worked in groups here and there throughout The Flats.

Anne's narrow summer kitchen teemed with apron- and kerchief-clad women and girls squeezing past one another to fetch and carry pots and kettles and wood to the stoves and oven. Outside the south half-wall, out of the drizzle and under the kitchen's extended eaves, others prepared the fruits and vegetables at the waxed-wood countertop dotted with puddles of water and juice.

Anne had chosen not to create a steam canner; so, vegetables were salted or brined or pickled in crocks for fermentation. As each new batch was completed and sealed, the stoneware tubs were hauled to the root cellar dug into the earth north of the foundation of the new west wing. Today, carrots and beans were doused with hot vinegar, while shredded cabbage was salted for kraut, cucumbers set to ferment, and tomatoes and cauliflower brined.

Small potatoes and beets went into the pot for supper. Herbs, lettuces, and greens would be gathered at the last minute

for salads, or for steaming in the bamboo baskets obtained in Chinatown.

Early apples, currants, and berries of many kinds and colours cooked slowly in syrups of juice and honey or water and sugar. Chattering girls stirred the sweet mixtures constantly, while their mothers flitted from pot to pan, keeping an eye on the process lest an inattentive daughter fail to recognize the signs of scorching.

No one needed lunch, for samples were tasted throughout the day, some blatantly and some surreptitiously.

∞

HAULING GRAIN again in the afternoon, Michael asked a fellow worker, "Do you know this man, Sloan? D'Arcy Sloan?"

The big, muscular man in grey trousers and sweat-stained green shirt who had introduced himself as Olaf Andersson picked up a burlap sack from the delivery wagon and hoicked it onto his shoulder. He spat on the ground before he replied, "Oh, that one." He cocked an eyebrow and said, "Careful o' that one you should be."

"Why?" Michael asked warily as he gave way to the other at the doorway.

"Likes to make trouble, that one," said the brown-haired Norwegian as he dropped his burden onto the pile already on the long rack that stretched from just inside the door.

"Any particular reason why?" Michael pressed.

Andersson shrugged and went back, lumbering slowly, to pick up another load of barley.

"Why you want to know?" asked Frank Visneskie, whose real Christian name, apparently, was unpronounceable, so everyone just called him "Frank." As burly as Olaf, he smelled of garlic and cheap wine and sweat, and he wore a jersey shirt with bold horizontal red stripes and with sleeves rolled past his elbows.

Michael shrugged and said lightly, "I met him earlier today and I just wondered. He seemed nice enough." *At first,* he added under his breath.

"Ha!" Frank hooted. "Nice," he chuckled, shaking his head. He said, "Nice like snake in bed."

He spat on the ground, a huge gob of slightly greenish phlegm. Michael wondered if that was a trait common to men whose job took them from a cool and windy alley to a warm, close malt room or furnace chamber and back again, over and over, all day.

Stepping around the slime, the Scot carried his umpteenth load of the afternoon into the building and deposited it on the rack. When he returned, he found another man, one he did not know, speaking to the two hauliers. On spotting the young MacGregor, the stranger shut up and quickly left.

"What was that about?" Michael asked.

"Ach!" said Olaf with a grimace. "He say you are big boss's son so we not talk to you."

Frank asked, "Are you big boss's son?"

The latter's tone seemed more curious that accusatory. Michael said, "Yes. I'm learning how the business works."

Olaf nodded approvingly. "You do work like us an' see what makes whisky."

"Yes," Michael confirmed. "In the Army, they say you cannot give orders until you learn to follow them."

"You were in army?" asked Frank, surprised.

"The British Army, yes," said Michael. "In Egypt and the Sudan, a few years ago."

"Sudan," Olaf repeated. "Not good place."

"Hot," said Michael. "And full of people who wanted to kill us. Not that they did not have cause, I suppose."

"Yeah," said Frank. "Army always in wars. You get shot?"

"Shot, stabbed, sliced, and beaten to a pulp," Michael replied. "But I think the flies and lice and heat were the worst of

all."

Frank grinned. "Yeah, you a soldier. Anybody else think to be shot worse."

All three big men chuckled at the irony, and the rest of the day passed in sporadic conversations about life in the immigrants' new country and work in Joseph MacGregor's employ.

∞

BY MIDDAY, the mizzle had tapered to a stop, though the sky loured, portending further rain to come. The women trod wet grass and herbage as they continued their harvest of whatever appeared ripe in the nearby yards. Wood-smoke drifted above chimneys as kettles boiled and, throughout The Flats, sheep and goats, cattle and chickens tentatively emerged from their respective shelters to forage once more.

In his usual brown vested suit and darker brown fedora, their shades lighter versions of his hair and eyes, Detective Morgan wheeled up and parked his bicycle outside Anne's front gate. He stood and appraised the foundation and plinth stones scarred by rain-streaked soot as Anne approached.

"Good afternoon, Detective. What brings you here?" she asked.

He pinched his hat brim and smiled in greeting. "Good afternoon, Mrs. MacGregor." He gestured toward the remnants of her house and remarked casually, "I hope you'll have a chance to rebuild soon, before the snows."

"I hope so, too," she replied. She waited.

After a brief hesitation, Morgan asked, "Did you see the poem in the newspaper?"

"Yes," she answered. "Clearly a message."

"'The price of eggs,' indeed," said Morgan with grim humour. He informed her, "Upon investigation, I have discovered that a man of the Russian count's description placed

it." He asked, "You wouldn't happen to know what it means?"

Anne said, "I believe it means that the purpose for which he came to this country has been accomplished, and the poem communicates that fact to one or more confederates."

She added, "If it's any consolation to you, I believe he will be leaving the country in a few days. He and the Prussian have already booked passage."

"So, they get away with their crimes," said the detective with a disgruntled sigh.

"I'm sure they think so," Anne said with a sly little smirk.

The detective regarded her a moment. His eyes told her he had decided not to ask what more she knew.

Anne's smile faded abruptly and she warned, "But they may commit a few more sexual offences before they leave, given the chance."

With a nod, Morgan replied, "We'll keep an eye on them. They'll have difficulty practising their particular perversions in this country."

Turning grave, he said, "We found the weapon that killed the boy, Geordie Monaghan."

Anne's gaze sharpened.

The detective revealed sadly, "The bullet came from the Irishman's pistol. I tested it purely for the sake of form, but it seems...."

He paused and shook his head before he continued, "I've found no connection with the demonstration in Mercer's Field. He may have known of it and used it to hide his crime, or the rifle shots occurring at the same time may have been pure happenstance. Either way...."

He did not need to finish. Anne closed her eyes against the renewal of tears, anger, and sorrow at the monstrous murder of a child to cover petty pilferage necessitated by the Irishman's own stupidity in losing his book and gem.

"There is one more thing."

Anne raised her eyebrows questioningly, though she was

not sure she wanted to hear any more when she noted the policeman's solemn countenance.

"We have not been able to identify the third man your boys described."

A shiver ran up her spine.

In farewell, Morgan grimly touched his hat again and bowed his head. Anne watched after the detective as he climbed aboard his bicycle and pedalled away toward the city. When he had disappeared beyond the bend, she trudged back to the summer kitchen, the joy of the harvest now supplanted by melancholy and by a foreboding she tried very hard to dismiss.

CHAPTER 29

Whisky business

T he table was set for company: the MacGregors' best white damask tablecloth and gilt brocade runner, gold candlesticks and platters, Hermione's finest crystal with graceful incised designs, elegant gold-rimmed cream bone china with a snowy filigree pattern painted along the edge, gold flatware with handles smoothly curved and adorned with tiny flowers, lace-edged napkins at each place setting, and crystal vases full of newly cut roses dotting the centre.

The table's extension had been inserted and extra chairs provided. The sideboards and doorjambs smelled of polish. The sconces gleamed, and all girandoles and candlesticks sported fresh tapers. The frames had been dusted and the still lifes and landscapes straightened with care. The usual burgundy draperies had been exchanged for gold silk damasks with bronze braid trim. No detail had been spared.

"What's the occasion?" asked Anne when she and the other MacGregor women returned from The Flats to find the staff in their best livery and the dining-room already being prepared.

"Oh, I forgot to mention it!" Hermione exclaimed. "Joseph has invited a few friends and associates in honour of Michael's joining the firm."

"I invited Mr. Ogden, as well," Elizabeth put in shyly. "I've asked him to take photographs to commemorate Michael's first day."

"That was very thoughtful," Anne responded, though she was certain her sister-in-law's motivations were more personal in nature. Elizabeth blushed, and Anne marvelled at the changes in the woman's attitudes and manner since the removal of Kenneth Armstrong from her life.

Hermione clapped her hands and urged, "Well, we must get ready, ourselves. Our guests will be arriving by eight."

Anne climbed to her room and gratefully lounged in the bath. In the water's enveloping warmth, she soon drifted to a doze until, at the sensation of rain upon her face, her eyes flew wide and fluttered in sleepy surprise. Instead of bona fide precipitation, though, she found her husband grinning and flicking droplets from long wet fingers.

"You're pruney, my wee faerie," he chided. "And I need the bath more than you do."

"So I see," she responded, noting the skin, hair, and clothes caked with dust and sweat. "Have they told you about dinner?"

"Yes," he said with a sigh of forbearance. "I'd rather eat a few sandwiches or bannocks and go to sleep, but instead, I must play the dutiful son and entertain father's guests."

"Should I have Harris spike your wine with coffee?" she asked, only half joking.

"No wine," he replied. "But I can certainly use the coffee."

"I'll see what can be arranged."

∞

FORD FUSSED and flapped about as Signore Abruzzi, dispatched by Evan, tweaked the black silk-and-wool-blend dinner jacket and trousers, and the white-silk shirt, tie, and vest that the tailor and his apprentices had spent the day feverishly sewing together. Evan had even sent along new patent-leather shoes and, as a joke, a pair of black-and-grey argyle socks to finish the outfit.

"Mmm," murmured the Italian as he tilted his head this way and that, assessing his handiwork. "It will have to do," he said resignedly. "A proper fitting would need more time."

"I am grateful for your hard work, Signore Abruzzi," said Michael with a slight bow. "I know you were given very little notice."

"We were *all* given little notice," muttered Ford irritably.

"Ah, well," said the tailor, "one must make concessions for such a special event."

"Thank you, again," said Michael as he showed the man to the dressing-room door. "Please send the bill to me, here."

"Oh, no, no!" said the Italian with grand gestures of negation. "The Lord Danford has already paid, Signore."

"Then, I must thank him," said Michael.

As Ford closed the door behind the tailor, Michael returned to the mirror and gave his hair another quick brush. On his way out, with Ford hurrying behind and whisking his shoulders with a garment brush, he mentally tallied how much Viscount Danford had paid and determined to send his friend the amount in full at the earliest possible opportunity.

∞

WHEN HE SAW Anne above, on the stairs, Michael caught his breath. She having dressed in their room with the help of one of the maids, he had had no opportunity to glimpse her until now. The viridian watered silk proved the perfect colour for her lightly

sun-browned skin and silver hair, and the gown cinched at the waist and curving over bosom and hips emphasized her increasingly round figure. Her tresses had been gathered and held with diamond pins borrowed from his mother. White satin gloves rose from her fingertips to just above her elbows. And the smooth, soft skin of her chest and neck, exposed by the deep neckline that hinted of the swell of her breasts, glowed in the candlelight, unadorned and perfect.

She smiled at him as she descended—that dazzling smile of white teeth and twinkling purple eyes and pink cheeks that always set his heart aflutter—and he wanted to take her directly back up the stairs to their room to make love to her until dawn. Instead, he let out a long, wistful breath and joined her, crooking his elbow as she stepped alongside. Arm in arm, they repaired to the drawing-room to welcome the guests.

Evan had arrived early, which he did occasionally just to maintain his reputation for unpredictability. He had been talking with Joseph and Hermione and a small punctual gathering when Anne and Michael entered. At once, he crossed the room and kissed Anne's hand in salutation.

"Dear lady, you look stunning!" the viscount exclaimed. He turned to offer his hand and a sincere smile, "And Michael, congratulations, dear boy!"

"Thank you, Evan," Michael replied as he shook his friend's hand.

Whatever the other guests may have thought, all followed Lord Danford's lead and greeted Anne courteously, if not warmly. Michael marvelled that Evan could treat the woman of whom he was admittedly jealous with such magnanimity. With shame, he realized he might not have done the same, had the roles been reversed.

Sometimes, he thought, *breeding does tell*.

∞

AT ANNE'S REQUEST, the kitchen had prepared cold, sweetened coffee to replace the wine at Michael's meal setting. For herself, she had suggested fruit juices in place of alcohol. The cook had happily obliged and set her assistants to preparing the benign beverages.

At table, Joseph and Hermione took opposite ends. Anne was assigned a seat next to Joseph and across from Evan, while Michael sat cater-corner to Anne, next to his mother. Sprinkled about between were Elizabeth and Mr. Ogden; middle-aged shipping magnate Nathaniel Bennett and his vacantly smiling wife, Marion; senior Justice Donald Edwards and his very young and attractive second wife, Barbara; banker Thomas Cavendish and his prim wife, Ruby; and—to Michael's surprise—late arrival Reginald Orwell, balding and portly father of Jaclyn Orwell.

During the soup course, conversation remained fairly neutral. Commentaries concerned the weather, with special emphasis on the recent freak storm; the state of the roads, again with remarks on the problems of travel during rainstorms; and mention of the strange earthquake of a few days before: Rain and snow could be anticipated and prepared for, but geological events must be classified as acts of God. That, of course, made them impossible to predict, regulate, insure against, or prepare to endure.

By the fish course, Reginald Orwell had drunk enough wine to erode his judgement, or perhaps merely to embolden him. Sitting in the middle and across the table from Anne, he eyed her lewdly. Although Michael could not see Orwell directly from his position, he had a clear view of Anne's diverted glances and cold glares.

He bent to whisper to his mother, "Who is Anne staring at and why?"

Hermione leaned unobtrusively to glimpse the entire tablescape. Momentarily, she whispered, "Reginald Orwell is behaving badly." Aloud, she called, "Mr. Orwell, I understand you have recently purchased a new carriage. A phaeton, I

believe. Are you enjoying it?"

The sudden use of his name drew his attention and Orwell inclined forward to blink at Hermione. He said, "A phaeton, yes. Jaclyn," at that, he glowered at Michael, "has been enjoying it immensely."

He leaned back and said loudly, "Of course, my Jaclyn is a girl of good breeding. Such pursuits suit her quality. Others," he looked at Anne and his voice dripped with disdain, "are better suited to riding...of a different sort."

"Indeed," Anne retorted proudly. "I'd much rather ride my husband."

Justice Edwards spewed his gulp of wine. Hermione's jaw dropped, a mirror of her husband's. Elizabeth squeaked and covered her mouth with her hand while Mr. Ogden blushed. The other guests gaped and looked from Orwell to Anne to Joseph to Michael.

Orwell fired a fresh volley: "Then, you must be a miracle worker, Madam, for I understand he is quite unable." He sneered, "With women, that is."

Joseph leapt up and shouted, "How dare you, sir!"

Orwell stood up to turn his venom upon his host. He replied, "I am quoting the city's whores, sir, the majority of whom seem very well acquainted with your son's ...idiosyncracies."

Joseph fired back: "I hadn't realized *you* were so well acquainted with the city's whores as to be in their confidence, Orwell!"

Michael had reddened to his scalp. His ears burned; his gut tightened; his breath shallowed; his hands curled to fists; his eyes cast about the surface of the table before him as his mind whirled, touching briefly on a series of memories, each too vivid with pain or too dulled by drink to recall clearly, and all swallowed in emotions from rage to terror to frustration to humiliation. He had thought whores discreet; clearly, he had been wrong. How long had his impotence been public

knowledge? He no longer heard the vituperations and vitriol between his father and Orwell. It was noise, now. Only noise.

Suddenly, he felt Anne's hands on his shoulders. He looked up to find her smiling fondly at him. She said, "You are the love of my life, Michael MacGregor."

He fell into the violet of her eyes for a long, long moment. Then, he stood and scooped her into his arms, and he carried her upstairs to their bed.

As Harris held the dining-room door open for him, he noticed vaguely that all the noise had stopped.

∞

BELOW, THE REMAINING visitors chattered in the foyer as they prepared to leave, their voices wafting up the stairwell. When at last the household settled, the family and their lone overnight guest sorted themselves into the bedrooms nearby and the sound of their mutters diminished with their footsteps along the corridor.

Propped on one elbow, Michael smiled at his wife as she lay nude in their bed, her hair and skin painted gold by the light of the guttering candle. He rested one hand on her belly as his gaze drifted from her face to her breasts to her belly and back to her eyes. It amazed him that he felt so utterly at peace when he lay with Anne. Their bed—whether a grand four-poster with goose-down quilts, like this one, or a patch of grass under a tree—was his sanctuary.

"Sounds like Evan's staying," she murmured.

Michael nodded. "The official announcement is to take place next week. He brought the invitations for our family, tonight. Apparently, the rest were mailed earlier."

"Will you miss him?"

With a thoughtful nod, Michael said, "Yes."

He pushed a lock of her hair behind her ear and admitted, "For all the separations through the years, when we were in

different schools or, later, on different continents...and for all the discomfort, the...strain...between us now, he has been my best friend for a long time. My only friend, in fact. The only one I felt I could truly trust."

His eyes focussed to the distance of the past as he recalled, "They hated me, most of the other boys...I was a Scot, I was a commoner, I was nouveau riche, I was...."

He released a shuddering breath and whispered, "They knew. Somehow, they always knew. A few—mostly senior boys—even figured it gave them licence."

He smiled wryly and added with a bitter edge, "Until I got big enough to make my presence felt in a fight even when I was outnumbered."

He sighed and shrugged fatalistically. "Then, I only had to put up with the professors and a few of their...'special friends.'"

"Like Skavronsky," said Anne.

"Like Skavronsky."

"He'll get what's coming to him," she said.

He smiled faintly at the certainty in her eyes. For him, knowing that someone would soon imprison or kill the man was hollow comfort.

The candle flame fluttered and went out. In the dark, he felt about for the sheets and quilts and pulled them up to cover the two of them. Then, under the cotton and silk and eiderdown, he snuggled with his wife and drifted to dreamland.

∞

FINE CAMBRIC curtains softened the sunlight penetrating the bow windows of the breakfast room. Draped in white linen with cutwork and embroidered scallops at the hem, the round table mimicked the curve and cladding of the snuggery. The green of the chairs' upholstered seats matched the leaves and vines of the floral wallpaper above the wainscot. And the oak sideboard, set

against the wall opposite the oak-mantelled fireplace, held the silver tea service and the *Country Rose* crockery and serving dishes the family always used for private meals.

"It was rather a pleasant evening once Reginald Orwell left," Hermione noted lightly as she took a cup of tea and a small plate of toast and jam from the buffet to the breakfast table.

"Bloody Englishman. I shouldn't have invited him," Joseph growled. Remembering their overnight guest, he looked from his sausage and biscuit to Evan and said, "Meaning no disrespect to Your Lordship."

"No offence taken, I assure you," said the viscount. "I feel the same way about men like Reginald Orwell."

"I'm afraid it's my fault things deteriorated so," Anne apologized as she sat down with a cup of tea and a dish of eggs, sausage, toast, and fruit. "I should have been more discreet."

Grinning, Evan said, "I'm glad you weren't, my dear. Justice Edwards's reaction was quite entertaining."

"It wasn't your fault," Michael told his wife contritely as he piled his plate from the platters and bowls on the sideboard. "It was mine. I have a long history of bad behaviour. It was bound to come back to me sooner or later."

Elizabeth spoke up indignantly, "I don't think it's your fault at all! Mr. Orwell was beastly just because he wanted to marry off Jaclyn and you didn't take her off his hands!"

"Well spotted, my dear!" said Evan. "He thought he'd marry into the MacGregor dynasty so he wouldn't have to buy into it."

Joseph froze, a bite of fork-impaled sausage halfway to his mouth. Suddenly pensive, he set down his utensil and the piece of biscuit he had held in the other hand. "Bloody hell!" he whispered.

Michael looked from his father to Evan and back as he took the empty place at the table.

Anne prompted, "Is there something you'd like to share, Joseph?"

Eyes downcast, the MacGregor patriarch said slowly, "I knew he wanted my business, but I didn't realize how far he'd go to get it." He pressed his lips tight and swallowed visibly.

Michael stared at his father a long moment. Perhaps there was more to the whisky trade than fermenting and distilling.

CHAPTER 30

Announcements

Signore Abruzzi and his staff had furnished an entire wardrobe of suits, waistcoats, shirts, overcoats, and even formal attire complete with silk-lined cloak and top hat, by the day of the British consul's party. Ford had pressed and brushed everything again, to his own satisfaction, and had buffed Michael's new shoes to a mirror shine.

Anne's closet and cabinets had been stuffed with silks and fitted finery purchased by Hermione despite her daughter-in-law's protests that the new garments would surely be too small all too soon.

"Mother's practising for the baby," Michael called to her from his dressing room as they chose their respective eveningwear for the event. "She'll spoil him rotten."

Anne set down the ribbon she had selected and strode to the adjacent room to put her arms around her husband's waist.

With eyebrows high, she asked teasingly, "What if it's a girl?"

Michael hugged her to him and replied, "Then, *she'll* be spoiled rotten." He bent to nuzzle Anne's nose and he grinned as he added, "And I'll do my best to give her a baby brother who'll put toads in her bed and hide her diary."

Now it was Anne's turn to grin. "Did you really do those things to Elizabeth?"

"Those and worse," he admitted with a remorseful smile. "I was a terror."

"Mmm," said Anne. "Then, I guess I'll have my hands full as *he* grows up."

At her playful pout, Michael kissed her. And kissed her again, deeply.

"Speaking of practising," he murmured as he moved to nibble her ear, "I'd like to practise making another baby."

Anne giggled. And wriggled. "Do we have time?" she whispered.

"We'll *make* time," he insisted as he brought her to the bed.

A tap at the door. Then, another.

"Not yet," Michael called, and he resumed his ministrations.

Footfalls faded down the hallway.

∞

WHEN ANNE and Michael arrived at Hampton House in a buggy for two, the rest of the family having gone on ahead in the coach, the couple found Evan Sydenham standing outside the entry.

"You're late!" Evan chided with a petulant moue when they alighted. A smile spreading across his face like sun coming from behind a cloud, he added, "But I can see why. My dear, you're radiant!" He clasped and kissed Anne's gloved hand.

She had worn pale-blue velvet, tonight, with matching

silk gloves and with velvet ribbon coiled in the chignon at the nape of her neck, soft blue ice wrapped in snow. Pearl tears dropped from her earlobes and a hint of rouge reddened her lips. From her shoulders, folds of velvet curved across her bodice, echoing the voluptuously gathered skirt.

"And I'm so glad you wore the blue gown," the viscount added as he produced from his pocket a pale ribbon of satin with a sapphire egg set in silver hung at its centre. A white asterism glinted in the lamplight under the *porte-cochère* as he held the necklace aloft.

Evan stepped round and tied it so that the stone nestled at the base of her neck. Touching it, Anne asked in astonishment, "This isn't...is it?"

Michael fingered the gem, leaning close to scrutinize it. "By Heaven!" he whispered. "It is!"

"Indeed, it is," Evan confirmed with a broad smile. "It seems the collector's prize vanished before he left the country."

Eyes narrowed in suspicion, Michael and Anne turned to the viscount.

Michael asked incredulously, "You stole it?"

"Well, *I* didn't," said Evan. "And technically, I'm just borrowing it until it can be returned to its rightful owner in Amsterdam." He smiled as he added, "But I thought it appropriate that you should wear it tonight, my dear."

Anne breathed a sigh of relief. "I'm glad it's only on loan," she admitted. "A gem like this is much more trouble than it's worth."

"As we've already seen," Michael added grimly.

When they stepped into the mansion's foyer, Anne asked, "But why not leave it under lock and key?"

"Because...." the viscount began; then, he scanned the area to assure himself they could not be overheard and lowered his voice to continue. "I have had word that a former possessor of the stone has also vanished."

"Skavronsky?" Michael whispered.

"Yes," said Evan. "The Prussian has gone missing, too, both last seen boarding a ship in Halifax."

Michael frowned, perplexed. "It's a lengthy trip across the Atlantic," he said. "How could they disappear from a ship in the middle of the ocean? Apart from being tossed overboard, of course. But how would you know of it already?"

Anne put in, "I doubt the Russians would kill Skavronsky before discovering who is involved in the plot."

Evan confirmed, "No, indeed. In fact, our villains did not actually remain onboard. Before the ship set sail, both were removed surreptitiously and placed on other vessels. Count Skavronsky is on a freighter bound for St. Petersburg as we speak. I do not expect he will be in the best of health when he arrives.

"As for Von Ratzenhausen," the viscount said as he stepped between Anne and Michael and turned to take an arm of each to draw them toward the ballroom, "he is on his way to New York. It seems the Fenian Brotherhood is well represented there. And the members do not take kindly to the murder of one of their own."

∞

THE CONSULATE'S ballroom glittered with polished marble, polished wood, polished mirrors, polished gilt, and the polished appearance of the social elite. Merchants, bankers, and judges chatted with Members of Parliament, Members of the Legislature, and members of the city's Council. Colonels and generals displayed medals and braid as fashionable ladies flaunted diamonds and pearls. Everyone who was anyone had been invited by the Earl of Heth to attend the farewell party for his eldest son.

Because of their dallying, Michael and Anne had missed the formal reception. Already, as they entered the grand hall, the centre of the floor whirled with waltzing couples.

"I insist that you allow me to dance with your wife, sir," Evan proclaimed as he held Anne's hand high. Michael grinned and bowed his head in acquiescence, and he watched as his friend paraded Anne to the centre of the room, clasped her waist, and spun her around the ballroom in an expertly executed grand waltz.

"She looks lovely, Michael," Joseph remarked as he came up beside his son with a glass of whisky in his white-gloved hand. Keeping his eyes on the dancers, he added softly, "And she makes you happy."

Michael looked down at his father, who did not look up. The MacGregor patriarch nodded to himself and walked away.

He has accepted her, Michael knew. *Completely and unreservedly.* He smiled to himself, and he watched again as his wife and his best friend twirled around the dance floor.

∞

THE ORCHESTRA rested while the British consul made the formal announcement of his son's appointment as diplomatic attaché to the embassy in Brazil. The clapping, some of it merely polite and some of it enthusiastic, mixed with a few disappointed ahs as some of the more ambitious young ladies realized their chance to marry an English peer was slipping away to South America.

Anne fluttered her silk fan toward her face, forcing a small breeze to cool her neck and her flushed cheeks. A waiter offered her a glass of wine, but she declined and asked for water.

"I must say, I am surprised," said a coldly casual female voice from behind her. "I'd have thought being married to a man of such...low character...would drive a woman to drink."

Anne turned to find Jaclyn Orwell and a clutch of young socialites, all of them frilled and feathered, staring at her with supercilious disdain.

The blonde daughter of Reginald Orwell injected a tone of

spurious pity into her voice as she continued, "But I suppose that, if one is too old to have a child, it would not matter if one's husband is...unable."

One of the others, a tall brunette in a rose-pink gown with enormous bouffant sleeves, added with a malicious smile, "And perhaps it would be a welcome relief to have a bed to oneself after a lifetime of sharing it with...strangers."

The waiter reappeared with water. Anne picked up the glass and smiled to the young man in white-jacketed livery. "Thank you," she said. "We pregnant ladies should avoid alcoholic spirits." The attendant nodded, his expression indicating he had made a mental notation to make innocuous beverages available to distaff guests.

Behind him, the spiteful Miss Orwell and her brood of sycophants gaped. When Anne snapped her fan shut to expose the star sapphire at her neck, their eyes and mouths flew wider still.

Anne smiled sweetly at them and said, "Close your mouths, girls. Gawking is most unattractive."

She turned on her heel, head high, and strode to her husband, who, being head and shoulders above the majority of the guests including the colonel of the Guards and the alderman with whom he was conversing, was easily found even in so large a gathering. When she stood beside him, he smiled down at her and automatically slipped his arm around her waist as he continued his discussion.

Across the room, Jaclyn Orwell pressed her lips together tightly and stamped her foot. When the blonde and her minions retreated in chagrin, one of the women, a brown-haired young lady in mauve, glanced back uncertainly toward Anne and Michael.

∞

"I SHOULD LIKE to visit Evan," Michael told Anne as she lay

next to him in the early morning light, glassy-eyed with contentment. He ran his fingers through her snowy tresses, even whiter than the sheets and pillow casings, and so opposite his own jet locks and stubble.

"Of course," she responded softly. "You must see him as often as you can before he sails for his new posting." She reached up and brushed his cheeks and jaw, ruffling the hairs grown overnight, and remarked, "You would look splendid in a beard, you know."

He smiled, realizing she saw in her mind's eye Alex—the other him—hirsute and wild. He had a vague impression that, besides the beard, he had had extraordinarily long hair. He chuckled softly at thought of it: He must have been the very picture of the barbarous Scot of English nightmares.

"You think the notion of a beard funny?" she asked.

Grinning broadly, he said, "I think that if I were to grow my hair and beard like Alex, I would frighten women, children, and wild beasts."

"Not half as badly as you would terrify men," she laughed, and he joined her in mirth.

As they settled once more, he suddenly recalled, "You haven't been sick for several days."

"I decided I had had enough of that," she replied with mock severity.

"Oh, it was as simple as that, was it?" he said, amused.

"Yes," she answered. "Well...almost." Her expression turning serious, she murmured, "More than anything in the world, I want to give you a child."

He studied her face, its curves and lines filled with love and longing. All at once, he knew: Their child was his greatest wish, as well.

CHAPTER 31

Diversions

E van had gone to the capital with his father and, despite
Michael's initial protests, Anne and Joseph had convinced
the younger MacGregor that a little vacation out of town
would clear his head and prepare him for the next phase of his
apprenticeship in the distillery. Anne arranged for neighbours to
harvest whatever ripened while she sojourned in the north, and
she assured her husband and mother-in-law that she felt quite fit
enough to travel. At her insistence, she and Michael packed
lightly for hiking and camping in the back woods. He had
thought her mad to wish to traipse through dense forests full of
wild animals and thick with biting insects. But he had relented
when she promised to bring a proven deep-woods insect
repellent and—giving him a suggestive wink—a tent just big
enough for the two of them.

As they disembarked from the coach that brought them

from the train to a village nestled beside a lake glinting gold in the afternoon sun, Michael breathed deeply of the clean air and wondered why he had resisted the opportunity to get out of the city's miasma. After a few more inhalations, he wondered how he would bring himself to return to the filth and stench they had left behind. Even the homely scents of The Flats could not compare to the tangy purity of this wilderness.

"I think I could live here," he declared as he followed his wife into the yellow board-and-batten inn with its white trim and gingerbread mouldings.

Anne turned back to him, grinning, and said, "You ain't seen nothin' yet!"

Once settled in their second-floor room, they joined their hosts and the other guests round a former family table to enjoy a dinner of roast beef and Yorkshire puddings with potatoes and kale, carrots and beans, and a sharply spicy relish. Few but Michael had room for the bumbleberry pie presented proudly by the plump Irish good-wife, and she pressed him to eat as much as he desired.

"You, too, my dear," she urged Anne as she set a plated piece of pie in front of her. "You're eatin' for two, and ye must keep up your strength."

No longer feeling ravenous, as she had for weeks, Anne managed half the wedge. Michael finished it for her.

∞

IN THE BLUE HOUR before sunrise, the world cool and tinted with a cerulean cast, Michael and Anne set out with most of their possessions strapped to their backs, some hanging from their belts. As he walked behind his wife, frequently admiring the view of her bottom displayed under a pair of loose culottes hemmed well below her knees and over boots but hugging his favourite portion of her anatomy, Michael found himself looking forward to the evening's activities too intently to notice any

discomforts caused by the day's excursion.

They trekked for hours, pausing occasionally for water or food or calls of Nature that Anne called "pit stops," until they reached a weathered log cabin squatting mere yards from a narrow river. Various boats floated nearby, fastened by ropes to the posts of a small, sun-paled plank wharf. More boats lined the sandy bank. Out on the water, a clinker-built dory lay at anchor and, in it, a man in a broad-brimmed straw hat sat dozing with pole in hand and fishing line dangling untended, his head drooping forward.

Anne cupped her hands to her mouth and shouted, "Yo! Beecham!"

The man started and shook his head at the sound of his name and looked about, eyes wide. When he spotted Anne, his creased and sun-browned face broke into a broad, toothy grin and he waved.

"Be right with ye!" he called as he pulled in his line and tossed the fishing pole into the bottom of his boat. A moment later, his anchor hauled up, he rowed back to shore and greeted his visitors. A hearty handshake for Michael, when Anne introduced him, followed close on a hug for Anne that lasted entirely too long for her husband's liking.

"Been a dog's age since I seen ye last," said Bob Beecham when introductions concluded. "Are ye goin' up-country?"

"Yes," Anne replied. "I'm taking Michael to visit my secret place."

"Ah, the 'secret place,'" said Beecham with a knowing air that set Michael's teeth on edge, the more so when the man winked at him. "Then, ye'll be needin' a canoe."

"That's why we're here," Anne confirmed.

Beecham pointed to the newest of his craft and advised, "Take Bessie, then. She'll get ye there and back, all right."

"Thank you, Bob," said Anne as she handed him a pouch that jingled when he accepted it. "We'll see you in a few days."

"Take care, then," said the man in farewell.

Michael removed his shoes, walked into the water, and slowly waded to where Anne had pushed "Bessie" out into the river. Assessing the small vessel, the Scot looked to the dory and back to the canoe, certain that the latter would not hold his weight. He suggested, "Maybe we should take the rowboat."

Anne smiled up from her perch in the narrow craft and said, "Don't worry, love. It's stronger than you think. Just don't jump into it."

After a momentary hesitation, Michael stripped off his pack and belt and handed them to Anne. After another, longer pause, he stepped very carefully into the canoe, and he let out a tremulous breath of relief when he found he had not put a foot through the bottom.

Once he had settled, Anne said, "I'll drive."

With that, she shifted to face the forward end, picked up an oar, and paddled away from the dock with an ease that astonished Michael. He smiled wryly to himself and shook his head. Life with Anne was not boring; she had a knack for surprising him.

∞

SEVERAL MILES downriver, Anne turned the canoe to a strip of shingly shore and disembarked. Michael lifted himself out of the craft into the water to help her haul the boat and their belongings to a thin patch of meadow edging conifer forest.

"We'll make camp here," she announced. "I'll fetch firewood while you set up the tent."

She wandered past the treeline, avoiding a patch of poison ivy, and she trod carefully under the towering pines and spruces lest she damage the delicate blossoms of pink lady's-slipper, or the three-petalled painted trillium that was rarely seen this far north. She revelled in the scent of sweet-fern as she gathered dry branches and twigs from the forest floor. The birds had hushed on her approach, and her footfalls crunched on the

carpet of dry brown needles and small twigs beneath the evergreens. She hummed happily.

Arms laden with her gleanings, Anne returned to the chosen campsite to find Michael hammering the last tent peg with a rock. Together, they made a shingle-lined hollow in which to build a fire and laid the twigs and sticks and larger branches teepee-fashion. As Anne watched, her husband struck flint to steel and instantly ignited the bark shavings he had scraped from one of the branches. She smiled: *Just like Alex.*

∞

A SWATH OF ORANGE clad the western sky immediately above the inky treetops as Anne and Michael prepared to bed down. Clouds of mosquitoes whined hungrily all about them, even inside the tent, but the voracious little beasts stayed out of biting range thanks to Anne's homemade lotion. Michael rubbed it liberally everywhere he could reach, and gratefully sat still as she applied it where he could not.

Tired as he was, with the fresh air and the food and the exercise, Michael was not ready to sleep: The day's imaginings had fuelled his desire for Anne. First, however, he needed to deal with the matter that had vexed him all afternoon and evening.

As he spread lotion over his wife's back, he decided to broach the subject. But instead of the casual inquiry he had intended and planned, he blurted accusatorily, "What is it between you and Beecham?" Immediately, he wished he could snatch back the words, or at least the tone, but it was too late. Why did all wit and resolve desert him when he was near her?

Anne turned to blink at him, nonplussed. Then, she narrowed her eyes and gave him a hard look. Finally, her face softened and she said, "There is nothing between us but acquaintance over several years." She smiled wryly as she added, "Though I cannot guarantee he would not wish for more."

Surprised at the depth of his relief, Michael licked his lips

and said simply, "Good...Good."

Anne could not hide her amusement as she encircled his waist with her arms and pressed her nude body to his. She batted her eyelashes at him in mock coquetry and taunted, "Jealous, are we?"

In response, Michael hugged her to him abruptly, gripping her buttocks and crushing her against his hardness. He whispered fiercely, "You're mine, Anne. Mine alone. And I'll prove it to ye."

He bent to kiss her passionately. Then, he lowered her to the mat laid over thickly needled pine twigs and manifested his ownership as she demonstrated hers.

∞

A SERENADE of avian song heralded the dawn. Michael woke to find himself stiff, in more ways than one, and Herself most provocatively pressed to him in slumber. Memories of the night's glories steeling him further, he ignored the twinges of muscle here and there to focus on tickling her nether lips. He smiled as he watched her sleepy little twitches and listened to her dreamy gasps and mutters. Soon, the motions of her pelvis and the rhythms of her respiration told him she approached wakefulness, and a probe with his fingers confirmed her readiness. As her eyes fluttered open, he slid inside her and resumed their wordless nocturnal conversation.

∞

SEVERAL HOURS' portage, hauling the canoe atop their heads through dense pine and spruce woods along a meandering rocky route that, astoundingly, Anne had described as a trail, brought them to another river. Michael examined the tears in his shirt and the scratches on his arms occasioned by encounters with hawthorn as Anne fetched water. He noted rips in her bodice and flared trousers, and a sanguine line much too close to her right

eye. He reached out to trace it gently and said, "You must be more careful, my love." He cupped her cheek. "I do not wish to see you blinded."

She rested her hand on his and smiled. "I will take more care," she promised softly. "And we will not be travelling such treacherous brush any longer."

As he sat on a downed tree, its top branches submerged in water as its roots rose withered and dry where they had been rent from the soil, Michael munched the mix of dried berries and nuts he and his wife had brought from The Flats. Absently, he watched the scudding clouds visible between and above the walls of conifers on left and right, until the harsh caw of a crow somewhere behind jerked his head toward the sound. He saw no flight and heard, thereafter, only the rushing of the water over pebbles and driftwood. The sun blazed hot, and the ambient scents, as sharp as the needles of the evergreens that produced them, wafted on the wind that soaked up the sweat trickling down his temples and the sides of his torso.

The Scot wondered what they would find at Anne's "secret place," and he curled his lips in amusement at the notion of his wife's laying claim, like a child, to a secluded spot here in the depths of God's Country. He shook his head at the thought, and he marvelled to discover, in the same person, the sagacity of an old woman and the playfulness of a young girl. Suddenly, it occurred to him that his father might feel the same of his mother. Was it always like that between a husband and wife? Memories of other couples of his acquaintance surfaced, and he realized some spouses did not enjoy each other's company. As he watched Anne hike her pants hems and squat to rinse her fingers in the river, looking much like a toddler playing in a puddle, he thanked Heaven once more that he had found her.

∞

AFTER THEIR BRIEF rest and refreshment, they followed the

shore two more hours past a series of rapids until they reached a stretch of clear water. There, they set the canoe into the stream and rowed on.

This time, Michael took up an oar and paddled with Anne against the strong current. Throughout the previous day, he had studied her motions and, now, his mind and muscles quickly adapted his old boating skills to this unfamiliar method of propulsion. After a time, he fell into a steady rhythm that matched hers, and he turned his thoughts to the beauty around him and to the drawing of a mental map of their journey.

The sun had started its descent well before they rowed up a tributary stream. Glowing ruddy gold, the heavenly orb touched the treetops of the western rise by the time they pulled ashore and made camp.

As if reading his thoughts, Anne said, "It's not much farther. We'll get there by midmorning tomorrow."

"And what will we find when we get there?" Michael asked at last, reining his curiosity no longer.

"Gold."

∞

ANNE CHUCKLED under her breath as, in her shift, she trod the upper reaches of the stream. She felt Michael's astonished gaze, and she remembered his flabbergasted gape of the day before, when she had told him what she expected to find. The water flowed, cool and smooth, over her feet and around her calves, and the pebbles shifted and crunched at her passage. Sunlight sparkled on the glassy ripples to obscure what lay beneath, but she kept herself between sun and streambed, her shadow affording a clear view of the bottom. Most of the rock bore the rusty tones of simple iron oxides, but here and there and from time to time, she glimpsed other hues: browns and blacks, whites and greys, and—just occasionally—gold or silver or the vivid colours of gems.

A dark patch drew her attention. She moved to cast shade upon it and bent from her hips to examine the detritus in and around the small basin. On the periphery, bits of brown and green jasper lay almost buried, and she picked a few of each to place in her waist-tied pockets. A chunk of smoky quartz caught her eye and soon joined the jasper in her cache. A piece of rutilated quartz shot with fine reddish threads, a small natural quartz wand that refracted the sun's rays into a tiny rainbow, and a sharp wedge of flint followed. Nearby, a pale glint and a hint of bright red led her to spinels, and she took a sample of the tiny gem trapped in a milky matrix.

She pressed on to sift through the fragments within the depression. Close inspection revealed matte-surfaced black calcite, the grey sheen of hematite, glossy black obsidian, and a shard of black Labradorite that glistened with blue iridescence in the light. She knew such variety was rare, and she wondered at discovering the last stone at all, but she had long since stopped questioning her finds, inexplicable though they might be.

The weight and bulk of her collection was growing, but Anne continued her search among the ferrous stones of the stream. After a time, cautious scattering of brownish cobbles and rounded gravel unearthed a gleam of bright yellow.

"Bingo!" she called as she stood appraising the nugget. She bent again and picked up several more of the precious lumps of metal. Moving downstream, she spotted another cluster.

When she had filled her pouches, she stood and stretched and, finally, looked about for her husband. She saw him fifty yards upstream, near a bend. His trousers and sleeves rolled up, he squatted near the bank and stared at something in his hands.

Anne waded toward him. As she passed a clump of cedars that grew mere feet from shore, a glint from the ridge above drew her gaze. A massive outcrop bisected the forest cover at the crest of the rise, the pale-grey slab stark against the dusky greens of the trees and the vivid blue of the sky and visible through a rocky channel that cut the holt from top to bottom. A

jolt of recognition shot through her and she swallowed hard at a memory. After a moment, she calmed herself and continued to her husband.

"What have you there?" she asked on her approach.

He held out a large specimen of clear quartz. Anne gasped when she saw it.

"A tantric twin," she whispered, gaping at sight of the pair of crystals, virtually identical, joined on one side and growing from a common base: a soulmate stone. Tears filled her eyes and her breath caught at a sudden foreboding.

Michael frowned. "Is something wrong?" he asked.

"Keep it," she responded, trying to smile. "It may come in handy."

∞

MICHAEL BRUSHED a strand of moonlit silver from Anne's face and regarded her as she slept. Something about the stone he had found today had disturbed her, though she would not speak of it when he questioned her, simply smiling and dismissing the matter as nothing of importance. But he had noticed her looking at it, and at him, frequently and with an odd expression. And she had made love to him, tonight, first with a ferocious passion and then with a deep tenderness.

As though it might be the last time.

He shivered. The thought had come unbidden from a dark recess of his mind, and he immediately shut a mental door upon it as tightly as he could to lock the notion away. *No, we will have many years together,* he told himself fiercely. *My Anne and I will grow old together.*

All at once, it occurred to him that he had no idea how old she was. Again, he suppressed a pang of fear and he kissed her softly before he lay back and closed his eyes.

∞

AS THEY PACKED their belongings for the journey home, Michael forcibly thrust to the back of his mind the questions that had plagued him the previous day. Anne would tell him in her own time if something was truly wrong, he told himself. But that certainty dissolved when, as he piled their bags and belts into the canoe, he caught her staring into the distance with a haunted look.

Abandoning the preparations, he strode to her, steeling himself for a confrontation. A few feet from her, though, he halted, licked his lips, swallowed, and decided to try a less belligerent approach. He stepped up behind and gathered her gently into his arms. Bending to touch his cheek to hers, he whispered, "Please tell me what troubles ye, my love."

Anne clasped the arms folded across her chest and leaned back against her husband. She murmured, "I'm sorry if I've been...off. I've...."

She sighed and then started again. "I've had the strangest feeling."

"Because of the stone," he said.

She sighed again. "Yes," she admitted. "I feel foolish, now."

He hugged her tighter and said, "We all get strange notions now and then."

"I know," she said. "And I know I should not dwell on them. It's just...." Yet another sigh.

Michael kissed her temple and said, "Perhaps you'll feel better if we go home."

"Yes," Anne replied. "But first, I must show you something."

∞

THEY DONNED their belts and sacks and left the canoe in the underbrush for a hike to the crest of the ridge that rose from the narrow beach across the stream. Rather than follow the tiny ghyll

that scored the rise, a meandering trough with treacherous footing, they kept to the woods.

It was a steep climb, made longer by detours around patches of poison ivy and trees so closely spaced as to form a barrier. When they cleared a huge outcrop, the forest suddenly opened on a breathtaking panorama: a short, sheer drop to a precipitous conifer-clad decline toward a wooded dell with a lake at its heart and a small island off-centre in the lake. Azure skies and white clouds reflected in the water, and drifts of white flowers under the trees of the vale mirrored the billows above.

"I don't see a way down," said Michael as he scanned the terrain.

"There is a way, but there is no need to go down," Anne replied. "I just wanted to show you the island."

Michael frowned and swallowed at a realization. "Is that...?"

Softly, Anne finished for him, "The point of power that brought me here to this time." Abruptly, she turned to him and clasped his cheeks. Her voice tremulous yet fierce, she promised, "If anything should happen to me, my love, I will find a way back to you."

For a moment, Michael could not speak, all breath snatched from him. Finally, and as fervently as she, he declared, "*Nothing* is going to happen to you, Anne. Do you hear me? *Nothing.*" He pulled her into his arms, willing with all his might that it should be so.

CHAPTER 32

Labour Day

Τhe MacGregors drove to the city to farewell Lord Danford as he embarked on his journey to South America. The coach driver waited as they alighted from the carriage in front of the main entry, and then reined the four horses around to find a place in the field beyond the newly built Union Station.

Joseph ushered his family under the great arch of pale-grey stone and through the open doors into the marble-floored lobby. One porter idled near the bank of ticket windows opposite the entry, and two clerks waited behind their wickets. The station seemed deserted, most people being at the fairgrounds or the Yacht Club or Rosemont Field for the festivities. (Labour Day had not yet been declared an official public holiday, though unions were pressing the federal government for acknowledgement of the contributions of ordinary workers. Nonetheless, an excuse to celebrate was always welcome, and sport *aficionados* across the

social spectrum applauded the opportunity to kick off the rugby season.)

Already familiar with the layout of the building thanks to recent business trips to Windsor and Montreal, Joseph shepherded his wife and grown children along the corridor to the east platform. There, as expected, Evan Sydenham lounged on a bench while his valet chivvied porters and checked luggage and trunks as they were deposited (not carefully enough, according to the manservant) into a baggage car. A large portmanteau and several valises remained on a porter's rack next to the viscount. Evidently, those items would be needed in his private berth.

Michael grinned. He called, "You never did travel light."

Evan rose and beamed at their approach. He retorted, "I'm moving to a foreign country for God-knows-how-many years and there may be none as skilled as Signore Abruzzi to dress me." He qualified the statement, "Or, at least it may take me some time to find a proper tailor."

A whistle blew and steam hissed from the long, wine-coloured iron snake that hugged the twin rails of the track.

"'Board!" called a conductor in that rising tone of command affected by many train attendants.

"Well, that appears to be my cue," said Evan with forced lightness as the valet hurriedly grabbed one of the valises and followed the porter who hauled the rest toward its destination in the sleeping car.

"I'm sorry we were so late," Michael apologized. He might have explained, but his friend held up a hand to stop him.

"I'm glad you were," Evan replied. "I hate long goodbyes."

The family quickly took their respective turns in farewell, Joseph shaking the viscount's hand, the three women kissing his cheeks. Then, they stepped away a few yards and waited as Michael and Evan stood wondering what to say to each other.

At last, Michael said simply, "I'll miss you."

Evan nodded, tight-lipped, and said softly, "And I will

miss you, dear boy."

The valet returned from directing the deposition of the portmanteau and valises, and he coughed discreetly.

With a sigh, Evan, Lord Danford, stepped back.

Suddenly, Michael lunged and hugged his friend firmly, closing his eyes against all he could not say. Evan reciprocated the embrace briefly and then pulled away. The viscount nodded, pressing his lips so tightly they blanched, and then he turned and climbed the steps into the train. He did not look back.

Anne approached quietly and took Michael's hand as the wheels began to rotate with piercing squeals and the train inched forward. It picked up speed as billows of smoke belched from the engine, and it clattered and rumbled and whistled away, farther and farther, until, beyond a curve, it disappeared behind rows of brown and grey buildings.

Michael took a deep breath and let it out slowly. Finally, he gave Anne a grimacing smile and a nod, and he hooked his arm with hers to walk back into the station.

He wondered if he would ever see his best friend again.

∞

THE ENTIRE STAFF had been given leave to spend the day as they chose. While most of the women had taken a bus to the fairgrounds, the men had decided to watch the first football game of the season at Rosemont Field. The Rugby Union had changed the rules again, and many enthusiasts were eager to discover how the game would be played.

As usual, Joseph and Hermione and Elizabeth had gone to the Yacht Club. There would be tennis matches and croquet, picnics in the gardens, a lavish dinner, and fireworks in the evening. And Elizabeth expected Mr. Ogden to be there photographing the highlights and the more illustrious personalities.

But Michael was in no mood for merrymaking.

In half-buttoned white shirt and hanging blue vest, sitting on a watered-silk burgundy wing chair by one of the drawing-room's three bay windows, he stared out through the open casements. A soft breeze blew whiffs of rose and mignonette into the house and fluttered the lace undercurtains drawn aside to bunch by the draperies at the edges of the bay. A rock dove cooed nearby, and the warble of a purple martin grew and then faded.

"We could take the buggy to The Flats," Anne suggested.

Michael smiled faintly. "No," he said. Then, he amended, "But you can go, if you like. I'll hitch up the carriage for you."

"No," she said. "I'll stay with you."

"I won't be good company," he warned softly.

Stepping behind his chair, she rested her hands on his shoulders and kissed his crown. "I don't mind," she whispered.

Then she said, "I'll be in the kitchen if you need me," and she left the room.

∞

MICHAEL TRUDGED down the aisle between the long black tables. All around, hateful eyes stared at him and malicious whispers taunted him.

Mist rose from the floor in whirling wisps that clung to and dragged at his legs, making each step heavier and slower. The cloyingly sweet vapours rose higher and higher to circle his neck with cold fingers that choked ever tighter.

Evan stood at the far end of the study hall, wearing his pale-blue silk robe and nothing more; he smiled and waved. Michael tried to call to him, but the fingers of the mist thrust into Michael's throat and cut off his voice. Reaching out, he attempted to gesture to his friend in a plea for help, but the smoky swirls of fog wrapped his arms and pulled them down.

Evan waved again and turned away.

Then, the mist devoured Michael whole while the voices

laughed.

∞

MICHAEL WOKE with a start, gasping and staring wildly. He swallowed hard, and he tried to determine where he was. Gradually, his gaze caught the shapes around him. He was home. In the drawing-room. Next to the window. The open window.

He pushed out of the chair, legs aching and trembling as they had in Egypt on a march through desert that went on forever. His sweat-soaked shirt clung to him, as it had then, and his hair matted on his sodden forehead. He reeked. And he hurt. And his mouth felt like sandpaper.

As his heart slowed and his legs steadied, he stumbled out into the foyer in search of water.

Something hit his head.

∞

HAVING WASHED the dishes rather than leave the task for the staff to come home to after their day off, Anne moved on to clean the floor. On her knees in the simple gingham gown and sturdy white apron she had purchased for such work, she scrubbed the squared stone slabs with brush and cloth, working in rhythmic circles down the length of the room from oven to larder. There, she opened the back door to let breezes speed the drying. And then, after hauling the bucket outside and tossing the filthy water near the dripline of the oak that lay twenty yards from the rear exit, she decided to make an early dinner.

Anne gathered plates and bowls, pans and spoons. She set water to boil and stoked the stove. Once she found the key to the pantry, she opened the room and scanned the shelves. Into a basket plucked from atop the kitchen's wide pine hutch she placed onions and eggs, bread made in early morning, and a small block of cheese to accompany the herbs and greens she had harvested from the kitchen garden on her way back from the oak.

Tea, she found in the row of canisters along the hutch, and fresh butter sat in a dish in the icebox.

The kettle whistled, and she emptied it into the waiting teapot to soak the fragrant leaves.

Now, she needed knives. Gazing into the drawer, she found a dazzling array of shiny, sharp blades with smooth wooden handles. Some were long, some wide, some curved, some serrated. She puckered her mouth as she decided which would best serve. A bread knife, of course. And—

She heard them: footsteps that did not belong to Michael. She had become familiar with the sounds and habits of the members of the family and of all servants of the household. These were the footfalls of a stranger.

She grabbed two of the larger chef's knives and dropped behind the work bench. Carefully, quietly, she pushed the knife drawer shut as someone entered the room.

∞

HIS FIRST URGE was to get up, but Michael resisted and remained sprawled on the terrazzo, the polished black-and-white-flecked stone cold against his cheek and ear and temple.

"Don't brain 'im, fool!" barked a man whose voice Michael did not recognize. "We need 'im alive to open the safe."

"Fuck that!" said another unfamiliar voice. "Why don't we just blow it like we planned?"

A sigh of exasperation. "Because, Dimwit, we don't have to take a chance o' blowin' ourselves an' the goods to Kingdom Come when this bastard can open it for us."

"I could do it right," the dullard protested. He muttered to himself, "Don't see why we need papers, anyway." Then, bolder, he said, "Let's jus' take the baubles an' get out o' town. They's gotta be worth more'n a bunch o' bloody papers."

"We said we'd get the papers an' we will," Tweedledee insisted with growing impatience. "The jewels'll be extras just fer

us."

"Well, all right, then," said Tweedledum.

"Go get the woman," Tweedledee commanded. "She's gotta be in back, there."

Michael's gut clenched as one of the thugs exited through the door to the servants' section. He heard the pacing of the other, nearby, and he knew he must see the ground before he could make a plan of battle. He groaned and made to push himself up weakly.

"Easy," said Tweedledee as he stepped back. "Nice 'n' easy."

Pushing up first to his knees, Michael glanced about quickly to count his enemies. So far, there seemed only the two.

His trembling was not feigned as he staggered to his feet, clutching the doorjamb of the drawing-room to steady himself. He put his hand to the throbbing spot on his head and felt wetness. When he looked at his palm, he found a streak of blood. He swallowed visibly.

A scan of his adversary revealed Tweedledee as a short, stocky, muscular man of about forty with the dark, furrowed skin of one who worked outdoors much of the time. A mat of greasy brown-black hair with a few streaks of white clumped under a flat brown wool cap. His nankeens were filthy, spattered with dark stuff (perhaps coal pitch; he did smell of it) and smeared with smudges where he had wiped his fingers on his pants. The hanging black vest and open brown cotton shirt displayed tufts of dusky hair up to his neck, and salt stained the cloth under his armpits. Judging by the sun-browned forearms, he habitually wore his sleeves rolled up to just below the elbow, as he did now.

The man reeked of sweat and whisky and pitch, with a hint of horse as well. And he held a Colt revolver pointed at Michael's heart.

∞

ANNE LISTENED to the footsteps to gauge which way to move. There was a grunt and a snort as the man—she was certain it was a man—stopped and stepped in place. *Looking about, no doubt,* she thought. When he clomped to the pantry where the door was still ajar, she scurried silently to the opposite end of the bench, grateful she had removed her shoes before washing the floor.

A clatter, a crash, and a few obscenities issued from the larder as the bull of a man stumbled about clumsily.

"Shit!" he exclaimed when he emerged from the dim little room. He stood a moment.

Probably thinking where to look next, Anne figured. Apparently, he was specifically searching for her.

The man wrenched the kitchen door open wider and stalked outside. With the knives gripped tightly in her fists, Anne scrambled to get a look at him before he returned. She knew she could safely hide in the pantry, now: He was not the type to search the same place twice.

What she glimpsed through the open back door was a tall man, almost as tall as Michael. Big and muscular, with no grace whatsoever. The sort who broke china cups as soon as he picked them up. He wore dirty grey trousers and a charcoal vest. The shirt would have been white, once upon a time; now, it was a dingy, mottled grey. He had the flat cap, rolled-up sleeves, open shirt, and dark tan of a labourer who worked outdoors. She had caught the smell of pitch, a substance often used as a sealant.

After a brief visual survey of the area, the man plodded back toward the house. Anne slipped into the pantry, behind the partially open door, avoiding crockery shards on the floor.

"Fuck!" he complained when he tripped on the threshold and barely caught himself in time. He stomped around the bench, opening a cupboard here and there as though he thought she could hide among the pots and bowls, and then he moved on to another room. It did not surprise her that he paid no attention to the evidence of meal preparation throughout the kitchen.

Heart pounding, Anne forced herself to think: Such a fool

could not be working alone. Someone was giving him orders, and that someone very likely lurked in the house. And must, she realized with a sinking in her belly, have already done something to Michael.

Were they merely robbers? she wondered. But if that was the case, why was The Unfriendly Giant searching for her? She answered her own question: *Because no one was supposed to be here, today, and they want no witnesses.*

∞

"CAN'T FIND THE BITCH!"

Michael relaxed ever so slightly. Closing his eyes, he silently thanked God.

"She ain't upstairs, so she's gotta be there!" snapped the other. "Look again!"

The bigger man puckered his mouth in a grimace of annoyance, but obeyed.

Alone again with Tweedledee, Michael demanded wearily, "What do you want?"

"Sump'n in your daddy's safe," sneered the thief. He grinned and added, "*All* o' what's in your daddy's safe, matter o' fact." He made a show of surveying the foyer and said, "Seems to me ye won't be missin' it much."

They locked eyes. Both knew that last statement could not be true: If it was hidden away, it must be especially valuable. Perhaps irreplaceable.

With a sigh, Michael dropped his gaze to the pistol. His belly twitched with a brief, bitter chuckle that came out as a snort. How many times had he hoped someone would shoot him? And now that he had something to live for, a man was ready to do just that.

∞

THE HEAVY FOOTSTEPS were coming this way again. Anne

turned back and ran down the hall into the kitchen. There, she ducked outside the rear door left open when the man had gone out earlier.

She did not want to kill him if it could be prevented. But should she?

His spirit was not very dark, but dark things might be done by relatively good people. If they were forced to it or tricked into it. Or just weak-willed and stupid, as she suspected this one was.

She must know how many accomplices were involved.

As the man banged about the kitchen once more, she sprinted round the rear corner of the house, past the laundry and utility sector. Cautiously, she peered into the breakfast room; it was empty.

After peeking inside to find no one in the formal dining-room, farther on, she crouched under the deep casements and crept to the library. No one there, either. She hoped the invaders were not upstairs.

At the bay windows of the drawing-room, Anne caught a glimpse of Michael standing in the doorway. His stance told her an enemy hovered nearby. From here, she could see nothing more. Could she climb inside undetected to pass him a knife? Probably not.

Frustrated, she crawled below the level of the bays to continue around to the front. At the corner, she found two saddled horses grazing contentedly upon the lawn. Two. That should be a manageable number. But what weapons did they have?

She realized that something in the way Michael had held himself had communicated more than she had first noted: The man with him must have a gun of some sort, not a knife.

Damn! she muttered under her breath.

She stole past the flower beds that bordered the house, clambered up onto the porch, and sidled to the leaded-glass window by the main portal. A thump and a hissed obscenity

alerted her to the approach of the large man. Jumping down to the soft earth of the garden bed and darting behind a bushy cedar for cover, she waited as he stamped up the stairs and threw open the front door.

"I tell ya, she ain't there!" he shouted to his confederate.

"Fuck!"

Michael lied, "Of course, she isn't. She took a horse and went to the party in The Flats." He added as though in afterthought, "I didn't want to go."

"We'd 'a' seen her leavin'," snapped the other man.

"Yeah," said the big one. "We was watchin' ev'rybody on the road."

"She's a good rider; she rode overland," Michael said equably. "But go ahead and keep searching, if you like. I've got all day." Anne heard the hint of strain in his voice, but he brazened it out, nonetheless.

She climbed onto the porch once more and tiptoed to the nearer of the windows flanking the door. Through its diamond panes, a long-barrelled pistol she saw in the hand of a short marauder. Anne leaned back against the fieldstone wall of the MacGregor country house and tried to think what to do. Sweat trickled under her chemise and down her temple.

A rich *cheer-up, cheerily* rose and fell as a pair of robins winged by. Cicadas whined in the trees. But there were no sounds of people who might help. How she missed The Flats!

A hiss of urination and a whicker issued from the horses. Suddenly, a mad idea occurred to Anne. She slipped the knives into her skirt pockets, grateful that the pouches sewn into her seams were deep. Hopping off the stoop, her landing muffled by the loose soil, she hiked her skirts and dashed across the grass to the equines, where she picked up the reins of one and vaulted onto the other.

With a loud "Hyaa!" she kicked her mount with her bare heels and galloped around toward the orchard with the second horse in tow.

A shot clipped the quoin of the house a split-second after she passed.

∞

AT ANNE'S SHOUT, the heads of all three men whipped toward the entry.

Tweedledee ran for the door. In that moment, Michael leapt toward Tweedledum and caught him with a right hook just as the man, gaping in surprise, turned his face into the blow. He staggered back, shook his head, blinked, and dropped.

Glass jaw, Michael realized. *Thank you, God!*

As he swung, Michael had heard the shot. But he had also heard, immediately after, the scream of frustration from Tweedledee. Now, the sound of the man's re-entering footsteps propelled the Scot over the body of the accomplice and through the door to the rear of the house.

There, he had a weapon of his own.

∞

ANNE REINED her horse to a halt just past the privet hedge that separated the lawn from the orchard, and she loosed the second horse to graze. She slid from her mount and tossed the reins over the saddle; if the beasts wandered off, that was not her concern. She abandoned the equines to the apple windfalls and strode past the espaliered grapes and the evergreen hedge to the rose garden. As she passed the first of the fragrant bushes, she heard a shot, and another, and her heart jumped to her throat.

Anne ran toward the house, her only thought, now, of her husband. *God, not again!*

She flew across the herbage, ignoring the sting of thistle leaves piercing her soles, the humps of uneven ground that threatened to topple her, the knife tips that had poked through the gingham pockets and now scratched her legs. Hurdling the bed of pink pansies and white everlastings, dodging around

more rose bushes and a trellis of honeysuckle, and squashing a clump of mushrooms in the grass, she raced around the corner of the house to smack into and bounce off of a six-and-a-half foot wall of flesh.

Suddenly, she was enveloped in Michael's arms and he was kissing her face, her neck, her eyes, her mouth....

∞

THEY HAD REQUESTED Detective Morgan by name when they called the police.

"Someone hired them," Michael explained to the eternally brown-suited detective. "The gunman told his associate in the other room that they had promised to get some papers and that the jewels they expected to find would be theirs alone. I doubt the accomplice will know anything of value. Perhaps not even who hired them."

"Do you know what papers they were after?" asked Morgan as he stood up from his inspection of the body in the hallway.

"I wish I did," Michael answered. "Surely my father will know."

Morgan nodded and Constable O'Toole made a note in his booklet as the coroner supervised the removal of the corpse.

"May I see the weapon you used?" the detective asked politely.

Michael reached to his back and pulled from his trouser waistband the service revolver he had brought home from the campaign in the Middle East. Handing it to Morgan, he said, "I wish I hadn't had to...."

The detective heaved a sigh and said, "I wish you hadn't had to, either." He shook his head and commented grimly. "Used to be I could take the day off on holidays."

Anne and Michael exchanged looks of remorse. Perhaps they should have accepted whatever officer was on duty, today,

in Rosemont, and left this poor man to his day off. With all that had happened the past few months, he must be thinking them the bane of his existence.

∞

THE STAFF RETURNED in dribs and drabs from wherever they had gone to spend their day off. The chambermaids, first to arrive, crossed themselves with eyes wide when they found Anne washing blood from the floor and wall in the hallway of the servants' domain and bleeding into the skirt of her dress where the knives had cut her thighs. The cook was horrified to find her larder violated, its floor sticky, sharp, and fly-ridden thanks to two broken jam jars. Ford was beside himself at the smudge of pitch on Michael's vest. And Albee Ross wanted to know what he should do with the strange horses that he had found watering at his trough.

Most of the footmen and groundskeepers were only interested in the score of today's game and argued vehemently over the merits of the new rules for rugby football, oblivious of the excited chatter of the women. But Harris brought order to the chaos and soon had the household operating as if nothing at all had happened on this Labour Day.

∞

HERMIONE, JOSEPH, and Elizabeth swept in the front door after midnight, flushed with the heat and gaiety of the day, and with the many bottles of wine consumed during the festivities at the Yacht Club. They found Anne asleep on the drawing-room sofa, her head in Michael's lap. He smiled faintly at their raised-brow expressions and put a finger to his lips as he stroked her temple. His family quieted abruptly and tiptoed upstairs.

CHAPTER 33

Ghosts

W hat the divil happened?" Joseph demanded as he entered the breakfast room. "Michael, Harris tells me there was an incident in the house yesterday. What's he talking about?"

Michael looked up from his bowl of porridge and said through a mouthful, "Thieves."

Hermione gasped and put a hand to her chest. Joseph's eyebrows shot up.

When he had swallowed, Michael elaborated, "Two men came to the house, apparently thinking it would be empty and planning to break into your safe."

"The safe?" Joseph exclaimed as he sat in his usual chair. A creature of habit, the patriarch had arbitrarily chosen a particular seat to be the "head" of the round table and he always sat there. Everyone else in the family merely took the nearest

vacant space.

"They wanted papers," Michael told him. "Someone had asked them to retrieve some papers from your safe. And they intended to take whatever jewels they found, as well." He asked, "Do you know what documents they wanted?"

Joseph frowned and blinked at Michael. Then, he stared at the tablecloth before him, searching his memory. An eyebrow cocked.

"You *do* know," Michael surmised.

Nodding slightly, still seeing something inside his mind, the patriarch said, "I think I ken. Perhaps."

Observing his father, Michael added, "The police will want to know. They'll very likely come around to the office, today."

Joseph nodded again, absently, and Michael narrowed his eyes as he watched the elder tap a forefinger on the table.

Elizabeth rushed in and asked eagerly, "Is it true there was blood all over the floor?" Her eyes sparkled with excitement; clearly, she had been talking to the maids.

At this, Joseph came back to the present time and place. "Blood?"

"I had to shoot one of the robbers," Michael replied. "But no," he said, pointedly looking to his sister, "there was relatively little blood."

"Was the man killed?" Hermione asked.

"Yes."

As she poured herself a cup of tea at the sideboard, Elizabeth thought aloud, "I wonder if we'll have a ghost, now."

Hermione looked about and asked, "Where is Anne, this morning?"

"I left her sleeping," Michael answered. "Yesterday's events were very hard on her."

"I don't wonder!" said his mother. "The poor dear must have had a terrible fright."

You don't know the half of it, Michael said under his breath,

remembering the panic in his wife's eyes that he might have been murdered. Again.

∞

MICHAEL WAITED until they were out of earshot of both house and stables before he broached the subject once more.

"Father, what papers did they want?"

Joseph stopped abruptly and sucked his lips between his teeth. He looked up at his son and said, "The deeds to my properties, the incorporation papers for the company, my shares in the shipping lines and other investments...."

Michael waited. He could see there was something more. Something...secret?

Joseph took a deep breath and then heaved a sigh. At last, he admitted, "And—perhaps—proof of wrongdoing in the Terence Bardon affair."

"Good lord!" Michael gasped in shock. "What do you mean, 'wrongdoing'?"

"Treason, theft, and murder."

∞

MORE THAN EVER, Michael wished he could talk to Evan.

According to the official reports, Terence Bardon had been killed in action during the Bhutan War, and Mrs. Bardon, devastated by the loss of her husband, had committed suicide soon after hearing the news. But Joseph believed his childhood friend, and the man's wife, had been murdered because the young officer had known which British soldiers had stolen a shipment of gold.

Treason and murder had occurred thirty years ago. And now, it seemed, those ghosts had come back to haunt the MacGregor family.

What should he do?

What *could* he do?

∞

ANNE LAY CUDDLED with Michael, one of her bandaged thighs draped across his leg, her arm across his belly, her head resting on his chest. Her nose twitched, tickled by one of the curling black hairs of his breast, and she shifted slightly.

Michael's fingers stroked her arm, tracing lazy circles round and round as he stared abstractedly at the ceiling, its smooth white plaster alive with tremulous waves of light and shadow from the fluttering candle flame.

"What are you thinking?" she whispered.

He sighed. "You think you know someone."

"We all make mistakes," she reminded him.

"Father thinks whoever killed Bardon and his wife may still be alive and has come here to retrieve the evidence against him."

"Then, why has the killer taken so long to come after the documents?"

Michael exhaled forcefully. "Good question."

Anne posed another: "Is it possible it has nothing at all to do with Bardon? Perhaps the thieves were meant to steal the deeds and shares. They're certainly valuable. And losing any of those documents would be, at the very least, a terrible inconvenience to your father. Someone like Orwell might commission the theft just to give your father grief."

"True," Michael admitted. "They've been sparring for years, Father and Orwell."

"Do you know why?"

Michael chuckled. "You may not believe this, but Father stole Mother away from Orwell, decades ago."

"Oh, my. That explains a lot."

"Indeed."

Michael squirmed to reposition himself. Facing her, he drew Anne in and kissed her nose lightly. Sliding his hand along her back to clasp her buttock, he said, "I know I'd be more than a

little put out if someone stole you from me."

Anne smiled and said softly, "That could never happen. I'm yours forever."

She kissed him, and he claimed his proprietary rights once more.

∞

THE SHOP was rather dark, despite the wide plate-glass storefront windows and chiefly because of the heavy dark wood of the cabinets and shelves, floor and service counter. All but the ceiling had been polished to a dusky gleam. The leather merchandise, plain or tooled, black or brown, lay in neat rows upon shelves, or dangled from hooks, or sheltered in glazed cupboards. And in one corner at the back, a single lamp illuminated a work station piled with heaps of leather and boxes of metal fittings.

"Hm-hmm." Anne cleared her throat loudly to get the attention of the man busily rummaging behind the counter. When he looked up, she said, "I have a special request."

The small man wearing a dark-brown leather apron, a hatless visor strapped and buckled behind his head and pulled down over his pale eyes, and a pair of brown cotton sleeve-guards stretched up to cover his white shirt-sleeves from cuff to elbow, quickly surveyed her attire and decided she could afford special requests. He pasted on a smile and came to greet her.

"And how may I help you?" he asked.

Anne set her basket on the countertop and reached in to retrieve the two knives, one of which she had purchased four streets over, and the twin derringers obtained from the gunsmith on Front Street. The metal blades and barrels shimmered in the golden lamplight, and the black handles shone dully.

"I would like special sheaths and straps for these," she informed the man. She produced a piece of paper from her reticule and handed it to him. "These are the specifications."

"Rather unusual request," he said as he picked up a blade and examined it. "A gift for your husband?" he assumed.

"Not exactly," she replied.

When he looked at her quizzically, she said, "They're for me."

At his shocked expression, she smiled and added, "I have found that even an ordinary woman like myself can have dangerous enemies."

The man gaped. Then he swallowed. In a wary tone, he said, "I think, Madam, that you are no ordinary woman."

Anne laughed. She replied, "I suppose that is a matter of perspective. I know my husband would agree with you." Sobering, she asked, "How soon can my order be filled?"

The man looked from the blades to the specifications and mulled a moment before he said, "I believe I can have them finished by the end of next week."

"Thank you."

∞

SAFELY BEHIND the closed door of the bedroom in Rosemont, Anne slipped out of her clothes and into the new harness for her knives. Cinched, the leather belt fit tightly at her waist and its long tail slid through a series of loops to secure it. But she had designed it for an expanding belly, and she now positioned the wide, sturdy, canvas shoulder-straps to take the weight of the leather and steel.

After adjusting the outfit and tightening the cloth cross-strap under her breasts, she donned her underskirts and dress once more. She pinned the side seams where she intended to create openings for access to her weapons. Then, she added the holstered pistols to her appurtenances, pulled on her jacket, and surveyed her appearance in the tall mirror. The guns protruded. She shifted them and looked again. *Too obvious*, she decided.

She removed the holsters and slid them lower on the

harness, where they would fit among the gathers of her skirt. Again, they protruded.

With a sigh, she said aloud, "I'll have to keep one in my purse and one by the door, I suppose."

She gazed at her reflection with cold determination. Pregnant or not, she would not be caught unarmed again.

CHAPTER 34

Risky Business

In the weeks that followed his first day in his father's distillery, Michael had worked in the malting, fermenting, distilling, aging, and bottling processes, spending long enough in each to learn every task and gain an appreciation of the nuances of fine distillery. Everywhere he went, D'Arcy Sloan and his coterie attempted to alienate the workers from "the boss's brat." And everywhere he went, men of The Flats, or men who knew of his marriage to Herself, befriended him and aided his education.

When he moved on to the company's warehouses, young Aiden Bannion took Michael under his wing and guided him through the inventory and storage procedures Joseph MacGregor had instituted. Then, Tom O'Herlihy explained the shipping arrangements and introduced him to the train loaders and dockworkers.

Along the way, Michael encountered Davey, Walt, and

Zeke, and a dozen other street urchins he had met before, as well as more to whom he was introduced. The lads generally ran errands, hawked wares of indeterminate origin, or just hung about with nothing to do. Some, he soon realized, had found ways to sneak into a few of the warehouses along the waterfront each night to bed down in relative safety.

∞

AN EARLY CHILL abruptly settled over the city. Geese flew the pale-grey skies overhead, their chevron formations maintained by the honking of the leader as they winged toward their winter sanctuary somewhere far to the south. Squirrels in yards and parks busily gathered nuts to hide away, their foraging now urgent as temperatures dropped.

From his father's office, Michael telephoned home and arranged for a wagonload of hot food in hayboxes and all the extra quilts that could be found. He waited at the distillery's front gate after the whistle blew, and he waved to departing workers. Sloan and company eyed him, their demeanour evincing the conflict between a desire to stay behind to confront him and a need to go home to hot food and warm beds. The need won out, encouraged by stern stares from the watchman; they melted into the crowd leaving the premises.

Alone at last, Michael leaned against the stone gatepost and watched the avian exodus above. Inside the locked iron gate, the night guard touched his cudgel to his hat brim in acknowledgement and walked on. A cold breeze whipped Michael's unbuttoned pea-jacket and he pulled it closer.

Finally, Albee Ross arrived with the buckboard, and Michael climbed on to direct him to the warehouse district. They negotiated narrow back lanes and wide tracts of wasteland among the buildings to pull up in front of the MacGregor stores.

Immediately, Zeke and Walt darted out from an alley as other eyes peered warily around buildings and piles of crates.

"Food and blankets, boys!" Michael called as he gave a haybox to each of the lads he knew.

When the smell of hot lamb stew wafted from the opened cartons and Zeke and Walt scooped mouthfuls with the wooden spoons provided, the road came alive with tatterdemalions scrambling for a share of the wealth. All the parcels were handed out, but there were not enough to go around. Michael counted the number by which they were short and sent Albee to fetch more food from a tavern.

"Don't worry, lads," he assured the stragglers as the groom drove away, "my friend will bring more, soon. In the meantime...."

He passed around blankets from the heap Albee had unloaded, two or three to each of the small groups that had formed as friends sat together to enjoy their feast. Michael said, "There won't be enough of these, either, but you'll be warmer sharing and sleeping back-to-back." He added, "That's an old Army trick."

"You were in the army?" asked a straw-haired child whose face, like the others, was so filthy the features were barely distinguishable.

"Six long years," Michael confirmed.

Zeke said, "You were an officer, I bet."

Michael smiled and replied, "No, I signed up as a foot-soldier. Didn't want to be an officer." The real reason being more than he wanted to go into, he said, "Too much paperwork if you're an officer."

"But officers is safer, ain't they?" asked a surprisingly plump boy. *Perhaps new to the streets,* Michael thought.

"You'd think so," the Scot answered him. "But bullets and cannonballs don't care what rank you are. And enemies often try to kill the officers first."

"Why?" asked a small one with blotchy skin stretched over fine bones.

Davey answered sagely, "'Cause the officers tell

everybody what to do. If they ain't givin' orders, the soldiers'll run around like chickens wi' their heads cut off."

Several boys giggled at the mental image.

"You're not wrong," Michael admitted. "Though sometimes soldiers are better off without a stupid officer to lead them into trouble. When everything goes to hell, the men can only hope a good sergeant will get them out of it."

For the benefit of those unused to military terms and ranks, he added, "A sergeant is like a foreman."

Several boys' ohs indicated understanding. Davey pursed his lips and nodded, adding this bit of wisdom to his repertoire.

"You're rich, ain't ye?" said one of the older lads. A statement, not a question. The boy tilted his head and fixed Michael with suspicious dark eyes. "So what ye want from us?"

Michael recognized the gamin's wary mien, much too worldly for his age. Deciding the honest approach would best serve him, he replied, "There is something I would like you to do."

The older one elbowed a lad next to him and muttered, "Told ye."

The boys regarded their benefactor, some expectant, some nervous, some suspicious. The plump one simply looked curious. *Yes*, Michael thought grimly, *he's new to this life*. He wondered briefly what circumstance had brought the child to such a state.

Getting back to the business at hand, he asked the lads, "Do you know the man named D'Arcy Sloan?"

"Yeah," said Zeke. "He comes around sometimes."

"Him an' them others," said Walt.

Davey said, "They come talkin' to the men around here. Sometimes askin' questions. Mostly talkin' about how the workin' men's gettin' cheated."

"Izat so?" asked the plump boy. "The workin' men gettin' cheated?"

"Some, yes," Michael admitted. "Not all businessmen are kind or just in their treatment of employees."

A lanky ragamuffin, all elbows and knees as he sat wrapped around his haybox, said, "That Sloan fellah says the Scotchman is the worst."

"Does he, now?" Michael inquired with cocked brow. "I suppose his friends say the same?"

"Yup," the gangly lad confirmed. "They says the bastard's payin' rotten wages and workin' 'em to the bone, besides."

"That ain't true," said Davey indignantly. "I got friends whose das work there, and they say that's ballocks!"

The spindly lad shrugged uninterestedly as he shovelled another mouthful into his maw.

The distrustful one demanded, "So, what ye want us to do?"

Michael took a long breath and replied, "I'd like you to watch him and his friends. And tell me what he does and who he talks to." He confided, "I think he's up to something. Men I've worked with say he's a troublemaker, and I want to know why he's trying to hurt my father's business."

"You figure he's workin' fer somebody," the cynic concluded.

Michael nodded.

"We can watch 'em fer ye," Davey agreed.

Several heads bobbed.

The older boy narrowed his eyes and pierced Michael with his mistrustful gaze. He queried, "Is that all ye want?"

Michael returned the stare and said, "That's all." He surveyed the group and added, "But be careful. I don't know how dangerous these men might be. Don't let them know you're watching them."

Davey asked, "Like them bastards what hurt Kevin an' Rob?"

Michael replied, "Yes, though these men may not be the same type. Nonetheless, they could still be dangerous; so, take care."

Albee lumbered up with fresh supplies, and those who had not yet eaten, the wary one among them, clambered aboard the wagon to grab their share of the food.

∞

AS THE URCHINS began to disperse to their respective hideaways with their new blankets, Michael stopped the older, more streetwise boy with a light touch to his shoulder. "I'd like to ask you something," he said.

The boy smirked sardonically and said, "Thought so."

Waiting until the others were out of earshot, Michael looked the boy in the eye and said, "You know what happened to Kevin and Rob?"

"Yeah." The smirk remained, though fear flashed through the lad's eyes.

Michael told him, "Two of the men are gone. Out of the country."

Now, the boy's countenance altered from cynical certainty to hesitant wariness. "'Zat so?"

"I'll let you know when I find out what happens to them," Michael promised. "But there was a third man."

The lad said nothing, but eyed him with a mix of caution and expectancy.

Michael inhaled a deep breath and asked, "Is it possible the third man is from the city?"

The boy replied slowly, "Ye mean, is there buggerers about what ain't foreign? Yeah."

Michael pressed, "Does it happen a lot, lads being raped?"

After a moment's rumination, perhaps deciding how much to reveal, and working his pinched lips up and down, the boy shook his head and said, "Not all the time. Mos' buggerers'll pay—though some of 'em'll cheat ye if they can." He added, "Gotta watch, though. There's a few are mean."

Michael nodded thoughtfully.

When the boy turned to walk away, the Scot said, "I'm Michael MacGregor. What's your name?"

"Dowd," the lad called over his shoulder.

"Dowd," Michael repeated to himself as he watched the insolent saunter recede into the distance. This boy seemed to weather life's storms better than the Scot had done at the same age. And much later, for that matter.

Or did he? Michael wondered what price the lad paid that no one could see.

∞

FROM THAT DAY, Michael and Anne frequently brought food, new clothing, shoes, and bedding to the urchins. Word spread, and girls, too, often appeared at the regular "drops," as Anne called them, to fill their bellies and wrap their bodies, as summer waned and autumn waxed. Anne dispensed medicines and bandaged wounds, while Michael clipped hair, doled out delousing powder, and distributed books.

Some members of the well-to-do frowned on what they saw as pampering of beggars. But after a series of articles in the *Evening Star* revealing the hazardous life of "the lost ones" (the report including a large photograph of the Four Horsemen, who proudly collected as many copies as they could find or afford), others within the city's gentry considered it their Christian duty to contribute money or materials to the cause of child welfare. A few, including Dr. Edward Hanes, donated their time and expertise, as well.

A shelter dedicated to such children had been proposed: supervised, yet allowing the urchins to come and go. But many considered the orphanages the best way to deal with them (out of sight and out of mind and, officially, someone else's problem). The debate among the elite occupied council meetings and social gatherings, but few turned their attention to the abuses of

existing institutions—some of which were owned and operated by prominent members of the community—and police officers were unofficially urged to "collect" any street children they found, to be "secured" in a facility. So, those urchins who would not be imprisoned in a workhouse or locked in an orphanage avoided and evaded the constabulary to remain at large. They came regularly to the designated pick-up points for food and other necessities, and most constables walking their beat chose to go elsewhere when the MacGregors pulled up in their laden wagon.

For Michael, these regular charitable activities had a particular benefit: No one thought twice when guttersnipes stopped to talk with him. Dowd and Davey had become his primary informants, bringing news not only about Sloan and company, but about everything going on in the distillery district, the docks, and the city in general (which is how he became aware of a brand new café opened by a couple of expatriate Russians). Now that he had joined his father in the office to learn the bookkeeping procedures and to meet suppliers and clients, the boys usually contacted him during his evening rounds with Anne.

∞

THE WHISTLE BLEW, and the men who were not required by the nature of their work to stay gladly headed for home as the small contingent of late-shift workers arrived. Cheerful calls filtered up from the labelling floor, below, and Michael set down his tooled mahogany pen and screwed the lid on the half-full bottle of India ink. At his broad oak desk in the office next to his father's, he leaned back in his chair, blinked, stretched his shoulders with a snapping sound, and rubbed his tired eyes. He stared balefully at the stacks of invoices and receipts and statements that seemed to grow, rather than shrink, the more he tended them: like black-speckled flowers.

When he glanced out the window, he found the sun had nearly set. Gold streaked through the double-hung panes to paint the ochre walls with squares of brighter yellow and to glint off eddies of dust stirred by a draught from the open door. Before him along the wall, photographs set in simple walnut frames and protected by glass—a few images in black and white and grey but most faded to shades of sepia—displayed the holdings his father had acquired over his lifetime: the dynasty Michael was to inherit.

But what would he give his son? he wondered. A borrowed legacy?

"Wish you were on the malt floor?" asked Joseph from the doorway.

Caught by surprise, Michael started and turned.

Joseph smiled wryly and admitted, "So do I."

"You could have fooled me," Michael replied.

"Being accustomed by the years of it does not make the paperwork more enjoyable," said the older MacGregor. His smile faded abruptly and he commanded, "Come. You have a visitor."

∞

DAVEY GLANCED anxiously at the guard who eyed him sternly from his position by the wide, double front door of the distillery. The man's dark uniform with belt and stand-up collar made the boy nervous, reminiscent as it was of the shape and deep navy blue of the constabulary's clothing. The boy turned as Himself appeared in a fine grey suit with the long frock-coat and silk tie of a gentleman.

Davey gaped. He had never seen The MacGregor so decked out, and it disconcerted him to find the man truly was a toff, not just a labourer as he had appeared before.

"What is it, Davey?" Michael asked gently. "Have you something to tell me?" Whatever it was, it must be important for the boy to come to the distillery, the Scot knew.

The ragamuffin's face contorted to a picture of desperation and he pleaded exigently, "It's our Dowd, sir. He's in a bad way."

"Show me," Michael commanded.

The boy raced ahead as Michael followed him, his extended strides easily keeping pace with the nimble gait of the gamin. They negotiated narrow alleys between buildings; a road barely dried from the downpour the day before, and rutted from heavy wagons; train tracks with charred ties and wear-smoothed iron rails; a meadow overgrown with disuse; another roadway; and an alley that brought them to Front Street.

"Over here, sir," Davey called as he darted among westbound and eastbound carriages.

Michael dashed after him, barely averting collision with a dray from Gooderham's laden with crates. Recognizing the label, it occurred to him how ironic it would be if he were to be crushed under a load of whisky produced by his father's primary competitor.

Safely across the street, he pressed on behind Davey. Abruptly, the lad stopped near the middle of an alley, on the far side of an old outhouse smelling strongly of its years of use.

"Oh, Jesus!" Michael breathed when he saw Dowd curled on the ground, bloodied and bashed, his face swollen beyond recognition.

"Fetch me a cab," Michael commanded as he squatted beside the injured boy.

Davey ran off toward King Street as Michael murmured, "It'll be all right, Dowd. I'll take you to a hospital."

"No!" the boy cried, the word immediately transforming to a groan of pain.

Discerning a note of terror in that plea, Michael placated the boy, "Well, I can take you to my home, if you like. My wife will look after you."

When no demur was forthcoming, Michael reached to help the lad stand. A stifled scream at his touch stopped him and

he asked, "Can you stand, Dowd? Can you move?"

Tentatively, jerking with each attempt and gasping with pain, the boy pushed himself up one-handed, very slowly. By the time he had got himself to a sitting position, Davey approached with Dan Doherty in tow.

Crossing himself as he spoke, Doherty exclaimed at sight of the boy, "Jesus, Mary, and Joseph!"

"Will you let us carry you?" Michael asked Dowd. He noted the odd angle at which the lad's arm hung, and he knew nothing could be done for him in this reeking backstreet.

"I-I-I can walk," the boy insisted, and he tried to get his feet under him. He had half-risen when, suddenly, he collapsed with a groan.

"Enough o' this!" said Doherty. The cabbie gathered the boy into his arms, despite the lad's cries, and trotted off to his waiting hackney with Michael and Davey close behind.

∞

THE WINDOW GLASS had not yet arrived, but the wood for the frames had been set in the pole shed erected to keep the construction materials under cover. Oiled cloths protected the roof decking because the shingles had not arrived, either. But at least the basic structure of the house had been raised and the doors had been hung. Most importantly of all, the privy had been rebuilt, complete with polished wooden seat and hinged lid and with muslin stretched across the window openings until such time as the casements could be assembled. In the meantime, Anne began to lay the bricks of her masonry heater designed in the Russian bell style that would not be invented for several decades.

Outside, Hermione chatted with the O'Reilly girls as foraging and harvesting, drying and canning continued unabated regardless of weather, house-raising, or pilfering wildlife. Inside, Anne set the solid first layer over the stove's foundation and, on

this, she began to place the initial course of perimeter blocks and firebox bricks. She had mixed mortar from the dust of fired ceramics and fine sand of the same types used to fabricate the rectangular blocks. Now, she trowelled the mud onto the base and pressed the bricks into it, one at a time.

The expectant mother hummed to herself as she worked, deeply contented and enjoying the Zen quality of the task. Her belly had begun to round, just a little, and she touched it lovingly whenever she thought of its occupant. How long she had dreamed of this: of creating new life with the man she loved.

The third course had been laid, and the fourth, when a shout came from outside. She wet her mopping rag and draped it over the mortar bucket before hastening to the door to find out what the ruckus was.

∞

WITH DOWD in his arms, Michael stepped down from the carriage, and he grimaced in apology and sympathy when the jolt wrenched a wince of pain from the boy. Anne came from the house, her apron, arms, and face mud-spattered and wisps of her hair flying wildly in the strong breeze. When she saw the bundle her husband carried, she rushed back inside, opening the door wide and ushering him in as Dan Doherty closed the gate behind him.

"What happened?" Anne asked as she cleared tools from the single chair in the partially finished lower storey. Michael brought the lad to the seat and set him down gingerly.

"I don't know, exactly," Michael told her as she peered into the boy's eyes and quickly surveyed the damage.

"Was a John, I'll bet," said Davey.

Dowd shook his head, but flinched at the motion.

Anne stood up and said, "First, we'd better take care of that arm."

"It's not broken," Michael told her. "I took the liberty of

feeling the bones on the way here. They're sound."

"Any idea how long he's been like this?" She glanced from Michael to Davey to Dan. All shook their heads and Davey shrugged.

"I won't ask you," she said to Dowd. "I expect a minute would seem like an hour, right now."

The boy grunted affirmation.

Anne grabbed one of her dry rags and carefully slid it under the limp arm. Knowing the procedure, Michael fetched a sizable block of stone from outside and brought it to Dowd. As he positioned it, he explained to the lad, "I'm going to put this into your hand, Dowd. The weight will help your arm pull itself back into place. Understand?"

The boy swallowed hard. He whispered, "Will it hurt?"

"Yes," Michael confirmed grimly. "But only for a moment, when the shoulder pops back to where it belongs. After that, it will hurt a great deal less."

The lad swallowed again, but curled his fingers under the heavy flag. Michael looked up to Anne. At her nod, he let go of the block as she pulled up on the loop of cloth. A sharp gasp from Dowd announced the shift. The boy dropped the rock, and Anne anxiously palpated his shoulder.

After the briefest of moments and with a sigh of relief, she straightened, smiled, and said, "You'll need to keep that arm in a sling for a few days so it will heal." She moved around and stooped to peer once more into his face, adding, "But right now, we need to deal with the rest of you."

∞

MICHAEL FETCHED the box of remedies. Hermione put a kettle on to boil and filled clean buckets with more water. The O'Reilly sisters ran home to rummage for blankets and clothing for the boy. And Dan Doherty drove Davey back to the city, along with several baskets of fresh fruit and nuts for the urchins.

Dowd sat silent and glum while Anne gently washed his face and Michael administered remedies every ten minutes. The boy's eyes followed Anne and she felt his stare, though she was not certain what emotions it held.

His brow, neither low nor high, had split at three gashes—one, nearly two inches long, cleaving his left eyebrow. A shorter slash opened over his right cheekbone. His chin had been cut, as well. Both eyes had nearly closed with the swelling bruises, and his lower lip had been bitten clean through. On top of all that, a pair of lumps on the back of his head had merged into one large one with two lacerations.

And she had not yet seen the rest of him.

When all the caked blood had been cleared and the fresh blood had been mopped, she said, "You'll need stitches to close these wounds, Dowd."

"No," he said.

Anne glanced at Michael, who told the lad, "If the wounds aren't closed, you'll almost certainly become infected."

"Don't care," Dowd replied.

Michael knelt to look into the boy's downcast eyes. He said, "Infection is painful. And it can kill you."

"Don't matter," said Dowd.

Again, Anne and Michael exchanged expressions of concern and bafflement.

With a deep inhalation, Anne asked gently, "Why doesn't it matter, Dowd?"

After a protracted silence, the boy revealed, "'Cause I'm poxed!" His eyes flashed with rage and he snapped, "So, I'm gonna die, anyway, all right?"

Anne blenched at his vehemence, but recovered to ask, "How long have you known?"

"A week, mebbe," the boy said sullenly. "Since just after the full moon." He snorted in a brief, mirthless laugh.

Michael spoke up, "Dowd, if Anne can cure the pox, will you let her—or a doctor—stitch your wounds?"

"Can't cure the pox," said the boy wretchedly.

"Yes, I can," Anne stated firmly. When he glanced up dubiously, she fixed the slits of his eyes with her own even stare and repeated, quietly but emphatically, "I can cure it."

He hesitated, now uncertain.

Michael said, "It's true, Dowd. She can."

Finally, the boy heaved a tremulous sigh and said, "Okay."

∞

HERMIONE PUCKERED her face squeamishly and looked away as she held the tray of sterilized needles and thread. Anne clasped one of Dowd's hands and Michael clenched the other as Dr. Hanes sewed young Humpty Dumpty together again in the light of a cluster of candles and an oil-lamp.

Having refused to be anaesthetized, Dowd sat stoically on the chair as the doctor worked, gripping one of Michael's fingers and two of Anne's and squeezing harder at each insertion of the needle. Anne wished she had thought to clip his long, ragged, filthy nails before the procedure: She knew he would have fresh wounds in his hands, as well, before this day was done.

As soon as the doctor had finished, Hermione set the tray of needles on the floor and ran out to vomit in the yard. Anne grabbed the large pan she had set aside earlier for the purpose, to shove it under Dowd's face. When he abruptly heaved a great deal of unadulterated stomach fluid, she guessed he had not eaten in a while. Once the lad had settled, Anne picked up the bowl of vomitus and started for the back door, but Michael swept it from her hands and disposed of it for her.

Old Lady Tulan, from down the lane, had waited outside the back door and now volunteered a jarful of leeches. Despite the doctor's protests, Anne fetched a pair of tweezers from the summer kitchen and applied the little grey blobs to the black bruises on the boy's face, neck, belly, and pate.

"Honestly, Anne!" said Edward Hanes as he shook his head in astonished condescension. "Leeches?"

Anne shot him a piercing glance and said equably, "There are more things in Heaven and Earth than live in your philosophy, Doctor."

Finished, Anne said, "There," and she smiled at the boy, who eyed her—as best he could beneath folds of bloated flesh—with as clear an expression of doubt as the doctor's.

Mrs. Tulan cackled and sauntered out to the back yard, scratching her backside as usual.

"How long will you let those things gorge themselves?" Dr. Hanes inquired.

"Until they fall off," said Anne. She explained, "This only works for fresh bruising. For older damage, remedies like Bellis and Ledum are best."

"And time."

"And time."

∞

MICHAEL RETURNED with Roquefort cheese from Miss Hetty, who now kept some on hand at all times, and with a jar of Mrs. Bucholtz's kefir to begin Dowd's pox treatment. Once more, the boy eyed his caregivers with skepticism, but he ate the meal laid before him and drank the milky liquid, just the same. He had been bathed, re-bandaged, clothed in clean trousers and shirt, and fed before Michael broached the subject of the attack.

In the moonless dark pierced only by the candlelight through the nearby windows, the lad sat in the hammock that hung between the maple and cherry trees, their leaves already turned to vivid reds and yellows. Seeing Dowd enjoy the swinging motions, so childlike as he pushed himself back and forth in the bed-cum-chair, Michael realized with a pang of sorrow how young the lad truly was under all his cynicism and worldliness.

The Scot leaned against the maple and watched a moment before he asked, "Do you know who did it?"

Dowd stilled his rocking, heaved a sigh, and stared at the ground. "Yeah," he said softly.

Michael waited.

After a moment of silence and another heavy breath, the boy said, "Sloan an' two o' his lads." He spat bitterly, "I hope they got the pox from me, the bastards!"

Michael closed his eyes and inhaled deeply, cursing himself for involving children in his family's business.

"I got sloppy," Dowd admitted, pounding his thigh with a fist in self-punishment. He looked up and rushed to assure Michael, "But I didn't tell 'em why I was followin' 'em." He amended, "Least not the truth."

"What did you say?" Michael asked quietly.

"Didn't really say nothin', but one of 'em figured I meant to pinch their wallets an' I let 'em think so."

Again, Michael cursed himself under his breath. Aloud, he said apologetically, "I shouldn't have got you involved. I had no right—"

"Weren't your fault," Dowd insisted. "If it hadna been them, it'd 'a' been somebody else. A John, maybe." He scuffed his heels in the ground and added in a low, flat voice, "There's not many as live long in the streets."

Michael swallowed hard and stared up to the sky, though he saw only the desolation of the people no one cared to notice: the homeless; the destitute; those reduced to selling themselves or hawking other people's belongings to survive one more day, one more night. And worst of all, the children with no one to care for them, no future to look toward, no joy in the moment.

How close had he come to that life, himself, saved from it only by God's grace...?

∞

Scotland, 1881

A COLD WIND blew from the north, driving needles of rain into his face as Michael MacGregor pulled his greatcoat tight at his neck and hunched his shoulders. He hated Glasgow. He hated the university. He hated his life. He hated himself.

Was there nowhere he could go to escape Professor Aldus Giles and his sodomitical cronies?

Or was it true that he drew such men to himself because he was, at least in part, like them?

In the dim light from windows here and there along the narrow street lined with old buildings of brick and stone, he caught movement overhead and recognized a swinging sign: *The Cock and Boar*. He hurried along the cobbles to the tavern and pushed inside.

The smoke of tobacco and of the coal hearth-fire filled the air with a grey haze that offended his nostrils and irritated his lungs, while the chatter of patrons and clatter of mugs and dishes assaulted his ears. A good place to hide from himself, he thought.

He proceeded into the taproom, its low ceiling and heavy, dark beams demanding that he sit and stay awhile among the wooden tables and chairs, the benches and pillars, the *habitués* and wanderers. Surveying the occupants as he scanned for a vacant seat, he noted no familiar faces, no leering looks. When he spotted an empty stool at the bar table, he made for it and reached into his pocket for his coin purse.

Placing a crown on the waxed wooden counter, he asked the publican, "How much will this buy me?"

Wordlessly, the podgy, redheaded, middle-aged barkeep set a glass and a full bottle before him. Michael filled the tumbler to the brim and downed it in one long gulp. The whisky seared his throat and flushed him with heat as it spread through his inwards and his blood. He poured another and tossed it back, as well. He had nearly finished the bottle and his eyes had become difficult to focus when a smooth, sultry voice with a decided Scots lilt said, "There's better ways to forget your sorrows, my

lad."

Michael turned toward the sound, and blinked, and forced himself to focus upon the pale round blur with its halo of flame. When he got his eyes under control, he found a freckled, red-haired woman with cool hazel eyes and very low-cut gown of brown wool that had seen better days. She smiled at him and ran a hand sensually from his elbow to his shoulder.

"I've a room upstairs if ye'd care to join me," she invited. She added peremptorily, "Bring the bottle."

Swaying on the stool, he watched as she walked away, slowly, her hips undulating beneath the layers of skirts. When she stopped and turned, waiting expectantly, he picked up the bottle and followed.

SHE PLUCKED the whisky from his hand, took a swig, and set the bottle on a small table in the corner by the door. Then, she peeled his coat, jacket, and waistcoat off while he stood blinking and staring. When she had draped the garments over a chair in another corner of the dingy little room lit by a solitary candle on an unvarnished chest of drawers, she deftly removed his pocketbook and took a couple of banknotes. She squirrelled them away in a drawer before she replaced the wallet and came back to unbutton his flies and pull off his suspenders.

"Would ye like me dressed or undressed?" she asked as she fondled his privates.

"I don't know," he responded with the honesty of drink and inexperience combined.

"First time, is it?" she surmised. "Well, then, we'll have to give you the full show, to be sure."

As he continued to bat his eyes and gape, she stripped away layer after layer of her clothing until nothing remained.

"Do ye like what ye see, lad?" she asked as she stepped closer and placed his hands on her small breasts.

In some remote part of his mind, he thought it ludicrous that she should call him a lad when he was surely older than she.

He guessed her no more than eighteen. But most of his mind ignored the observation, occupied as it was with remaining upright and with assessing the sensations in his fingers and palms where they brushed her milky mounds and her two little knobs that protruded, hard and pink.

"Come," she commanded, taking his hand and leading him to the bed. She whipped back the blanket to reveal crumpled sheets, threadbare and too rarely washed; in the fluttering light of the taper, the folds cast dusky shadows in sinuous bands. The young woman climbed into the bed, spread her legs wide, and waited for him to join her.

When he did not move for a long moment, simply swaying above her, she instructed, "Come and get on top o' me, my lad." She added with a grin, "Unless ye want to take a closer look, first."

At the suggestion, he realized he did want to get a better view of the mysterious bit of feminine anatomy of which he had heard many whispered tales and ribald jokes.

Grasping the nearest post, he stepped to the foot of the bed. Then, when he let go of the support, he all but fell onto the mattress and crawled to peer at the little auburn bush and rosy lips between her thighs. She smelled strongly of sweat and drink with a hint of urine. And a man's spunk, as well. But there was something else he had never scented before. In his drunken muddle, he could not decide whether he liked it or not. But he did decide that the reek of her previous client's fluids made him sick.

He scrambled up. Gasping, he glanced about urgently for a chamber pot. When he glimpsed one under the night table by the bed, he lunged and dragged it to him just in time to vomit.

"Well, that's nice!" the woman exclaimed in anger and disgust. "I suppose ye think you're too good for the likes o' me, eh?"

Sitting up and kicking his behind, she demanded, "Well, ye can just take your carcass on out o' here an' be damned wi' ye,

then!"

She stomped to where she had left her clothes and dressed hurriedly as he pushed himself to his haunches and wiped his mouth on his sleeve.

"I-I'm sorry," he stammered. "I-I-I...I'm sorry."

"Get out!" she shouted. "Bloody damn toff! Get out!"

She tossed his belongings at him, and a part of the coat fell into the muck in the pot. Clinging to his bundle of garments, he staggered up and blundered out of the room, tripped down the stairs, and ran into the night.

Cold rain pelted his face once more, now mixing with the hot tears that streamed down his cheeks.

HE HAD SQUATTED to swish his fouled coat-sleeve in a puddle before it occurred to him that the contents of the pool might be as bad as what he had rinsed off. He pushed himself up and stood in the rain, face to the sky and letting the water soak him. Only when he tried to walk again did he realize his unfastened trousers had sunk below his buttocks. Pinning the jacket, coat, and waistcoat between his arm and his body, he yanked the drawers and pants back up over his arse and tried to re-button, his efforts hampered by fumbling fingers and by bunches of fabric in the way.

"Don't bother on my account," said a voice from his right.

Michael started, jerking to face the stranger and stepping back. His heel caught a cobble, and he stumbled and sat down hard in a scatter of sodden wool.

The man chuckled and said, "Didn't mean to startle you." He offered his hand and added, "Let me help you up."

The streetlight behind blackened the man's face with shadow, but the cape and beaver-skin hat declared him a gentleman. Not that a gentleman was any more trustworthy than most, Michael reminded himself, but at least he was not likely to be a murderous footpad. Then again, if he were, would it matter?

The Scot took the gloved hand and got his feet under him.

He was steadier, now—still drunk, but no longer dazed and dizzy. Or perhaps not so steady after all, he realized when he bent to pick up his clothes and nearly fell again.

"Easy, there," said the man, grabbing Michael's arm to avert disaster.

When Michael straightened, his wallet fell to the pavement.

"I'll get it," the man volunteered, quickly stooping to pluck the leather pouch from the street. "Here you go," he added as he presented it.

"Thank you," Michael responded, grateful but wary. He had become acutely aware of the effect of the rain on his fine silk shirt: The fabric had melted to transparency save at the white of the folded seams. It clung to his skin, revealing his mat of chest hair and the muscular shape of his shoulders, and it left him feeling naked.

They both turned, and the streetlight revealed the stranger to be a handsome man of about thirty, average height, hair and eyes dark, lashes lush, nose sharp, and long face angular. His full lips and wide mouth drawn into an amused grin, the gentleman tilted his head and raked Michael's face and form brazenly.

"You're gorgeous," he declared, looking up into the Scot's eyes. "Despite the drowned-rat appearance."

Michael stuttered uncomfortably, "I-I'd better be going." Just then, a tickle in his nose triggered a sudden explosive sneeze that echoed in the narrow canyon of brick and stone and glass. He jerked his head aside barely in time to prevent spraying the man with sinus fluids; now, he snorted and shook his head violently to rid himself of the irritation.

"Good heavens!" The man whipped out a handkerchief and gave it to him. "We'd better get you inside before you catch your death."

"I'll find my way," Michael replied, wiping his nose and immediately handing back the square of fine linen. "Thanks."

With a gesture refusing the return of the handkerchief, the man said, "I have a flat nearby, and I insist that you at least get yourself dried off and take a hot bath and hot tea."

The gentleman grasped Michael's arm and pulled him toward Argyle Street. "I'm feeling quite chilled, myself," the stranger said as he dragged his reluctant guest to the boulevard and turned them west. "I'll have my cook make us some Athole brose, as well, shall I? I'm John, by the way. John Waverly."

Some minutes later, Michael found himself in the bright, marble-floored lobby of a small residential hotel. The building's plain outward appearance of unembellished stone and wood belied a lavish interior of polished oak, plush furnishings, and glittering silver fittings.

Waverly led the way to broad stairs that circled upward four flights, each level lit by silver girandole sconces with tapers that had recently been replenished. At the top, the man opened a figured oak door into a small entry hall that widened to a sumptuous apartment filled with exotic woods and rich silks.

A clap of the hands brought a middle-aged servant in deep blue livery and white gloves.

John Waverly announced, "My friend and I are in need of a hot bath and hotter tea, Hume. And ask Cook to make us some sweet brose, will you? There's a good lad."

The dour butler bowed slightly and said, "Very good, My Lord," before disappearing beyond an inner door.

"My Lord?"

With a dismissive gesture, Waverly said, "My father is a marquess. Let's get out of these sopping clothes, shall we?"

The young earl had already doffed his hat and cape and tossed them carelessly over a chair. When his guest vacillated, looking from his own dripping pile of grey wool to the expanding watermark on the pale Utrecht-covered fauteuil, the marquess's son said, "Do come along. I feel a sniffle coming on and I'd like to immerse myself in the hottest water I can stand."

Flustered and cold, Michael heaved his garments onto the

floor by the chair and followed his host to the bathing room. He decided: If he must endure another sodomite, at least he could warm his limbs and his belly for his trouble.

MICHAEL WOKE to the smell of tea and oatcakes and found himself in an enormous canopied bed with soft white sheets and heaps of pillows and feather blankets. He blinked and scratched himself as he glanced about trying to recall where he was and how he had got here.

When he attempted to rise, a stab of pain that threatened to explode his skull reminded him of the how. Gasping and clutching his head, he began to recall the events of the previous night.

Slowly, cautiously, he turned and rolled himself out of the bed. The door of the lavatory stood open, and he made his way there to relieve himself. When he returned, he collapsed onto one of the dove-grey plush wing chairs at the brocade-covered table under the window, and he poured himself a cup of tea from the waiting service.

A survey of the room revealed satinwood and mahogany, ebony and walnut, intaglio and parquetry, gilt-framed landscapes and still lifes, vases of flowers and bowls of fruit. But no John Waverly.

Glad of the solitude, Michael picked up the plate of cakes. He had started to munch an oat wedge when he glimpsed something odd: a fold of banknotes where the dish had been. He set down the china and cake and took up the money. He stared at it several minutes, recalling again and again the practised motion of the whore as she had deposited his cash into her drawer. He felt the paper, dry and crisp, its blocky official print and delicately curving calligraphy proclaiming its value.

Glancing around, he appreciated the luxury and comfort wealth afforded. Of course, his father provided him a substantial allowance, but it came with a price, and Michael often felt the man begrudged him the money despite his insistence upon

advanced education. At every failure or mistake, disappointment flickered in Joseph MacGregor's pale-blue eyes or resounded in the voice evoked by his handwritten missives, stabbing Michael with the knowledge of his insufficiency.

He looked again at the notes and counted them, awed by His Lordship's generosity, and wondering....

Then, he remembered the prostitute's wounded anger at what she had thought his rejection. And the small room and meagre furnishings, the worn garments, and the eyes so much older than her years. No, that was no easy life or quick route to riches and freedom.

He felt in memory the proprietary manner in which the marquess's son had touched him, and the same treatment, and worse, from others so many times before. No. No easy life. And no freedom.

He set the banknotes on the table and laid the plate over them. Then, he went in search of his clothes.

CHAPTER 35

The day was clear and warm, a fine September day.

A flight of geese honked overhead. Soon after, another flock flew southward in the familiar V configuration. Many of the smaller birds had already headed for their wintering grounds, their songs no longer heard, and the squeaky gurgle of cowbirds and the rusty screech of grackles foraging in the meadows and woods before embarking on the next leg of their journey heralded autumn as surely as the iconic call of the geese.

Michael had gone before first light to Stuart Avenue, thence to bring to The Flats a portion of his and Anne's wardrobes—hers primarily the working garments and smallclothes she had specified, plus a gown for Sunday, and his clothing weighted toward suits for his employ in the office. He and Anne had decided to gradually move back home, into the

north bedroom, now that the house was nearing completion. His mother had balked, at first, preferring that they remain in Rosemont. But Anne had not fainted in weeks; so, she coaxed and cajoled until Hermione agreed to the move—on condition that she or Elizabeth or both visit Anne daily while Michael worked in town.

As the glow of sunrise spread across The Flats, gold and glimmering, Michael returned with the boxes in Dan Doherty's rig. When they pulled in front of the gate, Dowd wakened in the hammock in the side yard, blinking and stretching. The boy untangled himself from the blankets in which Anne had wrapped him and, following his host, he eagerly fetched packages into the house, albeit one-armed.

Outside again, Michael smiled when he saw Dowd inhale deeply of the scents of the hot porridge and fresh tea that steamed in the summer kitchen. At first, the lad had not been happy that Anne insisted he stay in The Flats a few days to heal. Now, he seemed glad to enjoy a holiday off the streets. He sat still when she cleaned his wounds and changed his bandages, and he ate heartily of her home cooking. He did not even complain that his meals were always preceded by a large chunk of mouldy cheese, or that each evening ended with a glass of sharp-tasting kefir. But he resolutely demanded to sleep outside.

After a picnic breakfast of oats dotted with white apple chunks, red highbush cranberries, black crowberries, blue sweet huckleberries, the *mélange* topped with a pale pat of freshly churned butter, Michael pushed up from the grass, slung his frock-coat and lunch bag over one shoulder, and kissed Anne goodbye. He stopped at the gate and turned back, smiling as he watched his wife show the boy how to gather more ripe berries. He tilted his head and looked more closely when he noted the way she cupped her hand below her belly. She was rounder, now. Her cheeks flushed; her eyes sparkled; she shone like a small sun.

Reluctantly, he stepped into the lane and joined the men

heading into town. He hoped the day would go quickly, the sooner to return to his wife.

∞

IN THE EVENT, everything that could go wrong did go wrong.

A shipment of barley had been delayed. The wife of the maltsman sent word that he was ill and Joseph took his place, leaving Michael to inquire into the missing grain. The workings of the mash tun stuck and took almost an hour to clear. They were shorthanded in the fermenting room, and one of the washbacks overflowed, spilling yeasty foam over the floor. A portion of the wash-still had to be patched with new copper, delaying distillation. The barrel supplier had sent casks previously used for bourbon instead of sherry. And a delegation of ladies from the Temperance League demanded an audience.

When he realized he would be very late at the office, Michael sent Joseph's only secretary, a thin woman with permanently puckered lips, prematurely greying hair, and tall collars that covered her neck completely, to fetch supper from a nearby tavern. She balked at first, clearly assuming she would be manhandled in such a place, but he assured her that the owner of the *Golden Crown* was a good Anglican fellow who would allow no such shenanigans. When Miss Pettigrew finally acquiesced and accepted a five-dollar bill to pay for the meal (with the substantial remainder for herself), Michael sought Sean Quinn in the stillroom and asked him to inform Anne that he would not be home for dinner. On his return to his desk, the Scot decided it was time telephone service came to The Flats.

∞

THE TEMPERATURE dropped with the sun. As the indigo of twilight deepened to black, dense fog rolled in from the lake, pressing around Michael as he strode faster and faster along the city's streets. He had neither horse nor buggy, for he had taken

the streetcar, this morning. And he had missed the last one westward, tonight. Halfway home, he wished he had thought to hire a hackney carriage to take him from the distillery to The Flats.

He shivered. The waning moon would not rise until well after midnight and, when he left the thoroughfare just west of the bridge, he passed the last streetlight, its orange halo dimmed by the thick brume. He strode on, the shallow tracks of wagons and foot traffic his only guide for a long way once he passed the Bow.

In the darkness of The Flats pierced occasionally by dull-edged blades of light from windows or from the lanterns of self-appointed roving night-watchmen, Michael perceived the fog not so much visually as viscerally. He sensed it around him, and his rising fear clutched at his gut and tightened his buttocks and his throat.

All at once, a stern voice came from behind. "Evenin'." Not a greeting but a challenge.

Startled, heart in his throat, Michael whirled to find a figure approaching, the face masked by the glow of a raised lamp. All he could see clearly in the yellow light was a shillelagh poised to strike. He forced down his terror to reply politely, "Good evening."

"Ah, it's you, sir," said Alec Cohan, lowering the weapon and the lantern.

Recognizing the older man at last, Michael asked, "How is your wife, sir?" Mrs. Cohan had been suffering from bouts of rheumatism, for which both Anne and Dr. Hanes had yet to find an efficacious remedy.

"Oh, tolerable, sir, tolerable," Cohan answered.

Michael said, "I'll pray for her recovery."

"Oh, I thank ye, sir," Cohan replied. Then, he offered, "It's black as the Devil's heart, tonight. Would ye like me to see ye home?"

Michael nodded and said with relief, "That would be most appreciated, Mr. Cohan."

∞

THE COMPANY of the night-watchman from Willow Bend made negotiation of the winding ways of The Flats easier and quicker, and the man's litany of complaints about everything from his wife's condition to the politics in Ottawa distracted Michael. But underneath his courteous attentiveness, the Scot remained acutely aware of the malevolent vapours that closed in on every side. When finally he bade good night to the patrolman, he stumbled through the gate and raced to his front door, scrambling to open it. Once inside, he slammed the door against the demon that was his own dread, and leaned back against the oak, grateful for its solidity as he trembled and he gasped for breath.

At sight of her husband, Anne rushed to him, eyes wide and voice shrill with alarm. "What's wrong, Michael?"

He pulled her to him and held her tightly, trying to quell the panic in his own breast.

"What is it, my love?" Anne pressed, reciprocating the strength of his embrace in reassurance that he was not alone, whatever the trouble that disquieted him and caused his heart to pound as though it would leap from his chest.

Michael swallowed and took a long, tremulous breath before he whispered, "The fog."

"The fog," she repeated as she stroked his back soothingly. Thoughtful, she said it once more, "The fog."

Over a few minutes of holding each other and rocking together, Michael calmed ever so gradually. His heart slowed; his respiration deepened; his muscles relaxed. At last, he took his wife's face into his hands and he kissed her softly.

"I'm sorry," he whispered, ashamed. "I wish I were a stronger man. A better man. For you."

Anne's eyes flooded. They overflowed as she squeezed them tightly, her belly twitching with the sobs she suppressed. At her distress, he clasped her to him again.

"I'm sorry. I'm sorry," he repeated urgently.

Anne pushed away and said fiercely, "No! Don't you dare be sorry!" She closed her eyes, struggling for control, and then she opened them to look into his depths. Her voice quiet, clear, throaty, certain, she said, "You are MacGregor, son of the mist: The fog belongs to you. They stole it from you. Now, take it back. With me. Tonight."

She cupped his cheeks with her hands and said, her tone now entreaty, "Let us take it back together, my love."

She held his gaze, and he searched her eyes even as he plumbed the depths of his own heart. Finally, he nodded.

She took his hand and led him out into the night.

∞

THE MEREST SLIVER of crescent moon rose over the trees in the northeast, its light dispersed to form a curved patch of grey in the pitch black before dawn. He should be cold, lying on the ground in nothing but his shirt, the silk unbuttoned and fallen to his sides, and with only a thin blanket as covering. But he was not.

He lay with Anne snuggled close at his side, her head resting in the hollow beside his shoulder, her arm stretched across him, her leg entwined with his. Her exhalations stirred hairs of his chest as she breathed slowly, rhythmically.

His own heart beat steady and strong, and peace filled him.

Staring up into the dusk, Michael MacGregor felt the mist around him and knew it was his.

CHAPTER 36

Trust

A fter the usual Sunday services, the entire community crowded into the nave of St. Anthony's—Catholics, Protestants, and Jews alike—for the long-awaited wedding of Constable Patrick O'Toole and Mrs. Sarah Monaghan. The pair had been dancing around each other diffidently for two years and would now, finally, tie the knot.

The seating had not officially been divided into groom's side versus bride's side, but Miss Hetty and her ladies occupied the first two pews on the left while O'Toole's friends and family, most of them members of the constabulary, formed a block on the right. The people of The Flats insisted that the MacGregors take a place of honour at the front alongside Miss Hetty, and then they filled the remainder of the seats and lined the walls.

Her arm entwined with Michael's, Anne sighed as the bride and groom knelt before the altar. Her husband looked

down to her and squeezed her hand, and she smiled up at him. She reflected fondly that he had changed in the months they had known each other: He had grown into himself and become more comfortable in his own skin. And she was glad for him.

Constable O'Toole dropped the ring in his nervousness, and flower girl little Miss Becky O'Malley, her red hair mirroring the bride's, scrambled after the golden band that rolled past her. When the ring came to rest three pews down, Becky stooped to reach for it and bumped heads with Terence O'Grady's little sister, Joan, who had also tried to retrieve the shiny thing at her feet. Throughout the church, adults stifled snickers as both little girls whined and whimpered and rubbed their wee pates, and as Patrick O'Toole and Sarah Monaghan and the girls' respective mothers tried to sooth and quiet them. The other children laughed out loud at the kerfuffle, and immediately received shushes and stern looks from their elders.

At last, all the children settled and the ceremony resumed with bride and groom scarlet-faced and abashed.

When the rite ended and the newly married couple walked down the aisle together wearing expressions of relief, Michael whispered, "Do you wish we'd had a proper wedding?"

Anne fixed his eyes and replied, "We *did* have a proper wedding, under law." She insisted, "I do not need all the trappings. And I would love you and live with you, even without a lawful marriage."

Taken aback at the notion, Michael asked, "You would accept such a tenuous arrangement? You would risk abandonment and public obloquy?"

She caressed his cheek and said softly, "I trust you. And I need only you."

He clasped her hand to his face, searching her eyes; then, he pressed his lips to her palm.

∞

AS HE STROLLED along the sunny lanes of The Flats with his wife, following the throng that wended its way toward the Commons where the celebrations of the nuptials would take place, Michael contemplated Anne's statement: *I trust you.* A *frisson* had run through him at her words, and did again at their echo in his mind.

He glanced down at Anne as she waved to Terence O'Grady and the boy's old friends, Ian Murdoch and the Four Horsemen—all still students of hers, though her unofficial school operated only sporadically since the fire that had destroyed the original house.

She trusted him.

Again, a thrill flashed through Michael at the thought.

How rarely had he trusted anyone. And how rarely had others had confidence in him—or he in himself, for that matter. A memory stirred....

∞

Egypt, 1884

THE BLOODY SUN beat down relentlessly in this godforsaken country. Sand got into everything, even the crack of his arse and under his foreskin, and flies crawled into his nostrils, flew into his mouth, and left eggs in his food. The water tasted foul, the meat tasted worse. And everyone had the runs.

What the hell am I doing here? he groused under his breath. In bitter self-deprecation, he answered his own question: *Oh, yes. I got drunk and "volunteered" for service.*

He had found a coin in the bottom of his quaich that evening and, being by this time unsteady on his feet, he had been no match for the soldiers who had gleefully pressed him into Her Majesty's armed forces under the pretext that he had already accepted payment from the Crown.

And now, here he was: in Egypt.

His comfortable and tailored civilian suit of clothes had

been traded for an ill-fitting uniform that included a grey wool serge jacket and trousers, cotton shirt, and tightly woven suspenders that rubbed sand and sweat into his skin. Over his shoulder, he carried the grey greatcoat that hung heavy in the heat of the day but proved essential in the chilly nights. He was trussed up in a thick canvas webbing belt with vertical straps over his shoulders, cross straps as well, and various pouches—all of which he had managed, on the advice of an old-timer, to stain with tea to soften their colour from their original eye-piercing white. He had purchased a milky cotton towel to wear under his white pipe-clayed helmet, both to soak up the sweat before it trickled down his face and into his eyes, and to protect his neck from sun and from wind-blown sand.

According to the sergeant, they were marching west. That much, he had figured out for himself. Some of his fellow privates speculated that they were headed for battle; Michael MacGregor suspected they were merely sightseeing: Their officer, third son of a baron, was a student of history who constantly expounded ancient wars and the politics of dead civilizations.

Michael shifted the shoulder strap of his Martini Henry Mark IV rifle and pulled at an unfortunately situated fold of his baggy trousers.

In Alexandria, he had seen Highlanders sporting kilts under their scarlet or grey tunics, and he wondered if such garb was advantage or disadvantage in this climate. The kilt would leave all below the waist open to sand and insects. On the other hand, a man would have no encumbrance should he be caught short—a hazard as ineluctable as the maddening sand.

Michael's eyes hurt, despite squinting, for the sun now shone in his face directly. From horizon to horizon, there was nothing but yellow sand, and he was certain that they would not reach an oasis before nightfall. *Bloody hell.*

THEY HAD NO WOOD with which to make a campfire. They had no water but what remained in their bottles. All had the

issued Bovril tubes marked "dinner" at one end and "cocoa" at the other, and some had purchased tea and biscuits, but without water or fire there seemed little point in breaking open the packages of dry rations.

Not tasked with sentry duty tonight, the Scot simply picked a spot a little way from the others but well within the perimeter, and there he bedded down. From the start, he had kept to himself, especially at night. True, he had never been a social creature like Evan. And he had little in common with most of his fellow soldiers, he being university educated and many of them not even literate. But he had noted an aloofness in the other men that was born of more than his differences from them, he was sure, for he did not like the way some looked at him. At first, he had wondered if they were merely intimidated by his size—he, head and shoulders taller than all but two who were an inch or so shorter than himself. He did not want to believe these strangers could see in him the deviance that seemed to draw sodomites to him like flies to manure, but he feared perhaps they did.

Whatever the cause of their unfriendliness, he did not feel as comfortable among the men as they had become with one another over the weeks in England, at sea, and here.

Michael lay on the ground wrapped in his greatcoat and stared at the night sky shimmering with more stars than he had ever before seen. The one thing that could be said for the desert, he mused, was that it afforded a spectacular view of the heavens. At a shuffling nearby, he looked to find that a small lad a little younger than himself had lain three yards away.

Private Thomas Pendarvis was a nervous, pretty man who had been a bookkeeper before he had been pressed into service. By rights, he should have been sequestered in some London bureau to file requisitions or audit ledgers. But there seemed little logic in the Army's doings, and the fair-haired, pale-skinned, fine-boned little lad had been sent, instead, to march across deserts and fight England's enemies.

Michael sighed.

Every muscle in his body burned, as did every patch of skin that had remained unprotected. But the chance to lie down was pure bliss. His eyelids fluttered and closed.

IT WAS THEIR THIRD day out.

The bloody sand had already worn his socks to shreds, leaving his heels bare inside the grit-filled leather of his shoes. He wished he had puttees or spats; they might have kept out some of the dirt.

His nose had begun to peel from the daily sunburns. His armpits and crotch had burnt raw with sweat and sand. But at least he no longer had "Delhi belly," as the sergeant called diarrhoea. With little water and less food, there was nothing left inside him to pass, though an ineffectual urge still struck from time to time.

No one had a drop of water in his bottle. They should have reached an oasis by now, but Michael suspected the bloody officer had got them lost. They were not travelling in circles—he would have recognized it, and he thought the sergeant would, too—but perhaps they did not walk a straight course. With no landmarks, only miles of sand in every direction, it was difficult to tell.

FOURTH DAY, he wrote in his notebook in the last light before sunset.

> We found a well. The water is muddy and smells putrid, but it is better than no water at all. All of us have filled our bottles and eaten a little of our rations. God help us if we don't find an oasis soon.
>
> I wonder if the daft officer

is trying to take us to Siwa and the Temple of Amun.

"What you writin', there?"

Corporal Apted, Michael had quickly realized, was one of the illiterates who had found his true home in the Army. Rough and rustic son of a collier, he mistrusted anyone with schooling and any profession not entirely physical. In defence against what he perceived as the ridicule of all "toffs," he had adopted a reverse snobbery that branded anyone not like him suspect, and probably worthless.

Michael closed his diary around his pencil and stuffed both into his expense pouch. He said, "Nothing important, Corporal. Just a letter home."

As soon as he was allowed, Michael had sent a missive to his father and one to Evan explaining his unintentionally acquired career. He knew neither could intercede on his behalf, and he should have expected his father to write that a stint in the military would do him good. He should have, but he had not, and the words under the MacGregor Highland Distilleries letterhead had struck him like a slap to the face: yet another veiled accusation of inherent inadequacy.

Pushing the memory aside, he untied his laces—thank God they were not yet worn through—and removed his short boots and his socks to dry his feet before shoeing himself once more. In the field, one did not dare to leave one's footwear off overnight, else creatures would crawl inside, drawn to the lingering warmth and the moisture. Even in barracks, Private Johnson had been stung by a scorpion because he had failed to empty his boot in the morning. But perhaps he was the lucky one: He had remained in hospital in Cairo while the rest of the regiment had set off on this fool's errand.

On the western horizon, the glowing orange orb quickly flattened into a band and abruptly disappeared, leaving all in instant darkness and sudden cold. Michael pushed his arms into

the sleeves of his greatcoat and snugged the thick wool around him.

He missed the long summer evenings of home with their gradually diminishing light and their gentle warmth. A misgiving slipped into his thoughts: He wondered if he would ever see his country again. And he wondered whether anyone would care if he did not.

AT FIRST, he thought it was an illusion, a mirage. The blasting heat shimmered above the sand, giving an impression of sunlight reflecting off of water, and the soldiers had been fooled, before, into thinking they approached a lake. But this time, as they came closer, the lake did not recede in the distance, ever out of reach. Instead, it sprouted clumps of vegetation around it and grew more distinct with every step.

The last hundred yards, the men ran headlong to the pool, shouting and laughing as they splashed into the Heaven-sent Adam's ale. The officer blew his whistle and tried to regain control, but soon gave it up on the whispered advice of the sergeant.

They dared not cut down trees for fire, but there were fallen fronds from the palms, and bushes that could spare a twig here and there, affording enough fuel to boil some water for tea and cocoa. In the morning, once the turbidity caused by their exuberance settled, they would all refill their bottles with the lovely, clear water.

The weakness that had crept into their bodies for lack of sufficient food and water and excess of heat and exertion had begun to retreat. Already, after a wash, a hard biscuit, and a soup made of Bovril paste heated in water, Michael felt much restored. He lay down a few yards from his fellows, his unloaded rifle nearby, and he slept with a feeling of deep, albeit unwarranted, contentment.

He woke in the dark with a blade at his throat.

PERHAPS HE SHOULD have cried out. *But then you'd have had your throat cut, for certain.*

Perhaps he should have fought. *But then you'd have been gutted, with no weapon immediately to hand.*

The Scot snorted in self-derision: How many times had he wished he were dead? When presented with an opportunity to die, though, he had saved himself, instead. But for what?

Michael scanned their captors. Berber, he thought. Or Bedouin. Nomads of some sort, to be sure. Now that he saw them in light of day, barely dawn though it was, he realized his regiment had been greatly outnumbered and these men could easily have murdered all the English troops in their sleep— thanks to the four sentinels who had probably allowed themselves to drift off instead of remaining alert. At least, he *hoped* they had fallen asleep: The only alternative he could imagine was that they had been killed by the enemy and, although he felt no kinship with his fellow soldiers, he did not wish them harm.

Glancing to Private Pendarvis, the bookkeeper's hands bound by jute rope as Michael's were and the lad trailing a camel as he was, Michael saw the blue eyes with white all around and the utter terror in the young man's countenance. In an attempt at consolation, he said, "If they meant to kill us, we'd be dead already."

"Then what do they want?"

Michael could not reply. Of the possibilities that came to mind, none would prove a solace to the Cornishman.

For himself, he thanked God he had wrapped his head in the cotton towel he had purchased in Alexandria, its snowy fibres now shielding him from the brutal sun. As for his helmet, it and his rifle (unless the latter was stolen) would have been all the sergeant and officer found of him when they awoke, this morning.

IF they woke, he reminded himself grimly.

WHEN THEY REACHED the encampment (a clutter of faded tents stretched on poles to provide shade, most of them with sides rolled up rendering them open to the breeze that came from the north), Michael found that he and Pendarvis were not the only captives: Corporal Apted and the redheaded Private Blake had also been taken. The British soldiers were herded to a closed tent in the middle of the compound. A guard was stationed outside the entrance and, all around, tribesmen milled in flowing, if faded and dirty and somewhat ragged garb and in headscarves cinched with twisted cloth. In their belts, the raiders variously sported damascened scimitars; gleaming broadswords; long knives, some with jewelled handles; and pistols of assorted vintages. The odd rifle had been slung over a man's shoulder. The Scot recognized a Martini Henry.

After a time, a boy entered the small prison into which they had been shoved. The lad brought to each of them in turn a bowl of water, replenishing it as needed from a larger basin set outside. The prisoners drank with relish, despite the odour of the water and the well-used appearance of the clay dish.

Once they were alone again, Private Pendarvis asked in a low voice, "Corporal, what do they want of us?"

"Damned if I know," Apted replied. "Don't know why they didn't take the whole regiment. Or murder us all, for that matter."

"Do you think anyone was killed?" Michael asked.

"Not that I saw," said the corporal. He turned a gimlet eye upon Private Blake and added, "But seems the sentries wasn't seein' much, neither."

"They came on us real quiet," Blake protested. "I was awake, Corp, truly I was. But I didn't hear or see nothin' a-tall."

Apted snorted contemptuously, his disbelief blatant. Blake pouted, turned his gaze downcast, and scratched his crotch with one hand while the other, still bound to the first, wriggled ineffectually in the air. Everyone else followed suit, trying to relieve itches and rawness and folds of serge bunched in

uncomfortable places.

THEY HAD BEEN travelling for many days, west for the most part, though they had made detours to oases and wells and, presumably, away from disputed areas or other known hazards of the desert, such as the Badlands with their salt marshes and salt lakes. Red ridges appeared in the distance, and soon the migrants passed among plateaux and mountains. Michael realized they must be in Tripolitania. How far would they be taken? To Benghazi? To Algiers? To Casablanca?

The sun hammered them mercilessly; their faces had blistered and their lips had cracked. But at least they were not encumbered and chafed by their webbings and pouches. Their belongings had been rifled, and the captives had been left with nothing but their clothes. Not even belts or suspenders had been returned, making it necessary to improvise belts from underwear in order to hold their trousers up.

For water and food, and for protection from the creatures of the golden sands, they were forced to rely on their keepers.

No one had spoken to the British soldiers except for commands in the native tongue accompanied by gestures to indicate their captors' intent. Only on the march did Michael spot women. The females of all ages, shrouded in dark robes and veils, travelled in groups and, when the tribe was stationary, were sequestered away from men—especially the foreigners. The women never seemed to speak to anyone.

The caravan stopped near a ruins of indeterminate age and original purpose. An abandoned town, perhaps? A temple? Rubble piles of rust-coloured blocks lay at the foot of crumbling cubic shapes, all tumbled and sand-blasted and gradually being reclaimed by the desert.

A few hundred yards from the landmark, the tribe milled in the manner Michael had come to recognize as the precursor to the pitching of tents and establishment of camp.

"I wouldn't mind some o' that," said Private Blake with a

nod toward a flock of women shuffling past.

Corporal Apted spat upon the ground and warned, "Give ye the clap or worse, that would." With a chin wag toward men of the tribe, he added, "Mind, they'd prob'ly chop ye to pieces just for tryin'; so, I don't s'ppose ye'd notice a bit o' pox." He grinned at Blake, who sighed in a mix of resignation and frustration.

With sardonic lewdness, the corporal turned to Michael and Private Pendarvis to comment, "Don't s'ppose you two would give 'em any cause for concern."

Blinking, bewildered, Pendarvis asked, "What do you mean?"

Apted replied, "Think I ain't seen the two o' ye sneakin' off to be by yourselves of a night?"

The Cornishman gaped in surprise, stuttered incoherently, and reddened as Blake snickered and Apted leered at the little bookkeeper.

His eyes daggers, Michael said evenly, "We were just putting plenty of distance between us and *you*, Corporal. Wouldn't be safe close by, lest you should feel a need for company when everyone else is asleep."

Blake suppressed a giggle as Apted whirled and bared his teeth, about to respond with a volley of outraged vituperation.

Abruptly, one of their guards whacked Apted, then Michael, with a riding crop and shouted, "Yallah!" in a command that could mean anything from "Shut up" to "Move along" to "Faster" to "Eat," judging by their experience to date. Only when the man gestured did they understand he wanted them to go in the indicated direction.

INSTEAD OF BEING marched to their usual prison tent, the four were shunted to the far side of the ruins, where another encampment had been erected. They were taken directly to the largest tent, a white one that appeared almost pristine.

Inside, they were presented to a dark-bearded, brown-

skinned, and black-eyed man in snowy kaftan, jibbah, and keffiyeh, lounging languidly beyond the central pole on red cushions embroidered with gold threads. Jewelled rings adorned his fingers and thumbs, and gems encrusted the handle of the curved knife at his broad cummerbund. Even the knife's sheath proclaimed its owner's wealth, being embroidered and beaded in gold.

Incense burned in a brass bowl, oil in a brass lamp, and lust in the sheikh's eyes. Michael's gut tightened as the man appraised each of them, from Michael to Pendarvis to Apted to Blake and back again to vacillate between the Scot and the Cornishman. Finally, the Arab's gaze lingered on the fair bookkeeper.

"Come. Sit," their host invited with a honeyed smile and excellent English.

A servant set cushions before them, and another brought golden goblets of water. The four soldiers sat. Their wrists still bound, they held the gilt cups in two hands and drank delicious, clear water such as they had not tasted since they had set sail from England. Michael wondered where it had been obtained.

In an attempt to take charge of the situation, the now fortified Corporal Apted demanded, "Why have you abducted representatives of Her Majesty Queen Victoria, sir?"

The sheikh feigned surprise and responded, "I have abducted no one, sir, much less representatives of the great queen. You are my guests."

His smile benign, he added incidentally, "Though I cannot speak to how you came to be in my realm." Nonchalantly, he sipped from his own bejewelled chalice.

The corporal asked through clenched teeth, "Do you keep all your guests bound? And how long are we to *be* your guests, then?"

The sheikh said lightly, "That will depend upon..." he waved his free hand in a vague gesture, "how soon I can arrange to have you returned to your people. As for the bonds...."

At his signal, one of his personal guards sliced the ropes.

Apted seethed but said nothing as he rubbed his raw wrists. Blake glanced about nervously. Pendarvis stared into his cup. And Michael fixed the gaze of their "host."

AFTER ONE MORE drink and a light meal of grapes and dates, the involuntary guests were ushered to a nearby tent and provided basins and towels with which to wash, along with delousing powder. Through the opening in the grey of the cloth wall, the tent-fly flapping in the breeze, Michael glimpsed, beyond their new jailers, the leader of the wandering tribe that had captured them. As the brigand exited the sheikh's tent, he grinned broadly and carried away a small, laden sack.

They had been sold.

Michael glanced to each of his fellow prisoners, surreptitiously assessing them as he washed away the sweat and dust from his body. At the mere suggestion of sodomy, Apted would fight until they killed him, he was sure. Blake would probably do the same, though the Scot suspected the young redhead did not have the corporal's skill in combat. Pendarvis would resist as best he could.

If they were forced—as might well occur with the help of servants and restraints—the corporal and Blake would turn their shame and hatred into a relentless search for means to escape and, perhaps, to exact revenge. Pendarvis, on the other hand, would be broken in spirit by such an attack; of that, Michael was certain.

A boy brought clean kaftans. When the young Arab began to gather up their filthy clothes, Corporal Apted clung to his belongings and growled obscenities. But the guards intervened and the frightened child escaped with what remained of their uniforms.

Once more, Michael MacGregor surveyed his comrades. After a protracted study of Thomas Pendarvis, he came to a decision. He rose and strode to the tent flap.

"Where you goin'?" Apted demanded.

Without turning around, Michael replied, "I'm going to try to get us out of here."

Before the corporal could inquire further, the Scot pushed outside and gestured to the sentries that he wanted to go to the sheikh's tent.

"I EXPECTED YOU would come," said the elegantly dressed Arab with a knowing smile. He motioned to his attendants, at which all but one left. The warrior stationed himself close by.

"I want to make a deal," said Michael. He stood several feet from his reclining captor, aware of the vigilant eyes of the large, formidably armed guard.

"What is it you want? And what could you offer me?"

The black eyes shone with cold amusement.

Michael swallowed and closed his hands into fists in an effort to control his voice. "Let the others go, and I'll stay with you. I won't try to escape. I'll do as you wish."

The Arab's face split in a mocking grin. "But where could you go, should you escape? There is nothing but desert, and you with no water and no knowledge to guide you." He stated coolly, "You have nothing with which to bargain."

His belly transforming to mush, Michael said, "I'll...make it worth your while. I know...the ways of pleasure." He swallowed again.

The sheikh eyed him a small eternity and finally said, "As you wish." He added, "You will call me 'effendim.'"

"Yes, effendim."

MICHAEL HAD EMPLOYED every means he knew to please his new effendi, his master. Almost every means: He thought it wise to keep a few tricks in reserve lest the man bore too easily.

Afterward, at the sheikh's wordless command, the sentinel brought Michael back to the prison tent to sleep with the other British soldiers. Blake and Pendarvis had fallen into fitful

slumber, but Apted sat up and cocked his brows as the Scot entered. Michael said nothing. He simply lay down and turned away to finish himself as he contemplated a future servicing a man who took delight in tantalizing him and leaving him unsatisfied.

How long would the bastard take to release the others? Perhaps not long, he thought hopefully. He had seen a glimmer to the west and believed the Mediterranean to be close by. Surely Apted could lead Blake and Pendarvis to the coast and find means to return to Cairo?

THE SLAVERS remained, feasting and dancing on the far side of the ruins. Each day, Michael asked when his comrades would be set free and, each day, the sheikh prevaricated. Each day and each night, the Scot did whatever was required of him, and endured the Arab's taunts and toying before returning to his jail.

On the evening of the fifth day, the sheikh sent him as a gift to a visiting Ottoman officer camped with his contingent of troops a half-mile away. The colonel had started with him a second time when shouts interrupted the man's pleasure.

Michael could not comprehend the rapid report of the Turkish corporal, nor the quick commands of the officer, but there was no mistaking the gunshots from the direction of the sheikh's encampment. He pulled on his kaftan as the colonel struggled into his braid-decorated European-style uniform. At a run, no one bothering to stop him, Michael raced across the sand toward the shouts and the torchlights.

When he arrived, he found Corporal Apted and Private Blake sprawled, dead, halfway between the cramped grey prison tent and the commodious white dwelling of the sheikh. He ran into the portable palace and shouted, "You said you'd let them go!"

Casually dismissive, the Arab replied, "I cannot be responsible for the behaviour of your friends. They attacked me, and my guards took appropriate measures."

Barely reining his fury, Michael demanded with accusation and disbelief clear in his tone, "Why would they attack you, outnumbered and without weapons?"

The man shrugged and said insouciantly, "We will never know."

Behind the Scot, the two corpses were being hauled away. Before him, the sheikh waved his wordless demand for pleasure. Weighed by futility and uncertainty and helplessness, Michael stepped forward, his shoulders slumped and his whole being drained of the fire that had filled him moments before. He knelt on the carpet.

When the Turk entered in full uniform, his host explained away the incident and offered once more to share his plaything.

EXHAUSTED AND SORE, his balls aching and cock throbbing with unfulfilled need, Michael staggered into the grey tent at dawn. He dropped to the mat next to Pendarvis and finished himself so that he could sleep.

As he settled, he noticed something amiss, and he glanced at the curled form of the Cornishman, the young man turned away, his shoulders jerking in little irregular twitches.

"I thought you were asleep," he whispered to the private.

When no response came, he asked, "Do you know what happened? Why did they kill Apted and Blake?"

Again, no response. Michael reached out and placed a hand on the bookkeeper's shoulder to shake him. An instant wail and reflexive recoil told Michael everything.

"God damn him!" he raged, and tears of frustration and fury filled his eyes. He pounded the mat impotently, choking with renewed choler and gasping in ragged breaths.

Then, he pushed down his wrath, down into his gut, hardening it and steeling himself as he clenched every muscle in his body in resolve. To Pendarvis, he snapped, "Endure it!"

"I can't! I can't bear it!" the young man responded through his weeping.

"You can and you must," Michael replied imperatively. "You can, as I have since I was eleven. And you must so that we can find a way to escape."

Belly convulsing with persistent sobs, Pendarvis rolled over and gaped at him. "Since you were eleven?"

With brutal irony, Michael quipped, "The benefits of a classical education."

The young man blinked and mulled a moment, gradually quieting. At last, he nodded.

THE OTTOMANS went north. The nomads went west. And after a few days of tormenting his "guests" at the ruins, the sheikh ordered his caravan south.

They travelled for several weeks, stopping at villages perched by oases, skirting the forests of Barqah with their oaks and wild olives, and trading with other wandering tribes where their paths crossed. Michael and Pendarvis were always bound or guarded or both, though they complied with their demon's every whim. When the cavalcade swung east into a sea of reddish dunes, Michael noticed his companion now moved like an automaton, trudging wordlessly within the cluster of warriors that separated the prisoners from the members of the tribe. The bookkeeper's eyes had dulled, the glint of life dying within them.

"Thomas," Michael whispered. When the man seemed not to hear, the Scot sidestepped and gently touched the Cornishman's shoulder.

The smaller man looked up at him with sightless eyes. He blinked and then turned forward once more, marching on.

"We must endure. We'll find a way to get home," Michael murmured, though he knew the man no longer heard and the words were, in truth, an attempt to buoy himself.

IT WAS THE NEXT day that their chance came: One of the outriders on camelback had spotted on the horizon a column of travellers where there should be none at this time of year. When

he reported the anomaly, the sheikh ordered the tribe to halt while chosen warriors investigated.

Women and children, old men and sick ones milled in increasing anxiety at the unexpected turn of events, their mood infecting their dromedaries and goats. As the sheikh and his advisors waited for word from the scouts, attention within the caravan proper lapsed. A goat escaped and trotted away from its herder. When women and children chased it through the throng, someone dropped a knife on the ground as the pursuit ranged back and forth. Michael glanced about: Those eyes not drawn to the turmoil looked to the horizon. He shuffled forward and kicked sand over the shiny blade. Again, he scanned for observers and found none. He knelt as though to refasten his sandal, and he slipped the knife into his sleeve.

When the goat veered back, Michael jumped up and out of the way, pulling Pendarvis with him as the commotion passed. He looked toward the sheikh and his council and found the bastard regarding him with narrowed eyes. The Scot glanced quickly toward the horizon and, to his relief, in his peripheral vision he saw the Arab turn his scrutiny back to the distance.

A cloud of dust indicated the scouts were returning at speed. Anxiety turned to fear, and the crowd swarmed chaotically as the remaining warriors stepped forward and everyone else pressed in the opposite direction, grabbing up belongings and searching for children who had wandered during the caprine caper.

Shouts reached them from the returning party, and commands from the hierarchy set the Arabs into even more agitated motion. A towering wave of powdery dirt that obscured sight beyond a few feet arrived with the gallopers, and Michael used it as cover to drag Pendarvis behind an abandoned cart. There, he slid the knife from his sleeve to clamp it between his knees and slice his bonds.

As the sheikh and council conferred with the scouts and as the rest of the warriors listened and waited for orders, Michael

cut the bookkeeper's bindings, as well, and clasped Thomas's hand. He cautiously peered past the edge of the little wagon toward the tribe's leaders. From the riders, he caught the word "Senussi" several times. It occurred to him that the arrogant bastard may have angered the Brotherhood, the *de facto* rulers of this region of the Sahara. Had he been spying on them for the Ottoman's? Was that the source of the Arab's wealth? If so, it would certainly be a *casus belli* from the point of view of the Senussi.

When someone ran past, the Scot quickly pulled the hood of his jellaba over his head and hunched down against the cart. Before him, a curled corner of sackcloth bared the cart's contents and revealed the covered lumps within to be water casks with strings. *Thank you, God,* thought Michael as he reached inside and pilfered as many as he could loop over his neck and arms. He draped three over the bookkeeper's neck, as well.

"We're leaving soon, Thomas," he whispered. "It won't be long, now."

While the panicked women and children headed north with whatever they could carry, the warriors mounted horses and rode toward the column of strangers, bent on war. No one paid attention to the two British soldiers.

As soon as the billow of dust from the departing cavalry obliterated vision, Michael dragged Pendarvis into the red cloud and ran through the whirling, choking powder, praying that he could stay within its shelter long enough to foil possible pursuit.

A few hundred yards out, their smokescreen was thinning. Michael pulled Pendarvis down and blanketed him with sand to his neck. For himself, he managed only to cover his legs, and he made shift with burrowing as deeply as he could into the loose dirt around him. He still had the knife, but it would do no good against swords or pistols or rifles. And he was only one man against a small army.

He waited and he prayed.

HOURS PASSED. At least, he *thought* it had been hours. The sun had descended, but he had not paid much attention to it earlier and he was now not sure by how much it had sunk toward the horizon. The distant sounds of battle had risen and fallen, but the pounding of hooves toward the intruders had not been replicated in the opposite direction. Had the tribe been defeated? Or were the shiekh's warriors simply engaged in gathering prisoners and plundering a caravan?

He did not dare to lift his head to peek in either direction.

Thomas Pendarvis merely lay there and stared at him, and Michael wondered if the man had gone mad.

BEFORE THE SUN SET, a low rumble barely heard in the ground below him rose slightly and then faded away. The sheikh and his advisors and personal guards had decided to leave, Michael guessed. He wondered how long it would take the bastard to figure out his prisoners had run off. With his army captured or wiped out and the rest of his tribe scattered across the plain, perhaps the Arab would ignore the trifling matter of a couple of missing slaves. Nonetheless, the Scot waited until dark before climbing out of his shallow grave and leading Private Pendarvis toward the east.

ON THE FIFTH day after their escape, Thomas spoke. "Where are we?" he asked.

They had passed beyond a series of red granite massifs into a basin of yellow sand. "Somewhere in Egypt, I think," Michael answered. Uncertain as to the bookkeeper's mental state, he added, "On our way home."

"Home," Thomas repeated.

"I can't guarantee we'll get there quickly," Michael warned. "I'm steering as straight a course as I can, but without compass or watch, we may be meandering."

"You'll take us home," said the Cornishman quietly.

The certainty, the trust in the man's voice startled

Michael. And disconcerted him. In his own estimation, he had done nothing to earn it. For both their sakes, he prayed he could live up to such expectations.

IN THE END, they did get home, thanks to a caravan of Berbers eastbound from Algeria who traded in glass and mirrors rather than in slaves.

Once back in Cairo, their reports were reviewed and their status as deserters was eventually rescinded (though the paymaster took months to acknowledge the change). Even after their story was officially accepted, they were tasked with light duties in the city—duties that afforded plenty of time for repeated interrogations concerning their experiences and observations. Finally, everyone seemed satisfied that no more could be gleaned from them and they were put on the roster for regular postings.

Given the notoriety of the sheikh to whom they had been sold, Thomas Pendarvis's request to be sent home to England was granted without hesitation. Several officers urged Private MacGregor to return as well, but Michael chose to remain with the troops headed for war. He hoped that in battle he would find death despite his cowardice.

His unit not yet ready to depart for the Sudan, Michael was given permission to see Thomas to the train station. The smaller man had barely spoken since their ordeal, and Michael worried what would become of him.

"Here's your ticket," Michael told him as he handed over the boarding pass. "The colonel says a Sergeant Farquharson will meet you at Alexandria and get you onto the first ship home."

"Farquharson," Thomas repeated.

In the bustling station, where they were jostled by passing Egyptians and Bedouins, British soldiers and Highlanders and Bengalis, the two stood as though at the centre of a whirlwind and stared at each other.

Finally, Michael licked his lips, extended his hand, and

said, "Good luck, Thomas."

"Why aren't you coming home, too?" Thomas asked, perplexed, perhaps even melancholy. He did not take the proffered hand.

Michael considered a moment before answering, "I don't have one."

"They don't know," Thomas said with realization. "Your family, they don't know."

"No."

He was sure his father would not have told Mother and Elizabeth what Michael had finally, in desperation, revealed in his letters from school in England, so long ago. Father would have kept that shame to himself.

Thomas swallowed. He said softly, "I don't think I can tell mine, either."

The whistle announced the train's imminent departure.

Michael guided his friend through the crowd to a passenger car entryway and saw him onto the step as the iron wheels slowly began to rotate and the locomotive lurched to gradually pull away. Though he did not know why, Michael felt compelled to keep pace.

Holding a vertical pole for support as the vehicle lumbered on its tracks, Thomas called above the ambient noise, "Why can't we trust them to love us anyway?"

Michael stopped dead and watched the forlorn face of the little bookkeeper recede in the distance. He had no answer.

∞

Present day

TENDED BY the O'Reillys, as usual, tables of food and drink lined the north edge of the Commons under the shade of a row of evergreen balsam firs and spruces interspersed with red-leafed maples and gold-topped beeches and ashes. Miss Hetty played the dutiful hostess, seeing elderly people to benches and chairs

sheltered under a copse of white-trunked birches crowned with vivid yellow foliage, and directing guests to the food, the drinks, or the nearest privies as needed. The musicians of The Flats, joined by a few talented members of the constabulary, warmed up their instruments and began to play. Thus, the shindig in celebration of an improbable marriage got underway.

On their approach to the festivities, Michael stopped and pulled Anne aside, into the shade of an oak by the mews that housed most of the neighbourhood's horses. He cupped her cheek and gazed into her eyes as she smiled at him fondly.

He swallowed. And swallowed again. Then, at last, he said with fervour, "I trust you, too."

Anne caught her breath. Tears filled her eyes and she clasped his hand and kissed his palm. Then, Michael gathered his wife into his arms and he held her for a long, long time.

CHAPTER 37

Warnings

Though he had recovered quickly and gone back to the city, Dowd had become a regular visitor to The Flats and occasionally showed up to take lessons with the Four Horsemen and the other students. The new MacGregor house had been completed before the frosts and had been built bigger than its predecessor, but it was by no means large enough to accommodate the expanding group of children who came to learn their Three R's. Anne had, therefore, arranged to give daily lessons in the Protestant church.

Elizabeth often joined her in the new schoolhouse, bringing favourite books and copies of newspapers. Hermione provided slate tablets and chalk and pens and pencils enough to go around. Meanwhile, Anne taught the children to make their own ink and paper, skills which led to a great increase in the number of letters sent to relatives in "the Old Country."

The wedding of Constable O'Toole and the former Mrs. Monaghan had sparked new romances with the introduction of many of the city's finest young men-in-blue to nubile young ladies of The Flats. And the neighbourhood's very first telephone line now brought service to five houses between the wagon-bridge and Cedar Lane, and accompanied the establishment of two police call boxes this side of the Bow.

∞

HALLOWEEN DAWNED clear and bright, but even though a thin crescent moon set early, the day was eclipsed by the candlelit night. At every house, pumpkin faces grinned ferociously from windows and front stoops. Lamps hung from porch ceilings and squatted on fence posts and swung by the sides of wandering watchmen. In the gilded glow, excited children skipped hand in hand along the lanes and alleys of The Flats in search of candied apples, toffee, and other home-made treats.

The night before, a gypsy caravan had parked its colourful horse-drawn Vardos on the Commons, arranged in a half-circle. Now, the Romani travellers joined the All Hallows celebrations with music and dancing, juggling and fortune-telling.

Once the MacGregors' supply of tasty goodies had been distributed, Anne and Michael snuffed the candles on their porch and joined the younger adults and a few of the elders at the Romani encampment. The couple stood together, Anne's back to Michael's front, his chin resting on her head and his arms around her. They swayed together to the exotic music and watched the vivid whirl of gypsy dancers who cavorted around a campfire until, out of the blue, a young girl tapped Anne on the hand and beckoned to her to follow.

With a shrug to her husband and an air of amused perplexity, she allowed the child to lead her to one of the

wagons. Inside, a candle flickered on a small table and an old woman in classic costume of scarf and earrings, blouse and skirt, shawl and sash, all in bright hues, sat with a deck of tarot cards in her hand. She smiled and gestured for her visitor to sit opposite her on the stool provided.

Anne glanced about as she perched. In the cramped dwelling on wheels, boxes lined the lower walls to house the gypsy family's few belongings, while an arched roof curved above to keep out the elements. Everything was painted gaily and decorated with symbols full of significance to the wanderers. And once the night's festivities ended, she knew, the space would be transformed as by magic into a cosy bedroom complete with mattress and pillows, sheets and quilts.

At the fortune-teller's behest, Anne shuffled the well-used cards and handed them back. Then, she pulled a few bills from her wallet and placed them on the table. To her surprise, the Romni pushed the money back toward her. But Anne pressed it to her hand. The woman fixed Anne's eyes and stared a long moment before she took the cash and stuffed it into a pocket.

The tarot reader slowly pulled six cards from the top of the deck and laid them in two rows of three, face-side up to show their figures. She touched each in turn before she spoke obscurely of trial and triumph, terror and tragedy, and final reunion with Anne's one true love.

When she finished, the woman clasped Anne's hand and looked into her eyes, her own clear and dark and compelling. She said, "You are very brave, my dear. And very strong. Stronger than you know."

For no reason she could explain, Anne's breath caught and her eyes filled with tears. She left the Vardo feeling suddenly weak and tremulous and filled with a strange, vague mixture of foreboding and hope.

∞

ANNE'S WAISTLINE had finally begun to outgrow her skirts; so, she left Elizabeth and Hermione in charge of the schoolhouse and journeyed to the city to purchase appropriate maternity attire. In the very modern department store on Bay Street, she rode the elevator to the upper floor and wandered through the large retail space, level by level, surveying dishes and tools, furnishings and toys, pens and toiletries. She stopped to chat briefly with Terence O'Grady's eldest sister Evelyn in the kitchenwares section, and then with young Dennis O'Shaunnessey, who sold shoes. When at last she browsed the ladies' fashions department, she examined the array of garments with a critical eye and pursed lips.

"May I help you?" asked a young woman in fitted navy skirt and in simple white blouse with blue satin bow tied between the wings of a rounded collar.

Anne said hopefully, "I'm looking for maternity wear. Can you direct me to that section?"

When the chestnut-haired twentysomething thought a moment, Anne cocked an eyebrow, her eyes narrowing and her mouth curling into a cynical smile as she recalled the silly Victorian attitude toward body functions such as pregnancy.

Abruptly, the young woman cleared her throat and admitted, "We don't have clothes for...that purpose...exactly. Most ladies just buy a larger size, or perhaps buy fabric and make their own dresses to...hide their shape." Noting Anne's silk gown, she quickly amended, "Or have a seamstress fit them specially." She smiled uncomfortably.

Anne sighed. "Then, please direct me to the fabric department."

Relieved, the young woman ushered her past perfumes and millinery to find a wide assortment of fabric bolts stacked on shelves and another woman waiting to serve needle-crafters. Nearby, racks held threads and notions, while a display of sewing machines offered the newest technology. Anne chose several cottons and linens for undergarments, wincey for

nighties, calico for workwear, and two each of silks and wools for formal attire, and asked to have them delivered to Cedar Lane across the Bow. The address shocked the middle-aged clerk, and she hastily excused herself to consult the manager. When she returned with the man, his eyebrows rose sharply and he blinked several times as he gaped at Anne, nonplussed.

Finally, he said, "Uh, please excuse me, Mrs. MacGregor. I was not aware you lived...."

"In The Flats?" she finished for him.

"Uh, y-yes," he stammered.

Anne took a deep breath and said with all the patience she could muster, "It may not be the most fashionable neighbourhood in town, but it is home. And I quite enjoy the...*ambiance*." She pronounced the last word with her best French accent and smiled sweetly.

"Indeed," said the manager with more flustered blinking. "Ah...indeed." He turned to the clerk and said, "Mrs. Cotnam, please have Mrs. MacGregor's purchases sent anywhere she likes."

As she walked out of the store, Anne wondered where she had met the man. The answer came to her a few feet from the entrance: A boy with a bundle of newspapers under one arm flourished a freshly printed copy as he shouted, "*Evening Star* here! Get your copy of the *Evening Star!*"

That was it: She had not met him, personally. He had seen her photograph in the newspaper after the asylum incident. She grinned wryly and shook her head. Perhaps publicity had its uses, now and then.

∞

AFTER HIS FIRST day in the distillery, Michael had asked his father, "Why have you not fired D'Arcy Sloan?"

Joseph had gaped at his son in surprise and asked, "Why would I do that? He's a good worker. Never misses a day."

Michael had explained in detail what he had learned from D'Arcy himself and from the other workers. Joseph had frowned, bewildered and thoughtful.

"Him and others, you say?" he had asked.

"Several," Michael had confirmed. "I've been trying to discover all their names."

Joseph had nodded abstractedly and said, "Good, good." But he had said no more and simply returned to his ledger.

The following week, Michael had presented the names of all of Sloan's confederates, but his father had simply taken the list, nodding, and walked away.

Now, Michael approached his father once more. After shutting the door to Joseph MacGregor's office, he asked, "What do you plan to do about D'Arcy Sloan?"

Joseph set down his pen; rubbed his ink-stained fingers on the blotter, leaving a dark smudge; and then wiped them with a handkerchief that bore the permanent evidence of frequent contact with ink. He sighed wearily and looked up at his son.

"What *can* I do?" he asked. "Not one of them has done anything for which I can fire him."

"Not done any —"

Michael gaped at his father in astonishment. Then, he said, "They've been trying to persuade the men to strike. Or leave and find work elsewhere. And they tell lies about you and about the conditions here to everyone who'll listen."

Joseph asked point-blank, "Do you know why?"

Michael heaved a sigh and admitted, "No, I don't. I think they're working for someone, but I don't know who." He added with determination, "Yet."

"Orwell," said his father flatly.

Michael frowned and regarded the elder MacGregor warily. "Are you sure?"

"I canna prove it," Joseph acknowledged. "But I know." He rubbed his eyes and heaved another world-weary sigh. "I wish I did not."

Michael stared at his father, the man seeming suddenly very old and very tired. Closing his eyes and heaving another sigh of his own, the younger MacGregor decided to talk to Davey and Dowd again.

∞

ANNE HAD CHOSEN to take tea in a little café a few blocks from the department store. She sat by the window and looked out through the translucent muslin curtain to the passing pedestrians and carriages as a waiter placed a glass of water on the red-and-white gingham-clad table.

She smiled up at him and said, "Tea, please. Green tea, if you have it."

"We do, Madam," he told her. "Would you like milk and sugar? A scone, perhaps?"

"Just honey, if I may," she replied.

"Very well," he said, and he hurried away.

She gazed out to the busy street lined with wide-windowed shop-fronts shaded by colourful canvas awnings, some plain, some piped, and some striped. Painted ledger boards and lintels printed with black or gold lettering proclaimed the names of the shop owners while interior displays or exterior tables flaunted their wares. Well-heeled ladies and gentlemen wandered among domestics and labourers, urchins and hawkers, as a couple of constables strolled their beat with watchful eyes.

Horse-drawn wagons rolled by laden variously with barrels or crates, while buggies and carriages and hackneys conveyed passengers. An open-topped automobile roared around a corner and its goggled driver irascibly blared the horn when a pair of horses reared in startlement and fear at the noise of his contraption. Naturally, the honk only frightened the equines more, and the coachman was hard put to get the panicked beasts under control. Anne sighed and shook her head in disgust at the hubris and self-absorption of the man in the

mechanized vehicle. Then, she sighed again at the knowledge that those ear-offending, pollution-spewing, hydrocarbon-guzzling machines would soon fill the streets and highways and crank up society's pace to a frenzied pitch.

Her tea arrived. As Anne removed her gloves, a stirring beside her drew her attention to a young woman in pink silk dress and straw boater hat with matching pink ribbon. The girl's gaze combined diffidence and defiance. Anne recalled that she had seen her at Hampton House; the socialite had been one among Jaclyn Orwell's coterie: the one in mauve.

"Yes?" said Anne, curious.

The girl pressed her lips into a tight moue, stared hesitantly, and then asked, "May I join you, Mrs. MacGregor?"

Taken aback, Anne said with brows high, "If you wish."

The brown-haired young woman relocated to settle herself in the other cane-seated bentwood chair by the window, and she hailed the waiter to ask for tea with milk and sugar. Once the attendant had left, she leaned across the table and said in low tones, "There is something I must tell you. It's...."

She glanced about nervously at the other customers and, when satisfied they were engrossed in their own conversations, she turned back to whisper, "It's about the Orwells."

Anne cocked an eyebrow but said nothing. She looked closely at the woman, past her outward appearance to the soul beneath, and decided to trust whatever the girl said. *Not "girl,"* Anne chided herself; the brunette was surely in her late twenties.

After several tentative starts that ended in flustered sighs, the younger woman finally spoke plainly. "I overheard a conversation between Mr. Orwell and another man I did not recognize. And...I think they plan to do your family some harm."

This came as no surprise, but Anne asked, "Did you hear what, exactly, they intend?"

The socialite admitted, "No. Only that it has something to do with loans."

Anne frowned, perplexed. She knew Michael had no

outstanding debts. Did his father?

To the woman, she said, "Thank you for telling me."

Shyly, the young brunette said, "I know people have been saying many awful things about you and...." Straightening defiantly, she took a deep breath and declared, "And I think perhaps they are not true."

Anne smiled warmly. She said, "I do believe that is the nicest thing anyone has said to me in some time." She added mischievously, "Anyone apart from my husband, that is."

The young woman blushed. Then, with a chuckle and an air of conspiratorial naughtiness, she recounted, "Jaclyn turned positively purple when she found out Michael—your husband, I mean, Mr. MacGregor—chose someone else instead of her." She rolled her eyes and added, "She always thinks all the men belong to her."

Anne said drily, "I've met the type."

Abruptly, her eyes flying wide, the young woman exclaimed, "Oh, I forgot! I'm Grace. Grace Donaldson." She extended her hand.

Shaking the lace-gloved hand firmly, Anne said, "And I'm Anne. Very nice to meet you, Miss Donaldson. Grace."

∞

MICHAEL FOUND Davey and Dowd lounging on the docks, near the stone-and-slate Customs and Harbourmaster's station where Zeke had said they would be. The lads ducked or shifted occasionally to move out of the way of gruff, pea-jacketed longshoremen and out from under heavy crates swinging overhead as ships were loaded here and unloaded there.

The unofficial leaders of the east-end street boys grinned as the tall Scot approached with a bag of biscuits and a flask of tea in hand. They gobbled sweet treats and gulped the still-hot drink, passing the container between them, while he told them of his new plan: From now on, they would shadow Reginald Orwell

and find out all they could about his activities.

When he had given each of the boys a sheaf of drawings of Orwell, he sent them off to spread the word and the likenesses among the urchins. Soon, he hoped, he would know the nature and extent of the threats against his family's business.

∞

A LETTER arrived from Brazil. It waited on the kitchen table: golden-white parchment on the butter-yellow cloth covering the pine oval, with Evan's familiar angular lettering bold in black, and with postmarks blurred across the foreign stamp.

My dear boy, it read, and Michael smiled at the salutation that, he had realized only recently, had protected him at school and, later, in other circumstances, as well.

> *The tropical heat is even more dreary than your colonial winters, I am sad to say, though the Trade Winds sometimes make it bearable. Nonetheless, there are compensations: People wear much flimsier clothing that, as you may imagine, can be quite stimulating to the eye and the libido.*
>
> *Happily, I have found a tailor as skilled as Signore Abruzzi, and a competent hatter, and have begun to establish a wardrobe appropriate to the Brazilian climate. I have also developed a taste for a peculiar local drink made of sugar and lime juice mixed into 'cachaça'—a liquor similar to rum. I have even begun to learn a rather exotic dance called the 'samba.' I do believe it possible, given enough time, that I could 'go native,' as they say.*
>
> *With regard to a certain Russian, I have it on good authority that he is released to the angels, or devils, as the case may be.*

Unfortunately, my news with regard to a Prussian of our acquaintance is less specific; nonetheless, I am told he did arrive in New York and disappeared soon after the ship docked. Rumour has it that there is a custom, there, of making enemies a permanent part of newly erected structures, of which there are many in the expanding metropolis. Perhaps he now haunts the basement of some department store full of garden tools and ladies' habiliments. The notion cheers me.

I have asked Father and one of my friends in London to inquire into a strange report that has reached my ears of the purchase by Reginald Orwell of controlling shares in several companies with which I know your father does business. His source of financing is a man named Richard Howes, owner of a number of breweries and distilleries. Perhaps it would behove you to make your own inquiries. Orwell has never been a friend to your family.

Believe me when I tell you that I hope that this letter finds both you and your wife well. It pleases me to think of you as a father bouncing a 'wee lad' on your knee. The image is almost enough to make me consider marriage, myself. That would certainly please Father. But I am afraid my forays into that particular territory have met with little success and less enjoyment.

Know that, even at distance, I am ever your friend,

Evan

Michael's gut had tightened at the news from Anne concerning the revelations of Miss Grace Donaldson. Now, with

this information from Evan, it turned to jelly. His father had recently borrowed a substantial amount of money: to buy new equipment to replace a damaged mash tun and two washbacks that had mysteriously developed leaks, more copper for repairs to the stills and lyne arms and condensers, and new aging barrels. With growing anger and apprehension, he recalled that Sloan and two of the agitator's friends tended the washbacks, another serviced the mash tun, and three more worked in the still rooms.

They had sabotaged the equipment, he was sure.

He strode to the back room that he and Anne had furnished as a study, and he picked up the recently installed telephone to call his father.

∞

AT MENTION of Richard Howes, his father had remained silent long enough to prompt Michael to ask, "Father, are you still there?"

On the other end of the line, Joseph MacGregor said slowly, "Yes, Michael. I'm here."

At his tone, Michael's grip on the tapering base of the candlestick telephone tightened. He asked quietly, "Who is he, father?"

Another lengthy pause. Finally, Joseph said, "I'll meet you there. Hermione has taken Elizabeth to an amateur theatrical at the university."

His father hung up. Michael swallowed, set the black porcelain telephone on the desk, and replaced the receiver on its gleaming brass hook. Whatever his father had to say must be very bad, indeed.

∞

ANNE POURED TEA and placed it before her father-in-law as the man sat at her kitchen table, across from Michael. The elder

remained downcast and silent in the yellow-tinged glow from the lantern above. He reached for the milk pitcher and sugar bowl, both white and fluted and swimming in the ripples of brightness reflected by the wide, silver-metal shade that beamed light through the pool of golden oil in the glass base of the lamp hanging directly overhead.

Wordlessly, Anne placed a second cup and saucer before her husband and sat beside him, taking his hand under the table. She had seen Joseph MacGregor suspicious, arrogant, angry, outraged, shocked, saddened, concerned, determined, happy, and triumphant. She had never before seen him afraid.

Joseph swallowed and fingered the plain white saucer for several minutes as Michael's hand tightened with Anne's. At last, the MacGregor patriarch explained, "When I first started importing whisky into this country, Howes wanted me to sell his stock."

He looked up and continued, "There had been a scandal, ye see, and he couldn't sell a drop in England. He tried to bribe me. Even tried to destroy the warehouse where my merchandise was stored awaiting shipment, thinking he'd force me to take his swill."

He sighed and gazed into the teacup again. "He went bankrupt and blamed me."

"That makes no sense," said Anne. "Surely he had been refused by others, as well."

"Aye," Joseph confirmed. He glanced from her to his son, and back. "But ye see, he discovered it was me brought the Customs and Excise into the matter when I found his bottles under proof."

Michael guessed, "Diluted and re-bottled."

"Aye," said Joseph. "And it turned out the bloody stuff was not only diluted and the seals falsified, but it was poisoned as well. Accidentally, perhaps. But poisoned."

Anne assumed, "And people died. That's what fuelled the scandal."

Joseph nodded. Then, he shook his head and said in a tone of bafflement, "I dinna ken how the bastard managed to build himself an empire o' distilleries and breweries after that business. The Crown has a long memory."

Anne surmised, "Probably partnered with someone whose name appeared on all the official documents, thus fooling Customs and Excise."

"But he was bankrupt," Joseph insisted with a frown. "How could he have started over, even with a partner?"

"We may never know," said Anne. She thought aloud, "But he could have been funded through blackmail or smuggling."

Michael suggested, "Or partnered with a criminal who had the money but no expertise, and another man with a good name but neither money nor knowledge of brewing or distilling. If he could—and would—doctor his whisky and try to burn your warehouse, he likely had criminal connections already."

"Aye," said Joseph, nodding thoughtfully. Something now troubled him even more deeply, his mind working furiously behind his eyes. Anne saw it, and she recognized that Michael did, too.

Anne wondered, "Did his partner happen to be Reginald Orwell?"

Joseph regarded her sharply. Then, he swallowed visibly. He whispered, "Jesus, Mary, and Joseph, it could be so!"

CHAPTER 38

The calm...

Michael lay spoon-fashion with Anne, snugly bundled under a quilt of goose-down. He inhaled the scent of her hair and skin as he cupped her round belly in his hand. Here, with her, in the warmth of their home, the troubles of the factory and the world seemed countless miles away.

He had almost drifted off when she winced and gasped lightly. The movement and sound had been so subtle that he thought, at first, he might have dreamt them. But the rhythm of her respiration had changed.

Rousing, he asked anxiously, "Are you all right?"

She pressed back against him and placed her hand over his upon her belly. She whispered, "Yes," but said no more.

Her breathing slowed and deepened, evincing no pain or distress. Gradually, her steady suspiration eased his disquiet and lulled him once more toward slumber.

All at once, he felt it: a tremor that seemed a resonance rather than an actual motion...an infinitesimal stirring inside her.

"Did you feel it?" asked Anne, her voice hushed with awe.

"Yes," he whispered in wonder, hardly daring to breathe lest the spell be broken.

They lay in shared delight, marvelling at the motion of the tiny miracle they had created together, until the dawn and the need to face the day.

∞

INSTEAD OF TAKING his mount from the small mews in The Flats where Dan Doherty and others kept their horses next to the carriage-house that held the hackneys and many of the neighbourhood's wagons, Michael walked in the early morning with the men employed at the distillery.

When he revealed to them his suspicions of sabotage, Tsi-Guy Villeneuve asked, "You gonna fire 'em?"

"I have no proof," Michael admitted. "Only a suspicion based on too many coincidences."

David O'Byrne rubbed his sharply cleft chin and said thoughtfully, "That'd explain a few things, to be sure."

Aiden Bannion demanded, "What d'ye mean?"

O'Byrne glanced to left and right at his companions, his lips pressed together tightly and his eyes narrowed in uncertainty. He said slowly, "Well, I thought little of it at the time, y'understand...."

With a wry grimace, he explained, "I saw Reed and Coleman the day the first vat sprung a leak. I went below to fetch a bucket an' mop to clean up a bit o' spill, an' I saw 'em there. Seemed like they was talkin', an' I wouldn't 'a' taken notice but for them lookin' at me queer, like, when I come down. Like I was interruptin' somethin'. Somethin' secret, maybe. An' they clammed up tight till I went back upstairs."

He added, "After that, I was too busy wi' the spill an' then wi' the leak to think on it."

"Bloody bastards!" barked Sean Quinn.

"It's still not proof," Michael warned, recognizing the danger that the men might take matters into their own hands. "And proof is what we need."

Tom O'Herlihy piped up, "That, an' makin' sure they don't bung things up again."

O'Byrne vowed, "We'll keep an eye on 'em, then. They won't get away wi' nothin' from now on."

∞

WHEN ANNE and Michael drove the food wagon to the usual Front Street East drop site for the mudlarks, Dowd joined the boys and handful of girls that appeared as if from thin air to claim a bag of food or to ask for a blanket. The older lad winked at the Scot and climbed into the buckboard to help with the distribution. When the wagon was empty, he accepted the last of the sacks of fresh bread, walnuts, and apples and surreptitiously slipped a bit of paper into Michael's hand.

The MacGregors made two more round trips, but finally headed for home as the crescent moon set in the southwest.

"Thank God for Indian summer," Anne commented. The day had been warm, and the night promised to be mild, as well.

As he reined the horses round the corner toward Bridge Street, Michael replied grimly, "Yes, they'll have a few more days before the cold drives them into whatever holes they can find." He swallowed hard, his mouth drying at the image in his mind of Dowd, Davey, Zeke, and the others trying desperately to keep warm through a long northern winter. He whispered, "God help them."

Anne moved closer on the plank bench, reached around his waist with one arm, and laid her head against his shoulder. "There's only so much we can do," she said just loud enough to

be heard over the rumbling of the wheels, the creaking of the wagon, and the clopping of the horses' hoofs.

"I know," Michael responded glumly. He heaved a sigh and said, "I just wish we could do more to protect them."

Anne squeezed him and nodded understanding as they crossed the bridge and entered The Flats.

∞

IN THE KITCHEN, under the light of the kerosene lantern, Michael unfolded the tight little wad of paper Dowd had passed to him. It was one of the woodcut likenesses of Reginald Orwell, now scrawled with pencilled notations of places and times the man had been seen, and names or descriptions of people Orwell had met.

"Bankers," said Michael once he had deciphered Dowd's scribbles. "One is Father's banker, Thomas Cavendish, and the other manages the new eastern bank on Bay."

Standing by his chair, Anne peered at the writing on the page and noted, "Gooderham. I'm sure he has an interest in seeing a competitor put out of business. Especially one whose whisky is better than his." Her brows rose and a cynical smile curled her lips as she noted with irony, "And Sloan. Now, there's a surprise."

She squinted at the paper and added, "But I don't recognize this one." Reaching past her husband's shoulder, she pointed to a name in another hand: Bertram Honeysett.

"A shipper," said Michael. "Ian Fraser handles our imports through him."

"Deploying in preparation for the final assault," Anne remarked, a hard edge in her voice.

Michael cocked an eyebrow at his wife. She frequently used peculiar expressions: either very old sayings or, according to her, ones from the future or, strangest of all, military terms such as a soldier or general would use.

Seeing his look, Anne expounded, "It seems very likely he intends to put your father into a position where he borrows more than he can afford to repay—thus forcing Joseph to sell assets, perhaps even bankrupting him. Your father has already taken loans for repairs and supplies. And Orwell's probably ensuring that no extra credit will be extended. As for the shipper—"

Michael finished, "He is both creditor, who must be paid, and asset, in that Father owns a share of his company."

Anne pressed her lips together and narrowed her eyes in that odd way she often did when thinking—as if she were staring into some ethereal realm, unseen by mere mortals, where answers could be found. Speaking as though to herself alone, she said, "Now for the sixty-four-thousand-dollar question: Does Orwell plan to create a need for more money through further sabotage? Or does he have some means to precipitate a loan recall requiring immediate repayment?"

Or both, went unsaid but hung in the air.

The possibilities so disturbed Michael that he did not inquire why she had specified the large sum of sixty-four-thousand dollars, which, to his knowledge, did not correspond to any of his father's holdings or debts.

∞

A LOVELY, warm week, nearly a fortnight, passed without incident.

Sloan and company, now under the none-too-subtle scrutiny of their co-workers, were forced to behave themselves. Reginald Orwell took the train to Montreal. The new casks arrived safely. The equipment was all in fine fettle, and the malting and distilling went smoothly. A batch of fifteen-year-old single malt was ready for shipment, along with a full warehouse of the twelve-year-old.

With the help of the O'Reilly girls, Anne whipped together loose, comfortable underthings, as well as drawstring

skirts and laced bodices much like the eighteenth-century styles she had worn for so long. She did, however, make a concession to Victorian times by raising the necklines and adding moderately bouffant sleeves to her maternity outfits.

Another letter arrived from Brazil, this one cheery and full of tales of colourful festivals, delicious drinks, exotic beauties—Michael and Anne smiled to each other with the knowledge Evan did not refer to Latin ladies—and exciting intrigues in a country still deciding what sort of government it wanted after the fall of the monarchy that had previously ruled it. Michael sent a lengthy reply to his absent friend, keeping his tone conversational and light.

On Thursday, Edward Hanes and Anne toured the city's streets and tended everything from scraped knees to signs of syphilis. The children had grown to trust the white-haired lady who dispensed little drops of medicine and bandaged wounds without lecturing about religion or propriety and without making the waifs feel worthless or wicked. When one young girl presented her with a cut flower exactly like the ones sold by a nearby street vendor; Anne did not ask how she had come by it.

On Friday, the moon was full as it rose near sunset. The weather changed abruptly.

CHAPTER 39

...the storm

A wind from the northwest blasted away Indian summer and plunged the land uncompromisingly into winter. It carried the smell of freezing rain as it ripped the remaining red and gold leaves from their branches to fly through the streets and lanes and collect along fences and house foundations. Folk wrapped themselves tightly with their coats and cloaks and rushed into the shelter of their fire-warmed houses.

"This will be a long winter. What can we do for the children?" Anne asked when Michael telephoned from the distillery. "Will they come to The Flats if we offer?" An earlier meeting of the local residents had concluded with one accord that the families would take in as many street children as possible when winter began in earnest, especially the youngest and especially when temperatures plummeted well below freezing.

But the ultimate decision lay with the urchins, themselves.

"I don't know," he replied. "I'll go there now and put it to them."

"Perhaps I should go to Queen Street," said Anne. "Some have been hiding in the alleys, but they'll freeze there, tonight."

He did not want her out in this weather, but Michael knew his wife well enough to realize her mothering instincts would compel her out into this hellish night. Rather than balk at her proposal, he urged, "Dress warmly. And take the buckboard. You'll be able to bring back any who are willing." He added, "Be careful."

She heard the concern in his voice. She said gently, "I will, my love. I'll see you soon."

Michael replaced the receiver and set the telephone on his father's desk. As he donned the wool scarf and the coat Anne had insisted he bring with him this morning, he wondered how she had known such would be needed. Then, he remembered: *Beira* is the *Winter Goddess*; of course she would recognize the approach of the season of snows. He smiled to himself at his inclination to see her as magical, even now, in this century, in an age of reason and science. It must be the Scot, the Highlander in him, he thought.

He pulled on the gloves she had handed him despite his protests, and he headed for the warehouse district.

∞

EVEN AS WARM-BLOODED as he generally was, the wind chilled him to the marrow as Michael strode through the alleys and byways to the shantytown of discarded crates some of the boys had created for themselves between a pair of disused board-and-batten warehouses. Dowd often slept there, and he would know where the other lads lodged.

Not yet clouded, the full moon shone clear and bright, a cold mockery of the sun's warmth. Under it, Michael rounded the

corner of the old storehouse, turning into the north-facing alley to find the scavenged huts that squatted flat and colourless, without chimneys or roofs, doors or windows, or even proper walls: crude counterfeits of the homes the children had lost through misfortune and societal meanness. Yellow light flickered and wavered above the centre of the clutter. They had built a fire.

Michael called out as he approached, using the words the boys had chosen as their challenge to intruders. Even over the wind, he heard the scuffle as they readied for flight or defence. Then, when one of them recognized the Scot, the sudden tension transformed to relief and Dowd stood, holding his hat to his head with one semi-mittened hand and waving a welcome with the other, his digits poking through fingerless old woollen gloves.

To his surprise, Michael found that the force of the wind abruptly abated within the circle of dilapidated slab-and-slat boxes: A glimpse from this viewpoint revealed mud and grass chinking, and rags tacked on the exposed sides of the crates. The blaze of the bonfire threw off substantial heat—at least, within a certain radius. Perhaps those who chose to brave the storm would fare well enough, he thought, if the coming rain did not douse the fire. But the risk was high, and he knew the offer must be made.

The Scot sat on his haunches in the crowded little space by the makeshift hearth and said, "The people of The Flats will welcome you into their homes, if any of you choose to come and stay with us." At the sudden wariness in the eyes, he added, "Just till the weather clears. No one is going to force you to an orphanage or make you stay where you do not wish to stay. And they'll treat you as they treat their own."

When all remained hesitant, Michael suggested, "Why don't you talk it over amongst yourselves. I'll wait by my family's warehouses for your decision."

With that, he nodded to Dowd, rose into the gale, and left the lads to their discussions.

∞

AS EXPECTED, some of the east-end kids huddled in each of several back alleys between stone and brick office and factory buildings, with only gap-filled crates and rubbish and the blankets they had acquired to fend off wind and cold and the coming frigid rain. Anne found them shivering and wretched. When she offered a warm home, albeit a stranger's home, they agreed with alacrity.

"I don't see Maggie or Clarissa," she remarked as the urchins gathered their meagre belongings for the trip to The Flats.

"They's gone to live in the cathouse in The Warren," Denny Higgins reported. "The one run by the Eye-talian fellahs."

Anne nodded and sighed. Such capitulations were inevitable facts of urban street-life, but that did not make them any less regrettable.

"What about the others?" she asked. "I haven't seen Vince or Timmy or Little Jack, either." Little Jack was the six-foot teenager with the mind of a five-year-old who never strayed far from his younger and smaller but highly intelligent brother Timmy.

"I think they went to the train yard," said Denny. "Them an' another bunch figured they'd find a place in the station or in a car."

"Thank you, Denny," said Anne as she helped one of the smaller children into the wagon. "I hope they did."

By the time she had brought a full load of children to be sheltered in various homes in The Flats, Anne had discovered that the train station and several inner-city stables had been invaded by guttersnipes. At least the boys in the train station would be in a relatively clean environment. She prayed that those in the stables would survive the high levels of ammonia in the air of the filthy, poorly ventilated establishments dotting the downtown business district.

When no more strays could be found in the streets, those she had rescued had been billeted among her neighbours, and the few developing sniffles had been given remedies and hot tea, Anne drove the wagon into the city once more. Shreds of cloud blotted the moon's white light with increasing frequency as she crossed the bridge and headed for the distillery district. But another glow — a hot, red-orange one — had appeared in the east.

∞

MICHAEL HAD BARELY reached his family's holdings some hundred yards away when Dowd hailed. Turning, the Scot saw his young friend crossing the windswept open expanse with three of the smaller boys. The dirt on their faces made them unrecognizable even in the garish light of the full moon, but all three sneezed at least once as they approached. Michael smiled inwardly at the leadership he saw in Dowd. *A future sergeant,* he thought.

"These'll come with ye," said the urchin boss. "They need a warm bed more'n the rest of us."

"Do not," said one, stubbornly, and Michael recognized the high voice of Wee Mickey.

"Do, too," the self-named Spike insisted. He coughed in a deep, wet, racking spasm, and Michael hoped the lad had not developed pneumonia or tuberculosis.

Young Zachariah Jones piped up in pubescent squeaks, "Dowd says you got a bed in a tree. 'Zat so?"

"Well, yes, a hammock," Michael answered. "But this is no night to be sleeping in it." He grinned and declared, "The wind would freeze your balls off."

"Can we try it when the storm's over?" asked Mickey, now eager.

"Yes, as soon as the weather permits," Michael replied, and he felt suddenly abashed at the fatherly tenor of his own words.

Raising an eyebrow and eyeing each of the boys in turn, Dowd instructed sternly, "Now, don't be liftin' anythin' what b'longs to the nice folks."

The three younger lads nodded subdued acquiescence. Satisfied that they would obey, Dowd turned to go, but he stopped when he noticed Michael's behaviour. The Scot sniffed the air, and he looked questingly around and up at the nearby brick warehouses with their tin roofs.

"Dowd," Michael said, pointing to the MacGregor buildings, "are any of the lads sleeping in these warehouses?"

"None o' *my* lads would," the boy replied. "They'd all be drunk as skunks on the fumes by mornin' and have headaches, besides, if they was in the liquor stores. There's some new ones been hangin' around down here lately, though, might not know better. Why?"

Michael said, "And everyone knows not to light a fire in any of these depositories, do they?"

"Yeah," Dowd said warily, now scenting the air as well. He qualified, "Least, *my* lads do."

Zachariah exclaimed, "I smell smoke!"

Spike concurred, "Me, too!"

Heart pounding, Michael left the boys and darted among the buildings, scanning quickly for the source of the odour, for any sign of fire. From the corner of his eye, he caught movement and turned to peer after a man running away. He glanced to his left at the footfalls of Dowd and the boys catching up to him just as a roar erupted behind him. The wide, double warehouse door at his back exploded in a blast of planks and splinters and rent metal, and the concussion wave threw him to the ground.

Michael blinked hard and shook his head, dazed. But a sense of desperate urgency forced him to awareness and he lurched up to a stand. Flames and smoke belched from the door, the shattered brace of windows, and the eaves of the depot, but he gave this no more than a cursory glance as he stumbled to the boys lying on the ground nearby.

To Michael's relief, Dowd shook himself and shot up. Spike and Wee Mickey also stirred and pushed up to stare at the blaze, agape. But Zachariah Jones did not move.

"Zach! Zach!" called Dowd anxiously as he pulled the boy from his prone sprawl.

Michael knelt by the lad and felt his wrist, then his neck, hoping for a pulse, though the child's wide, sightless eyes told him he would find none. On inspection, he saw in the light of the fire the tip of a dusky sliver protruding near the adolescent's nape. A dribble of dark blood oozed from the wood-stoppered wound to stain the dirt-greyed collar of the lad's shirt.

"Zach!" Dowd wailed when he saw Michael's aggrieved expression. "No!"

Dozens of urchins had come running at the sounds. Michael called to them, waving them away, "Stay back! Stay back!"

The boys looked from him to the blaze to Dowd. But Dowd merely leaned over the body of young Zach and wept as Spike and Wee Mickey sat beside him, distressed and not knowing what to do.

Michael jumped up and dashed to the onlookers to herd them away from the conflagration. He shouted over the din of screaming tin to make them understand the danger of proximity, and he sent the taller lads to the nearest fire station for help.

Several watchmen arrived from wherever they had hidden from the weather, each carrying a lantern and glancing from the fire to the boys to Michael and back again. A second explosion and a third split the air as more buildings went up. Then came a distant series of detonations like the rapid fire of a Gatling gun, as not only warehouses but the distillery itself burst into flame.

Michael raced to the factory to find a guard unconscious near a rear door and covered in glass from the exploded windows above. The Scot ran around to unlock the gate, and he pulled the man outside of the fence. Then, he quickly surveyed

the trickles of blood here and there to determine the extent of injury. Satisfied the lacerations were minor and the bump on the back of the sentry's head survivable, he propped the man against the stone gatepost and ran to the stable to free his horse.

Eyes wide in terror, the dark-brown stallion squealed and kicked at the walls of the stall as the ground shook with the force of a nearby explosion and as the reek of burning grain and wood penetrated the mews.

"Whoah, boy, whoah!" Michael called as he hurried to unlatch the door of the compartment. When he flung it open, the horse bolted past and out into the night. Smoke seeped through the ventilator windows and the open door. Michael turned to the exit, but stopped when a stirring of straw caught his eye.

"Is someone there?" he called. "Come out. I won't harm you. We must leave. There's a fire."

The stable came alive with scurrying boys who climbed down from the hayloft and scrambled out of unused stalls.

Grabbing one of the strays by the arm, Michael inquired urgently, "Are there any more of you?"

The boy shrugged, and he ran after his mates when Michael released him. The Scot scaled the ladder quickly and cast about the loft, coughing convulsively in the thickening, acrid smoke. When he found no more children, he slid down the sides of the ladder to the main floor and checked the stalls, a handkerchief over his nose and mouth and his eyes streaming.

Hoping he had missed no one, he fled the stable as straw ignited, and he charged into the malt house, its door already blown off just as the warehouse doors had been. The intensity of the heat stopped him no more than a few feet inside and forced him back out. If any were still in there, he was certain they must be dead already.

Anxiously, he sprinted through each of the buildings in search of workers or watchmen who had not yet fled, but he found only fire and destruction until he reached the still-house. There, just inside the door, Sean Quinn lay sprawled, his clothes

aflame and shoes smouldering. Michael dragged him outside and smothered the burn with his coat. At Quinn's cough and groan, he said, "I'll get ye home, Quinn," and he hauled the man to safety beyond the fence before returning to the distillery for one more look around.

Firemen and water tankers pulled up in a clang of bells that pierced the roar of the inferno and the squeals of warping metal. When he staggered out into a freezing drizzle, coughing raggedly, his lungs scorched and his jacket smoking, Michael passed the volunteers and firemen desperately pumping water into the flaming doorways. Slumping next to the still-unconscious guard, the Scot checked the man's pulse once more and found it strong. Then, he scanned Sean Quinn and snugged his greatcoat around the man. Finally, he leaned back against the stone wall as Anne reined the buckboard's team to a halt thirty or forty yards away and climbed down to rush to her husband.

∞

IN THE END, the firestorm could only be quenched by the rainstorm.

The warehouses had been a lost cause from the start, their highly flammable contents beyond salvage. The untended fire in the boys' shantytown had caught the tip of a blanket and spread to burst into a second conflagration that destroyed not only their makeshift homes but the wood-clad warehouses on either side. Fortunately, the windowless structures had been so rat-infested that none of the urchins had dared to shelter inside; thus, only a few rodents failed to escape the blaze.

John Devereux had arrived early and pitched in with the professionals and the volunteers in their frantic but ultimately futile efforts to fight the fire. After a time, the exhausted men and boys simply stood and watched the collapse of roofs, and listened to the crumbling of the skeleton and internal organs of the distillery as its heated stone skin warmed the night despite the

chill of sleet and rain.

Anne had given repeated doses of remedy to Michael, to Sean Quinn, to the guard, to the injured boys, and to a few employees and firemen who had sustained cuts or burns during their attempts to save the distillery. Having tended the living, she then turned her attention to the dead: She asked one of the watchmen to bring the body of Zachariah Jones to the buckboard, and she carried the corpse to Mr. Jessop's funeral parlour. Upon her return, Anne sought her husband.

"Let's get you home," she said gently. "The boys, too."

Suddenly, the pagoda-shaped roof-and-chimney of the kiln caved in upon itself with an ear-splitting crash. His eyes bleak, Michael glanced at his wife and back to the ruins that, only hours ago, had been his family's pride and prosperity, and the source of income for so many other families. Now, all was lost.

Dowd and the rest of the urchins had crept as close to the radiant heat of the walls as they safely could. Their tattered clothes had soaked with sweat and precipitation; now, the boys shivered as sleet pelted them and raw winds whipped their rags. His sense of responsibility trumping his fatigue and desolation, Michael whistled. When Dowd turned, the Scot beckoned, and the boys gathered to him as one. The reports of the burning of their hovels had been relayed by one of the watchmen of the warehouse district: They were truly homeless, now, and the knowledge showed in their sullen faces.

"We'll get you to The Flats," Michael told them. "Let's put the smaller ones and the sick ones into the buckboard."

Dan Doherty's voice came from behind. "I can carry a few and so can Ian, here."

Michael and Anne found their neighbourhood's two hackney drivers approaching, their respective rigs parked in the meadow nearby. As John Devereux and a fireman helped Sean Quinn to the larger cab, Dowd took command of his troops and ordered Wee Mickey and Spike into the other. Sorting the boys by stride length and strength, the teenager dispatched the smaller

and weaker of his expanded company—including the newcomers from the stables and the warehouse and dock districts—into the waiting wagon and carriages and marshalled the rest to march as fast as their legs would carry them.

"As soon as we've dropped off this lot, we'll come back for you," Anne promised the children and the night-shift employees resident in The Flats as she wheeled the buckboard around toward the west.

Michael's whistle had summoned not only the boys but his stallion from wherever it had sheltered. The Scot mounted bareback and took two of the smallest children, one in front and one in back. Using nothing more for control than his affinity with the horse, pats on the neck in lieu of the touch of reins, and nudges of his knees, he trotted past the laden buckboard and hackneys toward The Flats.

CHAPTER 40

Aftermath

E very house in the neighbourhood was crammed with waifs by morning. And two husbands and one son had not returned from the distillery.

The exhausted guttersnipes lay sleeping as women stoked fires and cooked breakfast and as men chopped wood and performed the other necessary chores that started their day. A pall settled on The Flats when news of the distillery disaster spread from house to house. Many were now unemployed and knew not what the next weeks might bring. And three households had lost the irreplaceable: a loved one.

Katie and Patsy O'Reilly soberly accepted charge of the MacGregor household and its guests. The two teenagers had learned how to fire Anne's peculiar new stove, and they stoked it to prepare a breakfast for the houseful of ragamuffins while Himself and Herself headed into the city.

At the gate, Michael urged his wife once more, "You should stay and rest. You've had no sleep at all."

"Neither have you," Anne reminded him. She insisted, "This is a family crisis, and I will not shirk my duty at such a time. I will help in any way I can."

Michael smiled faintly and caressed her cheek. "All right," he said softly. "I know Mother will need support."

The usually loquacious Dan Doherty opened the door to his cab and waited wordlessly as the MacGregors climbed aboard. When he snapped his reins to urge his horses onward, the wheels of the carriage crunched along the thin layer of ice coating the grass and ground, and the sharp sound seemed a metaphor for the shattering of so many lives.

Anne held Michael's hand as they travelled in the pallid, bluish light under a low sky, from The Flats, through the frozen silence of the city, toward Rosemont. There was nothing to say, no words of comfort to assuage the shock and anguish.

When Dan reined the carriage to a halt in front of the house on Stuart Avenue and opened the door for them, Michael handed him the usual fee and tip. At the driver's earnest attempt to refuse the money, Michael fixed his neighbour's eyes and said quietly, "Take it while I have it to give, Dan."

After a long moment, Dan nodded, a slight and sombre motion, and he accepted the bills.

∞

JOSEPH HAD HEARD. They found him sitting in his nightshirt and dressing-gown in the study, elbows on the desk, head in his hands, disconsolate. When he looked up, eyes red with strain and face creased with weariness and hopelessness, Michael wanted to weep for him. The younger MacGregor sat across the bureau, Anne at his side, and waited for his father to speak.

At last, Joseph said in a whisper, "I haven't told your mother." He looked to his son and asked, "Have you seen it?"

Michael nodded. "Yes."

"Davis called. He said there's nothing left."

Michael confirmed, "Nothing but rubble. And three men dead. Sean Quinn is burnt, but he'll live."

He added under his breath, *I hope*. Remembering the effect of the scorching heat and searing smoke on his own body, he realized how he had tempted fate, and he thanked God again for Anne's ministrations and remedies.

His father asked plaintively, "How could this happen?"

Michael could see in his father's eyes that the elder knew the answer but did not want to believe it. He replied glumly, "I saw someone running from the warehouses. And Davis and other guards had been knocked unconscious."

Anne asked bluntly, "What will this mean, financially?"

Joseph pulled his lips into a bitter grimace. He spat dismally, "Bankruptcy. Years of work gone. Loans to be paid and no sales to cover them."

"So, you'll have to sell what you have left," Anne concluded.

Michael asked anxiously, "I know you moved the papers from your safe, here at home. Did you store them in the office?"

"No, thank God!" replied Joseph. "I placed them elsewhere."

"With Cavendish?" Michael asked, his gut clenching.

To his relief, his father said, "No. I decided to take them to a solicitor. A young fellow with an office on Parliament. I dinna ken why, exactly, but I thought it wiser than keeping them in my bank."

Michael revealed, "Orwell was seen talking with Cavendish, and with other bankers as well."

Anne said solemnly, "I know a safe place for your documents. Perhaps it would be wise to take them there today. Just in case."

"And then," said Michael, "we must figure out how much we need to sell off and how soon."

Joseph nodded, purpose giving him energy and determination. "Right, then," he said, rising. "I'll get dressed."

∞

THE DOOR to the office of William MacDonald, Barrister and Solicitor, stood open when they arrived at the building three blocks north of Queen Street. Originally a house, it now contained the offices of the young lawyer, an architect, and a man whose business was not revealed by the sign painted in gold lettering on his door. Joseph, Michael, and Anne entered as the grey-suited redhead rummaged through one among a bank of filing cabinets on the inside wall. Beyond, bookshelves with horizontal glass doors protected new leather-bound books of law. The man's tidy oak desk sat at an angle, facing the door while also allowing light from the pair of tall, narrow windows to slant across the writing surface. The smell of new leather and freshly polished wood combined with the dusty scent of paper and a sharp whiff of ink.

The young man glanced up and smiled. He said, "I'll be with you in a moment, sir. Please have a seat," as he continued to flip through the card-paper folders. With a triumphant air, he pulled a jacket and shut the drawer with a slam.

"Here we are," he said as he placed the documents, flapped accordion folder and all, on the desk before Joseph.

Extending his hand as he approached Michael and Anne seated in the two extra chairs against the only empty wall, the lawyer added, "I don't believe I've had the pleasure. I'm William MacDonald, and you must be Mr. MacGregor's son."

Michael shook the hand and replied, "Michael MacGregor. And this is my wife, Anne."

The solicitor nodded respectfully to her, and then returned to his own seat behind the desk, asking, "Is everything in order, sir?"

"It is," Joseph confirmed with relief and gratitude. He

added, "I fear I shall require a great deal of you in the near future, Mr. MacDonald."

The lawyer sobered. He said sympathetically, "The fire, yes. The city is abuzz with the news. Please accept my condolence, sir. This must be a time of great distress."

"Indeed," Joseph replied, his voice barely above a whisper. He stood and reached to shake the young man's hand. "I shall contact you as soon as certain matters are decided."

"Of course," said the lawyer. "I await your call."

∞

"HE SEEMS QUITE personable," said Michael as he helped Anne into his father's carriage. He rasped hoarsely, his throat and lungs raw, and Anne quickly produced a remedy bottle from her reticule to minister to her husband. When Michael took the seat beside her, she deposited a couple of drops under his tongue.

"Aye," said Joseph. "The only lawyer in town both a Scot and a Highlander."

Anne smiled and said, "I believe he can be trusted." She had examined the solicitor's aura and found it bright.

"To The Flats," Joseph called up to the coachman as he closed the door. He sat back in the seat facing his son and daughter-in-law, the files beside him on the plush bench. As the carriage got underway, he confided, "I'd rather this not be discussed at home. I've told Harris to see Hermione is not disturbed by calls or visitors. I want to tell her myself."

Directing his query to Anne, he said, "So, tell me about this hiding-place of yours."

Anne smiled: always pragmatic, her father-in-law. She answered, "In a hole in the ground."

Joseph's eyebrows leapt toward his hairline.

Anne's grin broadened mischievously. She said, "Locked; weatherproofed; safe from water, fire and vermin; and hidden from prying eyes."

Michael clasped his wife's hand and asked indulgently, "And what is it you have need to keep so safe?"

"The deeds to The Flats."

Michael stared at her, then looked to his father, the elder also agape. Anne's lips twitched as she stifled a chuckle at their astonished faces. She knew they were not sure whether she was joking, but neither asked.

∞

BY THE TIME the MacGregors arrived, the ragamuffins had wakened and seated themselves on chairs, on stairs, and on the floor, eating porridge sweetened with dried berries and fresh-churned butter.

"We'll be in the study awhile," Anne told the O'Reilly sisters. Of the urchins, she asked, "How are you all doing? Enough to eat?"

The children nodded happily as they continued to spoon the hot food into their mouths.

"Good," she said. "Perhaps you can play outside, later, while the ladies clean the dishes."

Again, the children nodded.

"I'll help," a little girl of perhaps six volunteered.

"Me, too," said another brown-haired waif, probably sister to the first.

Anne smiled and said, "Thank you." Then, she followed the men.

Behind the closed door of the study, the three MacGregors gathered around the oak bureau topped by three candlesticks of varied heights clustered in one corner, the telephone in the other, an ink pot and cup of pens between them along the outer edge, and a large square of thick green paper secured in a leather-bound blotter pad placed before the wooden swivel chair. Joseph opened the stiff card-paper case tied with string wound around a brass button. One by one, he removed the

documents and spread them across the table, sorting them into piles. A sheaf bound in red ribbon he put back into the case.

Joseph rested a hand on a group of papers on his left. He said, "These are the deeds to the properties downtown and in Montreal, and the deed to the house. These," he set his right hand on another raft of documents, "are the shares of various companies in which I've invested over the years." He pointed to another stack, "And those are the loan certificates and copies of invoices as yet unpaid."

"These?" Michael asked, pointing to a small central pile.

His father replied, "Whisky receipts."

"Your own recipes," Anne translated.

"Aye," said Joseph, shoulders stiffening with pride. "Like a woman with her pies and cakes, we makers of whisky guard our secrets jealously."

"Well, those won't be worth much here," she warned. "The Temperance League is gaining support and will soon have the political clout to make the business of distillers and brewers and vintners more difficult and less profitable."

"Ye think so?" Joseph replied dubiously.

"I know so," said Anne, her tone quietly assured and her eyes fixing his.

Michael interjected, "They have become increasingly bothersome, Father."

The elder Scot frowned uncertainly under Anne's intense gaze, and he glanced to his son. "Aye," he agreed. "They've been coming to the office and handing around pamphlets among the workers. Damn nuisance."

"Keep the recipes," Anne advised. "They will be more use in Britain than here. The Puritans have a greater hold on this continent."

Joseph sighed. He said resignedly, "Maybe it's a sign from God, then, that we've been forced out o' the business now." He added, "Still, I would have liked to go back to the Old Country a rich man, rather than have to start over." He looked at

Michael and smiled sadly, "Even with a fine son to help me."

Michael returned his father's smile. Then, he searched Anne's eyes as he asked, "Do you really think we'll have to leave?"

She answered, "If you want to remain in the whisky business, yes. But there are other pursuits you could try, if you wish to stay here."

Husband and wife stared into each other's eyes a long moment until Joseph cleared his throat and said brusquely, "Well, we'll have to deal with our losses, first."

With that, he began an assessment of the value of the remaining assets in comparison with the debts outstanding. As her men discussed their options, Anne excused herself to visit Sean Quinn and see to the treatment of his injuries. Money could wait; healing could not.

∞

IN THE STUDY, as he sealed the envelope he had addressed to Evan, Michael regarded his wife. He had noticed the way Anne often bent this way and that, lately. He asked gently, "Are you in pain?"

She stopped in mid-arch and straightened. Smiling fondly and rubbing her belly, she said, "Just giving my muscles a little relief. The baby has got heavier."

She looked so very tired, he thought. He said, "Go to bed, my love. There's nothing more you can do, today. I'll go with Father and return as soon as I may."

"I should be there," she protested. "For Hermione."

His eyebrows high in an expression that conveyed his intention to stand firm, he reminded her, "Who knows better than Mother you must rest, troubles or no?"

He stepped round the desk and took her into his arms to rock her a moment, a large hand cupping her head and pressing her to him as he kissed her crown. Snickers nearby drew his

glance to a trio of ragamuffins beyond the open door, sitting on the floor. He smiled and winked at them, but his smile quickly faded.

God, he thought, *however will we take care of all these children, now? They've come to rely on us, but soon we'll have no funds to feed them.*

He remembered the admonition of his family's cook, who had once warned him not to feed the birds in winter. "Let them fend for themselves," she had said, "or they'll starve if ever you're not there to care for them. Don't start what you'll not be able to finish."

The people of The Flats had families and troubles of their own. They could not be expected to take on this burden indefinitely. He closed his eyes and cursed Reginald Orwell.

As though she had heard his thoughts, Anne pulled away and looked into his eyes. She said with certainty, "We'll manage. What we need will come to us."

∞

WHEN JOSEPH and Michael arrived at the family estate, they found Benjamin Ogden walking with Elizabeth on the grass beside the lane. His sister waved to them as they passed, and Michael waved back. She knew. He could tell by her red eyes and pathetic expression.

Standing at the front door as the coachman drove the carriage to the outbuildings beyond the kitchen garden, Michael looked back and pulled his mouth into a lopsided smile when Ogden took Elizabeth's hands into his own and spoke to her earnestly. She leaned against him, cheek pressed to his chest, crying, and the man held her in a comforting embrace.

"Seems she's found a better one, this time," Joseph remarked. "Perhaps he'll take care of her."

When I cannot.

Michael swallowed, his heart wrenching at his father's

unspoken words. The elder MacGregor looked old and broken, and Michael forced back the tears that wanted to flood his own face.

Be strong, he told himself. *For Da.*

∞

IN THE DRAWING-ROOM, after dinner, Hermione and Joseph sat not in their usual wing chairs but on the settee, Hermione reading aloud the *Evening Star* article about the distillery fire as Elizabeth and Ben Ogden and Michael listened.

"He does have a way with words," Joseph said of the writer, John Devereux. "Almost makes me wish I'd been there."

"Trust me," said Michael, his tone haunted, "it's better you weren't."

No one spoke for several minutes until Hermione broke the silence. "How is Anne?"

Michael smiled faintly and answered, "Tired. She did not sleep at all, with caring for the injured and bringing children from the cold."

"How many did you rescue?" Ben Ogden wanted to know.

Michael shook his head vaguely and frowned as he estimated, "Perhaps six dozen. Maybe a few more, all told."

"So many?" his mother gasped, appalled.

"Those are the ones we found," her son told her. "More remained well hidden where they had discovered or built some degree of shelter."

"I had no idea," said Elizabeth, her voice hushed and tinged with a hint of shame. "I've seen the odd urchin now and then, but...it never occurred to me they had nowhere to go." She admitted, "I suppose I always thought they had families somewhere...and homes."

Ben Ogden said, "I suspect most people believe that."

"Or know better but don't care," Michael added grimly.

Hermione asked incredulously, "How can anyone not care?"

Michael's slight sneer was as sardonically bitter as his tone. "Do you think Reginald Orwell cares that he just killed three good men and a boy, injured others, and put dozens—no, hundreds—of men out of work, thus jeopardizing their families and perhaps sending some of them into the streets as winter approaches?"

At his mother's tears, he closed his eyes and cursed himself under his breath. Even the newspaper account had not revealed the extent of the disaster as fully as his thoughtless words. Now, she shed for others the tears she would have held stoically for the sake of her family. A glance at Harris, approaching from the doorway with a tray of tea, reminded him that the staff would all fear for their own livelihoods, as well.

Michael stood. He said, "I must go to Anne." As his father rose, he added, "I'll see you on Monday, as agreed."

His father nodded and escorted him to the door.

∞

ANNE HAD SEEN in his face when he returned home that Michael was exhausted. Yet he could not sleep. When he tossed and turned in their bed for the fourth time, she asked, "Shall I massage you, my love?"

He opened his eyes to behold her and he smiled tenderly, his features thrown into sharp relief in the light of the full moon: black shadows and black brows, bronze skin paled by the silver glow from the window, lapis eyes gleaming onyx. The lines of fatigue and worry softened as he gazed at her and caressed her silky tresses.

"Have I told you I love you?" he whispered.

She traced the shape of his lips with her finger and replied, "Not for at least an hour. You'd better remind me."

She pushed up and brought her mouth to his.

Lacing his fingers through her hair, his broad palm cupping the back of her head, he answered her tongue with his own. She lingered, first brushing his lips with hers and then stroking his temple rhythmically with her fingertips. His breath slowed and his hand gradually slid to her neck as he drifted to sleep. At last, she pulled his fingers from her mane and gently placed his hand upon his belly.

When she had covered him and lain at his side, keeping her bulge an inch away lest the baby move and wake him, she surveyed her husband's sleeping form. After a time, she sighed and whispered, "I love you, too."

∞

MICHAEL WOKE to find his wife turned away, her long tresses carelessly strewn across the pillow and flowing down her back, their whiteness gleaming gold in the sunlight. Some had wrapped around her shoulder to dangle over her breasts. He smiled and pulled the errant strands to join their fellows and ran his fingers through them, revelling in their fine, silky texture. Most women braided their hair for the night, but his Anne was a creature too wild for such restraint.

"Are ye awake?" he whispered.

She shifted slightly and exhaled a soft sigh.

He hurt like hell inside and out, but he did not care. He was already hard, and looking over her slumbering body stiffened him more. Slowly, carefully, he peeled away the quilt and sheet and slipped his hand beneath the hem of her nightshirt. Unlike other women, Anne wore a short gown to sleep, because a longer one would tangle uncomfortably between her knees. His wife needed freedom, even in bed.

His fingers found their way under the soft wincey and pulled it up to bare her sweet, round bottom. How he craved that lovely arse!

In quick, delicate strokes, barely touching her skin, he

tickled along the back of her thigh. Still sleeping, she inhaled sharply and curled her upper leg forward, exposing the other thigh and his true target: the oh-so-sensitive cleft between. He turned his attentions to it, petting lightly and eliciting little gasps and small twitches of her hips.

By her breathing, he knew she had risen almost to consciousness. He kissed her shoulder and then her temple, and took her earlobe into his mouth to suckle it.

"Mmm," she murmured.

"Are ye awake?" he repeated, knowing she was.

"Mmm," she moaned again. "I take it John Henry is very much awake, too."

"Aye, he is that," Michael admitted, exaggerating his Highland burr. "And he verra much wants to be inside ye."

She chuckled, a low ripple that stoked his desire. She said, "Then, perhaps we should see if the door is open."

At that, he slipped his finger into her entry and found it almost wet enough. He nibbled her ear and kissed her neck as he resumed his caresses below and found his own hips moving impatiently at the delay. "Lord, I want ye!" he whispered hoarsely.

He gently tapped her little knob. She sucked in her breath and her hips began to rock in a strong, beckoning rhythm. He slid his finger inside her once more. Oh, yes. She was ready. And so was he.

∞

RIVAL CHURCH BELLS rang out across The Flats (the little Protestant church having finally received a small but respectable brass carillon), the musical peals calling the residents to their devotions. Michael hugged Anne closer, unwilling to let even God part her from him, this morning.

"Let's stay home," he urged.

Against his belly, hers moved of its own accord.

"That's two votes in favour," he said with a grin.

"You think so?" she grinned back. "What about all the votes across the hall and downstairs?" The snores and snuffles of resident urchins droned in the background.

"Ah, weel, now," he drawled, "this bein' a Hieland hoose, only the chief and his heir and his wife get a say in the proceedin's."

Anne giggled. "Now I *know* you've been away from the Highlands too long!"

Sobering at her words, he asked, "Would you like to go back there? To go home?"

"Home is where you are," she replied softly, her eyes fixing his. Husband and wife held each other's gaze a blissful moment before he kissed her deeply and won her vote.

∞

MICHAEL GATHERED Dowd and the eldest boys and girls to the MacGregor house while the rest of the children in The Flats, local and urchin alike, cavorted in the freshly fallen first snows. Anne handed a cup of tea to each of the dozen teenagers and handful of adolescents seated cross-legged on the floor. Her husband, also sitting on the broad polished planks, called the meeting to order. Anne sat by the stove and took up her knitting as Michael discussed adult matters with children too soon forced to grow up.

After describing his family's financial straits, the Scot said, "So, as you may have already guessed, we will not be able to bring you food or to replace the blankets many of you lost."

Dowd realized, "An' the folks here can't afford us, neither."

"Not for long," Michael confirmed softly. "Especially now that my father and I cannot offer employment to those who once worked for us."

The kids looked from one to the other.

One of the boys suggested, "They could go west. I hear there's work out there."

"Perhaps some will," Michael acknowledged.

Always cutting to the core, Dowd said, "But that don't help *us*, none."

"'Less we go west, too," said a dark-haired young girl.

Anne warned, "The Prairies are very cold in the winter. Colder than here. And they get blizzards so blinding people become lost a few feet from their own door and freeze to death." She added gently, "If you were to establish yourselves in spring, you might manage out there, but going in winter would be suicide."

Michael said, "The west coast is milder than the Prairies. That would be an option, if you want to leave town."

A tow-haired lad said, "I hear'd that they's plannin' to make us all go into th'orphanage 'cause o' the fire."

Michael confirmed, "Yes, many people in the city think you would be safer there. You'd at least be fed and clothed and have beds to sleep in."

A second girl, a blonde with widely spaced blue eyes that now sparked with anger, spat vehemently, "I ain't goin' to no orphanage! If I hafta put up with men touchin' me, they's damned well gonna pay fer it!"

The brunette agreed, "Yeah! I ain't goin' to no orphanage, neither!"

"Nor a workhouse," said Dowd. "I ain't workin' my fingers to the bone and freezin' and half-starvin' so's some bastard who don't give us enough wood fer the fire nor food fer our bellies can get rich!"

Michael glanced to Anne and back to the children. He sighed and said resignedly, "Then, we must figure out an alternative."

∞

AFTER A SEEMINGLY endless day of discussions interrupted by meals and by the demands of younger children, the *de facto* leaders of the urchins decided to gather their flock in St. Anthony's (the only placed large enough to seat them all) to enumerate and debate the possibilities and to call for a vote. The workhouses and orphanages were, of course, ruled out by all from the start. Even the youngest wanted no part of such places.

Returning to the city, there to attempt to avoid being detained by the constabulary and forced into the most undesirable options was also vetoed by the majority, although a few of the more daring chose that as their path.

The oldest lad, a tall brunet who could pass for seventeen, decided to join the army. Some adventurers wanted to go west to the mountains and the seacoast, or east to the opposite coast, though there was no guarantee they would not be apprehended by authorities, there, and sent to a workhouse or an orphanage or worse. Two brothers chose, instead, to go north into the forests to live by the skills their father had taught them. A few boys and two girls asked to go with them to learn bushcraft and to live in the freedom of the deep woods.

Within a few days, weather permitting, all the children who had chosen to leave town would be gone and The Flats would become just a little less crowded.

The remainder of the gamins accepted an extraordinary idea: a self-run orphanage, built by their own hands, operated by their own rules, and sustained through the sale of their own garden produce and crafts. Anne showed them the land she would grant them, and Father O'Donnell vowed to urge the parish to help with the building and furnishing of the place. Michael promised to create a trust to channel funds from donors such as Dr. Hanes and his more liberal friends in order to get the new "Sunshine Farm" on its feet. And Dowd decided to canvass the rest of the city's street children to offer them a home.

∞

MICHAEL STEPPED up behind Anne and pulled her into his arms as they stood on the back porch and stared at the gibbous moon rising above the treetops. Clouds streaked across the sky and the moonlight blinked frantically. The Scot sucked in the wintry air. Its chill burned his lungs almost as painfully as the fire had, but it left behind a cleanness, as though it washed away the soot and grimy smoke he had inhaled.

With one more slow breath, he leaned to rest his chin on his wife's crown and said, "So, I married a rich woman after all." He could swear he felt her smile.

"Are you disappointed?" she asked facetiously.

He rocked her playfully and said, "Oh, aye, but I expect I'll make do."

His smile fading, he licked his lips and began in a hushed voice, "But I wonder...."

When he said no more, Anne guessed, "Why I didn't tell you sooner?" She turned in his arms to gaze up into his face.

Michael stared into his wife's eyes a long moment before he dared to ask, "Did ye not trust me?"

Anne smiled faintly as she traced the line of her husband's jaw with her finger. She said in a whisper, "I trusted you my love. But you needed to stand on your own feet and learn to trust yourself."

He held her gaze a breathless eternity as he recalled their first few days and weeks together: his piqued and prideful refusal to allow her to seek work, his fear that he would not be able to provide for her, his relief at finding employment, his rising sense of self-worth as he proved himself capable of earning a living and supporting a family.

He chuckled softly and caressed her cheek.

"My *Beira* is so wise," he murmured.

Then, he kissed her deeply and reminded himself why he had married her.

∞

THROUGH HIS FRIEND, journalist John Devereux, Benjamin Ogden knew that over the past week the police had found evidence of arson but nothing to prove who had committed the crime. Now a regular visitor at the house on Stuart Avenue, and occasionally in The Flats, the young photographer eagerly revealed all he had discovered, including the fact that D'Arcy Sloan and his confederates had suddenly disappeared.

Sitting in his usual chair by the hearth, Joseph closed his eyes and sighed at the news.

On the sofa, Michael curled his fingers with Anne's. The comfortably stuffed chesterfield had been pulled to its winter position next to the settee, each of the two long seats obliquely facing both the fire and his parents' wing chairs. At his father's woeful expression, the younger MacGregor asked, "What is it, Father?"

Joseph took a deep breath and said, "One of the warehouses in Montreal was robbed; the banks have called in their loans; and the creditors are demanding immediate payment."

"Orwell and Howes pulling the strings," Anne surmised.

Harris and the two footmen arrived with trays of tea and biscuits and set them on the long tables before the seats. Hermione had chosen the European style of high serving tables, more comfortable to use than the low ones fashionable in North America. Ever the dutiful hostess, she poured the steaming drinks and served the guests herself.

When she handed a cup and saucer to Anne, the matriarch's hands trembled enough to make the crockery rattle. "I must be more careful," she apologized. "I don't want to spill hot tea on anyone."

Anne grasped her mother-in-law's hand firmly and gave it a squeeze as she took the rose-painted, gilt-rimmed china from her. She smiled up at Hermione reassuringly, and the distaff head of the family pulled her lips into a stoic answer of gratitude tinged with fear.

More because of than despite his mother's distress, Michael pressed on, "How is Mr. MacDonald managing?"

Joseph smiled in relief as he replied, "Well, there is some good news." He nodded with satisfaction at his choice of the young Scottish solicitor and said, "With the help of his associate in Montreal, he has managed to sell the distillery there, as well as the warehouses. The men will stay on with the new company. And Ian Fraser has sold all the whisky stock remaining in Québec. That will cover much of the debt."

He continued, "As for the shares, I have asked young MacDonald to get what price he can for them all. He believes he can convert them quickly in New York."

Elizabeth piped up, her voice thin with strain, "Then what?"

Michael's gaze softened as he surveyed his sister's countenance: She had aged almost overnight. Her forehead now creased with apprehension, and lines sprouted between her brows. She had no idea how to live without the security of the wealth she had known from childhood, and it showed in the dark circles of sleepless worry under her eyes.

Joseph heaved a sigh and jerked his head at Harris. Obeying the wordless command, the servants left the room and closed the door as their employer bit his upper lip and braced himself to reveal the hardest news. Finally, Joseph confessed, "We will have to sell the house and let the servants go."

At Elizabeth's strangled cry, he explained, "We willna be able to sustain ourselves as we have, my dear." He gave his wife a melancholy look of rue as he continued, "Without such income as we have had through the business, we must be frugal. We can perhaps make do with a small house somewhere and live on what remains of our funds."

Ben Ogden took this opportunity to say eagerly, "I can take care of Elizabeth, sir." He turned to her to finish, "If that is agreeable."

The photographer knelt before her, taking her hands into

his and gazing into her eyes. "If you'll have me, Elizabeth," he said, "I would very much like to marry you."

Agape, the wetness in her eyes and lashes glinting in the firelight, she whispered incredulously, "Truly? Even if I have no dowry?"

He brought her fingers to his lips and kissed them. He smiled and affirmed, "Truly. I need no payment to make you my wife." He assured her, "And I have excellent prospects in my profession. I may not be rich, but I'll see you never want for food and a good home."

Joseph said, "If ye wish it, daughter, ye have my blessing." He smiled at his wife, whose joyful expression evinced her approval. Turning back to the young couple, the patriarch added, "And I'll see ye have enough to buy a house of your own."

When Ogden started to protest, Joseph dismissed the young man's objection with a wave and said peremptorily, "I want ye to have a good start together."

Looking from the elder to the younger of her in-laws, Anne spoke up. "There's certainly room in The Flats for two more houses, if you wish to build there." She grinned and added, "I have it on good authority that you'll have no trouble getting permission from the owner."

She angled her head to look up at her husband as she finished softly, "And it would be nice to have the family together."

Michael's smile mirrored hers.

CHAPTER 41

Changes

Michael telegraphed Evan in Rio de Janeiro (a stable telephone connection having been impossible to make) to tell him of the need to find work for some of the servants. Most of the younger men—grooms and groundskeepers— had decided to travel to the goldfields of the west to seek their fortune with train tickets purchased by their former employer. One of the footmen (the handsome blond who had briefly wooed each of several girls of The Flats) had gone to New York to make a life in the theatre; the other footman became a waiter in the Tuscarora. Two of the housemaids had found work in one of the department stores downtown, while one rode west in search of a little adventure and perhaps a husband. The younger of the scullery maids returned to her family home in Hamilton; the other gained a position in the kitchens of the Carleton Hotel.

The cook finally gave in to her long-time suitor, a local

farmer. Albee Ross returned to Scotland and Joseph's aging valet to his family in Wales. The coachman, Combie, used his savings to buy the largest of the MacGregor carriages as a hackney; for his years of service, Joseph gave him a substantial discount on both coach and horses. And Harris was snatched up by a young member of the Legislature wishing to establish himself in society.

But Ford, the lady's maid who had long served Hermione, and two of the elder groundskeepers floundered for a time.

Fortunately, thanks to Evan's wide range of social contacts, the valet and the lady's maid found themselves sailing to England and new employment in service to members of the peerage. The groundskeepers, though, waited several more weeks until a gruff Scottish laird, a friend of Lord Heth, decided he had had enough of half-witted youngsters who didn't know a roe deer from a Highland cow.

The manor on Stuart Avenue was sold through the young solicitor to a well-heeled farmer who had taken one look at the orchards and fallen in love. His wife's and daughters' eyes had popped at the silk wallcoverings in the dining-room and the enormous stove they would inherit, and his wife had immediately consented to make do with the fieldstone farmhouse of her wildest dreams.

Many of the furnishings had been purchased by the new owners (they having left most of their own to their only son, along with their previous home and farmland). Other effects were sold at auction for a fair price. The MacGregors took their beds and bedroom furniture, and their personal belongings, but little else when they moved to Cedar Lane. However, Hermione insisted on giving the best china and silverware, crystal and serving pieces to Elizabeth as a wedding gift. For herself and her husband, she brought to their temporary home the old, plain stoneware and cutlery used when the elder couple had first married; Hermione had kept it locked away in her trousseau chest since they had moved to Stuart Avenue. Soon, she would

use it once more in her new, much more modest kitchen. When he saw it, Joseph smiled to his wife, his eyes softening at the fond memories evoked by the rustic tableware.

With daily attention from Anne and frequent visits by Dr. Hanes, Sean Quinn was gradually recovering from his burns. The sentry, Davis, soon found a new job on the docks. Two of the other distillery guards joined the constabulary; one headed for Montreal; three more went west. And Miss Pettigrew gained employment in the new bank on Bay.

However, the rest of Joseph's former employees were not faring so well, and the MacGregor funds were quickly dwindling as Joseph and Michael tried to help those who had been set adrift by the Scotch family's misfortune: Three households now had no provider, and Sean Quinn would be an invalid and need costly medical attention for some time to come.

∞

MICHAEL LEANED BACK and rubbed his eyes. He had been poring over the accounts an hour in the light of a single candle on the desk, his broad oak bureau now crowded into the kitchen between the coat cupboard at the front door and a hutch full of dishes. His father snored in the former study, and Elizabeth padded in from the privy and up to her room where once the nursery had been. A half-dozen urchins remained, in the third bedchamber upstairs, but many of the lads had taken up residence in the mews to sleep in the hay, and some boys and girls had been accepted by families whose previous gamin guests had left the neighbourhood for good.

Michael had not heard her approach, but Anne's hands now massaged his shoulders and she asked softly, "What is it, my love?"

"We're running out of money," he said simply. Suddenly, it occurred to him to ask his wife, "Are you receiving rents from the residents of The Flats?" He turned his swivel chair to look at

her as she responded.

"Not rents, exactly," she replied. "Each family pays me a kind of mortgage. Many of them will soon own their homes outright. Some already do."

He frowned and squinted at her. "Then why were you working as a charwoman in the garment factory when I met you?"

Her smile widened and she said, "That was for me. My living. I have been using the rest of the money for other purposes."

"What purposes?" he asked curiously.

"Some of it is invested," she replied, stepping between his spread knees to wrap her arms around his neck as he gazed up into her face and she down into his. She stroked his glossy black hair, drawing her fingers through the silken waves.

She continued, "Some, I've been using to build and maintain the churches and mews here in The Flats, to buy useful items for the hospitals and orphanages in the city, and to help the odd person here and there. Recently, I have also set aside a fund for the children's new farm, and one to help the families who have so many extra mouths to feed since the storm. Another portion, I keep for contingencies."

She held her husband's eyes, cupped his cheeks, and added, "Do not worry, my love. We'll manage. My money is yours."

Michael encircled Anne's waist with his arms and rested his head against her bulging belly. He listened to the sough of her breath and the tiny, muffled sounds within her womb as the baby moved.

What angel had brought this extraordinary woman to him? he wondered. How foolish he and others had been to presume by her appearance alone that she was a poor peasant of no consequence. He was curious to know how she had come by the money to buy The Flats, but he would not ask; it did not matter. He smiled as he remembered the gold and gemstones she

had brought from the north. Who knew what resources his *Beira* might possess?

He looked up into her face once more and said, "Do you know how much I love you?"

She grinned, a playful twinkle in her eyes. "How much?"

He rose and gathered her into his arms to rock her and press her head to his chest. He said earnestly, "I love you more than words can express. And I always will."

"Ditto," she whispered, and he chuckled.

As they stood holding each other, he decided he must find a job. In Trevelyan's employ, perhaps. His pride would not allow him to live entirely by his wife's property. Yes, he would familiarize himself with all her holdings, but those might not be enough to cover the many obligations they had acquired—at least, not when the mortgage income diminished. He must contribute as best he could.

He nearly groaned aloud when he remembered how many men would also be seeking work, now. And some of those men were his neighbours.

Damn Orwell!

∞

WILLIAM MacDONALD had happily set up a trust fund for the children as Michael and Anne had requested, the redhead's own family history being filled with orphans of feuds and wars. He also hosted a soirée to solicit donations to what he described as a "children's relief fund"—the true purpose being too revolutionary for the conservative minds of even the more progressive among the city's elite.

Ben Ogden attended in order to photograph smiling donors and make note of conversations. Elizabeth giggled when she confessed to Anne that her betrothed enjoyed spying on the "toffs" and reporting back to the family. As it turned out, so did young Mr. MacDonald.

Seated at the kitchen table, hand in hand with Elizabeth, Ben said, "Reginald Orwell didn't attend."

William MacDonald interjected, "I did not invite him."

Ben continued, "But Mr. Cavendish complained that Orwell has been bragging about his new investments in the whisky business and how he's a much better businessman than Mr. MacGregor."

Anne put in caustically, "As if his force of personality could magically prevent disasters like arson." She looked at Joseph and grinned. "Let's see how he fares against the Temperance League. Some of them are crazy enough to burn a factory."

Frowning, Hermione wondered aloud, "Could it have been the teetotallers who destroyed the distillery, rather than Reginald?"

"No," said Michael. "It was Sloan I saw running away that night, just before the explosion." He added grimly, "I can't prove it, but I know."

Joseph clasped Hermione's hand in both of his at her distress. It was clear she considered the whole debacle her fault for having spurned Orwell so long ago.

MacDonald said, "I overheard a conversation between Thomas Cavendish and Nathaniel Bennett that tells me Orwell has been blackmailing them about something—something their wives would find offensive."

Michael's mouth curled into a sardonic grin. "Madame Maxine. He must have some proof they regularly enjoy her 'French lessons.'" He shook his head and tisked. "It seems her establishment does not provide the discretion she claims."

Joseph said glumly, "That's why they betrayed me."

His wife placed her free hand atop his. She said, "I'm glad I did not marry such a wretched man. I'm glad I chose you, instead."

Her husband lifted her hand to his lips and kissed her fingers. Ben followed his example and kissed Elizabeth's hand

tenderly, while Anne rose to stand with Michael and grasp his hand.

William MacDonald quipped, "I suppose I should get myself a sweetheart if I'm to be coming here often." He grinned broadly. "If I must fit in somewhere, better here than Madame Maxine's.

"As for the trust fund," he added grandly, "we have made a very fine start with nearly thirty thousand dollars in donations."

"Thank you, Mr. MacDonald," said Michael and Joseph together.

"Please call me Will," said the solicitor. "And I hope I may call you Michael and Joseph."

"First names all around," Anne declared. "It's only fair, now that you're effectively part of the family."

"In that case," said Joseph, "let us celebrate properly." He disappeared into the back room and re-emerged with a bottle of fifteen-year-old single malt.

"Well, now," said the lawyer with a chuckle after taking a sip, "I can see there are benefits to joining the Clan MacGregor."

∞

SOON AFTER BEN and Elizabeth persuaded her parents to accept a winter wedding, the little white church near the bridge filled, one bright December morning, with friends and family of bride and groom. To a fiddle's tune, there being no organ, Elizabeth glided up the aisle on her father's arm, draped in a blue silk gown with fitted jacket and a white gossamer veil that did not hide her shy smile and maiden blush. Ben, in his best grey suit, stood by the altar, trembling and swallowing visibly and appearing scared out of his skin as John Devereux whispered words of encouragement and firmly gripped his friend's elbow to keep him from bolting.

Both bride and groom stammered through the ceremony

and shook so badly that it took a full minute to slide the ring onto Elizabeth's finger. Anne wanted to jump up, grab the gold band from Ben, and shove it into place herself.

As soon as the happy—and very relieved—couple exited the church, Anne pushed past the crowd pouring into the aisle, raced by Ben and Elizabeth, and flew in a flurry of cherry-red wool to the nearby mews. There, she flung open the door of the privy and slammed it shut behind her.

"Damn!" she said aloud in the cubbyhole. When a small quantity of urine had been expelled, she repeated, "Damn!"

Emerging from the outhouse flustered and annoyed, Anne found her husband waiting and grinning. He said, "Ye had me worried there, a minute, the way ye squirmed in the pew."

"Junior has planted himself solidly upon my bladder," she complained crossly. She placed her fists on her hips, scowled down at her belly, and demanded, "Move!"

When nothing happened, she heaved a great sigh and looked forlornly toward her husband. He threw back his head and laughed a deep, rumbling guffaw that brought a petulant slap to his arm.

Anne retorted, "You wouldn't think it so funny if *you* had to carry a fifty pound Highlander around in your belly!"

"Oh, fifty pounds, is he?" Michael scoffed. "More like five, if that."

Anne groused, "Feels like fifty."

The Scot pulled his wife into his embrace and bent her back, cradling her in his arms. He said lasciviously, "Maybe ye just need a change of position."

Anne gasped, "Oh, God! Let me up!"

At her tone of desperation, Michael swept her to a stand. Instantly, she rushed back into the privy as he chortled behind her.

CHAPTER 42

Opportunity knocks

After a two-day honeymoon in a small inn, the newlyweds relocated to Ben's garret in the city, leaving most of Elizabeth's furniture behind, for the time being. Two feet of snow from the season's first blizzard persuaded the happy couple to wait until spring to begin building their new home. The orphans grudgingly made the same decision when the carefully positioned markers that described their future walls disappeared under the drifts.

Some of the ragamuffins moved back into the MacGregor house when Elizabeth's room became available once more. Five little girls revelled in the big four-poster bed with its silky sheets and feather comforters. Taking the opportunity to play hostess in their fairy-tale bedchamber, they held frequent sleepovers with friends.

The O'Reilly girls were now a part of the household,

coming every morning to cook and bake, launder and clean, and tend to the smaller children. Anne suspected the two simply wanted to escape the extreme crowding of their own home, the shrill admonitions of their mother, and the knowing eye of their grandmother. It had not escaped Anne's notice, nor that if the eldest Mrs. O'Reilly, that the same two young men turned up at the gate almost every evening to escort the girls to the mews with baskets of food for the urchins who remained there.

Christmas preparation and baking began in earnest with the arrival in The Flats of several wagonloads of flour, sugar, and spice. The fragrance of gingerbread and fruitcake wafted from every kitchen, and pungent wreaths of pine sprigs with bows of red ribbon circled every front-door knocker.

Under the combined direction of Father O'Donnell, Reverend Ferguson, Dowd, Hermione, and flame-haired Miss Alice O'Reilly, the children practised daily for a pageant and scrounged props and costumes. Dowd had succeeded in begging the ends of a couple of bolts of cloth from Anne when Michael crossed paths with him on the front porch. Casting a curious glance back over his shoulder as the boy hopped the fence and headed toward Sumac, the Scot asked, "What's Dowd up to?"

"You're home early," Anne noted as she greeted her husband with a quick kiss. In answer to the question, she added, "He's helping with the Nativity play. I have no idea why he wants the fabric. Costumes, perhaps. I gave him the last of the wincey."

Michael shed his snow-speckled brown wool coat, his lighter brown cap, and his green-and-blue plaid scarf and heaped them over one of the sturdy iron hooks by the door. He spread his fleece-lined leather gloves on the little wooden mitten-tree perched on the warming bench that jutted from the side of Anne's brick stove, and he smiled at the practical gadget she had fashioned from a twiggy branch of spruce. Then, from behind, he reached his long arms around to hug and hold her as she whipped a large bowl of batter.

Bending to her ear, he said, "That smells almost as good as you do."

"Mmm, flatterer," she pretended to scold, affecting a prim manner. "Methinks you would seduce me, sir."

He snarled lewdly and said, "Damn right, I would!" He tightened his grip around her raised waistline, just below her swelling breasts, and he whuffled at her neck in the way that always elicited shrill girlish giggles that delighted him. He and Anne carried on with their tickling game for several minutes, necessitating a pause in her baking preparations, until Joseph walked into the house.

Closing the front door, the elder MacGregor called loudly, "Didn't mean to interrupt!" His shoulders shook with mirth as he slipped his muffler over an empty hook by the door and peeled off his coat.

"Like hell, Da!" Michael rejoined with a grin.

"You're obviously in high spirits," his father replied. "Do I take it ye got the job?"

"Better," said Michael.

When his wife and father regarded him with brows raised in expectant curiosity, he announced, "Jake Trevelyan and I will be partners in a new stone- and brick-works off Front Street. We'll build a temporary shop to start, and we'll be hiring right away. Tomorrow, I'll arrange to transfer my savings to help fund the venture."

"That's wonderful, my boy!" Joseph exclaimed. The elder MacGregor rushed forward, extending his hand, and Michael grasped it to pull his father into an embrace.

When they parted, Michael added, "We'd like you to join us, Da. We could use your knowledge of accounts and contracts."

Joseph's face fell and he responded in a tone of dejection, "Ye don't need me, son. You've all the knowledge ye need."

"But I won't have the time," Michael insisted. "Nor will Trevelyan. Someone needs to manage the office while he and I do the stone-cutting and the brick-making and the building."

Knowing his father's mind, he entreated, "It's not charity, Da. We need ye."

Anne piped up, "Makes sense, Joseph. Especially for a fledgling business, there are so many things to be done at once."

The patriarch looked from Anne to Michael and worked his lips as he pondered the notion. At last, he agreed, "All right. Since ye need a little help to get started."

Michael picked his father off the floor in a bear hug that set the elder man to wheezing for breath.

∞

AFTER HER THIRD trip to the privy, Anne threw off her wool robe and climbed back into bed to snuggle under the quilts with her husband. For all his playfulness, he had become increasingly inhibited in the bedroom. There was no hiding her pregnancy: Her belly seemed to grow by the day, and her loose gowns often heaved with Junior's activity, to the amazement of round-eyed children and the dismay of some of the older male residents of The Flats. More than once, she had seen her husband's anxious glance at their child's acrobatics.

"I'm not made of glass," she murmured as she rolled toward Michael.

He turned to her and stroked her belly. "I know," he replied in hushed tones. "But I dinna want to hurt either of ye." Gazing into her face in the light of the candle he had not yet snuffed, he whispered, "Sometimes I scare myself, with what I want to do to ye."

"Like what?" she asked.

His mouth curved into a smile that did not reach his sorrowful eyes as he brushed strands of hair back from her temple. He warned, "It would not be wise for me to think on it, much less to say it."

He gasped and gaped at her when she reached beneath the hem of his nightshirt and traced the line of his thigh, slowly

and delicately. "Are ye mad?" he whispered. He pulled her hand away, but she replaced it with the attentions of its twin, and a minor skirmish ensued, to the sound of her giggles.

When she freed a wrist and encircled his stiffening member, he closed his eyes, panting, and groaned, "Jesus, woman! Dinna torture me so. I canna...I canna...." His verbal protests were belied by the broad hand that clasped hers but did not push her away.

Anne curled under the blankets and added flicks of her tongue to her manual caresses. He moaned, and he slid his fingers through her hair to urge her on. As she sheathed him with her mouth, he cried out, "Oh, Jesus!" and promptly ejaculated in spasms that left him breathless.

Her task accomplished, Anne released him and pushed up to behold her husband's sated expression. She murmured, "Better?"

"It'll do," he replied with a faint, abashed smile.

His mien suddenly anxious, he cupped her cheek and said earnestly, "Do you have any idea how much will it took not to throw you down and pound you into the ticking?"

Placing her hand over his, she said, "They say absence makes the heart fonder. But I can see abstinence most certainly makes your desire stronger." She kissed his palm and entreated, "Please let me give you pleasure, my love." With a grin, she added, "There are ways that don't require pinning me to the mattress."

He held her face and regarded her a long moment. Then, he pulled her into his arms and kissed the crown of her head. "I suppose you're right, he admitted. "But what about *your* pleasure?"

She lifted up onto her elbow once more and fixed his eyes. "I can wait," she insisted.

He tilted his head and studied her, pursing his lips thoughtfully. With a quirk of his mouth, he said, "Or, maybe I should return the favour."

Abruptly, peremptorily, he pressed his wife onto her back and dived between her legs.

∞

SHE WAS RIGHT, he thought as he pinched out the candle's flame and scooted under the quilts to spoon with Anne. Not that he wanted her less for having her more, but the past week of not making love to her had made the wanting more urgent. He sighed contentedly as he fit his front to her back and inhaled the fragrance of her hair. However had he managed without her? He could not imagine it, now.

Her breathing slowed to a steady rhythm and he knew she slept. His own slumber was not far off as his mind drifted to the events of the evening: When he and his father had offered employment, the reactions of the former distillery employees had included everything from Aiden Bannion's instant enthusiastic acceptance, to Tsi-Guy Villeneuve's cautious consideration, to Avery Chegwin's disgruntled refusal to consider a new trade. The MacGregors had assured the naysayers they would have the opportunity to change their minds if they found no work with which they were familiar.

Now, the Scot reflected, all he had to do was to start a new business...on a small budget...and with many untrained workers. *Piece of cake,* Michael had heard his wife say of similarly dubious undertakings. He grinned to himself at the breezy phrase that made light of a daunting task.

Just before he dozed, he hazily wondered where his father had been all day.

∞

"WELCOME, WELCOME!"

George Catesby rose to greet Anne expansively as she and Michael and Joseph entered his office. The jovial, beefy banker kissed her hand in courtly manner before extending his chubby

paw to Joseph and then to Michael. "And you, Mr. MacGregor...Mr. MacGregor. I am so pleased to see you. Do sit down."

He gestured to the leather chairs facing his desk, and he took his own well-padded swivel armchair behind the massive walnut bureau. To his rear, the red, white, and blue of a Union Jack draped from a pole in one corner while a potted fern effused in the other. Between those, a long walnut credenza squatted below a picture of the queen flanked by smaller portraits of the current prime minister and the governor-general. On his left, the wide, high casements along the outer wall filled the room with light and boasted a splendid view of MacDonald Park under its blanket of snow, while the windows on the opposite wall allowed Catesby to monitor the bank's workings.

Leaning forward, clasping his hands and resting his forearms on the pristine buff ink-blotter, Catesby looked to each of his guests and asked, "What can I do for you?"

Husband and wife momentarily exchanged a wordless glance of communication before Anne answered, "I wish to invest in my husband's new venture, and he and his partner, Mr. Trevelyan, have agreed to handle their business through your bank. My father-in-law, Mr. Joseph MacGregor, will be handling the day-to-day administration."

"Wonderful, wonderful!" Catesby enthused. "And how much will you be transferring?"

"Fifty thousand dollars," said Anne.

"Of course," Catesby replied as though such transactions were not at all unusual. "And when will Mr. Trevelyan—?"

"Speak of the Devil and he doth appear!"

Jake Trevelyan stood in the doorway with a Cheshire grin as a slender, bespectacled man in plain charcoal suit hovered at his side. When the bank manager nodded to the latter, the mousy secretary scurried away as Trevelyan stepped forward and met Catesby halfway between door and desk.

"Good to see you, Mr. Trevelyan," said the banker as the

two shook hands. "Please take a seat."

Several cups of tea and a raft of signed papers later, *Trevelyan and Company* officially opened their accounts.

∞

THE MACGREGOR PARTY alighted from the hackney as Jake Trevelyan dismounted and hobbled his horse near a public trough. Not trusting his wife's balance these days, Michael grasped Anne under her arms and lifted her out of the cab to set her gently upon the street: He had seen her step heavily from a carriage only the day before, when they had visited the young Scottish solicitor to incorporate the company, and twice she had nearly fallen while negotiating the stairs at home.

"Here it is," Jake announced with a gesture indicating the land between rail line and lake. "Bought and paid for," he added with satisfaction. "Now, all we have to do is build on it."

Michael's mouth curled wryly at his partner's cavalier dismissal of such a monumental endeavour.

The four stood a long moment, taking in the stretch of heath overgrown with shrubs and saplings, riddled with rills, and currently undulating under the layer of white powder that had fallen in the night. Chalky gulls squawked and soared in the pearl glow of the winter sky above, and a freight train chugged and hooted behind them as it rolled eastward, its rumbling undertone felt in their feet.

"Does it flood?" asked Anne out of the blue.

All three men looked at her in surprise. Trevelyan answered, "Not that I've heard. Most of the land's higher than over there in The Flats, and the water from rain and snowmelt will soon be channelled into the sewers, I'm told."

At the last statement, Anne shot Trevelyan a glance that Michael was sure included anger, though he could not imagine why. Her ferocity softened instantly, and she sighed in what he recognized as resignation, chewing her lips thoughtfully.

He leaned down to whisper in her ear, "What is it that bothers ye?"

She smiled faintly as she glanced up at him and murmured, "It's...." She shook her head. "We can speak of it later."

Trevelyan strode forward, picking his way along the uneven ground as he described his vision of the future stoneworks and brickyard. His two partners asked questions and suggested alternatives. Gradually the three men came to a consensus as to the best configuration for the site. Through it all, Anne remained silent, listening, and occasionally hiding behind an evergreen bush to relieve herself.

Despite his interest in the matter at hand, Michael glanced frequently toward his wife. It occurred to him that she must know something, some unforeseen outcome, some difficulty arising from their plans.

We can speak of it later, she had said.

Clearly, we must, he thought.

∞

WHILE JOSEPH and Hermione sat in the kitchen drinking tea and discussing their own plans for the future, Anne and Michael slipped out into the night air. Somewhere in the distance, young carollers belted out "Joy to the World" a little off key. Above, the crescent moon had not yet risen among the stars sparkling crisply against the cold black. Michael pulled the downy wool of her shawl snugly across Anne's bosom.

"I dinna want ye to catch a fever," he said with a slight scolding edge in his voice. He grasped her shoulders and smiled and pulled her close.

"Do you know that you sound more Scotch with each day that passes?"

He chuckled. "From bein' around Da and MacDonald so much, I suppose." He pushed a strand of her long, unbound hair

behind her ear, the pure whiteness of her tresses glinting gold on one side, in the light from the window, and silver on the other, in the starlight. He cupped her cheek. Tenderly, he said, "Do you know that ye look more like an angel with each day that passes?"

She placed her hand over his and beamed at him.

He stroked her cheek with his thumb, and his smile faded. He asked quietly, "What was it that distressed ye so, today?"

Anne inhaled deeply, her own smile melting away. She said soberly, sadly, "There are many things that have been done, and that will be done, that will prove harmful to the earth and to people. It will take decades for the effects to become obvious, and decades longer to understand the cause. Worse, those who benefit by the status quo, or who do not want to pay the price of their own or previous generations' folly, will not want to correct the problems."

"Like the filth in the Durham and the Bow," Michael realized. "If the Durham did not flow past the Yacht Club and a few other choice properties, Council might never have invested the money to clean it up. And they still have no plans to salvage the Bow."

"Indeed," Anne confirmed. "And when they finally decide to do something, their solutions to the many problems inherent in cities will create new, unexpected difficulties."

"Perhaps we can stop these things before they start," Michael suggested. "Do differently."

Anne smiled up at him, admiring his optimism. But knowledge intruded and her sorrow returned. She sighed and said, "I fear the forces driving us to that cliff are too strong to withstand."

At his crestfallen expression, she added more hopefully, "But while that may be so in the larger scheme of things, individuals and groups can still provide a better example that may someday be recognized." She fixed his eyes. "That *will* be recognized, once the lessons are finally learned by the majority."

Michael regarded his wife a long moment, wondering what this woman from another time had seen to fill her with such certainty of doom. He stroked her hair once more and asked quietly, "What would ye have us do?"

Anne glanced down and away, and she pursed her lips thoughtfully. Then, she returned her eyes to his and said, "Rather than rely on sewers, you could channel the excess precipitation to a pond that would both prevent uncontrolled flooding and give you a source of water for your operations. Or as a backup in case of fire."

"Aye, the site's big enough," he agreed. "And there are low spots toward the lake."

She continued, "And I could help you design the kilns to increase fuel efficiency and capture the smoke."

He frowned, perplexed. "Why would we capture the smoke?"

"Well," she explained, "there are several reasons: For one, the smoke is a pollutant of the air and, when the particles fall, of the land and water. Second, it contains heat that can be held in the system for other uses. And whether you burn coal or wood as your fuel, the creosote can be sold for extra profit."

Michael nodded thoughtfully as he pondered her advice. "Aye," he said at last, "all of those make sense." He grinned down at her and asked, "Anything else?"

"Well, now that you mention it, the contents of the privies could be very useful."

He threw back his head and roared with laughter.

CHAPTER 43

'Tis the season

When Ben and Elizabeth arrived, dusting flakes from their coats and hats and stamping their feet to dislodge the wet snow clinging to their footwear before stepping over the threshold, Anne recognized instantly the special glow that now lit her sister-in-law's visage: Junior—little James Alexander MacGregor—would soon have a cousin to play with.

Taking Elizabeth's coat and hanging it with care, she said, "Come warm yourselves by the fire." She gestured toward the chairs already set out for their guests from the city.

Jake Trevelyan perched on a tall stool, sipping some of Joseph's fifteen-year-old whisky and discussing matters of business with his new partners, while Hermione sat in the warmest spot in the house: the heated brick bench Anne had built into her stove. Next to the MacGregor matriarch, two of the smallest gamines, scrubbed and wearing honey-toned wool

sweaters over their brown dresses, practised knitting with their kindly grey-haired teacher.

Elizabeth shrieked in delighted surprise when she saw Miss Grace Donaldson sitting in a chair next to Hermione, stitching needlepoint by the light of the candles sprinkled so liberally throughout the room as to rival daylight. Miss Donaldson leapt to her feet, and the two younger women ran to each other and embraced with the affection of old friends long parted.

Ben, suddenly forgotten, shook his head and smiled with a combination of pique, amusement, and tolerance as his wife and her friend sat together and chatted excitedly about the events in the months since their last meeting.

"Get used to it," Michael murmured to his brother-in-law as he handed him a glass of single malt. "She loves you, but she always was a chatterbox." He added, "Besides, those two have been friends for twenty years."

Ben lifted his glass in a wordless toast and sipped. Then, he coughed a couple of times and his eyes watered. "Strong!" he squeaked.

Michael grinned, "It is that. I take it you don't imbibe much."

"I'm usually working when I attend parties and gatherings," Ben admitted. "And I don't drink at home." He noted the glass of water in his host's hand and said, "I take it you don't partake, either."

"Used to," Michael replied. "In fact, I was a drunk, as you may have heard. Now, I try to stay away from it."

"Must have been difficult when you worked in the distillery," Ben observed.

"Aye," Michael acknowledged. "I was sorely tempted when I worked the stillroom and warehouses, to be sure." His gaze shifted to Anne, sitting with Elizabeth and Grace Donaldson, and he said, "But I had reason to resist."

The two young men looked to the circle where Elizabeth

and Grace gingerly touched Anne's belly in fascination.

"I'm surprised your friend Devereux hasn't come," Michael commented.

"He's working," Ben told him, rolling his eyes.

Michael gaped in astonishment. "On Christmas Eve?"

"The man's obsessed," the photographer confided. "Seems he's discovered some conspiracy or other, and now he's like a hound that's caught the scent of a fox. He won't quit until he's hunted it to its lair."

"That could get him killed someday," Michael muttered grimly.

His brother-in-law started. But after a moment's sober reflection, he concurred softly, "Yes, it could."

At a knock, Michael opened the door to find William MacDonald slapping his cap against his thigh to remove snow accumulated on his walk from the mews. Entering, the lawyer said, "You've a fine stable and plenty of hands to tend the horses, Michael."

"Aye," said his host as he took the man's coat and hooked it onto the wall along with the snow-dampened muffler woven in MacDonald tartan. "Some of the lads sleep there in the hay. They say it's warmer than a house." He leaned in to mutter, "Personally, I think they just like being where no one minds if they don't bathe."

MacDonald let out a hoot and chortled as Joseph put a drink into his hand. "Slainte," said the redhead as he raised the cut-glass vessel and then put it to his lips. When he had downed the whisky, he uttered an "Ahh!" of pleasure and said, "Nothin' like fine Scotch whisky on such a night."

"Hear, hear!" said Trevelyan, raising his own glass and emptying the last of its contents.

Joseph circled the room, replenishing mugs of sweet spiced cider and glasses of whisky as Elizabeth eagerly ushered her socialite friend forward to introduce the newcomer. Across the room, Anne winked at Michael when young Miss Donaldson

blushed under the suave attentions of the Highlander. Michael lifted his glass to his wife and winked back before turning to corral the herd of youngsters that had burst in the back door, covered in snow and red-faced with cold and the exertions of play.

∞

IN THE HOUSE redolent of roast turkey and baked sweet potatoes, gravy and herbed stuffing, fresh bread and warm pie, dinner saw tables pushed together for the adults, the smallest children seated on and about the warm-bench by the stove, and the older children cross-legged on the floor or staggered up the stairs. While Grace chatted with Elizabeth throughout the meal, and MacDonald and Joseph discussed contract law, the rest of the gathering uttered only occasional murmurs of appreciation as they gobbled their festive fare.

When the plates and pans were finally cleared to the waiting tubs of hot, soapy water, and the scent of the pine wreaths and garlands that festooned the house began to overpower the odours of food, sleepy children, their eyes wide and blinking with the effort to remain awake, protested weakly as Michael and Anne shepherded them to their beds. Host and hostess rejoined the party a little later as Hermione placed fresh tapers in only a few of the candelabra, allowing the majority of the candles to gutter and extinguish themselves. In the softened glow, conversation hushed.

"You're a fine cook, Mrs. MacGregor," said Jake Trevelyan to Anne.

"I can't take all the credit," Anne admitted. She clasped Hermione's hand and said, "*This* Mrs. MacGregor did much of the work."

Her mother-in-law blushed when Joseph said proudly, "Just like when we were in the Highlands, my dear."

Hermione corrected, "Except we had mutton instead of

turkey, and turnip instead of sweet potatoes, and oatcakes instead of fruit pie."

Joseph chuckled and replied, "But you could make a sow's ear taste like ambrosia, my sweet."

Hermione reddened to her roots and slapped her husband's arm in bashful remonstration.

"I do not doubt it," said Trevelyan, raising his glass to her and adding to her pleased embarrassment.

Grace Donaldson piped up shyly, "I wish my mother could teach me to cook. But I don't think she has ever so much as boiled an egg."

Anne volunteered, "Then, you must let us teach you. After all," she winked at Elizabeth, "they say the way to a man's heart is through his stomach."

Michael grinned at his wife and countered, "There's a quicker route."

All females but Anne flushed at his blatantly lascivious suggestion. Ben Ogden and William MacDonald started and gaped at him, instantly turning pink and squirming awkwardly. Joseph snorted and gulped his whisky to suppress a chuckle.

It was Jake Trevelyan who rescued the youngsters by saying, "Ah, but it's pleasing a man's stomach that keeps him close to home for the long haul."

Elizabeth asked, "And you, Mr. Trevelyan. Have you no wife?"

"I used to," the stonemason answered, sadness sweeping across his eyes. "She passed some years ago."

"Oh! I'm so sorry!" Elizabeth exclaimed, hand to her chest, countenance sorrowful.

Grace Donaldson asked with sincere concern, "Have you found no one else?"

When the Cornishman downed his drink in lieu of reply, Michael said quietly, "For some of us, there *is* no one else." He cast a loving glance to his wife.

∞

WILLIAM MacDONALD insisted on riding alongside the sleigh all the way to Rosemont and the home of Grace Donaldson. He dismounted and offered her a hand out of the carriole when Michael debarked and opened the door for her.

Curious eyes peeked through the lace-curtained window of the sandstone mansion as Mr. Donaldson, dressed in black dinner jacket and brocade waistcoat, stepped out of his front door with, first, a look of anxiety and, then, of relief at sight of Anne bundled in the sleigh. Grace's father cocked his brow and eyed the redheaded stranger upon whom his daughter bestowed a shy smile, and he watched narrowly when the lawyer bowed and kissed her hand with a courteous "Good night." As Grace ascended the stairs, father and suitor briefly locked eyes. Then, a subdued William MacDonald turned to climb back into his saddle.

When farewells and season's greetings were concluded and the Donaldsons had retired to the warmth of their home, Anne called softly, "Give it time, William. You'll win him over."

The lawyer smiled diffidently and nodded acceptance of her advice as Michael snapped the reins and urged the pair of bays around the curve and back to the lane.

∞

LANGUID FLAKES drifted down to settle on their heads and shoulders and their blanketed laps as Michael and Anne drove home in the open sleigh. No wind blew, as though the world held its breath, and the susurrus of the runners whispered in the silence of the night. From the front of the vehicle, two lanterns cast enough light to steer safely along the road and sparked both sinking and settled snow crystals with gold.

With a contented sigh, Anne snuggled close to her husband, and she purred when he gathered the reins in one gloved hand and put his arm around her shoulder. They did not

speak. There was no need.

∞

BY THE TIME the bells of St. Anthony's rang, everyone in the MacGregor household had dressed and broken fast, ready for a day of celebration. Brimming with excitement, the children had gulped their bannocks and jam and their tea, eager to run to the church where the entire Christian community, Catholic and Protestant alike, had agreed to gather for a combined service before the spectacle the children had prepared.

When the MacGregors arrived, Anne and Michael smiled and nodded to the Hoffmans and the Golds standing discreetly in the back. The two Jewish families had asked permission to witness the festivities for which the gentiles of The Flats had so feverishly prepared and, though he had gaped in surprise and stammered, at first, the priest had consented.

No furnace was needed today as the ambient temperature rose with the sheer number of bodies crammed into the church. The pews filled to capacity, many children sitting on laps to make more room, and the younger men and teenagers lined the walls. Those who were not Catholic glanced about curiously, watching as Mrs. Buzzetti lit a candle for her late husband and, as always, Old Lady Tulan lit three.

The shuffling and mutters quieted when Father O'Donnell and Reverend Ferguson entered. Robed in white, the priest began the Mass as the minister looked on, and the Protestants mimicked their Catholic friends each time the latter knelt. For the Eucharist, the two congregational leaders attended their own flocks. And the Catholics listened courteously when Mr. Peckham read a passage from the bible and Reverend Ferguson followed up with a short sermon.

A sigh of relief issued from the majority of the children when the formalities were finally concluded. Now, it was their turn.

As the chosen young carollers replaced the choir to serenade the adults with Christmas songs, and as a few of the pregnant ladies made a hasty exit to the nearest privy or bush, the rest of the youngsters scrambled behind a screen that had been drawn across the apse to hide their props and costumes. With a great deal of whispering and giggling, and under the guidance of Dowd, Hermione, and Miss Alice O'Reilly, the little ones donned their cloaks and angel wings, haloes and woolly wigs, as the older children brought forth and arranged the set for the story of the birth of Jesus in Bethlehem. The preparations took long enough that most everyone stood to stretch legs and wandered outside for fresh air until Reverend Ferguson signalled them to return. Once the elders had settled back into their seats, Ben Ogden set his camera upon a tripod in the central aisle to immortalize the performers.

Robed in a sister's deep blue dress that brushed the floor as she walked, little Becky O'Malley played Mary, while gamin Joseph Horne portrayed his namesake in a fuzzy raw-wool beard. Seamus O'Reilly, in his diapers and christening gown, sat in the cradle-cum-manger and looked about with wide eyes and open, drooling mouth. When the baby spotted his mother in a nearby pew and reached out for her, Becky picked him up—a boy fully two-thirds her body weight—and rocked him as he howled in frustration. His mother patted the air at him from her seat and called soft reassurances, one hand fisted at her side with the effort not to run to her firstborn.

Father O'Donnell had nixed the notion of bringing live animals into the church; so, a couple of dozen urchins baaed and neighed and hee-hawed in their brown and grey and white wrappings as many more played everything from wise men to angels to stars complete with pointy paper headdresses.

The audience stifled giggles as the pageant progressed through explanatory asides, little ones rendering their respective roles with gusto and mispronounced words, Becky and Joseph attempting to placate the inconsolable Seamus as they called out

their lines, angel Giuseppe Cacciotti tripping on a sagging hem and falling with star Dorcas O'Herlihy in a tumble of white muslin and flying wing-feathers, and Joseph announcing loudly that the central character had pooped in his diapers. The last brought hoots and cheers as red-faced Sharon O'Reilly hurried to take her son from his temporary parents.

When the play concluded and the congregation ambled out into the churchyard, the Hoffmans and Golds, their cheeks stained with tears of mirth, milled with the Christians of The Flats and chatted awhile before heading home. In the wan sunlight, families collected their little Thespians and strolled to their waiting luncheons and a day of visiting with friends and extended family.

∞

ANNE AND MICHAEL lay facing each other, her belly filling the space between them. When the baby stretched and pushed her roundness into a misshapen mass, Michael pushed up onto one elbow and placed his palm gently over the protrusion.

"Does he hurt ye?" he asked, eyes and voice full of concern.

"Not at the moment," she assured him as she placed her hand over his on her abdomen. "It can be uncomfortable at times, especially if he kicks out suddenly, but for the most part, there is no pain."

"Good," he said, relieved. In truth, though, Michael did not look forward to the birthing of his son. He had heard many shocking tales of difficult deliveries, and he had witnessed the screams of Tsi-Guy's wife less than two weeks ago. He shuddered at the memory, and he knew he could not remain as calm at Anne's pain as the younger Villeneuve had seemed when his second daughter was born.

"She's jus' makin' a fuss," Tsi-Guy had said with apparent nonchalance at Michael's horrified expression. "It's her

way."

Tsi-Guy's brother, Mike, had pulled Michael aside and quietly told him, "'E like to tell 'imself dat so's 'e don' worry. But inside, 'e worry anyway."

As though she heard his thoughts, Anne said, "You needn't worry, my love. All will be well."

"Piece of cake?"

She grinned. "Piece of cake."

He dowsed the light and pulled the quilts snugly up over her shoulders and his own.

Piece of cake.

He wished he could be so confident.

∞

FINE SUNNY WEATHER and perfect fort-making snow combined to keep the children occupied throughout the week following Christmas. Each day, they tired themselves out making angels in the drifts, hurling snowballs at one another, and building elaborate fortifications complete with parapets and windows. Dowd and Jack had even erected little flags over their respective castles and waged white-cannon warfare across the Protestant churchyard-cum-schoolyard.

The fattening crescent of the moon cast long shadows over the drifts and around the play structures each night as it arced westward. Michael took a turn on watch, armed with a pistol and carrying a lantern through the quiet lanes. When he met other sentries, the men nodded wordless greetings to each other and continued on their rounds. The deep chill of January and February had not yet settled upon the landscape, but a slight dampness in the air sharpened the cold; it penetrated the Scot's woollen cloak and appurtenances, and its sting made the evening drag interminably.

The moon set and took with it the luminescence that had washed The Flats in silver and black. Its exit left only the pale

glitter of stars above, while below, the ruddy gold auras of the meandering lanterns remained as the earthly defence against darkness. His timepiece chimed midnight, marking the end of his shift, and Michael turned from one of the narrow bridges across the Bow toward home. He had passed beyond a hedge of cedar when he heard footfalls on the wooden planks behind him. His hand resting on his pistol, he strode back to the creek in time to confront Dowd and Zeke. He raised his lantern to illumine their faces.

"Been to the city, then?" he queried, trying without success to keep censure from his voice.

With abashed expressions, the boys muttered overlapping prevarications that told the Scot all he needed to know. He warned gently, "I know ye want to pay your way, but ye must take care not to get yourselves into trouble, aye?"

"We take care," Zeke replied with the confidence of youth.

Dowd added bitterly, "'Specially now they're roundin' us up ever' chance they get."

(The police had been given express orders to remove unsupervised children found in the streets to orphanages or, in the case of older urchins, to a workhouse if no parents could be found to take them home. Michael strongly suspected the owners of the workhouses had used their influence not for the welfare of orphans but for free—forced—labour for their factories.)

"Well, get yourselves to bed," said the Scot, letting his fondness for the lads colour his tone. He watched them scamper off toward the mews, raising his lamp above his head to show them the way for as far as the kerosene glow would extend.

As the pair disappeared, Michael turned to make for Cedar Lane. But a sense of danger drew his glance back to the bridge. At the far end, an indistinct shape moved against the blackness behind, and a *frisson* ran along Michael's spine. Instinctively, he reached for his weapon once more and he stepped toward the Bow, lifting his lantern again in hope its light

might reveal the threat.

He waited, tense and alert, hardly daring to breathe lest he miss some telltale sign across the way. At a sound of footsteps in the snow behind, he whirled to see who approached. To his relief, he found Patrick O'Reilly arriving to replace him on guard. As the elder came to stand beside him with his own torch and the Scot looked back toward the city, a shifting of shadows on the far side of the creek evinced a retreat. Michael swallowed with difficulty, his mouth suddenly dry.

The O'Reilly patriarch had seen the movement. "What is it?" he whispered.

"I don't know," Michael murmured. "But we'd better double the watch at the bridges and warn everyone to be extra vigilant."

"Damnation!" spat The O'Reilly. "What sort o' arsehole'd be out skulkin' about at this hour?"

A voice came from the recesses of Michael's mind, and its words chilled him more than the damp winter air: *Someone who knows the children are here.*

The Scot stayed at the bridge as Patrick spread the word to the other sentinels.

∞

UNDER THE HALF-MOON, New Year's Eve revellers ambled and danced along the lanes and alleys of The Flats without regard for the extra watchmen, each sentinel armed and wearing a whistle at his neck. Michael stood at the Alder Street bridge, nearest Cedar Lane, staring across the creek to the city on the far side. Anne observed him from the crossroads of Cedar and Creekside, where Calum O'Shaunnessey and the lad named Spike duelled musically, the former with fiddle and the latter with harmonica. Around her, dancers whirled and bystanders clapped, but her attention remained focussed on her husband, standing guard against a spectre. She rubbed her belly

protectively, her thoughts echoing his.

Not on my watch.

CHAPTER 44

New business and old

In the clear blue skies above the city, the sun's brilliance promised summer's heat but delivered only winter's cold as temperatures plummeted to settle in icy lows despite the usually mitigatory proximity of the lake. Frost clung to every breath, and every nose and cheek waxed rubescent as brows and fingers stiffened and paled.

"Stand up, hook up!" Anne called out. "Put these on your eyes."

At the order they did not know as a command for paratroopers (a species of soldier that did not yet exist) to prepare to jump out of troop-transport aircraft (that had not yet been imagined much less built), the urchins shuffled into ragged formation and waited their turn as Anne handed out strips of gauze. By way of example, she tied a single layer around the head of one of the little girls, knotting it at back and stretching it

across eyes and nose.

"We won't be able to see!" nine-year-old Eva Janus wailed.

"Yes, you will," Anne insisted as she wrapped the next boy's face. "It's thin enough to see through, but it will block some of the light so you won't get snow blindness." She added, "It'll help keep your nose a bit warmer, too."

As the rest of her brood exchanged uncertain looks, some shrugging acceptance of yet another peculiar adult demand, she said, "I know you had no difficulties in the city, but here in The Flats, there are large stretches of snow to reflect the sunlight straight into your eyes. In the far north, many a man has been blinded because he did not know enough to protect his eyes against the glare."

"Were you up north?" Eva asked.

"Not as far as the Arctic Circle," Anne admitted. "But far enough to have seen nothing but white in every direction and sunlight strong enough to hurt the eyes."

Joseph Horne asked, "Will them as went up to the Algonquian get blinded?"

"Not very likely," Anne assured him. "In the bush, trees—especially evergreens—provide a lot of shade as well as protection from wind."

"They just gotta watch out for wolves an' such," said Hugh Aitken sagely.

"An' find food," said Eva.

"An' build a house or summat," said Denny Higgins.

"They'll be fine," Anne affirmed with confidence as she snugged Little Anne's woollen hat over the makeshift sunscreen and around her face. "Boyd and Reese know what they're doing, and they'll teach the others well."

She hugged each of the ragamuffins on their way out the front door to play in the lanes, and she watched as the Four Horsemen, Dowd, Davey, and a half-dozen other self-appointed adolescent and teenage guardians shepherded the frolicsome

flocks of the neighbourhood, all of them wrapped and bundled and ready for fun.

In the kitchen behind her, Katie and Patsy helped Hermione prepare a mutton stew as the matriarch regaled them with tales of her childhood in Wales. Onion vapours wafted, overpowering the bland scent of turnip and faint sweetness of chopped carrot. Somewhere outside, the distinctive bay of Mose announced the flight of a hare or squirrel, giving rise to a chase the aging mutt would maintain until his wind gave out. Nearer, the squeals of happy children all but drowned the sound of the dog.

Michael stepped up and folded his red-flannel-clad arms around Anne as she gazed through the window. He kissed her crown and waited quietly, knowing she had something on her mind. Momentarily, she sighed.

"We'll be watching Wee Jamie play in the snow, soon," she whispered wistfully.

"Aye," he said, a smile evident in his voice. "And then he'll have a sister to play with him. And a brother."

Anne chuckled softly. "Just how many siblings are you planning to give him?" She shifted to look back and up into her husband's face and she cocked an eyebrow. "Hm?"

Michael grinned. "Weel, noo," he said in his broadest Scots accent, "'tis no' entirely up t'*me*." He dipped to nuzzle her neck, and he set her to giggling so vociferously that Hermione ahemmed loudly and called, "Don't you have somewhere to be, Michael?"

Turning himself and his wife to face his mother, Michael admitted sheepishly, "Aye, I expect Da will be wondering what I got up to."

Hermione smiled with amusement and replied, "I expect Da will know *exactly* what you've been up to, which is why he hasn't telephoned yet. Now, get yourself off to work, ye wee imp!"

Michael crossed the room in three strides to give his

mother an affectionate hug; then, he returned to Anne for a kiss before cloaking himself against the cold and heading into the city.

∞

MICHAEL RODE directly to the temporary stable-cum-carriage-house and dismounted to relinquish his horse to the care of Little Jack, a lanky urchin known to Dowd and Davey. The childlike lad who had an affinity for equines now lived with his brother and two others on the *Trevelyan and Company* property, officially employed and safe from the dragnet of workhouse owners masquerading as do-gooders.

The board-and-batten structure had been put together quickly, but sturdily enough to keep both horses and boys safe and warm while withstanding gale-force winds, should the need arise. On its sometimes-sunny south exposure facing the lake, a row of privies and an office added to the utility of the building, the former offering a comfort station that, though not warm, at least did not freeze a man's arse when he sat on the "throne," as Anne liked to call it. Michael chuckled to himself at the term as he made use of the facility.

Upon his exit, he found his father, in bowler and greatcoat, muffler and gloves, pacing in front of the office, the older man's face contorting alternately in frowning squints and raised-brow grimaces. Michael grinned and shook his head slightly at the familiar expressions of Joseph MacGregor deep in thought. Rather than disturb the man, he slipped round the side of the building and sought Jake Trevelyan among the men at streetside unloading wagons of timber.

The Cornishman greeted him eagerly when Michael, in sturdy blue dungaree trousers and heavy boots, brown short coat and tan sheepskin gloves, pitched in to help with the unloading. As the partners each grabbed an end of boards bound with strapping and hauled them to the staging pile, Jake said, "I've

been looking over the plans your wife drew up. Damn, that's a good idea! If her estimates are even halfway correct, we'll use a great deal less fuel that I expected. And Joseph's already got a list of buyers for the creosote."

He concluded, "We'll save money on one end and make it on the other. Damn, that's a good idea!"

Walking back to the wagons, Michael told his associate, "I've been studying the lay of the site and I think the west side," he pointed, "near that clump of cedars would be a good spot for the pond." He added, "We'll have to see in the spring just how wide the reservoir will be once the thaws and rains swell it. Then, we can determine the level for the overflow drain to the lake."

"Good," said Trevelyan as he grasped another stack of planks. "The less water we have to buy from the town, the better."

As Tsi-Guy Villeneuve and Patrick O'Reilly Jr. hopped out of the way of their employers and reached for the next batch of boards, Trevelyan asked Michael, "What was it she wanted to do with the privies?"

∞

LUNCH WOULD have been a cold affair had it not been for a pile of pinecones gathered from the roadside and a damaged beech that Aiden Bannion and Tom O'Herlihy had cut down. In a hollow in the lee of the lumber pile, the pair built a small bonfire that warmed the men and their sack lunches as it boiled a kettle of well-water hauled from The Flats in a wooden barrel for tea. Though the stove in his office kept him warm as he sat at his desk, Joseph joined the rest of the men in a spirit of camaraderie around the campfire. He sat on a broad chunk of the felled beech, pulled off his gloves, and spread his hands to soak in the warmth from the flames.

"We've got a contract to supply stone for the new city hall," he announced with satisfaction. "And I've put in our bid

for the office tower going up on Bay—it's going to be big, that one. Biggest in the country, I expect."

Michael asked him, "Is that what you were pacing about, earlier?"

Joseph looked up from the fire and frowned uncomprehendingly. "Pacing?" Realization dawned, and he glanced away as he said dismissively, "No, no. That was another matter."

The elder MacGregor reached into the muslin lunch bag Hermione had prepared for him, removed a sandwich, and unwrapped it from its paper protection. With affected nonchalance, he bit into his layered lunch, avoiding his son's eyes. Michael regarded his father a moment. Recognizing that no more would be spoken on the subject, he chomped into his own midday meal. But he eyed his father intently as he chewed, listening with only half his attention to the conversations around him. Tonight, he decided, he would revive the matter at home.

∞

THE MILKY half-moon had begun its descent toward the western treetops and a north wind had picked up, swaying the conifers and relieving their dark needled branches of the last vestiges of snow. As the biting currents whistled round the chimneys, scattering the smoky vapours and instantly snuffing the tiny sparks that rose from hearth-fires, Michael pulled the neck of his coat close and forged through the drifting snows to the well-house. Inside, he relit the hut's candle and waited.

Presently, Joseph opened the door in a rush of frigid air, and closed it as his son struck another match and lit the doused taper once more, this time setting a glass chimney overtop.

"What's going on, Da?" Michael asked as gently as his concern would allow.

Joseph stamped his feet, brushed away a swath of snow that had attached itself to his long charcoal coat, and smoothed

his windblown hair into place. After a moment of standing mute by the door, he said lamely, "It's surprisingly warm in here."

Eyeing his father, Michael replied conversationally, "It's built to stay above freezing. Even in the worst weather, it takes only a candle or a lamp to keep it warm."

"Good, good," said Joseph, looking everywhere but at the younger man.

After another minute of awkward silence, Michael sighed and demanded, "Are you going to tell me?"

Joseph glanced to his son and to his hands and to the floor. Finally, still downcast, he said, "Through old friends, I've been investigating Orwell and Howes."

Perplexed that his father would consider such an obvious move a matter of secrecy even within the family, he asked, "Why did you not say so?"

Joseph heaved a sigh and bent his head back to stare up at the junior MacGregor. With an expression that combined resignation, shame, and regret, he confessed, "Because I have come to believe there is a connection between Howes and Bardon."

"Jesus!" Michael whispered.

"Aye," Joseph said, bowing his head a long moment. With a deep inhalation, he looked up to regard his son once more and admitted, "I should, perhaps, have done something about the missive Terence sent me long ago, but in truth...."

The pause dragged on, but Michael simply waited for his father to finish. At last, Joseph said softly, penitently, "In truth, it was easier, then, to do nothing."

"Because you were afraid?" Michael said with a hint of accusation, not sure he wanted to hear the response.

His father's face hardened. The elder said sharply, "You're damned right, I was afraid! I had two bairns and a wife to protect, and nay family left to help me."

Trying to calm himself, he continued bitterly, "There'd already been two murders, perhaps many, and I'd nay reason to

believe a traitor would hesitate to kill me and mine, besides."

"Of course," Michael said contritely. "You're right, Da. It would have been foolish. I'm sorry." He licked his lips, considering whether to ask what he really wanted to know. Finally, he did.

"So, why go into it now? Because of the distillery?"

Joseph paced a moment within the confines of the small well-house, hands clasped behind his back. Then, he stopped and confirmed, "Partly, yes. But I also discovered recently that an acquaintance of mine has risen in the Home Office. Risen to a position that affords him scope to inquire thoroughly into Howes's and Orwell's dealings, past and present.

"At first, I did not have the ear of a man of consequence, and the papers Terence sent pointed to treason but did not implicate anyone specifically. I believe he had suspicions but no proof, yet." The elder closed his eyes, struggling with his past decisions, and then he looked to his son to say, "And then, the damned money was there, within reach, when I needed it."

Michael swallowed. Would he have done any differently in the circumstances? He took a long breath and thanked God he had not been so sorely tempted as his father. Then, he prayed he never would be.

Joseph went on, "But when I started digging on my own into the connection between Orwell and Howes, I discovered they had both been in Bhutan, near Deothang, just before the disastrous battle at the fort of Dewangiri."

At Michael's frown of uncertainty, his father clarified, "When British soldiers with modern weapons were soundly defeated by a rabble—not a real army, mind—a rabble armed with matchlocks and swords."

After another moment of pacing, he said, "And later, as I learned, both Howes and Orwell had been on the detail that lost 35,000 rupees in a raid. At least, they claimed there was a raid. They were the only survivors, and there was cause to suspect Sikkim or Bengali involvement; so, the matter was hushed up in

order to prevent stirring local tensions and embarrassing allies."

Michael wondered, "Surely all this was investigated at the time?"

"Oh, aye," Joseph confirmed. "And Terence Bardon was assigned to the investigating officer."

Michael guessed, "So, he found out enough to get him killed, and the evidence disappeared with him."

Joseph blushed. "Not all of it," he muttered. "Terence had sent the money—at least, the cache he'd found; it was only a portion—and copies of several documents to me." Sadly, he added, "I believe that's why they killed his wife: They thought he'd sent them to her."

Again, the elder MacGregor closed his eyes, wearied by the long-held secret and the attendant fear and guilt. Then, he glanced around the shed, shaking his head, and said, "There had seemed nothing I could do, at the time. But when I learned Orwell and Howes had been in Bhutan, and suddenly, on his return to England, Howes had had the funds to buy a distillery and warehouses...."

He concluded, "And Jeremy Forbes now has the wherewithal to put it all together; though what will come of it, I canna say."

Michael asked hesitantly, "Does Forbes know about the money you took?"

Joseph sighed and said softly, "Aye. He does. I've agreed to refund it, as I can."

"Anne would give you all you need," Michael reminded him.

"Aye," Joseph acknowledged. "But that wouldna be right. It was my...mistake...and I must be the one to pay."

With a determined huff, the MacGregor patriarch turned, opened the shed door, and sprinted to the house. Alone in the dark, the candle's flame again blown out despite the glass shield, Michael stood and pondered the life that would have befallen him and his family had his father not used stolen money to

finance the building of his empire.

∞

THE TRIAL of Kenneth Armstrong began on a Monday at ten o'clock, on Adler Avenue, in the grey stone structure that had served as courthouse for nearly half a century. The MacGregor family arrived just before ten, and all were quickly ushered to the row of seats immediately behind the Prosecutor, among the other witnesses for the Crown.

Tall windows set in the stone exterior wall cast pale February light across the benches and desks, chairs and empty dock, bailiffs and onlookers. Barristers for the accused, in court garb, riffled papers and shot occasional surreptitious, assessing glances toward the ranks of witnesses. Meanwhile, the Crown attorney sat blandly in his tightly curled white wig and his black robe.

The chamber filled, the sounds of shuffling and whispering rising with the numbers of spectators. At last, as a clock-tower bell tolled the hour, Oliver Anderson strode in to take his place at the polished oak altar of justice and uniformed bailiffs closed the courtroom doors. Once the judge was ensconced, the crier announced the session while a scribe at a small desk stocked with ink and pens and notebooks recorded the proceedings.

A side door opened. A burly bailiff in the dark blue of the constabulary escorted Kenneth Armstrong to the dock and then stood nearby as the crier listed the charges against the erstwhile lawyer and as the court reporter scribbled furiously. Armstrong, in grey prison trousers and shirt, and in a grey wool coat supplied for transport between jail and courthouse, glared at the MacGregors as the list of his crimes was proclaimed.

To everyone's surprise, the defence attorney immediately asked for a recess to confer with his client. Judge Anderson gave the man a gimlet eye, but allowed the interruption with the

proviso that it be very short. The bewigged barrister hurried to Armstrong and whispered advice that brought incensed hisses from the accused. When the argument dragged on and escalated in heat and volume, the judge pounded his gavel and brought the matter to an abrupt end.

The red-faced advocate stalked back to his table as Armstrong seethed in the dock. Moments later, the plea of "not guilty" was officially entered, along with the surprising choice of trial by judge instead of by jury. Then, the circus began.

∞

ANNE HAD TO HAND it to the defence counsel: He prodded every witness thoroughly in hope of finding means to cast doubt as to Armstrong's guilt. In the end, though, he did not stand a chance.

Several asylum staff members had seen Armstrong in discussions with Dr. Desmond. A janitor had overheard mention of abortion. Nearly three dozen people had witnessed the rescue of Anne MacGregor. All of this, of course, would not have convicted Elizabeth MacGregor's former fiancé, but the Prosecutor was only warming up.

The next Monday, Justice Donald Edwards took the witness stand and detailed the documents provided by Kenneth Armstrong that had caused him to sign commitment papers for Mrs. MacGregor in the belief that her family and physician had requested she be hospitalized for her own safety. The Prosecutor entered into evidence the documents confiscated by police. Then, Michael, Joseph, and Hermione, each in turn, flatly denied having made and signed such application, and Dr. Hanes disclaimed the medical report. The defence attorney had wisely avoided the question of Armstrong's motives in the matter, but Joseph managed to slip in his opinion on the subject, prompting protests from Armstrong's attorney, mutters from the spectators, and hammering from the bench.

The noose was tightening around the neck of the accused, and Anne had to wonder why on earth Kenneth Armstrong had decided to contest the charge. Was he so arrogant as to think he would get off? Or was it merely a desperate attempt to save himself?

Following the afternoon recess, Judge Anderson adjourned the trial until Wednesday for no apparent reason.

∞

"REGINALD ORWELL was seen speaking with Justice Anderson at the courthouse and, now, they are in conference at Orwell's home."

Ben Ogden's announcement stunned the family to silence. They gaped at him from their places at the kitchen table.

Gathering his wits, Michael asked, "How do you know?"

"John Devereux telephoned me," Ben replied as he held a chair for Elizabeth and then took a seat next to her. "He witnessed the two at the courthouse, yesterday, and saw Anderson enter Orwell's home this morning."

Michael's gut clenched and he set down his fork, no longer able to stomach a bite of Anne's delicious *ratatouille*. He concluded, "He's trying to suborn the judge."

"But why would Reginald do that?" Hermione wondered.

"To spite me," said Joseph. "It's as simple as that."

"That's a great deal of risk to take for such a petty purpose," said Ben dubiously.

Michael responded, "There are some willing to go to such lengths for personal vengeance. But I have to wonder, now, whether it was Orwell who put Armstrong up to courting Elizabeth in the first place."

His sister blushed and bowed her head at the humiliating notion.

Anne reached out to Elizabeth and clasped her hand. She said, "Fortunately, you were saved from marriage to such a

scoundrel." She smiled at her sister-in-law's diffident, upturned glance and added, "Saved for a better man. The right man."

At that, Elizabeth smiled gratefully through tears and turned to her husband, his expression fond and his hands enfolding hers in affirmation of love.

Joseph brought everyone back to the original topic of conversation by asking, "What could Orwell offer the judge? Money?"

Michael replied, "Knowing Orwell's history, it could be blackmail or threat. Orwell does not like to part with his coin if he can help it."

Anne mused, "Perhaps a counter threat would be in order."

Michael objected, "We cannot be seen to influence the outcome of the trial."

"No," Anne concurred. She turned to Ben and continued, "But John Devereux could interview the judge for the *Evening Star*."

Ben guessed, "And make it clear that Orwell's attempts to affect the outcome of the trial could be brought to light."

Joseph said hesitantly, "Perhaps there is something else the judge should know." He gave his son a meaningful look and jutted his lower lip meditatively.

"Are you sure, Da?" asked Michael anxiously. "Is there enough evidence?"

Ben Ogden looked sharply from his brother-in-law to his father-in-law.

Joseph admitted, "Perhaps not yet."

Ben suggested tentatively, "The implication that there is something else to know about Orwell, something...indictable?" He focussed a questioning gaze on the elder MacGregor, who nodded a wordless reply.

His supposition confirmed, Ben finished, "Might persuade the judge to ignore whatever Orwell has told him or threatened."

Michael smiled wryly at his brother-in-law's proposal. The man had a devious streak, to be sure—not unlike Orwell, himself. A string of memories of the latter's actions played across his mind at lightning speed and led him to warn, "But perhaps we should ensure that your friend is not alone when he speaks with the judge."

Joseph reminded his son, "None of us can go. You said it yourself: We canna be involved."

"No," Michael agreed. "But there are others who can stand watch." He ran down a mental list of available men and boys from The Flats as Ben rose from the table to telephone the *Evening Star*.

∞

WHEN COURT RESUMED, the Crown produced its star witnesses. Nurse Nasty and psychiatrist-cum-abortionist Dr. Felix Desmond tried to pretend innocence and to place the blame for the kidnapping and illegal detention of Anne entirely upon Kenneth Armstrong. Their protestations provoked vitriolic outbursts from the dock that disclosed previously unknown abortions and other crimes committed by the pair: The doctor, it was officially discovered, was in the habit of eliminating his sons' indiscretions *in utero,* and the nurse had been dismissed from a hospital in Moncton for negligence leading to a patient's death. Such revelations might have cast doubt upon their assertions that Armstrong had orchestrated the kidnapping of Anne MacGregor, had Dr. Desmond not identified the man who had brought Anne to the asylum. In his turn, the kidnapper testified that he had been hired by the lawyer who had once represented him in another criminal matter.

By the end of the day, the prosecution had rested, Kenneth Armstrong's defence had crumbled, and all that remained was the announcement of the verdict. Justice Anderson hesitated, shuffling through the evidentiary documentation, and

Destined

swallowed nervously. Finally, he looked toward the dock and said, "Kenneth Armstrong, given the weight of the evidence against you, I have no choice but to find you guilty as charged, on all counts."

The courtroom erupted as Armstrong shouted obscenities and the spectators responded to the convicted criminal's invective.

Pounding his gavel, Justice Anderson called above the tumult, "Order! Order! Bailiff, clear the court!"

When she stood and turned toward the exit, Anne glimpsed, beyond the departing crowd, Reginald Orwell standing at the rear wall, alternating the focus of his malevolent glare between the judge and the MacGregors.

CHAPTER 45

Vengeance is mine

As Anne snuggled under the quilts, resting her head in the hollow by his shoulder, Michael stroked her hair absently, remembering with a shudder the face of Reginald Orwell. The man had glowered hatefully from Joseph to Hermione to Elizabeth to Ben Ogden to him; then, his spiteful stare had come to rest on Anne and her belly.

"He's going to come after you," he said, and he grimaced when he realized he had spoken aloud.

"I know," she replied. "I'll be ready."

He looked down at her, seeing her only in memory, there in the dark. He wanted to protect her. Her and their child. But as much as he wanted it, he could not be with them every hour of every day for who-knew-how-long. His belly liquefied at the horrifying possibilities that surged, unbidden, to the front of his mind. And the memory of what another vengeful bastard—or

two of them—had done the summer past. He thanked God for the men of The Flats who had taken it upon themselves to create a nightly watch to protect their own. And he promised himself he would take more shifts with them.

He would rest when Orwell was dead or behind bars. He did not care which.

∞

ANNE ARCHED to ease her back and heaved a sigh as she surveyed the children crowded into the clapboard church-cum-schoolhouse. Soon, she knew, they would need a proper school with classrooms and desks, chalkboards and library. Perhaps one could be built in the coming summer, after the Sunshine Farm and the homes for Joseph and Hermione and for Elizabeth and Ben were completed.

She took her seat once more as the sharp click-click of abacus beads sounded above the muted roar of the masonry heater that had been installed in early winter to warm students during the week and parishioners on the weekend. She smiled as she contemplated the tall, narrow, white-tiled stove, its fire hidden behind an iron door and its ceramic chimney rising to the roof. It had taken four years to persuade the dour Protestant congregation to forgo righteous discomfort. Finally, they had accepted the notion that unselfishly heating the building for the sake of the children and their studies was more virtuous than stoically freezing their arses every Sunday.

Heeding a persistent call of Nature, Anne rose and waddled down the aisle, tapping Jack's shoulder on her way by to indicate he was in charge until her return. She stepped outside the inner door and into the vestibule. There lay the other innovation she had recently managed to incorporate into the building: a privy on one side of the entry and a row of coat hooks on the other, each illuminated by a window set a few inches beneath the ceiling. How she would have liked such a "luxury"

in the little house of worship she had attended in her childhood! With a chuckle, she remembered that the church in question had been built about the same time as this one. She opened the privy door.

Once finished her business, Anne straightened her clothes and washed her hands at the little porcelain basin occupying the corner beside the lavatory door. Above, an enamelled tank with a spigot provided water; below, a pipe drained the wash-water out to a pit filled with wood chips and straw set strategically among sheltering conifers.

As she dried her hands on one of the towels hung nearby, Anne heard the outer door open with a squeal: Damn! She had forgotten to oil the hinges.

At the sound of unfamiliar footsteps, quiet and tentative, the hairs on her arms and neck rose. Her heart pounded and her every muscle tensed as she reached through the slit in her right side-seam to unsheathe the dirk she had bought in late summer. Slowly, cautiously, she opened the privy door just enough to peek out. There, peering into the church, stood a strange man, one hand reaching under his coat. He was tall, perhaps six-foot-two, with ill-fitting clothes and boozy body odour. His dark-brown hair needed either cutting or binding; instead, it hung limp and greasy to his shoulders. He sported a badly trimmed beard, and his hands were calloused and bore the scraped-knuckle evidence of a recent fistfight. The bulge under his coat told her he gripped a pistol.

Knowing she could not move quietly enough, Anne abandoned any attempt at stealth and swung the lavatory door wide. "Dowd! Jack!" she called as she launched herself forward. The man started and turned, but she flicked the long blade of the dirk across his weapon hand, eliciting a yelp and drawing blood. Before he could bring the pistol to bear, she snatched it with her free hand and hopped back out of the way just as the boys charged into the stranger and slammed him to the vestibule floor.

"Out of the way, boys!" she ordered as she quickly

stepped back, swapped the weapons from one hand to the other, and aimed the gun toward the man.

When the lads rolled clear, Anne demanded, "Who are you and who sent you?"

"Fuck me, lady," said the man, "I was jus' lookin' fer my sister's kid."

"Oh?" Anne replied with eyebrows raised in disbelief. "So, you were planning to shoot your sister's child, then."

"Hell, no!" said the man, frantically trying to think of some logical explanation. "Uh, uh, I was jus', ah, ah—"

"Save it!" Anne snapped. "You weren't just uh-uh; you were trying to kill someone. Who? And why?"

She cocked the pistol one-handed and aimed for his crotch.

Hands spread before him and eyes round with panic, he exclaimed, "Shit! Wait! I'll tell ya!"

"I'm listening," Anne rejoined icily.

The man bit his lower lip below a nose that had been broken more than once, and he stared at the business end of his own revolver as it pointed to his favourite appendage. "Okay, okay," he said. "I was hired to kill some bi—"

Recognizing belatedly the poor choice of words, he amended, "To kill a woman with white hair, a schoolteacher name o' MacGregor. Man wanted it real bad."

"What man?" she demanded.

"Dunno," he replied. Panicking lest she not believe him, he hurried to say, "I swear! I dunno who the fellah is. He jus' paid me a whole hundred dollars to do it. Said it had to be today, in broad daylight."

Acutely aware of the boys standing on either side of the would-be assassin, and of the children crowded at the doorway, Anne pursed her lips in thought for a moment. Then, she said conversationally, "You realize that the first rule of assassination is that the assassin must be killed?" At his baffled blinking, she explained, "Meaning that the man who hired you would have

killed you afterward to ensure your silence. You do know that, don't you?"

The man's eyes widened once more and his eyelids fluttered wildly as he considered the previously unimagined repercussions of this line of work. He bit his lip hard and swallowed, his Adam's apple wobbling up and down jerkily under the skin of a rarely washed neck thick with dark stubble.

When she saw the recognition of his precarious position dawn, Anne continued, "Now, the way I see it, you have two options. Make that three." She pressed her lips together thoughtfully a moment and then went on, "First, I could let you go and—"

Dowd and Jack began to protest, but she held up her left hand, still holding the dirk, without taking her eyes or aim off the stranger. When the boys quieted, she resumed.

"I could let you go and you would probably not make it out of the city, perhaps not even out of The Flats.

"Second, I can kill you right here."

At a collective gasp from the little ones, she amended, "Well, perhaps outside, this being a church, after all."

She smiled without warmth, her eyes cold purple fire, and she said, "Or three, you can confess to the police and help them catch and convict the man who hired you. If you do that, you *may* avoid both the noose and the bullet that is intended for you."

Tilting her head curiously, she asked, "So, what's it going to be? Door Number One, Door Number Two, or Door Number Three?"

The man swallowed hard several times, his brain working feverishly behind his flickering eyes. At last, he whispered hoarsely, "Three."

"Boys."

Dowd, standing by the coat rack, grabbed his gear and Jack's. He tossed the latter across to his friend and the two of them headed outside to the nearby police call box, grousing resentfully that they had not been allowed to beat the bastard

senseless. Or better still, to watch Herself shoot him in the nuts.

Hearing the young lads speculate gleefully how much blood would have flowed from such a wound, the supine man closed his eyes and muttered a prayer under his breath.

∞

AS MICHAEL and Joseph and the other men of The Flats approached the bridge, Dowd and Davey and the Four Horsemen ran across, eager to tell the lurid tale of *Herself and the Assassin*. The six boys expounded and embellished, acting the parts and repeating with relish the conversation between the pistol- and knife-wielding white-haired lady and the nefarious giant—with frequent repetition of Davey's favourite new word, nefarious.

By the time he and his father arrived home, Michael did not know whether to laugh or cry or scream. He crossed the room in three strides and pulled his wife into his arms to hug her so tightly, she gasped, "Michael, I can't breathe!"

When he released her, he trembled visibly and closed his eyes, inhaling deeply and fisting his hands in an attempt to calm himself.

"You've heard," she stated the obvious.

Michael opened his eyes, cupped her face with both gloved hands, and said too loudly, "You could have been killed!"

"But I wasn't," she replied softly.

He put his forehead to hers, closing his eyes against both her logic and the vision in his mind's eye of the afternoon's events as portrayed by the boys.

"I'm all right," she whispered. "I'm all right and so is the baby."

"It's true then," said Joseph grimly as he came to stand by them in the kitchen. "Orwell hired a killer."

Anne informed them, "I suggested to Detective Morgan that he show the man a picture of Orwell along with photographs

or newspaper clippings of other men, and the ruffian picked Orwell out right away. Reginald Orwell is probably in custody by now."

Michael gathered her into his arms again and held her until she suggested gently, "Why don't you chop some wood, my love. It'll help you get rid of some of that nervous energy."

Now, Michael did laugh. And cry, tears hot on his cheeks. And he kissed his wife before he stalked outside to attack logs in lieu of Orwell and his bloody assassin.

∞

WATCHING MICHAEL from the kitchen window, Anne rubbed her belly to the rhythm of his ferocious, almost frenzied axe strokes. It occurred to her that she did not recall experiencing a single year as eventful as this past one, even with Alex during and after The Forty-five—though, to be honest, she had spent most of that war keeping the home-fires burning while he did the fighting. And in point of fact, even *he* had probably travelled more than he fought.

She suddenly wondered: Had they accomplished anything?

She sighed. That was a question for philosophers; though, even in future, few philosophers, much less historians, would entertain the notion of time travel and its impact upon events.

And what would be her effect here? She knew all too well the future of this city. How long could she ward off the pressures that would eventually destroy The Flats and scatter its inhabitants? Could she protect any of them? And what of the coming world war? Could she protect Michael and their child and their extended family?

Again, she sighed.

Michael had slowed his pace to a steady swing-chop-release.

The worst, Anne had to admit to herself, was her growing

unease, her difficulty in pushing away a nagging thought that invaded her mind at any time of day, and especially in the night: a dread that she would not live to see her child walk, play, run. She had known from the start she would not watch Michael grow old, given her own age. Was it too much to ask that she have the chance to be here as her son grew to manhood?

She flicked a tear from her cheek and began to set the table for supper. As she placed the plates, she told herself firmly, *I must be grateful for the opportunity to create a life from love, the opportunity that has so long been denied me.*

She knew prophecies of gloom and doom could be self-fulfilling; she must not dwell upon them. Yet, she also knew that her condition, the imbalances in her body, affected her mental and emotional equilibrium. Taking a moment to close her eyes and clear her head, she promised herself she would work harder to keep her thoughts bright. *All will be well,* she told herself. *It will work out for the best.*

∞

TWO DAYS LATER, Michael opened his front door to find grim-faced Detective Morgan and equally chagrined Constable O'Toole stepping onto the porch. Hermione poured them each a cup of tea as Morgan explained to the MacGregor family the foolish mistake of the inexperienced constable who had failed to confiscate all of Reginald Orwell's personal effects before placing the man in the jail cell at the precinct house.

Michael's hand on Anne's instantly curled and tightened. He demanded, "Are you saying the murderous bastard has escaped?"

"No, no," Morgan replied hurriedly, "I did not mean to imply that. No, sir, he did not escape." He drew a deep breath and revealed, "He killed himself."

Constable O'Toole added, "One of the older lads happened by and tried to stanch the wound, but it was too late."

Michael and his father both let out a long breath and exchanged a look of relief.

Frowning, Anne said, "I would not have thought him the suicidal type. Particularly given that he might have defended himself successfully in court."

"Perhaps," said Morgan. "The evidence of Mr. Knox, the would-be assassin, might not have been enough to convict him. But we had received word from London advising us to hold Orwell until he could be brought back to England for trial on charges of treason."

"We didn't tell him that, sir," O'Toole assured them. "But his solicitor may have done." He grimaced guiltily and divulged, "The man overheard some of the lads speculating what Mr. Orwell might have done to deserve such a charge."

"At any rate," said Morgan, "we informed London, but they say they're sending someone to speak with you, Mr. MacGregor." He looked pointedly at Joseph.

"Aye," Michael's father replied with a thoughtful nod. "I expect they'll want the evidence in my possession."

Detective Morgan looked from Joseph to Michael and back. With a slight shake of his head, he dismissed whatever he had thought to say and rose to take his leave. Clearly, this family had more secrets.

CHAPTER 46

A child is born

Things settled down once more, though Michael and his neighbours maintained the vigilance of the nightly watch that, with the help of a few unemployed men and older lads of the community, had been expanded to the day—dark coming so early in winter. From his own pocket, the Scot paid a small stipend to those willing to serve. Everyone knew Himself had fallen on hard times, his new business not yet profitable; no one complained about the meagreness of the remuneration. As for Herself, God knew she had enough to think about, what with a child on the way, and the attempts on her life, and her husband's troubles, and teaching the young ones most days, and the food she provided for neighbours and urchins alike, and so many underfoot until new housing could be built.

The sky cleared again after a big storm that had buried the entire region under three feet of snow on St. Patrick's Day,

though that inconvenience had done nothing to dampen the traditional festivities. Now, clouds rode high in the intensely blue sky, and the wind came from the west. The air did not yet smell of spring, but it no longer stung the nose with frost, and the sun bestowed warmth as well as light during the gradually lengthening days.

Anne brought the last basket of apples from the cold cellar to share with her students. The shrivelling pomes filled the room with their sweet perfume and none could concentrate on the lessons of the day. Seeing the children fidget and squirm and glance often toward the woven container, Anne grinned and announced, "Since your attention is not on your studies, why don't we have an early lunch?"

She chuckled at the resounding "Yay!" and the sudden scramble from the pews and benches. Leaving the youngsters to their own devices, she turned to her chair by the altar, but stopped. She pressed a hand to her abdomen and, recognizing an immediate need, spun back toward the door and hurried out with a glance toward Dowd as she passed him. He caught her eye and nodded as he watched after her abrupt exit.

In the privy, Anne sighed with relief at the purging that left her feeling wonderfully empty. She had cleaned herself and was about to stand when a clutching within her belly rooted her to the bench. The sensation lasted to a count of thirty. It was time.

After washing her hands and wiping them dry, she left the lavatory to grab her cloak. At the entrance, she called to the day's monitor, "I have to go, Dowd. The baby's coming. Please see the children home safely."

"I will," the boy assured her over the excited response of the students.

As she buttoned her cape and pulled on her mittens, Anne realized her brood had no intention of staying quietly to finish their lunches and their studies. Opening the outer door and stepping into the late morning's brilliance, she heard the clatter and mutter of youngsters behind her, all rushing to dress as

quickly as they could to follow. Even the boys wanted to attend the birth of Herself's child.

Anne had reached the first intersection on her way home when another, more powerful tension in her belly stopped her in her tracks. When the initial shock of it passed, she staggered a few steps to clutch a nearby fencepost and forced herself to breathe slowly as the children milled around her.

"She's gonna pop soon," said Eva Janus sagely.

Rob leaned to peer up into Anne's face and asked, "D'ye need us to carry ye?"

The contraction easing, Anne straightened and smiled. "No," she answered. "I'm sure I can make it home on my own. But thank you for the offer."

Larry Doherty said, "I wish Da were here. He could take ye in his buggy."

Waddling on, Anne admitted, "That would have been nice, Larry, but I'll manage. I just have to put one foot in front of the other."

She proceeded to do exactly that, with a growing escort, with shortcuts through a few unfenced yards, and with three more pauses on the way to Cedar Lane.

∞

JACK HAD BORROWED a horse from the mews and ridden bareback at a gallop to the worksite. "Herself's havin' the baby!" he called from hundreds of yards away, waving one arm as he reined with the other. He repeated the announcement several times on his approach and finally slowed to a halt to wait for Michael, who had abandoned his shovel and run for the stable. Moments later, the Scot appeared on his dark-brown stallion and raced homeward with whistles and shouts of congratulations fading into the distance behind him.

Across the Bow, with Jack following, Michael turned onto Sumac to find a crowd filling the crossroads at Cedar Lane. As he

neared, he saw past fences and leafless trees that the throng stretched around the bend that curved the street toward the east. At the intersection, he brought his horse up short and jumped out of the saddle, leaving the stallion to the lads hovering at the edge of the crush of onlookers. Abstractedly acknowledging the well-wishers and their greetings as he passed, he made his way through and beyond the host of neighbours and hopped over the fence to dash inside his house. There, his mother and the eldest Mrs. O'Reilly were boiling water and preparing towels.

"She's upstairs," Hermione told him with a nod toward the staircase.

Michael took the steps three at a time, completely forgetting his boots and outer clothes on his way to his wife's side.

The bedroom door lay open and Anne, in deep-blue gown of winter-weight wool, leaned against the jamb as Katie and Patsy, flushed with excitement, spread a sheepskin and extra sheets across the bed. Nearby, the quilts sprawled where they had been laid over the rocking chair set beside the cradle and changing table in the dormer nook. When the sheets were tucked into place, all was in readiness. Except for the expectant father.

"What-what...?" he stammered, his eyes searching his wife's. He was not sure what to ask, much less what to do. He dared not even touch her.

Anne reached up and cupped his cheek, smiling fondly, her eyes a soft amethyst glow. She said, "Come, my love. Help me get my boots off, will you, please?"

Grateful for a task, he brought her forward, one arm around her shoulder and the other hand gently clasping hers. Once she had perched on the edge of the bed, he squatted to pull off her felt-lined mukluks (as she called her loose, suede, Indian-style boots), removing them one at a time and setting them aside. Her stockings now hung half off, dangling from her toes; he removed those, as well. Then, he began to rise with intent to help her position herself upon the bed, but she held up a hand

peremptorily and clutched her belly with an expression of intense concentration. The rhythm of her respiration had changed to short gasps and repeated huffs.

Michael stood frozen in a crouch, not daring to move for want of knowing what to do. Eyes wide and fixed upon his wife, his own breath held, he waited for some sign, some signal, some word from her, as he was utterly at a loss to imagine how to proceed. At last, Anne relaxed and her breathing slowed to normal inhalations and audible exhalations. She smiled up at him in reassurance and grasped his hand.

"I'd better sit on the bed, now," she said simply.

"Should ye not lie down?" he inquired. Somehow, he had formed the impression that was the correct birthing posture.

"Sitting up is better," she told him. "But I'll need lots of pillows behind me."

Gripping her hand firmly, he waited as she heaved herself into the centre of the bed. She let go of his hand and pulled her garment hems out from under her bottom. Once she had settled, he pressed pillows, quilts, coat, mitts, hat, and muffler into service as a chair-like back support. When he had built a substantial mound, he stood back with a short-lived satisfaction.

Again, he observed the strange manner of breathing he had witnessed earlier as Anne's downcast eyes stared intently into some other world: Over and over, she pushed out her lips and cheeks to blow a series of short puffs before she drew air once more to start again. He hoped this behaviour was normal, for it had not occurred to him until now that a doctor's presence might be advisable.

Turning to the O'Reilly girls, their eyes wide and their gaze glued upon the labouring mother, he asked, "Has anyone sent for a doctor?"

It was Anne who replied, in a strangled voice, "No need."

He turned back to find her still in the grip of that unseen force and panting against it. He sat on the end of the bed, leaned toward her, and brought his face lower to peer up into hers. "Are

ye sure, Anne?" he asked anxiously. At her affirmative nod, he stood, not entirely convinced Dr. Hanes should not be fetched regardless of her wishes.

His mother and Mrs. O'Reilly entered bearing tubs of steaming water, with towels slung over their arms. Mrs. Bannion brought a knife and string. The women set the supplies on the baby's toiletry table and turned to observe Anne's progress. Spotting Himself's boots and the trail of small puddles he had left on the floor, Mrs. O'Reilly exclaimed, "And could ye not've left those great clod-hoppers below, man?"

"That's all right, Dottie," said Anne with a chuckle as she settled back. "The floor will survive."

Abashed at the O'Reilly matriarch's disapproving glare, one of her eyebrows raised and the other lowered over an eye narrowed in promise of retribution (an expression that, no doubt, regularly brought the members of the rambunctious Irish clan to heel), Michael hurriedly sat, unlaced and removed the offending footwear, and darted to set his wet boots outside the bedroom door. For an instant, his mouth curled into a lopsided grin at the realization that the muck that had caked his boots during the morning had been scraped off them when he had tramped through knee-deep snow from Sumac. If the woman responded so vehemently to a little water, he did not want to know what epithets would have issued from Dottie O'Reilly had he trailed mud about the house!

Hermione remarked, "There's no need for such a crowd in here." She waved dismissively to the O'Reilly girls, who blushed and scurried out. The MacGregor matriarch opened her mouth to send her son after them, but her daughter-in-law cut her off.

"I want Michael to stay," said Anne firmly. She smiled to him and added, "If you're willing."

Needing no other encouragement, Michael hastened to his wife's side and took her hand as Mrs. O'Reilly muttered grumpily, "Don't see why ye need a husband underfoot when

'e's already done 'is part."

Sitting next to Anne, Michael kissed her hand and brushed a wayward strand of her hair into place. "What must I do?" he asked in a whisper.

"Just be here," she said softly. "Although," she added in afterthought, "I could use a sip of water."

Michael raced downstairs and fetched a glass from the cupboard to fill it from the blue-striped stoneware crock with brass spigot kept on the counter by the back door. He had reached the stairwell when he recalled that his mother had taken hours to birth each of her children, according to the stories she had told from time to time. He returned to the kitchen to fill a ewer as well.

Once more taking three steps at a stride, he brought the pitcher to the bedside and sat as he handed Anne the glass. While she sipped, he gazed into the face of the woman he loved and mused happily that she was the most beautiful, the most perfect woman he had ever known. Then, his gut clenched as another spasm seized her and contorted her countenance.

∞

"I NEED TO MOVE," said Anne. "And I would appreciate a damp cloth to cool my face and neck."

Immediately, Michael sprang into action, and by the time she had stood and ambled half the length of the room, he returned from the kitchen to wipe her brow, cheeks, and neck with a cold compress.

"Should ye be up like this?" he asked uncertainly.

Anne smiled and answered, "I'm fine. Motion seems to help."

He walked with her, pressing the cloth alternately to her brow and nape. After one circuit around the room, she climbed back into the bed, this time sitting on her knees and leaning on her hands.

The contractions had become more frequent and they lasted longer. Despite her husband's ministrations, drops of perspiration trickled and tickled down her temple and cheek. Following a spasm, Anne unlaced the bodice and untied the skirts of her gown and peeled off the heavy blue wool. Her sweat-soaked cotton shift clung here and there, and hung limply everywhere else. She wanted to remove it as well, but her body overrode the mental impulse as an irresistible physical one took hold. Things were happening more quickly than she had expected.

When her muscles relaxed at last, Anne visualized the position of the baby, the coil of the umbilical cord, the squeezing of her abdominal muscles, the slackening of her cervix and vagina. She felt the weight of her child ease downward, his body's contours stretching her interior dimensions in new ways as he moved toward the outside and freedom.

Again, she felt a desire to reposition. Now, she pushed upright and squatted a moment before sitting once more.

She spread her thighs wider and leaned against the mound behind her as the pressure below grew. Hermione's confirmation was not needed to tell her that the baby's head was now visible, though it slipped back inside again. At Michael's widened eyes, Anne wanted to laugh. But other matters required her attention.

A burning sensation grew in her nether region as the child's head crowned. Though Hermione and Dottie and Fiona Bannion spoke encouragingly, Anne did not hear them. She looked into Michael's face, but scarcely noted the awe written there. What she saw clearly, in her mind's eye, was the further extension of her already enlarged lower passage as she pushed with all her might to propel her son into the world.

A brief pause to catch her breath, and she pushed again. At a sudden give, she knew the baby's head had been born. Hermione—or was it Dottie—inspected the little pate and neck, but Anne heard none of the chatter around her. After one more

short, panting respite, she put her back into it—literally, pressing deep into the heap of pillows and quilts as her muscles clenched—and drove the oblong mass that lingered within out into daylight with a long guttural grunt that ended abruptly as her child's shoulders, arms, body, and legs gushed forth at last.

"Let Michael give me the baby," Anne insisted immediately and breathlessly as she lifted the hem of her shift above her substantially flattened belly.

With utmost delicacy, Michael picked up his son, the child's tender skin slippery with residue. "Why isn't he crying?" he asked anxiously.

"Bring him, love," said Anne.

When he did, she reached into the baby's mouth with a finger to remove any mucus, and then turned the wee head carefully and bent her own to suck the nose clear as well. She spat something toward the floor and commanded, "Raise the legs."

As Michael firmly grasped the boy's tiny ankles and lifted his son's limbs while maintaining a hold of the wee chest and shoulders, water dribbled from the baby's mouth and nose. Then, Anne rubbed the little back with a forefinger and, all at once, the child's torso expanded. James Alexander MacGregor began to breathe on his own, and he uttered a howl that brought a happy smile to Mother, a proud grin to Father, giggles to the O'Reilly sisters waiting in the corridor, and chuckles of relief to the matrons looking on.

Anne sat back and gathered her shift in folds once more, pulling it up until her belly lay fully exposed. She patted her abdomen to indicate the child's intended resting place and said, "Put him here, please."

When Michael laid their son supine, Mrs. O'Reilly rushed forward bearing knife and string. With efficiency born of experience, Dottie tied and severed the umbilical cord as Hermione swooped in with towels to wrap the newest member of her family.

"Is it done, then?" asked the first-time father.

Dottie O'Reilly hooted. She said, "Hell, no! The afterbirth's still to come yet."

She gestured to Anne's privates, and Michael frowned at the bluish coil of rope trailing between his wife's outstretched legs. Yes, clearly that needed to be removed. After a moment's trepidation, he retook his place at his wife's side and gazed upon the tiny, vociferous life they had made together. Gradually, his son quieted and fell asleep under Anne's gentle stroking.

"I guess being born is tiring," Michael whispered.

Anne chuckled softly. She said, "Indeed. It certainly is for the mother, as well!"

Suddenly, she closed her eyes and inhaled an audible breath. When she opened them, she said, "Better take him, now. I have a little more to do."

∞

PAST SUNSET, as the waxing crescent moon hung above the treetops, Michael lit a fresh candle and watched his wife gather their newborn son into her arms. When she had settled in the bed, she opened her nightshirt and brushed her deep-red nipple across the baby's lips. Little Jamie whimpered faintly as she teased his mouth open wider. At last, she pushed her breast into his gaping mouth and a sucking sound announced that mother and son were firmly attached to each other.

An unfamiliar smell emanated from both, Michael noted. No longer the scents of sweat and blood and the wet, earthy aroma of delivery, nor the odd odour peculiar to the afterbirth: This was a sweet, homely fragrance that Michael imagined must belong only to infants and new mothers.

Downstairs, Joseph and Hermione entertained Jake Trevelyan, Elizabeth and Ben, and the remaining well-wishers from The Flats in subdued conversations that had dwindled over the last hour. Occasionally, the noise spiked with renewed

congratulations and subsequent farewells; then, the back or front door thumped shut and the gate hinge creaked as someone departed. Michael had considered joining his parents to greet guests, but had chosen, instead, to remain with his wife and child.

As the baby suckled, Michael slipped his finger into the little palm of his son. At the curling of Jamie's tiny digits around his large one, a *frisson* swept up his spine and he basked in a sense of joy and belonging so profound it almost hurt.

CHAPTER 47

One thing...

As the days lengthened and the soil warmed, the people of The Flats rivalled their bees in activity: Gardens and houses and sheds were cleaned, early seeds were sown, harvest of the first of spring's wild green bounty began, egg collection resumed, and foundations were dug for two houses and one orphanage. At the same time, *Trevelyan and Company* bustled with business and building as Jake supervised a new project on Parliament and Michael oversaw construction of the reservoir and brickworks.

Every day, Michael returned home to find his son suckling at Anne's breast and, every day, he bent to kiss both before shedding his filthy clothes and washing off sweat and grime from his labours at the worksite. Wee Jamie had grown already, in only three weeks, and he charmed everyone with his big blue eyes, his thick lashes and brows, and his little curls of jet

hair. No one doubted his paternity, and all remarked how quiet he was for an infant, rarely crying.

"Aye," Michael responded to such a comment from Tsi-Guy Villeneuve as they walked from the mews, stepping on the boards that had been laid to protect boots from mud and freshening grass from boots. "He's like his mother. She barely made a sound when he was born. I was amazed."

"Mebbe she can teach my Georgette dat," the former distillery worker replied with a note of envy in his voice. "Save my ears, eh?"

"I'll ask her," Michael promised, and he waved goodbye as Tsi-Guy turned toward his home on Poplar Lane. The Scot walked on, trailing the majority of his employees and the other men of The Flats. He always closed the company site personally, and today he had seen his father off to dinner in town, that repast to be followed by a meeting of the elder MacGregor's lodge brothers. Michael smiled at an image of his father in a silly hat, pronouncing peculiar words and phrases in a cryptic ceremony complete with gestures and handshakes. His smile faded as he recalled the one occasion on which he had joined such a group as guest of a man he had thought his friend. There, along with ridiculous rituals and costumes, he had found a nest of sodomites intent on recruiting him for the secret society they maintained within the larger league. The whole affair might have been risible had it not been for the laudanum with which they had laced his drink. Even drugged, he managed to escape, though he had never been entirely sure the nightmares he experienced for weeks after were merely opiate-derived phantasms.

He turned from Sumac to Cedar Lane. As he stepped through his gate, it squealed, reminding him that he had forgotten, again, to anoint its hinges. Today was the day, he decided, and he marched directly to the tool shed beside the well-house to fetch a can of oil. When he returned, he touched the spout to the winter-rusted iron and worked the gate several times to spread the fluid. When the squeaks faded and the motion

smoothed, he released the paling portal to clack shut and he went in search of other items in need of lubrication. Doors and windows received remedial measures. Tools were cleaned and oiled in preparation for the summer's gardening tasks. Finally, feeling pleased with the performance of his chores, Michael replaced the significantly lighter oil tin into its niche in the shed and stepped through the kitchen doorway to find dinner already on the table and Anne waiting for him.

"You've received a letter from Evan," she told him at once.

He glanced toward the desk, where a parchment envelope leaned against an ink bottle. "I'll read it later," he said, and he kissed her thoroughly. When he released her, he added, "First, I'll wash."

"First, you'll eat," Anne insisted. "Before your supper turns as cold as your nose."

He grabbed her round the waist and drew her in. "So, I'm cold, am I?" he responded. "Then, perhaps ye should warm me, eh?" He buried his nose in her neck and tickled her here and there as she squealed with laughter. At the ruction, wee Jamie began to howl.

"Now, you've done it!" Anne scolded playfully. "Your son wants to join in."

Michael gave her one more buss and a smack to the bottom before striding to the crib to pick up the baby and bring him to the table. "That's a fine bellow ye've got there, Jamie," he said as he held the child to his chest and sat to his dinner. "Ye'd make a fearsome drill sergeant, to be sure."

Of Anne, the Scot asked, "Where's Mother?"

"Gone to spend the night with her friend Amy Miller," Anne revealed as she sat to her own meal. "She says your father will be very late coming home from the meeting, and probably very drunk; so, she's decided to have a Girls' Night Out with Mrs. Miller and a few others."

"Girls' Night Out, eh?" he responded. "And shall I expect

to find ye cavorting all night with your friends one o' these days, now that you're an auld married woman?"

Something flitted across her face, some emotion he did not understand, but it fled and left in its wake a mischievous smile. "That depends whether I have something to keep me home, don't you think?" She twitched her brows and pouted her lips provocatively.

His voice a low menace, his eyes narrowed, Michael leaned forward and said, "I assure ye, my sweet, I'll keep ye home." He leaned back with a lingering, lascivious smile that threatened retribution for the mere thought of such escapades. Then, with his soothed son cradled in one arm, he turned his attention to the meal before him and wolfed down his stew of beef and potato and foraged greens spiced with herbs and pepper, onions and garlic. He had not realized how hungry he had become until the scents of the ingredients penetrated the reek of the lubricant still clinging to his fingers and nostrils.

"Delicious," he managed to say through a mouthful.

Anne grinned across the table. "Are you sure you can taste it?" she replied. "At Mach Two, I would think you'd barely get a whiff of it."

Michael frowned at her. "Mach Two?" he repeated when he had swallowed. "Ye said that before, I recall, but I dinna ken what it means."

"Twice the speed of sound," she clarified, eliciting a look of shock from her husband. With a raised eyebrow, she added, "And *you* sound more like your father every day."

Now, it was his turn to grin. "MacGregor, I am, 'tis true, lass. Ye should ken it weel by noo."

She leaned toward him, fixed his eyes, wrinkled her nose, and said softly, "And I'd have no other."

∞

AS ANNE WASHED and changed the baby, Michael opened the

envelope from Brazil and read. His lips curled at Evan's usual salutation.

> My dear boy,
>
> I am so very pleased to hear of the birth of your son. Please convey my very best wishes to your wife for her continued health and wellbeing. You must send me a photograph or a drawing of young James Alexander. I must say that I am curious as to the choice of name. Why James Alexander, rather than Michael? Not that the selection is not a fine one, but most fathers of my acquaintance prefer the vanity of self-replication. But what am I saying? You are in no way like most fathers, indeed, like most men of my acquaintance. I should not be astonished at your divergence from tradition, and I applaud you for it.
>
> On another matter: I was deeply surprised to hear of the death of Reginald Orwell. Surprised and particularly concerned. The man did not seem to me the sort who would commit suicide even in the face of so grievous a charge as Treason, with its attendant scandal and potential punishment. No, for that reason, I decided to press my own inquiries, already under way since my learning of the destruction of your distillery, and I have discovered that there may have been a third and, indeed, a fourth treasonous conspirator in the Bhutan incidents. Moreover, Richard Howes has also died suddenly, not five weeks past, run over by a carriage near Hyde Park before he was to be detained for questioning. I believe it entirely beyond the possibility of coincidence that two men die under

mysterious circumstances mere weeks after they have both come under investigation and days before they can be officially questioned.

Further, my man in London believes he has been followed since he made his own inquiries. This has the whiff of a powerful person or persons covering tracks. Your father would do well to distance himself from this matter at once—if indeed he can, if it is not too late.

I am sorry to be the bearer of such fearsome news, and I sincerely hope that further unpleasantness can be averted. Please take care of yourself and your family, and know that I am ever

> *Your friend and servant,*
> *Evan*

Michael set the letter on the desktop and stared at its familiar angular scrawl. *More conspiracies,* he thought bitterly, and he swallowed hard. *Lord in Heaven, will it never end!*

∞

ANNE LIGHTLY COVERED her infant son with the cotton sheet and down-filled quilt, quenched the candle, and crawled into bed next to her husband. She had noticed that Michael lay on his back, arms behind his head, staring at the ceiling meditatively. No—glumly. She moved closer and slid her arm over his chest.

"Surely those who were involved know only one of their own number can threaten them," she murmured hopefully. "If Joseph had known who they were, they'd have been arrested long ago."

Michael replied in a whisper, "I wish I could be sure they are that intelligent, that sensible." He tilted his head as if to look into her eyes, though he and his wife lay in blackness. "But whoever it is may feel that there is only one way to be certain."

Anne stroked his cheek, its black stubble rough on her palm. She could think of nothing to say that would ease his apprehension. Or her own. Instead, she decided to take his mind off the matter altogether.

She pushed up onto her elbow and dipped her head to kiss his chest, feeling and appreciating the way the past months' physical labour had sculpted his musculature as she explored his form by touch. Nuzzling him, his curly jet hairs tickling her nose and cheeks, she moved on to lave each of his nipples with her tongue. One of his hands came to rest on her head as she proceeded down across his belly, and farther, to the hardness below.

Slowly, delicately, her lips massaged the corrugated sac that had firmed with his desire. His scrotum smelled of her homemade cucumber soap and of his own musky masculinity, with a bit of perspiration. When she sucked a fold of skin into her mouth, he groaned, a deep, breathy moan of pleasure.

"Come," he beckoned, sliding his fingers through her hair and urging her upward.

She traced his phallus from its base with her tongue, eliciting another groan as she approached the head. "Holy Jesus!" he whispered when she eased her lips around it and sheathed him as far as she could. His hips rocked, unbidden, and his breath came short. Anne could almost feel the throbbing that she knew had grown in intensity. She wanted to bring him to fulfillment.

But he had other ideas.

∞

IF HE DID NOT stop her, he knew he would spill himself in a moment. Abruptly, Michael gripped Anne's hair, the tresses entwined in his fingers, and he pulled her up as he pushed himself down out of her mouth. He had no intention of letting her indulge him again without returning the favour.

He knew why she had become bashful in their bed: Her belly sagged, now, still stretched from its former burden. His mother had explained that the skin would tauten in time. But its current condition embarrassed Anne; she shied when he touched her there or tried to pleasure her.

But she had done without for long enough, he decided. Forcing her onto her back, he straddled her, on his knees, and then grasped her under each arm to slide her into a better position on the mattress. When he was satisfied with her placement, he bent to his task and kissed her thighs, alternating one to the other, from her knees to his ultimate target.

He inhaled the scent of her, a uniquely feminine mixture of earth and sea, with a hint of newborn-baby smell still clinging to her body. A trace of soap, a whiff of onion and garlic emanating from her fingers, a suggestion of cinnamon and walnut and apple, and the tang of sweat. Aromas with the clarity of colour, and he knew them all.

He revelled in the soft smoothness of her skin, picturing it milky in sunlight even as they lay in darkness. Each of his caresses provoked a tremor and a catch of her breath, and that, too, pleased him.

"You don't have to, Michael," she murmured as she reached between her thighs to comb his locks tenderly with her fingers.

"I want to," he said, pushing up to kiss her belly before returning to suckle her.

And when he had brought her to her finish, he united them once more as husband and wife.

∞

ANNE STIRRED and sighed. Not to wake her, Michael rolled carefully and looked into her dreamy face, haloed with silver hair in the pale glow from the rising moon. His *Beira* was back, lusty and loving as ever. When she smiled in her sleep, his heart felt

too big for his chest.

"Thank you, God," he whispered.

∞

HAVING BATHED Jamie in the white enamelled pan dedicated to the purpose and towelled him dry, Anne pulled the green wincey gown she had made for him over his head and guided each of his tiny arms into the sleeves. At a bleat she had come to recognize, she hiked his gown and grabbed him up, dashed to the chamber pot, and held him over it while he pooped. Because the procedure was invariably accompanied by a soaking of her front, she had taken to wearing a bib over her apron to absorb the spray of urine.

Once more, she wiped her son's private parts and his little behind, before fastening a diaper and slipping his feet into the woollen booties Katie O'Reilly had knitted for him. Now that he was dressed for the day, his mother wrapped him in a bundle and set him in his crib.

She brought her baby's soapless bath water out to the garden and poured it onto the ground beneath the herbs and vegetables meant only for him. That done, she emptied the chamber pot into the privy and rinsed it out. Then, she stepped inside the back door to set the porcelain potty by the crib in a corner of the kitchen. Finally, she donned a fresh bib and tossed the wet one into a waiting pail of vinegar water on the porch, that the baby's urine should be neutralized.

The sound of a carriage brought her to the front door. Hermione alighted from the hackney, opened the gate, and skipped up the walk in a sprightly dance, grinning from ear to ear. She looked ten years younger, Anne noticed, amazed what a brief respite from the everyday cares of the family had done for her mother-in-law.

"How is Joseph?" Hermione asked. "Is he hung over?"

"He hasn't returned," Anne told her. "If he is suffering

the effects of a night of debauchery, he's likely doing it at his office."

Hermione's face fell at the news. She said softly, apprehension clear in her tone, "It's not like him not to come home, however late."

Anne offered, "Why don't I call his office?" She tried to sound reassuring as she suggested, "Perhaps he spent the night there, rather than wake the household." Preceding her mother-in-law into the house, she hoped with all her heart that Joseph had, indeed, slept off an evening of overindulgence in the offices of *Trevelyan and Company*.

Anne jumped, and her belly, already tensed with concern, tightened further when the telephone rang just as she reached for it. Picking up both receiver and base, she said, "Michael?"

On the other end of the line, her husband said, "Aye, it's me. Is Da there?"

Now her whole body clenched as she answered, "No. I was about to call you to see if he had gone straight to work."

"No," Michael replied. After a moment's pause, he said, "I'll call Marcus Donaldson. I believe he's a lodge member. Perhaps he'll know where Da's gone."

"Let me know," Anne said unnecessarily.

"I will."

Putting down the telephone, Anne pressed her mouth into a thin smile that did not hide her emotions as she turned to her mother-in-law. At the worry plain on Anne's face, Hermione hurried to the nearest chair and collapsed onto it with hand to her heart.

"Michael will call as soon as he hears," Anne assured her, and she hastened to the stove to fetch hot water for tea. Her hands trembling, she put leaves into pot...steaming water over leaves...cup in saucer...spoon to the side...honey bowl on table....

∞

MICHAEL CALLED every lodge member he knew, but all said the same thing: that Joseph had left the meeting in fine spirits and headed home around midnight. No one had actually seen him hail a hackney or climb into one. Nor did anyone recall any other persons on the street when they had stepped out on their own way home.

His gut in knots, Michael called George Catesby and then William MacDonald to find they had neither seen nor heard from Joseph MacGregor recently. Next, he tried Ben Ogden's studio, to no avail. After several minutes' internal debate, he called Elizabeth, hoping against hope that their father had, for some reason, gone to her home instead of his own.

He had not.

Finally, Michael called Detective Morgan.

∞

THE POLICE STATION, in general, smelled of strong soap, ink, the constables' sweat and pomade, and a *mélange* of reeks from the various drunks, criminals, witnesses, and complainants who passed through its doors from time to time. Along with those odours, the detective's office also bore the scents of chemicals and metals and other substances used in his work.

Gadgets, some of unknown purpose and others familiar to Michael, cluttered shelves, tables, window ledges, desk, and even the floor in Paul Morgan's office, most of the objects crammed here and there next to substantial buckram-covered or leather-bound books. A large chalkboard set into a wheeled frame and overwritten with cryptic notes had been pushed against a bank of shelves on one wall, while a row of open boxes held file folders piled high enough to obscure the view out of the half-glazed wall opposite.

Morgan, on the far side of the desk and in the shaft of sunlight from a tall casement, leaned back in his wooden swivel chair and contemplated the tale of treason, murder, and intrigue

told by Michael MacGregor. Abruptly, he stood and stepped to the door, opening it to call Constable O'Toole.

"Find Joseph MacGregor. Check all of the hospitals and the other stations," Morgan instructed. "Hotels, as well. And let me know at once, whatever you find."

O'Toole nodded acknowledgement and strode to his own desk, calling to other constables for aid as Morgan closed his door once more and returned to his seat. Elbows on his blotter, the detective clasped his hands and pursed his lips a moment before he looked up at Michael and said without censure, "I wish I had known of this sooner."

The Scot exhaled a long breath, nodding, and replied, "I do not know what you could have done, Detective. Until I received the letter from my friend, I thought the matter all but concluded, wanting only my father's turning over to the Crown's agent from London what documentary evidence he has." After a pause, he added, "From what I saw in the papers he had received from Bardon, there really is nothing to point to a specific traitor. In fact, the evidence against Orwell and Howes is entirely circumstantial."

Morgan said, "But apparently compelling enough to warrant investigation of those men and any associates they may have."

"I can only surmise," said Michael, "that one or more of those involved in the treasons in Bhutan—and perhaps elsewhere, for all we know—used the ill-gotten gains to support a career in the halls of power."

"It would appear so," Morgan concurred. "Which leaves me doubting whether this agent of the Crown can be trusted."

Michael wondered, "Was there any indication from London that the man, upon arrival, would identify himself to local authorities?"

"It was not specified," said Morgan, "although, as a matter of courtesy, that would be the usual protocol." He mused, "Given the circumstances, perhaps I should contact London to

obtain the name of the agent and a description, as well as the expected date of his arrival."

The detective excused himself and left to send a wire. Meanwhile, Michael waited with all the patience he could muster, trying not to imagine his father face down in a gutter and bleeding out from a horrific wound.

He had examined every book in the office and had begun a nervous tattoo on the edge of his chair by the time Morgan returned. As the detective stepped into the room, Constable O'Toole dashed to the doorway to announce that Joseph MacGregor had been found.

∞

"OH, GOD, DA!" Michael gasped when he saw his father's corpse on the narrow morgue table. As Dr. Howard Thorne replaced the upper edge of the sheet that covered the length of Joseph's pale, naked body to hide his lifeless face once more, the younger MacGregor closed his eyes tightly to hold back tears. He fisted his hands against the rage that rose like a tidal wave and threatened to engulf him.

"It was a single bullet to the heart that killed him," said the coroner in a manner that managed to be at once businesslike and gentle. He refrained from mentioning the wounds sustained before the execution, but Michael had recognized the signs of a brutal beating.

Detective Morgan said softly, "According to the constables who found him, his wallet and watch were taken. We'll need you to identify what effects were found and tell us if anything else may have gone missing."

Michael opened his eyes to a watery view of the policeman. His voice strained, he stated with conviction, "This was not a robbery."

He held Morgan's gaze. After a wordless moment, the detective nodded concurrence.

∞

AS HE ACCOMPANIED Michael along the narrow alleys and side lanes back to the stationhouse, Morgan broke the silence between them with a confession.

"There is something I had not mentioned earlier," he began. "It had seemed to have no bearing, at the time, but given what I now know...."

After a pause and a long breath, he continued, "Shortly after Reginald Orwell was brought in for questioning, another man was arrested on a charge of Drunk and Disorderly and locked in one of our cells. It seems he had a visitor, that evening."

"Just before Orwell died," Michael guessed.

"Yes," Morgan confirmed. The detective waited until they had crossed the street before he went on.

"Under the circumstances, I will be reviewing all of that evening's events and questioning the constables on duty as well as the prisoner and his visitor."

If one or both have not disappeared, Michael said under his breath. His gut, already clenched, tightened to a hard knot.

CHAPTER 48

...and another

Michael wondered hazily if it always rained on the day of a funeral.

Somehow, he had never thought he would have to bury his father. He had seen the corpse in the morgue and, later, in the coffin at Mr. Jessop's funeral parlour. Now, he saw the simple spruce casket lowered into the grave. Still, his father's death held no reality for him.

He looked to Anne, beside him, and the baby asleep in her embrace, both in the shelter of Elizabeth's umbrella. His wife and son were real to him, but everything else—even his mother, clinging to his arm as he screened her—felt like phantoms from a strange dream, insubstantial and ephemeral.

Or perhaps, stated a cold, harsh, accusatory voice in his mind, *you merely WANT it to be a dream.*

Yes, I want it to be a dream! he replied angrily to that

internal critic. *I want my father back!*

And that steely part of him laughed sardonically at the thought: After all, he and his father—his adoptive father, to be accurate—had been strangers since he was eleven. They had begun to mend fences and become a family again only recently.

Perhaps, he grudgingly admitted to himself, what he wanted back was not his father but the innocence he had lost all those years ago. Perhaps he missed not truly the man but the father Joseph MacGregor had failed to be for so long. Granted, Da had not known what was happening to Michael. But logic does not assuage a sense of betrayal or soothe a broken heart, especially the heart of a child who feels loathed and abandoned.

Perhaps he still was a child, he mused. Perhaps he had grown only in body since that night so many years ago.

After a few moments' reflection, he decided, *All that may be true. But I loved him and I miss him.* He stifled a sob.

Jamie became restless. He squirmed in his mother's arms and whimpered fretfully. Brought back to the here and now, Michael stroked his son's brow and cheek gently and prayed he would never disappoint the boy.

I will take care of you, he promised under his breath. *I will protect you. And if I fail in either, I will be here for you. I will love you with all my heart and support you with all that I am. So help me God.*

∞

MICHAEL AND ANNE, Hermione and Elizabeth and Ben lingered at the graveside, watching Tim Peckham and Harry Hayes shovel wet dirt into the pit. Their work concluded, the mound that covered Joseph MacGregor smoothed, the two men tipped their sopping hats to the family, picked up their shovels and jackets, and trudged away.

After a shuddering sigh that seemed to expire her soul, Hermione turned away, but she stopped suddenly with a sharp intake of breath. The members of her family followed her red-

eyed gaze to find Detective Morgan and Constable O'Toole standing at the edge of the churchyard, waiting.

Michael said, "Ben, please take Mother and Anne home. I'll speak to the detective."

He handed his umbrella to Hermione with a smile that might have been reassuring had it not taken the shape of a pained grimace. He followed his kin to the gate, and he stopped when he reached Morgan.

"Shall we take a walk?" suggested the detective, raising his umbrella to shield Michael, though the rain's damage had already been done. O'Toole stayed behind with the policemen's bicycles, protected under the spreading branches of an old pine.

Michael and Morgan ambled in silence, allowing the distance between them and the MacGregor family to grow. Finally, when the others had disappeared around a bend, Morgan said, "I received a wire from London, this morning." He paused and Michael waited as they continued past the Commons where the O'Shaunnessey girls tended their family's new cow, two goats, and four sheep in a three-sided shelter.

Resuming, the detective said, "There was a delay in sending a man and the agent they dispatched is still at sea; the ship is expected in Halifax in three days. I have been given his name and description and have been assured his was instructed to introduce himself upon arrival."

"I'll give you the papers Da had held," said Michael. "Save you both time and trouble."

"Yes," said Morgan. "They will, perhaps, be safer in the station than in your possession. And your family safer, as well."

As they turned at the intersection, the detective said, "Regarding the other matter we discussed, it seems that the prisoner who had been in the cell next to Reginald Orwell's was killed in a drunken brawl the following evening. It happened in another jurisdiction, so I was not made aware of it earlier."

"Let me guess," said Michael. "No one knows who killed him, and his visitor has disappeared as well."

"I'm afraid so," Morgan admitted.

They continued without further conversation and Michael wondered if his father would have been spared had he turned the documents over to the police. Or had the die already been cast as soon as he began to inquire into the dealings of Orwell and Howes?

At the next intersection, they heard the scream.

∞

ANNE WAITED on the porch, bouncing Jamie as Ben and Hermione deposited the folded, dripping umbrellas on the plain pine planks and Elizabeth opened the front door. Her sister-in-law's screech stopped Anne's heart an instant, and she ran inside with her son clutched to her breast.

"Oh, my God!" she exclaimed at the mess of removed and overturned drawers, emptied cupboards, and toppled cabinets. Gathering her wits, she commanded, "Out! Everybody out!" and she whirled to dart back to the veranda, tugging Elizabeth by her sleeve.

A whistle sounded some distance away. Within minutes, Michael and Detective Morgan hurtled along the lane and over the fence.

"What's happened?" Michael demanded in alarm, holding Anne's shoulders and quickly looking her over to assure himself neither she nor Jamie had sustained damage. He glanced to the rest of his family for the same purpose as Morgan returned from his brief survey of the house to pull the whistle from his pocket and blow two more shrill notes.

"Jesus!" Michael swore in a whisper when he saw the destruction beyond the doorway. He looked to Morgan and asked in a low voice, "Could he—or they—still be inside?"

"We're about to find out," said the detective as he beckoned unnecessarily to O'Toole, who came toward them at a dead run, hurdling fences and cutting across yards.

"Here," said Anne, passing her wailing son to Hermione. She reached into her reticule, produced her derringer, and handed it to the detective. "Just in case."

Morgan accepted the pistol with a range of expressions that fleeted from shock, to censure, to a grudging appreciation, to determination. He checked the ammunition and nodded to O'Toole, who pulled his nightstick from its ring on his belt and forcibly steadied his laboured breath in preparation for possible confrontation. The policemen stepped cautiously into the house and scanned from the entryway before proceeding to the back room and then up the stairs.

"Thank God the children were not here!" said Anne, retrieving Jamie as Michael, wielding both closed umbrellas as though they were swords, peered round first one, then the other outside corner of the house.

Concerned neighbours, many of them employees of *Trevelyan and Company* who had been given the day off to attend the funeral, gathered in the lane, some of the men armed with shillelaghs and others with axes or shovels or pitchforks. Dowd and the Four Horsemen appeared among them, frowning and blinking and straining to see through the rivulets that flowed from their rain-matted hair.

Several members of the O'Reilly, O'Shaunnessey, and Bannion clans hopped over the fence and fanned out, weapons at the ready, to flush any intruders who might be lurking among the trees and outbuildings. By the time they returned, dourly disgusted that they had bagged no quarry, the police officers had reappeared to announce that the birds had flown.

"About those papers," Morgan called loudly to Michael. "Perhaps you should give them to me right away and I'll put them into the safe at the stationhouse." To O'Toole, he muttered, "Send for reinforcements, and tell them to open the armoury."

The constable headed inside to use the MacGregors' telephone. Meanwhile, Morgan carefully uncocked the little derringer and handed it back to Anne with a wry smile. As she

slipped it into her pocket, he said, "Given all that's happened of late, I should not be surprised that you feel the need of such precautions. Though I suspect you have long been no stranger to danger."

He pinched the brim of his fedora, picked up the umbrella he had abandoned open and upside down on the edge of the porch, and followed Michael around back to the tool shed, where the documents had been locked away in a thick ironwood strongbox inside a hidden compartment.

∞

ONCE THE CONTINGENT of armed constables had departed, escorting Joseph's documents to the safety of the precinct house, the urchins came out of hiding to reclaim their guest status. The ragamuffins wolfed down meals in the homes where they had been sheltered for the winter, and then ran back through the rain to their new quarters in sheds erected on the Sunshine Farm property. When her former lodgers chose to leave after washing the dishes, Anne made no demur on the grounds that a soaking in the rain was very likely the closest thing to bath and laundry any of them would manage before the orphanage's main building was completed. She smiled as she watched them scamper away. They had scrounged wood and stone, nails and tools with astounding resourcefulness. She did not doubt they would create a home for themselves, with or without the help of adults.

She stepped through her back door and closed its lower half, leaving the upper portion open to a slight breeze. Her house had been set aright, with everything put back into its place, but a sense of violation and insecurity remained. One or more men had managed to evade the watchmen who still patrolled the neighbourhood and to invade her family's home. True, there were fewer sentries during the day. And true, the doors had not been locked, though locks would not have stopped the sort of

people who would kill an elderly man for documents that implicated no one in particular. Perhaps they did not know that, she reflected. Perhaps they—whoever "they" were—believed the information sent by Bardon contained some clue to the identity of the traitors. Or perhaps, as Michael had suggested, they were simply being thorough. Coldly, calculatingly, impersonally thorough.

The things people do for money and power! she thought grimly. She huffed a brief, silent, mirthless laugh at the knowledge the Bhutan War had been nothing more than one in a long list of grabs for wealth and power in the guise of promoting national prosperity—prosperity based on the policy of bullying, thievery, and exploitation euphemistically called "Empire" that, in fact, served the ends of a small number of very rich people and effectively enslaved the rest of the citizenry to them. Closer to home, a similar policy had been labelled "Manifest Destiny."

"The more things change, the more they stay the same," she muttered to herself, knowing too well what evils would soon be perpetrated by those who would claim personal power and wealth at the expense of others' homes and livelihoods, even of others' lives.

"What's that?" Michael asked as he slipped his arms around his wife from behind and held her to him.

Anne leaned back against him and sighed. "Just reminiscing," she said.

"In a good way, I hope?"

Anne's mouth curled on one side and she murmured glumly, "I wish."

His voice serious, Michael whispered, "Do ye want to tell me?"

Anne turned in his arms and glanced up into his face. She shook her head and answered, "It would change nothing." She amended, "We could not change it."

Michael held her gaze a moment. Then, he stroked her hair, cupped both cheeks, fixed her eyes, and whispered, "But

you would not bear the burden alone."

As a floodgate burst behind her eyes, she hugged him with a desperate need.

∞

MICHAEL STARED at the ceiling and stroked his wife's back abstractedly as Anne pillowed her head on his shoulder. In ten years, the whole world would be at war. This country would be at war for five long years.

What neither of them had mentioned: He and most of the men they knew and counted as friends would quite likely be forced into the thick of it, ripped away from home and family. And for what? To fight, and probably die, on foreign soil for someone else's financial benefit.

A part of him wished he had not asked.

∞

DAMN! ANNE CURSED HERSELF. *Why am I doing this? Why am I wallowing in dread and fear? And worse, to have weighed Michael with knowledge that can only distress him to no good purpose.*

It's the "Baby Blues," she thought, remembering that many women suffer a period of depression during their bodies' postnatal readjustment. She sighed. Normally, these things started, and usually ended, within the first weeks after childbirth. She chuckled silently and sardonically to herself: When had she ever done anything "normally"?

Of course, their family tragedies were not helping matters any. She sighed again and deliberately, forcibly, turned her mind to a pleasant memory.

As she began to drift off, she suddenly recalled that she had told her husband that the Great War would come in ten years instead of twenty, and she wondered why she had made that slip. Her thoughts increasingly hazy, she tried to recollect the dates she had learned so long ago in school: *Nineteen...nineteen*

four...nineteen...four....

CHAPTER 49

Constructing the future

Olaf Andersson reached his long, bulky arms to help Anne from the buggy. She had secured Jamie into a basket and wedged it under the seat; now, she untied the wicker bassinet. Before she could pull it out, Olaf grasped and lifted it effortlessly from the carriage.

"Boss-man's boy big fellah," he grinned approvingly as he handed the bundle to her.

Lanky stable boy Little Jack peered into the basket curiously as his brother Tim joined him. When the mentally challenged teenager smiled and reached toward the baby, Tim instantly pulled his brother's hand away, at which Jack simply gave an eager little wave to the infant. "Lotta hair," he commented.

"Just like his father," said Anne, lingering to let her wide-eyed son gape at the strangers gathering to stare at him. The men

of The Flats had all seen Himself's child, but the stable boys and the employees resident in other parts of town had not.

Michael called out as he approached, "I see I'll have to have my wife arrested for disturbin' the peace." When the crowd parted before him, he lifted Jamie from the wicker cradle, clutched the infant to his shoulder, and swept Anne into his free arm to kiss her thoroughly, eliciting whistles and hoots from the men and blushes from the boys.

"Easy there, lad," Jake Trevelyan warned as he sauntered through the throng. "Much more o' that and she'll be up the spout again!" Bawdy laughter greeted the remark.

Michael winked lasciviously as he replied, "Ah, but she's wanton when she's whelpin'."

Almost hiding a smile, Anne slapped his shoulder and chided, "Behave yourself, ye silly Scot!" to the delight of their audience.

"It's good to see ye, Anne," said Trevelyan as he gave her a brief paternal hug. Getting back to business, he bawled, "All right, lads, show's over! Back to work!"

As the men drifted away and the boys unhitched the horse to lead it to the stable, Jake and Michael showed Anne around the site, from the reservoir pond to the wooden warehouses erected by the rail line to the temporary buildings that housed the stonecutters and the brickmakers.

"The problem is the heat build-up," said Trevelyan as they stood before the kilns. "Even with the special flues you designed, it's just too damned much." He added hesitantly, wishing to give no offense, "Or maybe because of them."

"Not that the men can't take a little heat," Michael rushed to say, "but we, that is, I hoped you might have an idea what could be done to improve the arrangement."

Anne pursed her lips and surveyed the offending ovens. Beside her, Jamie began to whimper in his "Feed me" fashion, and she absently took him from her husband, opened the front of her blouse, and pressed the child to her breast. Michael sucked in

a shocked breath; Trevelyan cleared his throat and turned away; several workers blushed crimson. Realizing his wife stood rapt and oblivious, Michael gently turned her away and removed his coat to drape it over her.

Anne glanced to the grey jacket that smelled of her husband, and then away, and then back to stare at it intently, tilting her head, frowning, and squinting.

Recognizing that look, Michael asked, "What? What d'ye see?"

"Stone dust," Anne replied in a faraway voice. She began to nod almost imperceptibly as she continued to gaze down, no longer seeing the garment or the dust.

"Stone dust," Michael repeated, with no clue as to the significance of the material to be found everywhere on the site.

Suddenly, Anne smiled up at him. "You need to make a laundry facility."

Michael and Jake Trevelyan gaped in astonishment.

∞

ANNE HAD TAKEN the baby to the privy. Studying the drawing she had made in the dirt, Michael marvelled and Jake said with awe, "If that isn't the damnedest thing I've ever seen!"

Michael looked up and pictured in his mind's eye the flues that would heat vats of water to clean the work clothes of the men, and the men themselves—one set of basins for brickworkers and one for stoneworkers in order to separate clay from rock dust. Soaking tubs placed nearby would allow the majority of the dust that impregnated their clothes to settle before the washing. Once the water was drawn off, the residue would be dried and the fines added to dust from the rest of the site, the lot to be made into bricks, mortar, and plaster. He smiled that Anne had even found use for the filthy water: Drains would draw it off to a man-made marsh full of cattails to filter the water and to add it to the reservoir. The residual heat would keep the

pond free of ice year round. And the cattails and reeds could be harvested for stable and privy straw.

Another flue extension with a damper would divert heat through the office to be built between the brickworks and the stoneworks, thus keeping it comfortable all winter. The sector dedicated to stone cutting could be warmed, as well, and in summer the flow through the office would be cut off so that the rock stores would absorb all of the excess thermal energy, thus allowing the administration rooms to cool.

Along each flue, accessible ports would facilitate cleanout of the creosote, which would be sold to local companies that use the oily residuum in their processes. Michael closed his eyes briefly in sorrow, remembering that his father had already listed the potential buyers.

When he returned his mind to the present, or rather to the future, Michael shook his head and smiled. Now, he understood the layout of their house and gardens. "Nothing wasted," he said. "Everything both product and resource."

Jake observed, "It'll cost us more time and supplies in the building, but it'll save us one helluva lot in the long run. Damned if I wouldn't like to meet the parents that taught her such things!"

Michael's smile faded. "Not possible," he told his partner.

"Ah," said Trevelyan, the single syllable encompassing realization, condolence, and apology. "That explains her soft heart for orphans."

∞

THE HOUSE at Sunshine Farm had begun to take shape. From sunrise to sunset, with brief breaks for meals, the children of The Flats—orphans and others—formed hemp-straw-and-clay walls between the posts erected earlier by the neighbourhood gentlemen. The youngest worked the wet clay, squealing and giggling with glee at the mud squishing between their toes.

Those a little older mixed the clay with straw. And the adolescents ensured proper proportions of ingredients, nailed forms into place, tamped the straw-clay around the timbers, and placed the frames for windows and doors. Dowd and Davey supervised the operations and put their backs into the heavier work, as well as seeing to the feeding and watering of the crew. Concurrently, the Four Horsemen scrounged materials, built windows and doors, and wheedled help from adults when necessary.

Busying herself in her grief, Hermione became everyone's grandmother, soothing scrapes, bringing baked treats, reading storybooks, and telling tales of her youth. Anne had, at first, worried that her mother-in-law used such activities as an excuse to avoid her feelings. One evening, however, she found Hermione with the youngest urchins, tears flowing freely as she described a dashing young Joseph MacGregor and his flamboyant courtship of a shy girl from Cardiff.

Remaining in the shadows of a clump of pines, Anne smiled sadly to herself as she listened, lamenting the loss of her son's grandfather and her husband's father. She had grown fond of the elder MacGregor and would have liked to know him better. When at last Hermione moved on to a folktale from her childhood, Anne slipped away, content that her mother-in-law had found her own method of mourning.

∞

GRACE DONALDSON arrived wearing a plain black dress that had clearly been borrowed from one of her family's maids. Elizabeth greeted her friend enthusiastically and immediately put her to work mixing mortar for the brick stoves Anne had designed for the Ogden home and the orphanage. An expanded work party of neighbours formed hurriedly, and they proposed to finish the masonry heaters, the walls, and the roofs of both buildings while the sunny weather lasted.

Always domestic, the O'Reilly sisters helped their mother and grandmother and the Donnelly women to prepare a feast for the house-raisings. In the meantime, other ladies of The Flats rolled up their sleeves and hiked their skirts to join the few available adult male participants in climbing ladders and treading scaffolds to form upper walls and to shingle roofs.

Eva Janus commanded the bucket brigade at the farm while old Tess Tulan, surprisingly spry despite her bent body, and cackling like a fairy-tale hag at whatever struck her as amusing, performed the same function on the Ogden property: bringing potable water to the workers.

Jack had come up with a plan to haul creek water for the clay slip in wheelbarrows, and he proceeded to form a barrow train between the Sweetwater and the orphanage. Meanwhile, early Saturday morning, Larry appropriated a wagon and draught team from the mews to fetch more straw from neighbouring farms, which left Erik Johannsen swearing in several languages when he could not drive to the dairy to sell his cans of fresh milk.

Having suffered a broken leg and been rendered temporarily unable to perform his paid employment, Calum O'Shaunnessey wheeled himself from one site to the other in the chair Johann Bucholtz had once made for Anne, and he serenaded the work crews with his fiddle. Before the sun set on Saturday evening, he had played, at least five times, every tune he had ever learned.

With Jamie strapped to her chest, Anne instructed the urchins and her sister-in-law in the building of the stoves. Elizabeth helped the children to trowel the mortar and lay the bricks for each of their heaters on Friday (they had decided six would be enough) and used the knowledge and experience to build one of her own the next day.

By sunset on Saturday, both structures had been closed in and capped, needing only a drying period before interior finishing and exterior embellishment began. The occasion called

for a party.

∞

THANKS TO surreptitious matchmaking by Elizabeth, William MacDonald had been invited to attend the shindig that spanned the length and breadth of newly named Sunshine Street, the short lane that terminated at the farm. He arrived with two friends recently come from Inverness, and the three Scots quickly doffed hats and jackets to join in the informal revelry. Mortified that he should catch her in a mud-stained maid's dress, Grace Donaldson tried to slip away, but the young lawyer spotted her in mid-flight and literally swept her off her feet into a reel.

"I foresee a summer wedding," said Anne as she sidled up to Elizabeth.

"More than one, perhaps," her sister-in-law replied as one of MacDonald's friends twirled Evelyn O'Grady and the other swirled Kenna O'Connell.

Ben Ogden stepped up behind his wife and sister-in-law to inquire, "Are you two conspiring to commit matrimony?"

"Just helping Nature take its course, dear," Elizabeth replied. "Ooh!" she exclaimed, eyes flying wide as she clutched her expanded belly.

"Are you all right, dear?" Ben asked anxiously, reaching his arm around her shoulders.

She smiled up at him and said, "I'm fine, sweetheart. I just felt the baby move, is all."

As Ben placed his hand on Elizabeth's bulge, Anne left them to their private moment and joined her husband at the food tables placed along the Buzzetti family's board fence at the T-junction of Sunshine Street and Redbud Road. With apparently indiscriminate abandon, Michael piled a plate with one hand as he held Jamie to his chest with the other. Their son, for his part, gaped past his father's shoulder at the shenanigans around him, enthralled.

"The lusty month of May," Anne commented as she speared new potatoes and placed them into a dish.

"Hm?" Michael asked. When she gestured toward the dancers, he said, "Oh, aye."

He stopped scooping food onto his plate to slip his free arm around her waist and pull her close. He murmured, "Plenty o' that to go around."

Jamie bounced himself excitedly and uttered little squeaks.

Anne smiled and said, "I expect he'll be very tired by the time we get home."

"Whereas I will not," said Michael, his hand drifting to her buttocks. He gave her a squeeze and added, "So, I'd better eat hearty to keep up my strength."

Anne chuckled and ladled a large spoonful of peas into her bowl. Across the table, Alice O'Reilly grinned and winked at her mother, beside her, as the women refilled platters depleted in Michael's wake.

∞

ANNE AND MICHAEL meandered through the throng of neighbours, bidding farewell as wee Jamie, his black-curled head on his father's shoulder, tried with intermittent success to keep his eyes open.

"Perhaps you should see that the little ones get to bed," Anne told Dowd, pointing out small lumps nestled here and there in the grass at the edge of the lane.

"We will," Dowd promised. "Looks like this one ain't long for his crib, either." He grinned at Michael and waved a little salute; then, he turned to press the Four Horsemen into service rounding up the sleepy younger orphans.

"A born sergeant," Anne commented.

"Aye," said Michael. "He is that. Though I dinna think an army captain would be pleased with his outside activities."

"Then, he's still prostituting himself," Anne guessed.

Michael nodded grimly and mused, "I suppose it's a hard habit to break when you've much need o' money." He looked into Anne's face to add, "And too much pride to beg or borrow."

"Yes," she concurred. "He does not recognize the many other skills he has to offer. Though perhaps most employers would not recognize them, either—seeing only the guttersnipe and not the capable, responsible young man."

Michael said, "If he were not needed here, I'd hire him."

"He needs an education," Anne declared. "He's learned to read and write, at least, in the past few months, but he will need much more in order to become a proper administrator."

"So, you've decided his career for him, have ye?" Michael remarked with raised eyebrows and with a hint of censure in his voice.

Anne replied, "I think he's decided it for himself: He's set himself to building and overseeing the farm. But he'll need help." She looked up into her husband's face. "From all of us."

"We'll teach him," Michael agreed. He bent to brush his wife's lips with a fond kiss, catching his son's head in his palm as the little pate fell back from his father's shoulder at the sudden change of position.

"It seems Jamie has lost his battle with Morpheus," Anne remarked with a smile.

"Aye," Michael replied. "The sooner we get him home...." He finished the thought with a grin and a wink.

∞

THE MORNING SKY loured, massed folds of sluggish grey cloud promising rain as birds soared and swooped in frenzied attempts to feed their fledglings before the flood. To east and west, church bells called parishioners to repent their revels, though many a bleary-eyed sinner already rued the intemperance of the night before.

Dressed in black bombazine and ready to attend church, Hermione looked to neither Anne nor Michael as she pulled on her black lace gloves and announced, "I'll be moving my belongings to Elizabeth's home."

After a moment's nonplussed hesitation, Michael said quietly, "Ye needn't rush, Mother."

Anne placed her hand on her husband's arm and said, "Elizabeth needs her mother, now, Michael."

At that, Hermione regarded her daughter-in-law with a grateful smile. "Yes," she confirmed. "She and Ben will need me, as you did." Downcast, and in a voice so low it was nearly inaudible, she added, "More so."

Then, with forced brightness, Hermione straightened and said, "And I'll be nearby should you need me, as well." Abruptly, she turned and grabbed a black umbrella from the stand by the door. Without another word, she stepped out and strode off toward the little Protestant church.

Michael looked to his wife, uncomprehending. She hooked her arm with his and stepped closer.

"She needs to be needed," Anne explained. "Now, more than ever." With a deep breath, she added, "And she's right: This is Elizabeth's first child and she needs help."

"Jamie was *your* first child," he reminded her.

Anne smiled up at him and replied, "But I was not as young and inexperienced as your sister. I could have managed alone, and your mother knows it."

Michael stroked her hair, neatly pulled back into a chignon. Fighting the sadness he suddenly felt, he murmured, "My *Beira* needs no one, I think."

Anne placed her hand on his and fixed his eyes to say earnestly, "I need *you*, my love. Never doubt it."

His eyes softened, their pain melting away, and he gathered her into his arms.

∞

HAVING HAD the foresight to pack a change of clothes, Grace Donaldson attended church with Hermione, Elizabeth, and Ben. The young woman wore a pale-rose silk skirt and jacket, the former revealing her fashionably buttoned, honey-toned ankle boots, and the latter embellished with embroidered shawl collar and peplum. A matching bonnet perched jauntily atop her brown hair, and her tresses swept up to a softly coiled bun, the position of which inclined the rear of the hat upward to display the spray of ribbon and silk roses with which it was adorned. She had even brought a parasol painted with rosebuds, which she twirled flirtatiously from the moment she saw William MacDonald and his friends returning, a little the worse for wear, from St. Anthony's. Telltale bits of straw in hair and jackets indicated that the young Scots had fallen asleep in the stable the night before, too drained by dancing and overindulgence to ride home.

The first drops of rain spattered their heads as the two parties turned into Cedar Lane from opposite directions. Squeals issued from the ladies as the seven scrambled to Number 10 and rushed inside the house with Anne, Michael, and Jamie close on their heels.

Hermione lit lamps and candles to dispel the gloom, while Michael kindled a fire in the stove and set a pot of water on the iron cook-top as Anne fed the baby upstairs. The guests seated themselves around the table, and conversation flitted from weather, to the price and availability of Oolong tea, to the Atlantic crossing endured by the young Scots weeks ago. Duncan MacPherson and Sandy Sinclair had attended law school with MacDonald, and they had finally, after much entreaty, accepted their friend's invitation to discover the New World.

"Do you plan to stay with us, gentlemen?" asked Hermione.

The two looked to each other and to William MacDonald, who merely shrugged at them noncommittally. Sandy (obviously named for the golden waves of hair that put Anne in mind of a storm-rippled beach of Loch Laggan) spoke first. "Well, Mrs.

MacGregor, it's a temptation, to be sure. But judging by the telephone directory I happened to peruse upon arrival, it appears there's no shortage of solicitors in your fair city."

Anne called from the stairwell as she stepped down and carried Jamie to his father, "*Good* lawyers are not so easy to find." With a grin, she added, "And I daresay a man could make a living suing unscrupulous lawyers who have committed misfeasance or malfeasance when the interests of ordinary folk have been at odds with the wishes of industrialists."

"Aye," said Michael. "If you've a taste for a little bloodless rebellion, this city will provide ample opportunity to indulge it."

Noting with satisfaction a spark of zeal that ignited in the eyes of all three young Highlanders, he broached a related subject. "We could also use what you might call lay teachers, to help common people learn about the law and how to apply it in their own lives. For example...."

He shifted Jamie to his lap, where the baby stared up at his father, mesmerized by the man's deep, resonant voice.

Michael continued, "We have a young man, here—you may have met him last night: Dowd is his name."

The three men nodded affirmation, and Michael resumed, "Dowd has taken it upon himself to run the orphanage we call Sunshine Farm for the benefit of the urchins who've been disabused of the notion that most such institutions are the havens of safety and beneficence they are purported to be."

Dark-eyed and dark-haired Duncan MacPherson interjected, "He's a bit young for that."

Frowning, Sandy Sinclair wondered, "Surely he canna legally own such a place—?"

Michael raised a hand and cut in, "He does not own the land; it has been granted for the purpose. But we are allowing the children to run it themselves under supervision from," he gestured toward Hermione, "my mother, the priest, the vicar, and others in the community."

The young men nodded and listened intently as Michael explained, "He's a responsible young lad, appearances aside, and he truly has the best interests of the children at heart. What he lacks is education."

Anne put in as she set cups of tea before Hermione and Grace, "We've been teaching him to read and write and he's picked it up quickly. But we were hoping you could provide him—and others—with a course of self-study in law and government, bookkeeping and the like, to guide them."

Michael added, "And perhaps, from time to time, you could answer questions and test their knowledge to ensure their understanding is accurate."

MacPherson said, "I take it ye dinna intend they be formally schooled."

Anne replied as she continued to offer tea and biscuits to her guests, "At this point, Dowd would not go even if he were admissible. He won't leave the children he's taken under his wing." She smiled wryly as she added, "And he's a little rough around the edges, as you may have noticed."

The young lawyers chuckled.

Michael said, "He may choose to go to university someday and I would be happy to help in that endeavour, but he is young, as you say. As are the other local lads and lasses."

William MacDonald offered, "I could lend some of my books, certainly. And I'd be willing to talk to the lad and ascertain how best to set him on the path."

Sandy Sinclair said, "I dinna ken if I'll be stayin' in this country, but if I do, I'd be happy to help as well."

"Aye," Duncan MacPherson agreed.

"You've given us a lot to think about, Mr. MacGregor," said Sinclair, rushing to acknowledge with a nod to Anne, "and Mrs. MacGregor."

"I hope we'll all be able to work together," Anne replied. "As they say, 'If you give a man a fish, he'll be fed for a day. If you teach him to fish, he'll be fed for a lifetime.'"

Will MacDonald, fiery red hair gleaming in the candlelight, raised his teacup and said, "To teaching them to fish."

∞

THE LAWYERS had farewelled the MacGregors and headed for the mews to fetch their horses a full hour before Marcus Donaldson arrived to pick up his daughter. The countenance of the well-heeled merchant expressed his relief to find her apparently without unmarried male company and chaperoned by no less than three "ladies of quality." As he offered his condolences to Michael and Hermione, Anne wondered how best to ease the man past his prejudices against William MacDonald. She was dismissing several unbidden ideas involving ropes and feathers when Grace's voice brought her back to the present circumstance.

"Oh, I almost forgot to tell you," said the young socialite, "Jaclyn Orwell moved to Montreal to take over her father's—her *late* father's business interests there."

Elizabeth commented uncharitably, "In other words, her social standing had plummeted and her chances of marrying a rich man had fallen to nil; so, she left town."

"Precisely," Grace giggled with guilty pleasure. "And I've heard from an acquaintance that she married a Frenchman." She hastened to specify, "Not of Montreal or Québec, you understand. A Frenchman from Paris. And she's sailing to France after he sells her father's holdings." She lowered her voice to reveal, "Apparently the man is positively ancient and a notorious rake who somehow managed to survive all those revolutions."

"Then perhaps he'll survive *her*," said Anne with a smirk, mentally slapping her own wrist—very lightly—at the comment.

Elizabeth and Grace burst into gales of laughter as the former's husband and mother and the latter's father looked on in tolerant bewilderment. When Michael cocked an eyebrow

suspiciously at her naughty smile, Anne responded with an almost chastened shrug.

∞

WORK TEAMS. That was what Anne had suggested: Men formed into self-regulating units, each man learning all of the skills required for the processes under the group's purview.

Amused at her description, Michael smiled to himself as he rode through sudden rain toward the factory. "Like a regiment of skirmishers," she had said. "Able to deploy and function on their own without waiting for orders from the commander. No 'right marker' or 'left wheel.' They just do the job the situation calls for."

What other woman would couch her explanations in military terms?

As he reined his stallion round a broad puddle dimpled by the pelting precipitation, he pondered the concept of a worker-run company: It reflected the aims of the Chartist movement that had scared the bejeezus out of many governments in the first half of the century, and it mirrored the goals of the successor Communist movement that currently struck terror into the hearts of bankers and industrialists and their pocket politicians.

Certainly, he mused, broadening the scope of workers' authority and responsibility gave them more stake in the success of the company and more pride in its products, whereas reducing men to mere cogs in the vast machine of a factory had a demoralizing effect that, often as not, resulted in shoddy work and even sabotage.

Taking the cross-training idea to its natural conclusion, every man could, in time, learn all the trades and workings of the company and thus be able to fill in anywhere. And a workforce that understood the purpose of every nut and bolt would be able to recognize trouble, entertain potentials for improvement, and

understand the need for occasional alteration. Eventually, the men themselves would be able, through regular meetings, to set goals, address difficulties, and basically run the operation without an owner's oversight. Indeed, the owner would become little more than another worker with his assigned tasks.

The notion of the company running smoothly without him appealed to his lazy side. But if he were not needed, he reminded himself, would it be fair that he received the lion's share of the profits?

He shook his head like a dog, expelling the water that dripped from his hair into his eyes and dangled at the end of his nose. Glaring at the sky, he wished he had brought his umbrella or worn his hat, though the latter would, perhaps, not have done him much good in this deluge. He heaved a disgruntled sigh, mentally kicking himself for having forgotten to note the weather as he left home. Another drop formed at the end of his nose. Flicking it away irritably, he returned to his cogitation.

Profits. Could the profits be shared? Perhaps equally? Surely one job was as important as the next in the greater scheme, rendering pay variations unjust. And could the company be owned by all the men—and women—who took part in its operation?

Such heresy flew in the face of conventional thought. But would it work? He must speak to Jake about this. Just how unorthodox was the Cornishman willing to be?

∞

MY DEAR BOY, Evan's letter began as usual.

Words cannot express my sorrow at news of your loss. I must confess I had thought of your father as rather like the sun: not immutable, yet decidedly eternal. I miss his dour countenance the more for knowing I will never see it again. But why am I dwelling on my own thoughts—

you do not need me to remind you of your bereavement. I leave this passage unexpurgated only to show you why you should not feel unduly distressed by my own great distance from you: I am nothing if not self-absorbed.

The investigation into the Bardon and Bhutan matters has officially been closed. Unofficially, I am, or rather, my friend is continuing to inquire discreetly. I assure you, dear boy, that your father's murderers will not go unpunished.

On a lighter note, I have been observing the politics of this rather exuberant country for some time, as you know, and have come to the conclusion that the devolution of power to local colonels and governors has, at least in some instances, proved beneficial for the peasantry. Such advantage, of course, depends upon the benevolence of the potentate in question, but I have discovered that, where such good will exists, the populace is better served by patronage of a leader both resident and accessible. A faceless king, even a kind one, who rules from half a world away cannot possibly understand or address the concerns of a farmer whose cattle have been stolen, or an artisan whose primary tool has ceased to function, or a mother whose child has died of fever.

Goodness! I do believe I am beginning to sound like a Chartist. Father would be horrified!

I have met a most intriguing Colonel Jorge de Las Cases, who has invited me to his villa outside the capital. I have been hesitant to accept, despite the continuing constraints and

uncertainties since the collapse of the recent insurrection, but as he resides in a high valley that he assures me is much milder in winter than Rio de Janeiro—it is odd to think of June and July as winter—with fewer of the mercurial changes in weather to which the city is subject, I have decided to set aside my reservations and join him after certain official matters are concluded. His address is written in postscript below, should you wish to write to me after June.

  Wherever I may be, I am ever your affectionate friend,

   Evan

Michael set down the parchment, his lips curving into a faint smile. He hoped, he sincerely hoped Evan's friendship with the colonel would bring him happiness.

∞

THE DOMINION DAY celebration in The Flats held special significance this year. As was the custom, the entire community gathered to the Commons for a patriotic speech from Alderman John McCallion, representative of the ward; for traditional tales of the origins of the infant nation as told by youngsters who pretended to be *coureurs des bois*, natives, missionaries, and pioneer farmers; and for songs dedicated to the land the immigrant families now called home. But on this occasion, there was one more event.

Master of ceremonies Rob Donnelly told everyone, "Before ye head for the tables, there, to fetch food and drink, Herself has somethin' to say to ye's all."

Michael took Jamie from his mother's arms and watched as his wife stepped onto the small dais and waved to Jack. The Four Horsemen marched forward with great solemnity, Jack in the lead holding an age-darkened wooden box, and they joined

her on the platform.

"As you know," Anne called out, "when I took possession of these properties and became your landlady, it was on a rent-to-own basis that the new leases were drawn up. Today, I am happy to hand over the deeds of ownership to the following families."

With a flourish, she unlocked and opened the box and produced a folded document.

"O'Reilly!" she cried.

Raucous shouts and hoots ripped the air as Patrick and Dottie O'Reilly walked arm-in-arm to accept the deed to their land and home. Rob Donnelly clapped the O'Reilly elder on the back and shook his hand as the usually unflappable Dottie wiped a tear from her cheek. When the couple walked away to rejoin their clan, all O'Reillys beaming, Anne called out the next name.

"Bucholtz!"

Again, cheers rose to congratulate those who had become full, legal owners of the property on which they lived. Michael watched the little ritual that brought so much joy to some families and hope to others. He swallowed hard at the lump that caught in his throat when he realized his friends and neighbours had never dreamed they could become landowners until Anne offered them the opportunity.

Most people of means, he knew, would have kept the land for themselves and forced others to pay all their lives for what everyone ought to consider a right: a roof over one's head and a little land on which to grow food. The wealthy too often enriched themselves at the expense of their neighbours, and whole nations plundered other nations, because few lived by any standard one could truly call civilized—ideologies and slogans, religious doctrines, and appeals to "patriotism" and "tradition" notwithstanding.

"Your mam's a very special lady," he whispered to his son. For the umpteenth time, he wondered how he had had the luck to find her.

CHAPTER 50

What rough beast

Though the actual distance as the crow flies was only a few hundred yards, moving Hermione's belongings through the meandering, rain-dampened lanes to Elizabeth's new house took two days. The substantial oak dresser and satinwood armoire, walnut writing desk and cabriole-legged *fauteuil*, silk-covered *récamier* lounge and figured oak linen chest were hauled in the buckboard, no more than two pieces at a time, and usually one, each strapped down, covered, and accompanied by Michael to ensure safe arrival. Too awkward to lug up two flights of stairs, the largest and heaviest pieces were hauled by block-and-tackle attached to a bracket built for the purpose up to the attic floor and in through the wide gable window. The four-poster bed required dismantling before removal from Cedar Lane and subsequent reconstruction in its new location under the steeply sloped roof of the house on Sunshine Street. Mattress and

pillows, bolster and cushions, sheets and comforters, curtains and valance all needed to wait for the end of a sudden shower before being carted to the Ogden residence. Finally, Hermione's books, clothing, and collection of hats in boxes made the trip in time for dinner on Saturday evening.

"The house feels empty," Anne observed as she washed and rinsed a plate and placed it in the drying rack beside one other.

Michael set down the tote full of wood he had fetched from the shed and began to lay the well-seasoned wedges into the storage niche of the stove. He, too, felt his mother's absence, and he recalled her face at their parting: a mixture of relief and excitement tinged with a trace of regret.

"The odd thing," Anne continued, "is that I lived alone happily enough for so long, yet now I feel bereft.

"Aye," Michael replied quietly.

Anne finished cleaning the stew pot, and then abandoned the pans of wash-water to kneel beside her husband. She placed a damp hand on his shoulder and said softly, "I suppose we've got used to the clamour of an overcrowded house. But now there is only you and me and Jamie, and it feels strange without the bustle and hubbub." In acknowledgement that there was more to it, she murmured, "She's a hop and skip away. We'll see her often."

Michael shoved the last piece of wood into the bay and turned to gaze into his wife's eyes. "I love you," he whispered.

Anne pushed up to stand on her knees and press his head to her breast. She held him in her arms. "I love you, too," she murmured, stroking his head gently.

He embraced her, clinging tightly, too desolate to put a name to what he felt.

∞

AT SUNSHINE FARM, all the youngsters of The Flats gathered

daily to help the orphans create and decorate their new home. It had become everyone's project, and the children felt a special pride in even the smallest aspect of it. They laid coloured stones and broken bits of crockery in mosaic designs on floors and paths, painted shutters and doors with homely images, hung framed photographs Ben Ogden had taken as well as pictures drawn by their own hands, and filled window boxes and vases with flowers.

Schooling now took place in the large open room known as The Library, where students of all ages sat at deal tables they had built for themselves and studied one subject at a time until they understood it thoroughly, helping one another with new concepts and unfamiliar language, and making good use of the dictionaries Anne had provided. True to his word, William MacDonald supplied books of law and statute, mathematics and accounting, philosophy and history. From time to time, he stopped by to answer questions and offer advice, before meeting Grace Donaldson in Elizabeth Ogden's parlour. His friends had returned to Scotland with the promise to consider emigration and, given that Sandy Sinclair corresponded regularly with Evelyn O'Grady, MacDonald had cause to hope that he would soon have one partner, if not two.

∞

EACH DAY, Michael rode away to the worksite to mould *Trevelyan and Company* into a model of efficiency and equitableness and, each day, Anne cared for Jamie and her garden and her house and her community until her lover and husband returned to their home. Nights, they spent in each other's arms, and they spoke of things mundane and momentous until they drifted to sleep in shared contentment.

∞

THE SUN SHONE clear in a sapphire sky and cicadas trilled in

the trees as The Flats settled into a summer languor between planting past and harvest yet to come. A sense of anticipation imbued the long, hot days—a waiting into which a shadow of foreboding had crept, unbidden and unwelcome. Everyone seemed to feel it: They spoke in hushed tones when they spoke at all.

Anne caressed her son's plump little cheek with her finger as he slept in his perambulator on the back porch. She smiled at the lush jet lashes and brows so like his father's. He had the piercing blue eyes; the thick, black head of hair; the strong build; and the natural heat of his father, as well. Replacing the fine tulle drape that protected the child from sun and wind and too-inquisitive insects, she returned to her laundry tub to clean the baby's sheets and clothing.

She had pegged the last of the washing on the line when a postponed call of Nature forced her into the privy. Finished, her hands washed in the little basin built into the corner, she emerged to a sudden sense of wrong. Anne strode three steps to the pram and threw back its cover to find it empty.

"Jamie!" she cried, scanning the back yard in alarm. Intuition drove her to dash to the front and check the lane. There, just beyond the fence, she glimpsed a man striding quickly with a blanketed bundle under his arm. Her heart pounding, Anne raced after him, leaping the fence and screaming as she hurtled toward the black-souled stranger who had glanced over his shoulder and promptly picked up speed.

At her desperate calls, neighbour women poured out of houses. O'Reillys and Donnellys filled the lane behind while O'Shaunnesseys and Quinns, Villeneuves and McGees swarmed in front, blocking the blackguard. Tess Tulan brandished her ebony cane, and Lil O'Shaunnessey wielded a dirt-smeared shovel. The Four Horsemen sprinted from the creek path followed by Mr. Tighe, hobbling as fast as he could with his hefty walking stick. The frock-coated kidnapper whirled, eyes darting from one opponent to another.

Now awake and frightened, Jamie shrieked and howled, thrashing and squirming in the unfamiliar embrace.

"Give me back my baby!" Anne commanded as she drew near.

The man's grey hair gleamed with pomade where it caught sunlight beneath his narrow-brimmed felt hat, and sweat glistened along the deep creases of his pallid face. Ignoring her, he pressed on toward the Bow, but the people of The Flats moved to intercept him. The stranger's mouth twisted into a vicious grimace and he pulled a pistol from his belt to wave it menacingly at the approaching adversaries. Some ladies gasped and retreated several steps; others stood their ground, glowering at the villain who had violated their community. Mr. Tighe tottered closer as the Four Horsemen spread out to circle the man. But the stranger fired a warning shot that barely missed Jack's foot, and he turned about, aiming this way and that as he hastily sidled along.

Anne ran after him, but he spun abruptly at her footfalls and levelled his revolver toward her. She stopped, her own heartbeat and heaving breath loud in her ears. She hissed through her teeth, "I said, give me back my child."

In the distance, three whistles shrilled.

The man she guessed to be in his sixties and aged by a life of excess scowled balefully and snapped, "You are not in charge here, bitch! I'm taking this boy and I'll do with him as I please. And make no mistake: I'll happily kill any slut who comes near me."

In a flash of insight, Anne recognized the man's vile intentions. She gasped in horror. *No! No, you will not!*

Suddenly, the man squinted and frowned, peering at her in recognition that she did not understand.

"I know you," he said slowly. Then, he demanded sharply, "How the hell did you get here?"

Anne stared at him, dumbfounded by the question that made no sense to her.

Pulling his lips into a sneer and flicking the hammer to cock his weapon, its fluted cylinder rotating into place to load a bullet into the chamber, he said, "I would have killed you then if that stupid Highlander hadn't interfered. But this time, I'll—"

A growl from his right turned him toward Jack once more, bringing the lad up short. The two glared at each other, both seething, teeth bared, as Jacob Gold and Reverend Ferguson came running from opposite ends of the street. Mr. Tighe lifted and shook his cane threateningly as he staggered forward a few more steps, and Dowd arrived carrying an axe.

Reckoning the distance, Anne realized the gunman could shoot her before she got close enough to use the knives strapped to her thighs. Even her derringer would have been useless, had she paused to snatch the nearest one; its effective range was far shorter than that of the man's pistol and she could not risk shooting her son. No, she needed something else, and she needed it immediately. Movement drew her eye from the bastard holding her baby to the flowering bush beside the lane. There, in an instant, she saw her answer.

Anne's slow smile bore no humour and her eyes held no mercy as she brazenly stepped toward the fiend. Her voice barely above a whisper, she said, "You won't have a chance."

He whirled and opened his mouth to retort, but halted abruptly. His head swivelled from side to side as he looked about, baffled and suddenly anxious. The low hum that had gathered momentum all around rose swiftly to an enraged drone when a dark cloud coalesced to attack the kidnapper. He screamed as he batted at the bees, and Anne sprinted and dived to catch Jamie as the baby fell from the man's frantically waving arms.

A loud crack rent the air.

As quickly as it had formed, the buzzing cloud dissipated.

The residents of Cedar Lane gaped at the fallen body of the stranger, every inch of exposed skin growing pebbly with the rapidly swelling bumps of bee stings. No one moved, as though

time had stopped.

An ear-piercing screech ended the standstill. Nearest, Alice O'Reilly reached Anne first and gently pulled the crying child from his supine mother's arms.

"She's bleedin'!" exclaimed Esther Quinn.

∞

SOMETHING WAS WRONG, but Anne could not quite understand what. She had lunged and twisted in the air to catch Jamie, she recalled. And she had landed hard while the bastard she did not know had reeled and danced nearby in an attempt to escape the swarm. Why could she not feel the baby in her embrace?

She heard muffled noises all about. Were the bees still there, above her? Her vision had clouded.

All of a sudden, she noticed pain. Terrible pain. And she knew something was, indeed, horribly wrong.

Someone seemed to be trying to lift her. In desperation, she cried out, "I have to stay! I have to stay here! I have to...."

...stay for Jamie and Alex.

No, not Alex. For Michael.

Cold. So very cold. Though she tried to focus, her mind wandered. It was so hard to breathe. It hurt to breathe. She wanted to sob, she wanted to speak out, but she could not summon the energy to do either. She looked about, but all was brightness and shadow, a blur of faces above her and forms around her.

I would have killed you then, if that stupid Highlander hadn't interfered. The words rang inside her skull, sharp and clear. *I know you. How the hell did you get here?*

Who on earth was that man? How did he know her?

His soul was as dark as any she had ever seen. Abruptly, a memory flashed through her mind: a blond preacher, an uninvited guest, staring at her unrelentingly during a feast in

Cluny Castle—a murderer who was thwarted when forced to leave the MacPherson stronghold. Why had he targeted her?

All at once, another vision came to her: She saw herself, but not herself, and a beautiful grey-haired man who as neither Alex nor Michael yet both. She and her belovèd husband stood together before the home that had been set afire by brigands. Knowing death to be imminent, they gazed into each other's eyes as a dark creature who called himself a "priest" screamed at the thugs who did his bidding, "Kill them! Hurry! Kill them at once!"

She and Mikhail had been pierced by blades and arrows, that the love they shared could be destroyed.

Now she understood: The kidnapper had been that priest, and that preacher, and perhaps many others besides. And though she knew not how, he had been reborn with the knowledge and intention he had carried through lifetimes. Insane though it was, the Black Souls wanted to erase Love, to put an end to Goodness and Joy, to encourage hatred and violence, and thus to bring destruction upon all Mankind.

No! I will not allow it!

Someone grasped her hand.

∞

MICHAEL'S HEART leapt to his throat when he saw Katie O'Reilly riding hell for leather on the grey mare Ian Farrell had bought a week ago. The girl's cries, her words indistinct in the distance but their desperation clear, propelled him to the stables. Not waiting for his saddle, he galloped bareback at breakneck speed to The Flats, across the Commons, over obstacles, and through yards to his home. There, he hopped off the horse and over the fence, leaving the stallion to trot off on its own. So intent was he that what he had seen in the roadway did not register in his mind.

Katie barely caught up on the grey as he dashed for the door. From Sumac, she called. "No, no! That way!"

Whirling to see her point eastward, Michael cleared the fence once more and ran to the cluster of men and women farther along the lane. Their faces, as he approached, tore his heart. He was half-blinded by tears by the time he reached his wife, lying in the middle of the street, a sanguine stain soaking her apron. Jamie sobbed in the arms of Alice O'Reilly. For an instant, Michael was torn between son and wife, but a faint groan brought him to Anne.

"She wouldn't let us move her," Tess Tulan told him as he knelt.

Someone had draped a woollen shawl across her shoulders and chest, and a dribble of blood now oozed from her mouth. When he took her hand in both of his, he felt the growing tremble and icy chill of her limbs.

She focussed upon him. "I'm sorry," she whispered weakly, a fine red spray erupting with her words. "I wanted...."

Tears trickled from her eyes to her temples, and Michael gripped her hand fiercely as though to force life back into her. "No!" he pleaded hoarsely. "Don't leave me, Anne!"

At a racking cough that bent her nearly double, bright blood spewed from her mouth as Michael watched helplessly. When the spasm subsided, Anne fell back and fixed his eyes with a stare that was only half of this world. She murmured, "I'll find you."

He saw the life leave her.

∞

A WAIL ROSE, seeming to issue from the very earth, and Michael was not sure if the cry was his own. He sat holding Anne in his arms and rocking, tears flooding his face—for moments or for hours, he did not know. His motions slowed, and when at last he stopped swaying to and fro, his eyes came to rest on a body nearby.

He frowned and squinted. A man lay dead a few yards

from Anne, he realized. With a detachment some part of him knew must be born of shock and pain and emotional exhaustion, he surveyed the figure before him: An old man. Well dressed. Strange, bloated lumps on his face and hands.

"'Twas him what kill't her," said Tess Tulan. She spat contemptuously upon the ground by the corpse and said, "Tried to make off wi' the babe an' bees got 'im. But 'is gun went off an' he kill't her tryin' to get away."

"Bees got him?"

Michael turned toward Detective Morgan as Tess confirmed, "Bees. Never seen a swarm like it, an' they didn't touch any but that bastard. Like magic, it was."

Beyond Morgan, Constable O'Toole and several other police officers waited, glancing from one to the other and back to the tragic tableau before them. How long had they been there? Michael wondered. He had not noted their arrival.

"Any idea who he was?" Morgan asked.

"I know who 'e is."

The voice was Dowd's, and Michael stared at him as the boy said, "I got a look at 'im just before the bees got 'im. A swell that likes boys, if ye know what I mean. One o' them bookish fellahs that talks a lot an' thinks 'e knows evre'thin'."

"I saw'm, too," said Kevin. "He's th'other toff what diddled me an' Rob."

Rob nodded confirmation.

Somewhere inside Michael's brain, fragments of information began to drift together to form a whole that filled his gut with a sick, sinking sensation. He laid Anne gently upon the ground, pushed to his feet, and staggered to the dead sodomite. The face was unrecognizable, but he spotted the ring on the man's right hand.

He wanted to vomit. He wanted to scream. He may have done both.

Morgan came forward and said something that Michael could not hear. Loud in the Scot's ears was the sound of his

laboured breath and his racing heart. With a roar that rose from a vast pit of rage within him, he kicked the body. Then, he kicked it again as someone grabbed his arm and tried to pull him away. He wrenched free and dropped to his knees to pound Aldus Giles until he could no longer lift his arms.

CHAPTER 51

Ever after

Michael looked up and asked vaguely, "What?"

"I said," Josiah Jessup repeated patiently, "I can leave the ring on her finger or give it back to you."

Michael stared at him and then stared down at Anne's hand, greyish-white and still, where it lay by her side in the coffin. His wife's last words echoed in his mind: *I'll find you.* He wanted to believe it. God, how he wanted to believe she could come back to him!

Tears forming again, he started to tell the undertaker to bury the ring with her, but he stopped, unable to speak those words, and pressed his lips together in an effort not to sob openly. At last, he gathered enough control to say, "I'll keep it."

Jessop nodded and pulled the purple band from the finger that could not feel his touch. Without a word, he handed it to Michael, who held it in his fist and closed his eyes against the

wetness that welled unchecked. His mother touched his arm, and he allowed her to lead him away.

∞

MICHAEL WATCHED the flame of the candle on the kitchen table, its incorporeal shape changing and wavering as the wax guttered. Beside him, in the pram, Jamie bleated faintly, a sound Michael knew to mean the child grew hungry. But there was no Anne to feed him.

"He needs a wet-nurse, Michael," Hermione told her son gently. "I've been inquiring, and Mrs. McGee and Mrs. Cacciotti are available."

When he looked up into his mother's face, his seemingly inexhaustible fount of tears gushed forth again. He made no reply, merely staring forlornly into her eyes. Hermione clasped him to her breast and held him as he wept helplessly, hopelessly.

The baby's cries grew louder. Michael's mother pulled away and cupped her son's cheeks. Speaking softly yet firmly, she said, "We must take him to Mrs. McGee, now. She is the closer."

After a moment, he nodded.

∞

BY THE TERMS of Anne's Last Will and Testament, she was to be buried in a simple shroud under the evergreen trees in the corner of the front yard. No one contested the choice: It would have been unseemly for the two churches to argue over which of their cemeteries should contain her final resting-place, and her home had always been her centre, her core. In her lifetime, she had been the cynosure of the neighbourhood, and all agreed that she should remain at the heart of their community in death, as well.

Reverend Ferguson and Father O'Donnell, along with Rabbi Azoulai from The Warren, each took part in officiating the

funeral held in the Commons. The people in attendance, come from all over the city as well as The Flats, filled the large meadow and spilled into the surrounding lanes.

Standing by the bier, Michael glared balefully at the sun, seething at its mocking brightness and at the cloudless sky that covered the mourners in a sham of order and normalcy, as if to say, "All is still right in the world." But all was not right, and he could not bring himself to believe it ever would be again. In his arms, his son lay quietly, as though the infant understood the solemn purpose of the rite and the depths of his father's sorrow.

With the completion of the rituals, the pall bearers chosen by lot from among the men of The Flats assembled by the shrouded form and picked up the bier to carry Anne to the grave that had been dug the day before. Michael walked behind, an automaton going through the motions of living, following the nucleus of his earthly existence, his spirit still bound to her.

Under the cluster of pines and spruces, the pall bearers picked up the broad straps of canvas on which she lay, lifted Herself from the wooden bier, and lowered her gently into the six-foot-deep rectangular cavity. Everyone waited expectantly as Michael stared into the maw that meant to devour his wife.

When seconds gave way to minutes, Hermione touched her son's arm and whispered, "We must bury her, Michael. Let me take wee Jamie." She grasped the baby and pulled him, gently but insistently, from his father's arms. Michael stared into her eyes, his own pleading. At his continued hesitance, she handed Jamie to Elizabeth, bent to pick up a handful of dirt, and held it out to him as she rose.

"You must do it, my son." In a whisper, she urged, "You must let her go."

The well that had dried instantly refilled and overflowed his cheeks when he slowly opened his palm to receive the clod. As though some force had gripped his arm, it extended and dropped the soil to scatter across the sheet-swathed figure of his belovèd. One by one, his neighbours and friends and people he

did not know silently stepped around him to grab a clump of dirt and toss it with a flower into the grave. As he watched, the white of the shroud gradually disappeared and the pit swallowed his Anne whole. By the time the last of the mourners had left, only his mother and sister and brother-in-law standing by, a low barrow lay at Michael's feet. He knelt and began to pat it down, as though he were tucking his wife into their bed to sleep.

"Ye must rest, my love," he whispered as he smoothed her covering. "I will be here if ye need me."

The sun had gone down and the crescent moon had set before Michael realized everyone had left him alone at the graveside. He had been firming the mound of soil for hours, neither eating nor drinking, and he suddenly felt wearier than he could remember ever being.

Jamie. He must take care of his son.

His mother would have the baby with her, he realized. He staggered to a stand and went into his house.

∞

HIS SLEEPING SON in his arms, wrapped in the small, plaid wool blanket Anne had woven for Jamie in her spare time, Michael stood in the doorway, staring at the bed with its smoothly tucked white sheets and coverlets glowing golden in the candlelight from the bed-stand. Their bed. The bed that would never again hold his wife in slumber, that would never again see their lovemaking or hear her sighs of pleasure and contentment. The pillows across which her tresses would not lie. And the quilt that would not keep her warm.

At a small motion of Jamie's tiny hand, Michael roused, stepped into the room, and gently placed the baby into the cradle. He gazed at their infant son, motherless in his fourth month of life, and he brushed a fresh tear from the corner of his eye.

He must go on for the sake of the bairn. But how could

he?

Turning away from the empty bed, he removed his coat and waistcoat and hooked them on the pegs behind the door. He leaned against the doorjamb to pull off his shoes and socks and set them by the wall, quietly so as not to wake the child. Then, he stood a long time, unable to bring himself to lie where Anne was not, until Jamie's restlessness and bleating alerted him to the imminent need for sustenance and a diaper change. How long had he been standing there?

He picked up his son and carried him to the kitchen to warm the breast-milk Mrs. McGee had supplied in a porcelain container to see the baby through the night.

∞

THE CANDLE guttered and burned out. In the dark, Michael trod carefully across the floor and set his son into the cradle once more. When the blanket had been secured around Jamie, he stepped to the bed and lay down, exhausted. It was easier, in darkness, to imagine Anne lying a few inches away in her accustomed spot. Easier to take his own place, as though everything had not changed.

On his back, staring into blackness, still dressed in his shirt and trousers, he waited for sleep to overtake him. Across the hall, his mother's soft snore droned, unceasing, and for a moment, anger stole into his thoughts at the unfairness that his mother survived, parted from her husband, while Anne had been stolen from hers.

From him.

He felt ashamed to have harboured such a selfish thought even for an instant. Of course, he was grateful that his mother remained to nurture her grandchild—grand*children*, once Elizabeth gave birth. The possibility of losing his mother, too, stabbed him, and he closed his eyes to force away the notion and the horror that had pierced his core alongside it.

Minutes stretched to eternity, marked by the rhythms of his mother's stertorous breathing. Nonetheless, he must have drifted off, because he woke to find himself curled, spoon-fashion, but with no Anne to cuddle against. A bright ray glinted at the window and flashed through the renewed wetness of his eyes. As he rolled onto his back to escape the dazzling sunlight, something pinched his hip. He shoved his hand into the trouser pocket and found a small, stony object.

Even before he felt the hole in its centre, he knew he held Anne's wedding band, the purple circlet of crystal he had placed on her finger a lifetime ago. And a lifetime before that. He turned it between his fingers, remembering the way she had twisted it upon her own finger, from time to time, and the lustre with which it had sparkled in sunlight, in moonlight, in candlelight. And he recalled the dreams of his youth, the visions of such a ring—perhaps, as she had believed, recollections of another self, in another life—that had given him hope that he might someday prove a man, the faint hope that had kept him from falling permanently, in despair, into the life of a catamite.

Jamie began to stir. Michael rose and opened the wardrobe where Anne's jewellery box still resided. He pulled it forward to unlatch the lid and caught a glimpse of something behind. When he reached to the back of the cupboard, his hands came to rest upon a cold, multi-angular hardness. Brought to the light, the twin crystals growing from a single base gleamed with a frosty whiteness, and a rainbow winked in and out as he turned the stone in his palm. Anne had told him to keep this. A soulmate crystal, she had called it. Would it, could it, bring her back to him?

You're grasping at straws, Michael.

He set the tantric twins against the back of the armoire and tenderly, delicately, slipped the ring over one of the points. Then, after he pushed the jewellery box in front of the crystals and closed the doors, he picked up Jamie and walked to the McGee house.

∞

THE INQUEST into Anne's death led to a sensational story about a cult of sodomite rapists unearthed by John Devereux. For several days, it eclipsed the latest news of the tensions in Africa, but was, in its turn, pushed aside for less disturbing articles about the new suburban railway, the merger of *The Mail* and *The Empire* newspapers, and the performances at the newly opened theatre.

The reporter's discoveries supplemented the investigations of the police, who had found among Aldus Giles's effects a train ticket and evidence the professor had booked passage back to England for himself and a widow he had hired to wet-nurse Jamie MacGregor. Relentless questioning brought Detective Morgan to the conclusion that the woman had known nothing of her employer's activities or intentions and had merely accepted an opportunity to return to Britain with her infant daughter. When the detective was satisfied and let her go, Michael gave the tearful mother the money to go home.

"I've been in contact with Scotland Yard," Morgan assured him. "And the local university has begun its own inquiries into the activities of its teachers."

"Good," said Michael. "I don't want to see any more boys hurt by such men."

"It's not just boys that are harmed, I assure you," said Morgan grimly. "Your friend Devereux has managed to find a brothel specializing in young girls, here in the city."

"Perversion takes many forms," Michael replied in a whisper. Closing his eyes wearily, he sighed and added, "And many victims."

Like poor Marco Buzzetti and Patrick O'Reilly Senior, who had taken guard duty that day. The O'Reilly elder and Marco had each been pistol-whipped and nearly killed by the bastard. Michael would not admit, even to himself, the anger he harboured toward the two watchmen for having failed to prevent

Giles's invasion of The Flats, the kidnapping of Jamie, and the death of Anne. But they were alive, and she was not, and Michael could no longer look his neighbours in the eye.

"Yes, many victims," Morgan agreed, sounding as sickened as Michael felt. He eyed the widower a moment before asking, "Why do you suppose he wanted the baby? Surely, he took quite a risk and a lot of effort to abduct your son?"

Michael regarded the detective as he pondered the question. Finally, he said simply, "I don't know."

"There is one other thing," said Morgan, looking deeply perplexed. "According to the witnesses, this man, Giles, seemed to know your wife—though, strangely, she did not appear to know him, they said. Apparently, he stated that he had tried and failed to kill her once before, and he intended to finish the job, when...."

He paused uncomfortably before he asked, "Do you have any idea why he wanted to kill her?"

Baffled, Michael squinted and frowned. Anne had been in this time only six years, she had said. Could Giles also be from another time? No, that did not make sense.

The Scot looked to the detective, shrugged in bewilderment, and said, "I cannot imagine how they could have met. As to why he wanted to kill her...." He shook his head and threw up his hands in a gesture of utter mystification.

∞

AS HE WALKED out of the stationhouse, Michael looked to the scattering of clouds visible above the rows of buildings and wondered if he had spoken truthfully. Evan had long ago noted the particular obsession the professor had developed for Michael. Had the kidnapping of his son been intended as some sort of revenge? Or was Jamie to be a substitute?

And was revenge why he had wanted to kill Anne? Or did they have some history, as the bastard's words suggested?

After a moment, he sighed wearily and hailed a hackney. He did not wish to dwell on the possible depraved motivations that had come to his mind. Aldus Giles was dead, and his cronies had begun to name and blame one another in the growing scandal that spanned continents. It made up for nothing, but at least his son and many other children were safe. For now.

∞

WITH HIS MOTHER'S help, Michael began to wean Jamie from Mrs. McGee's breast milk to fresh goat's milk purchased from neighbours. His son balked at first: The India-rubber nipple and matching valve of the banana-shaped glass Allenbury Hygienic Feeder bottle stank to high heaven. Experiments with a wooden nipple also failed for the sheer hardness of the carved teat. Finally, the baby accepted a rag in lieu of either artificial nipple, and a former wine cork with a thin piece of bamboo shoved into it replaced the malodorous rubber valve meant to maintain a narrow opening for air pressure balance.

Once accustomed to bottle feeding, Jamie drank thirstily of the alternative liquid, and he seemed to appraise the taste of each of the spoon-fed pasty substances his father and grandmother offered daily on a trial basis. By early October, when his cousin Joseph was born, his diet included thin porridge, fruit mash, vegetable broth, and creamy soups.

∞

THE SUBSTANTIALLY bigger James Alexander MacGregor gazed wide-eyed at his tiny, squirming relation nestled in the wicker crib that had once held Jamie, himself. Michael sat on the bare waxed floor by the cradle to introduce newborn Joseph Benjamin Ogden. He slipped his son's finger into the curl of the baby's palm; when the infant gripped it tightly, Jamie let out a squeal of delight.

Elizabeth smiled and said happily, "Fast friends already."

"Aye," Michael grinned. "They'll be stuffing frogs into your bed before ye know it."

Elizabeth narrowed her eyes at her brother in recollection of his childhood pranks. She warned, "Don't you dare teach them that, Michael MacGregor!"

"Ha!" he laughed. "Ye think anybody needed to teach me?"

"Ha!" Jamie repeated the sound forcefully, rocking in his father's arms and shaking his head. "Ha! Ha! Ha!"

"Now look what you've done!" Elizabeth scolded, trying not to smirk. She bent to the boy and said, "Your da's a wicked lad!"

Hermione objected, "Now, don't you be telling lies about his da!"

Her son admonished, "Mother, you know I was a wee demon."

Michael stood, and he lifted Jamie to sweep him up toward the ceiling, eliciting a thrilled shriek. "Aye, Jamie, your da was a wee demon."

After swinging and whirling the bairn several times, he clasped him to his chest and said to his son, "You're growin' fast and bright as a penny, aren't ye? You'll be terrorizin' your aunt and drivin' your da to distraction in no time."

Jamie said, "Da!"

Michael blinked and stared at his son. He murmured, "Aye, I'm your da, my boy."

Reaching out to his father's face, Jamie repeated, "Da!"

The elder MacGregor searched the child's eyes, certain he saw understanding within them. Michael kissed him and laid Jamie's head upon his shoulder, wishing Anne were able to witness their son's first words.

∞

TO EVAN SYDENHAM'S chagrin, he arrived concurrent with

the first snowstorm of the season.

"It is most unfair!" cried Lord Danford peevishly as he disembarked from the train. "I leave one winter to be deposited into another."

Stifling a chuckle, Michael pointed out, "You could have stayed in Rio de Janeiro."

Evan's face and voice softened. He said, "Of course I couldn't, dear boy." He apologized, "I'd have come sooner had I not got myself caught between opposing factions in the ongoing drama that is Brazil." Gravely, he fixed Michael's eyes and said, "I am truly sorry for your loss, my friend."

"I thank you," Michael responded quietly. "And I do appreciate the efforts—*all* the efforts—you've made on my behalf."

"No effort at all," Evan replied with a gesture of negation, the flush that came to his cheeks not entirely caused by the chill wind. As though suddenly noticing it, he regarded the woollen bundle in Michael's arms. "And this must be the 'wee lad,' himself."

Michael turned his son to face the newcomer and introduced them. "Evan Sydenham, Viscount Danford, may I present James Alexander MacGregor." Bending to the boy's ear, he said, "Jamie, this is your da's best friend."

The viscount reddened to his scalp, smiling with a diffidence Michael had never before seen in the aristocrat.

Evan's valet cleared his throat. When his employer glanced his way, the grey-haired and black-suited manservant said, "I have retrieved your luggage, My Lord."

"Well, then," said Lord Danford, turning raised brows to Michael, "shall we repair to The Flats?"

∞

SINCE HERMIONE had returned to stay with her daughter, both spare bedrooms lay empty. And spare they were, the valet's dismayed expression pronounced as he surveyed the divan bed;

the single small night-stand with unvarnished wooden candlestick; the simple, rush-seated side chair; and the narrow wardrobe in a white room with pale maple floorboards and three windows curtained in plain, milky muslin.

"Surely, you'd rather stay at the Carleton or at Hampton House?" Michael suggested. His friend had never spent a night in such humble surroundings in his entire life.

Evan dismissed the notion with a wave of his hand. He said, "Father has the most dreary guests at present, and I'd much rather stay here than be snowed into a hotel miles from you." He corrected quickly, "From you and your family." Lightly, he added, "After all, I did not come all this way to be obliged to spend days on end listening to the chatter of bourgeois merchants from some unpronounceable town in New England or Old."

His mouth curling into a wry smile, Michael cocked an eyebrow at the viscount and said, "Suit yourself. But I warn you, I've only the one extra bed, now, and I'll have to fetch a mattress for your man, there."

Evan turned a questioning gaze toward his valet to ask, "That will suit Billings, won't it? It will be like being on campaign."

The middle-aged man's expression unmistakably belied his words. "Yes, My Lord." He added with forced cheer, "Just like India."

Michael hastily turned away, choking back a chuckle. He knew that Evan had spent his service in India in a hotel that put the Carleton to shame, attended by his valet, by various orderlies, and by native servants. His father's influence had even extended to Evan's being diverted to diplomatic details whenever any trouble erupted, thus ensuring the safe return to England of the earl's eldest son when his official duty had been done.

∞

AN HOUR LATER, one guestroom was crowded with Evan's trunk, portmanteau, and valises, as well as the mattress and bedding for his valet. In the larger chamber Billings had assigned to His Lordship, a rocking chair with cushions was substituted for the rustic side chair that now occupied the valet's room.

Soon after, the long-suffering Billings accepted, albeit uncomfortably, a seat at the kitchen table with his host and his employer as they all dined on bread and soup, cheese and fruit provided by the O'Reilly girls, who had blushed and gushed at the honour of meeting an honest-to-goodness member of the peerage. But when Evan removed his frock-coat and offered to help Michael with the cleaning of dishes, the manservant nearly had an apoplexy.

"Your Lordship!" he protested vehemently. "You must not soil yourself with such tasks! This work is for women!" He glanced balefully at the back door that the O'Reillys had recently exited before he added, "Or for servants such as myself."

"Oh, Billings," Evan replied, "you never want me to have any fun."

"Bu-bu—!" The valet gaped, speechless, as Lord Danford proceeded to remove his cufflinks, roll his sleeves, and dip his hands into hot, soapy water to scrub a plate.

"Oh!" Evan exclaimed. "This is delightful. I don't believe my hands have been this warm since I left Brazil!" In an aside, he said, "The bathwater on the ship was barely above tepid, and smelled like rusty nails, to boot."

John Billings sat in a kitchen chair, looking as though his world had come to an end, while the younger men indulged in domesticity and reminisced about their school days. Then, the valet retired to the upstairs room, beside himself with consternation, after Michael placed the baby in Evan's lap and demonstrated how to feed an infant from a bottle. A short while later, the servant's eyes flew wide when he returned from the privy to find Michael and Evan cleaning little Jamie's appallingly dirty bottom in a pan of water on the kitchen table. He stood

agape inside the back door, listening as the viscount asked pertinent questions about the proper way to fold a diaper.

When his aging manservant climbed the stairs once more, muttering to himself, Evan confessed in a low voice, "I must say I do enjoy bemusing Billings now and then. The man is so stuffy!"

Michael grinned and reminded him, "Like the time you hid a toad in your valise so it would jump out at him when he opened it?"

Evan's slender shoulders shook as he chuckled at the memory. "Father locked me in my room for a week, after. Said I'd no business plaguing the servants so."

When the mirthful old chums headed upstairs, Michael placed a cleaned and sleepy Jamie into the cradle and tucked the blankets around him, growing sober as he did so. He swallowed hard as he caressed the temple of his dozing son, and his vision blurred.

"I miss her so," he whispered, and he began to weep, collapsing to his knees. He had buried himself in the day-to-day details of living, of caring for his son, and of managing the company. Now, he realized the wound in his heart was as fresh as the day he had found Anne lying in the lane.

Evan knelt by him, gently placing a hand on his friend's shoulder as he attended Michael in his grief.

CHAPTER 52

Promise

N o!" Jamie declared. His favourite word. "No, no, no!" he yelled, running away from his father as Michael loped after him and caught him up in two strides. The boy screeched angrily when Michael grabbed him from behind and lifted him high into the air, but the child's tone turned to squeals of glee when his father swung him to and fro and finally brought him down, face first, through a mass of grass and reeds and cattails to within an inch of the murky marsh-water at the end of the drain system.

"Smell that?" Michael asked his son.

Jamie wrinkled his nose and exclaimed, "Aagh!"

"Yes, aagh," said his father. "Stinky and wet and slippery; so, you must not play there."

The lad's grimace indicated grudging acceptance of his father's judgement, but opened to a fascinated gape when

Michael raised him once more and the child spotted ducks floating on the surface of the reservoir beyond the wetland. Though they swam dozens of yards away, he reached out to pet them and, in his wriggling, nearly escaped his father's grasp to topple into the muck.

Getting a tighter grip, Michael closed his eyes and cursed himself for bringing the boy to the brickworks, where there were so many ways for Jamie to get himself into trouble or outright danger. True, Mother needed to recover from the twisted ankle that would keep her off her feet for a week or more. And Elizabeth had her hands full with Joseph and his newborn sister, Marianne. And Evelyn O'Grady Sinclair had been suffering morning sickness day and night for a month. But Grace Donaldson MacDonald or one of the O'Reilly sisters would gladly have minded Jamie for as long as necessary. Even Dowd would have taken the youngster under his wing.

Sheepishly, the Scot admitted to himself that he had brought his son to work in order to ward off the amorous attentions of his secretary. Miss Eliza Franklin was a pretty girl, and capable, certainly, but he had no interest in her beyond her abilities with typewriter and telephone. He had hoped Jamie's wilfulness would dampen her affections, assuming the prospect of mothering such a rapscallion would appal her enough to turn her attentions elsewhere.

That had been the theory. Unfortunately, she seemed to have taken the wee imp's behaviour as proof Michael needed a wife. He sighed.

Setting his son onto his shoulder and walking back to the factory, he determined to keep the lad with him for the rest of the day and speak with the Misses O'Reilly after supper.

∞

MY DEAR BOY, read the familiar script.

I do hope this letter finds you and your

family, and especially wee Jamie, well and happy. My convalescence has been dreary and uncomfortable, and Billings has been clucking about like a mother hen, but the doctors seem hopeful that I will survive this wretched fever. Frankly, there are times I do not care to, though I must hasten to add, lest you worry for my mental state, that such depths of despondency are brief, and invariably occur at the onset of an attack.

After thought on the matter, I have come to the conclusion that your only recourse with regard to Miss Franklin is to find her alternate employment or a new love interest. Because the latter is decidedly less reliable and more difficult, I must recommend the former. Knowing that your sensibility will not allow you to turn her out into the cold, I suggest you find her another situation as soon as possible. Given her competence, that should require little urging on your part.

My relationship with Colonel de Las Cases has taken a turn, of late. But I cannot bewail our estrangement severely as I had begun to find his overbearing nature tiresome. And at present, I am far too weakened to distress myself over the loss of a lover.

Jeremy Forbes has disappeared, along with the substantial fortune he had amassed. Sadly, my friend in London has since found conclusive evidence of the man's connexion with the quelling of inquiries into Bhutan and other irregularities, and with the death of your father. But do not despair that the blackguard has got

away with his crimes. My man is in pursuit; so, I have little doubt Forbes will be brought to justice. In the event I am wrong, please take comfort, as I do, that the few places he can hide from the wrath of Her Majesty's government are tantamount to Hell on Earth.

And speaking of Hell on Earth—no, that is not fair; Brazil is a fascinating country with much to recommend it, despite my current predicament. However, I may not remain here much longer. My father has sent word that my name is on a short list before Lord Growe for an unspecified position. Normally, I would shudder at the notion of an unidentified posting, but, given my knowledge of Lord Growe's more clandestine activities, I believe I should accept such appointment with enthusiasm if it is offered.

Billings and my nurse are becoming dreadfully insistent that I rest, and I confess that I have begun to tire. Therefore, I end this letter with the hope that I will be hale and hearty by the time it reaches you. If not, know that, whatever my condition, I remain

  Your devoted friend,
  Evan

∞

"MOTHER, WE'LL BE FINE," Michael insisted. "Jamie's old enough now." He added, "It's only for two weeks, and we'll be staying at an inn. Don't worry."

"I'm your mother," said Hermione. "I always worry."

Michael bent and kissed her cheek. He said softly, "I know, Mam. But I've booked a room in a lovely little hotel; we'll

have pleasant day trips; and we'll spend our nights in the comfort of a bed."

He did not mention the likelihood that the guest-house's facilities included neither a modern toilet nor a pleasant privy like the ones in The Flats. Nor did he divulge that the bed in which he and his son would sleep would, most of the time, consist of blankets atop conifer branches under a tent. And he certainly did not dare to tell his mother that the "day trips" included long hikes into wilderness and travel by canoe on remote rivers.

When Hermione patted his cheek in resignation and returned to the kitchen to prepare supper, Michael continued his packing under Jamie's curious eye. More often than not, he had to repack items that his son retrieved for close examination, usually with questions as to their utility. The lad had reached the age at which his favourite word was "Why?"

Only after he had lightly swatted Jamie's behind and sent him down to help his grandmother set the table did Michael pull from the wardrobe the twin crystals and the purple ring, to wrap them in Jamie's swaddling blanket (the red-and-black cloth lovingly hand-woven by Anne in a traditional MacGregor tartan pattern) and place them in the valise. Finished, he closed the suitcase and set it next to the large sack of camping gear by the long mirror.

He paused before descending to the kitchen to join the others for dinner. Was this journey wise? Was he deluding himself that his belovèd could ever return to him?

He consoled himself that, whatever else might come of the excursion, experience of the wilds would be good for his son. Besides, two weeks without the relentless, albeit well-intentioned, matchmaking of his family and neighbours would be bliss.

∞

BOB BEECHAM looked exactly as he had six years ago. Michael found him in what appeared to be the same dory, wearing the same broad-brimmed hat, snoozing in the afternoon sun as his fishing line dangled in the river.

"Beecham!" he called, to the distress of several birds and the startlement of the dozing guide.

"Be right with ye!"

The man's skin was the same mahogany colour, though the creases might be a little deeper, the Scot observed. The blue shirt had the same faded patch on the right chest, and the trousers might have been the same nankeens. Michael shook his head slightly and curled his lips in amused amazement as Beecham rowed to shore. How was it that some people never changed?

As the guide moored his boat, Michael asked, "Is Bessie still available?"

Beecham looked up, surprised. He studied the visitor a moment, trying to recall the unfamiliar chap who had mentioned one of his canoes by its name. Suddenly, his eyes flew wide and he exclaimed, "Annie's fellah!" He strode forward with hand outstretched.

"Yes," Michael confirmed, taking the proferred hand. His smile fading, he looked down to Jamie and said, "This is our son."

"Hullo, there, little fellah," Beecham greeted Jamie with a friendly tousling of the boy's hair. "He certainly favours ye," he added, looking up to Michael. With a glance around, he said, "I see ye didn't bring Annie with ye."

"No," Michael whispered, astonished that, even after so long, tears suddenly blurred his vision at the admission.

"Oh, Jesus!" Beecham murmured, realizing the reason for her absence. After an abashed moment, he recovered to say sadly, "She was a good woman."

"Aye."

∞

JAMIE SAT in the bottom of the canoe, hands clutching the gunwales and head swivelling from side to side to take in every sight and sound and smell. His father's announcement that they would visit his mother's "secret place" had thrilled him, and he had prattled happily on the train and coach rides that brought them to the northern wilds. Now, the boy's excitement overflowed to the point of speechlessness as his exotic adventure unfolded.

Michael marvelled at how little the countryside had changed since his journey along this river with Anne. True, he had not paid much attention at the time, but the landmarks he recalled had endured unaltered: the outcrop of stone that resembled a tortoise peeking out of its shell; the clump of five pines growing together, leaning in a manner that suggested they whispered to one another; the stretch of water that zigzagged back and forth as though the river could not make up its mind which way to go; the shingly beach by a meadow, where he and Anne had spent their first night in the wilderness.

He paddled to the cobbled shore and hauled the canoe to the grassy strip that had narrowed since he had seen it last, the verge now encroached by saplings of birch and spruce. There, he set up camp as he had done years before.

As the sun went down in a blaze of orange, father and son roasted the small fish they had caught off the riverbank. Then, when darkness descended around them, leaving their campfire the only source of light and the focus of their world, Michael told Jamie of a day when the lad was a baby: the day that his mam had saved him from a bad man.

"But she was hurt," he concluded, "and she had to go away. That's why she's not with us anymore."

Instead of asking his usual battery of questions, Jamie stood up, climbed between his father's crossed legs, reached his arms around his da's neck, and hugged him. Michael embraced

his son, trying with all his might to hold back his tears and control his voice. "We'll be all right, my boy," he whispered.

Soon after, Jamie lay on their bed of spruce branches and cotton sheets and curled into his favourite sleeping position, undisturbed by biting insects thanks to Anne's repellent recipe. Beside him, Michael fell quickly into a dreamless doze, fatigued by sun and fresh air, exercise and emotion.

∞

DA ALWAYS TURNED sad when he talked about Mam. Jamie thought he remembered the lady with white hair that Giuseppe Cacciotti and Jack O'Reilly had described that one day by the creek. In dreams, he saw her, holding him and singing to him. She had always smelled nice, he recalled, and he had felt safe when she was near.

Da missed her, he knew. And he thought perhaps he did, too.

Closing his eyes, yawning and stretching out on the lumpy bed of spruce and balsam boughs as his father snored softly beside him, Jamie wondered what it would be like to have a mam, like Gino and Giulio and Giuseppe, and like Joseph and Marianne.

∞

CARRYING THE SACK of gear on his back and the small craft called "Trixie" on his head (Bessie had apparently been rented out the day before, and was not recommended for a one-man portage in any event), Michael was much relieved to find that the trail he and Anne had followed years ago had been worn wide enough to afford him and Jamie passage safe from hawthorn spikes and poison ivy leaves. There were a few close calls when one end or other of the canoe caught among vines or struck a tree-trunk because he had forgotten himself and turned at a sound, but he and his son made fairly good time even at a pace

comfortable for Jamie.

All along the way, the tyke asked the names of the critters he spotted scurrying in the underbrush or climbing trees, and of the plants that sprouted in profusion in the north woods. More often than he would have liked, Michael had to admit his lack of knowledge and, several times, to command his son not to touch a clump of unidentified mushrooms that peeked invitingly from under the herbage or grew from a tree trunk. Suitable resting places were few and spaced at odd intervals, and relieving oneself in the backwoods could be most inconvenient if not downright hazardous; nonetheless, both MacGregors enjoyed the trek.

Early evening, they made camp by the river at the far end of the trail. This time, Jamie told his own tales of adventures with his cousin Joseph and the younger Cacciotti boys. Though he smiled at the puerile stories expounded with innocent enthusiasm, Michael made a mental note to have a word with his sister and with Giovanni and Adella Cacciotti when he returned home.

∞

THE NEXT DAY, Michael once more donned his belt with its attachments of sheathed knife and small axe, shrugged into the straps of the sack containing the folded tent and other supplies, secured the valise into Trixie, lifted the canoe and its contents up to balance on his head, and pointed Jamie in the direction of their path. They followed the shore past the series of rapids he remembered, stopping repeatedly to rest and drink and munch dried fruit and nuts. Shreds of cloud scudded above, offering intermittent relief from the heat and from the glare of the summer sun. And occasional shallows in the river beckoned them to cool, barefoot wading.

Eventually, Michael recognized the region where he and Anne had taken to the water. From there, he paddled the canoe to

the mouth of the tributary stream that he and Jamie must follow on the morrow.

∞

THE MORNING SKY loured and threatened rain. Nevertheless, Michael deposited his son and their belongings into the canoe to head upstream; there seemed no point in huddling all day in a tent when they were so near their destination. A cool breeze blotted the sweat from his brow as he paddled against the current, and he noticed that his arms had already accustomed to the unusual use to which he had put them over the past few days. He smiled to himself, recognizing that his frequent stints of labour in the stonecutting shed and the brickworks had kept him fit despite the sedentary office work with which he was primarily occupied.

Before sunset, the Scot and his son reached the shallows beyond which boat travel was impossible. He pulled the craft ashore, and they walked the short way to the spot where Anne had found gold.

While building a fire in the very depression where he had lit one before, Michael felt a sudden shiver and glanced around warily. He called Jamie to him and commanded his son to stay close. Then, he stood and scanned every opening beneath tree and beside bush. When he could see nothing peering back and no movement caught his eye, he let out the breath he had not realized he had been holding. He waffled a moment, but decided to stay for the night despite his misgivings. With frequent glances toward the underbrush, he unpacked the tent as the flames of the campfire spread from tinder to small sticks in the little pit.

"We'll stay close to the fire tonight," he said more to himself than to his son. "There may be no wild animals nearby, but it's better not to take chances."

∞

THE FIRE SPUTTERED as, for the third time since morning, rain began and intensified from drizzle to shower. Michael sat watching it through the open flap of the tent as Jamie slept beside him. He could not shake the feeling that had settled in his gut since that sharp prickle along his spine, earlier. The ongoing tension held a sense of foreboding, but of what? Too vague to be a warning of imminent danger, it filled him with unease all the same.

Perhaps it was just the place, he thought. This was the spot Anne had first felt her own presentiment of death. At least, the first he knew. Looking back, he recalled instances when she had gazed at him with a strange, dolorous expression he had not understood. When questioned, she had dismissed the matter and distracted him. He smiled sheepishly at how easily she had deflected his attention.

Had she felt something like this? he wondered. Not knowledge, but apprehension? A foreshadowing that left a persistent pall of anxiety?

He shook his head to dispel the notion, and he watched the last flames fizzle and die to leave him in darkness.

∞

MICHAEL WOKE with a start. His heart pounded at the realization he had drifted off despite his attempts to keep himself alert. How long had he slept?

He crawled out of the tent and surveyed the sodden landscape. The stream had swollen to flow mere inches from the canvas covering, which now sagged damply from its supports. All around, the branch-tips and needles of the trees dripped, and beads and runnels of moisture glistened in the wan morning twilight. Birds cheeped and squawked and twittered in a cacophony of avian calls, and the air hung heavily, thick with the sharp scents of pine resin, damp earth, and wet rock. But there was no sign of danger.

When he saw no cause for concern, Michael relaxed, loosening the fingers that had been fisted. He recognized, too, that the strange apprehension that had seized him the evening before had vanished. In the fresh morning air, he felt a resurgence of optimism and anticipation.

After a breakfast of blueberries and juneberries gleaned from nearby, Michael left the tent up that it might dry out while he and Jamie continued on the next leg of their journey. In its stead in the sturdy muslin sack, he added from the valise a change of clothing for each of them, placed atop bedding essentials should he and his son need to bivouac before they returned. Among the softer items, he sheltered the twin crystals.

Gripped by a sudden belly-melting mixture of fear and hope, he stared long at the gleaming pair of stones nestled among the smallclothes. Finally, he stuffed the spare dungarees in after and wrenched the drawstring tight to tie it. On impulse, he slipped the purple ring, Anne's ring, into the pouch at his belt before he locked the valise. Once he had cached the canoe and suitcase in the undergrowth, Michael propped Jamie on his shoulders and headed to the ridge that rose from streamside.

∞

WHERE THE SLOPE inclined sharply, Michael set Jamie on the ground to continue the climb hand in hand, then to clamber in tandem over the steepest terrain with frequent stops to rest and drink. Their path meandered around patches of poison ivy, underbrush too dense to penetrate and, occasionally, trees so closely spaced as to form a barrier. They pressed on with naught but occasional warnings or directions from Michael, he intent on their goal and on his son's safety, and Jamie concentrating on his footing and sensing his father's urgency. Finally, as the sun approached mid-sky, they reached the top.

At the crest of the rise, beyond the pale-grey outcrop he remembered, the Scot scanned the valley that spread out before

him, draped in the bright and dusky greens of foliage and spangled with the whites and pinks, yellows and purples of summer blossoms. The lake below shone white with the reflection of the cloud-paled sky, and its off-centre island floated like a moss agate set in a silvery amulet.

Michael picked up his son to afford him a better view, and Jamie gasped at sight of the dell.

"Is that the secret place?" the boy asked.

"This whole area is her secret place," Michael answered. "The creek behind us is where she found her little stones, and the island in the lake, there, is...."

He hesitated, not sure what he should divulge. At last, he said simply, "It's special."

"Can we go there, Da?" Jamie entreated, his lapis eyes sparkling with eagerness.

"Yes," said Michael. He glanced with a sudden sense of vertigo to the sheer drop at his feet, and he stepped back as he added, "After lunch and as soon as I find the way down."

They rested on the rock and ate foraged berries to supplement the dried vegetables and the nuts Michael had brought along. Jamie chattered cheerfully, apparently oblivious of his father's silence. Michael's gut had tensed, for the closer they came to the end of their journey, the more the Scot questioned the belief that had led him here. Could Anne really come to him? Or was he deluding himself? Would arriving at their destination lead only to bitter disappointment?

Finished his meal, Jamie became restless in his impatience to proceed. With a sigh of resignation, Michael donned his pack and searched for sign of the track Anne had assured him led to the valley.

Abruptly, a stray shaft of sunlight penetrated the cloud layer to briefly illuminate the upper reaches of the switchback trail leading from the hog-back to the dale. As though God pointed the way, Michael thought when the beam revealed the path. Hesitant hopefulness solidified into certainty as he led his

son down the hill.

∞

OVERHEAD, THE CLOUDS drifted higher in a thin blanket that obscured sun and moon. His timepiece chimed five o'clock when Michael, holding Jamie in his arms, arrived at the smooth, sandy shore of the lake. Not a ripple marred the surface of the water, and the still air floated redolent with the perfume of honeysuckle, dogwood, and sweet-fern, and with the sharp tang of native evergreens. So near it seemed he could reach out to touch it, the island rose stark and haunting, its rocky base thrusting spikes of balsam, spruce, and pine toward the heavens.

The Scot surveyed the strand and discovered a promising driftwood log beached thirty yards away. "Tomorrow," he thought aloud. "We'll use that to cross the lake in the morning."

Smiling down to his son, he added, "In the meantime, we'll do a little fishing and sleep under the open skies."

∞

STARS WINKED at him and a full moon played hide-and-seek behind the clouds as Jamie snuggled next to his father on the mat of green needles. The droning of mosquitoes lulled him, the beasties kept away by the smelly lotion he and his father always wore in the bush, and his eyelids fluttered.

Tomorrow I'll see Mam's special place, he thought happily. *Me and Da will go and find her.*

He sighed and closed his eyes.

∞

AFTER BREAKING FAST, Michael strolled along the beach with Jamie running ahead in his excitement. On approach, the Scot observed the log that appeared to have been pulled up rather than washed up onto the sand. Eyeing it curiously, he noted axe marks indicating it had been felled and its branches and bark

removed. It was sun-weathered, yet it did not have the look of having rested long in water. Why was it here? he wondered. He scanned the area for footprints but spotted none, though he guessed that, if the chunk of balsam had been left some time ago, any traces would be long gone. With a shrug of his eyebrows, he chalked the matter up as one more example of serendipity helping him to achieve his goal. The thought sent a flutter of optimism through him.

Soon, Jamie sat atop the half-soaked log, holding the sack tied in front of him. Michael had laced their footwear together and slung the pairs over the balsam bole to dangle, one small shoe and one large on each side, the latter skimming the water. As his father pushed off and walked the length of roundwood toward the island, the boy giggled with glee and paddled with his little, bare feet.

The lake-bottom abruptly dropped away. Grateful for the buoyancy of the fir, Michael kicked to keep himself afloat and to propel the makeshift raft to its destination. His efforts soon brought them to a rocky shelf on which he once more waded beside the driftwood bateau.

The moment he set foot on the islet, he felt a faint prickle of electricity on his skin and up his spine. Now, with a shiver of trepidation, Michael recalled Anne's description of travel through time, and he again wondered whether he had chosen correctly in coming here. Deciding it was too late to turn back, that he must try to summon her while he had the chance, he lifted Jamie off the log and set him upon solid rock. Then, he unstrapped from the fir the sack containing their belongings and tossed their shoes onto the ground.

"Come put your shoes on," he said when Jamie turned to walk on. Reluctantly, the boy obeyed and, together, father and son sat and shod themselves. As Michael picked up the bag to open it and fetch the crystal that he and his son might gaze into the stone and call to Anne from here on the shore, Jamie dashed into the forest, calling, "Mam!"

"No! Jamie!" Michael cried, scrambling up and racing after the child in panic.

He darted among the trees, stumbling repeatedly as he tried to grasp the surprisingly swift boy who managed to elude him again and again. Abruptly, the woods gave way to a broad clearing containing a huge, slate-grey outcrop upon which even lichens did not grow. His terror deepening at the realization of what this place must be, Michael stretched his strides on the open ground and caught up to lift his son into his arms just as they stepped into Chaos.

∞

MY DEAR MOTHER,

If you are reading this, Jamie and I have failed to return from our vacation. I must apologize for my deceptions, cold and inadequate comfort as such apology may be under the circumstances.

In truth, my purpose in going north was never merely to take my son, your grandson, Elizabeth's nephew, on a holiday in the countryside. As mad as it may sound, as it surely must be if you are reading this, I have gone to a place Anne once showed me: the island whence she came, a place of a kind with Dùn-Draoidheil, where you found me as a babe.

As she lay dying, Anne promised she would find me again, and I hold her to her word. I take with me a special

stone—a soulmate stone—she once bade me keep in case I should need it, and I now take it to the island, that it may draw her to me.

As I write, I acknowledge this may be folly, even insanity, nothing more than the madness of my longing for her. Perhaps I should leave Jamie with you and risk only myself. Yet, I cannot bear to be parted from him as I can no longer bear to be parted from Anne. Nor can I bear the thought of leaving Jamie behind, to be orphaned if I should not return, even though I know and appreciate the love and guidance he would receive under your care and that of Elizabeth and Ben—indeed, of the whole of The Flats.

I have selfishly deprived you of your son and your grandson, and for that I can only beg your eventual forgiveness and take solace in the knowledge that you still have your true daughter and her children.

Of whatever other thoughtlessness and lunacy I may be guilty, I have at least made the effort to ensure a legacy: William MacDonald has in his possession my Last Will and Testament,

Powers of Attorney for you and for Jake Trevelyan, and other such documents as may appropriately transfer funds, property, and authority.

I have already seen to the disposition of the remaining Deeds owing to our neighbours, and the Landowners Association has authority and means to make decisions that had formerly been left to Anne, and later to me, including oversight of the Sunshine Farm. Dowd will soon be of age, and will then be able to take legal as well as de facto charge of the orphanage, and I know he is well aided by you and by many of our friends.

The company can run well enough without me, and you will retain a share of the ownership. The documents I have left in William MacDonald's keeping ensure my absence shall not disrupt business.

The favour I would beg of you, Mother, is to send the final letter I have addressed to Evan in London. Although he deserves better than I as a friend, our fellowship has been an important part of my life, and the least I must do is to bid him farewell, albeit posthumously.

For all the trouble and grief I have caused you in my lifetime, I wish you to know that I have always loved you, Mother, with all my heart, as Jamie loves you, too. I dearly wish we could have remained with you, and that I could have been a better son. But such words, too, are cold comfort and, perhaps, self-serving drivel. So, I will close with only my promise that I remain, even in death,

Your loving son,
Michael

AUTHOR'S NOTES

∞

| Draoidheil: | (pronounced DROO*ee-yah*) Druid, Druidical |
| Dùn: | (pronounced *doon*) hill, fortified hill, hill-fort |

∞

Trivia: While I started writing *The Ghost of the Highlands* first, I wrote and finished the story of *Destined* before I concluded *Ghost*. Not sure how to end the first story, I began catching up on a season of a television series called *Murdoch Mysteries*, set in Toronto in the late nineteenth and early twentieth centuries. Those episodes inspired me to set my own next tale in that time and place, and while writing the sequel I came up with the ending for the first book.

So, although *The Ghost of the Highlands* is the first book in the Ex Tempore series timeline, *Destined* (which was originally titled *Our Life Yet to Come* and intended to be the third book in the series) was, in fact, written first.

∞

Use of the word "Scotch": Please note that I have used the word "Scotch" to refer to a person because, even as recently as when I was a child, that was a common term — as opposed to the politically correct "Scottish" that is now used — and the term was not necessarily meant to be derogatory unless appropriate to the context.

∞

Why a Scottish hero? Simply, I like Scots and Scotland and I am proud of my Highland heritage. Moreover, my husband was of Scottish descent.

∞

Why are the bad guys homosexual? First, not all of them are. Second, neither homosexuality nor heterosexuality guarantees that a person is good or evil. Third, the bad guys in question are rapists; that they are homosexual rapists in this story does not reflect on all homosexuals, just as the fact that heterosexual rapists exist does not reflect the behaviour or all heterosexuals. Any offence taken by a homosexual or heterosexual person is in the mind of the beholder; none is intended by the author.

∞

Why time travel? First, the past intrigues me and lends itself to romance and adventure, in my opinion, while the future is a mystery to me. Second, I am admittedly old-fashioned in some ways, but I am a woman of the present century and so writing a character originally from this time comes naturally. Third, I have always been a science fiction fan; so, why *not* time travel?

∞

Why stone markers, etc. as the literary device for time travel? To my way of thinking, there are three possible methods of time travel: artificial, magical, and natural. Artificial methods would require machinery of some kind, and I did not wish to write a full-blown science-fiction novel replete with gizmos when I began this tale. Magically transporting oneself would be deliberate and reversible, and that did not suit my intentions, either. On the other hand, the possibility of stumbling upon a natural time portal fit my purposes perfectly.

Natural methods of time travel would have to be, in my opinion, somehow caused by the earth, itself, with or without a psychic component. For a very long time, dowsers have been using what are currently called ley lines, believed by some to be geomagnetic lines of force and by others to be psychic lines of

force. Further, points on the earth where odd things occur have long been recorded: Faerie and UFO lore are rife with tales of sightings and occurrences in the vicinity of dolmens, stone circles, "hollow hills," and the intersections of ley lines.

Scotland, Britain, and Europe have many stone and earthen monuments, henges, and barrows, as well as hills and islands associated with fey creatures. Why not one more type of phenomenon?

Certainly, if anyone of the past were to witness the sudden disappearance into thin air or appearance out of nowhere of one or more persons, the area in question would be considered cursed or otherwise best avoided. In a culture that prizes permanence, hazard markers could be monoliths or other stone configurations that would stand the test of time and remain as warnings (or portals for the curious and intrepid) forever.

Cultures less inclined to the use of stones and earthworks, or even solid timbers, would have to rely on legends and verbal warnings. The purpose of monuments or of verbal warnings might eventually have become muddled or even falsified, particularly when a new religion or political power replaced an old one and rising powers rewrote history and mythology for their own aims. Moreover, some natural event horizons might remain undiscovered.

∞

Why make time travel a scary experience? If it were pleasant, no one would avoid it. Moreover, it seems logical that travel through time or dimensions or universes, and even direct jumping from one point to another without passing through the space between—as by means of the "wormholes" of many science-fiction tales—would feel so foreign to our senses as to be terrifying.

Further, finding oneself in a time when the rules of survival and culture are vastly different, when one's family and

friends do not exist, would be a shock from which some might never recover.

ACKNOWLEDGEMENTS

I gratefully acknowledge the contributions to my work of:

Draft2Digital, a company that makes publishing independently possible;

Wikipedia and other online resources that provided information or led me to books, and the books I have read in my research including *Sherlock Holmes: The Complete Novels and Stories* by Sir Arthur Conan Doyle;

Friends and acquaintances who helped me and supported my work, including the very competent and kind staff of the Renfrew Public Library;

My family, whose skills and talents and accomplishments I have appreciated, though I may not have expressed it openly;

My Highland ancestors, whose call I have always heard;

And my husband, who taught me the nature of love and loyalty and honour, whose support and encouragement sustained me even in our lowest times, whose courage and fortitude I have always admired, whose real life outshone any fictional tale I have read, and who invariably looked delicious in his kilt.

Reviews help readers find new books they may enjoy. So, if you liked this story, please post a review on your favourite retail or review site.

EXCERPT from *THE WINTER GODDESS*

by Allison M. Azulay

MICHAEL HAD FILLED the flask and started to screw on its cap when he heard something coming through the underbrush, fast. He ran back to Jamie to lift him into his arms and hurry along the edge of the forest, desperately scanning for a hiding place or a defensible spot. He had spied a likely shelter, a screen of ferns, when his peripheral vision caught a pale flash erupting into the open. At Jamie's joyful cry of "Mam!" he stopped and turned back.

He stared. There, a few yards away, was a human being. At sight of the Scot, the other turned, and both of them blinked and shook their heads and then gaped at each other in wide-eyed astonishment.

Jamie squirmed in his father's arms and reached for the short figure in sturdy, round-toed, light-brown boots; red-rimmed, pale-grey socks; short, sand-coloured pants; matching shirt with dark buttons; pocketed khaki vest; brown leather belt with sheathed knife...and white hair peeking from under a narrow-brimmed khaki hat. At first, Michael had not realized this was a woman, but as she walked toward him, he saw the gentle roll of her hips, and her thighs' inward slope toward her knees. The vest of bulky pockets hid her upper attributes, but he guessed they were modest in proportion. As she came near, his

heart jumped to his throat and his eyes grew wider. The soft curve of her lips; the slightly square jaw; the smooth pink cheeks; the hint of upturn of her nose; the high forehead; and as revealed when she reached him, the purple eyes fringed with brown lashes: This was Anne. Younger, he thought, but his Anne.

∞

A HUMAN BEING! Two of them! How was it possible?

Cautiously, Phoenix ambled toward the tall black-haired man of muscular frame and long heavy-boned limbs. He wore button-front blue dungarees, brown hiking shoes, and pale-blue shirt. On his shoulder, he carried a sack like hers. He held a silver flask in one hand and, in the other arm, a child who was clearly his son and similarly dressed. Both sported brown felt hats wrapped in something white—underwear maybe? A knife in scabbard and an axe hung from the man's wide leather belt cinched with grey-metal buckle. Had they been camping before they landed here? she wondered. Something about the man told her he was no backwoods hick.

The boy wriggled in his father's arms and eagerly reached toward her.

Nearer now, Phoenix noted the man's solid jaw all but hidden by thick black stubble, his straight nose and moderately high cheekbones, his brushy black eyebrows and jet lashes, his high brow and slight widower's peak visible under the head gear that sat askew. When they were a few feet from each other, she saw the eyes that shone the colour of lapis lazuli.

Lord, he was handsome!

∞

"MAM!" JAMIE CRIED again. He grunted, trying to escape his father's relentless hold, and angry, now, that he was not being allowed to run to her.

It was her; he knew it. He saw the white hair. It had to be

her. Why wouldn't Da let him go to her?

When she came close enough, he grabbed her vest to pull her to him.

∞

"JAMIE!" THE SCOT SCOLDED as he tried to pry his son's hands from the woman while struggling to hold the boy lest he fall out of his father's grasp with all his squirming.

To the woman he dared not presume recognized him, he said abashedly, "I apologize for my son's misbehaviour."

"Why does he call me 'Mam'?" she asked as she stepped forward and pulled Jamie into her arms as though it was the natural thing to do. Immediately, the tyke threw his little arms round her neck and held on with all his might.

Michael could no longer hold back his tears, though he wrestled with his feelings, fisting his hands in an effort to control himself. Through the wetness that clumped his lashes and glinted in the sunlight, he saw her tilt her head and regard him curiously as he forcibly suppressed the sobs so long held against his never-ending grief.

When he did not speak, she asked, "'Mam' means mother, yes?"

Michael could only nod.

Her voice quiet, she guessed, "I take it you lost your wife recently. I assume I look like her."

Again, Michael bobbed his head as he continued his attempts to stem the spate of his emotions and tears.

"I'm so sorry," she whispered.

Michael squeezed his eyes tightly against the pain that engulfed him. As he had feared, his Anne no longer knew him.

Other Books by Allison M. Azulay

Short-story Collections

That Christmas Feeling
In Heaven and Earth
Fateful Attractions
In the Fast Lane
On Top of the World

Twin Tales Series

Propositions and Proposals
Fates and Furies

Ex Tempore Series

The Ghost of the Highlands

Other Stories

The Chalice of Forever

about the author

Stories of all kinds enthralled Allison M. Azulay when she was a child, starting with fairy tales read aloud by her parents and then Nancy Drew Mysteries discovered in the one-room schoolhouse she attended in her early grades. Since that time, she has devoured everything from romance and historical drama, to mysteries and crime thrillers, to chick lit and science fiction.

Though she wrote tales of her own in her youth, "adulting" put a damper on her creativity awhile.

Later, encouraged by her husband, she explored her talents and now writes romance and adventure novels and short stories, for the most part, though she dabbles in other genres as well.

"I try to give readers the sorts of thrills I get reading books by Diana Gabaldon and Jack Whyte."

Her website can be found at https://www.allison-m-azulay.ca.